The Psychic Dimension,
Part II

ii

The Psychic Dimension, Part II

BY

JAY DUBYA

www.bookstandpublishing.com

Published by
Bookstand Publishing
Morgan Hill, CA 95037
4139_3

ISBN 978-1-61863-868-7

Printed in the United States of America

For Dan and Karly

Other Books by Jay Dubya

Pieces of Eight
Pieces of Eight, Part II
Pieces of Eight, Part III
Pieces of Eight, Part IV
Nine New Novellas
Nine New Novellas, Part II
Nine New Novellas, Part III
Nine New Novellas, Part IV
Black Leather and Blue Denim, A '50s Novel
The Great Teen Fruit War, A 1960 Novel
Frat' Brats, A '60s Novel
Ron Coyote, Man of La Mangia
So Ya' Wanna' Be A Teacher!
The Wholly Book of Genesis
The Wholly Book of Exodus
Mauled Maimed Mangled Mutilated Mythology
Fractured Frazzled Folk Fables and Fairy Farces
Fractured Frazzled Folk Fables and Fairy Farces, Part II
Thirteen Sick Tasteless Classics
Thirteen Sick Tasteless Classics, Part II
Thirteen Sick Tasteless Classics, Part III
Thirteen Sick Tasteless Classics, Part IV
RAM: Random Articles and Manuscripts
One Baker's Dozen
Two Baker's Dozen
UFO: Utterly Fantastic Occurrences
Shakespeare: Slammed, Smeared, Savaged and Slaughtered
Shakespeare: S, S, S, and S, Part II
Snake Eyes and Boxcars
Snake Eyes and Boxcars, Part II
Suite 16
O. Henry: Obscenely and Outrageously Obliterated
Twain: Tattered, Trounced, Tortured and Traumatized
Poe: Pelted, Pounded, Pummeled and Pulverized
London: Lashed, Lacerated, Lampooned and Lambasted

Young Adult Fantasy Novels

Enchanta
Space Bugs, Earth Invasion
Pot of Gold
The Eighteen Story Gingerbread House

Contents

The thirty-seven novellas presented in *The Psychic Dimension, Part II* are works of pure fiction. The stories' themes deal with paranormal and psychic experiences. Any character resemblance to any living person on planet Earth in this work is purely coincidental.

"Multiple Choice"

As veteran Agents Salvatore Velardi, Arthur Orsi and Dan Blachford entered Philadelphia FBI headquarters at 600 Arch Street, the three black-suited government detectives had been casually discussing the amusing notion that their distinguished boss Chief Inspector Joe Giralo was indeed one hundred percent psychic. But as the chatty trio would soon discover, the astonishing and confounding "Multiple Choice Case" would become a perplexing development that would virtually confirm their speculative suspicions about their boss's seemingly uncanny paranormal abilities.

Chief Giralo was preoccupied sitting upon his black swivel chair behind his impressive Canadian oak desk, but instead of reading the early morning edition of the *Philadelphia Inquirer* as was his habit, "the Boss" was engrossed in studying certain words printed upon fresh computer paper. Joe Giralo instantly abandoned his introspection to acknowledge the expected appearance of his illustrious investigative trio.

"Glad to see that you three non-Musketeer sleuths could make our scheduled Friday morning appointment," the Chief greeted his commuting work staff. "Tell me Salvatore, how was the Eagles concert down at the Wells Fargo Center, I believe."

"It was absolutely spectacular!" Agent Velardi spontaneously exclaimed. "Don Henley did a terrific job singing 'Hotel California' and 'Dirty Laundry' and Glenn Frey was sensational doing 'Take It Easy' and 'Tequila Sunrise'. The three-hour show was fantastically great. Even Kathy now is an enthusiastic Eagles' fan!"

"Isn't Joe Walsh in that group too?" Joe Giralo asked, his timely query delving deep into his impeccable memory.

"Yes indeed," Agent Velardi indicated. "Joe Walsh is regarded as the comedian of the band, and just like Don Henley and Glenn Frey, the guy has a well-established solo career too. I especially like his rendition of 'Life Is Good' along with his performance of 'Rocky Mountain Way'. And the fourth member of the Eagles, a fella' named Timothy B. Schmit also sings a few solo hits of his own."

"The Wells Fargo Center has a super-tremendous sound system," interrupted Agent Arthur Orsi. "In April Carol and I had gotten tickets to a Fleetwood Mac concert and I have to admit, the show was truly exceptional. Stevie Nicks still has a sexy voice and Lindsey Buckingham is perhaps the best electric guitarist ever. And John McVie on bass guitar really jams, especially with two particular songs, 'The Chain' and 'Go Your Own Way', and of course," Agent Orsi prattled, "Mick Fleetwood is one of the premier drummers in all of rock and roll, going back to Bill Haley and the Comets in 1954."

"And how about you Dan?" the amused Chief inquired of Agent Blachford. "Have you and Bing lately attended any sensational rock concerts at the Wells Fargo Center?"

"No Boss, my wife and I had spent last weekend relaxing on the beach and walking the boardwalk down in Ocean City, Maryland," Agent Blachford answered. "We enjoyed the tasty Thrasher's French fries, had a few great meals in the Holiday Inn's Reflections Restaurant, and we also experienced smooth seventeen mile rides across Delaware Bay on the Cape May-Lewes Ferry. But tonight Bing and I plan on going to the July 16th carnival in downtown Hammonton. The colorful ritual's become an annual tradition that my wife and I have come to honor each and every summer."

Wily Chief Giralo then intentionally bemused and confused his three crime-fighting disciples by asking the frequent office visitors when was the last time they had taken a 'Multiple Choice' objective question test. Agents Velardi, Orsi and Blachford seemed momentarily bewildered by their boss's rather peculiar inquiry.

"In Mr. Tom Curley's Western Civilization class I believe, my junior year at Hammonton High School," Sal Velardi remembered and articulated. "Mr. Curley loved presenting labyrinth-length multiple choice questions, telling his lethargic pupils that it was too hard for him to read and grade alternative-type essay test items."

Next Art Orsi chimed-in to add his commentary to the new-found oddball conversation. "Mr. Bill Heston's tests on Herman Melville's classic novel 'Moby Dick' and on William Shakespeare's tragic play 'Romeo and Juliet' were somewhere between horrendous and abominable for an unmotivated senior like me to take and pass," the all-too-honest agent recalled and guiltily reported. "How I ever graduated from Hammonton High School was truly a minor miracle. I almost had to petition the New Jersey Commissioner of Education in order to successfully make it out of *that* renowned institution of scholarly endeavor."

"Well Boss, I had found Mr. Gordon Strycula's American History tests to be quite atrocious," Dan Blachford attested

2

without direct solicitation. "The guy's enigmatic multiple choice questions were virtually indecipherable, and by the time I got done reading the introduction to a test item, my total mind would be swimming in a foggy nebulous quandary. If I recall, there was a controversial issue always floating around the high school; whose arduous tests were more difficult, Mr. Curley's or Mr. Strycula's!"

"Fellas', I just have to mention that I also had the distinct pleasure of attending Hammonton High a full decade before you three Einsteins had ever evolved out of kindergarten," Inspector Giralo incisively driveled, "so naturally I had been exposed to teachers who had become retired prior to your undistinguished high school careers. But honestly, Mr. Neil Pastore's Chemistry multiple choice exams' were predictably quite challenging, and also, Mr. Jimmy DeFiccio's French tests had often made me wish I had taken Spanish or Italian as foreign languages instead."

"Forgive my burgeoning ignorance," a slightly vexed Sal Velardi piped-in, "but what's all of this crazy nonsense about high school academic multiple choice tests?" the inquisitive agent abruptly asked his often-vague and evasive federal government mentor. "As the Eagles allude to in the famous song 'Already Gone', 'I can see the stars but never see the light'."

"Well Gentlemen, now that we've supposedly discussed positively nothing in regard to our all-important FBI workload," Inspector Giralo mildly chided his three subordinates as "the Boss" slowly opened his top desk drawer and gingerly removed three duplicate pages ditto to the one existing before his eyes, "I wish to share something rather bizarre with you notorious gumshoes. Three weeks ago I had received *this* unusual item via certified mail and at first inspection, I had erroneously evaluated it to be a weird joke originating from a jealous prankster who despises government bureaucracy. But now as a result of recent current events, there's strong evidence to the contrary, the accumulating facts suggesting otherwise."

Joe Giralo then methodically distributed the three previously concealed identical papers to his more-than-curious underlings, requesting that the agents read and then render their individual opinions about the rather strange scenario being reviewed. The three investigators intensely and silently read the language and anxiously contemplated the five-item quiz selections, each loyal detective having a very serious expression appearing upon his face.

"Multiple Choice Quiz"
Figure-out the U.S. Cities

1. A) Buccaneers but not Pirates
    B) trouble brewing
    C) Marty Robbins saloon fight
    D) Lost Wages
    E) all of the above

2. A) KO
    B) Spanish for "that"
    C) mountain water tumbling, (hive-see-sea)
    D) BA, BA black sheep
    E) all of the above

3. A) AC/DC
    B) small diamond
    C) bashful girl
    D) elephants and marauders
    E) all of the above

4. A) hall of fame rocks
    B) Bulls and Bears
    C) metropolis in the fast lane
    D) Rice-A-Roni miners
    E) all of the above

5. A) arachnids in Virginia
    B) small fruit city
    C) remittances and payments
    D) evaders and heavenly creatures
    E) all of the above

Good luck Inspector,

The Puzzler

Chief Giralo perceptively examined the pensive expressions upon his agents' faces, allowed thirty additional seconds for document analysis and then imperatively informed his addle-minded men that "the Puzzler" was not just a mere clever practical joker but conversely, the treacherous anonymous rogue actually represented a major threat to both corporate and government security and that in the short span of two July weeks, the complicated case that was being described had quickly escalated from a minor nuisance caper into an urgent FBI matter, its essence uniquely characterized by the new-found issue's awesome, paramount significance.

"Well Guys, what do you make out of this fairly unorthodox riddle?" the Chief frankly asked. "I'll meticulously walk you through the first two sets. Now here's a definite starting point. You might want to discard your history and English teachers' multiple choice tests and exclusively concentrate on Mr. Charles Galinas' seventh grade Geography class quizzes."

"In my humble estimation, it reads like complete jabberwocky, total illogical gibberish to me!" Agent Velardi assessed and stated. "Run us through the first two answer groups Boss, and then Dan, Arty and I could possibly pick-up the style of thought being exhibited."

"Okay Salvatore, but please stay focused on the fact that we're dealing with certain American cities here and nothing else," the Boss emphasized. "Now deciphering the first set of prompts, 'Buccaneers but not Pirates' means Tampa and not Pittsburgh; and next, 'trouble-brewing' refers to Milwaukee and not St. Louis in terms of early month July events that I'll soon explain in detail, and then Marty Robbins saloon fight comes from the classic rock and roll song 'El Paso', and finally, 'Lost Wages' is a fairly awkward play on words for...."

"I get the pattern now!" reflexively boomed Agent Velardi. "Las Vegas, Nevada!"

Demonstrating splendid self-control, stoic Inspector Joe Giralo ignored Sal Velardi's excessive display of exuberance and proceeded to analyze the second set of tricky answers. The Boss decided to deflate Velardi's fantasy bubble by asking his main apostle what the abbreviation 'KO' meant.

"Could it be 'knock-out' pertaining to the sport of boxing?" Agent Velardi guessed, his emotions swiftly changing from giddiness to obvious uncertainty.

"Well now," Chief Giralo seriously lectured, "I'm a stockholder of Coca-Cola Company, and the soft drink outfit's New York Stock Exchange ticker-tape symbol is 'KO'. As you know, the company's based in Atlanta. But don't feel bad Sal. I've been busy dismantling *this* disturbing dilemma, or should I say 'conundrum' for two whole weeks now and have a better handle on its elements than you do at the moment. But here's a constructive hint to guide you along the illuminated Path of Knowledge. The whole second set of favorable responses all concern major U.S. Corporations."

Seeing that his three extremely befuddled agents were not adequate Wall Street stock market experts, Inspector Giralo continued elaborating on his rather astounding multiple choice quiz determinations. "And incidentally, the Spanish word for 'that' is 'eso', which relating to the popular Fortune 500 Corporations' index, magically converts into Esso, which exists in Europe as a separate entity but had been renamed in the U.S. as the appellation EXXON several decades ago. And very shrewdly, 'mountain water tumbling, hive-see-sea' could only signify the letters 'BCC', or Boise-Cascade Corporation, its international headquarters located out west in Idaho. And BA, BA black sheep automatically switches into...."

"Boeing Aircraft out in Seattle," Agent Arthur Orsi recognized and immediately vociferated. "My goodness! We're dealing with an evil genius villain here, whoever this crazed Puzzler is!"

Next, Sal Velardi accurately interpreted the third contrived set of clever items. "In the second series of choices, I'll conjecture that 'AC/DC' is not the legendary acid rock band, but I'll say that the decoded translation probably means Atlantic City and Washington DC, since the general theme being applied here is American cities; and naturally, next on the list, 'a small diamond' would be Little Rock and in the next intriguing example, 'a bashful girl' would be..."

"Cheyenne, Wyoming," Agent Orsi realized and contributed. "But Chief, how about this mystery of 'elephants and marauders?'"

"That same mystification had stymied me for a few hours, but then I theorized that the right answer would have to be Oakland, California, because the Oakland A's mascot symbol is an 'elephant', and the noun 'marauders' is an appropriate synonym of the word 'Raiders'. Now we're finally cooking with gas Men; our combined efforts shrewdly connecting all of the myriad geography, sports and economic dots. Our initiative is beginning to organize into a lucid plausible pattern."

Agent Orsi then volunteered to unravel the fourth multiple choice's possible answers. "Now I think that my mind is less cluttered and more honed-in to the exact thought process that's needed. First of all, 'hall of fame rocks' must associate with the city of Cleveland, where the Rock and Roll Hall of Fame is flourishing. And next Boss, 'Bulls and Bears' either refers to Wall Street in New York or to Chicago, the professional basketball

6

team being the Bulls and the corresponding Windy City football team being the Bears."

"Excellent observations given Arty!" Chief Giralo generously commended. "Newly derived information clearly supports your Chicago basketball and football hypothesis. And what about the odd vernacular 'metropolis in the fast lane'?"

"It's not that cryptic anymore!" gushed Arthur Orsi. "That's without a doubt referring to Rapid City, South Dakota." After glancing-down at *his* sample test paper, the suddenly enlightened agent then confidently declared, "Rice-A-Roni miners is indeed pertinent to San Francisco, since the old Rice-A-Roni TV commercial jingle maintained that the delicious food product was 'the San Francisco Treat', and the miners prompt given obviously has to do with the historic California Gold Rush of 1849, hence, the pro' football team, the San Francisco 49ers!"

"Fantastic employment of the Associative Law of Thinking!" Joe Giralo praised and congratulated Agent Orsi. "You're well on your way to achieving the title of Freshman Psychic! And finally Dan, try your luck at decoding the fourth set of the Puzzler's fairly remarkable quiz."

Dan Blachford was not to be denied earning relevant kudos from his Boss after disclosing that the esoteric phrase 'arachnids in Virginia' 'more-than-likely' meant the Richmond University Spiders, that the allusion 'small fruit city, tiny pop drink' was analogous to Minneapolis, Minnesota, that 'remittances and payments' apparently materially applied to Billings, Montana and finally, that the nomenclature 'evaders and heavenly creatures' dealt specifically with the National League Los Angeles Dodgers and the rival American League California Angels baseball teams."

But after Dan Blachford's brilliant deductions had been uttered, Agent Velardi required much-needed clarification from the coy FBI official seated behind the prodigious oak desk. "But Boss, although this outlandish Puzzler 'City Test' is quite fascinating and interesting, how do these weird play-on-words involve the element of crime in any way, shape or form?"

"Sal, have you noticed anything unique about the four choices provided in each set?"

"Well Boss, now that you've mentioned it," Velardi reluctantly replied, removing some summer sweat deposits from his brow, "in every set, each disguised city is situated in a separate geographic time zone. For example, in Set One, Tampa is in the Eastern Time Zone, Milwaukee is in the Central Time Region, El Paso is the only major Texas city located in Mountain Time, and Las Vegas is thriving in the Pacific Time Zone."

"Have you keenly observed any other noteworthy pattern?" the well-prepared Boss wanted to know.

"Yes indeed Chief!" Agent Velardi proudly shared and replied. "The correct response that's relevant in all five zany and absurd questions happens to be, in each case, Choice E, 'All of the Above'!"

"Tremendous cognition Salvatore!" lauded Inspector Giralo. "Now permit me to identify and describe the fundamental FBI problem here which Matt Riley down there at DC headquarters insists that *we* professionally resolve. This pathetically devious culprit, who is inconveniently known to us as 'the Puzzler', has maliciously hacked into various corporate, federal and state government computer systems and the dangerous felon has also wickedly pilfered invaluable company patent secrets along with top CIA and State Department highly classified methods of operation. This wanton criminal must be apprehended immediately and his defiant brazenness brought to justice! Do you three skilled detectives now fathom the full magnitude of *our* latest assignment?" the on-a-mission Chief rhetorically asked. "We'll meet again as soon as I acquire more pertinent background info' on this truly complex and quite embarrassing iniquity-in-progress! Our country's reputation along with the health of our great American economy remain in dire jeopardy until this pesky Puzzler villain is promptly arrested and expeditiously incarcerated!"

* * * * * * * * * * * *

A week later in July via e-mail, Inspector Joe Giralo hastily summoned his three agents to a breakfast meeting in the rear dining room of the Red Barn Restaurant, Route 206, Hammonton, New Jersey. G-men Velardi, Orsi and Blachford were all eager to learn more corroborative data about the sinister and unscrupulous mastermind known only to FBI law enforcement officials as "The Puzzler." After the Red Barn's proprietor Evelyn jotted-down the four customers' standard orders, the normally jovial Boss abandoned his ordinary preliminary smalltalk remarks and impetuously delved right into the vital subject matter at hand.

"I suspect that this slippery Puzzler fellow has organized a team of dedicated personnel, all deftly working for the prevaricator inside each of the four principal U.S. Time Zones,"

8

the Chief austerely declared in characteristic formal fashion. "I suspect that *his* employees must be sophisticated computer hackers that have profound animosity for the American capitalistic economy and also great disdain for the current massive U.S. Government bureaucracy."

"Is that why you've arranged this unscheduled morning conference?" Agent Velardi audaciously questioned. "What other germane information did Matt Riley and you manage to glean?"

Chief Giralo then opened a commonplace oak-tag folder and proceeded to distribute three of the four typed copies that had been contained within the newly obtained grammar school object. Much to the three agents' sheer surprise, the impudent Puzzler had sent their revered boss a second multiple choice test, which the adamant Inspector advised the conscientious agents to solemnly read and interpret.

"Second Multiple Choice Test"

1. The most popular black and white TV female singing group.
    A) the McGuire Sisters
    B) the Andrews Sisters
    C) the Lennon Sisters
    D) the Sisters of Mercy
    E) none of the above

2. Where would you rather not play a game of bridge?
    A) Dodger Stadium
    B) at a Golden Gate
    C) island West of San Diego
    D) Chesapeake Bay
    E) none of the above

3. Who was the worst U.S. President?
    A) Gerald Ford
    B) Grover Cleveland
    C) James Madison
    D) Andrew Jackson
    E) none of the above

4. Most dangerous animal species is:
    A) elephants in Alabama

B) birds in Maryland
C) rams in California and Missouri
D) bruins in Illinois
E) none of the above

5.   Name the city.
A) red stockings
B) Bengals but not Tigers
C) Lone Star dudes, no ranch dressing
D) Is your nickname 'Gino'?
E) none of the above

After several minutes of silent meditation, Chief Giralo sternly asked his team of astute agents exactly what they imagined the second multiple choice test meant. Sal Velardi was the first to provide an erudite response.

"It stands to reason in item Number One," the senior government squad member pointed-out, "the McGuire Sisters and the Andrews Sisters sang mostly on radio shows in the 1940s, the Lennon Sisters were mainstay feature artists on the Lawrence Welk Show in the '50s and 60s, and the Sisters of Mercy choice was a trick selection possessing no merit whatsoever. Therefore," Agent Velardi deducted, "the correct answer has to be 'E', 'None of the above'."

"Magnificent comprehension Sal!" commented Inspector Giralo. "There is a McGuire Air Force Base near Fort Dix just outside Trenton and there's also an Andrews Air Base outside Washington. Both McGuire and Andrews were nefarious canards specially designed to set us off searching for clues in the wrong direction. And now Arty, what do you make of the quiz's second item?"

"Well Boss, four bridges are rather coyly referenced: Dodger Stadium in L.A. became the future home of the Brooklyn Dodgers, so subsequently, we have the Brooklyn Bridge, and secondly, the incomparable Golden Gate is out west in the neighborhood of San Francisco. Thirdly, the Coronado Bridge connects San Diego with Coronado Island, and finally, the Chesapeake Bay Bridge had been constructed near Annapolis, Maryland, connecting the state's Eastern Shore to the mainland. I've driven over *that* lengthy span many times while going back and forth from Jersey to DC."

"Exactly Arty, but what is the only satisfactory answer to item Number Two?" interrogated a grim-faced Giralo.

10

"Why would anyone desire playing a game of bridge atop any of those four already mentioned architectural wonders?" Orsi volleyed back. "Just like in quiz Item One, the best answer is indubitably 'E', 'None of the above."

"Too bad we aren't at the 16th of July Carnival or else Arty, you would've won an authentic miniature-sized cupie doll or perhaps a rusty Dewey Button!" Joe Giralo very clearly enunciated. "And Dan," the Boss beckoned to Agent Blachford, "tell us in a short oral paragraph what you've derived from quiz item Number Three."

Dan Blachford maintained that question three involving United States' Presidents was also "a repulsive red herring mess" with Gerald Ford possibly mischievously referring to Ford Motor Company outside Detroit, with Grover Cleveland pertaining to the home of the baseball Cleveland Indians and the football Browns, with James Madison possibly alluding to Madison, Wisconsin, and lastly, with Andrew Jackson associating with Jackson, Mississippi. "I'm inclined to agree with Sal and Art and unequivocally state with total confidence that the correct choice is 'E', 'None of the above."

"Admirable evaluation Danny Boy!" exclaimed the Chief Inspector. "You're developing a masterful *psychic* acumen for skillfully deciphering annoying cryptograms!"

"And consistent with everything else we're discussing with this second Puzzler quiz," Agent Velardi awkwardly butted-in, "a definite relationship pattern that's in stark contrast to the first multiple choice test has been materializing. For instance, in item Number Four, elephants in Alabama refers to the University in Tuscaloosa (tusks are looser), birds in Maryland would rationally be the Baltimore Orioles, rams in California and Missouri would be the Los Angeles Rams football team, which later became the St. Louis Rams of today, and ultimately, bruins in Illinois would ostensibly be the hapless Chicago Cubs. And here's my stellar deduction from this second multiple choice quiz riddle. All of the items in Question Four are bogus illegitimate allusions, each one having little or no merit. And so Boss, Number Four is another plain and simple 'E', '*None* of the above'. In the first peculiar Puzzler test, the right response was always '*All* of the above'."

"Fabulous scrutiny and marvelous Socratic deduction rendered!" Joe Giralo verbally lavished. "And in the final irrelevant item, 'red stockings' would suggest the Boston Red Sox, 'Bengals and not Tigers' would mean the Cincinnati football team and not the Detroit baseball squad, 'Lone Star dudes without ranch dressing' probably denotes the Dallas Cowboys, and the nickname 'Gino' would easily synchronize with Eugene, Oregon. Gentlemen, this entire second Puzzler scenario that I had also received via U.S. certified mail obviously constitutes a grotesque exercise in futility."

"So Chief, tell us, why have *you* called us so early this morning to join you for breakfast at the Red Barn?" Sal Velardi bristled and demanded learning. "Was your sagacious purpose to have the three of us appreciate the true merits of a very disgusting Puzzler wild goose chase?"

Inspector Giralo then opened and again reached into his cheap nondescript oak-tag folder and next carefully removed four copies of a recent e-mail he had received at midnight from the diabolical Puzzler. Agents Velardi, Orsi and Blachford all sat there with their mouths agape, and the three listeners prudently read the electronically dispatched letter.

FBI Inspector Joseph Giralo,

Greetings there, you incompetent Government Bozo! By now you've finally determined that the second set of multiple choice questions has been deceitfully and adroitly assembled by me, your new-found formidable adversary, the inimitable Puzzler. Now Mr. Bureaucrat, to set you back on the right trail, you clumsy inept Dunce, I've just concocted a simple little joke for you to genuinely ponder. I now have you over a barrel Inspector, but unfortunately, not a barrel tumbling over cascading Niagara Falls.

Ask me if I'm an orange.
"Are you an orange?"
Yes I am. Now ask me if I'm an apple?
"Are you an apple?"
How can I be an apple if I'm an orange?

Have a good one Inspector, and please don't strain your minuscule brain from the rigors of thought overload!

Your Relentless Nemesis, the Ubiquitous Puzzler

"Besides being egregiously insulted, what can you conclude Boss from this ludicrous blabber?" Agent Velardi wondered and asked. "This insolent Puzzler jerk is playing advanced mind games with *us* while demonically denigrating *you*!"

"Yes Salvatore, but it's my objective opinion that the rotten scoundrel has now gotten to be too arrogant and too cocky for his own good, and I know from decades of experience that *that* sort of over-confidence usually means that he's about to trip himself up big time! The master of disaster will soon become the engineer of his own demise!"

"How Boss?" a perplexed Arthur Orsi injected into the dialogue. "Could you possibly be more explicit?"

"Well Arty, it's my educated gut hunch that the term 'orange' in the e-mail might be referring to William and Mary of Orange of England, and that possibly the William and Mary University campus in Williamsburg, or maybe *that* entire area of Virginia including Historic Williamsburg along with Busch Gardens Amusement Park has been ruthlessly targeted for mischievous computer hacking. Or perhaps the computer system at the Williamsburg Bridge connecting Manhattan and Brooklyn might also have been selected for its general vulnerability."

"What's the Puzzler's motive?" Blachford insisted on knowing.

"I don't believe that the condescending rascal is planning on blackmailing or extorting ransom money out of Uncle Sam in exchange for his purloined classified computer files," Chief Giralo maintained. "The insidious Puzzler's far too smart to pursue *that* risky avenue! Instead, I think he'll attempt selling the illegally acquired confidential information to either the Chinese or Russian governments! But it's always the sin of hubris that eventually brings these haughty punks down to Earth!"

"So what's our next strategic move Chief?" Agent Velardi requested finding-out. "Where are we three FBI pawns to be assigned on the government chessboard to perform our due diligence?"

"You Salvatore will be dispatched down to Williamsburg, Virginia to engage in some necessary surveillance work, and you Arty," Chief Giralo paused to inhale a much-needed deep breath, "your temporary job will be to stay on reconnaissance duty around the parallel Williamsburg and Brooklyn Bridges. And finally Dan," the now-inspired Inspector stated to Agent Blachford, "your vital role in this crucial mission will be to keep your vigilant eyes on the James Fenimore Cooper House at 457 High Street over in Burlington, New Jersey. That's all the productive business I have to offer and share for now Gentlemen! Oh terrific! Here comes ever-reliable Evelyn with our delectable breakfast orders!"

Bewildered and beleaguered Agents Velardi, Orsi and Blachford simultaneously and incredulously shrugged their broad shoulders, the awed trio staring at each other with blank expressions registered upon their pallid countenances, the "out of the loop" threesome surmising that their inscrutable superior was either becoming senile or was again experiencing one of his inexplicable psychic moments.

* * * * * * * * * * * *

At noon on Sunday, July 29th Agents Velardi, Orsi and Blachford were individually notified by their eminent superior that a summary teleconference session would be occurring at precise 3 pm to "unofficially wrap-up" the intricate high-priority "Puzzler Multiple Choice Test Case." The always-ready trio had been instructed by a cell phone voice mail message to arrive at respective government video facilities in Williamsburg, in Manhattan and in Trenton in order to participate in the Boss's urgently scheduled "group communication."

"Sal, what did you discover while curiously sleuthing-around down there in Williamburg?" Inspector Joe Giralo inquired, his solemn face displayed upon the three agents' video screens. "Was there anything extraordinary or irregular you had noticed or witnessed?"

"No Boss. Everything was tranquil in and around historic Williamsburg and also in and around nearby Busch Gardens," Agent Velardi verbally conveyed. "I'm afraid that my uneventful week-long presence down here in Tidewater, Virginia has been an exorbitant waste of taxpayer's money. I even got tired from riding the park's exciting roller coasters over and over again!"

"And how about you Arty?" Chief Giralo resumed his informal audio/video roll call. "Anything out of the usual occurring near the Willliamsburg and Brooklyn Bridges? Are any new trees growing over there in Brooklyn?"

"No Boss," Agent Orsi glumly answered in a melancholy, disappointed tone of voice. "The action on both sides of the East River was slim, not even qualifying to be described as mediocre! I'd have learned more just staying home and watching morning and afternoon soap operas with my wife! My true ambition in life is to be more than a lethargic couch potato or an ambitious Lazy Boy cucumber!"

"And tell me Dan, did anything exciting or dramatic transpire this morning on your critical assignment over there in Burlington at 457 High Street?"

"Why yes!" Agent Blachford jubilantly exclaimed. "But the boisterous commotion was not happening inside or outside the James Fenimore Cooper House. Your fearless pal Colonel Bob Bauers magically showed-up on the scene and swiftly led a Delta Force commando raid into a brick residence across the street, the designated house situated at 474 High Street; and the well-trained military team was accompanied by a well-armed New Jersey SWAT squad. Together the units easily arrested a short thin fellow and quickly escorted the suspect out to a parked unmarked black police vehicle, which then rapidly sped away, dark tinted windows and all!"

Instead of explaining the crux of the sudden 'suspect apprehension', Joe Giralo then boringly and monotonously elucidated about how Burlington, New Jersey was a historic town, that General Ulysses S. Grant had *had* his family live there on Wood Street for safety reasons during the culmination of the Civil War, and how the small city was also a welcomed place called home to famous Revolutionary War era novelist James Fenimore Cooper, celebrated author of classic American literature works such as *Leatherstocking Tales* and *The Last of the Mohicans.*

"But Boss, you've lost me somewhere in transit!" Sal Velardi nervously interrupted his all-too-garrulous mentor. "What factor does James Fenimore Cooper along with his former 457 High Street home have to do with finding and taking the elusive Puzzler, I presume, into government custody? How did you ever narrow-down the computer thug's location to Burlington, New Jersey?"

"I had theorized from the Puzzler's e-mail riddle that his true identity would either have something to do with Williamsburg, Virginia because of the very deliberate 'orange' allusion, or his operating base would have something to do with a 'barrel'. And because of my ever-dwindling annual budget, I didn't have enough men available to also send to Niagara Falls, to Cooper Hospital down in Camden or to Cooperstown, New York, the traditional home of the Baseball Hall of Fame. Incidentally Sal," Inspector Giralo paused and then orally deviated, deliberately extending his prolific monologue, "Cooperstown, New York had been named after James Fenimore's religious father, William Cooper. The aspiring novelist had lived most of his life in his native Cooperstown. Actually Men," Giralo elaborated, "*that* unique relationship of 'Cooper' with 'Cooperstown' happened to be the vital first step leading to *our* putting the cuffs on a certain Mr. Thomas Cask, otherwise recently known to FBI law enforcement as 'The Puzzler'."

"But Chief," a very frustrated and animated Arthur Orsi remarked, "what does this elusive trouble-making character Thomas Cask have to do with the James Fenimore Cooper House? Your nebulous accounting makes me feel dumber than a full sack of heavy rocks!"

"It pays to know and be influenced by American literature. That's how I'm aware of the works of James Fenimore Cooper and his early American hero, Natty Bumppo. I also owe my so-called psychic ability to Mr. Edgar Allan Poe's dark story, 'The Cask of Amontillado'," the well-rounded Inspector communicated to his still-stunned audience of three. "As you might know, Amontillado is a rare Italian wine, and a *cask* is not exactly a hogshead, but rather it's a sort of tightly sealed barrel used for storing and keeping wine until it's ready for consumption!"

"Now you've really stimulated my interest!" Agent Blachford aggressively stated. "But how did you ever equate the idea of a wine cask with James Fenimore Cooper and this repugnant electronic computer file thief, Thomas Cask!"

"That's quite elementary Dr. Watson!" Inspector Giralo replied, poorly imitating the legendary Sherlock Holmes. "As you know, I absolutely love etymology, the academic study of the origin of words. In colonial times, a *cooper* was a barrel maker, just like a tallow chandler was a soap and candle craftsman. Hence," the long-winded Inspector continued his comprehensive video lecture, "the existence today of last names like Carpenter, Chandler and Cooper populate our home telephone books. And when the self-indulgent Puzzler mentioned 'having me over a barrel' in his last tricky communication, my hungry mind instantly connected the word 'barrel' with the word 'cooper' with the word 'cask'. And when I instinctively executed a computer search of former federal employees' names, I soon uncovered that...."

"That this slick computer hacker, the pernicious Puzzler, had been a disgruntled former NSA employee who had become infected with vindictiveness because the jerk had been fired from his government job," hypothesized and offered Agent Velardi.

"Exactly Salvatore!" verified Joe Giralo. "And then this avaricious and inventive criminal Thomas Edison Cask, alias the now-jailed Puzzler, effectively recruited other disenfranchised former government and corporate computer systems' experts, all

16

hired to practice their illicit acts in the four separate U.S. Time Zones."

"Phenomenal and staggering, both in scope and sequence!" marveled and expressed Agent Orsi. "But Boss, I can't neglect citing my suspicion that you're at least partially psychic!"

"Truthfully Fellas'," Inspector Giralo courteously and modestly replied via the closed-circuit network video screens, "if I'm at all psychic in this particular FBI Puzzler episode, I owe it all to the venerable Edgar Allan Poe, to the illuminating James Fenimore Cooper, and finally, I owe it to my tough-minded high school English teacher who made me suffer through excessive grueling research on common word etymologies, Mr. Tom Alvino!"

"The Attic Television"

On *New Year's Eve*, December 31, 2001, John Peter Walker was celebrating his forty-eighth birthday with a bottle of his favorite scotch, *Johnny Walker Red*. The brand name of his most preferred whiskey had been chosen for consumption as equally by coincidence as it had by design. When on required business trips *Johnny Walker Red* was the introverted tycoon's most requested "on the rocks" drink in bars from Miami Beach to Honolulu. The tycoon was certainly addicted to that specific brand of whiskey.

John P. Walker was the richest man in Hammonton, and perhaps the wealthiest investor and entrepreneur in all of southern New Jersey. His good fortune all started with the acquisition of the family's road-paving materials' patent, which eventually led to lucrative contracts and enormous royalties from other area, national and international asphalt contractors. John's deceased father had acquired and owned the road sealant patent, but since the company founder had focused his energies on the day-to-day operations of his business the elder Walker never pursued the exclusive formula's economic potential. By 1990, John Peter Walker had taken over the firm and had amassed sufficient capital to finance a small army of equipment to honor major road-surfacing contracts all over the tri-state *Delaware Valley* region.

'Dad would've been mighty proud and happy about my many accomplishments,' Walker thought about his deceased benefactor as the son liberally poured several ounces of premium scotch over a glass containing four ice cubes. 'I've parlayed my father's small paving business into a financial monster having no serious rival firms within a thirty-mile radius of Hammonton. It's too bad you and mom didn't live to see *my* great success,' John P. Walker lamented as he raised his glass to his lips, respectfully saluting an oil portrait of his deceased parents on the mansion's den wall. Then the highway-paving mogul slowly sipped the rich whiskey, savoring its unique taste. 'Yes Dad and Mom,' the young man sincerely acknowledged, 'I'm grateful for my inheritance and I promise I'll be diligently pursuing the company's excellent reputation until the day I die!'

A rapping at the walnut-paneled den's door was followed by the entrance of Giles pulling a handle and Hillary pushing the rear of a metal squeaky-wheeled cart having an ancient table-model television on its top.

"Where should we leave it Mr. John?" Giles Wood, Walker's faithful butler politely asked his rather eccentric and presently apathetic employer.

"Next to that far wall near the electrical socket," Walker pointed and answered rather imperatively. "Right in front of that shelf of rare books."

"Don't tell me Sir that you plan on watching this old rather obsolete contraption?" Hillary Wood, the loyal Walker' maid jested. "This thing is as old as *you* are. In fact, it *is* exactly as old as you are!"

"You don't say," John P. Walker lazily replied. "Then that bulky museum piece would've had to be manufactured in or around the remarkable year 1954," he added realizing the unique parallel.

"That is correct," Giles affirmed with absolute certainty. "It was manufactured the same year *you* were born, exactly forty-eight years ago. What a curious coincidence! But I'm afraid that this antique has seen better days."

"They don't make *Emersons* any more," Walker seriously interrupted. "If I recall from my childhood this particular unit was one of *that* company's most popular items. It has a twenty-one inch bowed screen with a control panel on the left," the mansion owner recollected and related. "And I still vividly remember this relic from when I was a kid sitting on my Daddy's knee. My God Giles and Hillary, time marches on, doesn't it?"

"Many brand names have gone out of business since then in the television market," Giles recollected and mentioned. "Besides *Emerson*, I remember TV sets with extinct names like *Muntz, Philco, DuMont* and *Admiral*. Those TV products have all gone the way of the *Edsel, the Hudson* and the *Packard* in the post *World War II* automobile industry."

The very wealthy man contemplated his fleet of thirteen classic cars parked in a huge garage recently added onto his impressive mansion, one of which was a mint-condition '54 brown *Packard*. His reverie was interrupted as the conversation continued.

"And Mr. Walker," the maid courteously stated, "it was very kind of you to donate this exquisite *Emerson* television to the Hammonton Historical Society Museum. It's indeed a real collectors' item," Hillary Wood continued, "and it was only gathering a pound of dust up in the attic. My husband and I thoroughly cleaned it up from top to bottom before we carefully transported it to your den."

"That will be all for now," John P. Walker thanked his servants before gulping down another mouthful of his favorite scotch. "Giles and I will take it over to the historical society on Wednesday. Tomorrow's *New Year's Day* and I guarantee you no one will be there to accept this noteworthy treasure from the '50s. Giles," Walker continued his reminiscence, "do you remember us watching shows like *Ed Sullivan, Jackie Gleason, Milton Berle, Jack Benny* and *I Love Lucy* on this splendid device?"

"I most certainly do Sir," the straight-laced butler recalled, "and if my failing memory serves me correctly, we also had viewed many episodes of *Howdy Doody, Dragnet, The Life of Riley, American Bandstand* and *Ozzie and Harriet* too."

"*Ozzie and Harriet*," Walker indulgently laughed. "The perfect '50s American family. If only life today was as simple and laid back as it had been back in the nifty fifties. Of course," the multimillionaire continued prattling, "I've become filthy rich over the last dozen years," the road-paving baron boasted, "so I guess I can trade a little complicated existence and aggravation for a modern huge bank account. In the final analysis," Mr. John Peter Walker assessed, "the prospect of a prosperous and profitable 2002 doesn't seem that bad after all. Cheers to the *New Year*!" the wealthy fellow said as he lifted his glass.

"Anything you say Mr. Walker," Giles quite amiably agreed. "I must congratulate you! You must be a very intelligent man since you've made many clever strategic money decisions to expand the family' business in the last decade."

"Actually Giles, my decisions involved more luck than intellect," Walker reluctantly acknowledged to his butler. "It was more like being in the right place at the right time than anything else. But I want to thank you both for finding and bringing in this archeological artifact," the happy resident related. "Stop by after midnight and we'll celebrate the *New Year* by polishing-off the remainder of this fine bottle of scotch. See you both in about an hour right before the grandfather clock chimes strike twelve. And Giles," Walker said with a smile, "don't forget to grease those squeaky wheels on that metal cart."

"Thank you Sir and I promise you I won't forget," Giles pleasantly answered. Then the butler and his accommodating wife jointly exited the luxurious den.

John P. Walker was a self-confirmed recluse. He shied away from having close friends, thinking that they would be more interested in his prolific *Merrill Lynch Cash Management Account* than in the distrustful man's true companionship. There were hundreds of acquaintances in his computer e-mail address book, but his dependable friends could be counted twice on a thumb-less hand. 'A secret is only a secret when it belongs to me,' the slightly paranoid man reckoned. 'As soon as it is shared with one other person it's a secret in jeopardy.'

The self-made businessman poured another glass of delicious scotch and sat back on his cranberry-colored soft leather sofa. 'Materialism is great,' he thought. John P. Walker was tempted to grab his remote control and activate his large-screen television featuring stereo sound, but suddenly the middle-age gentleman felt a temptation to get up and casually saunter over to the early '50s *Emerson* set that was still situated on top of the squeaky-wheeled metal cart.

Then Walker chuckled as he had an inspiration. 'I'm going to plug this baby in to see if I could get more than static on the screen,' he laughed, placing his scotch drink on top of the convenient TV cabinet. 'I wonder if this antiquated thing still conducts electricity after sitting idle up in the attic for over forty years. I suppose I'll soon find that out!'

John P. Walker reached around the set and soon located the device's electric plug. Then he inserted the two-pronged object into the wall socket, meticulously turned the "ON/OFF" knob inside the control panel, adjusted the "rabbit ears" and impatiently waited to see if anything would happen.

In ten seconds the vintage *Emerson* TV's picture tube illuminated. John rotated the station selector to 1, noticing that the old set had thirteen channels on its dial. To Walker's delight and amazement, a news broadcaster appeared on the black and white picture tube. The mildly astonished man increased the set's volume on the control panel, lifted his scotch on the rocks from the top of the television cabinet and then returned to his soft cranberry-leather sofa.

"Why that's Douglas Edwards sitting behind a studio desk doing his nightly news program!" John P. Walker marveled and uttered. "This must be a '50s television rerun special or something," the viewer theorized and softly expressed. "That news show went off the air maybe thirty-five years ago, and Douglas Edwards is certainly now deader than a doornail, no doubt about it. Gee, nostalgia is a wonderful thing!" he said to no one but himself'. "Let's see what good old deceased Douglas Edwards has to report."

"In January news," Douglas Edwards began his broadcast, "the highly motivated Michigan State Spartans defeated the

22

UCLA Bruins in the annual *Rose Bowl Game* by a score of 28-10. The football extravaganza was played before a capacity crowd in Pasadena, California. Now moving on to some favorable economic news," Douglas Edwards said and paused as his hands shuffled to the next page, "*General Motors* has announced that the giant corporation is planning a one billion dollar retooling and expansion to its popular line of automobiles, which includes *Chevrolet, Pontiac, Oldsmobile, Buick* and *Cadillac*. In other jobs-related news," the serious-faced Douglas Edwards remarked, "on January 19th, the Senate will approve construction of the *St. Lawrence Seaway*. The new project is designed to..."

John P. Walker reckoned that he would step to the fascinating television set and perform an experiment by manually changing the channel. Returning to his soft leather sofa, the successful entrepreneur was more than surprised to notice that Douglas Edwards was also doing the news on Channel 2 as he had been presenting on Channel 1. Walker could not believe his eyes and his ears upon contemplating the bizarre phenomenon. The wealthy fellow settled into his comfortable seat, poured another generous measure of *Johnny Walker Red* onto the shrunken ice cubes in his glass, and started to imbibe more of the potent alcohol as he again scrutinized the black and white TV screen.

"On February 2nd of this year President Eisenhower officially disclosed for the record that the first hydrogen bomb had been detonated back in 1952 at Eniwetok Atoll in the Pacific," Douglas Edwards reported. "The bomb was extremely powerful, according to sources, and it..."

John P. Walker had again risen from the sofa and changed back to Channel 1 to test a theory that was swimming around in his half-intoxicated mind. The results of his effort proved rather disconcerting to his sense of rationality because the aforementioned Douglas Edwards broadcast was still in progress.

"In a special message to Congress," Douglas Edwards read from his teleprompter, which apparently was now functioning properly, "President Eisenhower today urged widespread modifications to the much-maligned Taft-Hartley labor law. It should be noted that our chief executive has staunchly advocated a return to flexible farm price supports."

The bewildered viewer switched back to Channel 2. Douglas Edwards was calmly reporting another pertinent event to his faithful American audience. "On February 23rd, Dr. Jonas Salk, the developer of a breakthrough serum against polio, administered injections of the vaccine to Pittsburgh school children. The inoculations are scheduled to continue for the remainder of the month and then the results will be evaluated throughout the course of the year," the news sole anchorman disclosed. "And now on the entertainment scene, *The Confidential Clerk,* a popular play by celebrated writer T.S. Eliot opened at New York City's Morosco Theater. The new *Broadway* production stars Claude Rains and Ina Claire as…"

'This is absolutely incredible!' John P. Walker imagined. 'Each channel seems to correspond to a different month in 1954. Channel 1 was January and Channel 2 is February. If my crazy theory is correct, Channel 3 will be March.' The man's head was dizzy from the shock of his stark observation and from the accumulative potency of the scotch whiskey.

Sure enough, Channel 3 was featuring the March 1954 news, so John Peter Walker tried twisting his neck first left and then right to shake out the loose cobwebs and to sober up a bit. Being thoroughly intrigued by the surreal mystery his eyes and mind had been interpreting, the extremely puzzled fellow returned to the comfort of his fine leather sofa.

"On March 1st," Douglas Edwards professionally indicated, "five Congressmen were shot by Puerto Rican Nationalists on the floor of the *House of Representatives.* All five are recovering from their gunshot wounds. In sports," Edwards conveyed, "Tom Gola led the *LaSalle Explorers* of Philadelphia to the NCAA Basketball Championship in a spectacular and impressive 92-76 win over *Bradley*. And on March 25th," the broadcaster continued in his standard monotone voice, "an *Academy Award* was presented to *From Here to Eternity* as the best motion picture of 1953 and an *Oscar* was earned by William Holden for his best actor performance in *Stalag 17.* Switching back to domestic and international events," the news' personality very deliberately proceeded, "on March 25th President Eisenhower revealed that a hydrogen bomb explosion in the Marshall Islands had exceeded all military estimates and government expectations. The blast definitively proved that the United States is ahead of Russia in the nuclear arms research and development race."

Being absolutely captivated with what his' mind was processing John P. Walker again stepped to the very extraordinary *Emerson* television and abruptly twisted the selector dial to Channel 4. The perplexed man poured another few ounces of *Johnny Walker* and mechanically chugged the whiskey down the hatch. 'Douglas Edwards was on the air even before Walter Cronkite!' Walker marveled and evaluated. 'This whole weird

24

thing is some sort of exceptional paranormal experience. It's too fantastic to be a clever prank or a practical joke!'

"On April 16th," Douglas Edwards announced with a stoic expression on his now-familiar countenance, "the *Detroit Red Wings* defeated the *Montreal Canadiens* in the Stanley Cup finals, four games to three. *Motor City* ice hockey fans enthusiastically celebrated the team's victory by…"

John Walker had again risen from his soft leather sofa and aggressively flicked the dial to the left back to Channel 3 to determine if the March of '54 news was still in progress. "On March 10th," Douglas Edwards said, "federal officials divulged that the Atomic Energy Commission approved plans for the *Duquesne Power Company* of Pittsburgh to construct the first nuclear power electric generating plant. The new facility is scheduled to go from drawing board to…"

The now-inebriated viewer hastily flicked the channel rotator forward from position three to four, or from March to April. John P. Walker staggered back to his seat very confounded by what his normally reliable five senses had been receiving and the astounded viewer was quite perplexed by what his' confused mind had been comprehending and reviewing. His common sense told him to deny all that was being perceived.

"Congress has authorized the construction of the *United States Air Force Academy*," Douglas Edwards confidently reported, "and it will be a first class institution that will rival similar military academies at West Point and at Annapolis. The site of the new school will be somewhere in Colorado, but the exact location will not be made public by the federal government until two months from now in early June."

The now-drunk and annoyed tycoon got up and switched to Channel 5 and then slowly trudged back to his comfortable leather den couch. He incredulously glanced at his quart bottle of *Johnny Walker Red*, which was now only half' full. The peeved and neurotic observer once again plopped down into the soft center cushion of his cranberry-colored sofa. The mentally disheveled fellow again reached over and filled his glass with whiskey and then blankly stared at the classic television situated directly before his eyes.

Douglas Edwards was peering into the camera at his loyal 1954 nightly television audience. "The big news in May is that the U.S. Supreme Court in a landmark decision declared that racial segregation is unconstitutional in the nation's public schools. The practice of 'separate but equal', prevalent mostly in the American

South up to the present time, will no longer be a viable argument to prevent the creation of racial integration into our nation's public schools." The famous anchorman cleared his throat and then resumed his long-winded recitation. "Most of you viewers already know that the 80th running of the *Kentucky Derby* was won by *Determine* in a time of two minutes and three seconds. Jockey Ray York was aboard the victorious thoroughbred as it triumphantly made its way to the *Churchill Downs* Winner's Circle. *Determine* will now attempt to achieve horse racing's most coveted honor, the *Triple Crown.* The next difficult challenge after the *Derby* will be the *Preakness,* which later in June will be followed by the ever-popular *Belmont Stakes.*"

Wholly intoxicated, John Peter Walker awkwardly stood and clumsily approached the ancient electronic mechanism. The annoyed gentleman anxiously turned the selector to Channel 6. "Well now I'll review some more ancient history," he slurred and stated to himself. "It all seemed so damned important back in 1954 but now it all seems so terribly haunting, so ugly and eerie. I always suspected that Douglas Edwards was a stern charlatan back when I was a kid. Now I realize the idiot must be an evil sorcerer. What on Earth has happened to sanity?"

The befuddled and distraught asphalt merchant slowly shuffled back to his familiar soft leather sofa. He instinctively imbibed another mouthful of scotch as the 1954 June news appeared on the *Emerson* television screen.

"According to *Air Force* Secretary Harold E. Talbott," Douglas Edwards aptly stated, "the site of the new highly anticipated *Air Force Academy* will be Colorado Springs, Colorado. Elated government official gathered today, June 6th to officially make the public announcement before..."

John P. Walker predictably rose and rushed to the fifties' table-model television perched on top of the metal cart. He roughly rotated the knob counterclockwise to May. On Channel 5, Douglas Edwards blandly declared, "The 38th *Memorial Day Indianapolis 500 Auto Race* was won by Bill Vukovich, who achieved an admirable average speed of 130.8 miles per hour. It was Vukovich's second consecutive *Indy'* triumph. Congratulations Bill from all across America! And now on to some regular news."

The very groggy viewer still standing in front of the *Emerson* shook his head in total disbelief. A puzzled look remained on his face and his fingers quickly gripped and advanced the dial ahead to Channel 7 to review some of July's relevant events. Walker

26

slowly sipped his glass without ever thinking about adding fresh ice cubes, which had all partially melted inside of an opened metal ice bucket disguised as a medieval knight's helmet. In disgust, Walker slammed the ice bucket's knight visor shut.

Douglas Edwards' grim face and penetrating eyes nearly filled the black and white television screen and presently occupied the full attention of its somewhat hypnotized viewer.

"The '50s were a time of black and white," Walker mumbled and maintained to himself'. "Sneakers were black and white, television screens were black and white, camera pictures were black and white, newspapers were black and white and segregation was black and white. What the hell is going on here? Devil, show yourself!"

"On July 13th," the grim-faced news commentator prefaced his narrative, "the Gross National Product for 1953 was officially announced. The Department of Commerce indicated that the *GNP* was put at 365 billion dollars and that this hefty statistic illustrates the prosperity of a growing and thriving American economic system. On the sports scene," the highly rated announcer read from his teleprompter, "the world tennis championships at *Wimbledon* are scheduled to resume today in merry old England. Vic Seixas and Maureen Connally are the men's and women's' favorites respectively. The annual tournament is a highlight of each summer, and participants are honored to enthusiastically compete in the prestigious classic each…"

The addled disbelieving viewer again habitually rose from his comfortable sofa and stubbornly twisted his wrist to the left back to Channel 6. "The June calendar is highlighted by the annual running of the *Belmont Stakes*," Douglas Edwards matter-of-factly articulated, "and *High Gun* won the highly-contested event with jockey Eric Guerin proudly escorting his champion steed to the Winner's Circle. *High Gun* dramatically won the racing contest with an impressive time of two minutes and…"

John P. Walker desperately switched ahead to Channel 8 to investigate into 1954 August news. The perplexed viewer's patience and prudence were eroding as rapidly as his fading sobriety. He stood slumped over, awkwardly leaning against the metal cart that held the now despicable obnoxious-sounding heirloom *Emerson* table-model television.

"On August 9th," the famous news broadcaster asserted, "Cooperstown's *Baseball Hall of Fame* inducted nine new members. Topping the list of new inductees was…"

Walker disgustedly and vigorously changed the station to Channel 9. He dejectedly reentered his spot on the still comfortable leather sofa and sank down into the cranberry-dyed central cushion. His heart, mind and soul were in a total quandary. 'This whole damned thing reeks of evil,' Walker thought, 'and I don't have the will or the strength to fight it. I'm a hapless victim and nothing more,' the afflicted fellow concluded as he instinctively swallowed down another quantity of scotch.

"Back on September 6th Vic Seixas and Doris Hart respectively had won the men's and women's' divisions *of The U.S. Lawn Tennis Association Tournament*," Douglas Edwards reported and reminded the nation's viewers on Channel 9. "And today September 24, the *United Steel Workers of America* banned all communists, fascists and card-carrying members of the *Ku Klux Klan* from its ranks. In other national news," the commentator competently continued, "the *U.S.S. Nautilus*, the first atomic powered submarine is slated to be commissioned at Groton, Connecticut. On hand for the momentous occasion will be…"

John P. Walker had just enough strength to wobble across the palatial den to the *Emerson* table-model television and savagely advance the selector to Channel 10. He leaned against the metal cart to support his almost limp anatomy with his left hand while holding his half-full glass of scotch with his right.

"Our news department has recently learned that on October 13th, the much-heralded B-58, our nation's first supersonic bomber was ordered into production by the *Air Force*," the commentator related. "And yesterday, October 15th, *Hurricane Hazel* ravaged the eastern coastline causing widespread devastation and loss of life. The most violent hurricane in decades has killed ninety-nine persons in the U.S. and another two hundred and forty-nine in Canada. Combined North American property losses are estimated at over a hundred million dollars," Douglas Edwards glibly disclosed. "And finally, in the dynamic publishing world, the literary community is looking forward to this year's *Nobel Prize for Literature.* The leading candidate for the coveted award is reputed to be Ernest Hemingway, whose most renown literary contributions were the novels *The Sun Also Rises*, *A Farewell to Arms* and *For Whom the Bell Tolls*. The announcement will be made October 28th at the *Nobel Prize* headquarters in…"

The now totally inebriated American "new money aristocrat" stooped down and rotated the channel dial one notch to the right.

"I still remember hearing about that damned destructive *Hurricane Hazel*," he muttered to his scotch glass. "It blew the roof off of almost every flimsy house in the Hammonton area. And that overrated author Hemingway was nothing more than a mentally sick perverted alcoholic."

"In the November 2nd national elections," Douglas Edwards austerely articulated, "the Democrats gained a valuable additional seat in the *Senate* for a narrow-but-important 48-47 majority over the Republicans. Meanwhile, in the *House of Representatives,* on-a-mission Democrats gained twenty-one seats to establish a 232-203 majority. President Eisenhower expressed his disappointment at the outcome of this year's...."

"Who cares about damned 1954 politics?" John P. Walker angrily exclaimed. "It's as dumb an activity as religion is, and both subjects are unworthy of public discussion or debate," the intoxicated man mumbled as he emphatically twisted the television knob to the left back to Channel 10. "I already know what happened in 1954," the disgusted viewer mumbled and complained, again slurring his words.

"The fifty-first *World Series'* best of seven games was decisively won in a surprising four games to none victory by the *New York Giants*, who easily vanquished the favored *American League Cleveland Indians* despite Cleveland's supposedly superior and invincible pitching staff consisting of veterans Bob Feller, Mike Garcia, Early Wynne and Bob..."

The road paving *CEO* managed to regain his equilibrium, traipse to the "haunted" television and switch the selector ahead to Channel 11, where the November 1954 news was still being delivered. Walker gawked down at the television set with his mouth agape.

"Yesterday November 4th," stern-faced Douglas Edwards formally announced, "the much-acclaimed musical *Fanny* opened on *Broadway*. S. N. Behrman and Joshua Logan have written the show, which is expected to draw..."

Realizing that the ongoing phenomenon he was witnessing had been verified by checking and re-checking the monthly events on various channels, John P. Walker frantically rotated the television knob to Channel 12. The now-apprehensive skeptic retreated to his soft cranberry-colored leather sofa and with a trembling hand poured the remaining contents of the *Johnny Walker Red* bottle into his ice-less crystal glass.

"Now it's finally December of '54," the asphalt contractor neurotically stammered. "This ought to be interesting. It's the month I was born, exactly ten minutes before midnight of the *New Year*. In fact the exact time is right now," Walker observed as he reflexively glanced at the handsome gold-gilded clock positioned on the den's stone fireplace's Canadian oak mantel. 'Let's see what materializes!'

But then the all-too-worried mogul felt nauseous in his stomach. "I feel like vomiting," Walker realized and admitted as he stared at the empty quart of *Johnny Walker Red* and then peered at his empty crystal glass, both now situated on an adjacent den table. "I was a fool to drink so much scotch just because of this bogus bothersome television set," the multimillionaire confessed to himself.

Douglas Edwards seemed to be waiting for John P. Walker's undivided attention. Then the news broadcaster proceeded with the irrelevant December of '54 news items. "Senator Joseph McCarthy of Wisconsin was condemned by his colleagues in a special session for his misconduct during *Senate* committee meetings over the last several years. The flamboyant Republican *Senator* had no remarks to make to the press concerning his recent formal reprimanding. In military news," Douglas Edwards proceeded, "*the U.S.S. Forrestal,* the largest warship ever built at almost sixty thousand tons, was christened and launched at the famous Newport News, Virginia shipyard."

At the sight of a champagne bottle being broken to officially launch the *Forrestal,* the mere thought of any type of alcoholic beverage made John P. Walker upchuck sour stomach juices from his upper digestive tract, which he sloppily wiped from his mouth. Nothing could now distract his eyes and the man's total concentration, all of which were intensely focused on the 'evil 1954 *Emerson* television screen.'

"On December 26th," Douglas Edwards matter-of-factly stated, "the *Cleveland Browns* convincingly defeated the *Detroit Lions* in the *NFL Championship* game, thus giving the Ohio city a much anticipated sports' championship that had eluded the baseball *Cleveland Indians* in the recent October *World Series* extravaganza. *Browns* owner..."

Suddenly, the Emerson television screen went blank and then showed a series of alternating and fluttering horizontal and vertical lines. "What's goin' on?" John P. Walker moaned in his stupor. "This old set can't quit before it gets to my birthday! What about December 31st?" he mocked as his troubled eyes witnessed the incessant flickering. "Come on you damned thing! What's next? Don't give up now!"

An image appeared on the television monitor but it wasn't the countenance of newscaster Douglas Edwards. Instead, a familiar voice from the past resonated from the *Emerson's* primitive speaker. "Hello, this is John Cameron Swayze bringing you the *Camel News Caravan*, brought to you by *Camel* cigarettes. I'd walk a mile for a *Camel*," Douglas Edwards' contemporary rival news commentator remarked.

John P. Walker foamed from his mouth as more sour stomach digestive liquid spewed-up from his esophagus. The millionaire was in shock as his form slouched-down in his comfortable couch and his ears half-heartedly listened to the new anchorman's enunciation.

"Our news program is coming to you tonight over Channel 13," John Cameron Swayze related to his almost incoherent audience of one. "Just before midnight tonight, December 31st, 1954, a deformed baby showing signs of mental retardation was born to Joseph and Louise Walker at the Atlantic City Hospital," the anchorman reported with little emotion.

"That's impossible!" John P. Walker exclaimed and then hiccuped. "As you can plainly see, John Cameron Swayze, I'm perfectly fine! Hic! Don't try demeaning me! Hic!"

"Upon being taken home, the imperfect infant was immediately switched with the baby of Giles and Hillary Wood, loyal employees of Joseph and Louise Walker," Swayze reported. "As a result, Giles and Hillary Wood are the biological parents of John Peter Walker, and slow-learner' stable-boy Johnny Wood happens to be the sole legitimate son and heir of the now-deceased Joseph and Louise Walker, the former owners of the lucrative Walker Asphalt and Tar Company of Hammonton, New Jersey."

"What!" John P. Walker balked at what he considered false news reporting. "My butler and my maid are my parents?" he gasped. "This terrible secret has been kept from me for almost forty-eight years!" he vociferously screamed at the ancient Emerson TV. "And my poor mentally challenged lame stable-boy Johnny Wood is really supposed to be me, the original John P. Walker!"

John Cameron Swayze's all-too-sober black and white appearance then instantly dissolved upon the television screen. A moment of static and vertical and horizontal fluttering followed. Then the set mysteriously turned itself off.

At three minutes before midnight Giles and Hillary Wood entered the mansion's spacious den. Giles was carrying a bottle of vintage champagne to officially celebrate the arrival of the *New Year*. The pair immediately rushed to John Peter Walker's aid when they noticed his limp form slumped down upon the cranberry-colored soft leather sofa.

"My God Giles! What in the world has happened to him?" the maid yelled.

"There's no pulse! Hillary, there's no pulse I say!" Giles Wood shouted as he desperately felt his employer's wrists and throat. "He's dead! My God Hillary! I think he's dead!" Giles panted. "Either he had a massive heart attack or had choked on his own vomit! My God Hillary! He drank an entire quart of scotch!"

"Our son is dead! Giles! Our son is dead!" Hillary deliriously shrieked.

"Yes, and we have both kept this ugly secret for too many years. Hillary, did you hear what I said?" Giles anxiously asked. "We've kept this terrible secret for too many years! We had promised *his* parents never to tell it. And now this family tragedy has ended it all!"

"I'll call the rescue squad. Perhaps they can revive him," Hillary Wood suggested to her all-too-formal husband. "Maybe *he* is in such a drunken state that it seems like his heart isn't beating!"

"No Hillary, not yet. Don't call the paramedics just yet!" Giles insisted. "I first have something I feel I must do. Our future deserves to be secure after all we've been through!"

Giles Wood swiftly paced out of the luxurious room, down the majestic wood-paneled corridor to the mansion's mammoth library. He swiveled a portrait of Mr. Joseph Walker to the right, exposing the combination knob to a huge wall safe. Putting on his clean white gloves, the knowledgeable butler repeated the combination he had memorized over the years, "Thirteen-left, thirteen-right, and now thirteen left."

"Giles, what on Earth are you doing?" flustered Hillary Wood demanded. "You're committing grand theft when *we* should be calling the rescue squad!"

"Hillary, all these pathetic years we've sacrificed and toiled for absolutely nothing," Giles ranted like a madman. "Our own son, our own flesh and blood has paid us shoddy minimum wages to be *his* exploited butler and *his* private domestic maid. At least his substitute parents showed us kindness and generosity in helping us send *their* physically impaired and mentally deficient son to special schools," the butler argued. "And all these years *we* have not been justly and fairly compensated for raising *their*

32

lovable *Johnny* in the servant's cottage. And for the past thirteen years *we've* had to labor for the selfish whims of *our* own son, this pathetic egotistical dolt, who treated *us* as if we were illegal aliens or common area indigents."

"Giles, what *you* are doing is evil!" Hillary screamed, revealing a trace of her own guilty conscience. "Put the money back, I tell you. Giles, please put the money back in the safe!"

"The perfect crime!" Giles cackled as his hands held the stacks of hundred dollar bills that had been cached away in the concealed safe. "This is our retirement, Hillary. Our honestly earned retirement ticket to tropical climates, do you hear?" Giles laughed deliriously. "This is finally our just compensation for what the diabolical Walker family has done to our lives this past half-century!"

"What should I do?" Hillary begged her husband. "Should I call the authorities now?"

"Wait another ten minutes until I hide this cash in the servant's quarters," Giles cunningly advised his wife. "Then you can notify the rescue squad of Mr. Walker's untimely but warranted and propitious demise!"

"You mean of *our son's* demise," Hillary Wood sobbed.

"No Hillary, I meant Mr. Walker's demise!" Giles maintained. "No decent son would ever treat his parents like John Peter Walker has treated us these past miserable forty-eight years!"

"The Timeless Sports Car"

Henry Johnson was very content with his station in life. The man was a successful lawyer in his hometown of Hammonton, New Jersey and was looking forward to early retirement. Johnson had married his high school sweetheart Lois and the couple had three grown sons, Howard, Harry and Hugh. 'Howard is now ready to take over the family law firm,' Henry Johnson thought as he stepped out onto the Bellevue Avenue/Horton Street pavement from *his* Attorney Office, 'and Harry is a prominent doctor at *Jefferson University Hospital* in Philly. And young Hugh is a prominent real estate developer in Saddle Brook up in North Jersey. What more could a 59 year-old man wish for?'

Once a month Henry Johnson would meet two cousins Charles "Chickie" Sceia and John Fallucca for lunch at a different pre-determined area restaurant. The three "Amerigans" would traditionally converge on a familiar convenient eatery on the third Thursday and enjoy each other's company over burgers and frosted mugs of thirst-quenching draft beer.

'Last month's cousins' engagement was at the *Mill Street Pub* over in Mays Landing,' Henry thought, 'and today's lunch is at the *Great American Grille and Pub* in Hamilton Township,' the lawyer reminded himself as he sauntered to his tan *Lexus* parked around the corner on Horton Street. 'This time was *my* choice in the rotation so I know exactly where the restaurant is located. I can't wait to see Chickie and Johnny and discuss and solve the world's perplexing problems,' Johnson mused as he clicked the remote control mechanism unlocking his luxury automobile's driver-side door. 'I actually look forward to these once a month get-togethers.'

Henry Johnson steered his expensive car down Horton, made a right onto Orchard and then another right onto North Third Street. He stopped at the red traffic signal and proceeded straight ahead across Bellevue, and where Third merged with Central Avenue at the yellow-brick *Hammonton Middle School*, the driver then took Central to *Route 30*, the *White Horse Pike*. In another five minutes the suave sociable lawyer was on Weymouth Road heading toward *Route 322*, the *Black Horse Pike*. 'I've ridden this highway at least three thousand times and know every inch of it,' Johnson mused.

Fifteen miles east on "the Pike" toward Atlantic City was a shopping center across from the newly constructed ultra-modern

Hamilton Mall, and in that shopping center were various shops and stores all having the same attractive red brick façade, with one of the larger establishments being the aforementioned *Great American Grille and Pub.*

'Today we're scheduled to get together at 3:15,' Henry thought as he inserted a music disc into his dashboard panel and then listened to the *Billboard Top Rock 'n' Roll Hits of 1956.* '1956,' Henry imagined with a nostalgic smile. 'What a wonderful year! And what a horribly tragic year it was also!' the lawyer recalled.

The tan *Lexus* cruised past the huge *Atlantic Blueberry Company Farm, Mays Landing Division* on the right, and just before the sentimental '56 oldies *CD* finished playing its last selection, Henry maneuvered his well-equipped vehicle right off of *Route 322.* Then the hungry man made a sharp left turn and next drove behind an *I-hop,* a *McDonald's* and a *KFC* franchise. Soon Johnson was in the designated shopping center that featured a fine mixture of brick-façade stores, supermarkets and shops.

Henry checked his wristwatch and compared the time to the clock inside his fabulous car. '3:05,' he thought. 'I'll sit and wait here until Chickie or Johnny arrives. They're both usually pretty punctual, actually more punctual than pretty,' the good-humored fellow mused and chuckled.

It was a warm April 24 day, and as Henry listened to his '50s music and adjusted his air-conditioning a few degrees cooler, he recollected the significance of the particular date. 'Lois and I were married on April 24th,' Johnson fondly remembered, 'and then there was that tragedy, that terrible tragedy that I don't want to think about ever again.'

The fastidious lawyer raised the volume to his 1956 oldies' CD and then after recollecting the horrible catastrophe that had occurred on April 24th of that same unforgettable year, Henry Johnson quickly switched the CD mode to a more contemporary John Fogerty album, *Premonition.*

Henry again checked his watch (impatiently awaiting the arrival of either Charles "Chickie" Sceia or Johnny Fallucca) in a nervous reflexive response to alleviate his temporary emotional anxiety. It was now 3:15, and neither cousin's vehicle had entered the parking lot facing the designated *Great American Grille and Pub.*

'It's very unlike either of them to miss our monthly appointment,' Henry reckoned as he attempted to make himself more comfortable in his light brown leather driver's seat. 'My cousins are both dependable fellas'. Something is definitely wrong here! But I'm not going to panic!'

Afternoon shoppers pulled into and others exited parking spaces to the left and right of Johnson, who now wondered what was keeping his cousins from promptly showing up. 'I'll wait here until 3:20 and then enter the restaurant,' Henry considered. 'They might already be seated inside enjoying cold draughts. But where are their cars? Maybe they came together in a new car I'm not familiar with?' Henry hypothesized. 'And in the past we've always had the courtesy of waiting outside in our autos' so that all three of us could enter together!'

Five more minutes elapsed and Henry was now feeling more than a bit apprehensive. He climbed out of his tan *Lexus*, paced across the asphalt and soon stepped onto the shopping center's sidewalk. The slightly concerned man opened the front door to the popular restaurant but only two patrons were seated at the bar and other customers were occupying only three out of the four-dozen tables in the dining room. After glancing around the pub's interior several times, Henry felt awkward when he suddenly noticed the bartender and a curious waitress staring at him, so without initiating a conversation Johnson quickly abandoned the premises and shuffled back to the security of *his* tan *Lexus.*

'I'll wait here until 3:45,' Henry confided to his image in the rear-view mirror. 'It's so unlike either Chickie or Johnny to forget about our habitual monthly luncheon,' Johnson thought as he double-checked the date carefully written inside his monthly calendar book. 'I feel so stupid every time I call to remind them about the monthly late-lunch session. And Chickie and Johnny always tell me to remind my clients about court appointments and depositions and not to lecture *them* about honoring *our* monthly restaurant luncheons.'

3:45 arrived but cousins Chickie and Johnny had not. Henry Johnson reluctantly fired-up the tan *Lexus* sedan's engine, backed out of his parking space and soon was heading west on the *Black Horse Pike* back toward Hammonton. As Henry approached the landmark *Palace Diner* on the left, he was struck with a sudden inspiration. 'I'll call cousin Johnny on *his* cell phone and give him a good friendly reprimand for failing to remember the *Great American Grille* lunch engagement. I got to get this weird anomaly out of my mind so that I can think straight. I hope that nothing unexpected happened to them!'

The somewhat distraught driver punched in the appropriate telephone number on his cell phone, touched the "Send" button

37

and waited through three rings. Johnny Fallucca answered his portable cell phone on the fourth ring.

"Hello!" said the call's recipient.

"Johnny," Henry began in an imperative tone, "where the heck were you? I was parked outside the *Great American Grille* from 3:05 until 3:45, and neither you nor cousin Chickie showed up!" Johnson admonished. "I had always thought that you guys were supposed to be reliable mature adults!"

"Henry," Johnny replied with a degree of astonishment, "Chickie and I are sitting at the bar in the *Great American G*rille right now still waiting for *you* to show up. We're now feeling pretty happy nursing down *our* fourth frosted mugs. We were beginning to worry about you. From where are you calling? *Outer Space?"* Fallucca mildly chastised.

"That's impossible!" Henry ranted into his cell phone's specially installed overhead microphone attached to the driver's side sun-visor. "What time did *you* get there? And how long have you two clowns been sitting there?"

"Cousin Henny," Johnny amiably said, "we've both been sitting here at the bar since 3 p.m. waiting for you. Are you trying to pull some sinister trick on us? I think you're a little old to be playing silly high school pranks!" Johnny Fallucca joked. "Now what's the story from your end?"

"Believe me Johnny, I had entered the restaurant, looked all around, but only saw the lady bartender talking to two old gents that looked nothing like either you or Chickie," Henry maintained. "And there were only three tables occupied in the dining area, and neither you nor Chickie were in there. Did you guys ever get up and step to the *Men's Room* by any chance?"

"No! Never! Our kidneys are still in good condition," Johnny facetiously replied. "We were at the bar all the time and nowhere else. We figured we'd spot you right when you entered. You were right about one thing," Johnny told Henry. "There *were* two old geezers flirting with the woman bartender on the opposite side and she didn't like it one bit."

"Is this some sort of weird practical joke you two guys are playing?" Henry interrogated like the prosecutor he often was. "If so, it's not-too-funny and it's now very impractical and has worn out its impact!"

"Honest Henny, we're all mature grown men, related by common relative's blood and not inclined to play stupid juvenile pranks on one another," Johnny Fallucca declared as his voice shifted into a more serious tone. "Maybe it's time for *you* to visit your optometrist?"

"I'm sorry Johnny if I falsely accused you," Henry diplomatically apologized, "but where were your cars? They certainly weren't in the parking lot, or if they were," Johnson defensively continued, "I surely would've recognized them!"

"That's a mystery for sure," his cousin conceded. "They're parked in the lot as sure as Chickie and I are sitting and drinking at the bar right now!"

"Perhaps I really do need to have my eyes examined," Henry Johnson admitted to his honest and trustworthy cousin. "I'll schedule an appointment for early next week. I'm heading back toward Hammonton now and will see you fellas' Wednesday, May 22nd at 3:15 p.m. for a late lunch at *Sweetwater Casino* on the *Mullica River*. It's still *my* choice! And let's not mess this one up! Write it down right now!"

"Okay, I'll tell Chickie," Johnny lustily laughed. "Sweetwater Casino, Wednesday, May 22nd at 3:15 as usual. But why don't you just turn around and head back to the restaurant? It's no big deal, ya' know!"

"Thanks Johnny, but it's also my wedding anniversary and tonight I'm taking Lois and the three sons out to *Venice Plaza* over in Berlin to celebrate!" Johnson mentioned. "The place has a great gourmet chef so maybe it's a blessing in disguise for my delicate intestines that I'm missing a delicious lunch. I certainly don't want to over-exert my sensitive digestive system! Maybe a rain-check with you guys is in good order."

"All right Henny," Johnny chuckled, "go out with the family and have a terrific time. I'll tell Chickie here your very strange-but-entertaining story. And please tell Lois and the boys we said 'hi', and don't forget about May 22nd, 3:15 p.m. at Sweetwater. Don't mess up this time! See ya' cousin!"

"Bye Johnny and tell that occasional alcoholic Chickie I said 'hi'," Johnson jested and answered while shaking his head in disbelief at the very weird non-meeting that had recently been discussed over the phone.

Just as Henry Johnson pressed *End* on his car phone, he realized that he had gone straight in the fork in the road, and instead of veering off left taking County Road 559 toward Hammonton, he was now en route to the village of Elwood.

"Oh well, I guess a minor detour is just what I need to top-off a rather peculiar afternoon," Henry said to his aging silver-haired reflection in the rear-view mirror. "Maybe the hamlet of Elwood has blossomed into a major metropolis since the last time I've been there," the driver snickered. "I haven't traveled this back country hick road in many years even though it's only eleven or so miles from Hammonton."

The rather disgusted fellow tapped the dashboard *CD* indicator to change his music preference from John Fogerty's *Premonition* album back to the *Billboard Top Rock 'n' Roll Hits of 1956*. Dark storm clouds were observable to the west toward Philadelphia along with occasional lightning flashes and peals of thunder rumbling in the distance. Johnson raised the volume to his '50s music to escape his present emotional perplexity and then he mentally navigated back to the year 1956.

'I seldom take this remote road,' Henry thought. 'In fact I can't recall the last time I had, possibly it *was* as far back as 1956. Oh well, and I guess I just have to accept the inevitability of occasional April showers.'

The tan *Lexus* rounded a bend on the right and the first object that came into Henry Johnson's view was a magnificent white 1956 *Thunderbird* convertible with a splendid *Continental* wheel cover on its back. The impressive shiny classic sports car was situated on the front lawn of an old white bungalow that was in desperate need of several coats of paint, appearing to have been built during the *WWII* era.

"What a rare beauty!" Henry gasped as he slammed on the brakes. "It's got red interior just like the one I had wanted back in '56, but Dad quickly put an end to my fantasy by making me drive his black '53 *Pontiac* around Hammonton."

Henry carefully backed up his tan *Lexus* in order to gain a better inspection of the marvelous white vintage automobile that appeared to be in mint condition. A handwritten poster attached under the left windshield wiper blade read "Like New: Only $20,000.00!"

The clever lawyer clambered out of his luxury vehicle to admire the white relic from *his* past. 'I've got to have this baby!' the examiner covetously thought as he stuck his fingers inside the convertible's interior and touched the well-preserved red leather upholstery. 'I couldn't own it back in '56 but I sure have the means to acquire this great roadster now!'

An old farmer in a checkered red and black flannel shirt and grimy blue jeans came ambling out to greet the prospective customer. "Howdy Mister!" the elderly whiskered gentleman said. "I'm Brent Wagner, the owner of this here perfectly reconditioned *T-bird*. Isn't it a beauty!"

40

"Sure is!" Henry marveled and concurred. "I really wanted one of these bad when I was a rambunctious teenager. Trouble was that my dad was a very frugal practical man, even though he could've easily afforded to purchase one for me. I'm not quite as economical as my Pop was."

"Well son, if you're that interested, ya' can have it for a mere twenty thousand," the old farmer stated. "And that's a real bargain, yes sir-eeee it is! This honey's only got seventy-three thousand original miles on it. Belonged to my brother-in-law who left it to me in *his* will," Brent Wagner emphasized. "Now I have no use for this classy toy so I figured I'd convert it into quick cash to spruce-up my dilapidated bungalow a bit."

Henry walked back to his tan *Lexus*, reached inside and shut off its engine. His desire was to negotiate a lower selling price to claim his heart's desire. 'I'm going to buy this *T-bird* if it's the last thing I do!' the man mentally promised his greedy eyes. 'Maybe I can haggle the old gent down a bit!'

The elderly man pulled a toothpick from his toothless mouth and uttered, "Say stranger, I'm gonna' start the engine up and you'll notice that this here baby purrs like a happy kitten. Still got a lot of zip, too, I must admit!"

"I'll give you eighteen thousand dollars for it right now!" Henry offered. "I'll gladly write you out a check for that amount right this minute! I always pay everything by check for obvious income tax purposes. That's why Mr. Wagner I always have my checkbook readily available."

"Wait a minute!" the shrewd old codger replied. "I wanted cash on the barrel-head, not a damned check! The *IRS* will take me to the cleaners with a check, yes they will!" Brent Wagner argued. "If ya' want to pay by check, the price is twenty-five thousand to allow for federal taxes."

"If it will start and can be driven, I'll give you twenty-five thousand," Henry reluctantly responded with a trace of regret in his voice for compromising *his* already set purchasing price. But in his heart, Johnson aptly knew that money was no object in realizing his fondest and grandest teenage dream come true.

The old gentleman entered the car, reached into his pocket and removed a set of keys on a ring, one of which he inserted into the ignition. With one twist of his right wrist, the white *Thunderbird* started up and sounded as good as new.

"I'll take it!" Henry enthusiastically consented as he watched lightning flashing and heard thunder rolling to the west in the direction of Philadelphia. "You certainly drive a hard bargain Mr. Wagner! I must say!"

"How do I know that this here check you're gonna' cut me isn't gonna' bounce?" the old man challenged. "I've been burned several times before with lesser amounts!"

"Because I'm a lawyer in Hammonton and I have a family name and a good personal reputation to maintain!" the attorney argued. "I can't afford to write a bogus check because then my last name would be Mud instead of Johnson."

"Johnson? Hammonton lawyer! I've heard of you," the old farmer acknowledged with a forced grin. "Ya' do have a good name around these parts, I'll admit to that. Show me your driver's license with your name and address on it and then I'll reluctantly sell this here precious jewel to ya'!"

Henry Johnson showed old Brent Wagner *his* bona fide New Jersey driver's license, which matched the identity the lawyer had originally claimed to be. The elated old backwoods resident stuck his head inside the sports car and opened the passenger side hatch and inserted a second key into the T-bird's glove compartment and then he removed the automobile's "Bill of Sale." "I was comin' out here to shut the windows just when ya' stopped because it looks like rain coming this way!" Brent Wagner informed Henry.

Henry Johnson was quite familiar with the transition of a standard car ownership document, and after the men signed the required signatures in the appropriate places, the deal had been officially consummated. Henry then wrote out a check for the prescribed amount to the now-ecstatic Brent Wagner, and the two men shook hands to recognize and verify the transaction.

"Ya' gonna' come back and pick it up?" the seller asked his euphoric new-found customer.

"Why yes," Henry confidently indicated. "I'll return later this afternoon with one of my sons and we'll pick it up and take it back to Hammonton. It'll be a glorious anniversary surprise for my wife Lois."

Henry eagerly walked the fifteen feet to his tan *Lexus,* opened the driver's side door and entered his distinctive automobile. Upon turning the ignition key, for some remote reason, the electrical system did not respond. Henry tried five times to start the engine but his efforts were to no avail.

The dismayed lawyer exited his auto' and noticed that Brent Wagner was still watching him. "These new cars and their sophisticated computer systems," Henry moaned to the backwoods shack owner. "Sometimes I think that modern technology is actually going backwards."

"I know exactly what ya' mean!" Brent Wagner attested. "Give me a four-barrel carburetor with a *V-8* engine any day over this here fancy fuel-injection *V-6* stuff! I ain't never had no problem with this here *T-bird* nor with my '53 *Chevy* parked behind the house. Say Mister," Brent continued, "how would ya' like to leave your *Lexus* parked on my lawn and drive the *T-Bird* home. Then you and a mechanic can return here and tow your fancy machine back to Hammonton."

"Terrific idea," agreed Henry. "I'll be able to skirt the thunderstorms because I'll be heading northwest toward Elwood while the thunder and lightning seems to be going southeast toward Williamstown."

Brent Wagner neatly folded the twenty-five thousand-dollar check in half and gingerly placed it in the upper-left-pocket of his red and black checkered flannel shirt. The two men then pushed the tan *Lexus* onto the weed-infested unkempt front lawn as Henry Johnson guided its forward progress by vigorously turning the steering wheel to the right.

After the *Lexus* had been moved a safe distance off the country road and onto the unkempt lawn, the two men again shook hands. Johnson forgot all about his disabled *Lexus*, opened the *T-bird's* door and eagerly leaped inside. The now-mobile-again lawyer waved "goodbye" to the grateful old fellow as *he* pulled away heading northwest toward the hamlet of Elwood.

'This fabulous *T-bird* is timeless!' Henry thought as he watched the seemingly accurate speedometer needle rise up to fifty. 'It's just as beautiful and graceful in 2002 as it had been back in '56. I'll be the envy of everyone in town!'

Henry casually turned the sports car's radio knob to determine if the device still worked. He was both rewarded and shocked when his ears perceived the familiar voice of a Philadelphia *DJ* from the past, *his* past. Joe Niagra's baritone said, "Thanks for listening to *WIBG*, Philly's top rock and roll radio station, and the only boss sound in town. This rockin' bird is about to fly. Now here's a blast from the past, a knocked-out Niagra nifty! Here comes Bill Haley and the Comets singing and playing the teen *National Anthem*, 'Rock Around the Clock'."

'This has got to be a commercial or a cruisin' record promo' of some sorts!' Henry Johnson imagined. His eyes briefly glanced at the radio and observed that the dial was set on *AM 99*, the exact position of *WIBG*, Philadelphia back in the nifty '50s. 'This just *has* to be a flashback commercial,' *his* naturally skeptical mind again thought.

In total amazement, the baffled driver turned the radio knob and found a news broadcast in progress. "And in entertainment news," the baritone-voiced announcer declared, "*My Fair Lady*, a smash hit musical by Alan Jay Lerner and Frederick Lowe is proving to be a fantastic box-office attraction at the *Mark Hellinger Theater* in New York. The popular *Broadway* play is based on George Bernard Shaw's classic story *Pygmalion*, and the terrific new musical features talented stage stars Rex Harrison and Julie Andrews. In other national entertainment news, …"

Henry Johnson turned the radio dial and momentarily heard Carl Perkins singing *his* famous rendition of "Blue Suede Shoes," and then the disbelieving driver quickly rotated the knob to another news broadcast. "The *Marine Corps* has finally finished investigating the drowning of six recruits at Parris Island, South Carolina while a platoon was on a so-called 'disciplinary march. Sergeant Matthew C. McKeon has been convicted of drinking on duty and found guilty of negligent homicide. His rank has been reduced to *Private*. In other news," the radio announcer continued, "the *New York Coliseum* is scheduled to open on April 28th. The new *Coliseum* will indeed be the world's largest exhibition building, covering over nine acres at a phenomenal cost of over 35 million dollars. In other current news, Victor Riesel was blinded when…"

Henry neurotically turned the radio dial back to *WIBG Radio 99* and heard Joe Niagra gleefully shout, "And now here's Elvis Presley's smash-hit recording of the classic rhythm and blues number Heartbreak Hotel!" Henry listened to the song's familiar intro', and then turned the *T-bird's* dial to "OFF."

'This is impossible!' the highly alarmed driver evaluated. 'I must be caught in some kind of time vacuum, a puzzling time warp! There's definitely one way I can prove that my theory is correct and I'm going to test my idea.'

Henry drove his new white *Ford Thunderbird* convertible (with the top down) into downtown Hammonton, which to his astonishment was downtown Hammonton, vintage 1956. 'Oh my God!' Henry thought. 'There's *Godfrey's Drugstore* on the corner. That business disappeared in the early sixties, and over there is *J.J. Newberry's* five and ten, and *Miller's Department Store*, and all of the soda fountains I used to enjoy so much as a kid. And look, the *Rivoli Theater's* marquee is visible down the street, and *Fire Company #1* is still in the middle of town and not out on

44

Lincoln and Passmore Avenues! And all of the cars on Bellevue Avenue are 1956 models and earlier.'

The astonished driver steered his handsome *Thunderbird* to the right and onto Central Avenue. He parked his 'wheels' on the street outside of *Olivo's Supermarket* and ambled across Central to his favorite teenage hangout, the *Gem Burger Palace.* Seated inside booths and at the counter were carefree *Hammonton High School* students' eating burgers, chatting the latest gossip and listening to jukebox tunes. The boys were wearing their white and blue trimmed lettermen's sweaters and most of the girls were costumed in blue and white cheerleader uniforms with black and white saddle shoes while other looser and tougher-looking young females were wearing pink and black *Poodle* skirts.

As Henry's eyes scanned the very active teen' scene he noticed his future wife Lois gossiping with *his* best friend, Tommy Davidson and *her* best friend, head cheerleader Candy Taylor. And also congregated inside the hangout were Bob Simpson, Chet Douglas, Dave Jensen and Jim Parker, all teammates of Henry's on the fearsome *Hammonton High School* 1956 football team, but none of them recognized their good friend's bearded face and silver-haired middle-age appearance.

Henry's mind was in a state of complete bewilderment as he approached the main counter where several of his old chums were sitting on stools discussing various topics. Mr. Clyde Dawkins, the gem's proprietor asked Johnson where he had gotten the "strange light blue jeans" *he* was wearing.

"Oh," Henry said with a smile and a blush on his cheeks, "my Mom put them in the washing machine and they faded when she used too much bleach. Maybe I'm starting a new fad?" he joked. "What do ya' think?"

"You're still living with your mother?" Mr. Dawkins inquired and criticized shaking his head in mock disgust. "Why Mister, I think *you* look like you're about sixty years old!"

Henry heard his former high school friends Bob Simpson and Chet Douglas laughing on their main counter stools in response to Mr. Clyde Dawkins' typical sarcasm. Feeling embarrassed and a bit disoriented, Henry Johnson rushed out of the establishment and hopped into his newly acquired *Thunderbird* as he heard Jim Lowe's "The Green Door" blasting from the *Gem's* jukebox speakers.

"I need more verification of my new reality!" the mentally disheveled driver said to himself. "Either I'm cracking-up in a major mental meltdown or I *have* already cracked-up!" The time-traveler turned on the ignition and motored around the block to another familiar old Hammonton haunt where he had bought dozens of automobile magazines and comic books in his youth.

Henry parked his *T-bird* outside of *Dan's Stationery Store*, which in 2002 had the designation *Tapper's Stationery*. He briskly stepped inside the establishment and checked the date on the newspapers, and it was indeed April 24th, 1956. Johnson glanced at the saleswoman behind the counter and at a customer purchasing a pack of *Lucky Strike* cigarettes. "That will be thirty cents Mr. Flemming," the woman politely informed.

'Why that's Mr. Flemming the local electrician buying the cigarettes and the lady behind the counter is Mrs. Martha Merlino, Lois's aunt! Those people died in the 1970s! I even attended Mr. Flemming's and Aunt Martha's funerals!' Henry remembered. 'I really *am* back in 1956!'

Johnson exited *Dan's Stationery Store* in a hurry. The date April 24th, 1956 was now a nagging nightmare that had been lingering in the back of the man's now-boggled mind. Henry's father, Dennis Johnson had been killed at precisely 5:30 on that date on Moss Mill Road while changing a tire. He had been struck by a speeding tractor-trailer that had veered off the roadway. 'If everything else is correct in this inexplicable time warp, I have more than enough time to make it to Moss Mill Road and save Dad!' the time traveler reckoned while intensely scrutinizing his wristwatch.

The driver of the '56 *Thunderbird* sped around the corner to Egg Harbor Road, briefly stopped and then turned left. Henry's new old car zoomed past *Hammonton Lake Park* where a *Little League* game was in progress and then turned left again onto Moss Mill Road. Soon Johnson had crossed the *White Horse Pike* (which now in 1956 had a 'Stop Sign' and no traffic light) and was instantly heading east toward Egg Harbor City.

When the auto's speedometer registered fifty-six miles an hour, the dashboard lights automatically and mysteriously flicked on and the time clock coincidentally indicated that it was nearly five p.m. 'I still have a half-hour to rescue Dad!' Johnson hypothesized. 'If I act quickly, I can save *his* life! I *will* save his life!'

Henry mashed his foot down on the accelerator and the *T-bird* responded with an swift burst of power. The driver recalled the year 1956, and a newsreel of events paraded through his unsettled mind as he sped east. Besides his father's accidental death, Henry had graduated *Hammonton High School* and had been accepted at

46

the *University of Pennsylvania's School of Law.* He had been aggressively dating Lois Morgano and the two had expected to be married in April of 1960.

'I still have plenty of time to prevent the accident,' the owner of the marvelous time-vehicle evaluated. 'I want to get the tire changed before that tractor-trailer arrives or before that thunderstorm on the western horizon hits Moss Mill Road.'

As Henry Johnson nervously drove further down the two-lane county highway he recalled that Dennis Johnson had only been thirty-eight years of age when *he* had met *his* tragic death. 'Dad would be eighty-four if he were still alive,' the determined son concluded. 'I'll make sure that *he* lives to see that age!'

Up ahead on the right a black '53 *Pontiac* sedan was situated on Moss Mill Road's right-hand shoulder. A middle-aged gentleman in a dark blue business suit was preoccupied jacking up the left rear-wheel. Henry halted his immaculate white *Thunderbird*, shut off the motor and got out to render his benign assistance. Saving his father's life was paramount in the time-traveler's mind.

"Hello," Henry greeted his beleaguered father. "I'll help you get that tire changed in a jiffy. You're in a business suit and I'm sure you don't want to get any grease or grime on it!"

"Why thank you Sir," Dennis Johnson answered, not recognizing his oldest son sporting a beard, mustache and a distinguished middle-aged appearance. "My oldest son wants a white *T-bird* just like yours," Mr. Johnson related. "I don't think he's quite ready to have such a fancy car yet, if ya' know what I mean. I don't want to spoil any of my sons by giving them what they can't actually afford to buy on their own!"

"I understand completely," Henry stated. "I had to work long and hard to get the money to purchase *my* new car. Tell your son it's well-worth having and saving for."

Henry picked up the lug-wrench off of the ground and loosened the nuts holding the tire to the wheel. Then he methodically jacked the black *Pontiac* up to the desired height, removed the rim's lug nuts and pulled the deflated tire off the wheel.

"Ya' sure know what you're doing," Dennis Johnson sincerely complimented. "I hope that all three of my sons grow up to be just as helpful and as courteous as you are!"

"One thing's for sure," Henry joked. "A flat tire's only flat on the bottom. But I'm sure your sons will grow-up to be fine outstanding citizens," Henry assured his appreciative listener.

"Apples and acorns don't fall far from the family tree! Are you on your way to a business meeting?"

"Yes, as a matter of fact I am," Mr. Dennis Johnson answered. "I'm goin' to Egg Harbor City for the *Atlantic County Bar Association's* annual dinner meeting. My wife has a *Civic Association* meeting over in Hammonton, so I'm goin' alone. Good thing she's missed all this flat tire aggravation! All because of one lousy misplaced nail I suppose!"

Soon Henry had the spare tire (that his father had already taken out of the trunk) onto the rear wheel. He placed and then tightened the new rim's lug nuts onto the corresponding protruding bolt threads and after lowering the black *Pontiac* to the road's shoulder, he finished tightening up the lug-nuts using the tire iron.

Severe lightning began flashing to the west over downtown Hammonton, so Dennis Johnson figured he'd lift the damaged tire and deposit it inside the automobile's trunk.

Suddenly a speeding tractor-trailer came loudly rumbling around the bend and Dennis Johnson yelled for the helpful middle-age citizen to "Get out of the way!" The driver of the gigantic truck blasted *his* air-horn and heavily applied the brakes. The enormous rig's tires screeched on the highway's asphalt as its air brakes locked.

Henry Johnson stood petrified for a moment and then attempted jumping out of the path of the oncoming monstrosity. The tractor-trailer's right front fender clipped the victim and then the *Good Samaritan's* body hurtled over the black *Pontiac* and landed twelve feet away inside the fringe of a pine forest.

A Hammonton ambulance arrived twenty minutes later and transported the unfortunate highway helper to *Atlantic City Hospital.* The victim was pronounced dead and the attending doctors on duty reported to newspaper journalists that the man had sustained multiple injuries that had caused massive internal bleeding.

* * * * * * * * * * * *

On April 24th, 2002 Dennis Johnson, an eighty-four-year-old retired attorney made a wrong turn after leaving the *Black Horse Pike* not far from a traffic light adjacent to *Palace Diner.*

"Dennis," his wife said, "you should have turned left at the fork and gone back to Hammonton. Now you're going to wind-up in Elwood."

"Big deal Lois!" the stubborn elderly man gruffly replied. "So what if I missed the hypotenuse of the old right triangle! We'll just detour five miles out of our way, Lois. I seldom travel this back road. That's all we'll have to do to get to Elwood and then we'll take *Route 30* west to Hammonton. Anyway my dear wife, I really enjoy driving my new tan *Lexus*. Ya' know Lois," Dennis Johnson proceeded, "we don't have many more years left on this Earth to relish the wonderful material comforts life has to offer."

"You're so philosophical," the wife observed and commended. "You've always been that way, even in high school. I think that's one reason I married you!"

A mile ahead old Dennis Johnson observed a white '56 *Thunderbird* convertible with red interior parked on an unkempt lawn in front of an old wooden-frame country bungalow. The elderly driver immediately applied the brakes.

"Why are you stopping?" Lois Johnson asked her suddenly rejuvenated husband.

"Lois, our oldest son always wanted a white '56 *Thunderbird* but I was too stubborn to buy one for him. And once a stranger stopped on this very day in 1956 and helped me change a tire over on Moss Mill Road. The poor man was killed when he was hit by an out-of-control tractor-trailer just before a terrible thunderstorm hit. I'll never forget that violent accident Lois and I'll never forget that horrible afternoon!"

"You never told me about a man being killed!" the wife returned.

"I was so upset that I never found out his name from the police and never even called *his* family or attended *his* funeral," the elderly man informed his wife. "And I've felt guilty ever since that day."

"Then you're going to buy that beautiful white car?" the wife asked in a very surprised tone of voice.

"I sure am Lois," Dennis Johnson verified. "I sure am!"

"Parallel Developments"

Twin brothers Frank and Fred Davies were 1981 graduates of Hammonton High School, North Liberty Street, Hammonton, New Jersey 08037. From their early youth the twins were complete opposites both in demeanor and in physical prowess. Fred Davies was always an extrovert and a competitive athlete while his twin facsimile Frank had a shy personality genuinely punctuated with humility and modesty.

In June of 1987 Fred graduated from Philadelphia's *Temple University* with a law degree and Frank evolved out of New Brunswick's *Rutgers University* with a master's degree in biology research. In the fall of 1991 during a dual ceremony Frank and Fred ironically married twin sisters Lois and Eleanor Cataldi of Bridgeton, a large town situated twenty-four miles southwest of Hammonton.

In order to celebrate their fifteenth wedding anniversary Frank and Lois booked a Mediterranean vacation featuring two nights in Barcelona and a seven-day-cruise aboard the resplendent Regal Adventurer. Coincidentally, Fred and Eleanor (through the same travel agency) also made arrangements on a similar vacation aboard the Regal Adventurer, but the former couple's scheduled dates were Wednesday September 13th to Saturday the 20th while the latter pair's sailing dates were several weeks later from Wednesday, October 4th to Saturday October 11th.

"How come Fred and Eleanor aren't going to accompany us to Europe?" Lois asked her husband as they waited for the van to pick them up for the thirty-mile drive to *Philadelphia International Airport*. "Do we have leprosy or something?"

"Certainly not!" Frank politely answered. "My brother and I mutually agreed that we should take separate vacations touring Spain, the French Riviera and Italy. We thought it would be too confusing for everyone we met or communicated with by having two sets of identical twins. And besides Lois," Frank persuasively communicated, "you honestly don't get along too keenly with Fred and quite candidly I don't hit it off too well with my loudmouth sister-in-law, er, excuse me, with your twin sister. And I do believe Lois that the eight people we're traveling with will be more compatible with us than Fred and Eleanor will ever be. In the final analysis that's the bottom line!"

"I suppose I have to subscribe to the basic wisdom you've just expressed!" Lois confessed. "Here comes the van now zipping down the Pike approaching our driveway! Let's carry our four pieces of luggage from the front porch."

"And as you know Lois, Fred and I have different sets of friends," the husband emphasized and clarified. "And as a matter of fact so do you and Eleanor. Warren and Melissa Mottola are much more mellow and gracious than Fred and Eleanor will ever be. And I want this trip to be as relaxing and comfortable as possible without those two garrulous nitwits ruining every meal and every sidebar excursion on our hectic itinerary!"

"Yes my dear Husband!" Lois verified. "We seem to harmonize better with retired science teachers and their accountant wives than we do with relative lawyers and their flamboyant spouses. Warren is studious and academic just like you are," the wife maintained, "and Melissa is generally quiet and likeable. I guess it's because she's always concentrating with numbers and figures at work. That's why she and her soft-spoken husband aren't wild and crazy lunatics like Fred and Eleanor are!"

The cranberry-colored van pulled into the two-story gray colonial home's U-shaped driveway and halted right where the cement walk bordered the asphalt driveway. Immediately the driver hopped out of the vehicle and introduced himself.

"Hi, I'm Tom Dixon!" the man cheerfully greeted. "Why don't you two hop into the van and join your friends! I'll take care of loading your bags into the back storage compartment."

"Thanks!" Frank politely acknowledged. "You look trustworthy enough Tom! It's great to see that courtesy hasn't gone completely out of fashion! My wife and I appreciate your fine gesture!"

Frank and Lois were immediately welcomed by Warren and Melissa Mottola, who were seated near their pretty office manager daughter Lisa and her handsome fiancé David Winters, a young and serious corporate jet pilot. Other passengers in the enormous cranberry van were Jimmy and Joanne Valerio, a construction contractor and an accountant respectively with Joanne being employed in the same CPA's office as Lois. Rounding out the party of ten Europe-bound-Americans were Dr. Rose Jeffries (an infectious disease specialist at Camden's Cooper Hospital) and her new-found friend Judy Marks, a comptroller for a large automobile agency in Marlton, New Jersey. Soon after Tom Dixon had carefully arranged the new baggage in the van's rear, he re-entered the vehicle, slammed the door shut, fastened his seat-belt and casually started-up the engine.

The thirty-mile drive from Hammonton to Philadelphia was quite pleasant. The late summer scenery still displayed deciduous trees with ample green leaves about to assume their predictable autumnal hues. The men's conversation focused on the latest professional baseball and football scores and the rising stock market while the ladies preferred exchanging dialogue on the best clothes to take along on the trip and the various sights to be explored on the general itinerary. In a short forty-five minutes the van stopped in front of the *U.S. Airways* terminal in the newly renovated section of *Philadelphia International Airport*.

After paying Tom Dixon the appropriate fee and tip for his vital services, the ten passengers hired a skycap to transport their twenty pieces of luggage inside to the *U.S Airways* ticket counter. That particular procedure was conducted rather expeditiously and after the necessary passports and photo' ID's were officially checked, five minutes later the ten anxious travelers passed through the airport's tight security check.

"I hate being treated like a terrorist!" Lois complained. "But Frank, you're so mild-mannered that it's just like water off a duck's back to you."

"Why get upset with taking your shoes off and having them scanned along with your other personal belongings?" the husband passively accepted and stated. "Why become neurotic about what you can't change! And since everyone flying out of 'Philly has to go through the same process, it's perfectly tolerable! After all Lois, we're not being discriminated against!"

"Sometimes you're so soberly philosophical!" the wife sincerely complimented. "That's one reason why I was so attracted to you when we first met at that wild party in Atlantic City! I really admired your calm disposition!"

"I'll try not to talk too much on the seven-hour flight to Barcelona!" the husband bantered tongue-in-cheek. "And I'll speak even less on the grueling eight-hour trip on the way back!"

"I can't believe we're actually going to Europe!" Lois jubilantly exclaimed. "I mean I've read about it in high school textbooks and in encyclopedias," the spouse marveled and said, "but now it's like a dream come true! Let's make the most of it! It might be a once in a lifetime opportunity!"

"Yeah Honey!" the normally laconic husband readily concurred. "After going eight times to the Caribbean and twice to both San Diego and Las Vegas, this long jaunt sort of represents a departure from the ordinary. Outside of a cruise boat stop in

Caracas, Venezuela, this is really only our second removal from the North American Continent. I hope we have a smooth flight!"

"I checked the forecast on the *Internet*," Lois assured, "and it's going to be clear skies all the way to Barcelona except for an hour of mild turbulence. I can't wait to leave the New World for the Old! Maybe next time we can do Madrid, Paris, London and Berlin instead of Barcelona, Marseilles, Rome and Naples!"

"Anything you say Lois! Anything you say!" the husband reiterated. "And just think! Thanks to modern-day airport security we only have to wait two hours before we finally board our wonderful airplane! We're scheduled to take off at 5:45 p.m. and then finally arrive in Spain at…."

"At approximately 7:45 a.m.!" Lois alertly finished Frank's sentence. "Already we're trapped in a time warp and soon destined to suffer significant jet-lag! But don't worry! We have the rest of our lives to recuperate!"

"You should do stand-up comedy even when you're sitting down!" Frank mused and expressed. "Now let's interact with our eight friends before they receive the impression that we're both anti-social in addition to being extremely introverted!"

The seven-hour flight from Philadelphia to Barcelona was *not* interrupted with an hour of rough air pockets (as Lois had predicted from reading various weather reports) and a two-hour movie, random magazine scrutiny and a decent chicken and rice meal had sufficiently distracted the passengers from their lengthy confinement and overall travail. A weak drizzle awaited U.S. Airways Flight 948 when it finally touched-down and landed on its destination runway on Spain's eastern coast.

The passengers had to be transported by bus from the tarmac to the Immigration and Customs Terminal, an adventure *not* characteristic of most major big-city U.S. airports. *That* specific inconvenience was followed with an hour-long-delay while waiting for the passengers' baggage to arrive on the Barcelona terminal's luggage carousel.

"I hope that this isn't indicative of the remainder of our tour," the usually reticent Frank Davies remarked to Jimmy Valerio. "I suppose it's true that we Americans are quite spoiled and too used to instant gratification."

"Yeah Frank!" Jimmy nodded and confirmed. "It could be said that Americans are like wristwatches, always thinking 'Get-there, get there,' while many Europeans are like grandfather clocks practicing the mantra 'Take your time, take your time!' Maybe we'd be happier with pacifiers in our mouths!"

"It's only 8:45 a.m.," an eavesdropping Warren Mottola reminded his male companions. "We have all day to squander if we ever escape this suitcase acquisition and retrieval area."

"You're absolutely right there Warren!" Frank diplomatically commented. "But I insist that it's over three-hours too early for the old Spanish noon-to-three siesta tradition. And as you've so appropriately suggested Warren, let's act like amiable and cooperative tourists rather than as typical dissatisfied and ultra-critical picayune Americans."

At last the luggage carousel was activated and the tired but now-rejuvenated Flight 948 new arrivals anxiously grabbed their suitcases from the rotating black belt slats. The multilingual Barcelona Customs personnel were friendly and professional in processing the several hundred folks through the initial security screening. After obtaining five luggage carts at the end of the "Immigration responsibility," the party of ten Americans hired a driver and a van to convey them to the Apsis Atrium Palace Hotel at 656 Gran Via de les Corts Catalanes, situated right in the heart of Barcelona's most elegant downtown shopping district. The twenty-five minute drive through the city allowed the ten Americans to view and evaluate the Spanish metropolis and compare it to certain American cities cataloged in their mental repertoires.

"They seem to have massive congestion gridlock just like New York, L.A. and 'Philly!" Warren Mottola observed and said. "But I'm especially impressed with their highway system and the use of tunnels. And everything including the buildings and streets seems to be well-maintained and really clean."

"I particularly like the architecture and how the four buildings at intersections are at catty-corners and not at right angles to the streets like they are in cities back in the States," Jimmy Valerio contributed to the conversation. "That unique construction pattern automatically makes each intersection more open and visible. Barcelona seems to be an urban paradise with lots of parks, fountains, monuments and museums," the observant building contractor added. "I do believe that the Europeans take more pride in their cities than Americans tend to do with theirs. Driver, what boulevard are we now on?"

"Las Ramblas!" the van chauffeur answered. "And that's the famous *Columbus Monument* we just passed! We're now only ten minutes from your cozy hotel."

"The sights are magnificent!" Joanne Valerio exclaimed. "We'll definitely have to take a double-decker bus tour and sit on top, weather permitting. I like the idea of open-air top-deck buses! I've already seen several dozen of them conducting tourists around this beautiful city!"

"And the shrubbery and flowers are really fantastic!" Lisa Mottola noted. "This part of the city is like one giant botanical garden! And they have lots of bougainvillea here just like we saw in…"

"In La Jolla and in residential San Diego!" corporate jet pilot David Winters remembered and finished. "And there's many sycamore trees along the boulevard too! Barcelona is very much like southern California except for the rain. I hope the sky clears up later today!"

"Yes it will," the driver authoritatively replied. "And I suggest that you take a stroll down the Passeig de Gracia after you become settled in your hotel rooms. It's a terrific shopping area just two blocks away from the Apsis Atrium Palace. I highly recommend it and I guarantee that you won't be disappointed. It's rather exceptional!"

After the ten new arrivals checked into the hotel, a bellboy escorted Lois and Frank Davies to the elevator and then up to their second floor room, which had a marvelous balcony view of the Gran Via de les Corts Catalanes. Frank was so happy to get to his room and take off his shoes that he gave the helpful attendant a generous five Euro tip.

"Hey, before you leave, how do we put the lights on?" Frank inquired. "These light switches don't seem to work!"

"Sorry Sir, my mistake for not telling you!" the bellboy instantly apologized. "You have to place the plastic room key in this wall slot here just after you open the door. The key insertion makes the lights go on. It's a measure we use to conserve energy and electricity."

"I see! Pretty nifty and practical!" Lois earnestly admitted. "Maybe we Americans could learn something from other cultures if we cease being so independent and arrogant. Thanks for sharing that important information with us!"

After the hotel porter left the Davies to their own privacy another minor crisis soon developed. Lois couldn't figure out how to flush the toilet.

"There's no flush handle!" Lois informed her equally puzzled husband. "There just has to be a handle somewhere! I feel so stupid and incompetent right now!"

After searching and experimenting for a full minute, Frank was surprised to discover the solution to the riddle. A flat rectangular silver metal wall plate (that appeared to be part of the bathroom's décor) served and functioned as a useful flush handle.

"Mystery solved!" Frank declared, pretending that he was a contemporary Sherlock Holmes. "I just wish the bellboy or the person at the desk would've explained that simple secret, or should I say *that* simple method to us! They just assume that we've been to Europe before and are familiar with the different habits and customs. Anyway, realistically speaking Lois, good old Yankee ingenuity and perseverance are difficult to stymie."

"Now you're beginning to sound haughty just like your obnoxious twin brother!" Lois facetiously kidded. "Nothing can defeat or stifle Fred! And now your inflexible attitude is contrary to acceptable!"

"And now you're starting to sound a lot like *our* overbearing sister-in-law!" Frank creatively joked. "If the slightest deviation is not a calamity, then it most certainly is a disaster! What a mental case Eleanor is and always will be!"

"Let a smile be your umbrella is indeed *not* Eleanor's favorite maxim!" Lois diplomatically assessed. "That vicious sister of mine possesses the combined personalities of Lucretia Borgia and Medusa the Gorgon! Need I say more to support my premise and your analysis?"

That afternoon the light drizzle subsided and the Davies took the airport van driver's recommendation and sauntered down the magnificent Passeig de Gracia, a splendid boulevard replete with spacious sidewalks, fabulous buildings, ritzy department stores and swanky fashion emporiums. The fascinating scenery was both overwhelming and breathtaking.

"This thoroughfare makes New York's Fifth Avenue look like an ordinary dump!" Frank sarcastically interpreted. "It's without a doubt the most excellent street I've ever walked along!"

"Now you're again sounding exactly like your disgusting brother Fred!" Lois quipped and benignly chastised. "Stop acting like a ruthless uncivilized cynical American barbarian!"

"And you're again sounding just like Eleanor!" Frank asserted. "Stop chiding and reprimanding me as if I'm a five-year-old wet-behind-the-ears kid! Please Lois, kindly show me some more respect and consideration!"

"Well, to change the subject," Lois Davies astutely said, "many of the structures on this fantastic avenue were designed by Antoni Gaudi, a world-renowned Spanish architect."

"Probably our English word 'gaudy' comes from the guy's name!" Frank deducted and articulated. "Everything on that building over there across the street seems exaggerated and garish!"

"I don't know about *that* uncharitable comment!" Lois replied. "But I had read about Gaudi in a brochure about Barcelona down in the hotel lobby while you were busy checking in. His work is still very popular here in Barcelona and actually the architectural genius has a huge reputation throughout Spain and Europe!"

"Look at that roof on the opposite side of the boulevard!" the mildly perturbed husband pointed out. "It looks like dragon scales accentuated with medieval fantasy towers. And that ostentatious apartment house on the corner looks like it belongs with the Flintstones back in prehistoric Bedrock! This Antoni Gaudi fellow was so out in left field that he's entirely out of the stadium!"

"You could never appreciate another person's artistic or personal expression!" Lois rankled. "Now your true feelings are fully exposed! Deep down inside Frank, you're an ingrate just like your hostile twin brother is!"

"And you're hostile and argumentative just like *my* vitriolic sister-in-law that happens to look exactly like you!" Frank volleyed back.

"Well, at least my problem is not partially genetic like yours is!" the wife caustically lectured. "Both you and Fred need the services of several priests and a squad of psychiatrists!"

According to Spanish custom, supper was not served in the hotel dining room until 8 p.m. During the delicious dinner Frank (out-of-character) got entangled in a minor wrangle with Dr. Rose Jeffries, a political liberal.

"These Spaniard natives all seem rather cold and indifferent to Americans!" Frank generalized with a frown on his countenance. "They mostly seem apathetic, not to mention pathetic!"

"I've seen equally unconcerned dispassionate people walking the streets of downtown 'Philly or New York!" Dr. Jeffries abruptly challenged. "I think you're being a little too judgmental!"

"You probably voted for John Kerry in the last Presidential election!" Davies vociferated. "I can tell by your tone and by your attitude that you're a devout left-wing liberal from the word 'go'!"

"How I vote is my own conscience," Dr. Rose Jeffries protested. "And I've learned from experience that nothing tangible can ever be achieved by debating either religion or politics! I suggest that *you* change the topic of discussion!"

"Why are you being so confrontational and belligerent?" Lois Davies disputed with her usually tranquil marital partner. "I'm becoming a trifle embarrassed with your new-found tirades and I don't condone them at all! It's all contrary to your general nature!"

"And I'm becoming pretty tired of *you* being non-supportive of your loyal husband!" Frank snidely affirmed. "Behind every man there's a woman, and that's exactly where she belongs!"

"Now you're proving that you're truly a right-wing male chauvinist!" Dr. Jeffries indicted her formerly mild-mannered philosophical opponent. "A dedicated conservative right-wing male chauvinist at that!"

"And Rose, you're probably a militant left-wing save-the-environment and save-the-whales advocate!" Frank angrily responded. "All you left-wingers have some perverted idealistic agenda to pursue like valuing animals over humans! You're all on the brink of abandoning capitalism and adopting socialism as an honorable way of life! Your history heroes are probably Karl Marx and Vladimir Lenin!"

"I see no reason to prolong this regrettable verbal altercation!" Warren Mottola interrupted the argument. "We're all here in Europe to have fun and recreation and not to verbally assault and attack one another! Now let's all drink to our newly engaged couple, Lisa and David!"

"Yeah David!" Frank unfortunately yelled while frivolously raising his glass in a mock salute. "The next time the *pilot* light on my basement hot water heater goes bonkers, I'll know exactly who to call!" Davies loudly said, deliberately insulting the young commercial jet operator.

* * * * * * * * * * *

Day two of the European vacation was much more harmonious and favorable for the Davies than day one had been. Frank had attributed his recent aberrant behavior to being overly fatigued from the seven-hour-flight. The rain had ceased and a cloudy blue sky had appeared over Barcelona's delightful sixty-eight degree temperature. After enjoying a hardy breakfast in the hotel's main restaurant the party of ten purchased tickets for the "city bus tour," which originated on the Placa de Catalunya, only four blocks from the aforementioned Apsis Atrium Hotel. The twenty-five mile bus excursion entailed twenty-eight stops where tourists could get off at their leisure, sight-see and next board another double-decker open-air bus on the grand circuit and then get off at another place of interest along the scenic itinerary.

"Look Frank!" Lois indicated as the bus passed from the Passeig de Gracia onto Calle de Cerdena. "There's the La Sagrada Familia (the Sacred Family) Cathedral. The tour pamphlet says it was designed by the great Antoni Gaudi in 1882. It's still under construction although Gaudi died way back in 1926!"

"It's marvelously built!" Jimmy Valerio recognized and attested. "As you know I'm in the construction business but I've never before seen anything quite like this terrific architecture! It's a combination of both primitive and modern! Just look at those unbelievable spires or towers or whatever you want to call them! They're worthy of any person's admiration!"

Evidence of Antoni Gaudi's brilliance was very abundant all over the bustling city as the tour bus passed by the Pare Guell, the Museum of Catalunyan Art, the Pueblo Espanol, the city's main university campus, the Maritime Museum and the Picasso Gallery. Not far from the waterfront the touring party exited the bus on Las Ramblas and stepped in the direction of the Gothic Quarter, an alluring section of Barcelona with buildings and residences dating back to the Thirteenth Century.

"Let's stroll up this narrow alleyway!" Lois suggested to the less rambunctious members of the group. "It looks rather intriguing and adventurous!"

"And the natives probably don't have clothes dryers because all of the laundry is hanging out of overhead windows!" Frank articulated, again finding fault with his environment. "Maybe they don't own washers either!"

"Regardless," Lois mildly countered, attempting to get the erratic exchange of words back on topic. "Let's see how far this alleyway extends! The walks on both sides are quite narrow and a compact car can barely squeeze by in the center!"

"That's why most of the people in this city have motor scooters and motorbikes!" Warren Mottola concluded and explained. "There's not too many large American SUVs speeding around town, that's for sure! And those new Mercedes Smart cars are now the vogue over here! Don't forget!" the science teacher elaborated. "Gasoline is around eight dollars a gallon and is sold in liters just like Coke and Pepsi are back in the States. That's precisely why most conscientious Europeans must be frugal and economical."

"Why do they call them Smart cars?" David Winters asked. "Do they have artificial intelligence generated by an on-board computer?"

"No!" Warren laughed and corrected. "Smart stands for Small Mercedes Art car! At least that's what I overheard a tour-guide telling a curious tourist on the bus!"

The commercial ancient alleyway (that was dotted with small neighborhood grocery stores and bakeries) stretched for over a mile, and upon leaving the very historic medieval area, Warren perceptively spotted the Roman Arch, a brick copy of the famous Arch de Triumph in Paris.

"The edifice is made out of Roman bricks," Warren academically told his exhausted companions. "The flat brick is about half as wide as those currently used in the United States and it *was* standard building material throughout the ancient Roman World."

"I thought you were a science teacher?" Joanne Valerio asked. "You seem to be an expert on history too!"

"Yes Warren," Judy Marks chimed in. "You must study dictionaries and encyclopedias both day and night to have knowledge of a trivial fact like that! No wonder why kids are bored in school!"

"I majored in science but minored in history at *Rutgers*!" Warren Mottola clarified. "But sometimes it's hard to divorce one subject from the other! For example," the erudite teacher elucidated, "architecture is a science that has a certain history! That's precisely when and where the two distinct disciplines integrate!"

"Barcelona is the most beautiful and most exquisite city I've ever toured and that includes Las Vegas and San Diego!" Lois Davies opined. "Even though the brochure I had read stated that it has a population of nearly two million, I haven't detected one slum or ghetto yet anywhere! It's truly unbelievable and exotic!"

The fatigued trekkers stepped into a small soda fountain and purchased Seven-Ups and Pepsi Colas to be drunk outside. Frank generously treated everyone to their beverages.

"You want to know something," the biology research specialist stated and complained, "they charge you extra if you drink the sodas outside. They sort of rent the table and chairs to you. It's a little different than how food merchants do business in the States!"

"Yes it is!" Lois agreed. "In the States soda fountains don't have twenty outside tables and sixty outdoor chairs! That's what I consider one of the main differences between Barcelona and 'Philly!"

Day two of the European vacation trip elapsed without any major incidents occurring. The travelers were satisfactorily adjusting to the six-hour time differential and were indeed becoming more social and less irritable. All ten American tourists were highly anticipating the seven-day voyage on the Regal Adventurer, the highlight of the trip being less than twenty-four hours away. The New Jersey visitors readily agreed that certain aspects of life were full of gratifying moments.

* * * * * * * * * * * *

Saturday September 16th arrived on the calendar and at breakfast Judy Marks announced to the group that the ugly three-day weather pattern that had hovered over and near Barcelona was now drifting east towards Italy.

"That makes sense Judy!" Frank acknowledged and commended. "Weather in the northern hemisphere moves from west to east and generally so does the jet stream."

"That's why our flight back to 'Philly will be eight hours, a full sixty-minutes longer than it took getting here!" Warren objectively added. "We'll be going against the headwind caused by the strong jet stream flow in the upper atmosphere!"

"Before we check out of the hotel at noon and meet our pickup van driver," Lois mentioned to Frank, "I want to go to the Passeig de Gracia and view its splendor one final time while I'll really be in quest of purchasing some decent postcards to put into a new photo' album."

The Davies did walk the magnificent Passeig de Gracia and had only two brief hours to inspect marvelous sights that hadn't been observed and explored before. Frank seemed back to his quiet-disposition self but then remembered an unusual scene he had witnessed on the balcony the previous evening (at midnight) while Lois was taking her hot shower.

"While you were getting ready for bed I stood on our suite's small terrace and was relishing the beauty of the Via de les Gran Corts Catalanes," Frank prefaced his observation. "The wide boulevard is really totally terrific when lit-up at night."

"Yes and it's so wide that it takes a full minute to cross," Lois recalled and exaggerated. "I especially like the double-lanes on each side and the corresponding wide pedestrian walk paths next to them before the crosser finally gets to the four main lanes. The

62

wonderful boulevards of Barcelona are not safe havens for careless jaywalkers, that's for sure!"

"Well anyway," Frank continued as the pair finally reached a newspaper and souvenir stand, "while you were in the shower I witnessed over three hundred midnight roller blade enthusiasts speeding by on the pedestrian walkway. It was pretty phenomenal! I counted each and every one of the three hundred and eleven of them. Instead of wild motorcycle gangs they must have roller-blade clubs here!" Frank humorously conjectured and revealed. "It's certainly less expensive than owning and driving gas-guzzling cars around Barcelona! Say Honey, here's a colorful book about the city to take home as a memento of our trip!"

"I don't want that one!" Lois emphatically disagreed. "I prefer this one!" she insisted as she handed the specific item to the souvenir stand proprietor.

"Allemagne!" the stand owner bellowed.

"He means the book's written in German and not English!" the husband recognized and interpreted.

"Entonces yo quiero uno en Engles, mismo eso uno!" Lois directed the salesman in broken stilted Spanish. "Then I want another one like the one I had selected in English!"

"Don't be ridiculous!" Frank strenuously objected. "The one I had wanted you to choose was all about the entire city and not just about the architectural works of Antoni Gaudi! Stop being so damned stubborn Lois!"

"You're again sounding like you're impersonating your rotten twin brother!" the wife steadfastly protested. "You're rapidly becoming the dispute king of American tourists! You've been far from hilarious lately!"

"And you're now evolving into a carbon-copy of that vicious viper Eleanor!" Frank accused his spouse in a bellicose tone of voice. "I suspect that somebody evil and jealous is putting a heavy wicked curse on our relationship!"

The volatile couple hardly spoke to each other on the van trip from the Apsis Atrium Palace down the picturesque Via Laietana, which led to the Passeig de Colom and ultimately to the docked Regal Adventurer. All ten tourists seated in the vehicle transport took a final stare at the elaborate lengthy and wide gray paver-stone promenade that accentuated the incomparable Barcelona waterfront.

Obtaining the required Sea Passes was easily facilitated once the ship's new passengers showed their passports and other relevant identifications to the courteous harbor terminal personnel. Everyone was allowed to board at 1 p.m. and the newcomers had six-full-hours to unpack and investigate all of the massive fourteen decks until the scheduled first seating supper in the Magic Carousel Dining Room at six-thirty (with the vessel's disembarking at 7 p.m. sharp).

In the grandly decorated Magic Carousel Dining Room the waiter and assistant waiter introduced themselves to the ten American diners at their table. "Good evening ladies and gentlemen! I'm Cem (pronounced Gem) and this is my very able assistant Tomas. I'm from Turkey and Tomas is from Czechoslovakia. We're here to cater to your every eating need!" Cem said in almost perfect unaccented English. "It will be our pleasure to serve you!"

Frank formally introduced everyone at the table to Cem and to Tomas and then ordered two bottles of Merlot for the assembled gourmets to enjoy. Soon the conversation turned to the other travelers aboard the ship after the well-trained waiters began attending to *their* individual duties.

In short time Frank Davies' recently acquired Dr. Jekyll and Mr. Hyde alternating personality again unexpectedly surfaced. "You all must know, some of these Europeans aboard this vessel are quite rude!" Frank began his impromptu criticism. "I was standing in Line H inside the harbor terminal acquiring Lois's and my Sea Passes when this nasty grumpy elderly Spanish man tried to wriggle into a spot at the Line G counter and then pushed me out of his way!"

"What did you say or do to the impetuous old fellow?" Warren Mottola curiously asked. "I'd think that his aggressive behavior would've warranted at least a perfunctory 'Excuse me'!"

"Well, I quickly raised my left elbow and deflected the old ill-mannered coot directly out of my standing space!" Davies bluntly reported, much to his wife's utter humiliation. "And besides that scenario Warren, this afternoon at lunch up at the eleventh floor Quarterdeck Buffet, Lois and I were seated at a table for four when a Hispanic lady signaled to me with sign language if she and her mate could sit down. I suavely said 'Si! Hable Engles?' and the snobby witch answered 'Portuguese!' Then neither the woman, I'd say she was in her fifties, nor her self-centered husband ever once again glanced at Lois and me during their entire meal. It was as if we were lepers or convicts or inferior beings or something! The only friendly people on this boat are good old Americans! You can pick them out in a second by their cheerful and happy demeanors!"

"Frank, I think you'd better stop speaking so loudly!" Lois rebuked. "You never know when you're going to offend someone sitting at another table!"

"Well, let them sue me for all I care!" Frank automatically and indiscreetly returned. "Let them sue me even if they're rude Europeans and not merely Sioux Indians!" the slightly intoxicated man awkwardly joked.

"Now just wait a cotton-pickin' minute!" Dr. Rose Jeffries boldly challenged her philosophical adversary. "I strongly suggest that you stop making unsubstantiated prejudicial statements and unfounded gross discriminatory stereotypical generalizations!"

"You're sounding too much like a cowardly liberal again!" Frank yelled across the table at the now-flabbergasted infectious disease doctor. "You're always crusading for a dumb cause! Get a grip on reality, will ya'!"

"And you're sounding more and more just like your haughty obnoxious brother Fred again!" Lois aptly injected into the three-way exchange.

"And I think you're deliberately mimicking Mrs. Eleanor Davies!" the indignant husband snarled back. "She's a venomous viper if there ever was one!"

"Folks! This is supposed to be a happy occasion for all in attendance!" Warren Mottola adroitly interrupted, acting like both a referee and peacemaker. "I'd like to now propose a toast to officially honor my daughter Lisa and her fiancé David's engagement! Let's all sincerely drink to their future health, wealth and happiness!"

* * * * * * * * * * * *

At 6 a.m. on Sunday morning Frank Davies opened the curtains to cabin suite 8322 and admired the superb view of the city of Marseilles. 'It's September 17th,' he thought. 'I vow to myself that I have to be more diplomatic and I must also stay away from initiating controversial subjects, especially with Lois and with that nasty despicable leftist Dr. Rose Jeffries.'

The passengers aboard the Regal Adventurer were given three separate tour options at each port-of-call. 'We could've toured Marseilles but instead Lois, Warren, Melissa and I have chosen the small fishing village of Cassis!' Frank reviewed in his now-somewhat remorseful mind. 'I'll try my best to make this day pleasant and enjoyable for all concerned! Wow!' Davies considered. 'There must be at least fifty tour buses lined up down there! You'd certainly need that many to accommodate the three-thousand four-hundred travelers aboard this super-mammoth ship!'

After a quick visit to the eleventh deck buffet for breakfast, Frank, Lois, Warren and Melissa assembled in the fourth floor Metropolitan Theater, were swiftly assigned to Bus #6, and then wearing small stick-on #6 badges, the four guests waited for their tour designation to be called.

"I think it's best if *we* hang around together on all five scheduled tours in France and in Italy," Warren privately suggested to Frank. "Lisa and David are lovebirds and only have romance on their minds and Dr. Rose and her roommate Judy tend to have radical political views that are diametrically opposed to ours. Otherwise we'll have to be constantly defending our conservative viewpoints! Dr. Rose has already labeled you and me 'Neocons.' I believe that in this specific case Frank, distance from that militant Marxist is the best remedy in order to avoid conflict!"

"I totally agree with your recommendation!" Davies instinctively answered. "Prevention is always better than cure! Even Dr. Rose must realize *that* obvious medical truth!"

The ship had its own sophisticated security-check system and the passengers' Sea Passes served as viable substitutes for the customary passports and photo' IDs. Soon the four friends were on Bus #6 and heading through Marseilles traveling from the "New Port" to the "Old Port," which featured numerous scenic marinas loaded with local fishing boats, Mediterranean schooners and extravagant yachts owned by the rich and famous.

"Notice that the residences' principal rooms all have three sets of shuttered windows facing the street," the French female tour guide explained in English. "Notice too that the city is built in a semi-circle. Marseilles presently has a population of around one million people and it remains the second largest metropolitan area in France. On your left is the classic Byzantine Cathedral, a favorite of tourists from around the world. And up on that hill overlooking our proud city and the gateway to the Mediterranean stands the impressive Cathedral of Notre Dame de la Garde with its magnificent gold-leaf towers," the knowledgeable guide described. "And soon we'll be passing by our Theatre National de Marseille La Criee. This part of the city with its many fancy stores and cafes looks very much like Paris's Champs Elysees, which incidentally in English means the Elysian Fields! Looking out toward the sea," the upbeat woman loquaciously stated, "you'll

66

notice a fort or prison situated on a small island. That's where the Count of Monte Cristo was held captive in the classic novel written by Alexandre Dumas, who as you know also wrote the book *The Three Musketeers*. And as we travel along the coast toward Cassis, please remember that the genius painter Vincent Van Gogh was often inspired by many of the area's olive groves and vineyards situated along that route!"

"This city is definitely beautiful but in my opinion, I still like Barcelona better!" Lois whispered to Frank.

"Me too!" came his rather convivial reply. "Everything looked a bit newer and cleaner on the Passeig de Gracia and on Las Ramblas compared to what we're now seeing in Marseilles."

Tour Bus #6 left the main highway and the skilled driver slowly navigated the vehicle along steep winding roads above rugged jagged cliffs until it stopped at the summit of the white precipices overlooking gorgeous Cape Canaille, a full 1,300 feet above the placid Mediterranean.

"The guide said that this spectacular view is actually from a higher elevation than the one from the top of the White Cliffs of Dover! In fact it's the highest cliff overlooking the sea anywhere in Europe!" Lois marveled and informed.

"It's truly sensational and breathtaking!" Frank confirmed. "Let's take some pictures of Melissa and Warren and then they can reciprocate! Just look at those fabulous homes with orange tiled roofs situated down there near the Mediterranean. I gotta' admit, it's all very enticing and extraordinary!"

The remainder of "Day 4" in Europe was inconsequential. The bus passengers were then taken with dispatch to the quaint fishing village of Cassis where they were left off on the outskirts of the town to be transported into the center while sitting in compartments of small trains on wheels pulled by cute diminutive locomotives of various colors. "The Mayor of Cassis insists that all tourists enter the village on these trams because of traffic congestion and pollution!" the tour guide explained.

"The Mayor sounds like another radical left-wing liberal environmentalist just like Dr. Rose Jeffries!" Frank complained to Lois. "He's probably an officer in Greenpeace and in PETA too!"

"Now, now Frank!" the wife giggled. "Let's not become cantankerous and let's simply pretend that we're normal tourists out to sample the exquisite fishing village, peruse its leather shops and then take some pictures of us standing in front of the fine waterfront cafes and restaurants. This is no time to act like a bullheaded contentious American, now is it?"

"I suppose you're right!" the husband reluctantly conceded. "This is no time to *harbor* any animosity!"

That evening Cem and Tomas served the party of ten delicious suppers of surf and turf followed by large portions of baked Alaska for dessert. "I wonder how the chef could fit an entire state like Alaska in his oven!" Frank jested with even Dr. Rose getting a brief chuckle out of his somewhat witty comment. At 9 p.m. everyone enjoyed the lively show "Broadway Sights and Sounds" staged in the Metropolitan Theater, which was followed by an hour's social activity at the Anchor Bar's piano lounge and then by some casual gift shopping along the ship's expansive promenade.

"Thanks for not being so verbally combative today!" Lois praised her spouse. "You're again mastering the art of being civil!"

"I'm trying my best!" the husband solemnly pledged. "Believe me Lois. I'm attempting to be calm and tranquil! I'm really working on it! But for some remote reason I'm finding it quite difficult!"

* * * * * * * * * * * *

On the morning of "Day 5" Frank, Lois, Warren and Melissa again stepped down the "gangplank" for the next stop on their wonderful sea odyssey. A "tender" would ferry two busloads of tourists to the mainland since Villefranche had no deep-water dock where the Regal Adventurer could moor and anchor.

"I always wanted to tour Monte Carlo," Lois began, "because it's where Grace Kelly married Prince Rainier in a fantasy-type storybook wedding! I can't wait to see the cathedral where the event took place!"

"We have to remember that Monte Carlo is the name of the casino in Monaco," Warren Mottola scholarly remarked and corrected. "People often get the two terms mixed-up and call one the other. Monaco and Monte Carlo are two different things!"

"It's too bad we had to make a choice between Monaco and either Nice or Cannes for our one-day shore excursion," Melissa piped-in and regretted. "Confidentially I'd like to visit and explore all three places."

"You could do this exact same cruise again and see totally different things at every port!" Lois Davies concluded and shared. "Perhaps we can do it again before we're...."

"Before we're all in wheelchairs having dual oxygen tanks on the rear while gasping for our last breaths!" Frank said while completing his wife's thought with terminology that showed a distinct insensitivity toward the handicapped. "I want my wheelchair to have chrome dual exhaust pipes!"

"That horrible statement was in poor taste and I hope you think things out more in detail next time before you again say something off-color!" Lois disciplined her husband. "You're more tolerable and less miserable when you're being introspective with your mouth zipped shut!"

"I swear that both you and Dr. Rose have no sense of humor!" Frank argued in defense of his vulnerable ego. "Neither of you know the definition of the word 'amusement'."

"Let's act a little more aristocratic now that we're mingling with highbrow society here in the French Riviera, even though in reality we're just middle class Americans and not Counts or Countesses!" Warren intelligently intervened. "I really never aspired becoming a wealthy snobbish aristocrat anyway!"

Tour Bus #5 stopped on the Avenue St. Martin near the Monaco Oceanographic Museum, the institute where Jacques Cousteau had conducted much of his essential nautical research. Not far from the very excellent museum was the Prince's Palace situated atop Monaco Rock, where the thoroughly enchanted tourists observed the hourly changing of the guard.

"The tour guide said that if Monaco were ever attacked by an enemy, then France would come to its defense!" Frank related to Warren. "When's the last time France ever won a battle? Was it before or after Julius Caesar?"

Although several eavesdropping American tourists found levity in Davies' assertive remark, Lois certainly did not. "You're again being very sarcastic and offensive!" the wife reproached as she approached her opinionated husband. "Do I have to tell you exactly who you're reminding me of?"

"No *Eleanor!*" the husband intentionally wrangled. "I wasn't making a public speech! I was merely whispering something in private to Warren! Why does every little conversation that I have elicit scorn from your lips?"

"Well, your boisterous whispers sound like they're being shouted into a bullhorn let alone into a megaphone!" the wife passionately countered. "Right now I believe that you're evilly transforming into your cavalier twin brother right before my very eyes!"

"Guys! Let's take a stroll over to the Cathedral where Princess Grace and Prince Rainier were married and are now buried!" Melissa Mottola wisely advised. "Then we can ramble over to the Monte Carlo Casino. We have two full hours to burn before we have to board the bus."

"The casino isn't open until this afternoon!" Warren recollected and quoted from a guidebook he had read. "And they charge you a ten Euros admission fee just to pass through the fancy doors! That's close to fifteen dollars! You're way behind even before you insert a coin into the first slot machine! I guess they want to keep all of the riffraff out!"

The foursome discovered a park located behind the city square that featured an array of colorful tropical plants, flowers and palm trees. Pictures were taken with digital cameras and then Warren noticed that all traffic in the square had been terminated to allow for the filming of a rap video in progress.

"Look, there's the famous rapper Bee_G being driven in that black Mercedes convertible. He's being chased by an anonymous villain in that gold and black Rolls Royce," Warren uttered in pure amazement. "This MTV video must be costing tens of thousands of dollars to film!"

"That lousy rap music is a scourge to America!" Frank opined. "It's corrupting the minds and hearts of our youth while it's eroding the very morality of society! And it's all done for the love of money! Bee_G doesn't care one iota about the damage he's doing to teenagers from Portland, Maine to Portland, Oregon. The hedonistic narcissist is a complete egomaniac. And the worst part about it is that rap music isn't even music!"

"Frank, please be quiet!" Lois simultaneously admonished and pleaded. "We're surrounded by Bee_G's film crew and several of his intimidating three-hundred pound Titan bodyguards and they're standing only twenty-feet away! Be more discreet! They might not savor what you're saying!"

"I'm tired of your perpetual uncouth character assassinations!" Frank fiercely reacted. "You're not exactly the most supportive wife you know! I'm only trying to explain myself to Warren!"

"I just don't want to see you causing a scene with your ongoing diatribe!" the wife emoted. "And I want you to know that for the first time the word 'divorce' has entered my mind! I find your behavior ever since this trip began most abominable!"

"Look! There's an ice cream parlor over there on the corner!" Warren nervously indicated. "Let's all cool off with some tasty treats! Vanilla cones might just do the trick!"

"I'm lactate intolerant!" Lois answered. "I can only eat yogurt, and that's on a full stomach!"

"That's not all that's wrong with my fickle wife!" Frank condemned and divulged. "In fact that's just the most minor flaw! Right *Eleanor!*" he alluded.

"You're mentally sick!" Lois yelled back. "You're a detestable disgrace to humanity!"

"At least I'm human!" Frank hollered back, getting the immediate attention of Bee_G's formerly nonchalant enormous bodyguards.

"It's going to be a long six mile bus ride back to Villefranche," Melissa accurately predicted. "Let's all please learn to temper our tempers!"

That evening after supper the normally compatible foursome attended a terrific one-man performance in the Metropolitan Theater starring Domenick Allen, a former member of the rock group Foreigner. All during the outstanding show, Lois and Frank sat mum and as still as statues. The Mottolas sensed and suspected that major conflict was about to erupt.

* * * * * * * * * * * * *

"Day 6" of the European trip was Tuesday, September 19. As usual Frank and Lois and Warren and Melissa met at the entrance of the Metropolitan Theater at 7:30 a.m. to await assignment to their designated tour bus and to obtain their associated bus badges.

"This was a really tough choice," Melissa began to test the waters and see if there was any apparent current riptide existing between Frank and Lois. "We could've gone to Florence but instead we selected Tuscany on the advice of our travel agent."

"Let's see what happens!" Lois blandly answered. "It's too late now to change horses in midstream."

"Tuscany's famous for Chianti wine, alabaster statue products, olive trees and excellent leather goods!" Frank said without any trace of rancor evident in his tone of voice.

"Yes, and I understand that many Renaissance painters found the Italian fertile valleys and the gentle sloping Tuscany hills as interesting backgrounds for their creative works," Lois Davies contributed. "And the weather's going to be eighty-two degrees, something between ideal and perfect!"

Tour Bus #8 traveled north from the port of Livorno along an elevated industrial highway stretching over several kilometers of marshland in the direction of Pisa. "I know many of you had desired to see the Leaning Tower and have elected to fore-go Florence to sight-see Tuscany. Believe me, you've made a wise decision and you won't be disappointed. Pisa and Florence are both located on the Arno River," their guide Maria said into her bus microphone, "which has over the centuries silted up. Thus Pisa, being situated inland, has over the years declined as a trading port and Livorno has risen. You'll all be totally enthralled and thrilled with both the medieval towns of Volterra and San Gimignano," Maria claimed. "Volterra even has some Roman ruins but actually during your short visit, you'll all feel like you're time-traveling back a thousand years into the past as you shop in narrow streets that haven't changed too much in appearance in the last millennium."

Stellar high poplar and cypress trees randomly dotted the many vineyards and olive groves as Tour Bus #8 was maneuvered around curvy bends while it ascended thirty miles inland up hill after hill on the gradual ascension to Volterra. Dreamy clouds wafted by in the valley below as the spellbound tourists feasted their eyes on the remarkable landscape. Frank, Lois, Warren and Melissa all felt as if they had wondrously entered a magical fantasy realm.

Volterra and later that morning San Gimignano were true medieval-type anachronisms, highly regarded special places to behold. The couples bought several leather belts, handbags and wallets in each town without any incidents, problems, haggling or dilemmas occurring. Lois was contemplating Frank's severe vacillating Jekyll and Hyde personality swings, but then she dismissed them as 'signs of manic depression' and was indeed glad that her husband's deportment appeared being 'back to normal.'

Since the total tour lasted a full ten hours, lunch was served at a remote farmhouse that specialized in tourist visitations. A full-scale three-course-meal was prepared and presented with the first dish being pasta, the second meat and vegetables and the third being dessert, all in small but very attractive servings. Chianti wine (grown and processed on the farm) was then poured into tall-stem glasses to complement the fine delicious food.

"The only negative feature of this place is that they only have two bathrooms, one in the adjoining room and the other in the farm's office," Lois perceptively stated to her friends seated at the long country farmhouse table. "It's a little inconvenient for forty-eight touring adults with overactive kidneys. But then again, this is Italy and not New York."

"It sure beats the lavatory facilities back in Volterra," Frank uttered in a non-threatening voice. "A fat woman sat behind a table and charged us a half-Euro each to use the toilets. This is one distinct advantage of public bathroom accommodations in the States as opposed to here in Italy. At least the two patron bathrooms on this farm seem to have some degree of privacy."

"And we had to waste fifteen minutes of our tour time standing single-file in a long bathroom line, at least the women did," Melissa Mottola remembered and offered. "What am I saying? It was a co-ed bathroom with a series of stalls! There were no gender designations! But over here they call them W.C.'s or Water Closets and not Men's Rooms or Ladies Rooms!"

"At least we haven't seen any holes in the floor with two feet painted on the cement showing the lavatory patrons where they have to stand," Frank pointed out to his listeners. "Several guys back in Jersey had told me that's what they had experienced at stops in certain parts of Italy. I'm glad we haven't discovered them yet!"

"Frank, I'm going outside to the farm's office to use the facilities," Warren judiciously hinted. "I'll beat the crowd, if ya' know what I mean!"

"Good idea. I'll go along and make sure you aren't molested by a savage poplar tree or by a demented chicken wandering around," Davies amusingly jested. "You might need my inexpensive personal protection."

After returning from the office's bathroom and then partaking of the delectable Tuscan meal Frank and Warren were surprised to see that the farm's two "multi-functional" office secretaries had moved to the gift shop to wait on customers from behind the counter because the diners all had to exit the building/restaurant into the gift shop area in order to return to the bus.

That evening upon the cruise ship was "Dress-up night" and everyone eating in the Magic Carousel Dining Room had to wear formal apparel. After dinner the party of ten enjoyed the Russian duo of Tara and Alexandre performing their professional ice-skating skills in the ship's spacious Ice Arena and the show's stars had a cast of twelve very talented skaters accompany them in enacting their very complicated maneuvers.

"This colossal ship has almost everything!" Warren bragged to his favorite companion. "Even an ice skating palace almost big enough for the Philadelphia Flyers to play an ice hockey game!"

"I had read where the Regal Adventurer is so huge that if you stood it vertically from stern to bow," Frank summarized and stressed without exaggeration, "the colossal ship would be as tall as the Empire State Building. Now that's what I call really thinking big! Hey Warren," the biology researcher related, "I can't wait to get out of this encumbering monkey suit!"

"Well good Buddy, glad to see that you're back on an even *keel*!" Warren Mottola merrily joked. "You had me a trifle worried there for a while and that's the honest-to-God truth!"

* * * * * * * * * * * *

Wednesday, September 20th was "Day 7" for the fully acclimated Mediterranean tourists now cruising aboard the ultra-modern Regal Adventurer. Again fifty buses were lined up at the dock at Civitavecchia, the modern-day gateway to Rome. Rosemarie, the gentle Bus #15 tour guide, was conscientiously explaining to her captive audience the overall layout of Rome. "The Vatican lies on the north side of the Tiber River, but on the south side is where the original Seven Hills of Rome are located along with the major shopping districts and ancient ruins. Our first exciting stop this morning will be the incomparable Vatican Museum."

The thirty-mile drive from Civitavecchia to Rome took an hour and a half due to heavy traffic congestion first showing itself ten miles outside the city. "Subways and underground parking are nearly non-existent because every time a construction crew begins excavating somewhere," Rosemarie educated her receptive listeners, "important archeological ruins are usually uncovered and work must be halted. Therefore as you might've presumed, there's little new construction going on in central Rome."

At the Spanish Steps a second gray-haired tour guide named Luigi was picked up who, like most Italian men, was an incessant chronic cigarette smoker. But the veteran host was quite experienced at shuttling his tourists through the Vatican area and his presence was well-known to the various security guards and Vatican attendants.

"Today the entrance line for the Vatican Museum is only four blocks long," Luigi mentioned to his assigned disciples, "but in another two hours it'll be eight blocks in length. Be happy that you've luckily arrived here at the most desirable time."

"I can't believe all of the beggars hanging around the outside wall trying to exploit the pilgrims and the visitors' good

74

intentions," Frank suddenly criticized to his wife. "It's astounding how people will sometimes use religion to achieve their selfish devious ends!"

"These are poor homeless people that have probably somehow evaded the welfare safety net and have inadvertently fallen between the cracks," an irritated Lois replied after solidly nudging her husband in the ribs with her right elbow. "Now please stop acting so uncultured and give your undivided attention to Luigi."

"I know that some of you have with difficulty sacrificed seeing the Trevi Fountain, the Pantheon, the Castel Sant' Angelo and the Forum for the sake of touring the Vatican and the Colosseum with me, but believe me when I say," Luigi appropriately pontificated and embellished with an Italian accent outside St. Peter's Basilica, "you haven't made the wrong decision. Perhaps sometime in the future you all can return to the Eternal City and see all that you've missed this first time around."

Luigi patiently distributed "Whisper Phones" to his assigned tourists so that they could place a plug into an ear and listen to his extensive narratives by turning up the volume. The lengthy line moved rather quickly and in forty-five minutes Luigi was conducting his "students" through the immense Vatican Museum, which exhibited long narrow galleries ornamented with huge wall tapestries and various invaluable marble statues. The highlight of the tour (beyond a doubt) was the incomparable Sistine Chapel, which possessed a tremendous arched ceiling displaying numerous paintings painstakingly created by the inimitable Renaissance genius Michelangelo.

"The frescoes were recently cleaned-up and they look as good as new," Luigi proudly explained to his tuned-in audience. "For your information Michelangelo also designed the uniforms for the Pope's Swiss Guards and in addition the Master had sculpted the famous Pieta, which you'll all see and admire later this afternoon inside St. Peter's Basilica."

"If they had Baptismal water basins in this church then it could be called the cistern chapel instead of the Sistine Chapel," Frank foolishly joked to his close male companion.

"Stop being so disrespectful and irreverent!" the eavesdropping Lois chastised her sardonic mate. "This is the Pope's favorite and most sacred chapel! Don't you have a conscience?"

"Shhhh!" two very stern-looking Vatican attendants reflexively implored as they held their index fingers up to their lips signifying the need for silence. "Shhhh!" they repeated.

"Sanctimonious Fools!" Frank uttered to Warren while effectively drowning out Luigi's voice on his Whisper Phone. "I wouldn't be surprised if God were to boot those snobbish 'Shhhh!' idiots right out of heaven!"

"Shhhh!" the Vatican attendants again reminded the talkative and impious tourists that were either standing or meandering about.

After leaving the awesome Sistine Chapel a tour guide and his group discourteously cut in front of Luigi and immediately the two all-too-proud leaders became embroiled in a heated disagreement. Luigi began hitting the other guide with his Bus #15 lollipop sign while several security guards deliberately ignored the saber rattling and quickly paced away from the minor imbroglio.

"Hey Pal, I'll give you a fat lip if you keep hassling my friend Luigi!" Frank yelled to the now-perplexed and flustered maverick tour guide. "Back off!"

"Frank, don't get involved!" Lois desperately pleaded. "You're behaving just like your lawyer brother Fred would in this situation!"

"Maybe I'm inheriting some of Fred's traits and he's getting some of mine!" Frank hypothesized and suggested.

"Don't be preposterous!" the perturbed wife answered. "That's totally absurd! I do believe that ever since this vacation began you're regressing in maturity instead of advancing! If you can't act your age, then please act your shoe size!"

"Shhh!" two Vatican foot patrol personnel characteristically breathed out from behind rigid index fingers. "Shhhhh!" they reiterated in animated fashion.

Two hours later Frank Davies somewhat redeemed himself by performing a good deed on the opposite side of the Tiber outside the Colosseum. A young black girl wearing a "Detroit" sweatshirt was running to catch-up with several of her friends (who wanted to take a picture with three men posing and costumed in ancient Roman soldier uniforms) when she tripped over a slightly raised cobblestone and landed hard on her right elbow. Frank rushed over, asked the girl if she could move her arms and legs and then clasped his fingers around her waist and swiftly hoisted the still-in-shock victim to a standing position.

"At least you still have an ounce of decency in you!" Lois chided after Frank had executed his admirable humanitarian deed. "You might actually be the chivalrous Sir Walter Raleigh reincarnated! Helping others was one of your better qualities

76

before we got married. Thank goodness you're once again a benefactor to society!"

"I'd do the same for you if you lost your balance," Frank retorted, showing a degree of rancor in his tone of voice. "I'm basically a gentleman and a Good Samaritan despite what *you* might think!"

"Thanks a lot!" an insulted Lois adamantly objected. "I would hope that you'd scurry over twice as fast for me! I guess I had just overestimated you!"

That sultry afternoon the passengers assigned aboard tour bus #15 devoured the traditional three course meal at an exclusive Rome hotel and then continued their tedious tour by returning to the Vatican for an inspection of St. Peter's Basilica.

"St. Peter must be a rich guy because he owns this vast structure plus hundreds of churches and schools all over the world!" Frank quipped. "He must be as wealthy as Bill Gates!"

"Frank, stop being so repugnant!" Lois disapproved, shrugging her shoulders. "You're rather repulsive and reprehensible at times!"

"Sometimes I just got to be candid! That's why they call me Frank!" the husband stupidly joked.

"Your sense of humor leaves much to be desired and is none too amusing," the wife fired back. "You're even more bullheaded than ancient Greek mythology's Minotaur! At least *he* had a lame excuse for his stubbornness!"

"Guys, let's all politely listen to Luigi's lecture even though it's now getting quite monotonous and boring!" Melissa Mottola proposed. "And just think. Tonight in the Metropolitan Theater the Regal Adventurer's multi-talented Singers and Dancers will be doing 'Hollywood in Motion.' Now that's something half-decent to be looking forward to."

At the first sitting dinner neither Cem's sumptuous fillet mignon nor Tomas's scrumptious "sorbet delight" could adequately cheer-up Frank and Lois Davies from their mutual enmity and from their obvious dual emotional depressions.

* * * * * * * * * * * *

On "Day 8" of the comprehensive European trip ("Day 6" aboard the Regal Adventurer) Frank, Lois, Warren, Melissa, Dr. Rose Jeffries and Judy Marks were all assigned to Bus #13, which they obediently boarded on the Naples dock.

"Where are Lisa and David?" Dr. Rose innocently asked. "Those two infatuated and hypnotized lovebirds don't mingle too much! They're too focused on each other!"

"They're more ambitious and adventurous than we are!" Melissa Mottola explained. "They're touring downtown Naples, then taking a ferry to the Isle of Capri and next taking another one from Capri to Sorrento where they'll be gallivanting around. They promised to meet up with us in Pompeii."

"That sounds like a pretty rigorous and exhausting day!" Judy Marks remarked with a smile. "I hope Lisa and David can avoid the notorious pickpockets and purse snatchers constantly patrolling downtown Naples! Those crooks especially thrive on ripping-off vulnerable American tourists!"

"They'll both be so tired that they'll probably miss having sex tonight!" Frank uncouthly and distastefully theorized and said as the group stood in a circle waiting to climb aboard Bus #13.

"That last comment was rude and crude and totally unjustified!" Dr. Rose sternly protested and challenged. "You should rinse your mouth out with *Lysol*!"

"Either that or learn to bite your tongue!" Lois verbally piled on. "I'm embarrassed to say that I'm married to you! You're becoming a pathetic excuse for a human being Frank!"

"I think you're all making mountains out of molehills!" Frank exclaimed like a true bona fide egomaniac. "Learn to lighten-up, will ya'!"

After everyone had clambered aboard Bus #13 Monica, the designated tour guide, diligently distributed the by-now-familiar Whisper Phones. "As the bus leaves the Port of Naples, which incidentally is famous for the invention of pizza, we'll be skirting the city and driving past Herculaneum and Pompeii, both towns that had been destroyed by the volcanic eruption of Mt. Vesuvius on August 24th, 79 A.D. to be exact. Then we'll be heading to Sorrento on the peninsula and taking the nearly forty mile scenic drive along the magnificent Amalfi Coast all the way down to Salerno," Monica expertly orated. "So just sit back and relax and be prepared for at least seven miles of walking before this invigorating ten-hour tour is completed."

The first stop just outside Sorrento was a local establishment called Miss Bellevue, a factory outlet that manufactured exquisite inlaid wood dining room tables with elaborate matching chairs, tea wagons and house furniture. The pieces exhibited in the showroom were quite intricately made and the tourists all marveled at the tremendous degree of craftsmanship that went

78

into achieving the highly sophisticated-looking final products. Frank and Warren were tempted to purchase appealing double-pedestal dining room tables (and matching upholstered chairs) that were listed at 3,500 Euros.

"That's about the equivalent of $4,700.00," Warren smartly acknowledged after doing a quick arithmetical estimate in his head. "That's what I call a bargain! You don't see stuff like this displayed at furniture stores back in the States!"

"But then you have to worry about shipping the set all the way across the Atlantic and who knows what condition it'll be in upon arrival back in Hammonton?" Frank objectively evaluated and maintained. "It's hard to return damaged goods when you're four-thousand or so miles away from the source!"

"Maybe on our second trip to Italy I'll have the courage to make the acquisition," Warren keenly answered.

"That's an un*warran*ted comment! You've never demonstrated a moment of courage since the day you were born!" Frank Davies arrogantly and caustically remarked. "You've been about as intrepid as an army deserter as long as I've known you!"

Warren Mottola abruptly left Frank's company to rejoin Melissa, who was preoccupied chatting with Lois, with Dr. Rose Jeffries and with Judy Marks, all concerned about Frank's annoying and insulting statements. A half hour had elapsed before the forty-eight tourists were instructed to again ascend the familiar steps into Bus #13.

"The classic song 'Come to Sorrento' was not a love melody," Monica matter-of-factly began her next memorized dissertation. "In fact the lyrics are a political message, a past sincere appeal for certain lawmakers and officials to return to the city to organize a new government."

"Doesn't that obnoxious witch ever shut up?" Frank said to Lois. "She's giving me an intense headache that won't quit!"

"Here, swallow down a couple of aspirins!" the wife insisted as she frantically opened her purse to retrieve a small plastic container. "How am I going to enjoy all of the exotic bougainvillea sprinkled in with prickly pear cactus and the totally gorgeous array of other flowers when you're chronically complaining and finding fault with everything and anything? Haven't you noticed the majestic trees flourishing throughout Italy?"

"What about them?" Frank acerbically reacted. "What's so damned special about the trees? Trees are trees, aren't they?"

"In Tuscany, in Rome and all along this entrance to the marvelous Amalfi Drive," Lois explained, "the trees' limbs have been sheared off at the bottom and in the middle to form handsome canopies. I suppose it's been done to provide ample shade because they don't have nearly as many woods and forests here in Italy as we do have back in the States. That's the only suitable logical explanation I can think of!"

"Maybe here in Italy they have a surplus of unemployed lumberjacks!" Frank unrealistically and indiscriminately joked. "Unemployment abounds here because they have plenty of lazy non-industrious citizens! That's what the heck happens when you have a mostly socialistic type of government. Dr. Rose must feel right at home here in Italy! Most of the parasitic people in this country despise capitalism and free enterprise! That's why they'll never be as prosperous as we Americans are!"

"You're being absolutely implausible and irrational!" Lois profoundly protested. "I think I'll be sitting with Melissa for the remainder of the tour!"

"Now you're again sounding like my bitchy sister-in-law!" the husband accused. "When we get back to Room 8322 be sure to check your passport and make certain that the name Eleanor Davies isn't printed on it! Better yet, examine your Sea Pass to determine whether or not your entire identity has been surreptitiously changed!"

"And closely check *your* passport and determine if the despised name Frederick Davies isn't typed on it!" the now emotionally disheveled wife snapped back. "You've become ruder than sin and cruder than petroleum!"

"We're now officially entering the world famous Amalfi Drive!" Monica exuberantly announced into her trusty microphone. "Many rich Neapolitans maintain resort homes here! Notice that some residents use their concrete roofs as their garages because their homes are built on the sides of the mountains overlooking the sparkling blue sea. Those types of homes are usually the most expensive! There's nothing like this physical beauty anywhere else in the world!"

"It looks exactly like La Jolla along the California Coast just above San Diego!" Frank shouted and disagreed from his sixth row seat, much to Lois's mortification.

"Thank you Sir!" Monica cleverly and graciously responded. "I'll make a note of that fact and definitely mention it on future tours!"

The panoramic view of the mountainside town of Positano was quite outstanding, appearing as if it belonged on canvas in a masterpiece painting as it nobly lorded over the serene Mediterranean. Buildings and dwellings appeared terraced, one on top of another, in some instances fifteen structures high all the way up the mountainside. Only one main street passed through the entire town and security patrol personnel with communications' radios stopped traffic in one direction for a full half hour so that vehicles could smoothly travel in the opposite direction. Then the traffic monitors alternated the procedure for a full half hour to accommodate and alleviate northbound congestion.

"They need some Yankee ingenuity around here to build some decent highways!" Frank thought and then impulsively blurted out. "In the States this over-populated town would be referred to as a ghetto or a barrio!"

"How are they going to possibly build parallel roads on this mountainous coast?" Lois incisively questioned her husband. "It would be a bizarre undertaking, that's for sure!"

"We American capitalists can accomplish almost anything! That's why we're the envy of the entire world!" Frank egotistically boasted. "We're born entrepreneurs!"

"Please be quiet and listen to Monica!" Dr. Rose Jeffries commanded from her seat directly behind Frank. "Show some courtesy! Your unsavory opinions aren't exactly being relished or cherished by the other passengers!"

"Your totally silly politically correct nonsense is contrary to the operations of the objective adult mind!" Davies mercilessly ranted to Dr. Rose, much to her chagrin and humiliation. "It's a revolting social sickness that rivals any infectious disease!"

The somewhat exhausted trekkers stopped in Amalfi (a large hillside town that resembled Positano in sublime appearance). The group ate the standard three-course lunch served at a posh hotel and then with renewed energy again boarded the tour bus for the anticipated trip to historic Pompeii.

"The traffic on this narrow street is quite horrendous, almost brutal!" Frank curtly mentioned to Monica. "And these people flying around the wicked curves on motor scooters are a definite hazard. This entire street is treacherous! How many turns did you say this winding road has?"

"Around two-thousand five hundred!" the effervescent tour guide recollected and confirmed. "Of course, that's an approximation!"

"That's about two-thousand four hundred and ninety-nine too many!" Frank negatively bellowed. "How do they get accident victims and emergency cases to the nearest hospital?" Davies relentlessly persisted. "This lengthy snake-like road is excessively dangerous!"

"By helicopter!" Monica replied.

"That makes sense because anyone in need of medical attention would otherwise die from traffic congestion let alone from lung congestion!" Frank condescendingly exhaled. "Where did you learn to speak English?"

"I spent three years living in Brooklyn!" Monica patiently replied.

"Shut up!" Lois reprimanded as she gave her husband another healthy dig in the ribs with her sharp left elbow. "Shut up! Stop asking so many irrelevant annoying questions!" she angrily parroted.

"You're hysterically overreacting!" Davies fired back.

The archeological treasures of Pompeii were quite exceptional, ranging from the well-preserved gladiator practice arena to the antiquated amphitheater, where Greco-Roman plays were once performed. Then Monica led the tourists on a walking trip around the "resurrected city" that Mt. Vesuvius had violently buried under thirty-foot of volcanic ash.

"Notice the elevated rocks in the center of the street!" Monica indicated. "Residents would use the raised rocks to cross the road because raw sewage had used natural gravity to flow down the street from the higher ground to your left to the lower end of the city to your right!"

"The ancient Romans didn't know crap about crap!" Frank boisterously nitpicked. "I'll bet that the Italians have learned *that* particular tradition from their primitive ancestors! The E-*truss*-cans all had double hernias, especially the men!"

Monica just stared incredulously at Frank Davies while *his* disbelieving wife dragged him to the back of the crowd to avoid potential friction in public. "The people of Pompeii had a fascination, or should I say a special fixation with sex!" Monica pointed out to her remaining listeners. "Please observe this bit of graffiti drawn on this wall. Look closely! It's an exaggerated male reproductive organ!"

"It's homo erectus, even if the ancient Romans weren't gay!" Frank boomed for all to hear. "That graffiti was probably drawn by a *porn'* again Christian!"

Monica was stunned and at a complete loss for words at the speaker's general audacity and brazenness. Lois then pulled her marital partner into an alley and again lectured him about his "total lack of decorum."

"Lately there's been nothing sentimental or commendable about you Frank! You've managed to deride many people including your good friend Warren on this supposedly wonderful tour!" Lois screamed out of control. "You're an insult to your country and to humanity!"

Frank intensely scrutinized his Sea Pass to verify his identity. "Truthfully Lois, I'm not myself. Today I actually think and believe I'm my ill-tempered brother Fred!"

* * * * * * * * * * * *

That evening Frank and Lois dressed for supper and hesitantly departed Cabin Room 8322. The couple remained non-verbal as they entered the vacant elevator that promptly conducted them down to the fifth deck Magic Carousel Dining Room. The emotionally distraught feuding couple obstinately entered the ship's restaurant not realizing that the whole place was virtually devoid of human activity.

When Frank and his peeved wife arrived at their familiar table they were appalled to see that Fred and Eleanor Davies were already seated there. Frank was the first to comment on the weird parallel coincidence.

"What are you two misfits doing here?" Davies exclaimed in absolute astonishment. "This is more of an ugly aberration than a blessed miracle!"

"Where are Warren and Melissa, Lisa and David, Dr. Rose and Judy Marks?" the virtually mesmerized Lois Davies asked, almost in a trance.

"This ugly encounter totally defies logic and reason!" Fred incredulously replied. "You two are on this ship two weeks later than you're supposed to be! This is supposed to be *our* European vacation!"

"Something's mighty peculiar here!" Eleanor Davies stated from her seat in a disconcerted tone of voice. "And I must admit that Fred and I have been acting rather strange lately. He's been sounding like *you* Frank and I've been sounding exactly like *you* Lois! *Our* confused minds just couldn't account for those crazy anomalies!"

Just then Cem and Tomas appeared to further complicate matters on the already-bewildering scene. "Welcome folks for your final dinner on the cruise!" Cem mysteriously began his odd-but-powerful discourse. "And today is Thursday, September 28th, 2006, what you four targeted passengers might consider a compromise date."

"You four dupes might think that Cem and I are working for the Regal Adventurer, but actually we're delighted to report to *you* four honored people that we have another even more successful employer!" Tomas obscurely and cynically stated. "This ship, or should I say this heinous trap, happens to belong to someone *you* commonly allude to as Lucifer!"

"Yes valued Guests, Tomas and I are shrewdly recruiting new clients and patrons for our awesome Master," Cem evilly informed.

"The terminology 'eternal slaves' would certainly represent and constitute more accurate language!" Tomas enlightened his rather astounded and appalled audience. "The four of you are now specimens, or should I say carefully selected participants in a new innovative *moral,* or should I say a new innovative *immoral* experiment involving the unique confluence of time and space. Congratulations Francis, Frederick, Lois and Eleanor!" Tomas diabolically declared and snickered. "You're all about to be dishonorably inducted into a most premier organization!"

"Now be ready to consume some delicious Deviled Clams for an appetizer, some Deviled Crab-meat for your main entrée and some Devil's Food Cake for your very palatable dessert," Cem confidently and confidentially related to his stunned prey. "You unfortunate nominees have no choice in this delicate awe-inspiring matter for indeed, all four of you naïve morons have just involuntarily surrendered your free wills!"

"No *Angel's Food* cake aboard Satan's favorite ship! Welcome to the enigmatic Prince of Darkness Regal Adventurer!" Tomas scrupulously clarified, much to the dismay and horror of his four victimized recruits. "Cem and I are greatly exuberant, way beyond *your* very limited human imaginations! This truly and undeniably is a most thrilling event! We've finally met our work quotas! We're now mercifully emancipated from perpetual drudgery! Freedom is finally ours! Thank you so much for *your* inadvertent cooperation!"

And then with an absence of ceremony both Cem and Tomas cryptically transformed into frightening zombies and next into incessantly laughing skeletons. In a matter of seconds and without

84

any indication of resistance, Frank, Lois, Fred and Eleanor obediently joined *their* un-illustrious and totally accursed damned company on a mysterious journey into infinity.

"Window of Opportunity"

The May Installation Meeting assigning new officers for the Hammonton, New Jersey Lions Club had just adjourned and afterwords, two recently appointed minor functionaries were discussing their basic roles with an elderly club member in the upstairs bar of Rocco's Town House on North Third Street. The all-too-garrulous District 16-C Governor had already departed the premises and Liontamer Mitchell Spencer, Tailtwister Michael Giberson and feeble Past President Julius Stetson were standing at the tavern's bar casually engaged in a genial conversation over their after-meeting cocktails.

"It's good to see new blood coming into the club and accepting active roles," eighty-two year old Julius Stetson praised the local Lions Club's two new energized recruits. "I was a charter member of the club way back in 1963," Julius informed his respectful listeners before sipping his cold *Southern Comfort* on the rocks, "and we had only a dozen members when John F. Kennedy was the country's President, mostly businessmen owning stores and properties up on Route 30. One guy had a liquor store, another guy was a produce broker, a third had a gas station and auto' repair garage and a fourth fella' owned a popular diner that stayed open until three in the morning," old Julius Stetson reminisced. "Those fun-loving guys are all dead now and I'm the only original charter member left. At the time the town's Kiwanis and Rotary were the top civic organizations in Hammonton and the fledgling Lions were like the town's orphan upstarts. After the Lillian-on-the-Lake closed for business," Stetson related, "our tiny club had to meet in the small back room of the Hacienda Restaurant while the hotshot and snobbish Kiwanis guys got priority and enjoyed their meals in the big dining area."

"Hacienda Restaurant?" Mitchell Spencer politely interrupted Julius. "I've never heard of it!"

"Where have all the years gone? The stucco Spanish-styled place used to be located at the intersection of Route 30 and Route 206 where the Rite-Aid Pharmacy is now situated," Lion Stetson nostalgically revealed. "The Hacienda was demolished back in the late 1970s, just a few years before either of you two whippersnappers were ever born let alone conceived."

"Were you a conscientious Lion?" Liontamer Mitchell Spencer courteously inquired. "I presume you must've been. I mean, I've never heard a vegetable vendor selling rotten tomatoes from his wagon! You had to be a true-blue Lion from the outset to have been a dedicated member all these years."

"Like yourself" Mitchell, I started-out as the lowly Liontamer, taking care of the club's banner, gavel, gong, microphone and table podium," Julius nonchalantly informed his avid audience of two. "Then I was promoted. The next year I was the Tailtwister, the club sheriff levying fines on members that came late to a meeting or who had forgotten to wear their club pin on their jacket lapel or who had neglected to wear their membership badge or have their Lions International Card in their wallet. And if they checked-out okay with those essential credentials in their possession," Julius bragged and prattled before imbibing a swig of sweet liquor, "I'd then fine them on the spot if the violators couldn't answer a simple question like 'Who founded Lions International in 1917?' or 'Who challenged the Lions to become Knights of the Blind at an early international convention'?"

"Melvin Jones was the founder of Lions International," Liontamer Mitchell Spencer proudly answered with an air of certainty evident in his voice, "and Helen Keller gave an important speech at the convention you had mentioned and got the first wave of Lions interested in becoming champions for the blind and crusaders for the hearing impaired. She also encouraged the Lions to help the less fortunate in their communities. But unfortunately," Mitch Spencer continued, "presently the government is taking over the function of charity through welfare programs and redistribution of wealth so the need for service clubs assisting the needy is rapidly diminishing all throughout the country."

"Okay Wise Guy," old Julius Stetson stated with a smile, "who was the first president of Lions International?"

"Melvin Jones?" Mitchell tentatively answered. "Obviously yes, I'm quite certain that it must've been Melvin Jones if *he* was the founder of Lions International!"

"No Mitch, it was a man named Dr. W. P. Woods, so that'll be a dollar fine!" knowledgeable club historian Julius Stetson joked and amply laughed. "And as the District Governor had lectured tonight, our international headquarters is in Oak Brook, Illinois, just outside Chicago. But over the years Lions International has grown to over 30,000 clubs in over 150 countries and our international membership now totals nearly one and a half million members," Julius reviewed. "In fact Gentlemen, in many parts of the world like in India and Japan for example, it's a distinct honor to become a philanthropic Lion."

"You must be pretty bored with all of the redundant routines and monotonous speeches after nearly a half century of involvement?" high school English teacher Mitchell Spencer asked his sponsor and mentor. "I mean, how many times do you have to hear the same rhetoric about membership drives, the value of newspaper public relations and the need for participation in club fundraisers?"

"Well, I gotta' admit," Julius replied and then paused to carefully select his next words, "over the years our charity fundraisers have switched around. In the beginning we had a Turkey Shoot and we also collected money donations out in front of a grocery store for White Cane Day. Then later on we had a Bike-A-Thon and sponsored a Tri-Ath-A-Lon mostly because four ambitious state troopers had joined the club and insisted on us having fundraisers that focused on physical fitness. Now of course," Julius paused and elaborated, "we have the Gold Raffle Dinner where we give away seventeen thousand dollars in cash and prizes and we also loyally sell muffins, pies, strudel and turnovers at the annual Blueberry Festival in late June. Those two events alone earn the club over twenty thousand bucks a year and I predict that someday both of you two greenhorns will be chairmen of those two highly profitable fundraisers."

"Well Lion Julius," Mike Giberson said before swallowing down the remainder of his cordial drink, "what in your whole recollection were the craziest things you can remember the local Lions doing back in the good old days?"

"Ha, ha, ha," aged Julius Stetson giggled and then smirked. "In the beginning when there were only men in the club, we did some nifty things. It was sort of like a fraternity for adult males. Once we hired a stripper to entertain us in the back room of an out-of-town bar to honor the achievements of an outgoing president. Another time twelve of us journeyed in a van down to Ocean City, Maryland and we paid a surprise visit to an enterprising club member who owned several thriving boardwalk businesses," Stetson recalled with a snicker. "The shocked fella' treated us all to a fantastic crab and spicy shrimp feast at Phillip's Restaurant. But the neatest occurrence I can recall involved a new member who had transferred into the Hammonton Lions from a club up near Yonkers, New York. Yes, that new member precipitated something special."

"Tell me quick what happened!" Tailtwister Mike Giberson insisted. "I have to soon get on the road and pick up my son at the elementary school after his basketball practice. I don't want to keep his coach waiting as a babysitter."

"Well, this new member, his name was Henry Thomas, had three of his old friends drive down from Yonkers, New York and lo and behold, the mischievous culprits stole our club bell. So eighteen of us Hammonton rascals rented a gigantic RV and drove up to Yonkers to retrieve the bell according to standard Lions' custom. The idea behind that kind of good-humored theft is designed and endorsed by all Lions' clubs to promote fellowship and subsequent visitations to other clubs in order to advance the cause of sharing a good time."

"Is that all?" Giberson asked in a disappointed tone of voice. "I was expecting something a little more dynamic! Did you guys ever retrieve your club bell?"

"You didn't allow me to finish my terrific story!" old Julius facetiously balked. "On the way up to Yonkers I was driving the mammoth RV on the New Jersey Turnpike. Traffic was bumper-to-bumper early that evening. The other guys were pretty inebriated by that time when we had reached the vicinity of the Newark Airport, and I must confess, including myself. In the midst of the massive automobile congestion," Julius expounded on his tale, "I awkwardly tried changing lanes and in the process I partially ripped-off the RV's back bumper when a stubborn tractor-trailer driver wouldn't let me switch lanes. There wasn't any noticeable damage to his big rig but the RV bumper was more than a trifle mangled."

"What happened next?" Tailtwister Giberson curiously asked. "Did you have to pay for the bumper repair? Did you have to buy a new one? Either way, it must've cost a decent fortune!"

"You're too impetuous and in my opinion Mike, your spoiled kid and his impatient coach can wait for you an extra five minutes at the school gym!" Julius chastised the recently installed club enforcement officer. "It was during the early '70s, yes, during the Carter Administration, and there was gas rationing and long gas station lines everywhere," Lion Stetson recalled and shared. "Anyway Fellas', on the way back from Yonkers we stopped near the north end of the Garden State Parkway to purchase gas. At the time a fuel crisis was rampant across the nation, and if your license plate ended in an even number, you could only buy gas on an even number day of the month. Well, it was an even number day and we had an odd number ending to our RV's license plate so the attendants refused to sell us fuel."

"How did you get home?" Liontamer Mitchell Spencer wanted to know. "This story is becoming quite intriguing. How did you avoid being stranded a hundred and twenty miles away from Hammonton in a gas-guzzling RV?"

"You're just as immaturely impulsive as Tailtwister Giberson is!" Julius Stetson merrily chided before imbibing another tasty gulp of sweet *Southern Comfort*. "The four audacious state troopers in the club, all of them thoroughly groggy from gulping-down hard whiskey, well, they showed the suddenly alarmed attendants their State Police ID badges, blatantly flashed guns from their holsters, told the petrified gas station employees that *they* would be accused of harmfully obstructing justice since the damaged RV was on a secret drug raid mission, and consequently, the totally intimidated gas station guys immediately filled us up without any further controversy whatsoever."

"Ha, ha, ha! That was rich!" Tailtwister Michael Giberson commended the old-timer. "I wish I had been in the RV to see the frightened expressions on the gas station workers' faces! But how did you ever get the rear bumper fixed!"

"Well now Boys, that's another fascinating tale that actually happened!" Julius merrily maintained. "When we eventually got back to Hammonton, the already drunk member who owned the large garage up on Route 30 got into the RV's driver seat, put the immense vehicle into reverse and then violently slammed into the cinder-blocked side of his service station. Miraculously, the bumper was pressed back into its proper place without any notice of ever being in an accident or ever being tampered with."

"That's really an incredibly nifty narrative!" Mike Giberson congratulated old Julius. "Sorry Guys but I gotta' split! Hope to see you both in two weeks at our next meeting."

After the newly appointed Tailtwister departed the sparsely populated Rocco's Town House bar area, Julius Stetson had a personal question to ask Liontamer Mitchell Spencer.

"Mitch, I'm a good judge of human character and I think you're a fine young man. I honestly believe that you remind me a lot of myself when I was financially struggling back in the midst of the 1950s recessions," Julius prefaced his odd and unexpected remarks. "I hear that you're thinking about dropping out of the Lions Club for money reasons. I know that you're an excellent high school English teacher and I'm also aware that you make just an ordinary income."

"Well quite frankly Mr. Stetson, I've accumulated considerable debts that I find myself drowning in," Mitch confided. "My divorce last year set me back big time, I have a tremendous mortgage on my home out on Second Road, I have to pay for my former wife's new condominium over on the bay in Brigantine, I must pay her alimony along with child support for our two kids now in her custody by the judge's ruling and finally, I have over forty thousand dollars in high interest credit cards. My overwhelming total debt obligations are in the neighborhood of…"

"A half million dollars," sage Julius passively declared before finishing his second delicious whiskey. "Like I said Mitch, I really like you and feel sorry for your unenviable plight. As you might know from town gossip, my wife is dead, I have no children of my own and I absolutely despise my still-living avaricious niece and greedy nephew on my deceased wife's side. I'm eighty-two years old and have bad cases of colon and prostate cancer. Confidentially, the doctors at Jefferson Hospital over in Philly' say that I have only a month or so left," the old gentleman frankly divulged. "It's too late for me to incorporate you into my will but should you happen to read my obituary in the local papers, I'm going to give you an extra back door key to my mansion over on Third Road. After my death, you must go to my residence immediately to avoid any complications with my money-hungry niece and nephew." The old man then reached into his pants pocket and exhibited a common key, finally surrendering its possession to the astounded wide-eyed young Liontamer.

"What will this key lead to?" Mitch marveled and uttered, scrutinizing the ordinary-looking object very closely. "Specifically, what's it really for other than to gain access to your home? Of what value is it to me?"

"Inside my cluttered master bedroom closet you'll find a big wall safe concealed directly behind my shoe rack," Julius indicated without showing any emotion. "In the safe I'm going to leave a half million dollars cash for you to pay off your massive debts so that you can start your life all over again and avert the grievous mistakes that have brought you to the threshold of bankruptcy. You'll find that *that* same key will open both the back door and the master bedroom closet wall safe."

"I can't believe your unexpected generosity!" Mitchell exclaimed, getting the attention of several idle tavern patrons seated on the opposite side of the oval bar. "Thank you so very much! You're an absolute Godsend!"

92

"But please listen carefully and fully heed my words," benefactor Julius Stetson whispered to his jubilant prospective beneficiary. "When I had been a flashy show business performer back in the late 1940s, I had amassed a fine reputation as a class-act magician. Inside my hall cedar closet I've painstakingly constructed what I call 'my Window of Opportunity,' which will become *your* 'Window of Opportunity.' Open the stained glass window leading to a hidden room and I promise that you'll discover additional rare treasures awaiting you!"

All that totally thrilled Mitchell Spencer could do was stand there at the bar with an astonished-but-grateful expression on his florid countenance while wildly imagining exactly what the mysterious 'Window of Opportunity' could actually be.

* * * * * * * * * * * *

Two weeks passed and the English teacher faithfully carried the 'gift key' in his pocket to Hammonton High School every single workday. 'Julius said that I must go to his home as soon as I learn of his passing and use this back door key immediately so that I can remove the half million cash from the closet wall safe and then determine what's behind the mysterious 'Window of Opportunity' in the cedar closet,' Mitchell kept reminding himself during seventh period while his advanced academic students were taking their *Hamlet* written examination.

That Tuesday evening Lion Julius Stetson did not attend the bi-weekly club meeting and it was reported that he was home suffering from a mild spring sinus infection and that the old gentleman seemed to be in good spirits when the distinguished elderly 'Past President' had called the club secretary and had informed the executive of *his* legitimate excuse for being absent.

An additional two weeks passed and another scheduled Lions Club meeting commenced at Rocco's Town House. After the customary Pledge of Allegiance, the opening prayer and the traditional Lions' Toast, during *his* introductory remarks the club president announced that revered Lion Julius Stetson had "suffered a devastating stroke" that afternoon and that the eighty-two year old multimillionaire had been rushed by ambulance to Mainland Hospital in Pomona, the renowned state-of-the-art medical facility being seventeen miles east of Hammonton.

'My cousin Helen Reynolds is a night nurse in the emergency room at Mainland,' Mitchell astutely and mentally associated. 'I'll quietly text message her during this boring meeting to learn more about Julius's condition. My cousin's very reliable. I'm sure that if Helen is not in surgery right now, she'll be able to give me an update on my benefactor's condition in the form of a prompt reply.'

Forty-five minutes later, just before the standard meeting ending "fifty-fifty drawing," Mitchell received a return text message from nurse Helen Reynolds stating that Julius Stetson of Hammonton had died at 7:35 p.m. that evening and that his next of kin were presently being notified along with a prominent Hammonton undertaker.

'It's happened! God rest *his* soul! The initial suspense is now over!' Mitchell sadly evaluated with perspiration appearing on his forehead just before he won the sum of thirty dollars in the fifty-fifty drawing. "I'd like to give the money I've just won back to the club!" Spencer articulated as the seated members unanimously gave him an appreciative round of applause.

Then an image of the prospective half-million dollar 'cash bonanza' focused inside Spencer's racing mind and the Liontamer's thoughts greedily contemplated the swift acquisition of his highly anticipated good fortune. 'I'll act calm and collected, pretend that nothing relevant has occurred and then unobtrusively leave the meeting and evade the subsequent small talk and chitchatting as soon as possible. Next I'll waste no time being off to Julius's mansion on Third Road to claim my spectacular windfall before his covetous niece and nephew or the Hammonton Police can beat me there.'

Every operational phase at the Third Road mansion smoothly developed and transpired just as Julius Stetson had accurately described to Mitchell Spencer only weeks prior to the old man's demise. The designated key easily opened the back door. After surreptitiously flicking on a flashlight to locate the master bedroom's closet, the eager interloper anxiously moved the vertical shoe rack and the ecstatic searcher easily located the wide-spaced wall safe. The key insertion worked perfectly and just as dependable Julius Stetson had predicted, the half million dollars in hundred dollar bills had been left inside the safe in a utilitarian white linen bag.

'Oh my God! My life has been rescued from disaster!' Mitchell Spencer euphorically reckoned. 'I'll never forget *your* compassion and your kindness! Thank you Julius! Thank you from the bottom of my heart! Now to find the Window of Opportunity in the hall cedar closet to retrieve my special bonus!'

* * * * * * * * * * * *

Mitchell hastily maneuvered his way down the straight light blue-carpeted hallway, and soon his curiosity found the object of his quest. In the center of the long corridor the highly-focused intensely sweating house-explorer quickly located the door to the prized storage room. 'It's locked!' Mitchell instantly recognized and regretted. 'Ah, the magic key also opens this closet door too! I believe that Julius forgot to mention *that* isolated fact to me! I'll close the door behind me, turn on the overhead light, saving the batteries in my flashlight. Then I'll carefully open that beautiful stained glass window at the other end of this closet. I see that it features two heavenly angels blowing their celestial golden trumpets. I can't wait to discover my promised bonus reward!'

After cautiously accomplishing those rather facile and elementary tasks, the perspiring searcher was so completely thrilled about admiring the singular and resplendent 'Window of Opportunity', and his totally engrossed mind never for one suspicious moment ever comprehended that his physical existence had been permanently locked inside the enormous rectangular cedar closet.

Firmly gripping and holding the linen bag containing the half million dollars, the obsessed young man gently lifted the bottom window frame and much to his utter shock and horror, Mitchell Spencer's body was instantaneously sucked inside the aperture by a powerful mystical supernatural force.

And before the frightened and petrified victim had a chance to either scream or shriek, the mystical Window of Opportunity quickly descended like a guillotine blade and the device forcefully slammed shut. Incredibly, the magnificent pair of handsome angels that had decorated the inimitable stained glass portal momentarily transformed into malicious-looking red-skinned demons, and then the wicked window that had been so maliciously constructed inside the cedar closet's back wall abruptly disappeared into oblivion.

* * * * * * * * * * * *

A dimly lit dense fog shrouded and enveloped a cold and barren subterranean swampy moor. The vigilant and awesome Black Angel of Death patiently awaited the arrival of the en route newly acquired transmigrating soul, for to the gargantuan immortal winged creature, time was not ephemeral and its mundane passage had no boundaries or particular definition. Finally the rejuvenated spirit and psyche personage of one wily Julius Stetson materialized on the hazy and nebulous moor, the space/time voyager's past personality now parasitically residing inside the physical appearance of its new host, Mitchell Spencer.

"I must compliment you on a most propitious and effortless spiritual transfer!" the austere-looking Black Angel bluntly stated. "I must confess that your diabolical Window of Opportunity trick has again been skillfully employed. The deceased spirit and soul of your targeted subject has been symmetrically aligned with and absorbed into your former eighty-two year old frail lifeless body and simultaneously, your former corrupt spirit, by virtue of *our* contract agreement, is now speeding on its way to Hell. Now Sir, alias Julius Stetson, your unscrupulous heart and mind, by virtue of your devious canard, have been meritoriously transplanted into Mitchell Spencer's vernal form and you've successfully earned a new extension to your mortal existence, and as you're well-aware, you've coincidentally inherited and obtained a vibrant new slightly used soul to complement your new virile body. And just to think," the thwarted and outsmarted Black Angel uttered and summarized, "our friendly relationship all started around three hundred and ninety years ago in Florence, Italy during the time of…"

"During the time of Galileo and the despicable Inquisitions when scientific thought was readily condemned by the unrelenting Catholic Church bureaucracy and thus, technological progress was deemed sheer heresy," the newly exchanged spirit of Julius Stetson answered the sinister Devil's Messenger, with the dead man's resurrected soul now-residing inside Mitchell Spencer's strong vernal anatomy. "That's when I felt compelled to sign my binding contract with *you*! But as is outlined in Paragraph One, *you* can only mortgage my soul when I fail to find a vulnerable substitute every six decades or so."

The Black Angel was somewhat perturbed that his subject had again evaded *his* relentless pursuit. "Wily Magician, I promise to apprehend your soul and escort it to Hell the first time you fail at performing your simple-yet-odious deception. Yes, but upon rehashing our odd history together Sagacious Sir, I recollect that our second devilish encounter had occurred during…"

"During the Great Age of the Illuminati in Southern Germany, yes Black Angel, in medieval Munich, and if I also recollect, a half-century later our third assignation, like the second one, had similarly transpired in this very same gloomy moor. That specific

96

third development had happened immediately after *my* dupe's death in Marseilles, France during that intellectual genius Voltaire's most splendid Age of Enlightenment."

"Affirmative, but please don't forget one significant detail Masterful Wizard," the solemn-faced and lugubrious Black Angel articulated with a frowning expression evident on its formidable-looking visage, "you're no longer Julius Stetson but technically, to the not-too-brilliant human world, you're now Mitchell Spencer, professional educator. Do you plan to continue your mediocre career as a high school English teacher?"

"Hell no Black Angel! As Mitchell Spencer, I'll wisely use up my remaining sick days and then I'll resign from the school district effective July 1st," the self-centered four-century-old re-formatted human being replied. "And of course, I still have in my possession my luxurious mansion, which naturally I had perceptively willed to myself (Mitchell Spencer) along with my five million dollars in my Merrill Lynch stock account and also my five-hundred thousand dollars in cash now concealed inside *my* upstairs cedar closet. The glorious and reliable Window of Opportunity, which as you've already acknowledged was really an exceptionally clever trap because it was *my* very necessary Window of Opportunity that was exclusively designed for *me* alone to live another fifty or so years inside this naïve gullible idiot Mitchell Spencer's youthful body. Perhaps I shouldn't criticize my new self so severely!"

"That's precisely why my immediate superior and awesome Commander-in-Chief Lucifer positively covets *your* calculated cunning so much, because Sir, your charming character is insanely disingenuous and you indeed are a virtual expert at executing marvelously heinous schemes!" the Black Angel commended his illustrious and very lucky mortal acquaintance. "Tell me now Triumphant One, will you be attending the dupe's, or should I say *the unfortunate victim's* funeral? After all, as bizarre as it may sound or seem, you will be *your* own fortunate heir."

"Yes, under the circumstances, *that* benign social gesture would be the appropriate and ethical thing to do since as you've just mentioned Angel Friend, I've been delegated as *his* sole and exclusive beneficiary!" the re-generated medieval alchemist and potent accomplished sorcerer cleverly remarked. "And soon thereafter Black Angel, I'll be moving to another unsuspecting community, that is, after I legally acquire and sell my inherited

Third Road mansion, ha, ha, ha! I think I'll try living in Italy again!"

"Well now," the contemplative Black Angel very respectfully addressed its human companion, who was apparently reveling in achieving *his* recently earned new lease on life, "you always accomplish your 'transmigration of soul tricking routine' within the required seventy-two hour parameters. I suppose that our next incidental meeting will be in approximately another fifty-to-sixty Earth years when *your* then decrepit spirit and debilitated psyche will again require replenishment, reincarnation and transmigration into a new body," the Black Angel matter-of-factly declared.

"That is absolutely correct!" the rejuvenated wily Alchemist wholeheartedly verified. "To be sure!"

"Indeed, Dracula and his vampires have nothing noteworthy over you!" the enormous Black Angel stoically admitted. "Good luck in scamming another unwary young male while you again gamble your already-damned soul. And I congratulate you for adroitly eluding your eternal fate! I feel obligated to inform you that my supernatural senses confirm the reality that my Satanic Colleagues now have the former Julius Stetson's body and soul in their custody while the former Mitchell Spencer's suspended pristine soul is presently on moral probation, comfortably residing inside *your* new young human form."

"So long my four-century-long Friend!" the most fortunate resourceful magician replied. "Truthfully, I think I need a change in venue from living in Hammonton, New Jersey. First I intend to move down to South Padre Island, Texas and begin a new fresh existence. But this time I think I'll join either the Kiwanis or the Rotary Club down there near the Mexican Border. When I tire of Texas, I'll then migrate over to Italy. I presume we'll again rendezvous in this same ominous swampy moor a half Earth century or so from now!" the mortal soul enthusiastically commented. "Over the centuries this Window of Opportunity bait idea has worked extremely well for me and as is my standard practice, I won't deviate one iota from again using it in the future! Fearsome Black Angel," the shrewd Alchemist declared, "my proven strategy might sound like an overused cliché, but the fact of the matter is 'Nothing really succeeds like success'!"

"The Music Portal"

Up until four months ago I had regarded my very ordinary life as being a dismal failure. My mediocre occupation ever since I was fresh out of high school has been that of a dissatisfied shoe salesman at Brock Shoes Outlet in Berlin, New Jersey. For thirty-one miserable years I would loyally commute each working day from my French Street home in nearby Hammonton, a flourishing agricultural community located twelve miles east of Berlin and also conveniently situated midway between vacation destination Atlantic City and bustling Philadelphia, Pennsylvania, the distances being thirty miles in either direction from my house to the East Coast gambling Mecca and to Benjamin Franklin's City of Brotherly Love.

The principal factor that I do remember about my former employment was that I absolutely loathed being a common shoe salesman, feigning cheerfulness daily, having to look at some very ugly feet over the course of the last three-plus decades, and unfortunately having to smell some horrible stenches emanating from the toes of people who apparently neglected taking frequent baths and showers and who evidently had little regard for the psychological needs of a disgruntled oxfords, loafers and sandals' salesman who never seemed to have the desired exact size and the precise color on the Brock Shoes Outlet's stockroom shelves.

And my family life (or lack thereof) also had immensely contributed to my chronic emotionally depressed condition. My materialistic wife Virginia had left me seven years ago for a more prosperous man, a prominent Hammonton blueberry farmer owning (through inheritance) a highly lucrative five hundred acre plantation on Middle Road. And to add to my quandary, my three children have disowned me, preferring to side with their now rich mother who continuously and generously dotes on them and helps the avaricious siblings with their high-cost college tuitions, with their monthly car payments and with their often-solicited recreation money.

Yes, all was utter despair in my lackluster financial existence, with my only real joy being the bad habit of blowing most of my spare money in various Atlantic City casinos. In time, *that* wretched addictive activity had become almost an uncontrollable obsession. Bally's Casino, Harrah's Hotel, the Showboat, Caesar's World, the Trump Taj Mahal, the Trump Marina, the Trump Plaza, Resorts International, the Borgata, the Claridge and the Hilton all provided my need for greed with basic gambling venue/entertainment while simultaneously confirming to my fragile psyche that I was a born loser and was surely destined to die as one.

But then last July 16th, 2008 (on a Wednesday if my undependable memory serves me correctly), I had attended the annual carnival feast of Our Lady of Mt. Carmel at the fair grounds on Third Street across from St. Joseph Catholic Church. Although I'm not the most congenial or convivial person in the world, I've always been a religious fellow and somewhat superstitious too, if I may mention *that* ancillary fact.

After attending the morning Mass that commemorates the festival, I sanctimoniously lit a candle next to the Hammonton church's altar and tabernacle. Then after stepping outside the building, I faithfully pinned a hundred dollar bill on the statue of Our Lady of Mt. Carmel in the traditional Italian noon street procession that immediately followed the sacred church observances.

Later that afternoon I indulged in swallowing-down two pepper and sausage sandwiches at the Assumption Concession Stand that had been erected in the St. Joseph Church asphalt parking lot to accommodate hungry feast-day patrons. Everything occurring on that particular July 16th day seemed normal, copacetic and consistent with my overall nondescript life.

Exactly one week later on Wednesday, July 23rd, the all-too-familiar brown UPS delivery truck pulled into my French Street driveway at 5:30 p.m. After exchanging a few casual pleasantries with the likeable driver, I carried my compact package into the house, a small carton weighing about two-to-three pounds. My curious eyes keenly noticed that the shipping address had been mysteriously labeled "Freiburg, Germany."

'This must be some mistake or error, or perhaps it's even a weird practical joke being played on me,' I initially considered. 'I don't know anybody that lives in Germany, let alone residing in a remote place like Freiburg. The town sounds pretty rural. True, my cleaning lady is from Germany and the janitor over at the elementary school is too, but outside of those two nice acquaintances,' I presumed and speculated, 'I have no other connections or associations with *that* particular European country.'

Before opening the unexpected brown-wrapped ordinary-looking package, I rechecked the mailing address to ascertain that the always- reliable UPS man had made an accurate drop-off.
100

Feeling satisfied that my assiduous inspection of the item's exterior had been complete, I ventured over to my den's book shelf and pulled-out *Encyclopedia G*. After leafing through the thick book's pages, my intensive research eventually located the "Population Distribution" map of Germany. After admiring impressive color photographs of the Rhine River Valley and of the architectural wonder known as Hohenzollen Castle, my cursory 'information investigation' discovered that Freiburg, Germany was located in the vicinity of the Bavarian Black Forest.

After completing my research, I eagerly tore away the package's outer brown paper covering and then meticulously opened the small carton, making certain not to damage the contents inside. Much to my curious surprise and wonder, a small computer-like instrument, comparable to a Blackberry hand-held device, had been neatly tucked inside, enveloped in wrinkled-up German language newspaper pages. With my fascination running wild, my eyes closely examined and then really scrutinized the very intriguing item of interest, its purpose at that specific moment representing an enigma to me.

'Let's see,' I pensively analyzed, attempting to objectively keep my volatile emotions in harness. 'I must not allow my heart to interfere with my mind's goal here. Here's a folded-up instructions' leaflet,' I astutely observed, 'and wow, by coincidence it's written in English too! I don't even have to consult the German-to-English dictionary on the *Internet* for an interpretation. All there is on the facing of this peculiar device is one 'On' and one 'Off' switch along with a standard liquid display readout at the top!'

Then I carefully read the directions to the remarkable "Music Portal Product," and all along my mind was unusually captivated with its new-found interest, the extraordinary object instantly manifesting itself as a unique source of personal wonder.

"Use this very special mechanism only in a dire emergency where your life might be in danger or in jeopardy. There are twelve relevant songs programmed into this very sensitive device, the purpose of each tune you'll be able to accurately hypothesize after your full usage of the 'Music Portal'."

Then I read a more vivid description. "The first ten songs will pertain to your ability to deal with unsavory people that might be endangering your physical well-being while the final two musical arrangements will be pertinent to your much-needed growth as an individual, helping you achieve mortal self-actualization and therefore affecting *you* to ultimately finding a genuine reason for directly participating in the efficacious development of your psychological/spiritual self-fulfillment."

I then finished comprehending the remainder of the given instructions. "It is strongly advised that you implement and use this wonderful gift wisely. Simply plug the accompanying earphones into the device, and when threatened, use the first ten tunes to eliminate your immediate problem. And then upon developing the necessary courage to overcome your ten adversities, responsibly activate the final two songs at your own volition and during the transition, courageously commence discovering your purpose-driven life."

Your sympathetic Freiburg friends

My re-energized thought processes contemplated the intricate invention's possible significance in relation to my monotonous dejected life. I truly wanted to avoid any potential discrepancies concerning the successful operation of the Music Portal while my fertile imagination considered what would actually happen upon my intentional activation of the 'very handsome-looking foreign made computer.' My captivated mind still being somewhat befuddled, I very deliberately thrice re-read the very explicit directions on how to effectively optimize my ownership of the newly acquired electronic object. It didn't take me too long to perceptively figure out the magical power associated with the exceptional miniature apparatus that I had by good fortune obtained via standard UPS delivery.

On Monday morning, July 21st I had to honor a scheduled 10:00 a.m. doctor's appointment at *Thomas Jefferson University Hospital*, Philadelphia. I drove my blue *Nissan Altima* from Hammonton to the Lindenwold High Speed Line Terminal just west of Berlin, purchased my round-trip ticket from the lady cashier and soon boarded the nine o'clock train into Philly'.

My scheduled appointment (and routine medical checkup) went smoothly and I was very happy with my heart doctor's favorable report. I exited the brick-façade 1600 Walnut Street Building and very warily strolled the several blocks east and then south to the Port Authority Subway Station at 10th and Locust. Without any warning, four young city punks wielding switchblade knives accosted me at the base of the otherwise empty subterranean station's steps.

Startled as I was, luckily I was holding the Music Portal Device in my right hand while wearing the accompanying

102

attached earphones. Instinctively I entered my survival/self-preservation behavioral mode. I forcefully pressed the "On" button and my auditory senses heard the 1974 ABBA hit "Waterloo" being played through my earphones. Instantly the four unsavory city thugs disappeared into oblivion, the fantastic event occurring as if they had never occupied that particular time and space. It was then and there that I superficially grasped the specific functionality of the most incredible Music Portal Device.

'I wonder if those four villainous creeps are actually right now at the Battle of Waterloo with Wellington's or with Napoleon's troops, or perhaps instead they've been marvelously conveyed to a 1970s ABBA concert,' I conjectured and assessed. 'In my opinion those future criminals need all of the history lessons they can get. Could it be that the Music Portal is indeed some phenomenal kind of sophisticated geography and time travel piece of equipment? Whatever the circumstances,' I thought with relief as my eastbound train approached the underground station platform, 'I'm really glad to have the amazing thing in my possession!' And after I boarded the train I reckoned, 'And I was never really a big ABBA and disco fan, always preferring to listen to classic rock and roll back in the flashy bell-bottom jeans, Strobe lights and polyester clothes' '70s era!' I mused and then chuckled as tunnel lights flickered on and off and metallic wheels screeched around a bend outside the train car.

After finally getting off the partially-filled High Speed Line train at Lindenwold, I slowly trekked a good distance to my trusty car, which was parked around a quarter of a mile away in the far corner of the massive lot. As I grabbed for the front door handle of my *Altima*, an armed robber (that was hiding behind an adjacent vehicle) suddenly appeared and demanded that I hand over my wallet. Being inspired after my former musical success in the Locust Street Subway Station, my right thumb adroitly hit the contraption's contact button and instantaneously, the shocked and petrified lowlife vanished into thin air. Simultaneously my ears discerned the familiar rhythm and beat of Jan and Dean's catchy 1964 car song, "The Little Old Lady from Pasadena."

'Could it be that the wicked nasty-tempered robber has been inexplicably transported to Pasadena, California?' I asked myself. 'If so, I hope he stays there and gets to see the next *Rose Bowl Game*! And if he's meandering around Pasadena right this second, is he in the year 1964 or is still in 2008? Oh well,' I concluded and shrugged my shoulders, 'that scar-faced fellow would be better off taking-up committing home burglaries instead of attempting bold-faced armed parking lot robbery as a chosen profession. In retrospect,' my mind reviewed, 'it's pretty hard for *him* to get teleported to a remote Golden State destination when nobody's there inside the place to operate a facsimile Music Portal mechanism to send *him* back here to Lindenwold! Maybe the relocated idiot will get to visit and tour 'Surf City' too while he's fully enjoying his unanticipated surprise West Coast jaunt!'

On Saturday morning I did my usual grocery shopping at the nearby Wal-Mart and ShopRite stores and then after unpacking and putting away my new food products in the refrigerator, inside the freezer and into various respective cupboards, I changed out of my blue denim jeans, donned my jogging outfit and drove my *Nissan* down the White Horse Pike to somnolent Oak Grove Cemetery. I had once checked the mileage on my car's odometer, and if I traverse the entire graveyard's asphalt surface twice, my diligent labor would result in a very beneficial cardio-vascular-friendly three-mile hike. Of course, my *Altima* was parked in its regular shaded location beneath a canopy of three tall oak trees, and I felt especially secure walking around inside the old cemetery carrying my Music Portal while performing my habitual weekend exercise routine.

As I was circling the caretaker's maintenance building situated in the center of the cemetery, six motorcycle villains drove their gleaming machines inside the graveyard to pay their respects to a recently deceased gang member. Seeing me innocently pacing in their direction, the tough-looking bikers all perceived me as being an easy target, first for blatant intimidation, and second for larceny. The Harleys speedily rumbled up to me, the riders thinking that I was unprepared to defend myself against their aggressive demands and against their spontaneously planned molestation. But I was fully ready to deal with any of their antagonism and prospective havoc.

"Okay, let's make this little encounter short and sweet!" the very arrogant head honcho belligerently declared in a gruff tone of voice. "Now Pal, just hand over your wallet and I'll gladly confiscate all your cash. Don't worry though!" the disgusting black-hearted maniac clarified. "We ain't all that bad! You'll get to keep your credit cards, your driver's license and all of your other personal ID! It's a lot better to be a live victim than a dead hero, that's what the hell I always say! Ha, ha, ha!"

The five other formidable-looking bikers all indulgently laughed at their leader's threatening comments and then mockingly applauded my apparent situational futility. Before any additional harassment could ensue from any of their lips, I nonchalantly touched the "On" button, and without any sign of hesitation or delay, the Music Portal played the melody and lyrics to the 1959 hit tune "Kansas City" by Wilbert Harrison. And before I could even begin to say '*Dick Clark's American Bandstand*,' the six nefarious derelicts that had been ridiculing me were miraculously erased from my presence, either swiftly being sent on their way to Kansas City, Missouri or to Kansas City, Kansas.

'I hope those desperate degenerates have enough dough to buy themselves some delicious Black Angus steaks,' I amused myself with a reflexive smile. 'Maybe they'll somehow be converted into bunkhouse cowboys working for a living on a sprawling dude ranch. I think that the flat-lands of the American Midwest would be a welcome change in scenery for those societal parasites when compared to the all-too-predictable South Jersey pine barren forest landscape that *they* no doubt have constantly abused in the past! Oh well, what could possibly happen next?'

The first Sunday in August, I was driving south to Vineland to have a delicious lunch at Esposito's Maplewood III Restaurant because I really think *that* establishment has the best tomato sauce and Italian pasta anywhere in South Jersey. After paying my moderate bill and leaving a generous tip, I sauntered out of the popular eatery and then hopped into my car, which much to my annoyance, failed to start. Upon opening the hood to diagnose the cause of the electrical problem, I recognized (much to my frustration) that the automobile's battery had been stolen. I angrily got out my cell phone and anxiously began dialing "Local Information" to obtain the name of the nearest road service that would dispatch a mechanic out to Delsea Drive to replace the vital missing part.

Suddenly three mean-looking Mexicans emerged out of nowhere, violently opened my car door and then signaled for me to exit my vehicle. I ceased my cell phone dialing and gestured to the triumvirate of wise guys that I was going to obediently follow their command.

I gingerly lifted up my Music Portal from the passenger-side front bucket seat and slowly inserted the corresponding earphones into their appropriate auditory positions. My index finger methodically made contact with the "On" button, and before I could blink an eyelid or even fabricate a wink, the three dumbfounded desperados vaporized into the separate spaces that they had been occupying, their astonishing disappearances all occurring in unison with the very identifiable sound of Marty Robbins' 1960 number "El Paso" being wonderfully discernible to my ears.

'Oh well,' I reflected and weighed with a huge sigh of relief, 'the song selection could've been 'Tijuana Taxi' by Herb Alpert and the Tijuana Brass or maybe even Ritchie Valens' terrific version of 'La Bamba' or perhaps even the good old-fashioned favorite 'The Mexican Hat Dance!' Those three missing-in-action Hispanic jerks were probably the same dastardly rogues that had stolen my car battery! Now they're probably already trying to get to the *Rio Grande* to come back to New Jersey and get even with little old *me*, their chief antagonist!'

I finally got my blue *Altima* operational again late that Sunday afternoon. On Tuesday after work I checked my refrigerator and noticed that I was completely out of beer. The *Phillies* were playing an important baseball game on television that evening so I decided to drive over to Canal's Discount Liquor Store on Broadway and *Route 30* and conveniently purchase a cold six-pack of *Coors Light*.

A desperate-looking fellow quickly entered the crowded store while I was checking out my beverage acquisition at the main cash register. The on-a-mission psycho' immediately pulled out a handgun and boldly announced that a holdup was in progress. Naturally I inserted the designated earphones and matter-of-factly hit the Music Portal's "On" button.

My ears instantly heard Elton John singing his 1975 smash hit "Philadelphia Freedom" and I assumed that the *Quaker City* was the audacious petty thief's appointed destination. 'The *Philadelphia Freedoms* were once a pro' tennis squad back in the long-gone 1970s and Elton John had written and dedicated the upbeat song to one of his closest friends, team captain Billie Jean King!' my non-photographic memory recollected. Then my very active mind conjured-up some additional spontaneous reactions.

'I hope that the criminal nutcase winds-up inside the 10th and Locust Street subway station and gets mugged by equally diabolical street hoods from the 'hood!' I creatively conceived and joked. 'One thing's for darned sure. Metropolitan crime is gradually trickling out of the urban areas and insidiously infecting the suburbs! If it weren't for this tremendous Music Portal Device,' I realized, 'I'd already be dead at least five times over!'

When I finally returned to my modest French Street residence, my rowdy immature neighbors were haughtily entertaining some of their very boisterous piney hunter friends at a "disturbing the
106

peace" backyard picnic. The raucous intoxicated rednecks apparently were quite disenchanted with my audacity because I had called the police to break-up several other clamorous next-door warm weather parties, one on *Memorial Day* and the other on the 4th *of July*. I was busy putting my lawnmower inside my outdoor utility building when all twenty-four inebriated revelers (that had been attending the loud backyard barbecue) trespassed onto my property and then insolently began badgering me with a barrage of disparaging insults.

"Look!" I diplomatically answered. "My ears are very sensitive! I don't like excessive noise and I don't relish the shooting-off of loud fireworks. Let's have some moderate behavior here! Why don't you kind folks just learn to be a little more civil and respect other peoples' rights! Then we could get along like good neighbors and not have this type of unnecessary cultural conflict all the time!"

"You're goin' to get the beatin' of your life!" my bellicose under-the-influence twenty-two year old neighbor/nemesis predicted. "Now I'm challengin' you in front of all of these witnesses here to act like a man and let's see how tough ya' really are when your very survival is at stake!" the incensed psychopath yelled as he angrily clenched his fists. The other defiant barbarians (assembled on my back lawn) shouted a bevy of brazen cheers and jeers in response to the offensive knucklehead's sarcastic comments.

Without wasting a second of precious time, I suavely activated the invaluable Music Portal and my ears eagerly listened to Glen Campbell singing his 1969 hit "The Wichita Lineman." The twenty-four baneful delinquents magically dissolved into thin air with not a trace or a vestige of anyone or anything (in their possession) remaining behind.

'Those drunken Jersey hillbillies frequently terrorize the Wharton Tract woods up on *Route 206* and the ruffians hang-out at the infamous Pic-A-Lilli Inn,' I remember thinking. 'They all belong to a deer club that just uses hunting season as an excuse to get drunk, to cause a ruckus and to commit perpetual gluttony. Maybe while they're trekking around out in Wichita, Kansas,' I mentally humored myself, 'perhaps those two dozen un-illustrious scoundrels will introduce themselves to the six obnoxious cemetery bikers that I had very conveniently teleported out to Kansas City while the talented Wilbert Harrison was singing his mantra-like verses!'

At that psychologically rewarding moment of proud triumph, I must confess that I was feeling rather superhuman and omnipotent. It did dawn on my awareness that the wonderful Music Portal Device must contain some revolutionary proprietary technology that if "the science" ever became available to the general public and then be universally used, the plethora of "magical music devices" would have everyone sending everyone else into different times and/or into different places, thus contributing to mass societal chaos and ultimately, possibly causing the end of civilization itself. 'Not everyone can be trusted possessing such a powerful device!' I academically surmised. 'Evil people cannot have access to such a marvelous disciplinary tool! I mustn't share the secret of this wondrous thing with anyone!'

Two more notable incidents had occurred later in August. Being totally bored with my less-than-mediocre shoe salesman job, I had driven forty miles from Hammonton up to *Six Flags Great Adventure* amusement park in Jackson the fourth Saturday in August for some leisurely diversion and to pursue a much-needed attitude adjustment. 'In terms of its structure, this Music Portal appears to be just another typical I-pod,' I remember thinking as I paid my hefty park admission fee. 'Whoever owns the patent to this electronic gizmo will certainly make an unbelievable fortune!'

Three drunken New Yorkers with heavy Brooklyn accents attempted to instigate a fight with me inside a crowded park men's room. Without uttering any derogatory expletives or counter accusations, I confidently hit the readily available 'transportation switch' and upon me hearing the introduction to Freddy "Boom-Boom" Cannon's 1962 top seller "Palisades Park," the trio of punks promptly vanished from my midst.

'Palisades Park was torn down years ago,' I later recalled as I chewed on a hot dog near the Batman Roller Coaster Thrill Ride. 'So if the three alcoholics were not time-travel-teleported back to 1962, then they're probably walking around Palisades Park, New Jersey right now in 2008 wondering what the heck had happened to them. The three tipsy bully maniacs more-than-likely now think that they've somehow been the victims of a mass hallucination!'

On Sunday morning I needed some relaxing diversion in my life so I attached my twenty-four foot long boat trailer to my 1997 red Ford 150 truck and towed the "Sea Daze" to a launching slip at a Sweetwater marina. A forklift operator soon lowered and then deposited my boat into the *Mullica River*. An hour later my small

Sea Daze was anchored in shallow water and I was quietly fishing in the vicinity of Crowley's Landing when three destructive wise-guy teenagers appeared on the riverbank and started cursing and throwing large stones at me. I activated my Music Portal and my ears heard the refrains of the "Bristol Stomp," a lively 1961 classic tune sung by the Dovells. 'Well,' I philosophically mused, 'those three despicable adolescents are probably now wandering on the banks of the *Delaware* in Bristol, Pennsylvania instead of bothering the daylights out of me here on the *Mullica!*' I logically concluded. 'Serves the roguish hooligans right! Maybe their little excursion into Bucks County, Pennsylvania will teach the discourteous instigators some much-needed manners!'

The second Saturday in September I felt an urge to drive thirty miles east to Atlantic City, stroll the world-famous boardwalk, buy some tasty salt water taffy, smell the fresh ocean air and blow five hundred hard-earned dollars at Caesar's World Casino. I parked my blue *Altima* on Pacific Avenue and while peacefully walking towards the A.C. Boardwalk I was accosted by a mugger who stopped me on Missouri Avenue to falsely ask directions to the *Steel Pier*.

Without thinking twice, Pattie Page's 1957 calming rendition of "Old Cape Cod" sent the annoying thug off to either Hyannisport or Provincetown on the famous Massachusetts peninsula. 'Maybe that vile fellow will be exposed to some New England culture, or more-than-likely he'll be manhandled by police and arrested for trespassing onto the Kennedy Compound,' I thought and laughed. Then my devil-may-care disposition changed to a more solid serious mode. 'The Music Portal's instructions indicated that I would have ten danger uses and then two additional personal growth uses,' I mulled over in my mind. 'That gives me just one more opportunity to dispose of harmful evil-minded individuals!'

Later that Saturday afternoon my gambling habit was rewarded when I hit a three thousand dollar jackpot on a Caesar's World nickel slot machine. While mentally reveling in a jovial mood, I drove from Atlantic City and stopped in at Tony's Bar on *Route 322*, the Black Horse Pike, to down some hard liquor shots and watch the featured go-go doll dance around a brass pole situated near the bar. The girl's boyfriend (who was also her pimp) tried soliciting me for a three hundred dollar hit, and feeling threatened by his obvious gruff demeanor, I sent the saucy fellow down to Southern hillbilly country when my ears heard the unique guitar riff to Lynyrd Skynyrd's 1974 smash hit "Sweet Home Alabama."

'Well,' I steadfastly thought, 'this last tenth episode has exhausted all of my Music Portal opportunities. October 6th is my birthday. I think I'll begin exploring my personal growth segment then. If my brain remembers the exact instructions,' I paused before I gulped down a second shot of 100 Proof *Southern Comfort*, 'I only have two future chances to reach self-actualization. I wonder what side of Nirvana *that's* on? Oh well, instant karma or no instant karma, I think I'll order another jigger of whiskey and then hit the road before the bartender and the go-go dancer finally notice that the pushy pimp is missing-in-action.'

The attractive go-go-dancer with Rockette-type legs approached me and asked if I had seen a "Tall, handsome muscular brown-eyed young man with a dimple in the center of his chin!"

"I think he's away applying to the *University of Alabama*!" I cleverly answered the voluptuous well-built scantily clad blonde. "Yes, I think he had mentioned something about being a freshman and drowning in the Crimson Tide!" I jested.

The knockout well-endowed girl just stared at me with her mouth agape as if I was an unstable mental patient that had just escaped from the nearby Ancora State Hospital high-security psycho' ward.

* * * * * * * * * * * *

I had reserved a non-smoking room for October 6th at Caesar's World Casino/Hotel so that I could quietly and privately celebrate my birthday. Since I had earned a Harrah's Diamond Card, I often enjoyed the benefits of food and room comp' privileges at the corporation's four Atlantic City properties: Harrah's, the Showboat, Bally's Casino and Caesar's World.

Inside the confines of my seventh floor suite, I felt motivated to take the time to again closely examine the amazing Music Portal Device. And then feeling a sudden compulsion to further explore the dimensions of my own "Self-actualization," I gathered my wits and courage and gently pressed the "On" button. Immediately I heard the harmonious Olivia-Newton-John song "Xanadu" and my suddenly disheveled mind found myself in a dazzling nightclub with several-hundred roller blade showoffs (along with equally skilled roller skaters) effortlessly whizzing by and all around me.

'Xanadu was definitely a weird movie about a romantic person's fondest dream of a romantic Utopia!' I thought as adroit roller skaters rushed by my stationary roller rink presence in all different directions. Then my overwhelmed brain found the wherewithal to recall a theory that I had once studied in a college psychology course. 'Maybe to reach my own special Utopia I have to explore my twelfth and final song and see how I can ascend to the very top of Maslow's Law of Human Hierarchal Development! Yes,' I decided, 'now I'm beginning to understand this rather puzzling phenomenon! Self-actualization should exist on a higher plateau than biological needs and *it* should also transcend emotional gratification too! *Its* awesome fruition should be the perfect culmination of all mortal enterprise, *its* manifestation represented in the full maturity of the human spirit, and in *my* case, *my* full emotional and mental maturity!'

After pressing the mechanism's "On" button for the twelfth time, my ears heard a familiar instrumental song which at first, my memory couldn't recall the melody's title. But in the meantime my fantastic Music Portal Device had magically transported me to a beautiful mountainous pine forest environment. Then my dizzy mind finally recognized the title of the rhythmic song, "A Walk in the Black Forest" by Horst Jankowski. 'Of course!' I jubilantly thought as I intensely gazed upon my stunning new-found surroundings. 'The houses on that hill over there and the architecture of those buildings in the town down in the valley are German in nature! I'll bet I've arrived near Freiburg!'

I hastened along a narrow dirt path until all out of breath I reached a remote monastery retreat. I stubbornly rapped upon the large wooden door and was reluctantly greeted by a monk who spoke English with a thick accent. Father Sebastian escorted me inside the medieval-looking stone edifice and after we were sitting in two hard wooden chairs that occupied a corner of his crudely furnished office, we discussed how I had been successfully "recruited" into the select ranks of "Music Portal assemblers."

"How will I be able to achieve self-actualization?" I inquisitively asked my laconic pious sponsor. "I understand that *that's* the principal reason why I've been guided and conducted here."

"You'll have plenty of time for introspection while doing your required daily *Bible* reading," Father Sebastian aptly and curtly replied. "You'll become most inspired reading essential assigned passages, especially those moral lessons organized throughout the

111

New Testament. That daily regimen will indeed accelerate your moral growth!"

My cynical side soon surfaced and its ego-based ugliness momentarily dominated my cerebral activity. My skeptical "outside world thinking" was not synchronized to my new self-examination reality. 'Father Sebastian and his fellow priests are isolated up here on this remote mountain and their narrow minds are trapped inside separate religious cartons!' I suspiciously conjectured. 'These holier-than-thou morons, or should I say these sanctimonious religious zealots, are quite ostensibly incapable of thinking outside the box!' I negatively and critically thought.

"You'll gradually learn self-discipline and after mastering that," Father Sebastian un-eloquently elaborated in an emotionless tone of voice, "you'll eventually rise above your propensity to vaguely communicate pessimistic ideas and also, at *that* juncture in time, you'll then finally conquer your affinity for being too liberally disingenuous!"

"Well then Father, what will be my assigned responsibilities here at this remote monastery?"

"First of all, you'll only be allowed to speak in sentences of ten words or less when sitting with others on our staff during our three regular daily meals, which are generally the only times that trivial conversation is tolerated," the no-nonsense priest informed me. "And starting first thing tomorrow morning, you'll be learning how to make Swiss cuckoo clocks and then also you'll be acquiring the art and science of beer brewing along with some preliminary exposure to botanical gardening, and after excelling in those basic mundane trades," the austere abbot continued his sermonizing, "we'll assign you at *our* discretion to help build sophisticated Music Portals that will be sent to psychologically depressed people all over this imperfect planet. But you'll be an expert at only one phase of the manufacturing process and will never know how to fully assemble a functioning Music Portal entirely on your own skill, and if I may add, no schematic of the entire design will ever be shown to you. Now then," Sebastian sternly stressed, "I'm a very busy man. Do you have any more curious questions?"

"Yes Father, will I ever be permitted to leave this cold all-stone monastery?" I inquired.

"After seven years of indentured labor, you'll be allowed to travel within a hundred fifty mile radius of this rather insular retreat," Sebastian objectively related to his new subordinate. "Once you prove your worth through self-discipline and once you demonstrate an enviable work ethic, you'll be able to travel all around what is known as Baden-Wurttemberg and if your enlightened *spirit* moves you, you'll eventually even be able to visit the Rhine River Valley and tour Hohenzollen Castle, which as you know Cinderella's *Disneyland* and *Disney World* castles were modeled after. You could even visit Munich and engage in an inspirational Octoberfest or two! But first, you must start at square one!"

Right after that initial mind-opening interview with Father Sebastian, my cerebrum realized one very salient concept. My mind and body had been transported in geographic space to Freiburg, Germany but according to the hanging calendar in the abbot's office, the date was still October 6th, 2008. Based on my utterly illuminating experience here in this solitary-confinement-like large monastery, *that* sage date observation simply means that all of the people that I had teleported (when I had felt threatened during the ten confrontations involving the Music Portal Device) probably also had been transported in space to new locations mentioned in the various song titles, but probably not dispatched into other times or into other distinct historical eras.

I'm finally becoming acclimated to (and actually now enjoying) the stringent agenda associated with my daily secluded monastic way of life, the discipline of which I strongly believe has been helping me elevate my former inferior self-esteem and deficient confidence levels. I'm happy to report in this strange-but-factual humble autobiography that I'm learning some rudimentary German words and phrases and now can almost fully interpret what the sagacious priests and my fellow resident craftsmen are saying in abbreviated sentences at meals and during morning Vespers. Most importantly, I've now become accustomed to abhorring and rejecting the traditional lavish lifestyles that are greedily pursued in the baneful outside materialistic world by mostly self-centered humans.

I've been diligently making Swiss cuckoo clocks and conscientiously practicing basic beer brewing and botanical gardening for two glorious months now, and my ever-growing *spirit* is enthusiastically awaiting my eventual assignment and transfer to the highly prestigious Music Portal Assembly Workshop Wing. I truly wish to help other moral and good-hearted depressed people all over the world and give them hope for self-actualization by rescuing them through "music geographic transfers" when they happen to discover themselves being in harm's way. That genesis phase of "melancholy re-location displacement," as I now fathom it, is the primary stage of "*Spiritual* Self-actualization."

In retrospect, as I author these final very realistic words, the package that I had anonymously received from Freiburg via UPS is now fully comprehensible and its ultimate implementation makes perfect sense. I can't wait to make my significant contribution to the moral stability of civilization by helping to manufacture new innovative and sensational "next generation Music Portals" at my designated workstation, and then, in the process, attain great satisfaction by having the finished products of my extensive labor delivered to deserving-but-despondent human beings all over this dangerous-but-wonderful world.

"The Multi-Faceted Diamond Caper"

On Wednesday morning, September 18th, 2013 FBI Inspector Joe Giralo patiently sat behind his solid oak desk inside his 600 Arch Street eighth floor office and silently listened to animated Agents Salvatore Velardi, Arthur Orsi and Daniel Blachford discuss the Philadelphia Phillies versus Miami Marlins National League baseball game that the three G-men had attended the evening before at Citizens Bank Park. The garrulous trio was thrilled that the previously hapless home team had won the close contest by a score of 6-4 and that the new interim club manager Ryne Sandberg had then achieved a respectable record of eighteen wins against thirteen losses ever since taking over the squad's helm from former beloved manager Charlie Manuel.

"Looks like dependable Roy Halladay is making a major comeback giving-up only one run and four hits in his fifth start following his return from right shoulder surgery," fan Sal Velardi observed and stated. "This season is basically shot, but if 'Doc' comes back next year in good health as the club's ace starter, he, Cole Hamels and Cliff Lee will make a really formidable pitching rotation."

"But also recovering from leg problems, my favorite player Chase Utley emerged as the hero of the game hitting a clutch homer and driving in four vital RBIs," Art Orsi melodramatically added to the general baseball euphoria. "According to the left field scoreboard, that fifth inning three-run smash into the right field bleachers traveled 404 feet. If first baseman Ryan Howard rebounds next year in tip-top shape from his foot injury and if *my* man Utley avoids being hurt again, the Fightin' Phils will definitely be Eastern Division contenders in 2014, I guarantee it!"

"That mighty blast was Utley's 217th homer of his big league career," Dan Blachford contributed to the unrealistic dialogue, "but I caution you Guys that Doc Halladay's fastball had only a maximum velocity of eighty-eight miles per hour on the official radar gun, but on the positive side," "Dandy Dan" emphasized, "Jonathan Papelbon was able to close out the Phils' victory by allowing only a scratch single in the 9th. Remarkably, it was the durable closer's twenty-eighth save of the season. That ninth inning guy's been tremendous ever since the Phils' acquired him from the Red Sox."

"I thought that the best part of the game was the terrific Philly' cheesesteaks and giant pretzels we swallowed-down after participating in the seventh inning stretch," Agent Velardi recalled and blathered, "and those TastyKake Butterscotch Krimpets you bought down in the stadium concourse Dan really made it a great evening! Tell us Chief, did Philly' have those giant pretzels and savory TastyKakes when Richie Ashburn, Del Ennis, Robin Roberts and the other 1950s Whiz Kids were playing in Shibe Park, later know as Connie Mack Stadium?"

Ignoring Sal Valardi's bothersome sarcastic drivel, formerly reticent Chief Joe Giralo decided to include some academic aspects into the mediocre conversation, and so the knowledgeable Boss suavely lectured his three subordinates, communicating that the stellar hurler Roy "Doc" Halladay's nickname actually was a gabby sportscaster's allusion to John Henry "Doc" Holliday, a notorious American Wild West gambler, dentist and lethal gunfighter who, most of his short life, suffered with (and eventually died from) a severe chronic tuberculosis condition, with the tough quick-draw's womb-to-tomb longevity "lasting only from 1851-1887."

"Historically speaking," Inspector Giralo boringly proceeded and prattled, "the original Doc Holliday was a close friend of lawman Wyatt Earp, their association often depicted in old '50s nightly black and white TV cowboy shows, and the invincible pair were involved in the classic 'Gunfight at the O.K. Corral' that had occurred in legendary Tombstone, Arizona. Now if the Phillies had another effective pitcher named Wyatt Earp," Inspector Giralo facetiously joked, "then *that* unimaginative sportscaster's play-on-names' coincidence between John Henry 'Doc' Holliday and Roy 'Doc' Halladay would really be a....."

"Er Boss," Agent Velardi very politely interrupted his encyclopedic federal superior, "I'm sure you didn't call this special meeting for the purpose of evaluating the Phillies' baseball prospects for next summer. What's on *our* agenda today? Are you taking us to the airport to vacation in sunny St. Thomas? Tropical Aruba or balmy Bermuda would be very nice too!"

"That type of extended excursion to any of those majestic islands would be more than adequate," Art Orsi chimed-in. "Strolling the Ocean City, Wildwood and Atlantic City boardwalks with my family for the past four months has become a bit monotonous and redundant!"

"I hope we don't have to travel south and work with Matt Riley and his overly ambitious true-blue employees down in DC headquarters," normally sedate Dan Blachford all-too-honestly opined. "Truthfully, I had labored diligently in *that* totally

116

stressful bureaucratic environment the first three years of my FBI career, and yes, quite frankly Guys, my memories aren't exactly super-fond ones whenever I recall me being perpetually hazed as a novice detective."

Growing intolerant of Dan Blachford's exaggerated sulking and unwarranted peeving, Inspector Giralo discreetly elected getting to the crux of the matter, offering an introduction that cited a series of aggravating diamond heists adroitly executed in assorted cities across the USA. Local police jurisdictions, state authorities along with the ordinarily competent Federal Bureau of Investigation had all been incredibly stymied by the lack of tangible clues available to the beleaguered and puzzled investigators.

"In April and May of this year," the Chief enunciated while carefully examining and slowly reading the print on a hand-held sheet of paper, "costly diamond thefts had been made in Atlanta, Miami, Cincinnati, New York, Cleveland, San Francisco, Phoenix, Miami again, Washington DC and Boston. The guys down in DC are extremely baffled, with my pal Matt Riley being especially embarrassed that the Friday, May 24th gem heist had occurred on his sacred home turf!"

"Miami was hit twice," Sal Velardi observed and confidently remarked as the alert agent scribbled-down the new pertinent information in his nearly full notepad. "That particular Miami repetition might prove to be significant."

"Maybe the perpetrators like warm weather," contributed Agent Orsi. "It's relatively hot in April and in May down in Miami, out West in Phoenix, down south in Atlanta, Georgia and sometimes over in Cincinnati. But on the other hand, San Francisco is either cold or cool during those two early spring months, and Boston, Cleveland, New York and Washington can be either cool or mild, depending on the Jet Stream's seasonal path!"

"The fact that only large cities are targeted is uniquely peculiar!" Dan Blachford logically expressed. "We all know that there are many suburban malls and wealthy rural communities that have well-stocked jewelry stores. This oddball random pattern that's been established does represent a sort of enigma."

Taking all of his agents reactions into consideration, the frustrated Chief then enumerated the cities that had been designated for diamond thefts during June and July of 2013. The list being reviewed read like a contemporary Homeric catalog: Milwaukee on June 8th, Minneapolis, on June 12th, Denver on June 16th, San Diego on June 25th, Los Angeles on June 27th,

Pittsburgh on July 3rd, New York on July 19th, St. Louis on July 25th and finally, Detroit, occurring on July 28th.

"Notice again Guys that New York had a huge gemstone larceny occur for a second time, just like Miami has had," Agent Velardi commented and then recorded onto his trusty hand-held notebook. "The crooks involved in this national crimewave must be enamored with Florida sunshine and with Big Apple Broadway plays, with Times Square and with the Statue of Liberty!"

"The fact that San Diego and Los Angeles are geographically in close proximity and the reality that Pittsburgh and Detroit are only within several hundred miles of each other might be fundamentally relevant," Art Orsi reckoned and shared. "But I still can't understand why American suburbia has been excluded from the pattern, if not ignored or neglected in this abominable rash of interstate felonies."

"There's little or no rhyme or reason to this implausible series of diamond pilfering," Dan Blachford assessed and said. "Other than New York and Miami being plundered twice each, my jumbled mind is swimming in a complete quandary."

"Well Fellas'," the equally befuddled veteran Boss vociferated, "here's the remainder of the metropolitan areas that have been victimized in August and then up to September 13th. We have Washington DC on Friday, August 9th, and Fellas', this second District of Columbia hit has Matt Riley and his team totally infuriated," Joe Giralo added with a broad grimace exhibited upon his chubby countenance. "And then Wednesday, August 14th in Atlanta again, Tuesday August 27th in Manhattan for the third time, Sunday September 1st in Chicago and finally, Friday September 13th in our Nation's Capital for the third time also, which naturally has the DC boys now fit to be tied!"

"There must be some obscure method to this out-of-control madness," a thoroughly addled Sal Velardi evaluated and voiced. "This colossal conundrum is far worse than sitting through the entire disappointing 2013 Phillies' season as a lousy depressed centerfield grandstand patron!"

"Wait a Philadelphia minute!" a now-motivated Agent Orsi enthusiastically exclaimed. "Boss, have *you* also perceptively discerned that none of the August and September crime dates had been performed on a Monday or a Thursday?"

Chief Giralo closely scrutinized his comprehensive Phillies' calendar list and then convincingly uttered, "Arty, what you've just mentioned about August and September is partially accurate and correct. You're right about Mondays being eliminated, but

118

according to *this* infallible documentation I'm now referring to, a prodigious diamond theft had occurred in Los Angeles on *Thursday,* June 27th and in St. Louis on *Thursday,* July 25th. But Arty," the Inspector paused and smiled, "I must commend your general acumen. Your keen mental dynamics concerning Mondays just might be valuably instrumental in cracking-open this very vexing mystery."

"Maybe the ambitious villains involved in the DC heists are really and truly infatuated with the Washington Monument, the Lincoln Memorial, the U.S. Capitol Building, the White House and the Smithsonian," Agent Orsi awkwardly jested. "We might have some patriotic felons on our hands, advanced citizen thugs who can't get enough of American history!"

"This is no time for preposterous amusement Arty," Dan Blachford rankled and reprimanded. "The very reputation of the Bureau is at stake here. These brazen diamond thieves are blatantly acting with impunity and making a grotesque mockery of our justice system."

"We know that we have a determined gang of diamond fanatics scouring every big city jewelry store and corporate gem exchange," Sal Velardi verbally summarized. "Boss, what do you think of these bewildering circumstances? You've remained rather laconic these last five minutes and from past experience, I just know that your brain is hypothesizing something major."

"Believe it or not Salvatore, your loose tongue has just given me a rather brilliant idea. Make that two rather brilliant ideas. I want to see you three Geniuses in my office at noon on Tuesday, September 24th. Yes Sal, I think that you're an absolute genius without you ever seriously contemplating that notion!"

"Boss, to tell you the truth," Sal Velardi then hesitated to contemplate an adequate clever response, "right now you've made me feel like a resurrected Neanderthal Man!"

* * * * * * * * * * * *

Tuesday, September 24th quickly arrived on the 2013 calendar and the three dedicated agents once again stepped from the 600 Arch Street elevator and promptly ambled across the corridor into Inspector Joe Giralo's walnut-wood paneled office. The three visitors were still somewhat emotionally distressed because the faltering Phillies had lost the past Sunday's afternoon baseball game played against the equally dismal New York Mets.

"Another ugly and pathetic Phils' defeat into the baseball annals," Agent Velardi pesimistically recounted his personal grief. "I really feel disenchanted about the team's inferior performance, and I'm seriously weighing whether or not I'm going to moronically purchase season tickets for next year."

"Well, the Eagles are off to a fairly decent start with new coach Chip Kelly," Agent Orsi ascertained and spieled. "I must admit: hope springs eternal during the beginning of football season just like it also does in the Phillies spring training camp down in Clearwater."

"Why are you looking so glum and pale Dan?" Chief Giralo asked Blachford. "Did your ferocious pet Doberman die after eating contaminated cat food or something?"

"No Boss," the seemingly disgruntled agent rather lethargically replied. "My wife's kitchen stove went haywire on Friday, and besides *that* irritating bummer, our overhead microwave needed rehab' too, so being good American consumers, Bing and I motored down to Appliances Plus in Vineland, and during our productive shopping spree we shelled-out two thousand bucks for a new GE range and accompanying overhead quick serve oven."

"Sounds like you negotiated a pretty thrifty bargain," Sal Velardi butted-in. "So why are you so melancholy and miserable if you and Bing got such a swell deal?"

"Well," Blachford indignantly answered, "when the aggressive salesman described the two products, he made it sound as if the devices were easy to install. 'Just rip-out the old range and the old overhead microwave and insert the new ones and next, simply plug them in,' the clerk claimed to us. But in reality, after the range and the microwave were delivered to Pleasant Street, it didn't work-out that way because...."

"Because Dan, originally you and Bing had had a custom-built remodeled kitchen professionally installed fifteen years ago," Art Orsi piped-up, "and I surmise that the space behind the stove and the area located behind the elevated microwave frame had to also be expertly modified to accommodate the newly obtained units."

Sporting a profound frown, Dan Blachford then painfully explained that it was soon required for him to enlist the capable skills of Hammonton builder David Noto to re-structure the dual stove and microwave areas, and next the premier builder had to commission the services of tile guru David Paretti to reconfigure the ceramic tile surrounding the original 'special range'. "But in addition," Blachford regretfully added, "Noto had to summon his

120

company electrician Mark Vaccarella to re-wire the new appliances to my electric circuits down in the cellar. The unanticipated supplemental labor eventually cost almost as much as the two new Appliances Plus ovens did!"

Realizing that more than enough valuable time had been wasted on commentaries about the Phillies, about the Eagles and about Agent Blachford's ultra-modern kitchen replacements, Inspector Giralo refocused the group's consultation on the ongoing skein of big city diamond thefts.

"Well Sal and Art, while you two Savants were attending Phillies and Eagles games and while you Dan were clumsily solving your kitchen appliance dilemma, I've been preoccupied wracking my brains out about this continuous coast-to-coast precious gemstone caper," Giralo reminded his loyal disciples.

"And exactly what did your splendid problem-solving efforts achieve?" Sal Velardi cynically inquired. "That the Phillies Phanatic has buried the missing jewels in the Citizens Bank Park baseball diamond!"

"Believe it or not Salvatore, your anemic attempt at ridiculous humor is not too far off base!" the Chief chuckled and punned. "You were close but earned no cigar or brass ring! Do you remember during our last session when *you* had remarked that the diamond thief must've been a fanatic?"

"Why yes!" Agent Velardi responded anxiously. "It was just an innocent utterance at the time, and nothing more!"

"Matt Riley and I now happen to believe that our anonymous diamond thief might very well be an avid Philadelphia Phillies fan who travels around the country picking-up stolen diamonds and then casually driving to other cities and selling the gemstones to Mafia and Cosa Nostra syndicates elsewhere. Quite possibly," Chief Giralo expounded on his surprise exposition, "our nameless subject might also be illicitly trading the purloined jewels for drugs in order to then barter the contraband for laundered legal tender."

"Your most fascinating theory rationally accounts for why no diamond heists had been committed on Mondays," Agent Orsi admirably marveled and verbalized. "But if that's the case Chief, if our unidentified suspect is a dye-in-the-wool Phillies fan, why haven't any related crimes happened right here in 'Philly?"

Joe Giralo then opened and slowly reached into his massive oak desk's center drawer and removed four copies of the 2013 Phillies baseball schedule, which the Mentor distributed, instructing his stunned agents to intensely peruse. "After examining the cities and related game dates Sal," the revered federal supervisor directed, "what American League teams are *not* on the Phillies Major League agenda?"

"Let's analyze this intriguing information for a minute," Agent Velardi requested. "Okay Guys, the Phillies this year have played every American League team except the Baltimore Orioles, the Kansas City Royals, the Oakland Athletics, the Seattle Mariners, the Tampa Bay Rays, the Texas Rangers, the Toronto Blue Jays, the Houston Astros and finally, according to the schedule, the always formidable New York Yankees."

"But the Phils' have played American League teams the Kansas City Royals, the Cleveland Indians, the Boston Red Sox and the Chicago White Sox at home in Citizens Bank Park," Joe Giralo recited, reading from his list.

"But the Phillies have played the Boston Red Sox up in Fenway Park on May 27th and May 28th," Sal Velardi divulged, "and they've also played another American League club you've just mentioned in an *away* series, the Cleveland Indians at Progressive Field on Tuesday, April 30th and on Wednesday, May 1st."

Art Orsi was inspired to remark that New York had already been hit with enormous diamond thefts and that Oakland was situated across the bay from neighboring San Francisco, which had already also been targeted for gemstone robbery.

"True Arty," Dan Blachford recognized and verified, "but besides the New York Yankess, who incidentally are categorized in the American League, the rival cross-town New York Mets are in the National League, so consequently, this is why the Phillies would visit the Mets in Shea Stadium more than once a summer, and also, *that* glaring detail possibly explains why the incognito Phillies fan/jewel courier would do business in New York City more than once a baseball season, and this is also why...."

"Why Miami, Washington and Atlanta have experienced immense multiple diamond thefts," Sal Velardi gasped in astonishment, "apparently because those three baseball bastions are stationed in the National League's Eastern Division, and obviously, the Phillies would visit the Marlins, the Nationals and the Braves for series' games more than once a summer, as would the unidentified person of interest, this phantom, itinerant avid Phillies fan."

Chief Joe Giralo again glanced-down and studied the Phillies schedule held between his chunky hands and his firm voice asked his three still-confused agents the significance of the following terminology: "Progressive Field, Fenway Park, Target Field and Coamerica Park."

After a half-minute of tense silence, Agent Blachford offered a suitable answer. "Progressive Park is where the Phillies had played the Cleveland Indians, Fenway Park is where the Fightins' later went up against the Boston Red Sox, Target Field is the newly constructed home of the less-than-devastating Minnesota Twins, whom the Phil's also played horribly against in mid-June, and last-but-not-least, Comerica Park is where the lackluster Phils' had a terrible series against the juggernaut Detroit Tigers in late July, but most importantly Boss," Blachford orally conveyed, "all four *away* opponents were American League teams."

"Wow!" exclaimed a suddenly enlightened Art Orsi. "According to the 2013 schedule, as we've already mentioned, the Phillies have played some other American League teams like the Chicago White Sox and the Kansas City Royals, but *those* other inter-league games were at home and not on the road. All of the accumulative evidence is now lending heavy credence to the Chief's outstanding guess that the main perpetrator we're wildly seeking is indeed also a bona fide Philadelphia Phillies fan!"

"Now the big picture all makes perfect sense!" Sal Velardi bellowed. "Notice on your schedules that sometimes there are week-long intervals between diamond heists and that other times the individual thefts are separated only by being several days apart. When the insular robberies are weeks apart...".

"The Phillies are coincidentally playing *home games* with Mondays off," Agent Orsi acknowledged and insisted, "but when the jewel felonies are only mere days apart...."

"Then understandably, the Phillies are playing *away games* in either National League or in American League cities with Mondays still off-days too!" an almost out-of-breath Dan Blachford excitedly blurted-out. "This ever-evolving baseball scenario is absolutely amazing! Boss, if you aren't ESP psychic, then you must be a genuine genius!"

"Matt Riley and I are still ironing-out the specific details of this rather challenging investigation," Chief Giralo calmly informed his three impressed confederates in law enforcement. "Next Monday morning, September 30th, we'll meet again in my office and confer about this case's most recent developments."

* * * * * * * * * * * *

The three blithe-spirited FBI agents eagerly returned to the Federal Building at 600 Arch Street to honor their pre-arranged September 30th rendezvous with Chief Inspector Joe Giralo, who contrary to his widespread parsimonious disposition, cordially greeted his award-winning team into his sacred bailiwick, treating the rambunctious trio to freshly-brewed coffee along with a selection of tempting TastyKake Butterscotch Krimpets, complemented by nine chocolate cupcakes and four small packages of TastyKake apple pies stacked on three individual trays.

"Sure beats ingesting sea gulls or bagels," bantered jovial Sal Velardi. "I'm glad I came in to work today. I don't regard eating sweet snacks as drudgery or punishment."

"I wouldn't even desert these desserts out in the desert," Agent Orsi added, ineptly entertaining himself. "Now Fellas', I honor the erudite person who had invented 'p-i-e' just as much as I value the ancient Einstein who had proficiently studied the esoteric composition of a circle and then accidentally discovered 'pi'."

"Enough frivolous quips from you, you equivocating, prevaricating wannabe' comedian!" rebuked Dan Blachford in Orsi's physical direction. "Let's confine all of the slapstick foolishness to the obsolete Vaudeville stage, and let's please limit all of the zany clown antics and semantics to Ringling Brothers, Barnum and Bailey."

"Say Boss," Sal Velardi articulated, desiring to change the totally ludicrous conversation from utter stupidity to more mature FBI concerns. "What new info' have you gleaned on the scurrilous Phillies fan turned Mafia messenger. We all know how the fearsome Cosa Nostra crooks along with dreaded al Qaeda terrorists are world-famous, or should I say world *infamous* for mendaciously killing the hired messenger!"

"That's positively true!" Dan Blachford confirmed. "The al Qaeda network is afraid of being monitored by their use of cell phones, so the vile anarchists solely utilize scouts and messengers to transfer letters and documents. Even in our daily lives, just about everyone in America is worried about privacy and about secret NSA electronic surveillance."

"Both the Mafia and al Qaeda are renowned all over the globe for doing deleterious and detrimental things to other doomed-by-decree human beings," Joe Giralo concurred. "But to be perfectly candid, we can't have disorganized law enforcement fighting organized crime, or we can't allow the existence of organized terrorists either. It's all just gotta' happen in reverse in order for

124

Jeffersonian democracy to survive and flourish in the 21st Century!"

The Boss, being in an extraordinarily favorable mood, next elaborated on how the evasive 'diamond culprit's ID' could probably be isolated by a national computer bank search, for the 'phantom' more-than-likely every year bought a brand new car with cold cash, since the 'person of interest' would naturally compile many odometer miles each summer driving from city to city all across the nation. And then, Supervisor Giralo again baffled his dumbfounded listeners by boldly pontificating that the anonymous transgressor probably conducted his year-round delivery enterprise by also being a fervent Philadelphia Eagles, Philadelphia Flyers and Philadelphia 76ers on-the-road fan.

"Well don't keep us wallowing in suspense!" Sal Velardi demanded. "Who is this pernicious felon who immediately needs the cuffs slapped on his wrists?"

"After painstakingly narrowing-down our nationwide dragnet search, we eventually honed-down to a slick individual named Melvin Michael Mitchell, who actually *is* a robust Phillies fan!"

"Sounds like the audacious knucklehead should've worked for the 3-M Corporation rather than being employed as a meager Mafia courier exchanging expensive diamonds for illegal drugs and under-the-table untaxed cash," punster Art Orsi summarized, much to everyone else's general chagrin.

"And ironically," Chief Giralo proceeded with his all-too-familiar litany while deftly ignoring Agent Orsi's rather inane babble, "our boys from the Atlanta office just successfully nabbed Mr. Mitchell."

"In the Turner Field parking lot?" Agent Velardi speculated and guessed. "That's where the Phillies wound-up their disastrous season yesterday, wimpily losing to the Braves,12-5."

"Correct," Chief Giralo readily affirmed. "Mr. Melvin Michael Mitchell was apprehended while exiting a 2013 red Lexus sedan having a suitcase containing a whopping $850,000.00 cash snugly deposited in the trunk. No doubt Mr. Mitchell shrewdly regarded his risky assignments as being too dangerous for him to be traveling through airport security checks, so the devious crook nonchalantly drove from city to city, specifically from Phillies away game to the next slated away game. And here's some true FBI serendipity for you Glorious Guys to savor. Mr. Melvin Michael Mitchell lives in New Castle, Delaware, also known as 'the Diamond State'!"

"And this slippery snake Mitchell even got to see the Phillies play the National League Arizona Diamondbacks out West in Phoenix!" Agent Orsi related and then guffawed.

"We still think that you're psychic Boss!" Agent Blachford opined.

"Fellas', I'm about as psychic as the phony ancient Oracle of Delphi was in the time of Socrates," Inspector Giralo maintained. "But in essence Men, it was the combined idea of the mischievous Phillies Phanatic coupled with the innocent reference to a 'baseball diamond' that got me whimsically thinking about a hardcore Phillies fan guiltlessly engaging in villainous criminal activity."

"Well Boss," hollered-out an almost delirious Agent Orsi. "It's too bad that this FBI investigation couldn't have happened twenty years from now!"

"Why's that Arty?" Inspector Giralo curiously asked.

"Because Boss, Phillies' fanatic Mr. Melvin Michael Mitchell's thrilling arrest outside Turner Field could've simultaneously occurred on *your* Diamond Jubilee Wedding Anniversary!"

"Soldier of Misfortune"

Dr. Angelo DeMarco had recently retired as the head psychiatrist at New Jersey's Ancora State Hospital so that he could devote his full time to expanding his private practice, which was located inside a second floor office suite at the southeast corner of 2nd Street and Bellevue Avenue, Hammonton, New Jersey. The psych' physician was perusing a letter received from Noreen Pearson, the wife of a twenty-five-year-old Army Corporal, and the distraught enlisted soldier had been complaining to his spouse of severe migraine headaches, of terrible repetitious nightmares, and also the afflicted young serviceman was often heard uttering "indiscernible gibberish" during his erratic nightly sleeps.

Dr. DeMarco considered the prospective case study of his latest accepted patient Jack Pearson to be quite novel and intriguing because in her curious letter of introduction and referral request, Mrs. Noreen Pearson had thoroughly described her husband's insistence that he had been suffering from symptoms of a baffling multiple personality disorder caused by regenerative experiences of 'organized chronological military service reincarnation.'

The psychiatrist's receptionist/secretary politely escorted Mr. Jack Pearson into Dr. DeMarco's spacious office where initial casual conversation gradually led to the standard doctor/patient interview. The mental health expert explicitly explained to Jack that all human beings were similar in that they respond to general fundamental needs and drives, but each person's relationship to his or her behavior being dynamically synthesized and expressed in a marked individual, unique and specific way.

"Frankly Jack, there are basically two types of needs," Dr. DeMarco pontificated to cooperative Pearson. "Physical needs such as the need for food, shelter and clothing to protect the body from the elements, and then there're also human psychological needs such as the need for approval, acceptance, attention, self-esteem and last buy not least, the need for love and security. And then of course Jack," the eminent psychiatrist sternly continued his introductory monologue, "there are those strong basic drives that often motivate and compel people to act, such as the characteristic hunger, greed and sex drives. Your unusual mental condition might very well be a combination of any two or more of the traditional needs and drives that comprise the 'typical human profile scenario.' Now Jack, your very concerned wife Doreen stated in her letter that you believe that you're over two hundred and fifty years old! Is her remarkable assertion true?"

"That's correct Dr.," the somewhat addled patient quite matter-of-factly answered. "But the stressful dreams that I've been having stay in my subconscious mind and I'm frustrated because I can never fully recall any specific details of my involvement anywhere from the beginning of my restless slumber to the end. All I can remember about my dreams, or should I say 'my nightmares', is that I'm predictably engaged in some kind of major war battle, but in each instance with all kinds of different enemies of various nationalities. Now please tell me, does that odd portrayal make any sort of sense to you?"

"I believe that I see what you're attempting to explain!" Dr. Angelo DeMarco stated, pensively rubbing his clean-shaven chin. "Since my ten o'clock appointment has canceled because *that* patient has developed flu symptoms, I'll have up to two hours to objectively observe your deportment under hypnosis and to also record and evaluate your verbal responses to my oral prompts. Now Mr. Pearson, I find the notion that you honestly think that you're around two and a half centuries old very fascinating indeed! I think that your abnormal nightmare events represent a distinct challenge to my general knowledge of human behavior and development. Let me ask you, are you now emotionally ready for me to delve into your psyche, your id and your ego?"

"Yes Dr. I've seen enough of this sort of stuff in the movies. I presume that I should first lie down on your leather couch over there," Jack indicated, pointing at the comfortable-looking piece of furniture with his index finger. "Honestly now, for my sake and for my wife's peace of mind, I hope that this experimental session turns out to be successful."

"If possible Jack, when you respond to a particular question, please inform me of the exact setting of your mental manifestation; that is," the psychiatrist stipulated and then paused to perfectly enunciate his additional words, "provide me with the exact or approximate year of the incident you're describing and also if you could, tell me the geographic location where the battle that you're directly involved in is taking place. I trust Mr. Pearson that you'll be able to do that simple task without experiencing any harmful duress or emotional stress."

Jack then voluntarily assumed his horizontal position upon the soft black leather sofa and in a matter of several suspenseful minutes Dr. DeMarco had effectively hypnotized Pearson using a

128

watch dangling and oscillating from a gold fob chain. When the soldier/patient appeared to be fully relaxed, the all-too-confident mind doctor commenced with his formal interrogation, which a remote camera was capturing on film.

"Please remember Mr. Pearson, you still possess your free will and should only verbally respond to my well-intentioned suggestions and comments if you so desire. Now then, as a brave and loyal soldier of history, where are you located now Jack and what time period is it?"

"I'm somewhere in Massachusetts in June of 1775," Jack began his bizarre recollection. "Yes, I'm helping in the effort to fortify the Charlestown Peninsula. The British barges are currently ferrying opposing troops across the river and my commander Colonel William Prescott has ordered me and the other men to make a stand and defend Breed's Hill. We had held our ground twice but now we've run out of gunpowder," the hypnotized subject expressed. "The redcoats are shooting at us, volley after volley. Boston and vicinity must not fall to the enemy! Oh my God!" Jack exclaimed. "I'm wounded; shot in the back while I was turned around and reloading my musket! My legs are paralyzed. The pain from my shoulders to my hips is excruciating! I'll never be able to escape the peninsula alive! I'm passing out! Everything's hazy all around me! I'm sure I'm dying! Goodbye cruel world!"

"All right Jack, you're safe and sound now and you've miraculously fled the enemy and your pathetic injuries have completely healed!" Dr. DeMarco declared as his eyes noticed that his patient's breathing was gradually becoming more normal and regular. "You've been safely evacuated out of the Battle of Bunker Hill and you've triumphantly endured *that* important-but-pivotal conflict of the American Revolutionary War!" the mind doctor loquaciously communicated. "I now recommend that you take ten deep breaths and then again tell me where you are and what activities are occurring in your immediate vicinity."

Jack had effectively calmed down from his initial ordeal and then the stabilized patient very deliberately articulated that the new date was January 8th, 1815 and that he along with other assigned riflemen were occupying an entrenchment while observing highly-trained units of British soldiers marching in neat rows directly into the pre-set American trap. General Andrew Jackson soon gave the command to "Fire!" and the ambushing American marksmen easily defeated the advancing hostile-but-surprised foreign enemy. But during the termination of the rather fierce engagement, a blast from a distant cannon sent Jack Pearson hurtling through the air, his fragile body being violently crushed upon impacting a sturdy tree trunk.

"I am an avid student of history and evidently, you had just participated in the Battle of New Orleans during the War of 1812," Dr. DeMarco immediately recognized and related. "But don't worry one iota Jack; you've apparently endured and survived your ordeal with flying colors! If my memory of history serves me correctly, the battle was unnecessary because a peace treaty had already been signed at Ghent, Belgium several weeks before the violent conflict had happened, but because of the lack of speedy communications across the Atlantic Ocean," the highly-skilled consultant elucidated, "neither the British commander General Edward Parkenham nor your own dauntless General Andrew Jackson were ever aware of the cease fire being in effect! You're doing quite excellent Jack!" Dr. DeMarco praised. "Where are you now?"

"It's February 23, 1836, although in truth, I haven't looked at a calendar or an almanac for several months," the amazing military patient prefaced. "There's this popular belief of 'Manifest Destiny' going all around America and presently Texas Territory is under Mexican dominion. I'm standing on a rampart so to speak, defending a Spanish mission, the Alamo, so I suppose that Davy Crockett, Jim Bowie and me are all 'on-a-mission' to fight to the death using our muskets as clubs, that is after our ammunition supplies have been used up. Oh how agonizing!" Jack Pearson anguished with conviction from his trance-like state. "A Mexican bayonet has just entered my chest and I'm bleeding to death and lying helplessly on the ground, my spirit about to exit my body. Oh Lord, please save me! Forgive me for my numerous sins and grant me life everlasting! Lord have mercy on me!"

'His entire narrative is positively incredible!' Dr. DeMarco marveled and contemplated. 'This very special man, at least according to this subject's extraordinary testimony, is an actual true-blue American patriot! And he's candidly and persuasively presented his recollection of virtually almost dying three consecutive times in precise chronological order, originating with the Revolutionary War, followed by the War of 1812, and now Jack's vividly describing his heroic actions during the quest for Texas independence at the Alamo in 1836, which if I recall from my knowledge of U.S. history was a major episode in the prelude to the Mexican-American War where General Sam Houston eventually vanquished Santa Anna at San Jacinto,' Dr. DeMarco's keen mind imagined. 'But how could Jack be possibly inventing such phenomenal fiction while being totally submissive and obediently compliant under professional hypnosis?'

Dr. Angelo DeMarco then hypothesized that according to the patient's exceptional 'already-established time line,' Jack would naturally next declare his personal association with the Civil War. The man's unique narrative was unlike any commentaries that the psychiatrist had ever before heard in *his* noteworthy thirty-five year professional career. To the astounded interviewer, Jack Pearson was like an addiction, and Dr. Angelo DeMarco wanted more of his subject's strange attestations.

"What's your next war adventure?" the captivated questioner courteously and suavely interrogated. "Verify for me Jack, are you fighting for the North or for the South?"

"Definitely for the Union Blue!" Jack emphatically confirmed. "It's September, 1862 I believe, somewhere in Maryland at a creek called Antietam near the town of Sharpsburg, and my commander General McClellan has vigilantly pursued the Grays there, but then backup Confederates have unexpectedly showed-up coming from the direction of Harpers Ferry, West Virginia and during the wild and bloody confrontation, I've just been mortally wounded and am rapidly losing consciousness. I've got enemy shrapnel in my arms, stomach and legs!"

"Well Jack, I have good news to relate. You've magically managed to survive the bitter Antietam altercation unscathed," consoled and comforted the veteran interviewer. "And you're fortunate to have come out of that formidable war zone still alive and able to speak! Your escape to safety is borderline miraculous. Over twelve thousand brave Union soldiers had perished in the wild siege," Dr. DeMarco, amateur historian, expounded in a soothing tone of voice, "all because General Robert E. Lee wanted to record his first victory on land that had been controlled by the North. But in the final analysis," the doctor indicated to his new patient, "Lee had to admit being out-manned and subsequently the Confederate General reluctantly retreated his exhausted army from Maryland back into Virginia."

The professional examiner was not especially skeptical of his new client's veracity but the mental health expert suspected that Corporal Jack Pearson might just have been suffering from delusional imaginings with certain ideas being spontaneously generated from *his* most creative subconscious mind. Dr. DeMarco accurately anticipated that his subject's next graphic depiction would entail *his* supporting role in the Spanish-

American War that had begun in 1898 with the sinking of the battleship Maine in Havana Harbor, occurring during Republican President William McKinley's Administration. The excited psychiatrist then expertly transitioned Jack into *his* new dangerous scenario.

"I had fought with Colonel Teddy Roosevelt's Rough Riders at the Battle of San Juan Hill but fortunately for us, only mostly enemy Spanish soldiers were killed during the brief encounter," Jack uttered and disclosed in a more relaxed oral delivery. "But because of poor sanitary conditions and camping-out in a mosquito-infested tropical environment, I did almost die in Cuba but not from any destructive cannon blast or gunfire. I had somehow contracted a repugnant case of Yellow Fever and then somehow avoided passing away on August 1st, 1898, exactly one month after Colonel Roosevelt and his rambunctious Rough Riders had basically run rough-shod over their intimidated Spanish adversaries."

"And if I may suggest your next wartime engagement, I suppose that twenty or so years later you were part of General John J. Pershing's advancing American Expeditionary Force in France," the knowledgeable history buff/psychiatrist asked his immobile mesmerized patient. "I've avidly read in various encyclopedias where over two million American soldiers had valiantly fought in France during the famous 'Lafayette We Are Here!' campaign. Did you ever sing *Over There*?"

"Yes I did sing that inspiring George M. Cohan marching song in the rural sectors of France in 1918," Jack rather lethargically confirmed. "I had gotten separated from my platoon after the left side of our trench had been demolished by a direct mortar hit. Bloodthirsty and aggressive German soldiers surrounded me near the Siegfried Line and I was immediately captured and tortured somewhere inside a dense forest without ever having a chance to raise my hands and formally surrender."

"Well, in the 1930s there was the Great Depression scourge along with Prohibition in America and then there was the infamous rise of Adolph Hitler and his Nazi regime in Germany in the mid and late '30s," Dr. DeMarco recalled and commented. "And after the Japanese squadron planes attacked Pearl Harbor, the United States responded to the belligerent assault by joining the Allies to fight the Germans, who were aligned with the Italians under Mussolini and also with the Japanese imperialists' fearsome military juggernaut. And don't forget the Jewish Holocaust too where over six million innocent people perished for no apparent

132

reason at all except for probably being Hitler's personal scapegoat!"

"World War II was an abomination, an absolutely atrocious ugly conflict waged against brutal and ruthless German fascists," Pearson uttered in a monotone voice from his trance-like state. "My Army unit was advancing north inside Italy and we were about to fight for control of Rome and then move on towards Florence in Tuscany. We were hunkered-down occupying a building in the town of Cassino, about midway between Naples and Rome," the perplexed man lying prone on the black leather sofa orally reviewed. "The Allies' planes then bombed the monastery at the top of Monte Cassino, thinking that it had been housing German and Italian troops, but then an errant shell landed squarely on top of the building I was in and I instantly was injured in my face and hands from what might be today described as 'friendly fire'!"

"Well Jack, after World War II the U.S. troops returned home and there was a tremendous industrial renaissance throughout the entire land with suburban communities and shopping centers popping-up outside and around every major urban metropolitan area," Dr. DeMarco lectured to his now quietly resting patient. "The short-lived peace was interrupted however with the initiation of the Korean War between the North Korea Communists and the United States. Was that particular war in your experiential repertoire?"

"No Sir, I don't recall any Korean War," the placid patient maintained. "Instead I remember the year being 1968. I was savagely wounded by a Viet Cong surprise sneak attack outside a coastal city called Hue. Apparently my platoon had wandered too close to an underground enemy tunnel hatch entrance and before I knew it," Pearson stammered and then regained his subconscious confidence, "three of my companions and I were viciously attacked and two of my buddies died, being cruelly maimed by several tossed hand grenades that landed near their American targets."

"And by virtue of deductive logic, because of a time sequence war pattern you've experienced over the last two and a half centuries, I reckon that you had to also be a participant if not a casualty in the 2003 Iraq War?" Dr. DeMarco speculated and conveyed. "Were you also a victim in that modern-era conflict?"

"Yes Sir, I did eventually die after receiving a bullet to my throat. I had passed away inside a temporary Kuwait military tent hospital after the sudden firefight I had been describing flared-up near the Iraqi border," pallid-faced Corporal Pearson divulged. "All together, I have accomplished dying or nearly dying nine times in nine separate American Wars, but each time, I had other last names than Pearson; names like Adams, Jensen, Douglas, Johnson, Burns and McFarland, but in each instance, my first name was always 'Jack'. I trust that my stated observations have managed to clarify certain important psychological concepts for you!"

Having to learn and ascertain another salient relevant fact, inquisitive Dr. DeMarco momentarily hesitated, his keen mind grappling with another interrogatory while his eyes gazed upon and studied inimitable Corporal Pearson, dressed in civilian attire, still lying flat upon the black leather couch. "Jack, in my professional opinion I find your unconventional multiple war lives' account to be both most absorbing and most incomprehensible. Now tell me, were you married during your nine former soldier existences and if so, was your wife's name Doreen in each instance?"

"Yes!" the subject affirmatively replied. "Yes, I had been wed!" Pearson confidently reiterated.

"Was your wife the same Doreen to whom you're presently married?" the now-enamored psychiatrist asked. "Think carefully, for *this* matter is of utmost significance!"

"No! Each time it was a different Doreen with red, black, brown or blonde hair!" the patient explicitly insisted. "But if I may add, each of my nine former wives was in her own way an intelligent beautiful woman, that I am sure."

"Well Jack, I've performed a bit of elementary math' in my head and have arrived at the statistic that, assuming that you were at least twenty years old when you had been wounded at the battle of Bunker Hill, you've lived approximately two hundred and fifty years as you've already convincingly asserted. And according to my calculation estimates," Dr. Angelo DeMarco conjectured and maintained, "most of the time intervals between the various wars that you've chronologically cited were on the average in the range of twenty-five years apart. I've achieved arriving at *that* temporal mean average length by simply subtracting twenty years from two hundred and fifty and then dividing the number two hundred and thirty by nine!" the authoritative mind and emotion evaluator declared. "The basic arithmetic tends to support and justify your claim that you're born again every twenty-five years, mature to adulthood like any normal adolescent would, and then coincidentally are injured or die in warfare just about every standard generation. This uncanny recurrent sequence means that…"

"Means that I'm on a schedule to soon be wounded or die for the tenth consecutive time," Corporal Pearson completed his perceptive mentor's statement. "Oh my God! I think my brain's entering into a panic attack! I'm being overwhelmed by a weird-feeling, a definite death anxiety!"

"Listen carefully to my strict directions Jack!" Dr. DeMarco imperatively instructed. "I'm going to count backwards from ten. When I reach the number 'one' I'll snap my fingers and you'll slowly come out of your deep sleep and then be as good as new. Ten, nine, eight, seven, six…."

* * * * * * * * * * * *

"Five, four, three, two, one…."

When Dr. DeMarco snapped his fingers, the office setting instantly became a thick dark fog and the next thing that the psychiatrist knew, he was occupying a bunker surrounded by a wall of sandbags and that he and Jack Pearson were in Army uniforms nervously preparing for imminent combat. Plumes of dense smoke were billowing in the background. Assessing the illogical situational anomaly, the alarmed and panic-stricken psychiatrist felt compelled to ask, "Jack, where the hell are we?"

"It's now April of 2017 and we're on a plain somewhere in northern Israel getting ready for the Battle of Armageddon! It's all very feasible and rational. The truths of Biblical prophecy must be fulfilled, you know!"

"What do you mean when you say that Biblical prophecy must be fulfilled? Are you totally insane or drastically inebriated?" the obviously incensed and apprehensive psychiatrist demanded a plausible explanation from his new-found companion. "Stop being so damned vague and evasive! Be more specific when answering me Corporal Pearson!"

"It's all a matter of exact Cosmic Divine Inspiration that is actually quite ubiquitous throughout the entire Universe!" Jack endeavored explaining to the thoroughly puzzled and perturbed mind doctor. "Believing is so much more vital to a human being than is the practice of abstract scientific thinking! Any avowed cynic or skeptic could engage in the simple act of doubting!"

"Your wife was right about your nonsensical verbalizations! Stop speaking this incessant ludicrous gibberish of yours! Explain yourself before I lose my temper and get violent!" the now-terrified mind doctor loudly yelled like an asylum maniac.

"I really don't fear dying at this particular moment like you do!" Jack cryptically and enigmatically answered. "The laws of the Universe prescribe that a person must die ten times to reach his or her ultimate destiny. After the final ninth reincarnation," the Corporal methodically articulated, "the individual's Karma has been finally attained upon rendezvousing a tenth time with the immortal Eternal Force. There's one thing I've neglected to tell you Dr. DeMarco. I want you to know that I've actually died nine times and *not once* as you currently believe, you frivolous Fool!" Jack Pearson solemnly informed his fit-to-be-tied listener. "So when we're both exploded into the hereafter Dr. DeMarco, I'll be emotionally content traveling to my ultimate destiny, commonly referred to as Nirvana, because Dr., *my* final spiritual examination will have ended and I will have then successfully passed the obligatory test. Don't you comprehend what I'm expressing? My ten assigned life-and-death Earth cycles will have been finally satisfied. My restless soul will have finally achieved harmony with the Great Universe!"

"But what about me?" the about to go berserk psychiatrist bellowed into the Corporal's serene-looking face. "What is to be *my* personal fate?"

"I've finally found you Dr. Angelo DeMarco, my gullible soul replacement, and you're now my foolish victimized substitute; you're futilely trapped in a three century series of future life/death reenactments," the Army Corporal apprised his greatly dumbfounded Army Private counterpart.

"But Jack, that's *your* eternal status! Tell me more about what's going to happen to *me*?"

"You must die nine additional times thereafter, that is, following your about-to-happen first expiration in order to fulfill your Eternal Karma. And then after you eventually die nine additional times as I will have soon accomplished, you'll progressively become spiritually purified so that your troubled soul can finally exist in total tranquility with the Endless Universe," Jack Pearson candidly conveyed to his still-astonished and totally alienated neurotic bunker mate. "Then and only then Dr. DeMarco, you and your pseudo-science psychiatry along with your immortal soul will at last be accepted by the omnipotent Powers-That-Be, and then your total being will be integrated as One' with the truth and wisdom of the Supreme Cosmos! Oh

God!" Jack joyfully exclaimed. "I just can't wait to die for the tenth and final time and majestically reach my Ultimate Karma!"

"The Rip Van Winkle Club"

William R. Stuyvesant unhappily lived with his domineering wife Gertrude in a magnificent Tarrytown, New York manor house situated on a palisade overlooking the majestic *Hudson River*. William often confidentially compared Gertrude (to male associates) to Dame Van Winkle, Rip Van Winkle's shrew of a wife who lambasted, browbeat and belittled the poor lethargic farmer every day from dawn until midnight. That is where the comparison between Gertrude Stuyvesant and Dame Van Winkle ends. William R. Stuyvesant was filthy rich and neither he nor Gertrude had to work another day in their lives to maintain their expensive tastes, selfish hobbies and extravagant lifestyles.

William Stuyvesant, just like legendary Rip Van Winkle, claimed that Peter Stuyvesant, an early Dutch governor of New Netherland (later New Amsterdam, and now New York) was one of his paternal ancestors. William had inherited a considerable fortune from his father, a shrewd shopping center and real estate developer in the New York City metropolitan area. The fortunate beneficiary was lucky enough to parlay most of his inheritance in the stock market's high technology "bull rally" in the 1990s into a fantastic financial bonanza. But William's prosperity, his mansion and the spectacular view of the *Hudson River* constituted meager consolation when equated with Gertrude Stuyvesant's petulant hostile disposition. William believed that he was on the brink of a nervous breakdown.

"Gertrude is much-too-demanding. She's never happy until she's made me feel inferior by nagging, embarrassing and berating me day and night, oftentimes in front of others," William divulged to Harry Jenkins, one of his business partners over the telephone. "And while she's been spending time out in Los Angeles shopping like there's no tomorrow on *Rodeo Drive*, I've taken the liberty of purchasing a nice home up above Hudson on the river. It's a little more than an hour's drive from Tarrytown Harry, and I plan to use my new dwelling as a retreat for myself and some new friends I intend to make."

"Oh really," William's partner and business consultant doubtfully said, "and how do you intend to acquire these new friends? Make sure you don't get involved with riffraff and swindlers! They're a dime a dozen nowadays. You might be putting your reputation in jeopardy so my advice is to be careful!" Harry Jenkins warned.

"Don't worry!" William R. Stuyvesant assured his apprehensive business contact. "Harry, I'll think of something to sift out the dirt from the gold."

William Stuyvesant was quite familiar with the stellar works of author Washington Irving and had often visited the literary giant's unique mansion *Sunnyside* located just below Tarrytown on the *Hudson's* eastern bank. The remarkable home, positioned just south of the *Tappan Zee Bridge* has been converted into a museum and is now open to the general public. Along with being an authority on Washington Irving's (1783-1859) mansion as well as on *his* biography, the multimillionaire also memorized virtually every passage in the author's works *The Alhambra, Knickerbocker's History of New York* and finally *The Sketch Book,* which contained Irving's most popular tales, *The Legend of Sleepy Hollow* and *Rip Van Winkle.*

"You really love the *Catskill Mountains*, don't you Bill?" the building/construction partner asked Stuyvesant over the phone. "My wife and I go up there all the time and stay at several plush resorts that we frequent. The *Catskills* are a great getaway in either summer or winter. We used to faithfully go to Grossingers and now we occasionally vacation at Villa Roma."

"Sure do love the *Catskills*," Stuyvesant quickly acknowledged and agreed, "and next to Ichabod Crane, Rip Van Winkle has to be my favorite Washington Irving character. I think it all started when I read as a young boy about Rip leaving his village with his faithful dog Wolf to escape the tirades of wicked Dame Van Winkle. The poor henpecked fellow ascended *Thunder Mountain (Mt. Dunderberg)* to seek peaceful sanctuary from his scornful wife."

"Is that why you've bought that place up above Hudson on the river?" the voice on the other end of the telephone line asked. "Do you compare in your mind Gertrude Stuyvesant with Dame Van Winkle?" Harry Jenkins mildly interrogated. "You better not let Gertrude find *that* little secret out. She'll have you wallowing in bankruptcy in no time."

"Yes Harry, as a matter of fact I believe I did buy that property for that particular reason," Will Stuyvesant readily admitted. "Gertrude's temper tantrums are probably even worse than any that old Rip had to contend with from *his* overbearing Dame Van Winkle. I hope to find refuge and asylum from my matrimonial misery, and I want to bond and commiserate with other wealthy men that have egomaniac-type wives out to fleece their husbands of their hard-earned fortunes. Say Harry," William paused and then continued, "do you know what term Washington Irving coined for public consumption?"

"No, I haven't the slightest idea! What?" Harry's voice politely asked.

"The almighty dollar! Ha, ha, ha!" William Stuyvesant loudly laughed over the phone. "Those other rich fellows are guaranteed to empathize with my plight because they'll be in the exact same predicament as I am: rich, despondent, abused and perpetually badgered!"

"Okay Willy, good luck," Harry Jenkins offered. "Let me know how your social experiment works out with your new friends. Gotta' go!" Click.

'Poor Rip Van Winkle had the right idea,' William pensively thought while rubbing his chin. 'Even though *he* was poor, the *poor* fool needed to escape constant verbal abuse. I can send Gertrude to California and around the world, and despite my great fortune,' Stuyvesant imagined, 'the witch of a woman still perpetually berates and haunts me over the telephone. I definitely need isolation from her relentless antagonism. Yesterday the witch called me from Palm Springs and was shopping up a storm on Palm Canyon Drive. Tomorrow she'll be ten miles south in Palm Desert and hitting all of the ritzy stores on El Paseo!'

Then William R. Stuyvesant's mind was struck by a sudden inspiration. 'That's what I'll do,' he instantly decided. 'I'll run a conspicuous ad in the business sections of *The New York Times* and *The Wall Street Journal*. I just want to see what kind of tangible results my lure will yield.'

The unhappy tycoon sat at his computer desk, went to his Microsoft Windows program and composed the following quarter of a page advertisement:

ATTENTION

Eligibility for admission to the prestigious *Rip Van Winkle Club* is now open. Candidates must be of Dutch heritage, must have a domineering, demanding and out-of-control wife, and must also show proof of annual net income of over a half million dollars. Benefits include male bonding and many lucrative business investment opportunities. All interested parties should submit documentation (*IRS* annual tax statement and a bona fide copy of birth certificate) to:

William R. Stuyvesant
P. O. Box 1783
Tarrytown, New York 10591

A full week passed without any meaningful responses to William Stuyvesant's unusual solicitation for qualified men to join the newly formed *Rip Van Winkle Club*. After ten days had elapsed from the publication of the *New York Times* and *Wall Street Journal* ads, the disappointed real estate developer thought that his "different idea" to form a social club of disparate and desperate wealthy male Dutch socialites had been both frivolous and futile. 'Perhaps I was a little too optimistic and naïve?' the multimillionaire thought.

But on the thirteenth day, applications began arriving at P.O. Box 1783, Tarrytown, New York, 10591. Twenty-four interested men sent in letters of introduction along with duplicate annual tax returns to validate minimum $500,000.00 net income along with accompanying copies of birth certificates to confirm authentic Dutch ancestry and heritage.

William was elated by the favorable response to his announcement. He immediately hired the services of a reputable private detective agency to investigate into the backgrounds and careers of all two-dozen applicants. After finding fault with some of the male applicants for either being a mere joint partner in the half million dollar net income specification or for having only one parent of pure Dutch ancestry, the final list had diminished down to the following twelve lucky individuals:

Arnold Tromp	Stockbroker, Company Vice President
Hans Duncan	Appliance and TV Chain Store Owner
Charles Andersen	Insurance Adjuster, Business Owner
Salavatore Von Velardi	Corporate Executive, Import-Export
Firm	
Andrew Kondrack	Builder/Contractor
Peter Van Brocklin	Law Firm Senior Partner
Jack Zeeman	Dentist, Investor
James Erickson	Author of Bestsellers, College
Professor	
Jesse Frank	Medical Doctor
Richard DeVries	Newspaper Publisher
Anthony Bosche	Accountant for *Fortune 500* Companies
Sam Vander Waals	Owner: Three Automobile Dealerships

'What an excellent list of fine distinguished entrepreneurial Dutch businessmen!' William thought and relished as he evaluated his final roster of names that had qualified for the newly amalgamated *Rip Van Winkle Club*. 'It's a wonderful cross-section of American free enterprise where honorable men of Dutch ancestry will exchange stock tips and share business investment opportunities while commiserating with one another the common bond of being continually badgered by bossy and dominant wives,' Stuyvesant thought and smiled. 'Gertrude's jet won't be flying home from *L.A.* until Sunday night. I'll have just enough time to schedule a cordial *Rip Van Winkle Club* get-together at my place for next Saturday afternoon. Then after *we* get acquainted, we'll have a small motorcade up to Hudson on the river and I'll show my kindred friends the newly renovated *RVW* club lodge, which will be available to any troubled member whenever *his* obnoxious wife starts to officially agitate and aggravate him.'

At six p.m. on Saturday the newly selected members of the *Rip Van Winkle Club* assembled at the Tarrytown palisades castle of William R. Stuyvesant. It was an interesting mix of unique personalities, but everyone shared one common denominator: *his* wife was a shrew who would incessantly browbeat her successful husband into "chopped liver."

"Will, are you sure thirteen is a lucky number?" joked Andrew Kondrack, the real estate developer's new acquaintance. "I always had a weird phobia about the number thirteen! Not that I'm basically superstitious or anything."

"Thirteen sure *is* lucky, Andy," William answered after closely studying the building contractor's name tag. "Just remember Mr. Andrew Kondrack how lucky the original thirteen colonies were to the birth of the United States of America. Thirteen might actually be the luckiest number in the universe for all we know!"

Everyone overhearing their genial host's remark laughed lustily after its utterance. Instant camaraderie abounded, and soon the phenomenon known as "male bonding" set in as the thirteen new *Rip Van Winkle Club* friends having common Dutch genealogies, incomes and interests discussed random subjects like polo, golf, tennis, business, world travel, but most importantly, their despicable leeching wives.

"My old lady Helen possibly makes Dame Van Winkle look like a novitiate nun," Richard DeVries, the flamboyant and effervescent newspaper mogul indicated to William and to Andrew Kondrack. "She's enough of a spitfire to make the Devil wish he was a blessed celibate saint! Helen's tongue must weigh more than three pounds, no exaggeration!"

"My spouse is so abominably nasty that our neighbor's three Doberman pinscher attack dogs are super afraid of her!" an eavesdropping Hans Duncan added to the conviviality. "She makes *mean* seem like *kind*! Once during *Halloween* trick or treat night my wife scared two adults dressed like Dracula and Frankenstein right out of our neighborhood, and that's no hyperbole, either!"

"Will," Salvatore Von Velardi butted in as things quieted-down around the semi-circular bar, "when are we victims heading up to the *Catskills?* I need a little mountaintop rest and relaxation right this minute so I hope we don't accidentally wind-up in the *Adirondacks*. I can't wait to see your glorious lodge up above Hudson! And judging by the elegance of this splendid mansion Will, I'll bet your little hideaway is pretty damned spectacular."

"After the third round of drinks have been imbibed," Will Stuyvesant promised his new wealthy friends, "we'll then all be on the same attitude adjustment wavelength and ready to begin *our* much-needed northern expedition. I'll lead the caravan with my sports utility vehicle," the host cheerfully volunteered and pontificated, "and I noticed that three of you men have 4-Wheel-Drive *SUVs* too. Use your four-wheel drive shift when we leave the paved road and have to climb up some steep terrain to arrive at my rustic sanctuary, or should I say *our* rustic sanctuary," Stuyvesant corrected himself. "It's thoroughly removed from all semblances of the hectic big city concrete jungle civilization!"

The now-liberated men all boisterously cheered William R. Stuyvesant's exaggerated bravado, and after the third round of mixed drinks had been swiftly gulped down by the jolly millionaires (assembled around the mansion's custom-made mahogany bar), the entourage was ready to embark on the first unprecedented weekend adventure of the newly formed *Rip Van Winkle Club*.

Quite soon the contingent of amiable half-intoxicated men left William's palatial residence and clambered into their respective vehicles. Four *SUVs* formed an impromptu mini-vacation caravan and William R. Stuyvesant led the jovial members in a military-type convoy north on *Highway 9,* which parallels the noble and serene *Hudson River.*

The small *SUV* fleet soon zoomed by *Sleepy Hollow High School* on the right-hand-side and shortly later down the busy road the autos' passed by Ossining, the infamous home of *Sing*

Sing State Prison. Buildings belonging to *West Point Military Academy* were soon seen on the opposite shore of the stately river, and as the cavalcade of *SUVs* meandered around rocky embankments northward in the direction of downtown Poughkeepsie, the highway inclines then became steeper and the picturesque landscape more rugged. All of the natural beauty brought out the "pioneering instinct" of the men sitting in William Stuyvesant's vehicle.

"Ah, communion with nature!" Will said to Jack Zeeman, his loquacious and very grateful front seat passenger. "*Henry David Thoreau* would certainly enjoy this impressive mountain excursion we're now conducting. Too bad the loner was a poor guy and wouldn't be ineligible for membership into our club if that *Walden Pond* fellow were still alive."

"Yes, I'm sure *he* would *Thoreauly* be thrilled by it!" Jack Zeeman imaginatively returned. "But I'm sure we'll certainly enjoy some Transcendentalism without old Henry's presence."

"Then Jack, you prefer this *Catskills'* outing to listening to your tempestuous wife ranting and raving all the time?" Will deliberately inquired to get a reaction out of Zeeman. "We'll have to have a contest to see whose wife is more vicious! But I must admit that yours sounds hard to beat."

"The Rip Van Winkle Club sure beats Martha chewing me out about returning home late from night *Yankees* baseball games," Jack Zeeman merrily replied. "Martha's *barbs* are more painful than barbed wire!"

Backseat riders Charles Andersen and Jesse Frank found Jack Zeeman's marital impressions extremely hilarious as they boisterously laughed in response to the all-too-true declaration by the henpecked dentist "riding shotgun" up front with Will Stuyvesant.

"Maybe your wife scolds you because she's an avid *Mets'* fan!" Jesse Frank amusingly suggested to Jack Zeeman. "There might be some hidden baseball vindictiveness there! Maybe Jack, Martha owns stock in the *Mets'* franchise without you even knowing about it. Ha, ha, ha!"

"Or maybe Martha is hard of hearing," offered Charlie Andersen, "because I know for a fact that people with severe hearing problems tend to yell when speaking to others so that they can then hear themselves talking! And that's no joking either! I'm bet Jack that your ferocious wife Martha has some sort of wicked hearing disability. Ha, ha, ha!"

"I don't think so!" the blithe-spirited Jack Zeeman chortled from the front seat. "If George Washington's Martha was anything like Martha Zeeman is, then the great *Revolutionary War* General would have become a *Tory* and jumped over to the *British* side just to get away from his wife's flagrant diatribe. Old George would've been a turncoat for the redcoats!"

"If that's the case," William laughed as he rounded a sharp curve in the road, "then Benedict Arnold must've had an overbearing savage wife very similar to your Martha!" Stuyvesant gleefully exclaimed to Jack Zeeman. Wild cackling and guffawing coming from the back seat resulted from Stuyvesant's sarcastic but acutely humorous comment.

The short procession of *SUVs* proceeded with *their* small expedition up *Route 9* and at late twilight passed through Hyde Park, rapidly buzzing by the historic and picturesque home of the revered Franklin Delano Roosevelt, the mansion/museum now converted into a popular national shrine. After driving past the magnificent Hudson River *Vanderbilt Mansion* situated on the left, the four-vehicle caravan continued on its itinerary heading north, the drivers' next destination being Rhinebeck, a town rich in tradition dating back to the early colonial era.

"I understand that good old George Washington once slept at the *Rhinebeck Inn,*" William informed his still giddy and amused passengers, "and it's really a pretty neat place to spend the night, even with *your* opinionated wife Jack! Maybe Gorge Washington's Martha is still in there," William joked to Jack Zeeman, much to everyone's delight.

"If Washington had slept at all these places that claim he had slumbered in their beds," Charles Andersen cynically volleyed from the rear, "then Washington would've slept his way right through the entire *Revolutionary War* just like poor exploited Rip Van Winkle had done."

"I guess that the signers of the *Declaration of Independence* put their money on Washington to be our nation's top general because they figured he'd be a real *sleeper!*" Jesse Frank obnoxiously hollered and punned from the backseat.

"You three guys are really a lot of fun!" William admitted as he stopped for a red traffic signal. 'I'm glad you all decided to get away from your nasty marital mates and get together for leisurely weekends up at my place in the *Catskills.* So far, you fellas' have been a real pleasure to be with," Stuyvesant commended his jolly passengers. "We all need to unwind from our daily stressful schedules and also need to evade our savage wives' negative bullying and intimidation."

Finally the four vehicles followed *Route 9* into the somnolent town of Hudson, where the highway converted into Fairview Avenue, which the caravan stayed on until the appearance of Rod and Gun Road on the left. After several miles of asphalt surface, William held his hand out of the opened driver-side window, signaling to the three trailing *SUVs* to enter four-wheel drive and then take a stone and gravel road up to *his* secluded mountain retreat lording over the dignified placid *Hudson River*.

"You know," William said to his alert and jovial companions in a philosophical tone of voice, "I can just picture poor Rip Van Winkle ascending these steep precipices on a cloudy fall day with his hunting dog Wolf just to achieve some much needed requiem from Dame Van Winkle's relentless tyranny. We all know poor Rip Van Winkle's burden all-too-well from local folklore! In fact Washington Irving aptly described Rip's unenviable plight as 'petticoat tyranny'! Ha, ha, ha!"

"Make sure our first toast at the lodge is dedicated to the fond memory of Rip Van Winkle," Jack Zeeman recommended to his merry colleagues. "All in favor say 'aye'!"

"Aye!" his three merry cohorts bellowed in raucous-but-sincere unanimity.

* * * * * * * * * * * * *

The good-natured men spent the night engaged in serious entertainment and whimsical amusement. They played cards, chess, checkers and dominoes. They drank expensive whiskeys, imported beer and vintage wines. After eating a late catered supper featuring fried chicken, baked ham and basted turkey, the new fraternity members of the *Rip Van Winkle Club* reminisced about past steamy romances and about exotic tropical vacations in Hawaii, the Caribbean and along the French Riviera. Will was elated that the members were all compatible, sharing and building a new-found camaraderie.

Next the club members conversed about the simple joys identified with the biological processes known as eating and drinking, and finally the topic of conversation centered upon the very unfortunate marital predicament of the newly organized club's special namesake, Rip Van Winkle.

"Rip drank the delicious Holland gin obtained from an enchanted barrel at Henry Hudson's wild mountain party," Will nostalgically recollected (and reminded his new-found friends) from the Washington Irving legend, "and the powerful substance put our favorite reveler to sleep for twenty long years. That's not such a bad sentence when you're married to an overbearing shrew like Dame Van Winkle, who sounds almost as treacherous as Jack Zeeman's toxic wife Martha."

"That twenty year sleep was more of a blessing than a curse," Andrew Kondrack steadfastly maintained. "Old Rip didn't have to confront or listen to his belligerent wife's ugly outbursts for two whole decades."

"Yes, most definitely a truism," Peter Van Brocklin chimed in, "but poor Rip lost twenty valuable years off his life where he could've enjoyed many satisfying draughts of ale at Nicholas Vedder's tavern. The impoverished Dutch farmer returned to his village twenty years later not recognizing a single inhabitant in the entire place."

"I really feel badly for the exploited gent, even if he was only a fictitious character," Anthony Bosche amiably qualified and contributed to the discussion. "First of all, we all sleep eight hours a day, so that means we really only consciously live around fifty years instead of the customary seventy-five-year average that biology textbooks and encyclopedias inaccurately state. One third of our lives is spent snoring in bed!"

"I see where you're getting at Tony," interrupted William R. Stuyvesant. "Rip Van Winkle was callously cheated another twenty years by Henry Hudson's cruel sleeping spell, so in effect, Rip was an old man at only thirty years of age. What a lousy bummer no matter how one studies it!"

After cleaning up the extensive waste the sumptuous feast had generated, the euphoric men strolled out to the four *SUVs* and removed their suitcases to lug into spacious "the RVW Lodge." Soon the sportive gentlemen all retired to their assigned quarters, satisfied and content, waiting for a morning of adventure following a restful night's slumber.

The next morning, dark clouds shrouded the distant mountain peaks, making that particular extension of the great *Appalachian* chain appear clad in a dull blue and purple-hued haze. Peter Van Brocklin, Salvatore Von Velardi and Andrew Kondrack were early risers that could have taught the area Hudson roosters a lesson or two in "dawn punctuality." The three new acquaintances were casually standing on the back patio deck of William R. Stuyvesant's "backwoods retreat" and were admiring the scenic tranquility of the passive *Hudson River* down in the valley while

148

contemplating and discussing the awesome *Catskill Mountains*. William R. Stuyvesant exited the expansive converted ranch-home-to-lodge overlooking the *Hudson* and soon joined his rejuvenated guests. The sightseers were carrying three pair of binoculars with a fourth very expensive pair being strapped around Will's neck.

"Here, use these peepers to survey the pristine beauty that surrounds us!" Will suggested as he handed his high-tech' high-powered binoculars to the three men casually stationed on the wooden platform deck. The four spectators took turns peering into the new ultra-modern magnifiers and with their elbows casually resting on a sturdy black wrought iron railing, the men gazed out at the wondrous environmental splendors all around them. Suddenly something highly irregular had been spotted.

"Hey guys," Andrew Kondrack observed and said in a mellow-but-serious tone of voice, "there seems to be some kind of ancient ship anchored out near that rock formation down there to our right. Can you guys see it?"

All four pair of binoculars instantly focused on Andrew Kondrack's rather curious sighting. William R. Stuyvesant, a student of Dutch antiquity, immediately recognized the identity of the object in question.

"Well I'll be a chimpanzee's first cousin!" Will emphatically marveled and exclaimed. "That ship down there in the river is a replica of *Henry Hudson's* prized vessel, the *Half Moon*. Has anyone read any recent newspaper articles about a model of the *Half Moon* visiting this area of New York north of Hudson? That's what that ship has to be, a replica!"

None of the men recollected reading any such journalism, so Will anxiously suggested that the *Rip Van Winkle Club* membership hop into the four *SUVs* and take a narrow side trail down the scenic mountainside to further investigate the strange ship anchored near the *Hudson's* shore.

The men inside the house were summoned from their shaving in front of vanity mirrors, from the breakfast table and from their beds, and in a matter of five hectic minutes, all thirteen adventurous souls scrambled outside the lodge and hopped into the vehicles. Will led the way in his silver *Ford Expedition* down the steep sloping trail to the vicinity where the mysterious ship had dropped anchor in the historic river.

Upon reaching a plateau overlooking the "facsimile *Half Moon*," the four *SUVs* halted one after the other in military parade fashion and the thirteen intrigued occupants got out in a hurry to satisfy their heightened curiosity about the handsome ship of yore and its crew. Much to their astonishment, three little men, each no more than four and a half foot tall, were climbing up an embankment and slowly approaching the men's location from below.

Each of the tiny grizzled-bearded men was dressed in the antique Dutch fashion that was emblematic of late seventeenth century haberdashery. Their extraordinary attire was comprised of cloth' jerkins, and below the short coats the cute but sour-faced fellows wore several pairs of baggy breeches that were handsomely ornamented with rows of buttons lined down each side. Each diminutive "midget Dutchman" (as Will Stuyvesant had labeled them) had been toting on *his* shoulder a small barrel, more of a cask than a barrel, and each fellow appeared quite encumbered by *his* object's weight. The little gents seemed preoccupied with their strenuous labor and were unperturbed by the sudden appearance and confrontation of the thirteen tall men recently arrived from the Rip Van Winkle Lodge.

"Hey little guys," Will Stuyvesant affably greeted, "let us help you carry your barrels up the mountain. We're just brimming with energy."

"This must be some kind of re-enactment of the *Rip Van Winkle* tale," Salvatore Von Velardi conjectured and articulated to all within hearing distance. "But if this experience is true and not a mass hallucination, then these tiny men will eventually lead us to Henry Hudson and his *Half Moon* crew."

Just then a loud rumble of thunder rolled through the distant mountains, and the noise was succeeded by additional low growling peals to the northwest.

"Legend says that that's Henry Hudson and his crew of little men playing a friendly game of ninepins up in the *Catskills*," Peter Van Brocklin related to anyone and everyone willing to listen. "If I'm not mistaken, these little men will take us to *their* leader just like they had done with Rip Van Winkle."

The thirteen visitors assisted the three wee individuals with *their* indigenous labor, thus alleviating much of *their* struggle and toil. About five hundred feet up a narrow rocky footpath, the head small Dutchman dressed in ancient garb solemnly uttered to a solid rock façade, "In Henry Hudson's great name, open a shortcut to *our* destination's game."

Amazingly, the dense rock façade slowly swung open as if it was a lightweight door on hinges. A long dark tunnel was immediately exposed and soon the sixteen human forms took
150

turns lugging the three liquor casks further into the dark hollow, which extended a thousand feet or so into the base of the mountain ridge.

A dull light was visible at the tunnel's other end, and upon exiting the dark cavity, the sixteen trekkers instantly perceived a beautiful ravine with rolling mounds and lush green grassy meadows. Luxurious sunshine radiated down on the splendid dell, and at least fifty other little men dressed in the same-style sixteenth century ancient Dutch costumes were idly standing around and engaging in small talk. But oddly, each tiny gent had a very melancholy expression on his face.

"Why are they all so sad looking?" Andrew Kondrack whispered to Will Stuyvesant after the two millionaires lowered their heavy cask onto a wooden platform that had been tacitly designated by one of the austere-looking diminutive fellows. "To use one of Jack London's favorite words, they all look 'lugubrious'."

"According to legend," Will speculated and whispered, "these little men are immortal. They are unchanging in age as time advances onward. Because they're all immortal," Will Stuyvesant continued his incredible explanation, "they're bored with their mortal existence and quite unhappy having to live forever. They've seen everything once too often and are not at all enamored with the monotony of life's repetitive events."

"And check out those other mischievous little imps partying over there," Jack Zeeman indicated to his companions with his right hand. "They're playing a game of bowling on the green and simulating the sound of thunder echoing through the mountains when the ball strikes the pins."

"Ninepins, not bowling," Will aptly corrected. "That game we're watching is often referred to as duckpins!"

Henry Hudson dispatched one of his chief wee English-speaking crew-members to the area of the thirteen spellbound twenty-first century Americans, and after a polite introduction, Heinrick addressed his former helpers.

"Thank you for assisting us in transporting the Holland gin to our big party," Heinrick began his impromptu speech. "As you gentlemen might know, every twenty years the crew of the *Half Moon* returns to the *Hudson River Valley* to review and celebrate our past explorations and expeditions. It's quite a treat for us despite our customary sad-looking countenances."

"Have you ever heard of a fellow named Rip Van Winkle?" Jack Zeeman nervously asked Heinrick.

"That's confidential information I'm not at liberty to discuss," Heinrick diplomatically answered.

"Well then, how come there're three barrels of Holland gin and not just one?" Will politely asked the peculiar-looking neurotic-sounding little fellow. "Are you intending to have a bigger party than usual this afternoon?"

"Well kind Sir," Heinrick defensively replied, "I strongly suggest that you listen attentively. The gin from each of the barrels will produce a different effect. One barrel's contents will have no effect on the drinker of its gin, one of the barrels will age the drinker twenty years, and a chug from the third random barrel will make the lucky drinker twenty years younger."

"Wow!" Hans Duncan (the wealthy appliance distributor) amply exclaimed. "It's sort of like a casino gamble on the wheel game with numbers one to three rotating around," Hans accurately interpreted. "If I choose correctly and can tack twenty years onto my life and simultaneously become two decades younger in the meantime," Hans hypothesized and declared, "then it's worth the gamble to be able to outlive my nasty wife."

"And even if *you* choose to drink from the wrong cask," Charlie Andersen guessed and explained, "then *you* still might choose the barrel that'll have no effect at all and still enjoy a cool refreshing mug of Holland gin. That's now reduced to a fifty-fifty chance."

"But fellas'," Will Stuyvesant cautioned his new-found comrades, "if someone selects the wrong barrel out of the three, then that person will be doomed to losing twenty years off his already pathetic life and will wake up an old man ready for the cemetery. Is that gambol worth the gamble?"

"Do you mean to say that *you* actually believe all this idiotic nonsense?" Arnold Tromp criticized. "This is the most preposterous hoax I've ever witnessed. It *is* in my fairly astute estimation and educated opinion that this farce is absolutely beyond a shadow of a doubt a silly college fraternity-type initiation prank of the greatest magnitude!"

"Then you Sir wouldn't hesitate to prove *me* wrong by taking the first sample," Heinrick offered Arnold Tromp as the gallery of fifty little men in attendance laughed exceedingly at their foreman's intelligent challenge to *his* dubious guest. "Would you care to sample a sip Mr. Arnold Tromp?"

"Well, I'll have to think about it and reconsider my options," Arnold Tromp uneasily conceded. "This is indeed a most difficult choice we're being pressured into making. Hey! How did *you* know my name?"

Again, the fifty or so little dwarfs roared out in laughter as the sound of a small rolling ball smashed against a triangular formation of duckpins on the ravine's lush green.

"I'll bet a cool thousand dollars with any of you that this decision Henry Hudson is presenting us with is for real," William R. Stuyvesant boldly offered the other twelve astonished members of the *Rip Van Winkle Club.* "Who's got the guts to put *his* money where his mouth is?"

All of the twelve other "party crashers" presumed and believed that the entire scenario was a "clever theatrical trick" that had been brilliantly contrived, paid for, sponsored and orchestrated by their illustrious host, William R. Stuyvesant of Tarrytown, New York. Salvatore Von Velardi was the first bold fellow to wager a thousand dollars, believing that Will would graciously reimburse him after the completion of "the chicanery." The other eleven meanderers all gave *their* pledge that they would pay William R. Stuyvesant a thousand dollars each should "the deception" indeed turn out to be a "functioning aberration."

William was nominated to choose first, so Stuyvesant drank a cup of Holland gin from barrel number three. Arnold Tromp, Salvatore Von Velardi, Peter Van Brocklin, James Erickson, Jesse Frank and Sam Vander Waals all were given empty mugs that were quickly filled and the "guinea pigs" eagerly quaffed down their draughts drawn from barrel number two.

The remaining six thoroughly entertained wealthy gentlemen all lustily drank down Holland gin from the cask labeled in plain English "Number One."

Will Stuyvesant began feeling dizzy, first losing his balance with wobbly knees and then acting irrational with planets, stars and galaxies spinning around inside his head. The intoxicated multimillionaire staggered and tottered about, clumsily and awkwardly gyrating from side to side as if he were a defective spinning top. The organizer of the *Rip Van Winkle Club's Catskill Mountain* excursion trudged off, walking between and around several jagged crags, gradually disappearing over the horizon as he cautiously attempted descending the rugged ridge while still under the influence of the very potent Holland gin.

Will Stuyvesant's twelve skeptical and traitorous apostles also staggered around like a bevy of soused alcoholics, desperately searching for a soft spot on the velvet-green-grass to take much-needed naps. Each man's fate was determined by the numbered cask from which *he* had selected a draught to drink.

Hans Duncan, Charles Andersen, Andrew Kondrack, Jack Zeeman, Richard DeVries and Anthony Boshe all unfortunately drank the Holland gin from barrel "Number One." Each man was destined to sleep in the mystical *Catskill Mountains* for twenty-years and thusly validating himself' as a true disciple of the inimitable Rip Van Winkle and also demonstrating that *he* was a dedicated member of the *Rip Van Winkle Club*. Upon waking up, Richard DeVries, the youngest of the first cask group would be age seventy-one in the year 2022, and Andrew Kondrack, the eldest among the ill-fated half dozen imbibers would be ninety-two upon awakening from his unanticipated slumber two decades later.

As for the visitors that partook of the second cask, Arnold Tromp, Salvatore Von Velardi, Peter Van Brocklin, James Erickson, Jesse Frank and Sam Vander Waals, all were miraculously rejuvenated with twenty years fantastically shaved off their ages. However, the sly and clever dwarf' Heinrick had not disclosed to the vain and gullible men that they would be assigned as cabin boys to perform myriad duties and drudgery-assignments on the good ship *Half Moon*. And regrettably, the six hapless victims of youth revisited were all now permanently destined to have futures laden with misery as servants of the no-nonsense taskmaster Henry Hudson and his disconsolate and temperamental crew of fickle little seventeenth century Dutch men.

As for William R. Stuyvesant, the foundering founder of the notorious *Rip Van Winkle Club*, his fate was not a benign one, either. The multimillionaire awoke (without aging) just before dawn on Sunday morning and found himself' lying on soggy turf between a termite-infested hollowed-out fallen oak tree and a clump of mountain sticker bushes and accompanying briers.

William immediately recollected his misadventure the day before with the irascible little ghostly Dutchmen in the very outlandish *Catskill Mountain* amphitheater-like ravine. The victim felt arthritis in his wrists and elbows and rheumatism in his back's lumbar area. Will's initial instinct was to feel for a long, shaggy gray beard', which would be evidence that he had been betrayed by Henry Hudson and *his* naughty crew and that *he* had indeed slept for twenty years just like his legendary mentor, Rip Van Winkle. Stuyvesant was glad to note that no lengthy grizzled beard had grown from his face and the befuddled man was never so happy to feel his whiskers' bristles.

'I wonder what happened to the others?' William meditated as he feebly rose to his feet and then brushed some skittering insects and loose dirt from his light-blue denim jeans and from his navy blue sweatshirt. 'I hope I can find my way out of this forsaken place and back to my *SUV*. Thank God I had only slept for one night!'

The addled fellow's head was still groggy from the potent alcohol he had consumed the prior morning, so Will' prudently shuffled down the ridge and soon recognized the verdant ravine where the games of ninepins had been played. 'This is also where I had made the mistake of taking the first sample of Holland gin from the third cask,' he regretted with a degree of guilt. 'This is like a nightmare revisited.'

Being distracted by his own vain thoughts, William accidentally stumbled over a log, fell onto the ground and then tumbled forward several hundred feet down a slope to the footpath that led to the dark tunnel shortcut that channeled through the base of the mountain. 'I think I know where I'm at now!' he remembered.

After Stuyvesant had rolled down to the base of the ravine, much to his consternation the tunnel exit was not observable, so Will recalled the rhyming language uttered by diminutive Heinrick at the long, hollow dank rock corridor's other end. "In Henry Hudson's great name, open a shortcut to *my* destination's game!" Stuyvesant shouted with his hands cupped over his mouth, his voice echoing throughout the ravine and resounding through the surrounding mountain precipices.

The rock façade slowly creaked open like a squeaky door with rusty hinges, revealing the same fabulous tunnel shortcut that the three dwarfs had led the loyal members of the *Rip Van Winkle Club* through the morning before. 'This tunnel is like a magical umbilical cord connecting the material world with a bizarre fantasy world,' Will's dazed mind thought and concluded. 'Now all I have to do is walk the thousand feet, get inside my *SUV* and drive back to civilization. I almost want to see and hear Gertrude again!' the disoriented explorer insanely imagined.

The secret tunnel was just as damp and dreary as it had been the day before, and upon entering the outside world dimmed by a dark cloudy overcast sky on the opposite end, the rock façade soon mechanically squealed shut much to Will Stuyvesant's awe and bewilderment. Then the solid rock door banged against the mountain base with a thud, quite effectively concealing its secret access to the secluded magical ravine.

Still stunned and mildly confused from his weird ordeal, William Stuyvesant cautiously descended the final three hundred feet down a ridge, the route leading to the aforementioned mountain trail where the four all-terrain vehicles had been neatly parked in a row the morning before. 'I must take it slow, for if I plunge down this last incline from this height,' Will assessed, 'then I'll risk breaking an arm, a leg or both. If I survive this arcane misadventure, no one's ever going to believe my sensational tale! And all four SUVs are still parked down there!'

With careful diligence, the man's aching legs finally carried his weary body down the remaining part of the ridge closest to his trusty four-wheel drive vehicle. The sky was still partially dark with the new day's sun ready to perform its daily resurrection on the black and pink eastern horizon.

Arriving at his *Ford Expedition*, Will frantically fumbled in his jeans' pockets for his keys but then he remembered that in his rush to make contact with Heinrick and *his* two dwarfish associates, Stuyvesant had inadvertently left the starting device in the *SUV's* ignition. 'Thank God it's still there,' Will thought as he opened the driver-side door and gingerly entered his beloved vehicle. 'Now to get out of here!'

The reliable *Expedition's* motor whined and then started and next Will methodically backed the vehicle up and swiftly turned the *SUV* around with his hood pointed in the direction of downtown Hudson. 'I should report the whole insane incident to the police,' Stuyvesant logically considered, 'but the cops would never believe me in a million years and accuse me of being delusional. The only thing I have going for me is my credibility and my track record of being a multimillionaire along with the fact that twelve highly successful businessmen will soon be reported missing to the authorities. I feel that I'm responsible for all of these extraordinary things happening!'

William had an inclination to turn on the specially installed *Bose* radio system to listen to the news but before he could honor his next impulse, the man's eyes instantly beheld a dark foreboding spectral image remaining stationary three hundred feet ahead. An ominous frightening figure sitting atop an enormous black horse stood directly in *his* path.

'Oh my God!' Will's mind immediately recognized and feared. 'It's the fabled *Headless Horseman of Sleepy Hollow*! What utter craziness! How could a fictitious character from one eerie legend

156

suddenly enter into the enactment of another? How horrendous! This torture is too surreal to be real! Not even Gertrude would wish such a cursed punishment on me!'

Will sat petrified like a contemporary Ichabod Crane in the front driver's seat of his dependable *Ford Expedition*, believing that *he* could outrace the formidable ruthless *Headless Horseman* once *he* could safely make it to a paved highway. The driver slowly inched forward, waiting for the right opportunity to gun the silver *SUV* onto a side gravel and stone winding road that paralleled the majestic *Hudson River.*

Showing marvelous timing and dexterity, Stuyvesant, out of his dire need for self-preservation, quickly rotated the steering wheel to the right and soon his vehicle was speeding down the mountain ridge trail with the jet black horse and its tenacious executioner closing the gap between William and the rider's speedy stallion. Stuyvesant had never before been so alarmed, so desperate, so endangered and so panic-stricken in all his life.

Will's reliable speedometer registered fifty miles an hour as he maneuvered around precarious curves and up and down treacherous terrain that would not ordinarily accommodate such high speed, but much to *his* trepidation, the well-conditioned horse remained close behind. Fortunately a mile stretch of straightaway was dead ahead for Will, so Stuyvesant again mashed his foot down on the accelerator, with the dependable *SUV* rapidly attaining a speed of eighty miles per hour. Still, the fleet galloping black steed was easily able to keep pace with the great instant velocity achieved by the silver *Ford Expedition.*

'This is impossible!' Will fearfully thought. 'Not even a gazelle or a cheetah could run this fast! This horrible anomaly is contrary to reason! It goes against both nature and science!'

The fantastic wildly snorting black steed with its determined headless rider in the saddle then incredibly pulled alongside the terrified *SUV* driver. A totally hysterical and delirious Will Stuyvesant took a brief glimpse at the shocking apparition, which suddenly removed a handgun from a concealed pocket inside its ghostly apparel and then aimed and fired the lethal weapon at the *SUV's* front wheel.

The bullets from the devastating blasts punctured the *Expedition's* left front tire. Will Stuyvesant abruptly lost control of the speeding all-terrain vehicle. The SUV swerved to the right and then skidded off of the already dangerous stone and gravel road, careened down a ridge of smooth weather-worn rocks and then violently plummeted into the formerly tranquil *Hudson River.*

157

Both William Reynolds Stuyvesant's life and the short-lived *Rip Van Winkle Club* had been fatefully and simultaneously erased from the face of the Earth.

Much to the shock of Hudson River Valley aristocrats, after Will Stuyvesant's corpse had been recovered from the cold river, his lengthy obituary appeared three days later in various New York City and Tarrytown newspapers. Accolades abounded in the various print media articles. William Reynolds Stuyvesant was described and praised as a "generous community-minded philanthropist" who will be deeply missed by his affectionate wife Gertrude Stuyvesant, who tearfully eulogized her husband during his somber church funeral service and then completely out of character, the normally stoic woman later cried incessantly at her husband's solemn burial.

"Fantasy Book Land"

Frank and Betsy Lanier were glad that the busy and hectic summer season was over at their well-established sixty-year-old South Jersey family business going by the all-too-familiar trade name of Fantasy Book Land. Finally it was time for the couple to enjoy a well deserved and relaxing fall hiatus, a getaway Columbus Day weekend. In South Jersey, the deciduous tree leaves were resplendently beginning to transform into their autumnal hues and to the needed-to-be-rejuvenated Laniers, a much-anticipated tour bus trip up to New Hampshire's White Mountains represented a most welcome departure from the continuous daily grind of adult responsibility.

"I'm glad we're again going with Ralph's Bus Tours up to New England," Betsy said to Frank as the husband pulled his black Mercedes into the Cape May Senior Citizens' Tour Bus Terminal parking lot. "The change in scenery will be most appreciated. We'll be able to forget our identities and duties for the next four days and be just two ordinary anonymous vacationers seeking asylum from grueling drudgery and accountability."

The Laniers were indeed rather fatigued from operating the thriving fifty-acre family business that catered mostly to young children ages four-to-twelve along with the kids' ever-doting parents. "Didn't we just go up to the Beacon Resort two years ago?" Frank grumpily asked Betsy as he pulled a heavy suitcase from the car's trunk. "On second thought, if my memory serves me correctly I did savor our last bus excursion up there. The food was excellent and I think we also got to see a baby moose entering a mountain pine forest. It's amazing that my mind is still functioning at 6 a.m."

"Yes Dear," Betsy calmly answered her jittery soul mate. "The fall foliage was simply spectacular! And as you've already recalled, so was the Beacon's irresistible food. But according to the latest brochure we had received in the mail, the resort's suites have been totally renovated with inviting Jacuzzis large enough to accommodate two weary loungers like ourselves. And on the menu at the lodge's Dad's Restaurant is prime rib au jus the first night, filet mignon for the second evening's meal and lobster tail will be feasted on for the third night's farewell dinner. Really Frank, I could almost taste the scrumptious food already. I'll just have to abandon my austere diet. All you can eat plus salad, the soup de jour and finally, a variety of tantalizing desserts too!"

"Not to mention three fantastic hardy breakfasts. Suddenly I've acquired a tremendous appetite!" Frank laughed and then beamed a broad smile upon his countenance. "Yes Betsy, my stomach is now demanding instant gratification!"

The anxious forty-eight passengers' patiently waited in a straight line and then slowly ascended the semi-spiral staircase into the luxurious Cape May tour bus where they were individually greeted by their cordial driver Mike. An hour later the excited-but-carefree adventurers were chatting and motoring past Asbury Park heading north on the Garden State Parkway, and sixty minutes later the mostly elder explorers would be stopping at a rest and snack station at Montvale. Frank's emotions had significantly transformed into a much more civil mood as the chronic worrier finally got his mind off of the family's Fantasy Book Land enterprise, which now was a distant memory, geographically a full hundred miles behind.

"I hope we're going to see some new and different New Hampshire attractions this second time around," Frank indicated to his devoted spouse, who was sitting closer to the aisle. "Somehow, I do remember the last time up there visiting a religious shrine near Dixville Notch."

"Yes Frank, that was the Our Lady of Grace Shrine up in Colbrook, and then of course right afterwards we had a fine lunch later that day at the classy Balsams Resort, which if you recall reminded us of the magnificent Hotel Del Coronado out in San Diego," the wife recollected and emphasized to her husband. "And if you remember Frank, the Balsams up in Dixville Notch is where the first votes are cast during each Presidential Election. They even had a special balloting room set aside to allow for the famous voting process. And only around thirteen citizens participate in the event."

"True Honey, that unique hotel is not too far from the Canadian Border," the South Jersey entrepreneur elaborated. "And then during that last trip we also went onto a pontoon boat and toured that decent-sized lake where the movie *On Golden Pond* had been filmed. I believe that it was called...."

"Squam Lake and the 1981 film you just mentioned starred Katherine Hepburn and Henry Fonda," Betsy Lanier politely lectured and informed. "But on this particular trip we'll be taking a ferry ride across huge Lake Winnipesaukee and then the bus will meet us at the other side to take us to see the incredible Castle in

160

the Sky mansion. And the numerous mansions built along Lake Winny along with the incomparable Castle in the Sky will be terrific attractions that'll make this a very memorable fall vacation. I'm glad that we brought along our video camera to document everything. It's your special duty not to lose it!"

"Montvale!" Mike loudly-but-courteously announced over the ultra-modern bus's intercom. "Now Folks, this is only a brief rest and snack stop so please be back inside the vehicle in thirty minutes. We aren't that far from the Tappan Zee Bridge going across the Hudson River, and then we'll be in New York State for less than an hour before eventually hitting Connecticut. And don't swallow-down too much junk food here at Montvale. Lunch will be served in approximately three hours at a pretty nifty Cracker Barrel near the Connecticut/Massachusetts Line."

After downing several tasty Dunkin' Donuts and big cups of much-desired coffee, Frank and Betsy re-entered the four-hundred-and-fifty-thousand dollar well-equipped motor coach and promptly resumed their propensity for civil marital conversation. Soon the bus and its occupants were zipping across the Tappan Zee Bridge into historic Tarrytown, New York, the site of famed American author Washington Irving's mansion Sunnyside, which was located on the north bank of the regal Hudson. And then fifteen minutes later the forty-eight riders were viewing and marveling at the impressive skyscrapers emblematic of White Plains, which indeed confirmed the fact that the wide-eyed riders were on the perimeter of the New York City metropolitan area.

"We're right on schedule," Frank confirmed to his wife and business partner, pointing to his Rolex. "I gotta' admit, Mike is a really skilled driver! He's the same guy we had two years ago."

"Yes Dear, and if there aren't any accidents or lengthy traffic snags along the way, we'll be having bacon and eggs at the Cracker Barrel in just two hours or so. And Frank," Betsy coyly added in a low tone of voice, "now that your father is turning full control of the business over to you as the newly appointed CEO, don't forget your chief assignment that you've been officially delegated. Pop wants you to be on the lookout for..."

"For a dynamic new attraction to add to Fantasy Book Land for the upcoming spring season," the husband astutely finished his wife's sentence. "And Pop's been quite generous in his expense allotment. Once the project's been approved, I'm allowed to spend up to a million dollars on the imaginative amusement park improvement, at least that's what the corporation has initially budgeted. I sure hope I get a miraculous inspiration while

161

meandering through the lackluster tourist traps up in the White Mountains. Holy Toledo Betsy!" the husband exclaimed. "What in the blessed world am I saying?" Frank chuckled and then reluctantly grinned. "Am I a hypocrite or what? I myself manage and operate a prosperous tourist trap just outside Atlantic City!"

As the thoroughly modern motorbus rumbled through the center of Hartford, Connecticut, Frank pointed out the shiny golden dome of the State Capitol Building and then Betsy pontificated that the last time they had journeyed on bus up to the Beacon Resort that three state capitol edifices had been observed: the first in Hartford, the second in Springfield, Massachusetts and the third one in Concord, New Hampshire.

"You must be a good buddy of the Sandman because you were sleeping both ways back and forth to and from New Hampshire," the wife mildly stated and complained. "Downtown Hartford I've seen before despite your incessant snoring. I even had to jab you in the ribs a dozen or so times to quiet you down. But getting back on subject," Betsy persisted in her harmless jabbering, "maybe you'd like to put miniature models of the three state capitol buildings inside Fantasy Book Land," the woman casually joked. "Or perhaps a small version of Mark Twain's famous steamboat-shaped home that had been built right here in Hartford."

"No Betsy, but I really need to come-up with a novel ride or exhibit for older kids and adults to experience," the more serious-minded and emotionally pressured husband replied. "I mean the Three Billy Goats Gruff and Troll Bridge scene is adequate, the Goldie Locks/Three Bears House is okay situated next to the fairly decent Three Pigs and Big Bad Wolf venue, the Giant and the Jack and the Beanstalk castle has been a hit ever since our amusement park was initially built back in the early 1950s' but I have to admit," Frank Lanier confessed, "the Hansel and Gretel Gingerbread House is getting a little old and obsolete-looking although it's still quite popular with the youngsters."

"I totally agree and think that we definitely need another transportation ride to go along with the train that makes a figure eight passage from one side of Fantasy Book Land to the station platform at the other end," Betsy constructively suggested. "I mean, don't get me wrong Frank! We have a merry-go-round, a small whip, a nursery rhyme haunted house, a small Ferris Wheel along with seven other moving kiddy rides, not to mention lively calliope music being played all over the park, but as you've stated, we don't really have something dynamic and intriguing to entertain and satisfy the twelve-year-olds and up."

162

"It's always far easier to borrow an idea than to actually invent a new one," Frank verbally conveyed. "This winter I plan to visit at least a dozen entertainment theme parks across the USA just to obtain and achieve that one special brainstorm I need. My glorious new structure will not be a pure plagiarism, but instead it'll be some cost-effective inventive modification of a functional ride that already exists somewhere else. All I have to do is discover the thought-evasive thing, but I assure you Betsy," the under duress spouse emphasized, "I'll readily recognize the evasive object I'm contemplating the minute my alert eyes perceive it!"

"What about a roller coaster, or mechanical horses on a track or perhaps a challenging miniature parachute jump ride!" Betsy Lanier diplomatically recommended. "Those types of sensational features helped get the Coney Island and Atlantic City boardwalks started back in their heyday. Or perhaps we could have a Swiss-style gondola skyway cable ride installed going north and south across the park while our current figure-eight train transports our customers east and west."

"A cable-driven Swiss sky ride? That's an excellent possibility," Frank sincerely maintained while scratching his head. "It's certainly worthy of consideration! Perhaps we can call it the Mother Goose Aerial Freeway and each gondola could have a different children's theme painted on it like Tom Thumb, Little Miss Muffet or Little Jack Horner."

The scheduled "brunch" at the Connecticut Cracker Barrel was delectable and after using the restaurant's lavatory facilities, Frank and Betsy sat on convenient-but-sturdy white rocking chairs on the establishment's front porch until an overhead speaker announcement was made that the "Cape May, New Jersey Senior Citizens' bus is now available for boarding."

"We're less than three hours away from gorgeous Lincoln, New Hampshire and the Beacon Resort," the wife reminded the husband. "I can't wait to sink my fork into the advertised four-course supper, and then later see the comedy show in the theater, sip some Merlot and then finish-off this evening's activities by stepping into the soothing warm water of our deluxe Jacuzzi."

Frank Lanier's mind was suddenly stimulated with his wife mentioning the utilization of a Jacuzzi bath. "Maybe my new incredible attraction will feature a terrific water park theme with huge cascading falls and an assortment of massive flume tubes for the older kids and adults to cavort around in and bravely zoom through," the husband imagined and expounded. "No Dear, on

163

second thought such a wild and dangerous monstrosity would be an absolute insurance nightmare. We need to consider something less exotic and much more mundane, something more practical. Have any solutions?"

"Well Hubby, sometimes an idea enters your mind when you're least expecting it," Betsy encouraged and supportively expressed. "That's exactly how many important discoveries have been made throughout history, many of them by sheer accident, chance or coincidence. Here's my theory for all that it's worth!" the wife enthusiastically exclaimed. "Just keep an open mind and have perceptive eyes and ears. I'm certain that the answer to your little dilemma will come when you least expect it!"

After arriving at the rather ordinary-looking Beacon Resort, room keys were distributed and then Mike the bus driver and two lodge employees delivered the passengers' luggage to their respective suites. Everyone arriving enjoyed the following two hours freshening-up, reading room literature and area guides and preparing for the highly anticipated dinner extravaganza, "The Prime Rib Luau." The comedy show that followed the extensive feast was especially hilarious, despite the abundance of slapstick comedy routines provided by the four principal entertainers, who in reality seemed old enough to be former Vaudeville stage performers.

The next morning the Laniers partook of the "New England *You Serve* Buffet Breakfast," and at nine a.m. the couple was again ascending the semi-circle stairway onto the "kneeling bus," which when stationary was lowered several inches by air hydraulics to allow riders to more easily board.

"What's on our itinerary today?" Frank inquisitively and curiously asked his lady companion. "Are we going to see Mt. Washington or Franconia Notch again?"

"No Dear. We're going to travel through the ultra-modern resort community of Meredith en route to a popular ferry landing known as Weirs Beach. Then we'll go up the gangplank onto a two hundred and thirty foot long ferry, the Mount Washington, named in honor of the highest and coldest peak in New Hampshire that you just mentioned," Betsy explicitly narrated as if she were the official bus tour moderator. "We'll have a delightful one and a half hour scenic cruise across famous Lake Winnipesaukee and we'll view myriad fantastic homes erected along the banks. I understand that some of the mansions have three door boat ports in addition to standard three door car garages."

164

"And are we having lunch on the boat too?" Frank innocently inquired. "Lately it seems that my stomach has been ruling my brain. I really should put off my next physical with Dr. Carver for a whole month after we return back to Jersey following this grueling vacation. My nasty cholesterol reading will be invading into diabetes warning territory!"

"Don't be so pessimistic Frank! You'll be able to relax and view the various sights after you consume, or should I say after you 'devour' some Italian stuffed shells, baby back ribs, boiled potatoes, green salad and apple pie that's listed on the ship's menu," Betsy reminded and related. "Unfortunately, it's all just what Dr. Carver didn't order!"

"The Mount Washington is coming around the bend right now," Frank said, pointing west with his index finger. "Listen to the whistle blasts! Why it's shaped sort of like a Mark Twain era Mississippi steamboat."

"Yes, and it's even older than Fantasy Book Land," the wife observed and elucidated. "Your grandfather borrowed money from banks, friends and relatives and began constructing the original twelve frame-house exhibits right after he had left the Army in 1947. Four years later, after much labor and aggravation, and after near bankruptcy, with admirable perseverance, your Grand-pop Tony finally got the park open to the public."

"I still remember what grand-pop always used to say," the husband nostalgically rehashed and shared. "He volunteered to go up against the Nazis to defend the world from Hitler's insanity and *his* private goal was to protect America in order to preserve democracy and to safeguard free enterprise. And Grand-pop Tony's strong American dream was to design and build Fantasy Book Land for young kids and for interested adults still young at heart. I feel that it's my obligation to continue the tradition!"

"And now we're both carrying on your family's wonderful business heritage," Betsy contributed to the dialogue as the Mount Washington slowly approached the crowded docking pier. "Oh well, the passengers are preparing to disembark and Mike has already given us our tickets. But we're not going to be returning to Weirs Beach," Betsy reminded Frank, who was still oblivious to the basic itinerary. "Instead Mike will be driving the bus over to Wolfeboro, a colonial town on the opposite side of Lake Winnipesaukee. We'll reunite with him and his bus there."

"Well Betsy, when we finally retire from operating Fantasy Book Land, you can be my personal tour guide when we eventually get to be elderly jet setters flying all around the world and staying at spectacular exclusive European, Asian and South American resorts. Say Honey, how big is this prodigious lake anyway?"

"The pamphlet I had read back at the Beacon described it as being seventy-two square miles and for your information, the article indicated that your favorite body of water, Squam Lake feeds directly into Winnipesaukee."

"It looks like you've done your homework and that you're already beginning your illustrious tour guide career right here and now in beautiful autumnal New Hampshire," Frank laughed and commended. "And Betsy, you'll probably point out and identify every singular island in this mammoth lake along with every canoe, every dock, every native bird and every fishing boat visible in the entire environment."

After the recently painted Mount Washington docked in Wolfeboro, the forty-eight chattering New Jersey travelers again boarded Mike's very comfortable bus and within ten minutes the driver was pleasantly on his way upland into Moultonborough. After ascending a second steep spiral grade, the wide-eyed riders were treated to a heavenly sight. High on a majestic mountain ridge was an exceptionally breathtaking view of Lake Winnipesaukee gleaming like a gigantic stretch of terrestrial splendor below, the calm fresh water sparkling like assorted diamonds in the radiant sunshine.

Then after the enchanted passengers were politely instructed to remain in their seats, Mike gave his riders a brief impromptu background description of the sensational Castle in the Clouds. "Construction on this eighteen room stone palace had begun in 1913 and it was financed and solidly built by a multimillionaire shoe manufacturer named Thomas Plant, who incidentally was a close friend of Theodore Roosevelt. The two pals often accompanied each other on hunting expeditions both here in New Hampshire and also out West. Anyway," Mike continued his thoroughly memorized oratory, "Mr. Plant had a fascination, or should I say 'a fixation' with the number five and only pentagon-shaped stones were used in the mansion's external facades," Mike further explained into his hand-held microphone.

"How many men worked on the project?" an old male passenger in the first seat second row opposite the bus driver asked.

"A thousand stonemasons were hired to complete the structure, the job finally terminating in 1915," Mike authoritatively answered. "This extraordinary estate consists of

166

five thousand acres of mountain land purchased by Mr. Plant, who was a very shy and introverted fellow that obviously valued his privacy. The Castle in the Clouds mansion was one of the first homes in America to have electricity, running water for sinks, toilets and showers along with telephone communications. Before you leave, be sure to visit and inspect the two octagon rooms that were deliberately built one on top of the other."

"Was Mr. Plant married?" a woman occupying a fourth row left side seat asked the standing narrator. "He seems to have been a very eccentric man for a woman to have to live with!"

"Yes he was married, but physically speaking, bashful Mr. Thomas Plant happened to be a very short fellow who probably suffered from a mild inferiority complex, if not a Napoleon complex. But when it came down to managing his noteworthy business accomplishments, Mr. Plant was an industrial giant, an economic wizard of sorts. Ironically though, he did have a tall wife, over six foot in height I believe. And at one time the short-in-stature gentleman had owned the largest shoe factory in the entire United States. And finally," Mike suavely and astutely summarized, "Mr. Plant possessed and frequently utilized a secret room, a sort of library/study strategically situated directly off of the living room where he often sought leisurely isolation from other humans dwelling or staying inside his handsome residence. But Folks, inside the mansion you'll have to stoop down low to fit through the opened portal wall panel to be able to enter the 'Secret Room.' If you frequently go to a chiropractor for back adjustments, I urge you not to bend down and enter the low portal."

"And I thought I had some annoying psychological hang-ups to deal with!" Frank giggled to his very perceptive wife. "Mr. Thomas Plant sounds like he required the full-time services of a trained psychiatrist. But Betsy," the amusement park tycoon added, "you have to admire somebody like this early twentieth century business genius Thomas Plant. The risk-taking capitalist overcame his beleaguering emotional phobias and throughout his life's ordeal, and despite his diminutive stature, the shoe mogul still managed to amass a sizable fortune."

'That's precisely what I always tell our three grandchildren," Betsy answered tongue-in-cheek. "If you can't act your age, then kindly act your' cotton-pickin' shoe size!"

* * * * * * * * * * * *

That evening the variety show in the Beacon Resort Theater was rather mediocre and the late-night Jacuzzi seemed like veritable paradise to the Laniers' aching joints and muscles. After sunrise, a wake-up call from the main office aroused the resort guests and in half an hour the bleary-eyed New Jersey tourists obediently assembled inside Dad's Restaurant, then swallowed down a "Hefty Country Breakfast" featuring tall stack pancakes and New Hampshire maple syrup, and after returning to their rooms for bus trip preparation, Frank and Betsy descended the lodge's wooden steps and slowly ambled over toward the awaiting bus.

"What's first on the agenda?" Frank energetically asked Mike. "I hope it doesn't involve too much walking. After yesterday, I think I'm developing a bad case of flat feet, not to mention aggravating my chronic arthritis and rheumatism."

"Well Mr. Lanier, first we'll be heading over to Cannon Mountain in nearby Franconia Notch, a popular ski area," Mike informed. "But the Old Man's face and head, the famous symbols of New Hampshire's White Mountain history, regrettably fell off down the mountainside several years ago." After *that* academic description, Mike adroitly changed his' subject matter. "Next I'll be taking you to a scenic and rustic local nature preserve. You'll walk down a winding trail and explore a forest creek and then enter the main building to browse through a gift shop and at the very end, you'll see a film about the area's geographic features and historic past."

"Are we then going to visit Loon Mountain?" Betsy asked Mike. "It's really pretty active during the winter. My sister Marge always comes up here with her family every January to ski and ice skate. Of course," Mrs. Lanier garrulously clarified, "they habitually stay at the Beacon while doing so!"

"Unfortunately the Loon Mountain Ski attraction is temporarily closed because of scheduled repairs and improvements, so *that* part of the tour has been scratched," Mike reported, much to the disappointment of Betsy Lanier. "That mountain as you might know was named after the local bird that can only land on lake water during the summer months. Its legs are too fragile to impact on ice during the colder months December through March."

"Well Mike, what have you planned as a replacement activity?" Betsy Lanier asked as a small crowd of concerned gossipy bus passengers gathered around the two conducting the dialogue. "I'm not looking for a refund but Loon Mountain was supposed to be one of the highlights of this trip!"

"Well Mrs. Lanier, I've contacted my boss back in Cape May and he's already arranged for us to zip over to DeClerk's Trading Post. It started out as a small general store but over the past thirty years the owners have expanded the property into a very impressive recreational facility. You'll notice exactly what I mean when we arrive there. I think you'll be quite surprised by what you'll see."

"Well Mike, sometimes it pays to be upbeat and expect the worse only to be gratefully satisfied later on," Betsy optimistically answered. "Now Frank, let's clamber up the steps before our perpetual questions cause a scene. As you know, I happen to abhor arguments and conflict."

Indeed, Cannon Mountain was not the same spectacle without the Old Man's Face protruding from its summit but a half hour later the late morning trek along the prescribed Franconia Notch babbling brook proved very invigorating to the opinionated and chatty bus tour patrons. After enduring (on soft cushion seats) the well-produced New Hampshire film in the nature center's vast recreation building, Betsy took several still pictures of Frank standing next to a family of giant stuffed brown bears, snapshots of him posing beside a ponderous-looking moose and close to a standard-sized deer, animals all indigenous to the serene White Mountains.

"Now we're off to DeClerk's Trading Post," Frank reminded his always-vigilant wife. "Quite honestly Dear, I want it to be better than it sounds. Now Bet, I don't desire to spend the rest of the day examining a bevy of key chains, souvenirs and knick-knacks. And Honey," the husband haughtily jested, "I don't wish to sound like a bragging wet blanket pest but *we* do have our own comprehensive New Jersey gift shop back at Fantasy Book Land."

"On our modified itinerary agenda it states that Mike will be distributing box lunches for us to eat at a designated picnic table pavilion," Betsy answered to allay her husband's negative attitude. "Who knows? Maybe DeClerk's Trading Post will be a marvelous substitute for Loon Mountain after all."

Situated only several miles south of the Beacon Resort, DeClerk's Trading Post had over the decades been expanded from a typical general store into a full-fledged family recreation/amusement facility. A dynamic steam locomotive was situated at the "Main Entrance" and was ready to take interested visitors on a circular train track adventure through a pine tree forest that surrounded the core entertainment area on three sides.

A village of small cute early 1900s-style houses, stores and municipal buildings had been constructed along a paved street. Parents, children and guests could saunter around and enter any of the very clean-looking "O. Henry era" places and experience the novelty of a turn-of-the-century firehouse, a nickelodeon-style silent cinema theater presently showing a classic Charlie Chaplin movie, a "Gay '90s" horse and carriage depot, a livery stable, an impeccable brick façade town hall, an archaic candy store selling all sorts of sweets including red and black licorice, a post-colonial apothecary shop, a mom and pop grocery store and finally an old-fashioned ice cream parlor.

An announcement was made over the park's loud speakers for all recently arrived guests to advance to the south end of the immaculately kept facility to enjoy the hourly "Trained Bear Show" that was slated to commence in ten minutes.

"After the circus-style bear performances, we'll go over to the shaded picnic tables and enjoy our box lunches," Betsy dictated to Frank as was her annoying habit. "Not to engage in plagiarism, but have you gotten any useful ideas from this novel park about how to improve Fantasy Book Land?"

"Well Bet, the Main Street sector was pretty neat but my conclusion is that it was too much like the Main Street district down in Disney World," Frank Lanier mildly criticized. "But overall, it's something for me to consider if we don't somehow stumble upon a more satisfactory utilitarian idea. I'm hungry and my stomach's growling for some peculiar reason. Remind me to swallow-down a hot fudge sundae at the Professor Harold Hill Ice Cream Parlor before we head back to the Beacon at 2 p.m."

"Didn't you tell me that it's a lot easier to borrow than to invent?" Betsy characteristically challenged. "I don't know how a bear entertainment show would fit into *our* plans but I do think that an early 1900s Main Street theme addition would be a definite plus for our aging Fantasy Book Land Park."

"It's something to consider and it's certainly within the realm of possibility," the predictably skeptical husband maintained, "but it's still not the million dollar panacea that I'm searching for! Oh well," the frustrated entrepreneur compromised, "let's sit through the bear show upon those hard metal bleacher seats. I'm glad that the animals are caged-in by that circular Cyclone Fence. And I suspect that the corpulent bears are muzzled and probably declawed too! I don't need to be viciously mauled and maimed five hundred and thirty miles from home!"

"Stop being so cynical just because you can't think of a new tremendous attraction for Fantasy Book Land!" Betsy balked. "I think that you're just envious that this DeClerk Trading Post rivals our Jersey theme park."

Much to the Laniers' delight, the bears and their trainers put on a very entertaining tricks' program, and next, the box lunches at the picnic pavilion were quite substantial and nutritious, and now it was time for the tourists to hop aboard an open-air carriage car (located behind the steam locomotive) and take a breezy ride through the dense pine tree forest.

"We do have the extra twenty acre pine tree woods behind the amusement ride sector of our park," Betsy said, comparing the present DeClerk scenario to a potential Fantasy Book Land upgrade. "Maybe *this* well-maintained railroad feature will provide you with the ideal solution you've been searching for."

"We'll see what transpires during the train ride," Frank stubbornly declared, disguising his eagerness. "If it's just a standard passage through the woods, then it'll be a little too mundane and commonplace. Let's look for anything in the 'unique department realm' that might have been cleverly improvised."

The train whistle sounded, signaling for everyone to "Climb aboard!" as the uniformed conductor bellowed and commanded. The noisy locomotive produced six puffs of steam and the loud machine slowly chugged away from the station platform. Soon the entourage aboard was being conducted over an enclosed New England bridge and the vehicle was now progressing into the interior of the dense pine forest.

A loud antagonistic and threatening male voice was quickly discerned by everyone's ears and from out of a "Gold Prospector's Mine Cave" stepped a bellicose-looking bearded and hairy mountain degenerate who boisterously introduced himself to the startled train passengers as "the Wolf Man."

"Betsy, capture all of this with our video camera," Frank demanded. "I like the hostile demeanor of *that* petulant barbaric fellow! By sheer pot luck I think we've just hit upon the magic answer that I've been pursuing."

"How do we hear the Wolf Man's bass voice inside the train?" the wife wondered and asked as she continued aiming her video camera. "It's really quite powerful and at first his ornery nasty tone was actually startling!"

"It's really a wireless remote microphone transmitting his voice from his location directly *here* into the overhead carriage car speakers," the husband explained. "Now the bellicose fellow is warning us not to trespass into *his* territory or else we'll have to face the dire consequences! I wonder if this bad-tempered Wolf Man lives over in Wolfeboro!" Frank facetiously joked as Betsy continued filming without ever breaking her concentration. "Look! Now the uncouth insulting guy is shooting his loud shotgun at us! I hope that thing's firing blanks! Ha, ha, ha!"

The steam locomotive and its trailing carriage cars then speedily passed through a woods' clearing on one side and the ubiquitous Wolf Man was now driving an old rusty and tarnished Model-T roadster and aggressively yelling new epithets and unflattering remarks at the thoroughly amused "trespassing" train passengers. This particular sequence lasted for a full minute until the pretentiously aggravated Wolf Man stepped on the accelerator and swiftly sped ahead while seated inside his remarkable jalopy convertible.

And just when the train (along with its harassed and amused passengers) exited another patch of woods, there stood the verbally taunting Wolf Man again firing his imitation shotgun and vociferously screaming a flurry of derogatory remarks and unsavory insinuations at the apparently thrilled riders, many of whom were documenting the series of incidents with their various cameras.

"That whole sequence of events was positively rich!" Frank euphorically exclaimed. "That's the miracle idea I couldn't seem to envision on my own!"

"It's always easier to borrow than to invent!" Betsy hollered back from behind her still-raised video camera. "It appears that the DeClerk Trading Post's wonderful Wolf Man creation has been the brilliant God-send you've been trying so hard to discover!"

* * * * * * * * * * *

Upon returning back to all-too-familiar southern New Jersey, out of family courtesy and professional ethics, Frank Lanier presented the idea of a Fantasy Book Land train ride through the property's rear pine woods to his father, the outgoing corporation CEO, and Mr. Joseph Lanier eagerly put his stamp of approval on the "most excellent proposal," which was then a week later unanimously endorsed at a hastily announced board of directors' meeting.

The necessary building permits were quickly acquired and an extremely competent and reputable job foreman was hired to oversee the intricate "architectural project phases" from beginning to end. Contracts were swiftly signed with major carpenter, plumbing, electrical and mason unions, the acquisition of materials was rapidly initiated and construction on 'Phase One' of the colossal "train and rail project" was begun in early March with the final rendition to be completed and subsequently open to the general public a full calendar year later.

"We came in just two hundred thousand dollars over our original budget," Frank ecstatically told Betsy Lanier on the long-awaited morning of the grand opening of the Fantasy Book Land Overland Express. "And guess what Honey?" the exuberant husband rhetorically asked. "I've managed to get the real Wolf Man from up there in Lincoln, New Hampshire to come down to South Jersey and play the role of Piney Jack terrorizing *our* prospective about-to-be-mesmerized train passengers."

"How did you manage to pull that fantastic deal off?" the wife curiously asked. "Have you been studying hypnotism, black magic or voodoo without my knowledge?"

"I made the former Wolf Man a very tempting overture that he couldn't refuse. I offered the talented bearded fellow a ten-month contract worth twenty-five thousand bucks more than he was making petrifying people way up there in the White Mountains, and I also guaranteed Piney Jack, alias Wolf Man, an additional two months employment and an extra salary bonus with full benefits to labor as a maintenance worker from January to the end of February when the park is closed."

"Well Dear, I must confess that you've always been a shrewd businessman," the wife reluctantly congratulated her very successful spouse. "Maybe things won't be so nondescript around here in the future. Oh my!" Betsy exclaimed, pensively staring at her diamond wristwatch. "The park's going to open for the new season at noon and it's about ten a.m., time for the Overland Express to have its first official run through the pine woods."

"Piney Jack's already in his Pig Iron Bog Lair, or should I say 'Cave Hideout,' and here comes Pop now ready to help us commission this ceremonial train trip."

Soon all invited family members and dedicated park employees climbed into the first open-air carriage and then Sam the Engineer strongly blasted the steam whistle three times.

Seconds later the brand new shiny black locomotive tugged the trailing cars out of the recently built and colorfully painted "Victorian Train Station."

"This fine train was a really terrific addition Son," Joseph Lanier amply complimented his chief heir and descendant. "I'm quite proud of your creativity Frank, and I'm happy to note you having the wherewithal of conceiving a superb attraction like this very desirable Overland Express. I assure you that it'll be the envy of all amusement venues within seventy miles of Atlantic City."

"Well Dad, I did spend plenty of cerebral time taxing my brain and I finally settled on the Overland Express idea," the red-faced son less-than-modestly answered. "Indeed Pop', this ride will be a tribute to the Lanier name for many decades to come. But just wait until you see the stunning surprise that Betsy and I have planned and arranged! I just know you'll be getting a grand kick out of it!"

The blustery locomotive picked up speed and advanced down the tracks, gracefully rounded a bend, traversed across a wooden covered bridge and then soon entered the posterior thick pinewoods. From out of his Pig Iron Bog Works Foundry Building came Piney Jack, a frightful-looking New Jersey facsimile of the New Hampshire backwoods Wolf Man. Much to the riders' emotional delight and excitement, a very antagonistic and hysterical Piney Jack articulated a series of threats and complaints directed at the fascinated passing train passengers.

"That fellow's absolutely terrific! Very animated and hilarious too!" Joseph Lanier hollered and clapped his gloved hands. "I must say that he looks mighty vindictive, mendacious and dangerous, even though we all know that he's harmless and only acting!"

"I knew you'd absolutely love his routine!" Frank confidently replied. "It's loaded with exaggerated histrionics! I know that I did relish the whole melodramatic routine when I had first seen the guy perform up in New Hampshire!"

"This whole scenario is totally captivating!" Betsy aptly agreed. "Even our usually bored grandchildren are enthralled with the wild man's crazy antics!"

Piney Jack rapidly fired six rounds of blanks from his signature shotgun as the maiden-run train completed its semi-circular pass through a clearing and then resumed its journey on the rails that bisected the thick coniferous forest. At the next break in the woods Piney Jack's voice was clearly discernible as he

174

drove his customized dump truck convertible out of the Pine Barrens Saloon's swinging doors and then the souped-up vehicle followed a dirt and gravel path that intentionally was designed to parallel the train tracks. All of the cheering passengers stood up to catch a full glimpse of Piney Jack's frantic gestures and to attentively listen to his booming barrage of barbs and preposterous denigrations.

"This has got to be the ultimate in family fun entertainment!" Joseph Lanier marveled and exclaimed. "Bravo Frankie! Bravo I say!" the elderly man hooted as he removed his felt hat from his noggin and then wildly waved the object above his head.

Before Frank could organize a plausible and grateful response, a second vehicle was detected speeding out of the pine tree thicket and ambitiously pursuing directly behind the fleeing Piney Jack's chopped-off-roof dump truck, and seated inside the modified Corvette convertible was a dark red-faced hideous-looking figure dressed in the exact appearance of the notorious Jersey Devil, who was persistently and intensively chasing the panic-stricken nefarious personage currently disguised as Piney Jack.

"Why this is really most bizarre and extraordinary!" Joseph Lanier instinctively praised his pallid-faced son. "Frank, you're a first class impresario, that's what you are! A veritable genius I say!"

"Betsy!" an excessively shocked Frank Lanier uttered to his equally perplexed and horrified wife as the thrilled grandchildren jumped about, screaming and shrieking with unbridled satisfaction. "Is this some kind of bizarre hallucination I'm witnessing? Did you by any chance hire a costumed Jersey Devil performer behind my back for the expressed purpose of scaring the living daylights out of Piney Jack!"

"No Frank!" the still-awed wife uttered in total disbelief. "It obviously appears that the real Jersey Devil doesn't at all like the now-cowardly Piney Jack encroaching and trespassing onto *his* sacred pine barren territory!"

"Superstitions"

Real estate broker James Brewster was elated, not because he had just completed reading Dale Carnegie's best-selling book *How to Win Friends and Influence People* for the fifth time, but because in March of 2009 the wheeler-dealer had shrewdly purchased a three-year-old beachfront three-story home (with an elevator servicing each suite) on the Boardwalk and 16th Street in Ocean City, New Jersey for the ridiculously-low sum of 1.5 million dollars, acquiring the residence as a vacation home but more importantly, owning and leveraging the dwelling principally as a seasonal investment-return rental property.

'I didn't even need Dale Carnegie's sound advice to negotiate this handsome bargain!' Brewster joyfully reasoned. Being a born-opportunist, the risk-taking entrepreneur wanted to take full advantage of the in-progress economic recession and then in three years, capitalize on the presumed 2.25 million dollar value of the three-year-old beach home should the country's money cash-flow scenario improve back to normal.

'Gosh, how I love these sacrifice home sales, especially when the victimized sellers need cash right away to cover for their divorce allotments or when a family will settlement or estate liquidation occurs. Yeah, Susan and I could make a quick three-quarter million bucks' killing if the weak economy ever manages to cure itself,' Jim thought as he shaved his twenty-four hour whisker growth off while diligently staring into the large master bathroom mirror. 'Or I might just elect to keep the beautiful beach house for entertainment purposes or for the family to use. Even in today's depressed market, fancy Ocean City beachfront rentals go for around seven thousand dollars a week per floor,' Brewster's imagination realized with a brief smile appearing on his face. 'That's a sweet twenty-one grand a week times ten weeks for the June, July and August beach season and now we're talking about an annual income of over two hundred thousand a summer. The entire place could be paid-off in around eight years should I decide not to sell it,' the real estate broker ecstatically considered. 'No matter how I assess the Jersey shore deal, whether I keep it or whether I'll be able to unload it in the future at a handsome profit, it's without a doubt a win-win situation regardless if the national economy rehabs' itself or not! And it's conveniently located and quiet there too, right where the boardwalk narrows at the south end!'

"Jim, who will be manning the Hammonton office today?" Susan yelled up from the downstairs front door foyer. "Is it you or our beloved son?"

"Jeff's gonna' be commanding the 12th Street office and I'll be over in Cedar Brook getting some newly arrived furniture into our new office arrangement," Jim Brewster answered between razor swipes. "Some desks and counters had been delivered yesterday and I gotta' map out where to situate them inside the six re-modeled rooms. That's the last time I'm ever goin' to buy a house and convert it into a commercial building. The township and state bureaucratic red tape was a bit too extreme."

"Yes, the construction costs, zoning fees and licenses were rather tremendous but you've told me on many occasions that that 1950s Cedar Brook home was the only land available along that busy stretch of Route 73!" Susan accurately reminded and yelled up to her forgetful husband. "As you always redundantly state, 'Location, location, location'!"

"What's on your schedule this morning?" the husband hollered down, sticking his head around the bedroom corner so that his wife could see his partially lathered face.

"A woman's work is never done! I'm going to first empty the clothes hamper and then throw the dirty laundry into the washing machine," Susan informed her less energetic spouse. "And Jim, please drive the red Nissan SUV over to Cedar Brook and leave the green Toyota Avalon for me to use. I have some light grocery shopping to do and after returning home from the supermarket, later on this morning I'm going to take a thirty-five-mile trip to Ocean City and inspect every room of our new beach home," the wife revealed. "I want to see if all of the major appliances are working and also see if I have to buy any new bed-sheets, towels or blankets for our highly anticipated eager-to-spend summer rental guests."

"Okay Honey," the husband readily and cheerfully acknowledged. "I'll take the red Murano. It has satellite radio and I can listen to my favorite oldies hits from the '50s, '60s and '70s on the jaunt over to Winslow Township. Do you have any errands you want me to run while I'm gallivanting around this part of South Jersey?"

"Well yes now that you've mentioned it!" Susan replied. "There's a list of ten items' that I want you to dispose of once and for all down at the Hammonton dump. I've decided that I have too much activity on my plate and I don't have the time to conduct a yard sale to get rid of all of the abundant junk that's accumulated in our garage, in our attic and in our cellar."

"You know Dear that I positively love old relics and that I'm a worthless object collector at heart," Jim laughed, hiding his underlying apprehension. "A lot of the stuff I've kept over the years has a definite sentimental value to me. You know Susan, they're all sorta' like living nostalgia to me! I just have difficulty throwing things out ever since my father disposed of my '50s baseball card collection, and from a strictly emotional point of view, I hate to part with personal things that I'm quite especially fond of!"

"Well Jim, you'll just have to get over it this time!" the wife imperatively insisted. "You can study the items' list that I've prepared over your morning cup of coffee. I couldn't sleep last night so I got out of bed, marched to the computer and started hammering away at the keys," Susan attested. "Truthfully Jim, I was quite surprised to observe that the printer was working again. You'll find the ten items typed-out on a sheet of paper and placed on the kitchen table. I'm really tired of looking at them scattered all over the residence! As the woman of the house, it's my firm position that those ten useless things have to be thrown out once and for all!"

Jim finished washing-up, put on a pair of jeans and a blue cotton shirt along with his casual black loafers and then descended the stairs and cheerfully sauntered into the kitchen. After concocting his instant coffee and adding his standard two sugars and cream, James Brewster sat down in his usual chair and closely examined the prescribed list of objects.

'Susan can't be serious!' the husband immediately thought. 'These ten things each have a very special meaning to me. Oh no! Here are several bits of nostalgia occupying space in the garage. First is my two-tone brown pair of ice skates from the 1970s, second is my initial set of golf clubs and accompanying bag, the set left over from the late '80s and third, Susan's itemized my twelve cartons of books from when I tried my hand at self-publishing my helpful manual of real estate tips. Too bad that the 1992 literary work only sold three-hundred copies, mostly to family and friends who felt obligated to buy them hot off the presses.'

Five other items stored in the garage and in the attic further disappointed the reader. 'Susan wants to throw-out the fall harvest farmer stand that I put on the front porch steps every October 15th. And then there's the taillight cover to my old yellow Volkswagen convertible, *our* first car after we had gotten married. How could she do this to me? How could she do *this* to *us*?' the husband regretfully concluded. 'And furthermore, Susan indicates that the token spare snow tire hanging on the left garage wall has to go. I love that memorabilia even though snow tires are no longer in vogue. And then there's Aunt Millie's disassembled bed that's stored in the attic. And oh no, the 28 inch by 28 inch old bathroom mirror from the guest bathroom that had been replaced just two years ago. That twenty-five year old mirror is still along the left wall in the garage and it's leaning against the sheet-rock right below the spare snow tire.'

Finally Jim's eyes arrived at the two remaining objects placed on the list that still remained stored down in the cellar. The rusty English racer bicycle that Brewster had owned and had proudly ridden in his glorious youth along with a bent screen (once belonging to the front storm door) that incidentally has been collecting cellar dust for over two decades.

"Susan, you can't be serious about me throwing this wonderful stuff out this morning!" Jim Brewster exclaimed to the kitchen table rather than face his tenacious wife, who had just coincidentally entered the room. "You're asking me to eliminate plenty of rich history here! Plenty of *our* rich Brewster family history!"

"Either the ten things go or I go!" the on-the-move wife loudly threatened her false ultimatum from the laundry room just off the den. "And if I go, I get the Ocean City beach home as part of the general divorce settlement and you can keep this two-story colonial and live happily ever after right here in Hammonton!"

"Okay Honey!" Jim reluctantly conceded. "I promise to dispense with the assigned ten things in about an hour!"

* * * * * * * * * * * *

One of the main principles of Dale Carnegie's informative book *How to Win Friends and Influence People* maintains that the consummate salesman must first cleverly get the prospective customers talking about themselves. Eventually the targeted client feels self-conscious about his or her personality dominating the conversation and then he or she will ultimately request vital facts and money statistics from the congenial sales person. But ironically, Susan's 'austere rubbish edict' had Jim not talking about himself but instead, talking *to himself*. 'I'll pull the red SUV out of the garage, lower the back seats to allow for more room and then sadly fulfill Susan's inflexible command,' the now-melancholy man of the house organized his 'surrender for marital truce strategy.'

After swallowing down a bowlful of wheat cereal and milk, the emotionally disheveled husband obediently gathered the ten specified articles from the garage, attic and cellar and after using his imagination, distressed James Brewster carefully loaded and methodically arranged the assorted objects inside the rear of the red Nissan Murano. Soon the disenchanted object gatherer, with sweat beads trickling down his forehead and cheeks, was seated behind the wheel and making a left turn out of his Valley Avenue driveway and motoring on his way to the town's Eighth Street dump.

Then feeling vanquished and disappointed, Jim's mind began reviewing the history of each of the ten items that his wife had firmly wished to be discarded. 'This undesirable process will cost me at least a hundred dollars town dumping fee!' the anguished man behind the steering wheel lamented. 'And the municipal garbage attendant at the gate will act like it's a difficult burden and a tremendous chore for him to dispose of the ten random things, each of which means something special to me.'

But then the *down-in-the-dumps* broker's mind realized that he had not only kept the ten dispensable items for their 'sentimental value,' he also had kept them for various worrisome 'superstitious reasons.' Slowly the individual pieces of the man's mental jigsaw puzzle began to re-form into a plausible configuration that now vividly suggested to the SUV driver that a sense of overwhelming bad luck would soon result from the ten items disposal.

'The two-tone brown ice skates were from my youth when my family had lived in Levittown, Pennsylvania. That winter I was with two friends skating on a frozen creek. We were having a friendly competition, racing towards the finish line, a bridge that was under Edgely Avenue. Each of us had to duck down in order to cross the imaginary finish line but then I recklessly lost my balance, foolishly believing that I was winning the contest. I abruptly collided with the bridge's concrete structure going at full speed and wound-up with a concussion. Being only semi-conscious and my mind in a daze, my two fourteen-year-old companions instantly panicked, rushed to a nearby house and had the owner call for an ambulance,' Jim recalled. 'That's the last time that I've ever gone ice skating and it all now seems like a terrible recurring nightmare even though the near-tragedy dramatically happened over thirty years ago!'

Then Jim's mind concentrated on the rusty golf clubs and the dirty plaid red and black checkered carrying bag. 'I was playing golf with some Rotary Club business friends over at the Pine Crest Country Club on Folsom Road. After the ninth hole, we decided to take a lunch and beer break. I casually called Susan at home only to learn that Aunt Vera and Uncle Leo had just been killed in a violent automobile accident down in tidewater Virginia, not far from Uncle Al's place at Sandy Point on the Potomac. The old golf clubs and bag along with the two-toned ice skates are all negative omens that if trashed, might again unleash a bad event or even a series of bad events to occur and interrupt tranquility in my life.'

As Jim Brewster made his habitual left turn onto Bellevue Avenue, his mind recollected the twelve cartons of unsold books neatly stacked directly behind the driver's seat. An hour after the twelve cartons had been delivered via UPS, an electrical fire had broken-out in the garage when one of the boxes had been pressing against an electrical cord used to operate the car doors. 'It's a good thing I keep a fire extinguisher attached to the garage's back wall or else the minor blaze could've erupted into an inferno and destroyed the entire house!' the real estate broker recollected and concluded. 'To this day I believe that there's a distinct cause and effect relationship between receiving those boxes of books and putting them in the garage and igniting the consequential blaze that resulted,' the failed author believed.

The horizontally packed straw hat fall farmer figure attached at its base to a blue-painted half cinder block was the SUV's item number four. 'Yes, right after the colorful outside fall decoration piece had been purchased at the Berlin Farmers Market back in the '70s, the stock market had simultaneously collapsed because of the oil and gasoline crisis. That's when Susan and I lost over a hundred thousand dollars in our mutual funds' portfolio and *that* sizeable investment was never recovered,' Brewster disconsolately remembered as his right clenched fist hit against the padded leather steering wheel. 'I don't need a similar financial disaster such as an expensive law suit coming out of nowhere or a crisis involving an unforeseen legal problem with the new Ocean City beach house. But certainly,' the very superstitious driver recognized, 'nostalgia is not the main reason for me desiring to keep the ragged-looking autumn four-foot-tall porch farmer. I absolutely fear the consequences of getting rid of it.'

Upon passing his 12th Street real estate office and then making a left turn at the next traffic signal onto First Road, Jim's mind

182

thought about the yellow taillight frame that had been hanging from the right wall pegboard in the garage. 'That Volkswagen was my first car and Susan also loved driving the convertible around town on shopping errands and on quick excursions to the pizza parlor and to the custard stand,' Brewster recalled as he drove his red SUV past Greenmount Cemetery. 'But the same day that my wife had a fender-bender while being rear ended at a stop sign at French Street and Packard, I had fallen off of the side porch roof. Our son Jeff had thrown a Frisbee up there and when I went to retrieve it using an aluminum ladder,' Brewster's memory rehashed, 'I slipped and then tumbled down, taking the entire rain gutter with me. Fortunately my only injury was a sprained right ankle, which still aches whenever the barometer's mercury fluid falls. Well, as a result of my tumble, at least I can predict certain approaching rain patterns with the aid of my prognosticating right foot!'

The obsolete snow tire that had been hanging from the left garage wall ever since the early 1980s was the next thing to be mentally assessed by the now-paranoid lugubrious driver. 'That February day I had bought a set of snow tires at Pep Boys over in Berlin,' Jim's memory accurately reminded him. 'That evening Susan and I had gone to Philly' to see the play *Man of La Mancha* at the Walnut Street Theatre. When we eventually returned to the parked car after the performance had ended, the front passenger side window had been smashed and the vehicle's interior vandalized. The right snow tire had been slashed with a knife and the one in the back of the SUV is the only remnant remaining from that snowy winter night's horrible discovery,' the driver remembered. 'Naturally, the Philadelphia cops never were able to apprehend any suspects and my insurance company did pay for the damages after I had submitted a carbon copy of the comprehensive police report.'

Aunt Millie's bed that had been faithfully preserved in the house attic was another cause for the neurotic fellow's concern and distress. 'How could I ever forget the negative significance associated with that bed?' Jim, who had never walked under a leaning ladder, who never stared more than a second at a black cat or who never intentionally stepped on a sidewalk separation crack apprehensively evaluated. 'That brisk late September morning I had to borrow Uncle Bill's truck to drive down to Aunt Millie's stone home in Bridgeton. During that early fall afternoon I managed to successfully re-assemble the bed in the upstairs spare room when I learned from Susan that Grand-Pop Tony had died at

183

his winter home in Miami, Florida. Grand-Mom Anna had an extremely hard time making arrangements to fly his body to Philadelphia and the poor woman had to be a passenger on the same jet plane in which her deceased husband was being flown as human destination cargo from Miami to Pennsylvania.'

Upon alertly turning from First Road onto Eighth Street, Jim thought about his symbolic superstition connected with the large garage mirror that had once occupied a space above the dual basin vanity in the guest bathroom. 'Back in 1994, after the mirror had been removed by carpenters and replaced with a new one, I had taken my mother to Harrah's Casino in Atlantic City to treat Mom upon celebrating her seventy-fifth birthday. Much to my utter shock and anxiety, Mom had suffered a simultaneous heart seizure and low sugar attack and when I turned around, she was lying unconscious on the casino's carpeted floor. Thanks to quick action by on-duty paramedics and nurses, an ambulance was soon summoned. Mom was rushed to the Atlantic City Hospital on Ohio Avenue and her life was fortunately saved. But honestly,' Jim nervously deduced, 'I don't savor the idea of getting rid of that mirror out of fear that something even more terrible and horrendous might be set into motion. I gotta' salvage that ominous thing, one way or another!'

At the intersection of Eighth Street and Second Road, Jim Brewster remembered the last regrettable time he had ridden the rusty English racer bicycle that later had been stored and forgotten in the cellar. 'I was riding ten miles from Hammonton to Batsto in a Kiwanis Club charity fund-raising event. I had raised over a thousand dollars from various friends and relatives who were generous enough to sponsor me in participating in the annual 4th of July event. While not paying particular attention and experiencing some mild exhaustion, my front tire inadvertently hit a stone on Pleasant Mills Road and before I knew it, the bike had careened into a swamp and I had been flung off the seat, landing in a briar patch and thus later requiring seven stitches to patch-up my annoying wounds. But needless to say,' Brewster analyzed, 'I was deeply embarrassed from my cycling misadventure because I was unable to finish the ten-mile-long course and obviously, my delicate pride had been injured much more than my aching body had been!'

Finally, as Jim's shiny sleek red Murano ascended the bridge going over the six lanes of heavy Atlantic City Expressway traffic whizzing by below, the anxious driver contemplated the relevance of the screen from the front storm door that had been leaning against the basement's cinder block wall for the past fifteen years.

'The same April 1995 day that a wicked mini-cyclone micro-burst cut a swath across my property, I noticed that the screen to the front storm door had been bent from the violent swirling winds,' the fidgety SUV navigator remembered. 'After I had removed the screen and then assessed the extensive tree damage on my front and back lawn, I dashed upstairs to change my clothes and get into some more appropriate work jeans, for I intended to use my chain saw to cut-up the downed tree branches into smaller pieces. After changing my attire, I astutely observed a column of termites emerging from a crack in the master bedroom wall and I spent the next three hours vacuuming the swarming bugs as the destructive army of insects exited the wall's floor molding one-by-one in a single file procession. That monotonous vacuum cleaner task I steadfastly performed rather than attending to the many downed tree limbs populating my front and back yards.'

As the red Nissan Murano finally approached the very remotely located Hammonton Town Dump, the saddened driver reviewed and summarized his superstitious instincts. 'Each of the ten articles in the back compartment represents something foreboding or problematic that had occurred in the past,' Jim subjectively hypothesized, 'and I have a good deal of anxiety building-up inside my heart that tells me that something bad is going to happen if I surrender the ten useless items to the town refuge center. I know what I'll do!' Brewster excitedly determined as he halted his vehicle at the main gate entrance. 'I rent and keep a storage unit at the 'Hammonton Self-Serve Lock and Go Depot' over on Egg Harbor Road where the old Hammonton Farmers Market used to be. That's where I store all of my lawn real estate signs and I just happen to have plenty of room inside there to accommodate all of the junk in the SUV's back cargo area. I'll just squirrel-away the ten treasured relics inside my rental unit rather than transfer the items to the Town of Hammonton for a hundred bucks expense. Call it a weird phobia haunting my mind but I feel that I must protect my family from some lurking imminent danger. I dread that something sinister or malignant is about to occur as a result of me honoring Susan's command to get rid of the ten bad-luck relics!' the real estate man irrationally theorized. 'Then after I safely deposit the ten cherished articles at the Self-Serve Lock and Go Depot, I'll hurry over to the new

Cedar Brook office on Route 73 and start figuring-out where the recently delivered walnut desks and counters have to go!'

* * * * * * * * * * * *

"Hey Mack, you've come to the right place. It looks like ya' got a hundred bucks worth of junk to discard," the Hammonton Dump's garrulous gatekeeper estimated and quoted. "That's what the town charges for either an SUV or a half ton pick-up truck full. And don't worry Pal! I'll give ya' a receipt whether ya' pay me cash or pay me by check or credit card."

"That's okay Sir, but I've just changed my mind and have decided to keep the old heirlooms," Jim apologetically replied. "Perhaps my wife will have a late spring garage or yard sale. We could always use the extra cash."

"Well now, that's the first time I've ever heard *that* story!" the grimy-looking heavy-set gate attendant laughed, then roughly wiping some excess chewing tobacco juice from his lips with his left hand. "Are ya' sure ya' don't want to part with that antiquated English racer bicycle ya' got back there? I restore antiques like that as a hobby. I'll give ya' twenty-five bucks for it right out of my own pocket. With a little elbow grease and a can of spray paint I could make that baby look like it was brand new!"

"No thanks!" Brewster explicitly answered. "Maybe the bike shop on the Pike near the lake can rehab' it for me a few years from now and I could save it for a future grandson, whenever I finally have one to give it to. In fact Mr., I used to ride this bike when I was in junior high. I think it was sometime during the Richard M. Nixon Administration! Ha, ha, ha!"

The real estate man slowly backed up, turned his handsome SUV around on the dump's gravel entranceway and then headed north on Eighth Street toward downtown Hammonton. 'Susan will never know that I've deliberately relocated the ten items inside my private utility shed. I'll just fib a little bit and tell her that I had religiously followed her exact instructions and that the undesired ten items are no longer in the garage, attic or cellar.'

Five minutes later James Brewster pulled into the wide asphalt driveway where he could access his individual twelve by twenty-five foot rental space at the seldom busy' Hammonton Lock and Go Storage Depot. No sooner had the superstitious fellow stopped his shiny red vehicle that his cell phone rang and the readout indicated the phone number of his Hammonton residence. After

186

awkwardly fumbling with the electronic device, Brewster's right thumb finally pressed the correct button.

"Dad!" an out-of-breath Jeffrey Brewster yelled. "I just stopped at your house to ask you a few questions. All of the doors were locked so I used my old house key to gain entrance via the side laundry room door. When I got to the front foyer," the son huffed and puffed, "Mom was lying there near the front door, unconscious with the half-full dirty upside-down clothes-basket laying on the tile right next to her, and then I noticed that the empty grocery bags were still on the kitchen table. I quickly dialed 911 and thank goodness the Hammonton Rescue Squad just arrived at the house; the paramedics put her on a stretcher and now she's riding in the ambulance on her way to the best area hospital."

"What do the paramedics think is wrong?" Jim loudly asked. "Did she have a stroke or a heart attack? Does she have a concussion?"

"I don't know!" Jeffrey responded in a stammering tone of voice. "The rescue squad guys said that Mom's vital signs were weak but they believe that they stabilized her before she was transported in the ambulance. They're now taking her to Virtua Hospital in Berlin! That's' where I've going right now after I finish talking with you!"

"Listen Jeff! I'll meet you at Virtua in about twenty minutes so that in the meantime you can get an update on your mother's condition! Talk to the doctors in the emergency room suite and see what you can find out after she's admitted! Those doctors at Virtua are among the best in South Jersey. If there's a more serious problem that needs prompt urgent attention, we'll have your mother transferred to Thomas Jefferson Hospital over in Philly'."

"Okay Dad!" the son comprehended and agreed. "It's a good thing that I dropped by or else Mom would still be lying there on the cold floor completely knocked out! I'll see you at Virtua just off Route 30 in Berlin as soon as you get there." Click.

The superstitious father hastily stepped on the accelerator and sped out of the entrance-way of the modern private storage facility. His prime destination was his white two-story colonial home on Valley Avenue where he would swiftly-but-carefully place the ten items back in their precise former locations in the garage, in the attic and in the cellar. After speedily accomplishing *that* reversal of 'bad luck harbingers' to his personal satisfaction, the now-paranoid real estate broker began driving the twelve miles west to Virtua Hospital.

'I'm glad I honored my sixth sense instincts and decided to keep the ten accursed objects rather than throwing them out at the town dump!' Brewster reckoned as he speedily veered out of his driveway onto Valley Avenue. 'It's my duty and responsibility to reverse my wife's bad luck incident that ironically Susan had convinced me to initiate. And now that I've returned those ten items to their exact former places,' the omen-believing man reflected, 'I'll confidently hightail it over to Berlin and relish the fact that my loyal and loving wife has fully regained consciousness.'

Ten minutes after the ten 'evil articles' had been returned to their definitive positions in the garage, attic and cellar, Jim's cell phone again rang and Jeffrey was once more on the other end of the line. The stressed-out motorist immediately pulled over to the busy highway's shoulder to answer the call.

"Hello Dad! Don't rush getting here! Mom's all right and has snapped out of her precarious state!" the relieved son disclosed in his normal-sounding voice. "The doctors think that she had suffered a mild concussion as a result of her blacking-out and falling!"

"That's absolutely fantastic news!" the jubilant father yelled into his cell phone. "I promise I'll be there Jeff in approximately fifteen minutes. I'll look for you in the visitors' lounge waiting area."

"Okay Pop! See you there, er, I meant to say 'here'!" the son exclaimed. "There for a minute Dad I had thought that our family had been subjected to some really bad luck!" Click.

'I'm really happy that I trusted my suspicious judgment and decided to keep the ten articles I had placed inside the SUV,' Jim Brewster determined as he cautiously observed the reduced speed limit while passing through Atco. 'If it wasn't for my superstitious nature, then who knows what terrible fate might've been awaiting Susan? I'm never going to get rid of those ten special objects as long as my home remains standing and as long as I'm alive and strong enough to safeguard them!'

"Trestles, Overpasses & Blue Skies"

Inspector Ned Carson sat at his office desk on the third floor of Philadelphia's Race Street "Round House," casually watching vehicular traffic flowing in both directions across the Ben Franklin Bridge connecting Pennsylvania with New Jersey, the span being a mile-long distance across the historic Delaware River. Carson's reverie was instantly broken when his office partner Detective Timothy Ransom entered the room carrying two fresh cups of coffee and then respectfully handed one of the steaming Styrofoam containers to his thirty-year-veteran colleague.

"Tim, every March right before spring arrives on the calendar I get the strong urge to get out of the congested city and use a week of my treasured vacation time to go either hunting or fishing with you," Inspector Ned Carson mused and said. "But I gotta' confess that our good wives have been quite understanding in allowing us to participate in some valued male bonding at suburban bars, and Jenny trusts me when I'm away from town at a distant convention with you for a week or so."

"Joanne feels the same way when I'm far away from the dregs of downtown Philly' hanging out in Maine or North Dakota with none other than you," Detective Tim Ransom amiably agreed before taking a sip of just-brewed java from his hot cup. "Ned, do you remember last year when we were on our last adventurous escapade up in Maine hunting big-buck deer? We bagged us two terrific trophies that our taxidermist Gordie had stuffed and mounted for us. My twelve-point buck head and accompanying antlers is now proudly displayed hanging over my brick fireplace as a souvenir of that terrific expedition into the wilderness."

"How could I ever forget *that* madcap excursion we had up North?" the Inspector replied with a smile. "Our hilarious hunting guide claimed that *his* grandfather had a left leg that was wooden between the knee and the ankle while the thigh section along with the foot were genuine normal flesh, blood and bone!" Ned Carson gleefully exclaimed. "And after listening to that old-timer's exaggerated travesty, I reckoned that *we* were all much more than a little smashed from drinking six rounds of boilermakers and so I was the first to call it quits and march off to my cabin to seriously prepare for the next morning's hunt. Quite frankly Tim, I enjoy hunting dangerous criminals as much as I do wild animals!"

"And after you were snoring and sounding like a wild unconscious boar in your bunk sack," jovial Detective Timothy Ransom reminisced, "our illustrious guide was giving me a tin ear about how he had proudly voted for James Buchanan when he had turned twenty-one and finally became eligible to cast a ballot. I told the old animal scout that it was impossible for him to do what he had maintained and swore he had performed because James Buchanan was the fifteenth President of the United States just before Abraham Lincoln, and *his* lackluster administration was even before the Civil War ever started at Fort Sumter," Ransom embellished his story. "But the demented and totally soused guy was adamant and then poured himself another full glass of whiskey."

"Well, how did you counter the intoxicated fool's outrageous and preposterous statement?" Inspector Carson wondered and asked. "Did you put the cuffs on him before he became violent? I must've slept through the whole weird fiasco over in the other cabin. There's only so much stupidity I can endure, ya' know!"

"Well Inspector," the amiable Detective chuckled and then proceeded with his recollection, "I felt obligated to tell our eighty-year-old drunken bearded guide that our English word "okay" had originated from another nineteenth century American President named Martin Van Buren, who incidentally was often called 'Old Kinderhook' because he had originated from Kinderhook, New York. Anyway," Tim Ransom continued with his extremely boring anecdote, "when Van Buren's aides would agree with *O*ld *K*inderhook they would often say 'O. K.,' and that's precisely how the birth of our simple word 'okay' came to be."

"Did *our* inebriated guide buy the factual tale you were selling him?" Inspector Carson deliberately asked to keep the ludicrous dialogue going. "Certainly he must've been impressed with your great storehouse of accurate-but-trivial knowledge. You were once a history major in college I believe."

"Well Ned, all the old geezer did was indulge himself and flagrantly gulp down the remaining six ounces of cold rye liquor in his glass, put the glass on the table and say 'Okay' to me. Then the old fossil-face lowered his chin and entered into the deepest sleep I've ever witnessed," Detective Ransom humorously elaborated. "Quite candidly Ned, I've never been so entertained in all my life! Say Inspector, what do ya' say that after work we have a temporary change in venue from our ordinary humdrum existence. We'll call our wives and tell them we're workin' a couple of hours late on next year's tight budget and then get out of town and drive across the bridge over to Jersey. There's a new hot stripper from Arkansas performin' her act over at the Aquarius Club just south of Camden, in fact, not too far from the Walt Whitman Bridge. I think the broad's stage name is Daisy Maisy and that her fantastic erotic dance routine is Daisy Maisy Gone Crazy!"

"Great suggestion Tim but my bowling team's havin' an important championship match tonight over in Penndel and I gotta' be there since I'm both the captain and official cheerleader. Ha, ha, ha!" Carson loudly guffawed. "I'm the captain tonight at the bowling alleys but at the moment I'm merely a rank inspector sittin' behind my desk here at humdrum police headquarters. But confidentially, I like your tempting Jersey stripper club idea so ya' gotta' give me a rain check for one sunny day next week."

The two amused center city working chums next momentarily discussed their upcoming planned July deep-sea white marlin fishing trip to Ocean City, Maryland that was slated to commence out of Captain Bill Bunting's Bayside Marina and they also reviewed the prospect of going down to semi-tropical Miami the following summer to try their luck at the more formidable Atlantic Ocean blue marlin fish variety.

"Great idea Tim!" the Inspector appreciatively complimented. "The blue marlin off the coast of Florida can be twice the size and weight of the white marlin we get off the coast of Maryland. We can arrange a week-long trip and take along the chatty wives and pesky kids. There're plenty of activities to keep our two tribes busy while we're out in the ocean meetin' the challenge of reelin' in the big blue game fish. I'll bring-up the subject with Jenny and the kids over the supper table," the thirsty-for-thrills Ned Carson promised his loyal friend. "All we have to do is get our boat captain and his mates a little smashed like we did with the hunting guide up in Maine and then have ourselves a real misadventure getting lost out there somewhere in the middle of the Bermuda Triangle."

* * * * * * * * * * * * *

Attractive office secretary Karen Stone brought in the morning's mail and city edition newspapers for the Inspector and the Detective to read. The *Philadelphia Inquirer* headlines were quite depressing with murders, robberies, assaults and rapes running rampant throughout the more dangerous police precincts in the metropolis. But one particular mail item was specifically addressed both to the Inspector and to the Detective, the peculiar postal delivery being a small square package having no return address, and the strange object caught the Inspector's immediate attention. Using his handy penknife, Carson casually slit open the plain brown wrapper and the co-recipient was surprised to examine what appeared to be a computer-made recording disc, which he then placed onto the D Drive tray of his desktop Hewlett Packard tower.

"This is pretty unusual!" Inspector Carson mentioned to his crime-fighting colleague. "Some gutless incognito person has sent us an anonymous disc. I'm not *that* computer literate Tim but I don't think it's a video DVD. Let's see exactly what it is and what kind of message it might contain. Perhaps it's just a blank hoax of some sort or some misinformation specifically designed to steer us in the wrong direction! I'm pretty sure that it's home-made and not professionally or commercially produced in a recording studio, at least that's my initial opinion at the moment!"

"My normally latent curiosity has suddenly been stimulated!" Detective Ransom exclaimed as he casually reached for his Styrofoam coffee cup on the Inspector's gray metal desk. "This must be some sort of wacky practical joke being played, that's my first perception. Who in their right mind would take the time and trouble to send that mediocre-looking disc to you, er, I mean to *us*!"

After inserting the circular item into the appropriate computer tray, several seconds later the familiar popular music tune of the Monkees 'Take the Last Train to Clarksville' blasted through the device's speakers. The two befuddled law enforcers looked incredulously at each other and then burst out in merriment at trying to decipher the minor mystery that had unexpectedly interrupted their congenial conversation. Carson and Ransom's brief period of entertainment was soon negatively affected by a disturbing news flash coming over the police bulletin wire.

"Is this a lousy coincidence or what Inspector?" Detective Ransom dubiously asked his department superior. "A murder victim's body has been found dangling from a railroad trestle on Flemming Pike, Winslow Township, New Jersey and the person had been smashed by an unsuspecting farmer driving a truck along the rural road at fifty-miles an hour and going beneath the isolated overpass. How gruesome and heinous!"

"Especially if the victim was still alive when the wicked impact occurred," Inspector Carson evaluated. "Could you imagine the intense terror that the dangling human must have experienced?"

"I hope it wasn't that gorgeous Arkansas stripper that's doin' her dancing-routine thing over at the Jersey Aquarius Club!" Tim Ransom awkwardly replied to try and break the room's moment of gloomy depression with an element of levity. "But Ned, I presume that the deceased *person* is a male. Do you suppose that the culprits were the South Philly' Mafia? They have plenty of ties with unscrupulous Jersey junkyard dealers, especially in the Hammonton and Winslow Township areas. And also Inspector, this kind of callous premeditated killing tactic does seem to fit *that* Mafia syndicate profile perfectly! And the poor innocent farmer driving the truck under the train trestle feels really guilty for accidentally crushing the dead guy's anatomy and simultaneously sending *his* tortured soul to the afterlife!"

"Yes Tim, I lean more towards the South Philly' Mafia being the perpetrators rather than let's say area street gangs like the Crypts and the Bloods or let's say even further, a cell of organized Islamic jihadists too!" Ned Carson concluded.

"But Arab terrorists are now concentrating more on smaller targets because the larger ones are so well protected," Detective Ransom speculated and declared. "That's their radical change in strategy on how they're conducting their clandestine heinous terror acts. Their new philosophy is to create public panic by ruthlessly and brutally killing individual citizens in bizarre ways rather than by sensationally blowing up national monuments, tall skyscrapers and the like."

Karen Stone re-entered the office with another square brown-wrapped package in her hands. "Inspector, I had forgotten to deliver this piece during my last rotation around the offices. It's addressed to both you and Detective Ransom."

The attractive secretary then handed the second sealed music disc to the somewhat startled Police Inspector, who anxiously unraveled the external covering and then hurriedly placed the new homemade object into the D Drive computer tray.

After Karen Stone had departed the office, the men's ears readily discerned the lyrics and accompanying rhythm to the catchy 1940s Glenn Miller Orchestra song 'Chattanooga Choo-Choo.' And to add to their overall astonishment, a female news reporter instantly appeared on the right wall's flat screen television and the young lady began describing an incident that had recently happened a mile south of the Tullytown/Levittown train station platform near Edgely, Bucks County, Pennsylvania. A

193

man's body that had been suspended-by-ropes had been obliterated beyond recognition by a speeding New York to Philadelphia AmTrak train. Additional relevant details concerning the commission of the dastardly and egregious crime were currently unavailable, but it was next announced that the Bucks County Sheriff's Department was feverishly working on the case.

"There's a definite pattern being established here and I think that someone's trying to implicate *us* into this bizarre series of nefarious events!" Inspector Carson theorized and conveyed to his devoted associate. "Tim, I think I'm developing a distinct aversion to popular train songs! I'm never going to take the Jersey Transit train from Philly' to Atlantic City again! Nor for that matter, the always dependable SEPTA High Speed Line transit across the Ben Franklin into Jersey!"

"I know the exact same feeling you're presently experiencing Ned!" the seated grim-faced Detective concurred. "Could *we* be prospective earmarked sitting duck targets on the hit list? I'll run a quick background scan of all possible Mafia figures that either you or I have put behind bars during our distinguished law-enforcement careers," Ransom instinctively indicated. "I dislike mentioning this glaring detail Boss but we're no longer third party investigators searching for or examining evidence and attempting to convict nefarious suspects. Really Ned, I believe that we're now marked men on the targeted victims' list and I think that we're being deliberately harassed and stalked by professional hit men! Here's what's bothering me in a nutshell. The whole thing is like *they're* the dominant cats maliciously toying with and taunting *us* vulnerable mice before arbitrarily deciding to eliminate our puny butts from mortal existence."

* * * * * * * * * * * *

The next several weeks Ned Carson and Tim Ransom had received five additional homemade CDs from the mysterious anonymous source: 'Midnight Train to Georgia' by Gladys Knight and the Pips, 'Mystery Train' by Elvis Presley, 'Peace Train' by Cat Stevens, 'Love Train' by the O' Jays and 'Freedom Train' by Lenny Kravis, all of which materialized into five corresponding victims dying after being dangled by ropes from respective train trestles and overpasses in Pleasantville, Camden and Burlington County, New Jersey and in Croydon and also near Norristown, Pennsylvania. Inspector Carson and Detective Ransom became even more baffled and apprehensive as each successive horrible incident was being vigorously investigated.

"This sequence of major felony incidents is too sophisticated to be a wave of easy-to-solve atrocities caused by local Crypts and Bloods' gang-related feuding," Inspector Carson insisted. "Most of the train sacrifice victims have been upper middle class suburban whites that apparently seem to have no significant city or regional gang affiliations."

"And the bodies were in far worse shape than being merely dismembered or wickedly decapitated as you've already alluded," Detective Ransom rendered an appendix to his partner's murder-motive theory. "I hate to sound too visceral but the corpses were severely mutilated, no, they were more-than-likely gruesomely pulverized with blood and tissue disgustingly smeared and splashed all over the concrete trestles and overpass column supports. Whoever is behind this heinous skein of sadistic killings must have an evil black heart," the detective ascertained. "What about Arab or Muslim terrorists? Do you see any valid connection there?"

"No, I don't think so at this point," sleuth Ned Carson answered. "It's not their type of M.O. The jihadists want to create terror by dynamiting historic monuments or famous places like Times Square or Yankee Stadium where tens of thousand of innocent people congregate or would spontaneously die. The hateful al Qaeda mindset is bent on causing widespread devastation and each primitive act of terror must always be bigger and grander than the barbaric preceding ones! Remember too Tim," Carson paused and emphasized. "You and I are now intimately connected to this hideous crime surge so it's pretty hard for us to be completely objective about cracking the insidious train trestle and overpass pattern. Either the victim is killed by a truck or bus zipping by under a train bridge, or the still-alive person is suddenly pulverized as a locomotive zooms under a signal support structure. Could you imagine the psychological damage that the diabolical incidents must have on the unwary train engineers after the poor fellows commit involuntary manslaughter at some cowardly thug's volition?"

"Then obviously you don't think that these abominable events are random crimes being committed," Tim Ransom surmised and expressed. "Well Inspector, what about the ruthless Philly' Mafia?" the worried detective rhetorically asked. "I've got the names of ten villains that either you or I or both of us have had incarcerated in the last fifteen years. We have Marco "the Brute"

Benedetti, Sal "Knuckles" Panachelli, Oliviero "Monks" Bruno, Giovanni "Undertaker" Perna, Pasquale "the Equalizer" DePalma, Antonio "Digger" Campanella, Angelo…."

"I know who all the treacherous South Philly' Sicilian punks are!" Inspector Carson angrily yelled as he thrice pounded his right fist upon his metal desk. "The ruthless scumbags even play Robin Hood and secretly sponsor several string bands in the annual Mummers Parade! But Tim, I gotta' confess that we have no concrete clues to adequately pursue. Every music disc that we've received has no fingerprints except for those belonging to postal employees handling the mail," Carson reminded Ransom. "And as far as the post office of origin is concerned, all the CDs were separately mailed with the necessary correct postage stamps from different public mailboxes in seven different locations in three states that comprise the entire Delaware Valley region."

"This whole problem is a dilemma of major magnitude!" Detective Ransom exclaimed as contempt mingled with fear occupied his soul. "What does the top brass say about it, you know, the Chief and the other moronic bureaucrats occupying key positions at the upper echelon?"

"They think that you and I are incompetent imbeciles because we're apparently clueless about where to begin," the flustered and thwarted investigator related. "Square One can't be found! And if you want to know my inner feelings," Ned Carson boomed, "I don't personally savor the notion of being suspended by ropes from a train trestle and then being mangled beyond recognition a mere six months before earning my lucrative retirement pension and corresponding social security benefits that I've worked all my adult working life to amass."

On the following Thursday morning pert and proper Karen Stone nonchalantly entered the third floor Round House police office and handed Inspector Carson a half dozen square packages sent from six different New Jersey, Pennsylvania and Delaware suburban post offices. The nervous duo very meticulously began opening the newly arrived suspicious items, being very careful not to contaminate potential evidence with their own fingerprints.

The first two CDs opened and played by Inspector Carson had undeniable tractor-trailer themes with C.W. McCall singing 'Convoy' and the second associated tune featured Dave Dudley's rendition of 'Truck Driving Man.'

An apologetic and embarrassed Karen Stone then re-entered the men's office and guiltily claimed that her memory and sorting skills were becoming diminished. "Here's one more piece of mail that I had somehow overlooked," the prim-looking normally reliable department clerk said to Carson as she handed him another plain-wrapped CD, which after being unraveled turned out to be the Eagles singing 'Take It Easy,' a lively song which also personified the truck driving big-rig theme.

The remaining already-delivered packages that had been later cautiously identified by Detective Ransom had (when played via the desktop computer) an observable change in subject venue switching from eighteen-wheeler semi' rigs to familiar bus themed songs. The first rendition was the classic 'Bus Stop' by the Hollies, followed by 'Magic Bus' by the Who, 'Barney's Adventure Bus' kids' song vocalized by a variety of unknown chorus singers and finally, 'Ramblin' Man' vocalized by the Allman Brothers, which much to Carson and Ransom's consternation and chagrin featured the famous lyrics: "I was born in the back seat of a Greyhound Bus, rollin' down Highway 41."

"What do you make of these new CDs?" the Inspector asked his dumbfounded assistant. "You don't suppose that...."

"That the method of death has instantaneously transformed from train, trestle and overpass murders to deaths caused by tractor-trailers and buses!" Detective Ransom sagaciously assumed and concluded. "This would be an extremely fascinating case if you and I weren't directly involved as intended victims! We're dealing with an unscrupulous surreptitious antagonist, that's for sure!"

"As the Eagles often sang in 'Take It Easy': 'Don't let the sound of your own wheels drive you crazy," the about-to-retire crime fighter advised his very upset partner. "Tim, what's that new info' appearing over there on the wall TV screen?"

"Two local tractor-trailers have just exploded killing the drivers in separate accidents fifty miles apart," the now-neurotic detective stammered as he slowly read from his own computer screen atop his own cheap metal frame desk. "The first one was going north in Philly' around the Academy Street Exit on I-95 and the second one was demolished on Route 322, the Black Horse Pike in Mays Landing, New Jersey."

"Two distinct-but-simultaneous incidents about fifty miles apart from each other!" Carson repeated to his shocked and exasperated underling, desperately attempting to connect a few dots. "True, the South Philly' mob syndicate is involved with the freight drivers' union and perhaps we're looking at a couple of stool pigeon whistle-blowing drivers that possibly knew too much info' about internal union affairs. I think that this coincidence

197

might be a blessing in disguise, the two new tragedies finally leading us in the right direction," the Inspector stated with a glimmer of wishful resolution prevalent in his raspy tone of voice. "I hope that we can soon locate and arrest the dirty skunks responsible for these horrific crimes before you and I become deceased entities listed in alphabetical order on the morning papers' obituary page."

"Hey Boss, an Eyewitness News team over at Exit 5 on the New Jersey Turnpike is now reporting on the flat screen TV that a bus with forty-three passengers aboard has just exploded and has burst into flames outside Burlington. Initial reports say that there are few if any survivors. It didn't take too long for the media focus to go from tractor-trailers to buses!"

"This is really serious business Tim!" Inspector Carson yelled to his already beleaguered subordinate. "Let's get off our rumpy carcasses and get in touch with the Jersey authorities about the recent bus turnpike calamity and then we'll head on over to Academy Street and I-95 and glean some essential data about the horrendous tractor-trailer inferno. I'll tell you one thing Tim. I refuse to be eliminated from this precious Earth before I'm fully retired and safely living in self-exile somewhere on a remote South Pacific island."

* * * * * * * * * * * *

Early the following Monday morning Inspector Carson and Detective Ransom were drinking their standard cups of morning coffee and reviewing their slate of responsibilities for the upcoming day's agenda. Carson was peering out the window and nonchalantly viewing a Septa High Speed Line Train rumbling across the Ben Franklin Bridge towards Camden, New Jersey.

Meanwhile garrulous Tim Ransom was commenting about a suspect line-up scheduled downstairs at ten-thirty and a press conference for "annoying media print and TV reporters" slated for after lunch. But introspective Inspector Ned Carson's mind was in a sullen depressed mood since his department's investigation into the series of trestle, train, tractor-trailer and commercial bus-related homicides had (over the span of the last month) become a veritable exercise in futility.

"Ya' know Tim," the frustrated Inspector began his brief monologue while still staring out the office window at the Ben Franklin Bridge, "some investigators look for a needle in a haystack while other gumshoes search for a haystack in the eye of

198

a needle. But is this perplexing sequence of despicable events really a series of planned murders?" Carson muttered, showing a degree of repulsion in his tone of voice. "Despite all of my time and effort, I can't even find an ordinary-sized haystack or a single needle with which to base a lousy flimsy hypothesis upon."

"I happen to share your disappointment," Detective Tim Ransom sympathetically remarked. "None of the regular punks that *we'* frequently rely on for ratting aren't opening their mouths. They're all afraid of being knocked-off themselves in this crazy and totally savage murder spree caper. They're all like craven scared-to-death pigs with intimidated mass laryngitis; they just aren't squealing!"

"Have we gotten any sort of DNA evidence back from the local coroner's autopsies?" Ned wanted to know. "Perhaps some new-found scientific data could lead to a breakthrough, a dramatic moment of enlightenment."

"The only DNA traces that had been recovered at the area crime scenes have been samples of the victims' tissues and blood and much to my bafflement, nothing tangible pointing towards any particular suspect has been uncovered," Tim Ransom sadly conveyed. "Say Ned, Hudson over in homicide canceled-out on the Police Convention in Denver on Thursday because of a nasty bout with bronchitis. And guess what? I've been assigned to take his place so I'll be rooming with you for a few nights in Rocky Mountain country. How's that for an inspirational surprise?"

"Unfortunately Tim, I won't be able to fly out to Colorado until Thursday morning," Carson indicated, disdainfully twisting his head back and forth to demonstrate his overall disenchantment. "I have plenty to attend to right here at my desk in terms of backlogged paperwork so Good Buddy, I hereby predict that I'll see you at *our* already-booked Denver hotel late Thursday evening."

"Sounds copacetic to me!" the seldom-pessimistic crime-combating assistant pleasantly stated. "Maybe a change in environment will get our minds synchronized and thinking on the same wavelength in regard to this rash of insane homicides happening to innocent dangling train trestle victims, to the lives of random tractor-trailer drivers and to the horror of unsuspecting bus passengers. Karen's made all of the arrangements and I'm flying west at 6:15 a.m. tomorrow morning. But I have to be at the airport at 4:10 in order to be processed through the security cattle line. You'd think Ned that I'd get some sort of privileged airport priority since I'm an honorable veteran police department professional."

"Okay Tim!" Carson robotically answered while ignoring his partner's general dissatisfaction with airport security measures. "It's all settled. Thanks to reservations obtained by Karen, I'll be checking into our Denver hotel late Thursday night. Be sure to set your watch back two hours. I'll buy you a couple of drinks at the lobby bar, that is, after I unpack, and then we'll rack up delectable late suppers on our individual expense accounts."

* * * * * * * * * * * *

On Thursday morning Ned Carson was seated at his desk reviewing the *Inquirer's* front-page headlines about the inability of the metropolitan police to put together the myriad pieces of the "reprehensible trestle bridge, tractor-trailer and commercial bus conundrum." The Inspector was sipping his steaming cup of coffee when Karen Stone entered his office and efficiently delivered the morning mail, and much to the recipient's displeasure, six separately wrapped and shipped CD music discs were very evident and distinguishable, all present in the morning post pile.

After energetically ripping off the external brown wrapping paper to the half dozen discs, the thoroughly aggravated police investigator was soon immensely horrified upon listening to the opening bars of the newly obtained six haunting song lyrics.

'Oh my word!' Carson anxiously thought. 'Tim's in immediate jeopardy but I can't call the airport because they'll think that I'm crazy inventing a plane crash prediction based on several homemade musical CDs I've just received. The Chief and the bureaucratic brass will want me to undergo a psychiatric examination and I don't wish to endanger any of my pension benefits if some quack shrink declares me being mentally incompetent if no plane disaster had ever transpired over Denver! Hopefully there wasn't any major headwind resistance and Tim's plane has already safely landed!'

Carson seriously pondered his psychological dilemma for a moment and then jotted down the theme-oriented song titles and performing artists connected with the six mentally haunting musical discs. 'Let's see now, there's five that had been addressed to both Tim and me and those five are 'Snoopy and the Red Baron' by the Yuletide Singers, 'Come Fly with Me' by Frank Sinatra, 'Jet Airliner' by the Steve Miller Band, 'Leaving on a Jet

Plane' by Peter, Paul and Mary and the last one was 'Volare' by Bobby Rydell.

Finally the fazed and crazed Inspector jotted-down the title to the one song disc that had specifically been sent to *him*: the 1940s' hit 'Blue Skies' by Bing Crosby.

The morning talk show gossip on the side-wall flat screen TV was instantly interrupted with a reporter having a very melancholy expression on his face announcing that five fatal jet airplane crashes had occurred simultaneously in various parts of the United States. "The first one being reported happened thirty minutes ago over the Air Force Academy in Colorado Springs. The flight had originated from Philadelphia International Airport and had been scheduled to land in Denver. The second jet crash ironically occurred just north of Boston's Logan International Airport and first responder rescue crews are now on the scene and we'll provide you with additional details as they soon become available. The third mysterious and amazingly coincidental crash has happened in the bay near New York's LaGuardia…"

Being very disturbed and emotionally rattled, Inspector Ned Carson grabbed his remote control and fearfully turned-off the wall flat screen television. Perspiration beads rolled down his forehead, cheeks and back. The affected aged man was on the right side of the law but yet malignant-minded devious underworld adversaries were arbitrarily sentencing him to death. Immediately Carson summoned brunette Ms. Karen Stone to his office to do him a special favor.

"Karen, I'm not feeling too well at the moment!" the appalled police veteran declared. "I think I must be having some serious flu symptoms coming on. Please call the airport and cancel my round-trip plane tickets to and from Denver. And while you're at it," the ashen-faced Inspector paused and stammered, "cancel my Denver hotel reservation too! And tell the Chief I believe I need immediate medical treatment and am driving myself over to Thomas Jefferson University Hospital right now."

"The Evil Force"

I, Colonel Cliff Dawson am accurately recording this incredible account into my personal electronic journal and not into the official ship's log for reasons that will obviously be self-explanatory later on in this narrative. Captain Jeremy Parker and I have been on a courageous ten-year space mission exploring outer space and methodically charting our landmark discoveries for the International World Coalition. Our well-publicized mission was described in the world's media as "an awesome enterprise" and quite basically, I've always been attracted to the prospect of being one of the first 'daring humans' to find intelligent human-like life thriving elsewhere in the nearby Milky Way Galaxy.

Our lengthy expedition started out from Earth in the year 2534 A.D. and it is now, according to our ship's reliable instrument panel May 5th of 2542. The Newton III is now ready to lift off and leave the planet that Captain Parker and I have labeled EL-741, which is an *E*arth-*L*ike sphere rotating around a Sun-Like star that my cohort and I have named Mater Seven.

But plenty of exceptionally weird and eerie phenomena have happened since our momentous landing on EL-741 approximately forty-eight hours ago, and thus, my guilty conscience would not allow the Newton III to take off until all of the pertinent details have been precisely documented into my personal diary and not into the ship's authentic log.

Captain Parker and I have been close friends ever since our dual graduations from the American Space Force Academy in Cape Canaveral, Florida in June of 2520. Jeremy happened to be a veritable wizard at understanding and repairing complex matter and anti-matter equipment and my 'space partner' was very adept at proficiently fixing warp drives whereas I am highly regarded back on Earth as being an academic expert at comprehending the intricacies of astrophysics and biochemistry.

Throughout our glorious odyssey trek across this sector of the Milky Way our general relationship on the Einstein III had been both cordial and compatible and my comrade and I satisfactorily shared navigation responsibilities and Captain Jeremy Parker and I had cooperatively alternated slumbering inside the spaceship's one and only Deep Sleep Hibernation Compartment, which over the course of our decade-long expedition efficiently slowed down our mutual biological aging process by five years, thus effectively halfing our breathing and our heartbeats.

Captain Parker and I had quite different motivations in volunteering for this very vital space mission. Jeremy had experienced marital difficulties and was divorced without any children and my co-pilot possessed a zealous spirit for adventure and challenge and also, my ambitious comrade always wanted to become historically famous. Jeremy's core aspirations were always goal-oriented and it would be an understatement for me to suggest that throughout his career Captain Parker possessed both the dream and the drive to achieve his valued objective.

As for myself, I am happily married to the former Carol Anderson and we have two wonderful kids, Tom, now age seventeen and Denise, now age thirteen. I had applied to participate in this historic journey because first and foremost, I consider myself an American Union patriot and quite truthfully, I despise all of the mundane conflict existing back on Earth like war, famine, pestilence, political wrangling, drought, disease and human envy, jealousy, greed and abundant spite too, which I assess to be the fundamental roots of all human evil.

Tending to have an introverted nature, I have always preferred to be a loner and as I now recollect, my personality was never very gregarious and convivial at military social events and at gala receptions. And besides, I had reckoned that *our* significant space voyage would be only five years in duration and not ten because of our body-preservation time spent in suspended animation inside the very essential Bio-Chemical Deceleration Chambers. Indeed I have greatly missed my family during this extensive space voyage.

Although Jeremy and I have visited, explored and thoroughly documented fifty-three unique planets during our current expedition, more importantly, we have successfully located and ambitiously cataloged three special planets very similar to Earth on our interstellar maps, but the only evidence of life prior to our recent comprehensive investigation into EL-741 had merely been primitive microorganisms, new strains of bacteria and various types of peculiar protozoa. Generally speaking, everything seemed rather normal on our galactic 'Interstellar Study' until we had eventually entered the most remote solar system of the Constellation Pegasus.

Upon approaching Mater Seven and eventually orbiting EL-741, Captain Parker was uncharacteristically excited to report that the Earth-like sphere had an atmosphere very similar to that of our native planet, seventy-five percent nitrogen, twenty-two percent oxygen and three percent hydrogen, along with minute quantities of other rare gases. My eminent co-pilot had always been quite eloquent in expressing himself.

"And Colonel Dawson, there's an excellent ozone screen filtering out traces of ultra-violet and infra-red rays so *that* important condition means that the possibility of plant and animal life existing on EL-741 is dramatically heightened," Captain Parker observed and communicated. "This is pretty thrilling Cliff both in scope and in sequence! A good chance exists that over the eons life has migrated from the planet's rivers and lakes onto land just like it had done back on Earth hundreds of millions of years ago," Captain Parker euphorically articulated to me. "Just imagine what kind of fantastic evolution might have occurred over the ages here on EL-741! Just the contemplation of such an evolutionary miracle is absolutely mind-boggling!" my friend indicated. "This extraordinary planetary encounter might be the first genuine human contact with alien life forms in outer space," Jeremy enthusiastically gushed and giggled. "Neil Armstrong should've been so lucky as *we* are right now! That ancient astronaut's biggest accomplishment as an audacious space pioneer was to set foot on the lifeless crater-pocked Moon. We have a terrific opportunity to become internationally renowned back home on good old Mother Earth!"

"Yes Jeremy," I passively answered, trying my utmost to contain my emotions from running rampant, "but I recommend that you now carefully study the topography of EL-741's surface. There aren't any oceans or seas as far as I can determine; just evidence of various irregular coastlines forming one enormous circular-shaped continent, if you like."

"But look Colonel!" Captain Parker ecstatically yelled to justify his total fascination. "There's an abundance of beautiful rivers and lakes on that one vast global continent that you've just so aptly described. And there're bountiful forests and trees and vegetation and deserts and mountains too, all fairly similar to those features existing on Earth!" my close friend anxiously vociferated. "The entire planet reminds me of depictions I've read of the American west before the invasion of the Conestoga wagons that traversed through Colorado, Utah and sunny California."

"Well Jeremy, it's always better to be safe than being either sorry or dead!" I objectively and rationally replied. "I'm not setting foot upon the surface down there until we perform a complete and comprehensive atmospheric analysis and finish a general land elements' probe. But Captain, I must admit that the present daylight surface temperature of seventy-five degrees and polar readings of twenty below zero are indeed favorable and possibly conducive to supporting advanced life forms."

"Okay Dr. Caution!" Parker promptly jested. "Let's look before we leap. *That* expression ought to be our new motto!"

"It would be nice if we could investigate without having to don our cumbersome space suits," I casually noted, trying to impress my colleague with my calm self-discipline. "But after landing, let's be patient and wait a few hours before we initiate our examination of the physical elements of EL-741. Who knows? We might be able to add a few more chemical items to the standard Periodic Table and become scientifically famous in addition to historically famous!"

Most of the minerals that we had identified on EL-741 were similar to those prevalent on Earth and on other foreign planets that we had recently explored and surveyed: iron, phosphorus, potassium, sulfur, sodium, aluminum, potash, quartz, silicon and gold were in good supply. More remarkably though, certain chemical compounds were commonly detectable in the form of carbon dioxide, sodium chloride along with measurable sugar molecules.

The evidence of carbon dioxide strongly suggested to us that plant life could exist and thrive, and *that* fortuitous factor could consequently support natural food growth through photosynthesis, specifically provided by radiant orange-glowing Mater Seven, which incidentally happened to be a very favorable hundred and twenty million miles away. That intriguing coincidence of satisfactory conditions promoting the possibility of EL-741 surface life represented a distinct and encouraging prospect, and both Captain Parker and I were highly motivated to commence our essential quest, searching for indigenous plant and animal life.

Twenty-four hours after landing on EL-741 (which incidentally rotated on its axis every twenty-six Earth hours), and after determining that the planet's atmosphere was indeed conducive to breathing and walking without the use of space suits and the need for any artificial aid apparatus, Captain Parker and I next intrepidly exited the Newton III's air lock chamber and then bravely stepped down the access ramp, eventually audaciously setting foot onto what later was defined as the "Planet of Evil Force."

* * * * * * * * * * * *

I am not a particularly religious man but I have always viewed my conscience's value system as being one founded on strong moral convictions and upon discreet ethical principles. Throughout my adult life I've generally assessed organized formal religion as being something analogous to superstitious and primitive prehistoric thinking, that is, until I had made certain incidental interactions with the mysterious "Evil Force" that I soon learned dominates EL-741. Now as the Almighty is my witness, I am convinced that some diabolical omnipotent power pervades and controls this God-forsaken planet that Captain Parker and myself had randomly-but-intentionally encroached upon.

Please allow me to articulate the astute recounting of my experiences, all of which I maintain will adequately justify and defend my seemingly implausible and fictitious testimony, for I now believe that any goodness that exists in the Infinite Universe is conversely counterbalanced with a diametrically opposed Evil Equivalent, a contemptible Evil Equivalent that has wretchedly pushed my mind to the threshold of insanity. I shall now be more specific in my elaboration.

After intensively analyzing the remarkable planet's atmosphere and thereby determining that the air was consistently safe enough to breathe, Captain Parker and I boldly exited the Newton III and steadfastly ambled out into what appeared to be a pristine New England environment abounding with late springtime forest deciduous and pine trees, the overall physical landscape exhibiting assorted strange-looking green leaves, branches, pinecones and accompanying needles.

About a half-mile distant from the Newton III we soon encountered a swift-running brook and the two of us followed its rocky meandering path until we eventually arrived at a gorgeous grove comprised of what appeared to be wild peach and apple trees interspersed with random bushes laden with red berries that seemed to be a combination of a raspberry and a blackberry, that is, in their physical three-dimensional appearance.

"This is what I truly love about EL-741," Captain Parker opined and declared. "It's pristine and astronomically remote and now there's definite evidence of delicious-looking luscious fruit growing here. Perhaps there're some human-like inhabitants residing nearby in this desolate vicinity too! Colonel Dawson, I don't want to sound too optimistic but right this minute *this* observation could be the all-too-elusive cosmic missing link that we've been desperately searching for, the crucial connection that decisively proves once and for all that Homo sapiens are not the only cerebral creatures populating our enormous galaxy."

"Jeremy, I want to do a complete property molecular inspection of this alluring fruit before we ever attempt devouring it," I suspiciously answered my best friend. "Ah yes!" I exclaimed as I gazed at the gauge reading being registered on my bio-chemical spectrometer compound-measuring mechanism. "Elements of fructose, glucose, chlorophyll and carbon-related compounds are quite prevalent inside the odd-shaped lavender peach and also inside the purple apple and inside the distorted-looking red and black berries too. I confidently deduct that they're all devoid of harmful toxins or poisons and I'm convinced that the fruit is edible and nutritious as well as being digestive tract friendly."

"This is truly wonderful because I'm sick of all the monotonous processed food meals, artificially flavored juices and all of the tasteless energy tablets we've been swallowing-down for breakfast, lunch and supper," my dependable space associate eagerly stated. "I just can't resist the temptation any longer. With your permission, I desire sampling the berries and the apple facsimile right away. But honestly, I've never liked the taste of peaches ever since I was a youngster, thinking the fuzzy produce to be too sweet for my sophisticated palate. I think I'll pass on eating the peach."

"Okay Jeremy," I amenably acknowledged. "I'm going to try the lavender peach and the purple apple while your fussy taste buds can enjoy the apple and the red berries. According to the spectrometer's readings," I observed and plainly stated to my companion, "the three kinds of fruit growing here in this valley almost seem to be of chain store quality."

The edible fresh fruit we consumed was positively mouth-watering and I made a mental note of the grove's location and considered it 'a must responsibility' that I should visit the wonderful wild fruit orchard again simply to satisfy my voracious appetite. After simultaneously synchronizing *our* solar-powered watches, Jeremy and I decided to separate and explore north and south respectively and we agreed that we would rendezvous at the aforementioned orchard in an Earth hour. Hence I wandered south while my conscientious partner conducted his separate exploration north along the brook.

After trekking for twenty minutes, my wandering arrived me at a double ridge that was divided by a deep valley. Realizing that my forward progress was impossible, I stubbornly trudged my way back to the vicinity of the exotic peach and apple tree grove.

'I know what I'll do,' I deviously imagined. 'I'll proceed north and meet-up with Jeremy' as he's returning south along the fast-flowing stream. My adventurous co-pilot will be surprised to see me prematurely trespassing on *his* turf!'

As I exited a nondescript patch of pine trees, I noticed my friend stooping down and collecting what appeared to be some sparkling gold nuggets from the brook's bank. 'I'll see if Jeremy is honest enough to tell me about his treasure trove find,' I wisely thought. 'It'll be like a little character test! Surely the gold bonanza will have no special value to either of us until we return back to Earth. Precious metals and paper money are absolutely meaningless commodities up here on EL-741.'

After filling his deep white collection sack with the precious mineral, Jeremy oddly headed west along a dirt trail and then paced through a small woods and much to my astonishment and bewilderment, he entered a house that was an exact facsimile to mine back in Vero Beach, Florida, inadvertently or deliberately leaving the stucco rancher's front door open.

My palpitating heart became filled with anxiety and curiosity. I surreptitiously ascended the three brick steps and next distrustfully ducked-down on the front porch. Not detecting Jeremy's presence inside, I stealthily entered the foyer, turned right past the living room and then nervously hesitated before entering the master bedroom. Furtively sticking my head through the portal, my disbelieving eyes caught a glimpse of Captain Parker making love to my formerly faithful wife Carol.

'How could this possibly be reality?' I skeptically speculated. 'It must be some perverted illusion or inexplicable hallucination, or perhaps some ugly mental manifestation! Anger is raging inside me! Could the same repulsive scenario have happened in the past on Earth without my knowledge?'

My mind was incensed. I furiously left the area of the familiar-looking house and headed directly for the peach and apple orchard. An innocent-looking Captain Parker showed-up fifteen minutes later than the designated grove rendezvous time, and Jeremy had the unmitigated audacity to offer the lame excuse that his attention had been diverted when he had perceived a giant human-sized frog catching a huge flying insect with its sticky tongue.

I pretended to accept his exaggerated tale as being truthful, but on our long hike back to the Newton III, not once did my avaricious and baneful colleague mention to me either the white linen collection sack full of gold nuggets or his sinful adulterous love affair with Carol.

'Ever since our academic days ay the Space Academy, my rival Jeremy's always been exceedingly jealous and especially envious of my numerous accomplishments and awards,' I selfishly conjectured in defense of my faltering ego. 'He's without a doubt greedy, arrogant and spiteful and will do anything malicious to pilfer my pride and ruin my good public reputation! My moral standards have been impugned by that conscience-less maniac!' I lividly concluded. 'Captain Parker is going to pay dearly for violating my wife's fidelity to me and he'll suffer dire consequences for not demonstrating military honesty and integrity in regard to his recent gold discovery! I swear I'll get my just revenge on that unscrupulous traitor and marriage-wrecker! I've never loathed anyone as much as I now wholly abhor detestable Captain Jeremy Walter Parker right this very minute!'

* * * * * * * * * * * *

My disheveled mind had difficulty fathoming how my transplanted Vero Beach home and how my cheating wife happened to realistically appear on Planet EL-741, which logically was over ten light years away from Earth in the constellation Pegasus and furthermore, where were the remainder of the homes in my Florida neighborhood?

On our arduous amble back to the Newton III Captain Parker and I exchanged few words but midway during our three-mile ramble, I did remove from my jacket's pocket and then munch on a lavender peach that I had previously pulled from the strange-looking orchard tree. The entire way back to our spacecraft I felt both resentment and hatred toward my betraying co-pilot.

That evening, after exiting the ship's shower compartment and then drying my body off with a soft towel, I dressed into clean clothes and silently stepped into *our* sleeping quarters. Intense acrimony filled my spirit when my alert eyes detected Captain Parker assiduously searching through my wallet and at that point in time, I instinctively suspected that the sneaky thief was brazenly attempting to pilfer my identity.

Never before had I ever felt such antagonism towards another human being. Feeling grievously violated and deceived, I quietly retreated to the galley's pantry to sit at the table and drink down a cup of ice-cold water, but all the while my offended mind was strategically contemplating my next move.

'Why is Parker rummaging through my personal belongings?' I asked my confused self. 'I know! He's jealous of me, desires to steal my wife and probably also covets my expensive vacation hacienda in Andalusia, Spain! But money and gold have no particular value out here on this desolate end of the celestial zodiac! Property and wealth are irrelevant here on EL-741 too! According to the astronaut's manual,' I continued thinking and evaluating, 'with the exception of military rank during an emergency, all basic relationships between Parker and me away from Earth are supposed to be egalitarian in nature! Now everything's changed for the worse!'

My poisoned mind actually believed that I possessed the uncanny capacity to fully perceive every aspect of Parker's sinister intent. 'The greedy scoundrel envies my rank, despises my ability, resents my integrity, loathes my fame and curses my success,' I irrationally concluded. 'He's now my one and only adversary who is wickedly planning to either harm or kill me! That's why I must plot to destroy the demonic wretch first!'

My ears heard Captain Parker's shoes casually shuffling into the ship's library and then five minutes later they discerned 'my nemesis' striding into our sleeping quarters' chamber. 'Parker must be eliminated because I fear he's secretly preparing to execute me in cold blood! I'll wait here in the craft's library for a half hour pretending to be chewing on a snack and then when he's later slumbering in his bunk,' I cunningly contemplated, 'I'll swiftly perform my wicked deed!' I deviously schemed and determined.

An hour later I rose from my soft chair and very quietly walked to our small bedroom. 'Forget about implementing the paralyzing stun mode!' I shrewdly decided. 'My avowed enemy must be instantaneously eradicated from mortal existence! Parker's soul is defective and the villain must be eliminated!'

I slowly and meticulously removed my trusty ray gun from my waist holster and while Captain Parker was soundly sleeping under the blanket inside his lower bunk, I mercilessly pulled the trigger and zapped him with the weapon's potent laser beam.

The following dawn I dragged Parker's limp lifeless body into the heavy equipment room and next awkwardly lifted his heavy corpse into the 'All Purpose Digger's' passenger seat. After pressing a button on the sidewall control panel, thus opening the ship's exit portal, I started the machine's engine and then

211

fanatically drove the versatile vehicle down the Newton III's back ramp.

Not far from the now familiar peach and apple grove I used the machine to dig a six-foot-deep hole, deposited my vanquished foe's remains into the hollow and then skillfully manipulating the device's levers, I competently covered the makeshift grave with ample dirt. Before departing the vicinity, and exhibiting no sign of remorse, I hopped off the All Purpose Digger and forcefully plucked a ripe lavender peach from the nearest fruit tree. Appeasing my sudden hunger, I ravenously ate the juicy fruit.

On my short excursion back to the Newton III, I was confronted with several inexplicable threatening situations. First a ferocious lion-like creature crossed my path but I managed to adroitly maneuver my All Purpose Digger and scare the awesome fierce beast away with several laser volleys from my handy ray gun.

I next encountered a giant hungry anaconda-like snake and honoring my need for self-preservation, I deftly escaped its imminent danger by adroitly speeding away in my swift reliable contraption. But then a seven-foot-tall squirrel accompanied by a ten-foot-high rat accosted me and in a flash, I shot at and chased away both apparent existential threats during the height of the emergency.

Soon a bizarre idea registered inside my addled brain. 'Parker said that he had witnessed a huge frog eating a very large insect,' I neurotically recalled. 'Perhaps he wasn't lying or hallucinating after all! Or maybe he was simply fabricating a tall tale to conceal his guilt for having an adulterous affair with Carol? There must be some lucid logical explanation to account for all of these abnormal crazy things that are occurring on this hellish planet! What is causing these very disturbing evil aberrations to happen?'

When I eventually returned the vehicle to the Newton III, I raised the segmented entrance ramp and next systematically closed and locked all exit portals. I was happy to note that the ship was still there at the landing site and that it had not somehow been stolen or damaged, but when I curiously looked inside Captain Parker's white linen collection sack, it was totally empty and much to my amazement, no glittering gold nuggets were hidden inside.

* * * * * * * * * * * *

As I impatiently sit here in the Commander's Chair ready to take off from EL-741 in always reliable Newton III, I am pensively reflecting on what exactly had provoked me to act like a savage felon and callously and maliciously murder Captain Jeremy Parker.

My co-pilot had eaten the apple and the red berries and I had consumed the apple and three peaches and had avoided sampling the berries. These relevant factors should be germane for me to better comprehend the true moral dimension of the Evil Force that capriciously governs the myriad strange events transpiring here on EL-741.'Possibly the purple apples eaten by Jeremy and me had caused *us* to independently hallucinate or imagine certain surreal fantasies,' I conjectured.

'Either the purple apple or the lavender peaches caused me to see certain illusions and delusions,' I keenly realized and hypothesized. 'The peaches were more of a hallucinogenic drug than were the purple apples and the red berries. And Parker had tasted the purple apple and the red berries while I had eaten one apple and three peaches. Therefore,' I pondered, 'I had imagined that the incidents I had witnessed involving Jeremy and the gold nuggets at the stream, his affair with Carol along with his scrutiny of my wallet in our ship's bed chamber all were illusions generated as a result of the effect of the combination peaches and apples I had digested. Parker only ate the single apple and a few berries, so *that* action caused him to envision *one* mammoth frog feasting on an oversized bug.'

I next theorized that a chemical synthesis of the ingredients that constituted the peaches and the apple had influenced me to behave like an evil person temporarily possessing a criminal mindset. Somehow the accidental chemical compound mixture in my body had a similar effect to that of the Lotus Plants in Odysseus's extraordinary adventure in the Land of the Lotus Eaters where *his* recalcitrant crew ate of the potent flowers and soon refused to obey their king's incessant commands to leave the idyllic paradise. Because of *this* noteworthy analogy between my zany adventure on this evil planet and the weird Lotus Flower episode described in Homer's *Odyssey*, I have decided to rename EL-741 'Lotus 1.'

'Those golden nuggets, along with the deceitful love affair and also the oversized lion, the immense squirrel and the huge snake were all distracting illusions that my fertile mind had projected into my physical surroundings,' I considered. 'This postulation of mine must be true because the Evil Force on this planet does not know that a lion is many times the size of a squirrel and that a frog is not the same size as a human being. That formerly perverted scenario that I had imagined all makes perfect sense now,' I finally comprehended. 'But the stark reality is that I have murdered Jeremy and now my conscience deeply regrets my grotesque and misguided misdeed. His death was no mental manifestation! It was truly real! I am now a bona fide wanton criminal all because I could not readily distinguish Lotus I fantasy from Lotus I reality.'

After I had started the atomic thrust engines and lifted off the remarkable planet's surface, according to my ship's compass and gyroscope, my course was heading due west. My sensitive pupils then observed a squadron of UFOs flying and then hovering over a gleaming city having enormous skyscrapers and spectacular obelisks along with stunning round and pyramid-shaped majestic edifices. Also quite conspicuous were a plethora of lustrous mass transportation tubes connecting the various outstanding vertical glistening structures.

'My scanners have determined and verified that those distant objects do not in reality exist!' I perceptively realized. 'The vivid visions are only products of my active subconscious imagination being diabolically projected into that distant fantasy environment, all somehow caused (I believe) by the tempting fruit, or fruit combinations that I had eaten on Captain Parker's EL-741. Naturally I'll have to mimic what most dishonest businessmen do when they keep two sets of books: one for the government agents' scrutiny and the other documentation exclusively for themselves. There's no way that this visual rendition that I'm presently observing is going to be entered into the ship's official log. In my own defense, the aberrant and outlandish story of the Evil Force that exists on 'Planet Lotus I' will forever remain a closely guarded secret solely preserved in my personal journal.

As the mythical Satan is my witness, according to *this* Devil's Advocate, Captain Jeremy Parker had died from a lethal unknown virus on Planet Lotus I and out of traditional human sympathy and my' sense of duty, I had respectfully buried his remains somewhere on the alien planet.

"Rapid Crystals"

Harry DeLareto sat erect upon his black leather swivel chair behind his desk in his walnut-paneled Elwood, New Jersey insurance office. The broker was preoccupied making a ten percent depreciation adjustment to the 'inflated claim' submitted by the Nesco Volunteer Fire Department that had recently and ironically burned to the ground in a raging inferno.

On Harry's desk were random additional claims from Mrs. Rhonda Leonetti of Atsion, who had just been involved in an automobile accident, Arthur Noto of Hamilton Township, who had recently collided his motorboat with a Mullica River marina dock and another one from Jennifer Friel, a Sweetwater resident who had experienced severe flooding into her house when the normally tranquil Mullica River had overflowed its banks during a torrential three-day downpour. As DeLareto was fumbling through the assorted bureaucratic paperwork that was frustrating his mental health, the gentleman's very capable secretary Nancy Davenport suddenly buzzed his desk from the adjoining room.

"Harry, Mr. And Mrs. David DeLaurentis had to cancel this afternoon's appointment because their son Alfred has crashed his motorbike into a barn on a blueberry farmer's property over in Hammonton and they're now at AtlanticCare Hospital in Pomona. The boy's all right but that'll definitely be another injury insurance claim appearing on your desk within the next few weeks," Mrs. Davenport advised her employer. "If you have no objections, I've already conveniently rescheduled them for next Friday at 2 p.m. The afternoon time slot happened to be available on your calendar's weekly planner."

"That's fine with me Nancy as long as there aren't any time conflicts," Harry replied into his desk speaker. "But right now I'm overwhelmed with a deluge of claims we're having so I've decided to take the rest of the afternoon off since as you've just mentioned, the DeLaurentis appointment has been postponed. My wife misses her old police and rescue scanner that she had kept for years on *her* kitchen counter and she has discovered it laying in our cellar storage area during her annual spring housecleaning."

"Yes, Sylvia's a fanatic when it comes to certain things. Does the device still work?" the friendly secretary curiously asked. "My husband and I listen to ours all the time. We get to know what's happening all over Mullica Township and vicinity and it keeps us informed about burglaries and house fires."

"Yes but if I recollect, only two of the eight crystals in our set are still functional," Mrs. Davenport's encumbered boss related. "In fact I have the scanner in the trunk of my car so I think I'll take a drive over to the Berlin Farmers Market. There's an electronics store just inside the main entrance that might just have updated replacement crystals for the eight channels on the scanner. It's worth a shot in the dark, anyway!"

"Okay Harry, it sure beats hanging-out at that raucous Pic-A-Lilli Inn over in the pine-barrens on Route 206! I'll lock-up the office at five for you," the faithful and trustworthy secretary assured her appreciative employer. "Good luck on making your important crystal acquisitions. The new digital scanners cost around two hundred bucks; at least that's what mine did!"

Harry drove the twenty miles west from his rustic Elwood insurance office to the bustling Berlin Farmers Market in less than a half hour. Ten minutes later the man was engaged in a congenial conversation with Mr. Phil Curreri, the affable proprietor of Modern Digital Communications.

"What have you got here?" the storeowner wanted to know as he carefully examined the ancient electronic scanner handed to him by Harry. "This relic looks like it belongs in the Smithsonian Institute or the Ford Museum. Pardon my amusement, but I haven't seen one of these rare babies since the 1970s. It's an Allied Patrolman Pro-7 VHF Scanner Receiver that you've brought in here. Ya' know," the merchant prattled, "these types of volume and squelch dials have been obsolete for a couple of decades now. Everything today from cell phones, to Blackberry handheld computer devices to standard police scanners happens to be digital! Was this machine given to you by the stars on *Bonanza*?"

"Well Sir, I hope I'm not wasting your valuable time," Harry politely answered after clearing his voice box out of sheer embarrassment. "Six of the crystals don't work at all and I'd like to replace all eight of them. Do you have any suitable crystals in stock you can sell me?"

"Where do you live?" Phil Curreri questioned his prospective customer. "I might be able to assist you."

"In Elwood, over in Atlantic County between Hammonton and Egg Harbor City," DeLareto informed the very accommodating store proprietor. "If possible, I'd like to get the essential fire department and rescue squad transmissions that are geared to my residential zone. My wife's very fond of this particular relic and confidentially she would like to see it working again. I always try to keep the Mrs. happy, ya' know."

"I'll see what I can do for you," the businessman assured his potential patron. "Just browse around the shop while I perform some basic inventory research."

Harry casually sauntered around the attractive store nonchalantly looking at various cell phones, cameras and electronics' merchandise exhibited inside old glass display showcases. Five minutes later Mr. Phil Curreri exited his cluttered stockroom with eight shiny crystals held in his right palm that he testified would definitely work in the antiquated scanner that Harry had brought into *his* electronics' establishment.

"Let's see now, we have one for the Hammonton Fire Department and Rescue Squad, one for Egg Harbor City, one for Mays Landing and one for the Folsom State Police Barracks," Mr. Curreri merrily articulated. "And here's one for the Hammonton Police, one for Mullica Township Police and one for the Egg Harbor Police Department. Now to fill out the entire eight slot channels, here's one crystal that's not been labeled. It might be for the Atlantic City Police or maybe perhaps it's tuned-in to the Camden cops. I really can't clearly identify it, but not to sound too cynical or sarcastic," the store owner awkwardly continued his explanation, "it'll give you another workable channel to listen to when things get too drab and monotonous in your rather dull existence over there in Metropolitan Downtown Elwood!"

The impressed and optimistic customer insisted that the eight already described crystals be inserted into the unit to ascertain that the archaic scanner was indeed operational. Upon hearing the Hammonton and Egg Harbor City dispatchers' voices and their associated instructions being conveyed to fire personnel and municipal police patrols, Harry was elated and satisfied with the very evident successful results. In fact it was fairly difficult for the fellow to control his gushing euphoria.

"How much for the eight crystals?" the customer anxiously inquired. "Please give me a good decent price so that I don't have to negotiate, haggle or dicker."

"What about fifty dollars for all eight, which would also include my three-minute crystal installation fee?" the proprietor offered. "That modest price would include the sales tax of course!"

"It's a deal!" the insurance broker readily and enthusiastically agreed, extending his right arm for a firm handshake. "You've saved me a ton-load of grief this dreary Friday afternoon! If my wife Sylvia's happy, then naturally *that* scenario makes me perfectly contented too!"

On the Route 30 drive from Berlin east to Elwood Harry cheerfully listened to the song 'Da Doo Ron Ron' by the Crystals on a popular Philadelphia FM oldies radio station. The tune's stimulating upbeat rhythm put the driver in a most favorable mood and Harry DeLareto imaginatively interpreted the cute coincidence of the female recording group's name and of his recent Modern Digital Communications purchase to be a very good and propitious omen.

* * * * * * * * * * * * *

Sylvia was thrilled that Harry had gotten the eight replacement crystals for the police scanner and her husband excitedly plugged in the device, which worked like new that Friday evening. Saturday the couple spent the late morning visiting their son Jake, a scholarly freshman at Rutgers University, New Brunswick and the close-knit family enjoyed the afternoon and a late dinner at a crowded Charlie Brown Restaurant

The DeLaretos didn't arrive back home to Elwood until eleven that night so Harry and Sylvia, suffering from mild exhaustion, didn't turn on their refurbished scanning device, electing to retire to bed and spending a half hour watching the eleven o'clock news before shutting off the tabletop television and going to sleep.

The couple spent Sunday morning attending church services in Hammonton and then having breakfast at Mary's Restaurant, which was situated directly across the highway from *their* parish, St. Anthony of Padua Catholic Church on Route 206. The afternoon hours had Harry and Sylvia strolling the newly renovated Hamilton Mall where on impulse the wife purchased a dress and an umbrella; and then later Sunday evening the pair partook of some adult entertainment by gambling at the blackjack tables and playing the nickel slot machines at Harrah's Casino in Atlantic City where the frugal DeLaretos had booked a complimentary room the week before and then stayed at the popular gaming resort overnight.

When Harry returned home from his insurance office late Monday afternoon, Sylvia had a strange look of consternation on her face. Showing genuine concern, the sensitive husband first consoled his wife with an embrace and then was very diplomatic in his verbal approach and subsequent inquiry.

"What's wrong Honey?" DeLareto sympathetically asked. "Are you upset that we lost a couple hundred bucks at the casino last night? Please don't worry about that trifle! It wasn't any tremendous loss to be concerned about!"

"No Harry," Sylvia nervously returned. "It's the police scanner that's gotten me all upset. The first seven channels work really well and I heard all about a minor traffic accident on Route 30 in Hammonton, several ambulance emergency calls and four police patrol transmissions in Hamilton Township along with a false fire alarm that had been reported over on Philadelphia Avenue in Egg Harbor."

"Well, I imagine that the voice jargon is still basically the same," the husband supportively comforted in a bland-sounding voice. "Stuff like where's your twenty means 'give me your location' and 'ten-four' probably still means something akin to 'okay, over.' What's so darn unique and special about Crystal Number Eight? That mysterious one happens to be an extra bonus that the guy at the electronics store had added in to close the deal."

"Harry, I was listening to the scanner around noon and on Channel Number Eight two men were wildly arguing," the very concerned wife related. "The first man was loudly accusing the second guy about making amorous advances towards *his* wife and he threatened to injure the second fellow if he ever tried flirting with her again. It was like a melodramatic afternoon TV soap opera scene and I felt as if I had been guiltily eavesdropping on a private conversation."

"Let's see if something similar happens tonight on Channel Eight," Harry constructively suggested. "I'm pretty intrigued myself now too. Your story has really piqued my curiosity. If your description is correct, my theory is that Channel Eight somehow picks up random cell phone conversations and then makes them public and accessible to our refitted police scanner. We'll wait and see what happens with the refurbished scanner tonight."

Around seven that evening enigmatic Channel Eight transmitted a vociferous cell phone exchange between a boisterous man and an infuriated woman. The incensed female accused the self-indulgent man of philandering and not paying his numerous debts and the livid husband acknowledged that he was in the process of filing for bankruptcy while the wife was intermittently screaming that she would soon be filing for permanent divorce. It was a very tempestuous and heated conversation that eventually made Harry raise his eyebrows and compelled Sylvia to cover her offended ears.

"Do you see what I mean about that oddball scanner?" the wife emotionally stated. "That weird Eighth Crystal must be removed and destroyed. It's sort of like an unauthorized wiretap that's randomly intercepting personal conversations that are not intended for public audience."

"Sylvia, I recognized the man's voice in that nasty dialogue we just heard," the husband almost apologetically revealed. "It belonged to Mr. Peterson, a struggling merchant who owns a hardware store over in Mays Landing. I had just purchased several gallons of exterior house paint from his place of business last week. Apparently his marital life is on the skids," Harry surmised and stated to his still shocked wife. "I know from local barber shop gossip that Peterson spends a lot of time gambling at boardwalk casinos and at Monmouth Race Track and that both he and his wife are chronic alcoholics. One glaring truth in this matter cannot be denied," the husband continued his revelation. "Things are not always quite as pleasant as they appear on the surface when it comes to certain marriage relationships."

"I still don't like Crystal Number Eight and I recommend that you remove it right away," the wife adamantly insisted. "Call it woman's intuition if you'd like, but I have a serious aversion about that unethical receptor. It's a definite intruder into other people's lives. It's almost evil!"

"I promise that I'll take the Eighth Crystal out of the police scanner tomorrow morning," Harry pledged, raising his right hand as if taking a solemn oath in a courtroom. "Now just remain calm and patient. Let's see if any other interesting discussions will occur. You gotta' admit Honey, Channel Eight is comparable to being a local gossip page gazette!"

Twenty minute later Channel Eight picked-up a frantic cell phone dialogue whereby a distraught high school girl informed her stunned boyfriend that she had become pregnant and that she wanted him to pay for an abortion immediately. Wanting to keep the newfound knowledge confidential, the suddenly distressed boyfriend agreed to the crying girl's impetuous proposal and stated that he would pay for half of the clinical procedure as long as their parents never learned about their mutually unsavory situation.

"That scanner device is positively abominable!" Sylvia yelled at her now-fascinated spouse. "We should not be privy to such disturbing private matters, even if the upset girl had been

220

consoled. Who knows what that wicked scanner is going to divulge to us next? A murder plot?"

"I recognized that girl's voice we had just heard. It belongs to Gene and Phyllis Riley's daughter over in Devonshire," Harry reluctantly declared. "The girl's name is Carolyn and she was involved in a small fender-bender over on the White Horse Pike in Hammonton just last month. Her parents had her sitting in my office just last week to review the settlement of the insurance claim on her mother's compact car."

"But having an abortion without their parents' knowledge or consent is far different than having a trivial Route 30 auto' mishap," the shaken wife countered. "Harry, that Channel Eight frequency is borderline Satanic! I demand that you dispose of it right this second! It can only bring more harm than good!"

"First thing tomorrow morning," the husband conceded and responded, shrugging his broad shoulders. "Here's my opinion on the matter Sylvia. If I listen to the scanner all night I believe I'll have accumulated enough juicy material to be able to author a decent best-selling novel."

A half hour later the re-activated police scanner conveyed a very private verbal exchange involving a local man and woman planning a secret extra-marital love rendezvous at the Hammonton Motor Lodge. Sylvia instantly recognized that one of the voices belonged to her close friend Dorothy Bronson of Vine Street in downtown Hammonton and from evaluating the extremely intimate dialogue, it was easily determined that the male voice belonged to a prominent minister who was the pastor of a familiar church with a large congregation on Bellevue Avenue in the same community.

"Yes, you're absolutely right Sylvia," Harry confirmed. "Your friend Dottie has a splendid alto singing voice and she's the soloist in *that* church choir. And that obnoxious sanctimonious preacher is a totally hypocritical fraud! What ever happened to moral authority where the devout minister piously leads his flock by setting a fine example?" DeLareto rhetorically asked. "You must admit that this disgusting reverend's immoral behavior is horribly irreverent! He's guilty of being a devious creep! And your friend Dottie," Harry concluded and alleged, "well she's nothing more than a modern-day Jezebel, a cheap harlot!"

"Harry, I insist that you either unplug the police scanner and put it back in the cellar or remove the Channel Eight Crystal and toss it into the garbage container underneath the kitchen sink," the mentally disheveled wife hollered, almost sobbing. "Don't you understand? We're hearing personal confidential private information from people that we happen to know and it's not intended for our ears."

The next Channel Eight transmission captured two female teachers that were employed at a nearby public high school. Unaware of any eavesdropping, the pair was discussing their steamy bisexual love relationship separate and apart from their husbands' knowledge. The voices belonged to Shirley Burgess and Darla Swift, former senior year classroom teachers of Jake DeLareto.

"This entire complicated mess is wholly deplorable!" normally serene and passive Sylvia bellowed as she slowly wept. "Harry, this baneful scanner is an instrument of the Devil. It can only bring malicious disgrace for others and also detrimental problems into *our* lives now that we're learning all of these terrible personal secrets. I strongly urge you now, take the scanner into the garage and crush it with your sledgehammer!"

"Who would ever suspect that those two reputable high school instructors were practicing bisexuals having a sultry lesbian extra-marital love affair?" Harry replied with his left hand vigorously scratching his head in disbelief. "I mean Dear, in my mind a person is either a homosexual or they're straight! There's none of this lousy in between stuff going on!"

"And I always thought that Mrs. Burgess and Mrs. Swift were excellent classroom teachers, each possessing outstanding character!" the wife added before wiping her eyes with a handkerchief. "They've both gotten Teacher of the Year awards. I've seen their photos' last June in the Press of Atlantic City and also in the two local newspapers."

"And Mrs. Burgess is married to a no-nonsense police chief rumored to have a terrible jealous and spiteful disposition!" DeLareto commented to his already appalled and rattled wife. "Yes Honey, if the Chief ever found out about his wife's odd and morally unacceptable infidelity, knowing his personality, he'd do something drastic about the scandal! That guy has a notorious volatile temper when he goes off the deep end!"

"Please Harry! I beg you! Throw out that despicable Crystal Number Eight before it causes serious trouble! I think it's more dangerous than the proverbial Tree of Knowledge that's described in the Book of Genesis. I don't like making innuendoes or hurtful accusations! But I don't want us having any outside conflict by either you or me accidentally slandering anyone's name!"

"Sylvia, I just want to hear and savor one more cell phone transmission!" Harry implored his mate. "Then I pledge that I'll remove the diabolical Eighth Crystal and get rid of its tempting functionality once and for all. But just to be on the safe side of truth," the husband stipulated, "I'm going to tape record the final cell phone transmission and immediately erase it if it's simply a mediocre frivolous personal conversation!"

At nine-fifteen the police scanner's Crystal Eight intercepted an extraordinary cell phone dialogue, which Harry instantly recorded on tape. The unique oral language exchange was between two chatty Arab high school students.

"Abdul, have you finished the part about blowing up the school gym," the first Muslim teenager inquired. "Don't forget the bombs in the auditorium and also in the library too!"

"Yes Saddam," the second juvenile answered. "And are you working or the cafeteria horror devastation enactment? Hand grenades and AK-47s along with rocket-propelled grenades would have the best graphic impact. Kids and faculty members that luckily survive the loud lethal blasts will be gunned down by terrorists with machine guns waiting in the high school's exit corridors."

"Great idea Abdul!" Saddam complimented and acknowledged. "This fantastic massacre will make Columbine High School look like a mere grade school picnic! Soon the clever jihad will be completed. See you tomorrow morning in homeroom and we'll discuss any additional details that need to be included."

"Okay Saddam," Abdul verified. "I'll see your ugly face tomorrow morning in homeroom!"

Harry and Sylvia sat in their den with their mouths agape. Then the introspective insurance broker remembered that their son Jake had often mentioned the two new Arab kids that were now juniors at the local high school so the father gave his pride and joy a 'surprise phone call' to the Rutgers freshman's dorm room.

"Jake, do you remember the full names of the two Arab boys that enrolled in the high school last year? I think they'd be juniors now and ready to graduate next year. Your mother and I couldn't remember their names."

"They are Abdul al Jameel and Saddam Kareem Habash," Jake lethargically answered. "Pop, I thought you were calling to tell me that you're gonna' buy me a car for my sophomore year. I'll be able to live off campus and could use a decent set of wheels to impress the Douglass campus chicks up here."

"Okay Jake, I'll discuss the issue with your mother and we'll see what we can work out for you over the summer months!" the father diplomatically responded. "Good luck on your two new courses! Take care now Son!" Click.

"Harry, what are you going to do with that tape recording you've just made?" Sylvia asked in a very alarmed tone of voice. "Are you planning to take the tape over to the Atlantic County Sheriff's Office?"

"No Sylvia. This is a definite terrorist conspiracy in progress and one of those Arab boys lives only a block away from my brother Ted on Cypress Lane. Yes, I'm first taking the tape over to the local police chief and get his professional opinion about its content," the husband nervously answered, his forehead breaking out in a sweat despite the den's effective air-conditioning. "And don't worry Sylvia! I'm not going to mention a syllable about the police chief's wife having a licentious lesbian love affair outside the sacred institution of Holy Matrimony!"

* * * * * * * * * * * * *

A week later Chief George Burgess summoned Mr. And Mrs. Harry DeLareto into his police headquarters' office to review certain aspects of the department's investigation into a possible terror plot involving suspected radicalized Arab students at the local high school. The Chief's attitude and general demeanor seemed to be austere and businesslike.

"Well Folks, you seem to have stirred up a bees' nest controversy of sorts at the high school," Chief Burgess began his dissertation. "Even the school board has gotten involved. First of all, did you follow my instructions and bring along that police radio scanner's Eighth Crystal that has apparently generated all of the current hullabaloo?"

"Yes, here it is!" Harry softly replied, handing the shiny object to the police authority. "But the conversation and all of the plotting between the two Arab boys that my wife and I had heard was captured on the tape recorder. You have the smoking-gun evidence in your possession."

"That it was, or at least seemed to be!" the Chief agreed and qualified. "But I wish you'd leave the gumshoe detective work to the police department and not go free-lancing and pretending to be Dick Tracy or Sherlock Holmes on your own. Are you sure that you hadn't heard any other cell phone transmissions besides the one between young Abdul and this Saddam kid?"

"Well Chief, Sylvia here had heard one other chat before I had arrived home," Harry awkwardly fibbed, "so then I figured I'd try an experiment and see if I could tape a cell phone conversation just for verification purposes. But in the final analysis, it seems that I had obtained much more than I had bargained for!"

"Well Mr. DeLareto," the Chief firmly said, "when a private citizen tapes another private citizen's cell phone conversation without the second party's approval or permission, then that deed could technically be construed as a violation of federal law. But don't panic because I'm not going to get the county district attorney's office or a federal prosecutor on your case to pursue any felony charges against either you or your wife. I'd prefer to have a peaceful solution if it's at all possible!"

"Why thank you Chief Burgess!" Harry commented, then taking a very deep breath. "Now please explain what the Arab kids were doing by talking about a terror act that they were scheming to commit."

Chief Burgess calmly explained that Abdul al Jameel and Saddam Kareem Habash were writing a fictional contemporary play for their English teacher Mrs. Darla Swift over at the regional high school. The 'terror play' was to be entitled "American Home-Grown Jihad," and the school principal had been caught between a rock and a hard place over the First Amendment rights of the Arab students and the high school's 'zero tolerance policy' in regard to students' allusions and references to acts of terror, especially those exhibited as graffiti on school corridor walls or visible as incendiary emblems and insignias or students' tee-shirts, jackets and coats.

"Mrs. Swift teaches on the same faculty as my wife Shirley does," Chief Burgess stated. "And as you can now plainly see," the high-ranking law-enforcement official solemnly revealed, "Abdul and Saddam were only collaborating on a school assignment project, but even ultra-liberal Mrs. Swift felt uncomfortable about their academic jihad play proposal. She did eventually get the support of the school administration and superintendent, and as a result the short two-actor play will be performed fourth period in her senior English classroom next week."

"Sometimes things don't turn out to be as they appear on the surface," Harry remorsefully confessed in a phlegmatic and lugubrious tone of voice. "Chief Burgess, I'm sorry that I've caused you so much duress and I feel really bad about making the false allegations against the two Arab-American boys."

225

"Well now, their sensitive old-tradition parents were extremely upset about these bizarre circumstances and have threatened to press charges against you for bearing false witness against their sons but I think I've adequately smoothed things over if it's all right with you Mr. DeLareto."

"And what do I have to do to make amends without having to hire a defense attorney and then appear in court and suffer a burdensome load of ugly newspaper and television news publicity!" Harry wondered and asked. "What a dreadful prospective nightmare *that* humiliation would be!"

"First Mr. DeLareto, write two letters of apology, addressing one each to Abdul and Saddam. Then next, simply go to Joe Italiano's Maplewood Italian Restaurant on the White Horse Pike in Hammonton and purchase two one hundred dollar meal certificates, one for each of the boys' families," Chief Burgess confidentially directed. "The two kids and their parents absolutely love Italian cuisine, especially spaghetti and meatballs! Finally Mr. DeLareto, deliver the two letters and the pair of hundred dollar Maplewood food certificates to my office no later than next Tuesday! Then leave the rest to me!"

"Wow Chief! Thanks for getting me out of a vat of hot boiling water!" Harry gratefully exclaimed. "I really feel relieved. My wife and I are very indebted to you for your assistance and cooperation."

"And one final thing Mr. DeLareto!" Chief Burgess remarked with a feigned dour expression evident on his countenance. "It's a good thing you never recorded any of my family's cell phone conversations while using your police scanner's magical Eighth Crystal!"

"Dream-On"

.

Hammonton, New Jersey resident Samuel Charles Dexter was both depressed and despondent. His recent divorce from his ultra-dominant wife Sharon left the man's mind in an emotional state of shambles. Sam's friends at the Vineland, New Jersey plastics manufacturing company where Dexter was employed as an accountant suggested that the numbers guru should seek professional therapy counseling. One of his fellow co-workers had highly recommended Dr. Adam Neville, a reputable psychiatrist whose practice was at the corner of Landis Avenue and Third Street in downtown Vineland. Samuel Charles Dexter honored his June 7th, 2010 "get acquainted appointment" and was cheerfully escorted into Dr. Neville's office by Miss Emily Jensen, the psychiatrist's secretary and bookkeeper.

"Mr. Dexter, you say in your letter of introduction you've been having peculiar dreams lately that seem to be compounding your mercurial emotional instability," Dr. Adam Neville diplomatically commenced his narrative. "And your well-documented medical records that have been forwarded to me indicate that you tend to be an introvert, that you don't mingle and socialize with others too well, that you have a noteworthy gift for organizing and manipulating numbers, that you have an aggressive Alpha-type personality when threatened or challenged, that you love popular music and that you tend to be a melancholy loner who frequently feels isolated from mainstream society. I suppose that you attribute your overall alienation to your recent divorce."

"That's correct," Sam candidly told Dr. Neville. "Oftentimes I feel jittery and nervous. I've even suffered several anxiety attacks, but fortunately, the terrible onslaughts were at home in Hammonton and not at my workplace in Vineland."

"I see!" Dr. Neville perceptively answered as he quickly jotted down some relevant notes about his initial interview with his new patient. "I believe I can help you Mr. Dexter but your meticulous psychological treatment will require at least one full year to complete. My very competent secretary Miss Jensen has already checked with your insurance company and I'm pleased to inform you that your visits will be totally covered. I'll convincingly report to your employers that you're undergoing light hypnosis to help you deal more satisfactorily with middle age adjustment along with the gradual therapy promoting your general relaxation. Don't fret one iota Mr. Dexter!" Dr. Neville routinely explained. "I'm not going to divulge to your company's management team the exact specifics of our confidential relationship or the precise nature of your mental health *problems,* or for that matter, your 'personal *issues'* as we now like to call them. Is that clear?"

"I appreciate your skilled handling of my rather bothersome condition," Sam replied with a weak smile. "You appear to be very adequately experienced at dealing with corporations and with insurance companies' red tape."

"That particular expertise comes with the territory. Now then, we'll begin your comprehensive treatment sessions starting next Monday at 7 p.m. and we'll continue our remediation program every Monday thereafter for a full year," Dr. Neville related to his new patient. "And Mr. Dexter, I want to again emphasize that our relationship is strictly professional and confidential. Please don't discuss any details of our dialogues with anyone else! I believe strongly in the 'doctor-patient privilege'."

"Don't worry Dr. Neville!" Sam sincerely declared. "I'm an introvert, remember? I seldom talk with anyone either at home or at work. Even my mother still thinks I'm shy!"

"That's quite fine and perfectly acceptable!" Dr. Adam Neville replied with a forced smile. "Your records from your regular physician show that you have a tendency to feel lethargic. Oftentimes emotional stress can sap a person's energy and enthusiasm, making *that* individual virtually phlegmatic. Now Mr. Dexter, I'm going to briefly put you under hypnosis for just one hour to measure and study some of your vital subconscious responses. This initial step is very important for me to better understand your underlying subconscious motivations."

"Okay Dr. Neville," Sam Dexter readily agreed. "Let's get started on guiding me back onto the road to recovery."

Session 2

On Monday June 14th, 2010 Sam Dexter honored his scheduled appointment with Dr. Adam Neville and at 7:10 the troubled accountant was lying prone on the psychiatrist's black leather couch and the patient's mind was already in a hypnotic state.

"Now Sam, just relax and tell me about your latest dream," the veteran examiner instructed. "Has it been a vivid one?"

"Why yes!" Dexter answered from his subconscious trance. "Every night this past week I've had the same redundant dream, or perhaps it could be better described as a nasty redundant nightmare. I dreamed that I had been trapped all alone in this truly gigantic department store that had three floors connected by escalators and elevators, and each floor never ended. Each department store level was infinite! I roamed, searched and wandered around from department area to department area but there were no exits to any outside or external mall area, no overhead skylights showing a blue sky or even night stars, and also there were no doors or windows to escape my overall entrapment. I felt totally powerless and needless to say, very apprehensive even though the enormous store was illuminated by translucent ceiling light panels. The entire experience was surreal to say the least."

"Did the store in which you were lost have any brand name like Macy's, Penney's or Nordstrom?" Dr. Neville curiously asked.

"No Dr. It was just a colossal-sized endless department store having tremendously stocked areas!"

"Was there any voice over the intercom directing shoppers to various locations or sections where bargain sales or discounts were going on?" Dr. Neville asked.

"No, in fact there weren't any other shoppers walking around inside the gargantuan department store nor were there any other customers randomly browsing about the various inventories besides myself'," Sam described his imagined-but-troubling emotional dilemma. "And no announcer's voice was ever heard discussing sales or giving directions to non-existent store personnel. But there definitely was background sound. Yes, now I remember. Music was being played over the sound system; yes, the same song repeated over and over again, 'Dream-On' by Aerosmith."

Sam Dexter then went on a lengthy Homeric-type catalogue of all of the departments that he frantically rushed through trying to find an avenue of escape from his illusionary mammoth store's captivity. His frenetic pursuit of freedom had the delirious hostage rushing around like a maniac on all three endless floors, his circuitous odyssey taking him through Men's Clothing, Women's Apparel, Children's Attire, Handbags and Accessories, Jewelry and Watches, Sporting Goods, Shoes Department, Lingerie and Nightgowns, Perfumes and Cologne, Furniture and Beds, Kitchen Appliances, Dishes and China, Bed and Bath, Wallets, Belts and

Men's Gifts, Towels and Washcloths, Electronics and TVs, Cameras and Photography, Toys and Games, Linens, Cosmetics and Lipstick, Luggage and then into Stationery Goods."

"Sam, calm down for a moment," Dr. Neville soothingly instructed. "You're working yourself up into a sweat. But I do find your general depiction to be most fascinating. Take ten deep breaths and then resume your most interesting story."

After honoring Dr. Neville's direction, the patient continued with his recollection. "Well, the monotonous and annoying Aerosmith song 'Dream-On' was constantly playing in the background as I desperately dashed from department to department in a wild frenzy," Dexter revealed to the very intrigued mind doctor. "It was an absolutely horrendous recurrent marathon nightmare as I visited each department on all three floors at least three consecutive times! Then I finally arrived at the thrice visited Hardware area, picked-up a large tool and immediately started smashing the cinderblock walls with the heavy sledgehammer I had discovered."

"Did you manage to shatter the wall?" Dr. Neville wanted to learn. "Did your great effort yield any tangible results?"

"No, the wall was impenetrable and the repetitious Aerosmith song was making me both mentally crazy and physically exhausted as I futilely hammered away in total frustration. And when I eventually collapsed from fatigue onto the fantasy store's tiled floor," Sam proceeded to communicate, "in reality, I had actually fallen out of my bed and then groggily woke-up upon impacting the bedroom floor."

With the patient then being gently guided out of his subconscious state, the knowledgeable psychiatrist next rendered to bewildered Sam Dexter his initial evaluation about the man's emotional condition and postulated *his* theories about its root causes.

"Mr. Dexter, my interpretation of your fantastic department store dream is that you were lost and helpless among all of the myriad merchandise in your imagined environment simply because you probably felt a degree guilty about being a loner and also you probably feel somewhat guilty about being too materialistic," Dr. Neville hypothesized and related. "Sigmund Freud has proven that subconscious human guilt is often responsible for overt external behavior. As you might know, man's mind is like an iceberg, one sixth above the surface, which represents the conscious mind, and the other five-sixths below the surface, which obviously signifies the subconscious mind," the

230

Ph.D. psychiatrist lectured. "This of course is only a preliminary conclusion and it might in actuality be too premature for me to state it definitively, but I conjecture that you're possibly feeling a burden of self-shame because you've deceived yourself into thinking that you're fundamentally selfish and possessive; hence, you've defensively isolated yourself from mainstream American civilization. I believe that your very graphic department store dream is a creative manifestation of your accumulated subconscious guilt."

"What do you recommend I do Dr.?" Sam asked. "Is there any hope? Is my condition treatable?"

"Like I said, it's really too early for me to give you any thorough or comprehensive professional advice," Dr. Neville evasively stipulated, "but you might want to search for and acquire a spiritual identity; not necessarily a religious orientation Mr. Dexter, but I'm referring to a spiritual identity that affords you an element of joy and satisfaction nonetheless! Better self-esteem will eventually lead to a higher self-confidence level."

"Thanks Dr. Neville," the impressed patient gratefully acknowledged. " I like your style and your disposition. I'll see you next Monday evening at 7 sharp."

Session 3

After Sam Dexter arrived at Dr. Adam Neville's modern-looking Landis Avenue office on June 21st the cooperative patient was again promptly hypnotized by the psychiatrist, who had effectively used a large watch dangling and swinging from a gold fob chain. Dr. Neville was enthused to learn that Samuel Dexter had been having a rather different nightly dream that did not relate in any way, shape or form to any immense and super-capacious department store setting.

"Sam, tell me about your marvelous dreams this past week," the curious interrogator suavely asked. "I know you have plenty to share. Were your dreams exotic? Were they drab? Were they the same repeated dream each and every night?"

"I have dreamed the same thing or theme every single night," Dexter muttered and disclosed. "This might sound ridiculous or absurd but I dreamed that I was the only male on a hot desert island beach and I had been wildly chased through the surf by a thousand or so beautiful native women. But ironically," the subject clarified, "some of the alluring dolls on that anonymous tropical isle were brunettes, some were blondes and some were

231

redheads. But none of the girls were naked. All of the gorgeous ladies were wearing similar red bikinis."

"Did they pursue you through any giant department store on that remote desert island?" Dr. Neville asked his restive subject lying horizontally on the black leather couch. "Forgive my direct questioning Sam, but for verification purposes I'm just trying to connect a few dots and I need some additional information."

"No, there wasn't any department store on that remote island; just some sex-starved really aggressive beautiful girls, all of whom had definitely gone through puberty."

"Did you hear any music in the background when you were being intensely chased?"

"Yes, come to mention it, the Aerosmith rock and roll song 'Dream-On' was perpetually being played over and over, which of course tended to make me very anxious!"

"This is all very fine and understandable so there's no need to be alarmed by a simple fantasy phobia," Dr. Neville communicated to his mildly agitated but still hypnotized patient. "You have a good separation of spatial fantasy because you were on a remote island and not lost inside a colossal-sized department store surrounding. And you seem inspired to be running away from any lengthy relationship with a woman, but as I see and interpret your complex emotional needs, despite your major adversity known as bashfulness, in the end you still desire being pursued and found to be attractive and interesting to the opposite sex."

An hour later Sam had been skillfully shifted out of his trance-like state and brought back to full consciousness. The doctor and the patient then engaged in several minutes of meaningful conversation.

"Sam, I believe that your subconscious mind has constructed a parallel fantasy to correspond with the fears and anxieties of your conscious brain, a sort of below-the-surface reality-coping mechanism, so to speak," Dr. Neville ascertained and shared. "And this past week you were dreaming where you're being hunted by a thousand lovely women; well now, that suggests that you desire to have a trustworthy love-mate but you feel isolated and hurt by your recent divorce misadventure. And the fact that the women chasing you in your fantasy dream were not nude reveals to me that your mind still possesses a degree of Protestant morality prudishness," the psychiatrist logically deducted and concluded. "But both your department store dream from last week's conference and your remarkable island dream of this week

232

have the Aerosmith song 'Dream-On' being played from some unknown source in the distance. This strange combination of ideas is all rather puzzling, rather perplexing too, since you've already maintained that you like music, especially '70s rock and roll."

"Are *we* making any significant progress Dr.?"

"I've already told you that any vast improvement won't be noticeable until after a full year of continuous therapy," the psychiatrist evasively answered. "No doubt you've often heard of the familiar expression 'No Man Is an Island?' Well Sam, *that* island comparison I've just articulated and brought to your attention shows me that you don't want to be completely detached from other human beings, especially gorgeous women. I believe that deep down inside your psyche," Dr. Neville hypothesized, "you really crave being connected to a sympathetic female and I suspect, despite your apparent reclusive nature, that you're now in the process of actively searching for the right lady friend, unless *she* finds you first. That's where the bizarre department store scenario is creatively invented and applied by your fertile imagination. You're desperately trying to find someone reliable to assist you in escaping your loneliness, a lady friend," the psychiatrist theorized and verbalized. "And the fact that a thousand stunning voluptuous women are infatuated with you on that desert island only confirms to me that you're in quest of a supportive female companion, but it has to be the right lady out of a pack of a thousand eligible ones. And Sam, don't let the tropical island environment represented in your dream throw your reasoning off course. It's quite evident to me that you're not being too selective either because you don't seem to prefer whether your next mate would be a brunette, a blonde or a redhead."

"Then I'm not going insane or anything drastic like that?" the somewhat relieved patient asked his newfound mentor. "That's what I truly fear the most!"

"Quite frankly Sam, I think that you have difficulty dealing with women in every day reality so the situational island dream theme is how your ever-active mind's fabrications have accommodated *that* ostensible inhibition that's quite prevalent in your fantasy subconscious realm," Dr. Neville elaborated. "Idealistically speaking Sam, your sensitive ego has been egregiously damaged by your recent devastating divorce, but in your starving soul, I believe that you still desire contact and affection from a lady friend. That's my theory at present, but *that* speculation of mine may change as our weekly sessions continue."

The examiner next asked his easily influenced subject if he had any other dreams in the past month that the paranoid accountant could recall besides the extraordinary department store entrapment and the incredible recurrent island paradise nightmare.

"Yes Dr.," the trusting patient all-too-honestly replied. "I'm the only passenger sitting on a huge jet airplane without any stewardesses or male flight attendants aboard. But now that you drew *this* particular remembrance to my attention, the familiar song 'Dream-On' was repetitiously being played over the plane's intercom system."

"Well Sam, your unusual tale makes excellent sense and as a matter of fact it's quite self-explanatory," Dr. Neville comforted and consoled. "The prefix 'Aero' in Aerosmith means 'airborne' or 'in flight, or it could also mean 'gasses in the air,' so *that* notion supports the idea that you're riding on a jet plane. And the word 'smith' refers to a working trade like a blacksmith, goldsmith or a silversmith, so *that* particular word connection accounts for you attempting to solve your emotional crisis in your subconscious mind by cleverly inventing disguised symbolic references and graphic terminology."

"Gosh Dr., I'm sure glad that I've decided to consult your skilled services," Sam praised his erudite dream interpreter. "I can't wait for our next session to commence next Monday. These formerly puzzling dreams are beginning to make plausible sense."

Session 4

Sam Dexter was not tardy for his slated Monday, June 28th consultation. Dr. Adam Neville did not deviate from past practice and employed the same administrative therapy pattern as had been applied in the first three sessions, and soon the receptive patient's mind had entered into a deep-but-comfortable hypnotic state. Much to the sagacious doctor's satisfaction, the easy-to-manage subject had recalled several very exceptional dreams conjured-up during the bygone week and then the passive subject accurately related them in full detail to his alert physician.

"I was participating in a crucial archeological expedition-dig on a western state's Indian Reservation and I accidentally discovered some ancient remains that presumably had once belonged to the nomadic tribe's shaman," Sam disclosed from his relaxed prone position on the black leather couch. "And all

234

throughout the entire excavation, the very entrancing Aerosmith song 'Dream-On' was being played somewhere in the prairie background. I believe I'm really starting to hate that catchy song."

"You could be uniquely combining and relating words like 'Aero' with 'arrow' and 'smith' with a colonial-type person or possibly with a pioneer-era craftsman," the psychiatrist pondered and summarized. "Your amazingly analytic mind does demonstrate *that* sort of co-relative propensity!"

"Yes, and on last Tuesday night I dreamed that I had been driving, well actually speeding eastbound on the Atlantic City Expressway and heading toward my destination, the Wild, Wild West Casino on the boardwalk," Samuel Dexter recollected and then conveyed. "Well anyway, all along the thirty-mile distance from Hammonton to the shore the enchanting song 'Dream-On' by Aerosmith was featured over my car's radio, no matter what station on the AM or FM bands I was listening to."

"You seem to have a fixation or some odd infatuation with the talented rock group and also with their catchy rock and roll tune," Dr. Neville commented. "Any other peculiar night fantasies to report at this time?"

"Well, on Wednesday night I had been dreaming that I was driving to New York on the New Jersey Turnpike for no special reason at all and I eventually reached the last toll booth without any money in my pocket or cash in my wallet," Sam uttered in a disconsolate tone of voice. "And no, I didn't have any EZ-Pass transponder attached to my inside windshield either. The macabre-looking toll collector was in the form and dress of the hideous Grim Reaper and the frightful specter was wielding his scythe close to my vulnerable face when I gratefully woke-up from that hideous nightmare, my entire body soaked in a cold sweat."

"I don't think you have a death wish Sam, and I profess *that* specific belief based on my broad expertise reviewing hundreds of different case studies and then comparing the sum to your exact situation. Now please remember, was the redundant song 'Dream-On' again playing at the turnpike toll booth?"

"Yes, and the sound of the lyrics was very unsettling to say the least," Sam abruptly answered, slightly shivering and squirming. "Very distressing indeed!"

"It could be Sam that you're cloaking your deepest thoughts and dreads and subconsciously revealing to me now that you have a distinct fear of dying," the psychiatrist predictably guessed and assessed. "And your morbid Grim Reaper association could very well also mean that you're afraid of living and are concurrently afraid of genuinely expressing your true emotions, always masking *them* with other phony contrived feelings. These problems could have their stem origin way back in your early childhood. And the song 'Dream-On' could be the essential link or thread that your hyperactive mind has chosen to meld together all of your latent anxieties and apprehensions," Dr. Neville cogently explained. "Now then Mr. Dexter, do you have any other pertinent dream recollections in your memory data banks that are worthy of mentioning?"

"There's one more," Sam offered from his subdued and now placid state-of-mind while still mentally hibernating in his classic reclined position. "In this new nightmare I'm describing, I'm lost for hours inside a baffling tall hedge maze quite similar to the one I had once whimsically explored behind the Governor's Mansion in Colonial Williamsburg. Just as I had been confused and disoriented in the department store labyrinth," Sam realized, compared and intelligently expressed, "I couldn't find my way out of the meandering passageways until the irksome song 'Dream-On' finally finished after around three horrible hours. Then rather coincidentally, I had thankfully awakened from my atrocious nightmare."

"Have you ever read the book *Aerosmith* by Sinclair Lewis?" the eclectic-minded multi-faceted doctor asked. "It's one of my favorite fictional works. The main character is a unique fellow named Martin Aerosmith, a dedicated genius in quest of a permanent cure for a certain deadly bacteria that often causes worldwide plagues and pandemics. At any rate Sam, this marvelous scientist Martin Aerosmith had gathered sufficient facts to author a profound research paper of paramount importance and later he delivers his vital information in a lecture hall presentation that had been given to prominent members of the inept medical establishment of the time. Getting back to my initial premise," Dr. Nevile insisted, "have you ever heard of or read the breakthrough novel *Aerosmith* authored by Sinclair Lewis?"

"No, I'm not at all acquainted with that novel although I have heard of the author," Dexter tersely answered. "I believe he was one of those famous *Depression-era* muckrakers."

"Okay Sam, in another hour I'm going to snap you out of your fourth hypnotic trance," the mind doctor casually indicated to his obedient client. "Then just as you've always done after our past meetings, you'll resume your normal adult life routines for a full seven days and we'll see you again next Monday for our upcoming very essential rendezvous! Now then, let's get on with our fourth interesting interaction."

* * * * * * * * * * * * *

Session 5

Conscientious Miss Emily Jensen had meticulously finished her record-keeping duties as usual at precisely 7:30 that following Monday evening and the secretary had left the psychiatrist's office soon thereafter. After loyal patient Samuel Dexter had departed the Landis Avenue premises at 9:10 p.m., Dr. Adam Neville walked over to the small refrigerator located in the side room, plunked five ice cubes into a clean glass and then concocted a jigger of vermouth mixed with three generous jiggers of sweet liquor to make a mouth-watering Southern Comfort Manhattan cocktail. Next the tired-but-gratified psychiatrist sat at his desk and concentrated on dictating some exceptional notes into a microphone. The recorded information the mind doctor was about to state would be later entered as a relevant document file into his personal desktop computer.

"I only have about ten more years to become famous in the psychiatry field and finally receive full federal grant funding in order to make my great aspiration come true, my revolutionary contribution to social science," the crazed plotter fancied and said into the microphone. "It is my steadfast goal and desire to become equally as acclaimed as dear old Sigmund Freud himself. My batch of eligible patients is now complete. At last I've accumulated ten good candidates to participate in *my* landmark experimental dream program," Dr. Neville vociferated as he then paused and slowly sipped an ounce of his potent mixed drink. "My psychiatric study will be published in a slue of prominent mental health journals and my valuable literature will be acknowledged and recognized as a major scientific work for many years to come. A vast array of medical experts throughout the world will place absolute credence in my indispensable research study."

The egotistical alcoholic paused for a moment to sip his liquor and then again activated his tape recorder, methodically speaking into the microphone, carefully enunciating each stellar word. "Yes, I've now successfully amassed ten 'Music Dream Study' patients, to all of whom I've diligently played ten different songs for sixty minute durations during each separate two-hour therapy session; of course, the ten individual songs were played on my desktop computer while each subject was under my strict hypnotic control," Dr. Adam Neville proudly articulated before again imbibing an ample swig of his delicious Southern Comfort Manhattan.

"Mrs. Angela Shaner keeps hearing the song 'Dream a Little Dream for Me' by Mama Cass, Mrs. Agnes DeLeo insists that she hears 'Dream Baby' by Roy Orbison, Mr. Vincent Cramer knows all about 'Dream Lover' by Bobby Darin, Ms. Helen Garrison is an expert on 'Dreamin' by Johnny Burnette and Miss Gina Wolfe claims she listens to 'Dream Weaver' by Gary Wright during the hysterical woman's constant nightmares."

After casually glancing inside a readily available oak tag folder, Dr. Neville gulped down another mouthful of his powerful mixed drink before resuming his momentous dictation litany. "And number six on my list is Mrs. Carla Franchetti who simply loves Stevie Nix and Fleetwood Mac's version of 'Dreams,' number seven is Mr. Jason Vaughn, who is enamored with 'Dreaming' by Cliff Richard, number eight Mr. Maurice Dugan truly enjoys the rhythm and beat of 'Dreamtime' by Daryl Hall, number nine Mr. Nigel Pierce finds great merit in the lyrics to 'Dreamer' by Supertramp and now at last my tenth candidate for inclusion into my federally funded program is Mr. Samuel Charles Dexter, who is totally captivated with Aerosmith's outstanding rendition of 'Dream-On.' And all of this preliminary groundwork has been cunningly and fantastically organized and accomplished by little old me, the soon-to-be internationally renowned Dr. Adam Neville, ha, ha, ha, and all of my secret goals have been furtively achieved, even without my very capable secretary Miss Emily Jensen's suspicion or knowledge."

The obsessed psychiatrist ceased his tape recording oration and then softly placed his microphone upon his very neat and clean side office desk. The half-intoxicated devil-minded doctor again tasted some more of his cold mixed liquor and then in the very midst of his narcissistic catharsis, the fanatic gloated and reminisced for several moments, leaning back in his black swivel chair and then arrogantly smiling at the overhead translucent ceiling light panels. Neville soon self-indulgently contemplated and assessed his own great shrewdness.

'My important study will certainly be the most wonderful and productive achievement of my entire life,' Adam Neville considered and relished. 'I'll be busy touring the whole country and be in demand lecturing at every major university in the United

238

States, and later as my reputation expands,' the maniac further schemed, 'I'll be speaking at colleges all across Europe too. So what if I had mischievously rigged and stacked the deck of cards in my favor! I'm going to win this high jackpot poker game and my good name will be acclaimed and revered throughout the whole-wide world!' the exhilarated madman imagined. 'I only hope that Mr. Sam Dexter and my other nine weak-minded case studies don't go psycho with their numerous dream delusions before my invaluable research project has been consummated and published. Ha, ha, ha! I don't wish to see my ingenious documentation suddenly turn into a tawdry scandalous debacle! Who cares about the fate of my mediocre gullible doltish patients? None of my ten idiotic dream subjects can be allowed to ever ruin my soon-to-be coveted prestige and fame!'

"Ship of Fools"

Philip Greco was born and raised in Hammonton, New Jersey but in the 1970s the elderly gentleman absolutely loved vacationing for a full week every August in sun-kissed Ocean City, Maryland. Phil Greco had memorized every commercial retail business in the inlet's five-block section of the boardwalk starting from South First Street right up to North Division where the Route 50 Bridge over the bay channeled automobile traffic into town. Trimper's Rides, the Red Apple Treats Stand, Dayton's Chicken, Marty's Playland Arcade, Sportland Arcade, Dumser's Ice Cream, The Purple Moose Saloon, Thrashers French Fries, the Alaska Hot Dog Stand, Dollie's Popcorn, Bull on the Beach Roast Beef Sandwiches, the Atlantic Hotel, the Glassblowers Shop, Fisher's Caramel Popcorn, Lombardi's Tower of Pizza, Dealers Choice Poker Game Arcade, the Candy Kitchen Shop, the Psychedelic Shop, The Sea Shell Emporium, The Dutch Bar, Telescope Beach Pictures and the Courtesy Gift Shop all held dear spots in the visiting South Jersey man's heart. And during his annual week-long hiatus Greco loyally patronized all of the mentioned popular boardwalk establishments.

Another Ocean City, Maryland place that Phil Greco was especially fond of was Happy Jack's Pancake House, which in the summer of 1973 was situated on Baltimore Avenue directly behind the landmark Atlantic Hotel. Greco and his Hammonton buddy Anthony Esposito were avid deep-sea fishermen and each summer the two friends would charter a boat out of the bay-side White Marlin Marina, but before each big fish ocean adventure, the New Jersey pals would always eat a hardy breakfast at the famous Happy Jack's Pancake House, which displayed on its four wood-paneled walls two-dimensional ship models that were offered "For Sale" to the public. The creative works were produced by an area artist named Captain James, and one particular post-colonial era warship (mounted on a dark ivory burlap background) immediately caught Philip Greco's attention.

"I really like that black warship hanging on the wall directly above your bald head," Phil sarcastically-but-affectionately told Anthony Esposito. "The vessel looks like it's late eighteenth or early nineteenth century, most probably from the War of 1812 era. And the black strings connecting the three masts really contrast nicely with and complement the dull white background. And Tony," Phil elaborated before gulping down a mouthful of delicious hot coffee, "I really like the rolled-up canvas sails too! If the price is right, I'm interested in acquiring it!"

Anthony Esposito turned his head and briefly studied the impressive-looking framed battleship rendition on exhibit. "That baby's got seventeen cannons facing us," Phil's friend and confidante counted and announced. "That means the real one that existed way back then carried thirty-four total cannons that could be booming and blasting away at enemy ships."

"I'm going to call that terrific beauty the 'Ship of Fools'," Phil laughed, "and I intend to buy the piece of art and hang it in my den if I can get it for under a hundred and fifty bucks. Let's see the asking price."

Philip Greco did negotiate for and finally purchase Captain James' "masterpiece" for "a Ben Franklin and a Ulysses S. Grant" and three days later the jubilant man transported the treasured item back to Hammonton, New Jersey where the owner proudly displayed the 'conversation piece' on his family den's largest wall.

But in June of 2006 Philip Greco died of a massive heart seizure and his loyal son Gino Greco inherited the "classic and decorative" Ship of Fools, which the beneficiary prominently hung in *his* modest French Street home's family den to specifically honor his father's intense love of the sea.

* * * * * * * * * * * *

Following in his father's footsteps, Gino Greco had graduated from the Philadelphia College of Pharmacy and took great pride in operating the family business trading under the name "The Apothecary Shoppe" on Bellevue Avenue in downtown Hammonton. Keeping with the European-style appellation of the establishment, the owner often referred to himself as "a chemist." And just like his garrulous father, the congenial proprietor was well-respected by virtually everyone he knew in the community and always conducted his "father figure" ownership capacity with both courtesy and integrity, constantly having the welfare of his customers and the dignity of his employees in mind.

"Harry," likeable Gino Greco pleasantly ordered his Apothecary Shoppe manager, "I'd like you to please check all of our inventory in the stock room. An independent pharmacy like this one has to always keep one step ahead of our more prodigious competitors Wal-Mart and Rite Aid Drugs." And then the "chemist" requested of his counter person, "Jill, since we aren't too busy this morning see if you could restock the over-the-
242

counter patent medicines' shelf. And after refreshing the candy bar selections, remind me to call my wife in a half-hour if you can. My memory is becoming as unreliable as an old sole-less worn-out shoe. I think we need a few more *Snickers*, *Hershey* and *Three Musketeers* bars in those half-empty display boxes. And oh Kathy," the fussy storeowner hollered over to his newly hired cashier, "can you please replenish the soap and deodorant rack next to the alternate cash register?"

At noon on Friday August 13th, 2010 Gino Greco phoned his always on-the-go wife from his Bellevue Avenue pharmacy office to see if Diane was home from her early morning grocery shopping at Bagliani's Market on 12th Street. The wife answered the landline call after the third ring.

"Yes Gino, I've just finished putting all of the dairy products into the refrigerator," Diane informed. "I've also bought you a half-gallon of your favorite ice cream, *Breyers* vanilla fudge. If you want to know the truth, I really miss Jimmy and Denise helping me. Pretty soon our little urchins are going to be entering those ugly early teen years when their acne-dotted faces look awfully grumpy and then a year later their peevish behavior will become terribly uncooperative most of the time."

"How much longer are the kids staying up in the Poconos with your sister Francine?" the forgetful husband inquired. "Are they coming back to Hammonton tomorrow? What's the name of that kids-oriented resort where they're now hanging out?"

"Jimmy and Denise are coming home to Jersey late Sunday afternoon and if you recall, they're rooming with their young cousins at a nifty place called Great Wolf Lodge up in Tannersville," the wife re-educated her husband. "I understand it's a pretty fantastic resort that's designed to accommodate kids of all ages. Good old Francine must be having a real ball babysitting, er, I meant to say 'chaperoning' four little hellions!"

"Remind me early this coming winter that we have to take an excursion up to Tannersville and do some skiing with our children at Camelback Mountain," Gino suggested. "That's probably the neatest ski mountain in the Poconos. The last time we had spent a weekend up there we all had a blast. And that Tannersville Inn has some really excellent food on their menu. What's the name of that other restaurant that we like?"

"It's the Smugglers Inn located right across the highway from the Tannersville Inn," Diane Greco remembered and informatively answered. "Every hot action place in that town is within a mile of the other sensational attractions. And the newly constructed Mt. Airy Casino Hotel is not too far away from Tannersville either."

"Say Honey, speaking of casinos, the kids are out of town, right? What do ya' say we' take a thirty-mile ride east to Bally's Casino tonight. If we lose our money too quickly at the green tables and on the slots, we can always stroll the boardwalk and reminisce our first movie theater date we had in Atlantic City."

"Splendid idea Hubby!" Diane robustly exclaimed over her kitchen phone. "That means I won't have to cook dinner and that'll also give me enough time to do some much-needed housecleaning and a little interior decorating too. The day's jobs will go by much smoother if I know we're going out on the town tonight over in Atlantic City."

"Great Doll! We'll be leaving Hammonton about five this afternoon," Gino enthusiastically said. "Of course, we'll have to contend with the heavy Friday night Philly' traffic on the Atlantic City Expressway heading down the shore, but I think I'll be able to navigate my Lexus through all of the turmoil and congestion. My EZ-Pass transponder attached to the windshield makes going through the toll plazas almost a pleasure. The Governor's TV ads are right. That useful electronic device is a real time-saving convenience and I'm glad I got it."

"See you around five Handsome!" Diane verified. "Now as soon as we hang up, I'm off to complete my basic housekeeping and to then hang a few items on the outside clothesline. As they've said and often repeated for many centuries throughout history, 'A woman's work is never done'!" Click.

* * * * * * * * * * * *

At two that afternoon a delivery truck dispatched from Frank Mazza Furniture Store pulled into the Greco family's French Street driveway and the elderly driver rang the front doorbell and after the portal was opened, then the company employee gingerly lugged the new mirror (that Diane had secretly purchased) from the foyer, through the hallway and kitchen areas and finally into the house's den. After unwrapping the gilded gold-framed mirror, Mrs. Diane Greco gave her nod of approval and eagerly signed the yellow "Customer's Copy" receipt. She next politely handed the appreciative driver a five-dollar tip.

"Thank you Mrs. Greco," the furniture store truck/delivery employee said. "In this day and age, every dollar counts!"

244

"You can spend the money at my husband's pharmacy," Diane giggled. "But better yet, stop and buy yourself a hamburger and a Coke over at Burger King."

"Would you like me to help you hang the mirror?" the suddenly extra-courteous driver volunteered. "I'm quite experienced at it since I do that sort of minor job all the time, especially for good customers like yourself."

"No thanks Johnny," the woman of the house replied. "I think I can manage the task all by myself. If you remember, my dad was a hard-working ambitious carpenter in town and he was a dependable builder too you know, and from him I learned how to use a hammer and nail at a very young age. Working at odd jobs around the house as a tomboy, well, that sort of activity kept my brothers and me from becoming juvenile delinquents," the woman exaggerated. "Anyway, thanks again Johnny for being so extra careful while carrying that expensive mirror all the way from the front steps into the den. It's a real beauty, isn't it?"

* * * * * * * * * * * *

Diane Greco thought that the out-of-place three-and-a-half decade-old "War of 1812 Battleship" was incompatible with the remainder of her modern den's décor. She felt that the 'obsolete spectacle' had to be removed from the most used room in the residence and then relocated to an empty wall in the upstairs computer room so that the 'eyesore' would be less conspicuous to visiting guests.

'That 'Ship of Fools' as my late father-in-law used to call it is an interesting artifact left over from the early 1970s but it really doesn't match the rest of the den's motif and I think it's much more suitable for the spare room upstairs. Gino and I never did have that third child as we had originally planned when we had built this house. And I don't think that my understanding husband will mind me replacing it with this splendid new gold-framed mirror,' Diane presumed. 'It's not like the all-too-gaudy 'Ship of Fools' room ornament is haunted or cursed or anything like that. Honestly, I'm not throwing Gino's treasured item into the rubbish bin. I'm merely transferring it from the den wall to the upstairs computer room wall. I'm sure my compassionate husband will easily adjust to the new arrangement.'

Mrs. Greco stood and balanced herself on a sturdy wooden kitchen chair and reached-up and removed the two-dimensional out-of-date framed battleship from the den wall. And after descending from her elevated position to the floor's carpet, the wife immediately grabbed onto the recently acquired mirror, stepped up on the chair again and proceeded to skillfully hang the 'Frank Mazza Furniture piece' of merchandise (using the accompanying back wire) onto the old wall hanging clip.

After that simple task had been finished, the on-a-mission wife carried the heavy "Ship of Fools" upstairs and using a spare chair from daughter Denise's bedroom along with an available hammer, wall hook and nail obtained from the hall closet shelf, the wife managed to find a convenient stud in the computer room's designated wall and then very adroitly hung and leveled Gino's beloved Ocean City, Maryland Captain James' Happy Jack's Restaurant memento.

With *that* challenging job being fulfilled, the satisfied wife returned the aforementioned chair to Denise's room, put the hammer back on top of the upstairs hall closet shelf and then slowly descended the thirteen steps downstairs in order to return the borrowed wooden chair from the cozy den back to its normal place in the kitchen nook area.

Upon re-entering the tidy cozy den to admire her exquisite mirror, the wife curiously glanced at a series of old black-and-white pictures positioned in a neat row on top of a corner flat table surface, and upon gazing more intently, Diane Greco was dramatically and literally shocked out of her mind when she noticed that the now-deceased six people that had appeared in the old photograph were presently missing.

'Oh my God! How could *this* possibly be true?' Mrs. Greco alarmingly thought. 'This photo' from the 1950s is supposed to have all of Gino's aunts and uncles in it, but all that is now visible is the beach, the Ocean City Maryland lifeguard stand and the turbulent Atlantic Ocean in the background! Over the years I've looked at this nostalgic picture at least a thousand times,' the astonished wife frightfully realized. 'How arcane, creepy and eerie! Aunt Elena, Uncle Jack, Aunt Vera, Uncle Stan, Aunt Marie and Uncle Joe, all six of them have somehow mysteriously vanished!'

And then Diane Greco's attention was drawn to another old sentimental 1950s' black-and-white photo' that previously had shown now-deceased cousins from Gino's family standing outside the main entrance to the world-famous Phillip's Restaurant in Ocean City, Maryland. But much to her dismay, only the widely acclaimed Philadelphia Avenue seafood house was represented in the snapshot without any trace of the vacationing six cousins Judy

Greco, Anita Greco, Richard Greco, Donald Greco along with married Eleanor Jenkins and Joanne Everitt. Those half-dozen familiar faces had been mysteriously erased.

A third black and white '50s Ocean City, Maryland photograph exhibited upon the same flat den table ordinarily featured four family members that upon closer scrutiny, had also strangely been eliminated. In the original framed snapshot, Diane's deceased father-in-law Philip Greco should have been standing in front of the grand old boardwalk Atlantic Hotel with his wife Ruth and his father Antonio Greco along with Gino's younger brother Russell, who years later had horribly died from drowning in the Ocean City, Maryland surf. Russell's untimely death explained why Philip Greco abruptly stopped visiting Ocean City, Maryland every August after the 1974 family tragedy.

'Sixteen family members missing, all of whom are dead and buried in local cemeteries!' Diane fearfully recognized, her frenzied mind entering into a heightened panic-attack state. 'There's only one vital thing I think I must do to reverse this living nightmare! I must run upstairs to the computer room and exchange the 'Ship of Fools' with the mirror I have just received. If I do that superstitious deed without delay, perhaps everything will return back to normal. Most certainly,' the distraught woman thought, 'I don't want to disturb or upset the Powers That Be, especially Death! I must let the poor sixteen dead souls rest in peace and I believe that the Ship of Fools relocation is the key!'

Diane frantically dashed up the familiar thirteen steps, obtained the nondescript chair from daughter Denise's room, rushed and carried the secured object into the spare computer room and then nervously stood upon a den desk, all the while carefully scrutinizing the hanging accursed Ship of Fools.

The result of Diane Greco's frantic labor was emotionally devastating to her. Much to the perspiring woman's horror and terror, the various heads of the sixteen deceased relatives belonging to Gino Greco's ancestral family were now blatantly represented, each with his or her diminished miniature face sticking out of the 1812 battleship's first sixteen cannons that were situated directly below the vessel's starboard-side gunwale railing.

And then Mrs. Greco screamed loudly and deliriously upon observing that her own head and face had punctured through the remaining seventeenth cannon's opening. While viewing the ghastly phenomenon, the petrified woman's knees buckled, the den desk wobbled and the wife lost her balance.

Still shrieking from her macabre ordeal, Diane Greco fell from her standing position upon the rickety den desk and then swiftly plummeted to the hardwood floor. A minute later the terrified soul stopped breathing. In stark reality, Diane Greco had been literally frightened to death!

* * * * * * * * * * * *

Since Diane Greco had died at a relatively young age, an autopsy had been ordered performed, and according to the subsequent toxicology report, the cause of death was determined to be "trauma to the head from violently impacting with the floor."

The following week a well-attended but extremely sad Wednesday evening viewing was held for Mrs. Diane Greco at the Carnesale Funeral Home on South Third Street. On Thursday morning a solemn mass for the deceased was celebrated at St. Joseph Catholic Church on North Third. Burial for the aggrieved chemist's wife occurred at high noon at the Greenmount Cemetery on First Road with a reception for family and friends following immediately thereafter at Illianos Restaurant on 12th Street.

When all of the flowers, condolences and traditional funeral distractions were over, a very melancholy and sorrowed Gino Greco sat at his desk in the upstairs computer room staring at and studying the 'Ship of Fools' that *his wife* had moved to its new upstairs location. The somber griever's heart remained inconsolable. The despondent pharmacist was wondering why his spouse had purchased the downstairs den mirror and had transferred the 'family heirloom' to the spare room upstairs without first consulting him.

'I suppose that Diane was just going to surprise me with the newly purchased mirror and in the meantime flaunt her notorious home decorating skills,' the emotionally disheveled chemist regretfully thought. 'Oh well, it's time for me to go and get Jimmy and Denise at my sister-in-law's place. It was nice of her to take the children over to her house for a few hours so that I could gather my wits with a little peace and quiet. Meditation and some basic soul-searching can certainly often be constructive.'

While standing in the upstairs computer room and upon scrutinizing the Ship of Fools more analytically, Gino Greco noticed 'an anomaly' that he thought was very peculiar. He then glanced out the middle window to clear his saddened mind for a moment and then again apprehensively peered at the framed 1812 era string-sailed battleship.

The impressive vessel was still mounted on its dull ivory burlap background but oddly enough, Captain James' signature was now on the left-hand-side and not the right where it had always appeared before. And the 'haunted ship' was now reversed in its orientation, the bow pointing in the opposite direction with the seventeen consecutive empty port-side cannons (situated just below the gunwale railing) now facing the appalled ashen-faced viewer.

'The Ship of Fools throughout sea lore legend was reputed to be a legendary ghost vessel,' the very nervous widower recollected from a college professor's literature class lecture. 'I wonder if this cherished Ocean City, Maryland heirloom had anything to do with Diane's untimely accidental death?

"Stairway to Heaven"

I had suddenly died in my home's master bedroom's bathroom while I had been staring into the vanity mirror after finishing shaving. A sudden pain spread from my left arm to my chest and the last thing I remembered as a human being was collapsing upon the brown-tiled floor. There is no doubt in my mind that my body had ceased functioning and that my awareness had slowly exited my form and then transferred into a strange energy-spirit state. I don't remember any spectacular catharsis when my soul had been ejected from its human shell.

Next I can remember, I was somehow cognizant of hovering over my lifeless corpse and a moment later my senses were aware of my wife's delirious screams as she frightfully bent over to touch my neck feeling for a pulse. 'So much for her being a veteran R.N.,' my still intact consciousness sarcastically thought. 'She does really love me after all!'

To my fallible knowledge I never traveled through any dark tunnel to any ethereal bright light destination. I believe *that* scenario is what some minds fearfully manufacture when brain cells are rapidly deteriorating and nerve endings are desperately transmitting the wrong information because of severe oxygen deficiency. So I firmly believe that after the spirit evacuates the body at the moment of the heart's cessation, the actual process of dying has just begun, for every cell in the human form must then soon die off one by one after breathing has permanently stopped. But still, conscience, mind and spirit survive the momentarily painful ordeal quite satisfactorily outside *the host* that had once sheltered *those* entities. I steadfastly maintain that death can be best described as a combination spiritual/biological process that has occurred.

The next event I remember was that my weightless atom-less spirit vertically floated through the ceiling and then right through the house's roof as if both physical objects were porous intangible imaginary masses. At that moment I felt as if I had been a scintilla of light penetrating through two transparent thermo-glass window panes. I recollect drifting around fifty feet above the ground and my *new* keener senses detected a crowd of curious neighbors dashing out of their homes. Soon an ambulance with red flashing lights entered and screeched to a halt atop my former dwelling's driveway.

As a scene of mayhem developed both in and around my Hammonton, New Jersey ranch-home, my ghostly consciousness began gliding slowly downward in the direction of a gray limousine parked at the curb across the street from my residence. I passed through the density of a tall tulip tree like water rushing through a teabag. While my *intelligent spirit* was descending, the limousine driver, a facsimile of the Grim Reaper (wearing a dull brown robe), opened the back door.

My soul easily entered the vehicle and my three hundred and sixty degree consciousness was acutely aware that all participants and eyewitnesses involved in the pandemonium in front of my Valley Avenue home were totally oblivious to my ghostly departure. However, many spectators grieved, sobbed and gasped when *they* observed two strong paramedics carrying my listless form out of the house on a Hammonton Rescue Squad stretcher. All attempts at reviving my body with special electric shock equipment inside the ambulance had failed.

My awareness felt no grief, remorse, shock, pain or anxiety from my sudden death. My mind remained calm, curious and alert as the gray limousine gradually moved forward and passed right through four people standing on Valley Avenue without them one bit knowledgeable about the 'spiritual hearse' or the phenomenon that was occurring.

"I suppose the afterlife is not governed by the laws of physics," my *spiritual intelligence* said to the macabre driver, who passively ignored my attempt at initiating a telepathic conversation. All the Grim Reaper duplicate did was stare menacing at me in the rear-view mirror. My chauffeur's face featured giant voids in the hollowed-out bony cavities where its eyeballs should have been. A hood covered the forehead part of the driver's skull above his grotesque-looking skinless face. The chauffeur's super-white teeth appeared twice as large as the average human's would be. I remember how futile and stupid it seemed contemplating escape from my alien captivity.

I dared not speak to my eerie escort again but instead my cognizance used my *intelligent spirit* to scrutinize the passing environment I remember perceiving while somehow looking out of dark-tinted windows without possessing any functioning human eyes. 'I must remain rational and try to make some sense out of this new world I've entered,' I nervously thought. 'After all, everyone is going to eventually die and go through the whole same experience too.' I did find some comfort in making that conjecture, even though I had believed that the process of dying

252

was quite singular to the individual that was doing the perishing. 'Death seems to be much more morbid and harrowing to the survivors of the dearly departed than it does to the deceased,' I concluded while prematurely evaluating the nature of my own recent demise.

As my reticent driver's non-palpable gray luxury sedan zoomed down the White Horse Pike my perceptive spiritual intelligence suddenly made a rather stark observation. All of the automobiles on the highway in my new dimension were limousines and they were of three colors, black, gray and white in their order of frequency. Instantly my astute mind-spirit concluded that the black ones were on their way to hell, the gray ones heading to purgatory and the few white ones en route to heaven.

Then I became a little more sober about my fascinating excursion because I was certain that my destination was going to be purgatory. 'It's logical that the bulk of people are heading for hell, a small percentage to purgatory and only a select few to heaven,' my mind-spirit surmised. 'I could have and should have led a better life,' I shallowly lamented without any evidence of heavy guilt, remorse or regret. It was more as if I was being disappointed rather than being angry with myself', and my soul was now resigned to accepting whatever fate awaited me without objection or without endeavoring to rationalize fanciful excuses in defense of my past actions and misdeeds. I felt as if my entire free will had been sacrificed and surrendered.

My foreboding chauffeur stopped at the traffic signal at Fairview Avenue and the White Horse Pike. I remember thinking that he really didn't have to stop, so he must have halted for a specific purpose designed to enlighten me about some aspect of the afterlife. A black 'hearse/sedan was visible approaching on Fairview directly behind us, and as *our* limo' turned left on green, I noticed the black hearse turn right in the general direction of Woodlawn Avenue, apparently heading to Valley to make a pick-up at my former home. 'Fools,' I mentally criticized *their* human enterprise. 'That's only my limp body lying in the ambulance over on Valley Avenue. I'm now in this immaterial non-visible gray limousine, you hapless money-hungry incompetent morticians!'

I then saw the facsimile Grim Reaper driver nastily stare at me in the rear-view mirror and my spirit became quite uneasy when I realized that *he* could read my innermost thoughts that, in the conundrum-like dimension I had entered were now public knowledge (at least to him) and were no longer secret notions exclusive to myself.

'We're now coming to Old Forks Road, and there's the new Hammonton High School up on the left abounding with vibrant adolescent life,' I genuinely thought. Soon the gray limousine made a left-hand turn into Oak Grove Cemetery and the unearthly vehicle first stopped at a recently dug grave with *my name* inscribed on the granite headstone. 'I'm now glad I had the foresight to buy grave plots and an en*graved* headstone,' my awareness concluded. 'But I'm sitting without any sensation of sitting in this sleek gray vehicle and only an expensive bronze casket (as specified in my will) containing my embalmed remains will be deposited into that lurid one-fathom-deep hollow.'

Then I realized that time-warping was a unique characteristic of the afterlife I had entered since I had just died what seemed moments before and I now recognized that my grave-site had already been excavated and a vault had been snugly placed inside. I stared at the vault's gilded golden lid as the gray limousine next moved slowly forward on the cemetery's narrow leave-strewn asphalt lane. I recalled I had died in early autumn, October 15th to be exact. 'One always knows the month he or she is born but the individual seldom if ever considers which month he or she will die,' I philosophically pondered.

As the Grim Reaper (or his replica) drove me around the various twisting roads of all-too-familiar Oak Grove Cemetery, I soon realized that at age sixty I knew more people that had already died than individuals who were still alive. But I still could not accept the notion that *I* had made any dramatic transition at all and had *crossed over* to anywhere except to Oak Grove Cemetery as a translucent passenger now dressed as a two-dimensional ghost in a now white-shaded black suit and tie I would be buried in.

My eerie-looking escort stopped at a particular grave-site and then an ominous newsreel flashed onto the video screen located above the limo's back seat. Mark DiMeo was a good friend of my son Steve. Mark had been killed in a tragic automobile accident. The teenager's parents had also been killed in an automobile accident twelve years earlier while crossing *Route 30* in a jeep. The young man had to be raised and mentored by his grandfather and I would often take Mark home after school events or when he had visited my abode on Valley Avenue. I say *my* abode? How absurd of me! When a person dies, he or she has absolutely nothing: no home, no money, no possessions, no capital gains' assets and certainly no material comforts. The richest man in the world isn't worth a mere brown penny once he succumbs to death.

254

The gray-shaded limousine driver very deliberately maneuvered the vehicle down and around a tree-lined oval lane and halted at the headstone of a former business associate. Our partnership had not been an amiable one, and I had outsmarted Jack Merlino in our one-sided business settlement. Merlino had bought me out and then went bankrupt ten years later. The sequence of events did not have to be reminisced because the incidents involving Jack and me had all been captured on tape and then mercilessly shown to me on the back seat video screen. But being cleverer than Jack Merlino now all seemed quite irrelevant and meaningless.

Apparently the visual representations on the television screen were not being presented in chronological order. A vision of me taking a final college exam' flashed upon the unique video monitor. I had needed an A on the difficult final to pass the "Educational Psychology" course and graduate, mostly because I had squandered valuable time absent from class relaxing in the student lounge playing poker and pinochle. A fraternity brother had stealthily and illicitly acquired the professor's final exam', and he and I spent two entire nights figuring out the seemingly enigmatic answers to the instructor's stolen "objective questions." I easily aced the final by cheating, but now I was specifically being supernaturally reminded of my unethical transgression that had somehow been mysteriously captured on some inexplicable arcane videotape.

Then it finally occurred to me that this uncanny itinerary through the cemetery was really a brief review of the good and the bad that I had contributed to civilization during my short lackluster tenure upon the Earth. An unsettling feeling drenched my spirit as the apparition of a female suddenly appeared sitting next to me. The woman's stone-cold face was horribly ashen and as she turned her head to stare at me, her distinct image was that of Persephone, daughter of Zeus. I recalled from a myth I had read in college that she had been abducted to the Greek underworld to be the companion of its heartless ruler/tyrant, Hades.

Persephone's grim and ghastly facial features then transformed into the countenance of Connie Morgan, a beauty queen I had dated in college, but then I had cruelly dumped her in favor of my present wife. I did not feel any guilt about my past un-meritorious deed. 'My comprehension of our college relationship is rational, objective and coldly analytical, just as my judgment by the *Powers That Be* will probably be conducted,' I hastily

255

hypothesized, instinctively accepting the uncertain fate that awaited me.

Connie Morgan's image then magically transformed back into Persephone's face and form, which gradually crystallized, vaporized and soon vanished into thin air. 'My entire past has been systematically recorded on tape to be used against me on Judgment Day,' I logically concluded.

The next cemetery stop was at my younger brother's grave-site. My grandmother had left me an inheritance and I neglected to share it with Tony, who had a not-so-easy life struggling to make ends meet. Then scenes of me' enjoying myself at Atlantic City casinos, going on expensive Caribbean vacations and cruises with my wife and children and next buying new house furniture with stock market earnings appeared in my brief visual biography. I rationally concluded that every good and bad behavior of my preempted life had been systematically recorded and documented by invisible camera crews using indiscernible equipment. 'If excessive pride and hubris were convicting criteria for eternal condemnation, then I'm definitely a prime candidate for such a deserving sentence,' I uncomfortably generalized.

'But these are only venial-type sins I've been witnessing!' my consciousness rationalized. 'Certainly any type of after-world justice would have to weigh all of the good against all of the bad,' my spiritual existence determined and justified, 'and undoubtedly I have performed much more of the former in my earthly existence than the latter. These are *not* serious mortal sins I'm observing here!' my uncomfortable *spirit-intelligence* mentally editorialized.

The hideous-looking driver moved ahead and passed by the grave-sites of my father, mother and my maternal grandparents. I was surprised that the limousine operator did not stop to haunt my mind with videotaped episodes of the insolence and defiance I had exhibited toward any of my dearly departed ancestors during my wild rebellious adolescence.

Then the gray limo' stopped at a Catholic priest's (who had willed to be buried with his family) tombstone. I recollected the name Father Thomas Randazzo, who had officiated at marrying my wife and me' in St. Joseph's Church on Third Street. Upon the now-familiar video screen appeared the image of my wife and three young sons sitting in a church pew without their father during a Sunday service. I quickly understood how futile and flimsy my argument had been that I hadn't been shown on the video screen any mortal sins I had committed. 'My six decade life was not without deviation from expected behavior. In many respects, a model father I was not,' I too late recollected and decided.

Another tableau appeared on the monitor and depicted me indulging in food and drink at a local restaurant. Gluttony had been practiced by myself' on numerous occasions, and according to inflexible church teachings, *that* bad habit was not exactly a stellar virtue. Now I immensely missed food and drink and I no longer have a body that requires biological sustenance. 'Physical pleasures and sensations now have to be sacrificed to allow for spiritual growth to occur,' I reckoned.

Ever since graduating high school, I believed that sin had merely been an invention of religion designed to instill in worshipers a promise of eternal reward that functioned as a cultural mechanism capitalizing on making churchgoers dread the possibility of eternal damnation. I had always thought that organized religion exploited one's hopes and fears to make individuals conform to certain austere and rigid codes of deportment. Now I was being graphically confronted with the strong chance that I had been erroneous in my assumptions and that the church's prescribed teachings (that I had liberally violated) had been infallibly right.

My mind was preoccupied pondering the nature and the structure of the overall afterlife my spiritual intelligence had been gauging. 'Humans live in a parallel dimension, an alternate illusion to the fantastic actual mysterious reality I have entered. This *is* the real world that the material world wrongfully thinks is an illusion,' I theorized, 'and the real world is truely the fantasy experience and the after-world venue is really the actuality of existence.'

My back-seat limousine imagining was interrupted by my awareness that *my* gray 'hearse/sedan was finally leaving Oak Grove Cemetery. In the distance I observed a westbound funeral procession heading toward Oak Grove from downtown Hammonton, and then it dawned on my powerless soul that the automobiles in line were filled with family and friends assembled to pay their final respects to *me*. 'I always thought that there would be more than just twenty-two cars,' my restless spirit protested as I counted the automobiles entering the graveyard. 'I suppose I wasn't as influential on others as I had wrongly imagined!'

Apparently time in the after-world had the ability to expand and contract, for it had seemed like only fifteen earthly minutes or so since I had suffered a fatal cardiac arrest to the moment when my mortal remains were about to be buried in Oak Grove Cemetery. Obviously my corpse had been taken to the mortuary, been embalmed, had a viewing and a funeral mass while my underdeveloped soul was being given preliminary exposure to phase one of the afterlife. This knowledge led me to suspect *too late* that the body and its attendant pleasures were but irrelevant distractions in both corporal life and to temporal death. I finally realized *too late* that one's soul, one's spirit and one's conscience were the only important factors in all human activities.

My morbid gray limousine turned west (left) on the *White Horse Pike* just as *my* slow-moving funeral procession entered the main gate into the century-old cemetery. The grim chauffeur's creepy mouth seemed to sullenly smile in *his* rear-view mirror reflection, but I imagined that the ridicule was simply a manifestation that my addled mind had conjured.

The Grim Reaper's duplicate sped without detection through a police radar trap in Chesilhurst. My escort zipped through a traffic light in Atco while simultaneously filtering through a bus, two cars, a dump truck and a tractor-trailer stopped at the congested intersection. He then passed through the towns of Berlin and Clementon with the speedometer registering a hundred and ten. Under ordinary conditions, I would have been petrified and panic-stricken at the dangerous speed but since I was already deceased, my faculties had evolved beyond normal fear and I no longer was awed by anyone human or anything that had been produced by humans. My ride was all rather surreal but in retrospect, quite humdrum because all along I knew I was already dead.

The gray limousine then turned right onto Linden Avenue beyond Clementon, and I was just meditating about how much fun I had had as a teenager at Clementon Lake Amusement Park when my frightening-looking skeleton operator abruptly pulled into the *Lindenwold High-Speed Line's* huge parking lot. The train service conveniently connected southern New Jersey to Philadelphia and it carries over forty thousand commuters daily to the *City of Brotherly Love* and then in the late afternoon transports them back home to suburban towns situated east of the *Delaware River*.

The robotic-like wretched chauffeur stopped the limo' in front of the main terminal entrance and as I curiously glanced around, I noticed that the entire parking lot was filled with other nondescript empty gray limousines rather than the usual standard array of domestic and foreign cars and trucks.

Two celestial-looking gentlemen converged on *my* vehicle and the taller specter opened the back door. I obediently stepped out, and then after the door was slammed shut, remarkably without any accompanying thud, the Grim Reaper casually stepped on the gas pedal, evidently dispatched to journey and pick up his next assigned unfortunate trans-migratory spiritual passenger.

'Hello!' my consciousness greeted, for I no longer possessed a functional tongue, throat or voice box.

'Welcome to a higher echelon!' the first figure returned in a weird sort of mental telepathy. 'I'm Gabe, and my companion's name is Mike.'

Immediately I felt inclined to query whether my new after-world acquaintances were the archangels Gabriel and Michael but I did not have the audacity to pursue that particular presumption upon initial introduction. I did not perceive any fluffy white wings on their shoulders, any flowing radiant gowns around their forms or any dazzling halos around their dual transparent heads, so I did not wish to appear facetious or foolish during that initial encounter even though the two immortal beings ostensibly knew exactly what I had been thinking and evaluating.

I glanced up at the sky and perceived that it was overcast, and *that* impression instantly suggested to me a general mediocre dull atmosphere that appropriately corresponded to the thousand or so stationary empty gray limousines in the giant parking lot, and my casual observation reinforced the notion that *they* had been symbolizing purgatory. When my spirit endeavored to initiate a mental exchange of ideas, I quickly fathomed that Gabe and Mike could understand me completely, but I could not comprehend or decipher their inter-angelic communications. The phenomenon was analogous to high-pitched sound frequencies dogs could hear and identify that happen to be out of the limited range of human auditory perception.

'Is this still the Lindenwold Station?' I mentally transmitted. 'I used to ride the High Speed Line from this terminal into Philly' to take my wife shopping downtown, attend plays at the *Walnut Street Theatre* or to visit *Thomas Jefferson University Hospital* for physical checkups.' The mere thought of my devoted wife made a trace of sentimentality surface from my *subconscious spirit*, which I suddenly fathomed was an important extension of (or a substitution for) my *subconscious mind* in the afterlife.

'You no longer have a free will to do whatever your hedonistic mind pleases or desires,' Gabe mentally informed, 'and your undernourished soul must now undergo massive cleansing and

259

purging until you're ready to be reborn and live a better life than the uninspired lame one you've just left.'

'Do you mean that I haven't been resurrected?' I mildly balked. 'Now *you* are telling me I have to be reincarnated after I am somehow sanctified by penance and anguish. Don't you have any good news to report?'

'We don't like that obscene word reincarnation!' Mike corrected. 'Be careful of your nomenclature! Let's just use the terminology *regenerated.* It's much more accurate, discreet and appropriate. There are entirely too many esoteric facts that an un-evolved dolt such as yourself must master. I advise you to learn to pay attention and to ignore your own limited mental impulses!'

After mentally trading several additional curious comments, I finally understood that this first phase of the afterlife was comparable to what humans do to *refuse* like paper, plastic and metal cans; they recycle them. That creative supposition was significantly consistent with what was happening to me and to all other passengers arriving in gray limousines under very dull and gloomy cloudy skies. *We* were in the sorting-out phase of being recycled before being washed and treated, but much to my bewilderment, the applicable acceptable vernacular was 'regenerated' and not 'reincarnated.'

'Well then,' I cautiously persisted in my inquiry, 'where is God the Father, Jesus and the Holy Ghost? Will I get to meet Them'?' I innocuously and presumptuously desired to know.

'You ask too many impertinent questions for a lowly neophyte,' Mike mentally reprimanded, 'but if you really want to know, you're not evolved enough to have *that* kind of special audience. Don't try running when you haven't yet conquered the art of crawling! Sorry, but I had to relate the advanced concept to you in mental language you could readily grasp.'

'Are we going to board the next train?' I rambunctiously asked. 'I've never been an advocate or a practitioner of *mass* transportation. Are we going to a Catholic Church or to a religious tribunal?' I awkwardly mentally joked.

'You must learn to temper your curiosity, your impudent sense of humor along with your rash opinions,' Gabe admonished with grim features showing on his angelic face. 'If you keep your soul open and receive knowledge and wisdom rather than send out wild flurries of cynical questions, then you'll finally comprehend the abstract nature of your new environment. That kind of discipline must be fully realized by you before you can ever evolve to a higher rank,' Gabe telepathically elucidated. 'Don't

260

expect *us* to volunteer information on demand. You'll soon be on your own and have to journey through the emotionally grueling ordeal of final atonement all by yourself.'

The two enigmatic angels then grabbed me by the arms. The three of us effortlessly floated across the parking lot above the gray limos' to the High-Speed Line's eastern terminal entrance ramp. I looked up above the concrete platform's pavilion and read the designation: "HA" where the lettered appellation "Lindenwold Station" should have appeared on the overhanging shingle.

'What *on Earth* does HA indicate?' I mentally asked Gabe, who in truth seemed rather bored and annoyed with my perpetual inane inquiries.

'Why you really aren't too imaginative now, are you!' he thought- transmitted. 'HA is an abbreviation, or more specifically an acronym for Heart Attack Station. All New Jersey humans that have died of heart attacks and who must be purged of past misdemeanors and indiscretions must ingress to the next stage of their eternal existence from *this* particular platform.'

'Let's get on board or else *our* supervisors will warrant more menial jobs for us to complete,' Mike mentally declared to Gabe. 'I don't want to be demoted from management to labor! Not with all of my accumulated on-the-job experience!'

'There's just as much stupid bureaucracy in the afterlife as there is in real life,' I thought to myself, forgetting that my mind was being eavesdropped upon. 'I hope there isn't any work, or any prying government, or any abominable *IRS* to contend with!'

'I warned you to keep your grandiose pin-headed opinions to yourself!' Gabe chastised. 'Try to impress us that you're more than the imbecile you boastfully appear to be!'

The three of us stepped into the nearest car, and within what must have been thirty earth-seconds, the doors closed and the train rapidly advanced on its rails in the direction of what used to be Philadelphia. I surveyed my surroundings and quickly discovered that I had been the only heart attack victim to get onto the death train at the former Lindenwold Station terminal.

'This' is a pretty inefficient system,' I critically evaluated, again neglecting to remember that my private thoughts were now public. 'This entire train is operating just to transport one passenger to some obscure destination. This confounded world is even worse than the one I had just escaped!'

'You'll never adequately comprehend your new dimension until you abandon your propensity for fabricating ludicrous and inconsequential impressions!' Mike mentally chided. 'I strongly advise you, try respectfully learning your new environment rather than merely engaging in all of this boring childish critiquing!'

Three miles down the track the train jerked to a stop in front of what used to be the Ashland Station, which now bore the identification 'C,' meaning Cancer Station. Four unfortunate doomed passengers were escorted onto the train by well-dressed supernatural beings that coincidentally looked like mass-produced carbon copies of Mike and Gabe.

'Well, I think the authorities oughta' have a crab up there on the sign to symbolize Cancer,' I mused while forgetting that my two companions and the eight new archangels could easily intercept and interpret my caustic ruminations. 'Perhaps the next heavenly station will be Libra or Aquarius.'

'Show more compassion and sensitivity, you blundering ingrate egomaniac!' one of the new angels who looked similar to Gabe mentally rebuked. 'No wonder why you have to be regenerated, you repulsive self-centered conceited cretin!' the very intimidating form pontificated.

It didn't take me long to ascertain that each new station had as its name a new disease or a particular cause of death. Those passengers that boarded with their angels at the next 'SD' platform (formerly Woodcrest Station) had suffered from strokes and had perished from drowning, Haddonfield was now renamed 'DMD' (The Drugs and Murder Death Station), and what was previously Collingswood now had the ominous title 'AND' (Accidents and Natural Disasters Station).

I glanced around the half-full car and counted a total of twenty-nine newcomers escorted by fifty-eight very competent-but-bored angel guides. The next stop on the unorthodox train route was ordinarily Ferry Avenue Station. I wondered if the stop's name would remain the same with boating accident and ship sinking victims entering through the train's ominous portals. Mike again criticized me for being too arrogant and too immersed into my own thoughts rather than empathizing with the new admissions to 'the Purgatory Local.'

The new Ferry Avenue pick-up destination had the appellation 'GDW' (General Diseases and War Station). A horde of misery-faced victims and their divine escorts patiently waited on the cement platform and when the doors opened, at least a hundred ghoulish-looking new riders were promptly escorted aboard.

'Why don't *they* simply pass through the doors rather than just stupidly standing there and be waiting for the portals to open?' I skeptically thought. I noticed infants that had died from birth

262

defects being pushed in baby carriages by somber-faced guardian angels, and many of the deceased appeared to have been terminated by chronic neurological maladies like multiple sclerosis and Lou Gehrig's Disease. The specters of six fatally wounded soldiers also entered accompanied by *their* twelve nonchalant and apathetic angel hosts.

'Why must death come to innocent babies and patriotic warriors?' I considered. 'It all seems so wicked and unfair!'

'Your reckless words border on heresy,' Gabe very deliberately transmitted and pointed out, 'and if you persist in continuing your abusive absurd remarks, you'll soon discover that you're only extending your stay on this perpetual elevated train ride.'

'It all seems like random arbitrary selection,' I imagined and inadvertently communicated. 'It's like we were all put into a worldwide lottery and each unlucky recipient happened to wind-up a victimized duck in a giant shooting gallery. I wonder who's been taking the rifle shots that are eliminating each of us from our happy earthly status?'

'You definitely are going to be made an example out of!' Mike mentally predicted and accused. 'Moral justice in *this* dimension is much more decisive and conclusive than political justice was in your former world. There are no appeals' courts in this afterlife you've entered after the sand in your *life-glass* had expired. You'll soon discover the profound significance of my statement. Now stop being so *damned* opinionated!'

I must confess I always had a proclivity for being frivolous during crucial situations. For example, I had a tendency to always want to crack a joke at a funeral or at a viewing and had to exercise self-discipline not to do so, my spirit recalled. 'At least half of the people on the General Diseases and War platform must have succumbed to debilitating *terminal illnesses.'* Then Gabe adroitly intercepted my most recent ludicrous brainstorm.

'If you persist in attempting to be an obnoxious comedian,' my ethereal companion's flawless superior mind conveyed, 'then Mike and I will be required by forces greater than ourselves to put you on a southbound *black* train at the next station. And believe me! You don't want to go there! Lucifer Prince of Darkness absolutely and positively loves tormenting and torturing pretentious morons such as you happen to be'.'

'I'm sorry,' my suddenly guilty consciousness automatically apologized. 'It was just my sanguine disposition surfacing from my subconscious mind, er, I mean from my subconscious spirit,' I mentally answered. 'I know I tend to be facetious and sometimes playfully sarcastic, but in this new dynamic mental environment, I must admit, I'm definitely at a disadvantage.'

'Control yourself! Harness your frivolous impulses, you pathetic excuse for a human being,' Mike critically cautioned, 'and just absorb everything that your spiritual eyes witness. Otherwise, your actions will not only have severe consequences. They'll also be the genesis of diabolical results you'll long regret.'

Gabe informed me that he had to attend to another assignment and was scheduled to get off the phantom train at the next designated station. I did not possess sufficient courage to ask him to describe his next mission, so my two-dimensional form sat solemnly in my seat and contemplated the general morbidity of the other deceased and melancholy purgatory-bound passengers. The speeding train entered the familiar tunnel just before what used to be the Camden City Hall exit and before Gabe departed my company, he handed me a gray pen to be utilized soon in 'your next major post mortem enterprise.'

I politely bade 'farewell' to my radiant angelic chum, who then casually sauntered onto the former Camden City Hall platform, which now bore the reference 'ND' (Natural Death Station). Depressing apparitions with wrinkled elderly faces cluttered the subterranean platform, and many of the new arrivals crowded aboard the thirteen unlucky cars that constituted the 'Purgatory Express' as I had now preposterously labeled it. I imagined that the phantom express could hold over a million ghosts if it had to, since all of us lacked anatomies or forms to occupy real physical space, and *we* could have easily been stacked on top of one another like sheets of construction composition board or otherwise simply crammed inside.

'Does this underground tunnel we're now in represent some sort of a birth canal in reverse?' I mentally asked Mike. 'Am I reentering the womb, so to speak, er, I mean so to think!'

'You are undoubtedly and indisputably a completely annoying dunce!' my all-too-perturbed escort reproached. 'It isn't like *that* at all. It's more like when light travels from air into water. It sort of gets warped or bent going from one predictable medium into another. That's exactly what's happening to you right now. You're going from one medium to the other.'

'What happened to what used to be the Broadway Station in Camden?' my curious spirit inquired to my austere host.

'Oh now, you must be referring to the Limbo Station,' my illustrious guide matter-of-factly replied. 'LS is temporarily out of commission because it's under repair and having drastic renovations being done to accommodate all of the horrible abortions being performed and all of the unfortunate still-borns being delivered back on Earth. Just look at all of the unnecessary work you daft former humans are causing the already-overtaxed eternal staff!'

The high-speed train surfaced from its subterranean cavity and next crossed what used to be the *Ben Franklin Bridge* into what used to be center-city Philadelphia, but now the connection had the designation *Crossing Over Bridge.* I looked at the traffic on the span's seven lanes and readily determined that it consisted exclusively of white, black and gray limousines conducting novice ghosts to their more permanent destinations. A second more-deliberate analysis determined that there were only a few white limousines traveling on the mile-long span, suggesting that Heaven was indeed under-populated.

The first underground Pennsylvania stop, which should have been Philadelphia's Eighth and Market Street platform, was now listed as 'CN' (Celebrity Notoriety Station). Transparent images of deceased rock and roll singers, movie stars and political and historical figures were standing around and idly conversing on the concrete walkway. I observed Elvis Presley interacting with John Lennon, John Wayne exchanging thoughts with Marilyn Monroe, Franklin Delano Roosevelt mentally mingling with Harry S. Truman and Dwight D. Eisenhower and Edward G. Robinson sharing ideas with Abraham Lincoln and J. Edgar Hoover. Many other famous specters were visible on the dismal platform including Daniel Boone, Charlie Chaplin, Thomas Edison and Edgar Allan Poe, but I had insufficient time to recognize the identities of all the distinguished phantasms.

'I have to get off at the next stop,' Mike imperatively stated. 'Here's a small gray notepad that you can write some of your impressions upon. I'll allow one written communication with a past acquaintance so that you can then successfully forget about your former world and concentrate on being processed into your new *medium*. Do you have any final relevant questions? This is your last opportunity to ask them!'

'Er yes,' my spirit telepathically stammered. 'How do I mail this document after I have authored it?'

'Oh, pardon me for the silly oversight,' Mike courteously responded. 'I'm usually much more thorough and dependable. I suppose I'm suffering from chronic mental fatigue! Use the gray pen Gabe had given you and jot down your thoughts and reactions

265

inside the gray notebook. Here's an official gray envelope. Address it to whomever you wish and then drop the correspondence into the gray *Inter-Dimensional Mailbox* you'll occasionally see at selected underground train platforms.'

'But I won't have enough time to write down all I want to describe!' my adamant spirit hastily communicated in a frustrated mood. 'Are you deliberately trying to aggravate me?'

'On second thought, seal and drop the envelope into the postal box's slot at the next station when the subway train again gets there sometime in your eternal future,' my guide suavely and convincingly advised. 'You must remember that you have all the time in the world to randomly scribble-down your notes in this book, so you don't have to foolishly rush. Practice good penmanship if you wish. Notice that adequate postage has already been attached to the standard gray mailing envelope.'

I was sage enough not to doubt the angel's veracity. 'My only alternative is to trust *his* instructions,' I logically decided. Then the train slowed to another subterranean halt.

Mike exited the perfectly noiseless and quiet train at the vacant 'SH' (Stairway to Heaven) platform. I attempted to rise from my seat to take an instant shortcut to paradise, but some supernatural force field prevented me from accomplishing my selfish pursuit. I again tried standing up. I experienced a sensation akin to a sleep paralysis I had once undergone while my mind was emerging from a strange dream. I could not move a muscle, feeling as if I was being subjected to a potent enchantment that completely enslaved my will and easily manipulated my spirit. 'Oh well,' I surmised. 'I have the entire future to be introspective and objective. I'll take my time in organizing this important narrative.'

The eternal high-speed train pulled-out from the rather fascinating brightly lit' empty Stairway to Heaven Station, which in my prior life was known as 10th and Locust. The next stop of the High-Speed Line Express, which ordinarily was the last one, was 15th and Locust. I again tried to rise from my seat but was thwarted by that same indomitable spiritual force's resistance. I glanced around the filled-to-capacity train and confirmed that all of the other more compliant passengers were assiduously writing down notes into *their* small gray tablets. I figured it was time for me to abandon my intractable disposition and finally conform to Gabe and Mike's expectations and obediently imitate my fellow passengers' appropriate example.

I then peered-out onto the platform from the window above my seat and read the name of the last station, which was peculiarly labeled 'FJ' (First Judgment Station). Standing on the platform were twelve individuals wearing long gray robes with accompanying gray-haired wigs positioned above their ashen-colored foreheads. The dozen jurors were all dead persons that I had wronged when they and I were living our independent lives back in Hammonton, New Jersey.

I objectively speculated that the twelve Solons would be judging my candidacy for probation from my dull uninspiring subterranean purgatory. I theorized that if I eventually passed *their* verdict, I would be assimilated into Heaven's lowest denomination once I had finished filling the small notepad and mailing it whenever the train were to again stop at a platform that had a convenient *Inter-Dimensional Mailbox.* Then, I assumed, my contributions and transgressions would finally be re-judged by a Superior Intelligence on *Judgment Day.*

'My arrogance and my defiance must be discarded in favor of humility and modesty,' I sincerely vowed. 'I will eventually escape this wicked underground punishment and hopefully qualify to ascend the *Stairway to Heaven* and be able to finally appreciate and 'see the light.' That is now my utmost aspiration in this mystical but monotonous and tedious underworld train afterlife. I feel like a groping lost charlatan in quest of admission to a world belonging to sage wizards.

'I will not send this manuscript to my wife,' I judiciously decided. 'I'll mail the package from an *Inter-Dimensional Mailbox* to Marilyn Jenkins, my editor and publisher at cyberread.com. She'll know precisely what to do with this vague glimpse of eternity so that in the future others can benefit from its content.'

"The Better of Two Lives"

People make many crucial decisions from several years after exiting their mothers' wombs right up to entering their cemetery tombs. Men and women usually encounter at least a dozen crossroad events in their lifetimes where important choices are made, some good, and perhaps some not so fortuitous as originally planned and hoped for. Major decisions about marriage, who to marry, career choice, real estate acquisitions and investments complement a person's numerous minor preferences such as which high school sports to play, who to ask to the senior prom, which college to attend, and what kind of house should be purchased. Such a plethora of mental challenges affect millions of Americans daily and continue to reap rewards and consequences throughout their mortal lives.

Richard Henderson was no exception to the law of human choices. The jack-of-all-trades and master of none had always desired to become a successful businessman, be a renowned author, and finally, thrive as a loving husband to a devoted wife who fully believed in emotional reciprocity. Those very noble aspirations represented Henderson's wishful goals and lofty ambitions, but quite often, obtained results seldom match the sincerity of initial intent. Richard Henderson's youthful fantasy and excessive idealism rapidly deteriorated into shattered hopes and crushed dreams.

Approaching age sixty, Richard critically evaluated his life's lackluster accomplishments. The distraught fellow's assessment led to feelings of guilt, depression and frustration. The despondent man had not achieved what he had set out to attain, even though he had always given his efforts "the old college try." Rather than seek professional counseling, Henderson allowed his sense of futility to govern his mental and emotional health. Dejection and despair dominated Richard's heart, his mind and his spirit.

On the morning of April 24th, 2002, Richard Henderson climbed into his brand-new leased red-colored *Toyota Avalon.* The saddened homeowner pressed the automatic portal's remote control, exited one of two garage doors leading into his two-story white colonial house, methodically lowered the left enclosure, backed-up in 'reverse', shifted into 'drive' and then turned left out of his U-shaped driveway onto the four-lane *White Horse Pike.*

'Things haven't exactly turned-out the way I had expected,' the man-behind-the-wheel thought as Henderson passed by *Oak*

269

Grove Cemetery on his short excursion into Hammonton, a somnolent agricultural community in southern New Jersey famous for its summer blueberry crop. 'It's Jennifer's and my thirty-sixth wedding anniversary,' the saddened driver lamented, his vehicle accelerating past a cement truck, which was en route to the new high school construction site situated across Old Forks Road from the stately cemetery. 'If only things had worked-out differently, or should I be thinking worked-out 'better',' the distressed 'failure' regretted. 'Oh well, it's now all water over the proverbial dam!'

A dominant negative disposition ruled Richard's mind as the self-labeled 'failure' steered his sleek swift automobile off 'the Pike' onto Bellevue Avenue, Hammonton's main thoroughfare. Henderson's fertile imagination assessed the past three and a half decades of his undistinguished life, his defeated mind wishing that he had made other choices in those ever-present "*old forks* in the road," and then wondering and speculating what outcomes would have culminated from alternative paths the vanquished dreamer might have taken.

"I'm worth more dead than alive," the disgruntled fellow muttered to his middle-age appearance in the car's rear-view mirror. 'The only tangible thing I have to show for thirty-six years of labor is a house without a mortgage,' Richard mentally reviewed with regret. Then a passing thought tinkered with the driver's better judgment. 'If I kill myself by smashing into a tree or a telephone pole, Jennifer and the kids could collect the balance of my pension. I have three hundred thousand dollars remaining in my pension account, and if I suddenly disappear from this dog-eat-dog Earth, then at least my wife and kids will be able to receive a half-decent estate when you throw into the mix my quarter million dollar accidental death insurance policy. I don't know why it's called life insurance if it exclusively involves death, in this case 'my death.'. I suppose that the notion of life insurance is one of those popular euphemisms that glib television commentators talk about all the time.'

Richard's self-deprecating daydreaming was abruptly terminated upon his eyes perceiving flashing red lights up ahead and then noticing the Bellevue Avenue railroad crossing gates descending. As the *Toyota* owner restlessly waited for the *New Jersey Transit Express* from Atlantic City to Lindenwold to swiftly pass through downtown Hammonton, Henderson's out-of-kilter mind rekindled several of its latest warped suppositions. 'I draw thirty thousand dollars a year out of my pension,' Richard recalled and theorized, 'and I'm still four years away from

270

collecting Social Security. That's another eleven thousand a year. A motley forty-one thousand dollar total retirement package. What a terrible wasted life!'

The *New Jersey Transit Express* train whizzed by, the Bellevue Avenue gates ascended back to their vertical positions, and soon traffic again was crossing the landmark railroad tracks. Instead of stopping at his primary destination, a commonplace town convenience store, Richard forgot about his morning newspaper and doughnuts and coffee and progressed straight down Bellevue Avenue, which then became Twelfth Street, and finally a mile further south, the road with many names transformed into State Highway *Route 54*.

'I've valiantly tried, but I've failed over and over again!' the mentally disturbed man concluded. 'My marriage and my career haven't quite turned-out as I had planned. I've been rejected and been a non-achiever much more than I can cope with. I should've never become an English teacher for thirty-four inglorious years of classroom sacrifice along with the added misery of dealing with scads of annoying student discipline problems. I could've gone into business many times, but I always foolishly put family needs first. And where has it all gotten me? To the brink of insanity, that's where!' the emotionally distressed driver angrily generalized.

As the merlot-color *Toyota Avalon* left the town limits, the state road expanded from two lanes into a four-lane dual highway. The retired English instructor expressed his emotional dissatisfaction by mashing his right foot against the car's accelerator. The auto's speedometer was now registering sixty-five miles per hour. Tears formed in the anguished driver's eyes and several rolled down his cheeks. Richard reflexively wiped the excessive dampness away from under his bifocals.

'I could've bought my parents' farm market,' the disgruntled fellow recalled, 'and I could've married my college sweetheart Carolyn Williams instead of hitching-up with haughty Jennifer Ranere. I could've bought several boardwalk businesses in Ocean City, Maryland, and I should've invested my savings into gold during the seventies major oil crisis. Could have, would have, should have!' Richard irately hypothesized. 'That's the story of my hapless life! One continuous pattern of inaction and unhappiness!'

The disconsolate *Avalon* driver glanced below the dashboard at the speedometer, which now indicated eighty miles an hour. 'And I tried turning things around,' Henderson regretted and

271

sobbed. 'I borrowed heavily on my credit cards, raising them to their limits, accumulating thirty thousand dollars in debt to e-publish my ten novels. My *Internet* web sites have gotten over a hundred thousand hits but it's just like owning a gift shop getting thousands of browsers but no paying customers. What a horrific nightmare my life's biography is! A complete financial disaster!'

The troubled speeder was becoming more and more delirious as Henderson then unfortunately passed an idle state police car while the *Toyota* was doing ninety miles an hour. Immediately the red flashing lights on the state trooper's roof illuminated as the officer initiated his hot pursuit of the radar gun violator. Richard stared into the rear-view mirror and observed the cop trailing *his* exceptionally fast 255 horsepower automobile.

'I can't take it anymore!' Richard grieved as the self-appointed failure put the pedal to the metal. The speedometer was now reading a hundred miles an hour, and Richard hopelessly wondered if he could get the vehicle up to its maximum miles per hour reading. "Sold only two dozen books on the *Internet!*" the driver screamed to no one. "Not even my friends and family have bought any of my damned books!" Richard shrieked as if he were an obsessed asylum maniac. "Nobody really cares about me, absolutely nobody!" the inconsolable speeder yelled to his uncaring apathetic dashboard in total frustration.

The merlot *Toyota Avalon* swerved back and forth, weaving from lane to lane, and then the out-of-control machine just missed having a head-on collision with an oncoming tractor-trailer as the highway bottle-necked down to two-lanes again. The driver of the diesel eighteen-wheeler was blasting his air-horn as the red *Toyota* recklessly zoomed past. The fancy luxury car skidded and then veered off *Highway 54* and next quickly crashed into a small cluster of evergreen trees, the automobile collapsing from the tremendous impact like a compressed accordion.

'I refuse to be doomed to dismal mediocrity! I would rather die!' were Richard's final contemplations before slowly lapsing into unconsciousness.

* * * * * * * * * * * *

A fantasy of momentary bright lights in the form of blinking red, green and blue colors prevailed around and above the accident scene, and then for Richard Henderson's emancipated spirit, there was a high velocity entrance into a narrow dark tunnel, his new existence heading towards an array of glimmering

272

and shimmering sparkles. Soon Richard's spiritual perception became aware of his body experiencing a sensational floating sensation as the man's escaped soul was now hovering over his corpse lying on the ground next to his totally demolished *Avalon*. The state trooper and a team of paramedics were frantically administering *CPR* to *his* lifeless form, and then after *that* attempt had become unsuccessful, the first responders were next futilely trying to revive *the accident victim's* vital signs with the implementation of a portable defibrillator.

'At last, it's all over. Instantly and painlessly over!' Richard marveled at how ingeniously easy it had been to die. 'If I had to do it all over again, that's exactly the method I would choose and use!'

"That's what *you* think!" challenged a winged figure clad in a white silk gown. "Richard Henderson, that's what you think! You ought to be ashamed of your cowardly sinful suicide act!"

"Who are you?" the semi-dead fugitive from life asked the bothersome illuminated figure.

"I'm your conscience, possibly your guilty conscience," the celestial being rather emphatically answered. "You have wished you could have made other more fruitful choices in your lackluster life that would've guaranteed you certain material rewards. You've relentlessly complained that you've dedicated your adult life to the betterment of your high school students Richard Henderson, and I must give you ample credit, indeed to a certain extent you have. *The Greater Power* has assigned me to afford you the opportunity to alter your final unwise choice, which was to evilly end your mortal existence," the radiant winged being communicated and explained. "This special pardon has only been conferred because you, Richard Henderson, have selflessly given of yourself helping over four thousand teenagers master the mechanics of English grammar and the development of a certain love for classic literature. Otherwise, your mortal sin suicide violation would never have been reviewed."

Richard Henderson's spiritual cognizance stared fifty feet down at his motionless body lying on the damp ground, the medical personnel and the police officer all completely unaware of *his* (or the benevolent angel's) overhead supernatural presence.

"Now Richard, you shall accompany me through a half century of relevant space and time, to a much simpler period, the specific era being your post high school years," the magnificent celestial creature predicted. "I suggest that you relax your heightened anxiety and enjoy your brief sentimental excursion into your past!"

The brilliantly-illuminated angel mystically whisked its right hand and almost instantaneously, Richard was enveloped in a swirling whirlwind, more like the benign eye of a hurricane than an actual violent tempest. When the revolving clouds and the accompanying eddying haze gradually vanished, the astounded liberated mortal was shown a memorable and nostalgic depiction by his new-found heavenly ambassador.

"Does this particular scenario ring a bell from your past?" the most excellent radiant being rhetorically asked. "It ought to Richard Henderson! You had an opportunity to purchase your parents' place of business," the marvelous angel aptly declared.

Richard Henderson's new cerebral awareness eavesdropped on a conversation that was taking place around an all-too-familiar dining room table. His very worried parents were seated at either end, begging their eldest son to buy the family roadside farm market.

"Rich, your father has suffered a damaging heart attack," Martha Henderson declared, "and the doctors say that the next one could be fatal. Your father and I have decided to sell our business, but we'd like to offer you the first chance to acquire it."

"That's right Son," Jack Henderson agreed and verified. "Your mother and I have decided to make you a worthy proposition. Buy the farm market from us for forty-thousand-dollars," Mr. Henderson pleaded. "You could have the best of both worlds. Teach school and put up with the board of education and your administrators' demands for nine months and then enjoy being an independent self-employed businessman during the summertime. We'll even help you out by working part-time at the market the first few years."

"But Dad, I don't want to go into debt and carry a heavy mortgage for the next ten years. I plan on marrying Jennifer Ranere next spring and will need money for a diamond ring and a down payment on *our* first house," Richard all-too-candidly replied without giving the important family business matter a second thought. "And besides, I think that Jen's father is going to eventually give me a high position in his fabulous furniture store."

"Okay Son, if that's what you want," Mr. Jack Henderson sadly answered. "Your mother and I were just thinking about keeping the fruit and vegetable market in the family before selling it to strangers, that's all. We wanted to give you first preference, but now your mother and I know your negative position on the subject."

"Thanks Dad. I appreciate your concern and your offer," Richard sincerely stated, "but right now I see more opportunity and more potential for advancement in the furniture business world. And if *that* prospect falls through, I'll always have teaching to rely on for basic job security."

Richard stared directly into the guardian angel's rich sparkling blue eyes. "But I've often wondered what would've happened if I had bought the farm market from Dad and Mom," the temporarily resurrected dead human curiously inquired to his very sage and seemingly omniscient guide. "Would *that* have been the proper decision? I think so, but I'm still unsure right up to this very minute!"

"Nothing ventured, nothing gained or lost Richard," the philosophical angel logically commented while once more waving his right hand, erasing the family dining room scene and magically replacing it with another familiar tableau that was still gradually coming into focus.

"Could you be more specific?" Richard respectfully inquired. "I need to know what would've happened if I had gone into debt and purchased the farm market."

"If you had acquired the premises for forty-thousand dollars, your loving parents would not have charged you any interest on the principal amount," the heavenly creature calmly revealed. "Four years later you could've sold the property four sixty-thousand dollars, and counting your twenty-five thousand dollar equity in the business, you could've amassed a stellar forty-five thousand dollar profit, which in 1970s money converted into today's inflated figures would be a whopping four-hundred thousand dollars. What do you have to say for yourself now?"

"I now realize *that* was a huge mistake I had selfishly made," Richard Henderson acknowledged and shared with the very knowledgeable immortal being. "I should've listened to my parents and heeded their judicious advice about Mr. James Ranere and the tantalizing furniture business. The grass is always greener…"

"And the furniture polish is always shinier on the other side," the clever angel rather amusingly finished. "And in the spring of 1966, April 24th to be precise, you had married Jennifer Ranere at St. Joseph Church on North Third Street."

"Against her father's wishes," Richard admitted with a frown instantly appearing on his two-dimensional pallid countenance. "I now understand that it's a mistake for a man to marry someone above his social status. I was too naive and immature to make that judgment when I was a foolish young man. Mr. Ranere rejected me and my personal ambition concerning my involvement with the furniture store right from the start. But as I've already mentioned Kind Angel, I was too young and too unsuspecting to catch on to *that* ugly reality at first."

The seemingly sympathetic angel once more motioned his right hand and then miraculously, several showroom displays inside a large furniture store appeared before their perceptive eyes. "You believed back in 1966 that you and Jennifer were both teachers and could make a comfortable living with you also being employed in her father's reputable retail store during the summer months, didn't you Richard Henderson?" the beautiful graceful being asked its current ward.

"That's right," Richard candidly confirmed while intensely staring at his guide's brilliant spectrum-hued halo, "and I was sure that I could've made a valuable contribution to my father-in-law's prosperous enterprise. But Jennifer was unhappy and fully stressed-out over teaching kindergarten after thirteen tough years, and then she foolishly handed-in her resignation. Her father hired her as a record-keeper working in the store's office. I think that her covetous father was trying to create stress in our marriage and ultimately break-up *our* initial loving relationship!"

"And in the meantime, Jennifer and you had the first of three sons," the magnificent glowing angel interrupted, "and you were sensitive about Mr. James Ranere incessantly picking on you and treating you meanly if not cruelly in front of your impressionable children. Is what I said correct?"

"Your statements are true and very accurate," Richard Henderson fully concurred, nodding his head, "and while I was supposed to be in charge of the retail department, my father-in-law made me deliver all of the furniture to customers' houses, often all by myself. And then when he supposedly put me in charge of the shipping department," Richard rankled and cringed, "I still had to deliver all of the furniture to customers' houses like a common flunky laborer. Jennifer's old man really put the screws to me good and the wicked miser seemed to savor every moment when he could harass me."

The angel summarized and orally conveyed that Mr. James Ranere was determined to break-up his oldest daughter's marriage so that Richard Henderson would be thwarted from cashing-in on any future lucrative inheritance Jennifer might receive, and also, the ambitious son-in-law would be cleverly preempted from obtaining profit money from operating the prosperous furniture store after Mr. James Ranere's future death.

"You were given a salary that amounted to a mere dollar above minimum wage," the majestic creature reminded Henderson, "and your paltry bonus came to only two thousand dollars a year. That was a meager pittance, even by 1966 standards!"

"And my wife was under instructions from her jealous father that I had to pay all of the family bills including house mortgage, insurances, utilities, property taxes and vacations," Richard argued in pitiful defense of himself. "I was never able to save anything, while Mr. James Ranere advanced his loyal spoiled-rotten daughter thousands of dollars annually under the table. All of that malice just to spite *our* marital relationship and to curry loyalty from Jennifer! My wife and kids always had money while I had to struggle and sweat simply to make ends meet. They were always favored, and I was always disfavored, perceived by all the Raneres as the intrusive avaricious distrustful outsider!" Henderson grieved.

The radiant angel then reminded Richard that *he* had dated another pretty girl in college, an attractive co-ed named Carolyn Williams, a beauty pageant contestant who had won the distinction of *Miss Brigantine*. When Richard imagined what would have transpired if he had married Carolyn Williams instead of Jennifer Ranere, the seemingly omnipotent all-knowing escort adroitly intercepted the mortal's mental transmission and immediately and very intelligently related *his* remarks to the essence of Henderson's conjecture.

"Brigantine is such a pleasant and cozy resort town just above Atlantic City," the clairvoyant creature suavely articulated. The resplendent being then again waved his magical right hand, thus eliminating the disturbing furniture store scenario and adroitly substituting for it a Jersey shore funeral parlor in its stead. "You had attended Carolyn's father's viewing," the angel alertly and perceptively reminded his accident victim.

"That is correct," Richard confessed with a trace of remorse evident in his quivering mental voice transmission, "but Jennifer went with me to the funeral parlor and stayed in the car. Just two weeks before Mr. Williams' death, Jennifer had made me promise her that I would not see Carolyn any more or else *our* relationship would have been through. I should've known right then and there that Jennifer Ranere's demand was a flagrant red flag warning for future conflict and power struggles between *us* and between her all-too-arrogant father and me."

And then the splendid angel made Henderson recollect how *he* often had violent disputes with Mr. James Ranere. One day the son-in-law had left the furniture store in a huff and drove down to Ocean City, Maryland where a fellow teacher had a summer job managing a boardwalk amusement arcade.

"My good friend hired me on the spot as the assistant manager for a hundred fifty dollars a week," Richard reminisced and confided to the angel (who already knew the entire story), "and right then and there my good buddy offered to share his two bedroom apartment so that I could live rent free for the summer."

"And then still in 1967, you gave Jennifer an ultimatum," the guardian angel deftly injected into the dialogue, reminding Richard of certain related past events. "That action did require a degree of courage on your part. You said, 'Either' come down to Maryland and live in the seashore apartment with *the baby* or else our flimsy marriage is doomed to divorce'."

The angel and the sorrowful mortal next discussed how Jennifer had conceded and had brought baby Jimmy to Ocean City, Maryland to also live with the helpful teacher/arcade manager/friend and *his* wife. The following summer Richard had borrowed money from his parents and grandparents and became a proud partner in the aforementioned Ocean City, Maryland boardwalk amusement arcade, and Henderson operated the popular establishment from 1968-'81 until the enterprise was knocked out of business by a Gaming Device Tax imposed retroactively by the extremely heartless *Internal Revenue Service.*

"That's right," Richard remembered and verified, "they wanted to make the gaming device tax retroactive for from 1968-1981, the lousy year that the *IRS* made the outrageous claim against my business. The government had actually knocked me out of business maintaining that thirty poker machines I had owned were gaming devices operating by *chance* when actually they were amusement devices operating by the *skill* and the eye-hand coordination of the players," Henderson recollected and accurately described to the receptive angel. "But I had to prove the wretched government wrong, and the greedy lawyers I had to compensate for their top shelf' services, which amounted to another enormous expense in addition to the unwarranted federal tax being imposed, along with tremendous   *IRS* penalties and interest debts that had accumulated. I didn't know who the bigger crooks were at the time, the ruthless *IRS* agents or the hired vulture lawyers! One was worse than the other!"

"Here's exactly what would have happened if you had married Carolyn Williams instead of linking-up with Jennifer Ranere," the angel objectively remarked as *he* symbolically gestured his hand and changed several vague shadows into identifiable female characters present and standing in the once-familiar Ocean City, Maryland boardwalk arcade.

"Wow! I'm now married to Carolyn and I still have the Ocean City, Maryland business going. The year must be around 1968, and we both seem very happy," Richard rejoiced upon viewing the new set of circumstances prevailing in the very lucid 1968 summer seashore visual vignette.

"Happiness, just like human existence, is very temporal and most ephemeral," the empathetic angel plausibly indicated. "Carolyn would've been very supportive of you until around mid-1974. Right after your dad passed away from a massive heart seizure, your wife Carolyn would have begun practicing random infidelity. You stayed the course, however, and in this alternate reality existence you lucked-out by selling your thriving boardwalk enterprise for two hundred thousand dollars," the informative angel divulged to the astonished listener. "That all happened in 1975, a year before *your* unfortunate sale victim that had purchased your arcade paid you that handsome sum. Then the heartless *IRS* knocked him and his partners out of business instead of you."

"Oh my God!" Richard bellowed, slapping his flat numb snow-white face in recognition of what would have transpired if he had married Carolyn Williams instead of Jennifer Ranere.

"Kindly watch how you say those *holy* words 'Oh my God'," admonished the semi-supreme being, "and be especially careful when and how you say *them,* for there might be unforeseen consequences for *you!*!"

"So then, if I had gone the alternate route and had married Carolyn," Richard introspectively reviewed, "I would be ahead of the game by at least two-hundred and forty-five thousand dollars between the farm market sale and the subsequent Ocean City, Maryland boardwalk arcade bonanza."

"But Carolyn would've been constantly unfaithful to you, and that kind of overwhelming grief cannot be measured in terms of dollars and cents," the stellar illuminated celestial guide convincingly advised. "Not everything in mortal existence Richard Henderson has a monetary value. But I must admit," the sagacious angel elucidated through sophisticated thought telepathy, "money is the root of all evil, second of course to having no money at all and then resorting to criminal activity to acquire it."

Next the helpful caring angel reminded Richard how *he* had gone into a second amusement arcade business with his former Ocean City, Maryland store managers in Atlantic City in 1977. But when the New Jersey gambling industry entered the picture in the late seventies, the Missouri Avenue boardwalk lease was lost (by a small-print clause in the tenet/landlord contract) to allow for the construction of the elaborate *Caesar's World Casino and Hotel*. The defunct Atlantic City, New Jersey amusement arcade venture had set the enterprising Richard Henderson back a hefty twenty-five thousand dollars.

"What a complete lousy bummer!" Richard recalled and nastily answered his heavenly mentor. "You show some motivation to work and a desire to get ahead, and then either the *IRS* or a stipulation in your greedy landlord's lease makes something valuable suddenly become absolutely worthless in a matter of seconds."

"Over the four year period Richard, you had lost over twenty-five thousand dollars in the Atlantic City venture, or should I say misadventure," the fact-oriented angel reminded the always aspiring entrepreneur, "and your meager profits barely paying for two-thirds of the gaming equipment and pinball machines you had obtained to adequately run the Atlantic City business. Mechanical poker machines are no match for electronic casino slot machines, that's for sure!" the angel objectively deducted and opined. "I'm glad I was never a human, to tell you the honest-to-goodness truth. The pitfalls and dilemmas are entirely unbearable and quite honestly Mr. Henderson, just too pathetically numerous to endure!"

"And then my problems were compounded when I bought two one acre vacation lots I couldn't afford near Bushkill up in the *Pocono Mountains*," Henderson recollected and disclosed. "The Ocean City federal tax debacle, my strained marriage, along with the stupid Atlantic City and Bushkill ventures all combined proved to be enormous 'white elephants' in disguise. Bottomless money holes, that's all they were! And I had no lucrative cash cows to satisfy the huge debts incurred by those all-too-deep money pits!" Richard soberly elaborated to his sublime audience of one. "I still had to pay taxes on the empty Bushkill. Pennsylvania properties in addition to expensive community

280

maintenance fees and ever-rising community association dues," Henderson sadly informed (confessed to) the all-knowing angel. "I could never afford to build a house on either of those two very burdensome one-acre mountain lots, not with Jennifer Ranere as my non-supportive wife!"

The growing weary slightly sarcastic angel then proceeded to intensify Richard's aggravation by disclosing that if *he* had purchased the farm market, had married Carolyn Williams, had sold the Ocean City arcade in 1975 (with intelligent investing in utility stocks and safe mutual funds), then the quixotic dreamer would now easily be a distinguished multimillionaire. "You would have wisely invested your ready cash in gold during the *OPEC* oil crisis in the seventies, and then your shrewd investment would've within two decades proliferated into a neat and tidy two million-dollar windfall."

"Now you tell me!" Richard's spirit mentally and pessimistically replied. "Hindsight is always more accurate than foresight, that's for sure. And Carolyn would probably still have been unfaithful, even after I would've bought her mink coats, precious jewelry and a white *Mercedes.* But who would have cared? I would still have been rich enough to afford her lustful infidelity! I could've learned to live with Carolyn's unfaithfulness and with the very desirable two million cold-cash dollars that would've allayed my marital problems!"

"But you and Carolyn would never have had any children," the angel cautioned and seriously maintained. "There is always a downside to any relationship, you know!"

"No children translates into having less headaches during a legal divorce," Richard ineffectively argued, "and besides, my three sons have all been brainwashed by their mother and by *her* greedy parents. 'Daddy's a no-body. Grand-pop gives us all *we* want. Daddy's unimportant in this family.' But I insist Angel that all I ever did was pay all the bills, that's all, while my carefree wife Jennifer extravagantly spent, spent, spent her father's token money!"

"Now you're being a little too cynical and self-defensive," the angel effectively reprimanded. "Humans all have their faults, you know, and unfortunately Richard, *that* rather simple eternal principle also includes you."

"But I seemed to never learn a good lesson," Henderson confessed. "In 1981 I needed money so I ate humble pie and went back to the furniture store to give it another try. What a disaster that horrible economic experiment turned out to be!"

"That's right," the supernatural guide amiably verified. "Your father-in-law made you work like a donkey loading and unloading trucks filled with heavy sofas, dinettes, bureaus and beds. In the meantime *he* promoted and made your oldest son Jimmy your superior in the firm, your immature kid constantly and obnoxiously telling you what to do and how to do it."

"Jimmy was a mischievous fifteen years old at the time," Richard remembered and sobbed, "and I was so infuriated and humiliated that I went and worked for a small rival furniture company located down the highway. I built that wimpy business up fifteen times its original size, but then..."

"But then the owner said that he didn't require your services any longer and terminated your commissioned employment as manager. You were motivated by spite to make Mr. Ranere's competitor succeed," the angel accused. "You wanted to show your covetous father-in-law that *you* were competent enough to build-up a nothing business into an awesome rival concern, a definite competitive threat to Mr. Ranere's financial base."

"Yes, but then my ecstasy was short-lived when old Mr. Jackson gave me the royal heave-ho. That's what you call gratitude for my invaluable contributions! An ugly pink slip!" Richard Henderson vehemently complained to his very wise listener. "Jackson gave me a swift kick in the butt when *he* should've sent praise and compensation my way! I was foolishly naïve to trust Jackson's promises on a handshake rather than specify the actual terms to our original agreement in black and white on legal paper."

The very erudite angel presented a contrary point of view, explaining that Henderson had been able to sustain himself from the bonuses and commissions *he* had earned at the crafty Mr. Jackson's suddenly competitive furniture store. The heavenly visitor also reiterated how Richard had continued teaching and slowly was adding to his modest pension during those five years of employment in Hammonton furniture-land, and how Richard had "miraculously" preserved his somewhat rocky marriage to Jennifer while winning the begrudging attention of his spiteful and vindictive father-in-law.

"And so after all of those years of toil and calluses, all I got to show for it is a house with three unappreciative sons that have been spoiled rotten by their arrogant grandfather," the retired English teacher protested to the merciful and somewhat sympathetic angel. "What would've happened if I had married Carolyn? At least my head would've still been above water and I

282

wouldn't have felt I needed to commit suicide in a desperate attempt to avoid bankruptcy and to escape harsh reality!"

"Just the opposite," the angelic being confided as the glistening creature again waved his hand erasing the two rival furniture store images and then his superlative magic forming an authentic-looking power struggle inside of a judge's chamber with two smiling lawyers sitting at opposite sides of a very long formal-looking oak table.

"Carolyn found and latched onto a wealthy corporate tycoon, a top executive in the computer industry," the angel informed his now-livid and jittery spirit companion. "But that arrangement didn't stop her from getting a four-hundred-thousand dollar settlement from you, basically your life's savings Richard. And then," the heavenly guide continued his revealing exposition, "the stalking *IRS* finally caught up to you to tax your capital gains from your gold stock sales during the *OPEC* generated oil crisis. You had slyly figured that since you didn't receive any dividends or interest payments on your gold stock investments, the government computers would never catch-up with your fantastic capital gains' return on investment mischief. But they eventually did! Yes Richard, they certainly would have if you had married Carolyn Williams!"

"Well, that means I would've been no better off whether I had married Carolyn instead of getting hitched to Jennifer!" Richard Henderson exclaimed in utter astonishment. "Either way, my mediocre life was nothing more than one continuous gigantic mis-adventurous sham! At least now Angel I truly know what would've happened if I had chosen different options."

"True, but only to a certain extent," the affable and obliging angel concurred. "But there is one final hypothetical irony to this crazy parallel girlfriend dilemma that must be disclosed regarding your distant past. After Carolyn soaks you for your life's labor in the second parallel scenario," the sagacious being divulged, "you go absolutely bonkers. You borrow heavily on your credit cards and invest in ten novels you've industriously spent the last twenty-five years desperately writing and refining. You Richard must be the ultimate idiot in the whole human race! Yes, your disastrous ill-fated novel publishing endeavors! That's what eventually pushed you to the threshold of bankruptcy and suicide in both marital scenarios!"

"I see," Richard softly answered in a definite defeated tone of voice. "I finally *see the light*, if you'll pardon the pun. I would be in the exact same monetary abyss regardless of whether I had married Carolyn and not had any children or had married Jennifer as I obviously did and had three not-so-wonderful sons. Either way, my pathetic life would've been fraught with failure, misery and discontent. I'm basically a born loser Good Angel, and that's essentially the long of it and the short of it!"

"It seems like you're magnetized to attract harassment and to lure mortification resulting from constant and continuous failure," the eternal angel merrily chuckled to the not-too-thrilled human chronic loser. "So now that you know what would've happened to you if you had chosen the other forks in the road, would you now care to re-enter your former body and continue-on with your rather abominable mortal life?" the celestial messenger amazingly asked. "I have three other jobs I must perform this earthly day, so I hereby strongly request that you provide me with an immediate logical and rational response to my offered proposition as long as it lasts."

Richard Henderson seriously weighed his winged colleague's proposal to return to his former mortal existence. The retired teacher considered how *he* had invested a thirty thousand dollar inheritance in the late 1980s' and how he had recklessly squandered it for the sake of an upstart computer company that contended it had a black box that could integrate and interpret all computer languages. 'A fool and his money are soon parted!' Henderson laughed to express his genuine reaction to an impromptu self-satire. 'And I really don't know whether I'm now heading to heaven, to hell or to purgatory!' the deceased fellow promptly assessed and considered.

"Well Richard , I'm waiting!" the on-schedule angel insisted and demanded. "I'll give you only one minute more to decide."

"Let Carolyn be married to that fat-cat hotshot corporate computer honcho and let her reside in her opulent suburban mansion," Richard firmly uttered like an obsessed madman, "and let Jennifer and my three defiant sons delight in exploiting my friendly masochistic nature. I want to return to life on Earth and savor every penny of my miserable thirty-thousand dollar a year pension and then gratefully relish the pleasure of anxiously awaiting the arrival of those meager monthly Social Security checks starting next year," Henderson snickered to his new-found supernatural acquaintance.

"Then you mean you truly plan to return to life in Hammonton, New Jersey on the morning of April 24, 2002," the heavenly dispatched angel reaffirmed.

"Yes, that is my will!" the relieved and elated human confirmed rather enthusiastically. "I want to continue living as a mere mortified mortal!"

* * * * * * * * * * * * *

"We have a pulse! We have a pulse!" the head paramedic of the Hammonton Rescue Squad shouted. "Let's stabilize this lucky soul and then get him into the ambulance. Notify the Emergency Room at Kessler Hospital that we're sending a rewired *flat-liner* over. This incredible man is nothing short of a major miracle! He must have a powerful guardian angel looking over him!"

Three weeks recovering in Kessler Memorial Hospital's *Intensive Care Unit* enabled Richard Henderson's condition to be up-graded from "life-threatening" to "critical," and after another week of hospitalization had elapsed, the rejuvenated man was finally classified as "in stable condition" ready for immediate discharge upon doctor's approval.

After spending a month at home monotonously roaming the confined areas between his bed, his bathroom and his comfortable recliner chair, Richard Henderson finally summoned enough gumption, courage and stamina to shuffle down the upstairs' hallway to his spoiled-rotten son Jimmy's old bedroom. The faded gaudy wallpaper had recently been torn-down and the walls had been spackled and then resurfaced with a tan coating of paint. The bedroom had been converted into "the computer room" right after the Henderson's oldest son sought independence of parental (fatherly) supervision and had moved-out of the residence to live in his own condominium, of course fully subsidized by his benevolent doting grandfather, the egocentric Mr. James Ranere.

Reluctantly, Richard Henderson slowly entered his cherished captain's swivel chair and anxiously pressed the button in the center of his computer tower. His effort activated the system's monitor and the operator awaited the appearance of his *Internet* service provider's icon along with the other accompanying symbols about to show on the all-too-familiar start-up screen.

"Wouldn't it be wonderfully great if I've sold another two dozen books between the time of my near death experience and my discharge from my extended hospital stay," Richard Henderson wishfully said to the inanimate screen situated before his eyes, the device stationed on top of his office's ancient-looking cherry wood desk. "I'm still surprised that two dozen strangers had taken the time and the energy to individually buy twenty-four of my idiotic novels in the first place. I guess I'm not a total failure after all!"

Richard's modem dialed into the *Internet* and he immediately visited the *Yahoo* search engine screen. The researcher typed-in his pen name and waited for the appropriate information to appear. The curious mortal scrolled-down the list of items under "R.H. Factor" and was instantly astonished. One hundred and twenty items were neatly cataloged, and the first listing at the top of the web-page conspicuously read "R.H. Factor at *Amazon.co.uk.*"

Henderson hastily traveled to *Amazon.co.uk* and was shocked to see all ten of his books listed in "Best Selling Order." The excited author anxiously clicked on the first title, which showed it had an *Amazon.co.uk* sales ranking of 2,570. All of his other nine titles had impressive sales rankings also, ranging from ten thousand to one hundred thousand, among from over three million online products.

Richard Henderson's heart was beating rapidly as the Internet investigator visited *Amazon.com, Amazon Germany, Amazon Japan, Amazon France, Barnes and Noble.com* and *Mobipocket.com,* and the jubilant writer quickly came-up with similar high rankings for all ten of his creative novel masterpieces..

The now-astounded author sat dumbfounded before his computer screen, incredulously analyzing the inexplicable turn of events that had recently transpired. After decades of futility, travail, hardship, disappointment, failure, frustration, rejection and an attempted suicide, fame and fortune had at last been inexplicably accomplished. The totally thrilled man simply passively sat there and emotionally delighted in the well-earned sweet taste of success.

"I'm now rich and famous, thanks to my Guardian Angel's intervention into my sinful death," Henderson mumbled to his image reflected in a 1940ish wall mirror hanging above the five-year-old computer monitor. "Thank God I have a second chance at life! It pays to follow your own instincts and not rely on anyone else to make *you* a success or a failure."

Footsteps were heard clambering-up the colonial-style home's steps. The bedroom door flung open and young Jimmy Henderson was somewhat startled to see his father sitting before the out-of-date desktop computer inside *his* old bedroom.

"Oh, hi Pop," the oldest son hesitantly greeted. "Hope you're feeling better this morning," Jimmy insincerely stated. "I just

286

came by to get a few compact music discs I had left on the shelf in the closet before I moved out."

"Go right ahead Son," Richard Henderson urged, showing no vitriol in his soft-toned voice. "Take your time Jimmy. When you get to be my age, you tend to value and appreciate every precious little second."

"Pop, why do you waste your time writing useless stories on that dumb obsolete computer?" insolent defiant Jimmy Henderson disrespectfully criticized. "Grand-pop Jim is right. You'll never sell more than two dozen stinkin' books for as long as you live. Grand-pop Jim says you're a born loser!" Jimmy Henderson sarcastically stated and then ungraciously sneered.

"I guess *you* and Grand-pop Jim have every aspect of my dismal life all figured-out," Richard Henderson coyly answered with a broad grin. "I wish I were only half as smart as either one of you two brilliant genetic geniuses!"

"Youth Revisited"

One August 2001 Monday morning Frederick Richard Barker drove his sky-blue *Buick LeSabre* east on busy *Route 30* to the *Blueberry Crossing Shopping Center*. The retired Hammonton, New Jersey brick and stone mason was a seventy-year-old health fanatic who was fighting a valiant battle against the onslaught of everyone's eventual common nemesis, old age. Fred parked his recently washed automobile in a convenient space and then strolled from the asphalt onto the pavement and ambled into the *Health Tree Nutrition Store* to purchase a re-supply of Vitamin E and a new bottle of potent *Multi-Vitamins and Minerals*.

"Hi," Fred politely addressed the preoccupied young girl standing behind the counter presently attending to the needs of a demanding customer. "Where's Sharon? She usually takes good care of me."

"Mrs. Bertino is in New York attending a health products trade show," the conscientious girl answered before ringing-up the fastidious customer's acquisitions on the cash register. "She'll be back in town on Wednesday unless my boss begins that *Pocono Mountains* vacation she's been talking about."

"Thanks for the info'," the regular patron replied with a forced smile. "Where's Bill, the manager? He always knows exactly what I want and need."

"Oh," the pretty blonde teenaged employee said, "Bill had complained that he's gotten another expensive speeding ticket and right now he's over at Town Hall paying the fine. He's worried about losing his license."

"Yeah, that makes a lot of sense," Fred answered in a disappointed tone of voice. "Bill's always buzzing around in that new red sports car of his. I guess that's what happens when you take too many vitamins," the twice a month *Health Tree* patron joked. "All that energy must go directly to *your* right foot. Maybe the notorious 'Billy the Kid' can bribe the cop with a few bottles of cholesterol tablets designed specifically for chronic coffee drinkers and avid doughnut munchers."

The pleasant young lady smiled in response to Fred's jovial demeanor and mild sarcasm and then focused her attention on another fussy customer's nutritional needs. Fred Barker casually sauntered over to a retail display rack and instinctively selected the two familiar bottles of vitamins and minerals the shopper had been in quest of. Then the health store visitor stepped to the main counter and placed the items next to the cash register. The fresh-out-of-high-school summer employee was a bit overwhelmed and quite flustered simultaneously waiting on two customers while nervously explaining to a third her mantra about where Sharon and Bill were.

Fred Barker then remembered he had only a half bottle of *Cava Cava* left on the kitchen counter at home, so the customer figured he would try and locate it himself until the pressured rookie store attendant could get caught-up on *her* rather challenging sales' responsibilities.

For several minutes Fred systematically searched the display racks to no avail, concluded that the *Health Tree* had sold out of that particular product, theorized that the girl behind the counter was unfamiliar with the retail outlet's diverse inventory and then, resigned to failure, Barker returned to the vicinity of the cash register. The attractive-but-impulsive novice cashier already had Fred's two acquisitions totaled-up and tucked inside a bag.

"Anything else Sir?" the freckle-faced young lady courteously inquired. "I'm trying to get caught-up with sales. I usually handle the stock room inventory and just occasionally work up here helping people during an emergency retail rush."

"I was looking for some *Cava Cava* but I guess I'll buy it next time around when either Sharon or Bill happens to be here," the purchaser casually remarked. "I still have half a bottle of the stuff at home, and that should tide me over until the next time I'm in the vicinity."

"Thank you Sir," the clerk sincerely stated. "Bill said I wouldn't be rushed when he left the store, and then around twenty customers have come in and bought vitamins and health foods in the last fifteen minutes. I'm still trying to figure -out all of the special discount keys on the cash register!"

"That's okay, I understand perfectly," the retired mason calmly said. "You'll catch-on in a hurry. Just charge me for the two bottles I had placed on the counter. I'll buy the *Cava Cava* in two weeks when my supply runs-out. Like I had said, I still have half a bottle remaining at home."

"*Cava Cava*," the girl laughed. "That's my favorite rock band. I didn't know it was a health product too! I learn a lot of real interesting things working here!"

"It's very good for calming the nerves and soothing one's restless spirit," Fred patiently explained to the *Health Tree* apprentice. "When you're my age Young Lady, you'll know that you need to stay relaxed. I'm trying to outdistance the *Grim*

Reaper and his relentless buddies who are in hot pursuit on my trail! It's a futile struggle we all lose in the end, ya' know!"

"Sir, that'll be a total of $22.95," the blushing self-conscious girl announced. "Thank you for your consideration during my minor rush trauma!"

Fred amiably paid the prescribed total and then ambled out of the busy store, holding the glass door open for some more clientele who were eagerly entering the *Health Tree* establishment. Barker drove home smiling, wishing his body were seventeen again and charming enough at *that* ripe pristine age to ask the pretty *Health Tree* girl for a malt shop date.

"Time passes more swiftly than we humans realize," Barker spoke to his wrinkled face in the *LeSabre's* rear-view mirror. "Where have all these years gone?" the driver mildly complained to his aged reflection as a traffic light at the intersection of Broadway and *Route 30* switched to green. "We're all vulnerable to the advance of time no matter what kind of physical shape we're in! I'm just trying to cheat Mother Nature out of a few additional years, that's all!"

Upon returning to his well-maintained Peach Street red-brick rancher, Fred was slightly peeved when opening the plastic bag on the kitchen table and then noticing that his purchases were not exactly the same items he had selected from the store shelves. The Vitamin E bottle was similar but of a different company make than the brand he had chosen, but the Multi-Vitamin and Mineral purchase was definitely not the same packaged item Barker had desired.

'The young girl must've gotten my sale mixed-up with another customer's order when I had gone to the back of the store looking for *Cava Cava,*' the rational fellow immediately suspected. 'I should've known that she was inexperienced and working under duress. Instead, I stupidly tried flirting with her when I'm old enough to probably be her great-grandfather,' Barker regretfully thought while simultaneously shaking his head and smiling about *his* own abundant shallow vanity.

The somewhat discouraged resident removed the Multi-Vitamin and Mineral bottle from its outer packaging and carefully inspected its unique label. '120 tablets. Take one daily every morning. Guaranteed to make you *feel* more youthful,' the reader skeptically comprehended. 'Manufactured by the *Eternal Youth Corporation*, Young, Arizona.' Then Fred reflected for a moment and generalized, 'This product sounds like some sort of rip-off to me!'

Intrigued by the plastic bottle's label, Fred paced to his den and removed *World Book Encyclopedia A* from a dusty bookshelf. Much to Barker's amusement and fancy, his curiosity and his research discovered that a place named Young, Arizona actually existed in the center of the state, and interestingly enough, the designation had no population statistic provided in the encyclopedia.

'Probably a fraudulent ghost town without a bona-fide *Zip Code* too,' the man mused, roughly returning the A encyclopedia back to its proper place. 'But I'm so fascinated by the claims of these *Multi-Vitamin and Mineral* tablets that I'll give them a try,' the "health-freak" decided. 'It also says on the label '*For Men Only*'. Now that's a laugh and a half,' Barker cynically imagined. 'We even have specialized vitamins and minerals for each gender. Now I really suspect that those tablets in that ordinary-looking brown plastic bottle are a real scam.'

Fred swallowed-down a Multi-Vitamin and Mineral capsule every morning for several weeks and soon forgot about the peculiar coincidence between Young, Arizona and *Eternity Youth Products, Inc.* The elderly but still-muscular fellow soon noticed the gray areas of his hair disappearing amidst expanding black hair growth, and the tablet user also happily observed the regions of his male pattern baldness thickening and regaining a healthy and fuller youthful texture. 'I no longer see the overhead bathroom light reflecting off my naked scalp,' the astonished man realized.

The structural tissue of Fred Barker's biceps, shoulders and arms began exhibiting vernal muscular definition, fat was rapidly vanishing from his midriff, and telltale old age wrinkles were being marvelously replaced by smooth skin all over his streamlined body.

"This product I'm taking is absolutely miraculous!" an exhilarated Fred Barker informed Sharon Bertino over the telephone a week later while heralding the terrific results. "I want to order a whole case of it if you have the item in stock! Whatever ingredients are in those tablets are awfully effective Sharon. I haven't felt and looked this swell in over thirty years."

"But the name you've provided me with, 'Multi-Vitamin and Mineral Formula from *Eternal Youth, Corporation* is nowhere in the *Health Tree's* extensive inventory," the confused store-proprietor answered in a rather uncharacteristic puzzled tone of voice. "I'm now checking my computer database and there's no evidence of any such product anywhere," Sharon conveyed to her disbelieving listener. "Fred, please look on the bottle and see if a *Health Tree* price stamp is on there. Maybe this item can be traced *that* way. Can you do me that favor?"

"Actually Sharon," Barker authoritatively said, "the sticker on the bottle reads $12.95 but it's just a typical-looking pink label with the cost typed on it, but the label isn't green and it doesn't officially read the words *Health Tree!*"

"That's very strange indeed," Sharon Bertino commented to her caller. "This sounds like some sort of prank and you're the unwary victim by purchasing the vitamins by sheer accident," Sharon speculated and revealed. "If you'd like Fred, you can bring the vitamin and mineral bottle back to the store and I'll give you a full refund," the businesswoman indicated in a fairly embarrassed tone of voice. "We do have a record that you obtained the item here."

"That's perfectly all right Sharon," Fred optimistically remarked after considering all circumstances. "I'll take my chances with this sensational product," the happy retired mason vociferated as the fellow proudly admired his vernal appearance in the den mirror situated over the fireplace mantel. "I have a four month supply so see if you can locate a distributor that handles this remarkable item," Barker requested. "I'll take out a loan and buy a fifty-year re-order if I have to."

"Okay, I know you're exaggerating but I'll thoroughly investigate the matter," the somewhat perplexed store owner returned. "But I assure you Fred, I've been in this business for over twenty years and I've never heard of such a company as *Eternity Youth Products, Incorporated* of Young, Arizona."

"All right Sharon, I believe you. Just keep me posted on your progress or lack thereof," the bewildered caller insisted. "Maybe it's psychological or perhaps simply mind-over-matter," the retired senior citizen claimed, "but quite truthfully I have complete faith and confidence in this wonderful product I'm now religiously taking."

A full month elapsed and Fred Barker was soundly conquering the persistent nemesis commonly known to all humans as "the dreaded aging process.' 'Now I can temporarily put the hospital geriatrics ward on hold,' Fred imaginatively thought and grinned, 'and I won't need the services of a wheelchair or oxygen tank for at least fifty more years if I can get my hands on more of these tremendously wonderful tablets. And with my insight, experience and maturity,' the elderly gent further whimsically pondered, 'I could avoid the social and peer pressure problems of the younger generation and besides that, I'll have no major financial obligations now that the first and second mortgages on the house have been satisfied. I just haven't stopped aging. I'm actually getting younger!'

The affable retired tradesman climbed into his *Buick LeSabre* and drove over to *A.T. Auto Clinic* on the corner of Fairview Avenue and *Route 30* to honor the car's next scheduled three-thousand-mile servicing and oil change.

"Gee Mr. Barker," Anthony (one of the brother co-owners of the auto' clinic) began, "you're looking much younger than you did the last time I saw you. Are you dyeing your hair? It's hard to keep a thing like that a secret with all of the snoopy people around this town perpetually gossiping non-stop day and night!"

"Anthony, thanks a lot for the unsolicited sincere compliment," Fred gratefully acknowledged. "For some peculiar reason, I do feel more masculine and more virulent than I ordinarily do. Maybe I'm entering my second childhood or catching my second wind, or something weird like that!"

"You almost look like you're a college student," Lou (the other mechanic on duty at the auto clinic) interrupted. "Fred, I can't believe how youthful you look," Anthony's older brother said. "I'll bet a lot of eligible single women and widows you know are keeping close tabs on you."

"Tell you the truth Louie," Fred communicated with a broad smile, "I do notice a certain sparkle in their eyes when they say 'hello' to me now. It's almost like I'm some sort of *Hollywood* celebrity or someone special like that! Or, it might just be my wild imagination at work."

"Have you discovered what that guy *Ponce de Leon* was searching for?" Anthony butted-in as was his bad habit. "You know Fred, that legendary Florida *Fountain of Youth* thing we've all studied about in school?"

"Well Tony, sort of," Fred Barker answered after clearing his throat. "Maybe I'm going through puberty for the second time around. It just might be an extraordinary case of glandular revitalization, hormone intensification or something strange like that! But frankly, I'm happy as long as I believe I'm getting younger and not older."

"When ya' finally find-out exactly what it is," Lou insisted, "bottle the secret formula and sell some to me. I feel like I'm eighty already and I'm still fifteen years away from receiving my first damned *Social Security* check!"

After leaving *A.T. Auto Clinic,* Fred drove east on *Route 30* to *Dunkin' Donuts.* Betty Martin, a seventy-year-old 1949 *Hammonton High School* classmate and former Hammonton High School prom queen was standing in line directly behind Fred at the main counter, waiting to be served.

"Why Fred Barker!" Betty ecstatically exclaimed. "My word, I haven't seen you in years. Ten years since our last reunion," Betty continued as the former beauty admired her junior class heartthrob, "and with Mr. Pastore passing-away last fall, all of our former teachers are now planted in the cemetery. But you," Betty Martin declared in what constituted more-than-mild astonishment, "you look like you haven't aged since we dated during the *Vietnam War* way back in the early '70s. How have you managed to cheat the daily assault of the fearsome aging process?"

"Oh hi Betty," Fred nonchalantly said when he finally recognized the identity of his longtime admirer. "I attribute it all to clean healthy living, laying off of tobacco and alcohol, and also, I give credit to drinking three tall glasses of milk and three double glasses of water daily. That's been my strategy for combating my inevitable admission into the geriatrics ward."

"Anything else?" the formerly beautiful woman anxiously asked. "I have a bit of vanity left in me too!"

The doughnut purchaser stared directly into Betty's pathetic-looking eyes and then gazed at her wrinkled countenance. "Yes Betty," Fred fabricated, "I also believe in sleeping and eating and going to the bathroom at the exact same times every single day and aggressively practicing yoga breathing exercises and *Transcendental Meditation* too!" the Dunkin' Donuts patron facetiously stated. "And oh yes Betty. I eat plenty of tacos and spicy Doritos too!"

"I'll have to try doing those things you've just suggested," Betty agreed, "because the results you've now obtained are absolutely convincing evidence to me. Forgive my candidness," Betty Martin proceeded and confided, "but you're probably the most talked-about and sought-after seventy-year-old man in all of Hammonton, and I mean that comment as the honest-to-God truth!"

"You're very kind and I'm quite flattered," Fred said while winking at his female acquaintance with an apparent twinkle in his left eye. The patient man received his three delicious double-chocolate doughnuts from the dark-complexioned foreign woman attendant and then haughtily paced-out of the popular junk-food eatery, feeling both smug and admired.

Later in the day the retired brick and mortar specialist had ordered a "small pizza with extra-thick crust and extra cheese" from *Bruni's Pizzeria* on Twelfth Street. Sam, the new owner of the pizza palace, felt compelled to praise Fred on his remarkable youthful appearance.

"Mr. Barker," Sam articulated as the genial Italian momentarily paused from kneading dough and then flipping the rounded mass high into the air, "you're looking more and more like *Hercules* every passing day. And your hair is no longer salt and pepper. How do ya' manage to keep yourself in such incredible shape?"

"Sam, please don't say that ridiculous comparison," the pizza purchaser blandly balked. "I'm a serious student of mythology and I wholeheartedly assure you that *Hercules* has been dead for over three thousand years! I'm insulted Sam! I plan to be around for at least two decades more!"

"Regardless," the pizza parlor proprietor persisted, "how have you managed to recapture your youth? If not *Hercules* reincarnated, are you some sort of sorcerer or alchemist?"

"Oh stop it Sam!" Fred chuckled. "I just believe that a healthy mind and a strong body go hand-in-hand," the former brick and stone contractor shared, inadvertently quoting the ancient Greek scholar *Plato*. "Take care of yourself, eat three square meals a day including plenty of Bruni's fabulous pizza, and don't watch annoying afternoon television soap operas. And oh yes Sam; stay away from ugly bossy women of all nationalities! That in a nutshell is the essence of my successful reclusive bachelor lifestyle."

"I'll have to remember that sage advice," Sam acceded in sheer wonderment. "If I can look like you do right now, I'd be the envy of every pizzeria owner in New Jersey; make that in the entire United States! I'd even join a monastery or a convent if I had to!" Sam joked as the owner's Sicilian wife standing at the cash register shook her head in disgust.

That night after consuming his small tomato and cheese pie, Fred mentally reviewed the significant details of his mediocre life. Children Jeff and Jill were each happily married, the son living with *his* wife in San Diego and the daughter being a single professional real estate/stock broker residing in uptown Manhattan. Wife Dottie had contracted breast cancer in the late 1980s and succumbed to the insidious disease in February of 1995. Barker was now free to find another woman, and since his seventy-year-old body had mystically been replenished and

296

restored to one seemingly belonging to a thirty-year-old male stud, the retired fellow was ready to again go hunting for a suitable mate in the wild and crazy American social jungle.

'I long for female companionship,' the melancholy man admitted to his now clear conscience. 'I'll try my gamble at romance at the gaming tables over in Atlantic City and see exactly what *Lady Luck* has in store for me. Life and love are just as much dangerous gambles as roulette wheels and blackjack tables are,' Fred Barker aptly concluded. 'And if Atlantic City falls through, there's always Las Vegas to explore.'

* * * * * * * * * * * *

The following Saturday night Fred Barker decided that he was adequately prepared to venture-out on "woman scouting patrol" at *Harrah's Casino* on the northern boundary of Atlantic City that bordered the family resort town of Brigantine. 'I remember taking Dottie to the boardwalk back in the early '50s, eating salt water taffy, and going to dances on the *Steel Pier*,' Fred recalled as the nostalgic fellow motored eastward on *Route 30* in his sky metallic blue *Buick LeSabre*. 'My God! How things have changed since the fabulous 1950s! Who would've ever thought that casino gambling would resurrect Atlantic City back into the '*Queen of Resorts*.' Wildwood, Ocean City, Cape May and Seaside Heights have to really struggle to try and keep-up with A.C. just like my other old flame Betty Martin has to struggle to try and keep-up with me!'

Barker piloted his *Buick* off of the *White Horse Pike* and soon was heading up Brigantine Boulevard past the opulent *Borgata Casino Hotel* and the *Trump Marina* towards all-too-familiar *Harrah's*. The glitter and excitement of the hectic casino filled the driver's mind with anticipation as Fred turned the steering wheel in the direction of the hotel's newly remodeled valet parking area.

After entrusting his nondescript vehicle to a nondescript casino attendant, the casino guest entered the flamboyant world of chance, gamble and potential romance. The man's pulse increased as the love adventurer boldly strode inside, his feet keeping a cadence to the rhythm of a Chuck Berry '50s rock and roll tune blaring from *Harrah's Casino's* twenty-four-hour non-stop background music system, the catchy tune blasting-out amidst the clanging of bells, buzzers and coins falling from slot machine tumblers and then being deposited into deep metal trays.

'I'll try my hand at the blackjack table,' Fred thought, seeking first the Queen of Hearts followed by the Queen of Diamonds. 'The odds are much better there than at the money-hungry slot machines. And besides,' the anxious visitor in quest of a seat further evaluated, 'I can sit-down and hopefully, a beautiful woman will suddenly appear like magic in the chair right next to me,' the aged dreamer imaginatively mused and fancied.

The robust casino gambler meandered past several active roulette wheel counters and then conveniently stationed himself in a comfortable black leather chair at an available poker table. A swarthy-skinned attractive Polynesian doll was the dealer at the ten-dollar minimum per game venue.

Fred's luck was mediocre for the first half-hour, playing the house almost even. Then his fortunes changed for the better when a knockout blonde approached and swiftly sat in the seat to Barker's right. Soon the energized man struck-up a friendly conversation with the gorgeous bombshell.

"Hi," Barker instinctively greeted the fantastically built alluring young lady. "Are you a magazine cover girl or a New York model?" the amateur gambler praised. "You certainly look like one or the other. What about a *Miss Universe* contestant?"

"Hardly!" the terrific-looking woman replied while checking-out Fred's stellar build and handsome young face. "I'm just a school teacher from Ventnor trying my luck at a little poker. I got a bit lonesome tonight so I figured I'd give *Harrah's* a whirl."

"Well, my name's Fred Barker," the impressed man introduced himself with a serious blush evident on his cheeks. "Can I buy you a drink? What's your pleasure?" the gambler said as a scantily clad free-drink attendant came sauntering by carrying her empty tray.

"Yes, a pina colada would be just fine," the luscious blonde declared while waiting for the beverage server to come around to their gaming location. "My name's Jessica Hughs. I'm a widow. My husband died in a terrible automobile accident four years ago this very night."

"That's really too bad Jessica," Fred Barker answered in a feigned sympathetic voice that satisfactorily camouflaged his overall delight at his new acquaintance being unattached. "My wife Dottie died of breast cancer a while back and I haven't quite gotten over the shock yet. It's a difficult and lonely existence once *you're* used to being married and then suddenly finding yourself jolted into isolation. Stark reality can be quite discouraging at times. Wouldn't you tend to agree Jessica?"

"I know exactly what you mean," Jessica Hughs readily admitted. "It hasn't been easy for me either. Loneliness can become a self-destructive torture!"

"Are you Scandinavian?" Fred perceptively asked as he glanced at Jessica's fair white skin. "You look exactly like that blonde chick that used to sing in the Swedish disco group *ABBA*. Agnetha was her name, I think!"

"Very astute of you to make *that* observation," Jessica bashfully stated and complimented. "Not about the name Agnetha, but about me being Scandinavian. My maiden name was Olson, and my parents were both Swedish immigrants. So, I suppose that now my real name again is Jessica Olson although I still officially go by Jessica Hughs."

The formerly preoccupied friendly cocktail attendant finally wiggled her way over to the poker table to take orders. "Give us a pina colada and a scotch on the rocks," Fred assertively declared to the well-proportioned lady clad in a skimpy cocktail waitress outfit. "And please have the bartender make the drinks extra-large. Here's a twenty dollar tip for your presumed cooperation."

"Why thank you Sir!" the cocktail waitress gratefully exclaimed. "Since the drinks are on the house, the bartender will surely fix your orders to your specifications after I tell him how generous your tip was! Incidentally, the bartender's my husband and he'll get ten bucks of this nifty twenty!"

Fred and Jessica were compatible right from the very start, and the two were quite jovial after losing two hundred dollars each at the blackjack table. After three rounds of drinks the half-inebriated twosome left the boisterous casino area and wove their way through a throng of raucous people, finally finding sanctuary in a main lobby cocktail lounge where the new friends chatted and listened to oldies' song lyrics performed by a talented *Elvis* impersonator. Soon their budding relationship was flourishing into mild romance.

"You know Fred," Jessica earnestly mentioned as the vivacious blonde slowly sipped her fourth pina colada," I really wish I had lived back in the more sedate 1950s. It seems like such an innocent decade from various movies I've seen and from the innocent songs of that era, years before the widespread use of drugs and before kids were exposed to sexually transmitted lethal diseases like AIDS."

"I know where you're coming from," the blonde's new-found escort aptly agreed. "I've often wished the exact same thing. I've always dreamed about going to *American Bandstand* and about slow dancing at sock hops! And I only wish I had lived during the time of Elvis, Marilyn Monroe, Natalie Wood and James Dean."

"Kids back then seemed more honest and sincere than today's teens do," Jessica Hughs astutely added, "and generally speaking, the children had more respect for family, for country and for good old-fashioned American traditions."

"You're absolutely right," Fred concurred, slurring a few of his words. "From what I've read, it was a very special era where people were more genuine, more civilized, more human! I mean," Fred rambled and slurred-on despite his addled mind's ulterior intentions, "I mean to say Jessica, that's what I've also concluded by watching old movies, by seeing *Ozzie and Harriet* TV reruns and by listening to the style of music from that incomparable time period."

The two new acquaintances were now indeed gravitating toward becoming more emotionally attracted to one another. At first it was a renewal in their hearts of the strong animal magnetism that is associated with "love at first sight," but soon thereafter it was a melding of kindred spirits and the definite presence of a powerful heartfelt emotional connection. This was the resurfacing of vital important feelings that both Fred and Jessica had longed for ever since the deaths of their beloved spouses. Now that fervor for opposite-sex companionship had ironically been rekindled, simply by a random chance blackjack table encounter, and so, Mr. Fred Barker and Mrs. Jessica Hughs were now thoroughly enjoying their outstanding compatibility.

"How about a date?" Fred impetuously proposed. "And please, 'Don't Be Cruel'!" the half-intoxicated fellow clarified as Barker alluded to and then mimicked the lyrics of the *Elvis* tune being sung twenty-feet-away by the suave side-burned impersonator.

"You Ain't Nothin' But a Hound Dog!" the slightly bombed blonde bombshell merrily reacted. "You Can 'Be My Teddy Bear'!" Jessica cleverly and creatively improvised. "How could I possibly resist your magnetic-like charm?"

The first gourmet restaurant date led to a second, and in a matter of a month, the enraptured pair was having an intense love affair. Fred would stay four nights at Jessica's place ideally situated on a Ventnor beach block, and then the gorgeous Swedish

300

doll would reciprocate by spending the rest of the week at Fred's cozy and secluded Peach Street Hammonton abode. Each love session became more intense than its predecessor had been, and the passionate couple openly shared years of suppressed feelings in the form of lovemaking and mutual affection.

The Friday before Palm Sunday Fred surprised Jessica with his announcement of an April vacation for two to Las Vegas. "I've booked a *United* flight out of Philly' for six nights at *New York, New York*," the euphoric courtship gentleman told his totally elated new soul mate. "Jessie, have your bags packed for a Monday flight departing from *Concourse C.* We're gonna' paint the town red and every other color of the rainbow too! Be prepared for the time of your life. And of course Jessie, I'm treatin' and payin' all the total expenses."

"What great timing!" Jessica enthusiastically noted. "It's the week of Easter vacation, well, we teachers call it Spring Break now, and I won't miss a day of school!"

The new lovers' smooth flight arrived without any hitch at Las Vegas's *McCarran International Airport* and then the two "almost newlyweds" removed their four suitcases from an airport rotary carousel and were soon transported by a hotel shuttle transfer service to 3790 Las Vegas Boulevard, the dazzling *New York, New York Hotel and Casino.*

"Wow! Just look at that replica *Statue of Liberty*, the authentic-looking New York City fire-boat in the water and the magnificent skyscraper façade!" Jessica verbally marveled. "It's almost like being in the *Big Apple* way out here in the Nevada desert!"

"And don't forget that scale-model rendition of the *Brooklyn Bridge* walkway decorating the front of the hotel," Fred most merrily added. "This whole adult fantasy world Jessie is like a wonderful dream come true!"

"I read in the flight magazine on our *United Air* jet that the casino is designed to give the appearance of *O. Henry's* turn-of-the-century New York. Everything is fashioned as if it were 1890 again," the excited blonde revealed. "Even the restaurants, the sidewalk cafes, the reproduction *Central Park* setting and the really unique retail stores sentimentally reflect the vintage 1890s' theme."

"And I had read in a brochure that *New York, New York* has scale models of a *Central Park* bridge, of 1890s' *Time Square* and of *Greenwich Village* homes and shops ,all exhibited as part of the general casino atmosphere. I'm glad I had booked this place for our memorable Las Vegas vacation!" Jessica's new-found lover exclaimed. "I find the whole place rather invigorating! Basically, quite rejuvenating!"

"Tell me, are there any other specific casinos you'd like to visit after our first few days at *New York, New York*?" Jessica asked, seeking as much tourist adventure as possible. "I hear they're mostly situated on the Vegas Strip!"

"Yes, as a matter of fact there are a few I plan on visiting," Fred answered his sweetheart rather emphatically. "Several buddies back in Hammonton told me that *Binions Casino* in Old Downtown Las Vegas has the best steaks and prime rib dishes in the world. *Binions* is definitely a must toward the end of our Nevada hiatus."

"Minions still go to *Binion's!*" jovial Jessica jested.

After checking-in at the stately *New York, New York* "mahogany-paneled Registration Desk," a bellhop led the couple over to the elevator lobby. "This incredible place even has an active *Coney Island*-style roller coaster circling it!" Fred disclosed as the three entered the lobby-level elevator. The helpful laconic bellhop quickly pressed the button for the tenth floor. "After we unpack our things we'll have to investigate all of the sights in this neat hotel and then we'll stroll by and perhaps tour some of the other palaces and castles on the glitzy 'strip' after tonight," Barker suggested to Jessica.

"You're so well-organized," Jessica Olson Hughs politely complimented as the elevator doors finally slammed shut. "I knew I was immediately attracted to you for some obvious reason!" the voluptuous widow said as the accommodating bellboy raised his eyebrows, wishing that he were lucky Fred Barker.

The first evening inside the glittering fantasy-land was spent touring the more popular *New York, New York* attractions. The pair enjoyed having supper at *Gallagher's Steak House*, seeing the fantastic stage-show "Lord of the Dance" in the thousand-seat *Broadway Theater,* and then casually strolling along the simulated boardwalk in the authentic-looking *Coney Island Pavilion.* Finally the New Jersey couple unsuccessfully experimented "unproven gambling theories" with several games of chance that were easily accessible inside the enormous casino.

"It's as if we're both kids again," Fred declared. Barker had never been completely honest with Jessica, keeping his true age a secret and pretending and claiming that he was a robust and ambitious thirty-five-year-old prominent brick and stone mason that had recently sold his prosperous business to a large corporation.

"If that's the case, I hope we both remain kids for the rest of our lives!" Barker's female supporter bantered back. "If only we could freeze this week in time!"

"Maybe some day a clever scientist will invent a formula that'll allow us to live to be two hundred wonderful years, our lives full of youthful vim and vigor," Fred deliberately conjectured and shared. "Anything's possible nowadays you know, thanks to the modern marvels of science and research!"

"Yes, I really hope so," Jessica solemnly attested, "because I haven't felt so enthusiastic and so positively thrilled about something since I was an eager bright-eyed teenager exploring the many sights of the *Atlantic City Boardwalk* for the very first time."

On Tuesday the New Jersey couple toured the major gambling premises along the Las Vegas strip, visiting such magnificent edifices as the *Bellagio*, the *Mirage,* the *Venetian* and the *Treasure Island* hotels and casinos. Jessica and Fred had already used-up two rolls of film just capturing the volcanic eruptions outside the *Mirage* along with the entrancing dancing fountains that were situated near the front gardens of the majestic and palatial *Bellagio.*

"I really enjoyed the pirate battle outside *Treasure Island*," Fred confessed. "It's as if I was a twelve-year-old freckle and acne-faced kid again," Barker confessed to his new lady inspiration. "I always wanted to be a buccaneer when I was a kid but soon changed my impractical ambition of being a swashbuckling pirate to desiring to play baseball for the *Phillies* when I turned ten."

"I want you to promise me that we'll return to Las Vegas at least once every five years," Jessica insisted as the doll wrapped her arms around Barker's slim waist and gave him a peck on the cheek in front of the *Venetian's* simulated *Campanile* clock tower. "This whole place is an absolute adult fantasy world come true, and I want to sincerely thank you for booking it."

"You have my word of honor that we'll return here again and again," Fred promised his special woman. "I love Vegas because there are no clocks in the casinos and time seems to stand still, or for that matter Jessie," Barker garrulously elaborated, "time seems completely irrelevant and unimportant wherever we decide to roam in this magical concrete and neon paradise."

The merry twosome discussed touring downtown Fremont Street later in the week and viewing the fantastic laser light show projected hourly onto an overhead domed screen serving as an outdoor pavilion exclusively designed for tourists. And the original familiar old time casinos were an alluring attraction when the spectacular colorful nighttime laser light presentations were not in progress.

"Several blocks of Fremont Street have been closed-off to allow for a mall-like pedestrian atmosphere," Fred informed Jessica, "and according to a pamphlet I had picked-up in the *New York, New York* lobby, the phenomenal nighttime laser show features cartoon characters dancing to *Motown* songs and jet fighter planes flying the length of the three-block-long outdoor screen with accompanying authentic sound simulation."

"And don't forget about your juicy steak at *Binions Casino*," Jessica Hughs reminded Fred Barker. "I understand that the whole downtown section of the old original Vegas casinos has been revitalized, just like our spirits have been rejuvenated too!"

Early on Wednesday morning the couple booked a tourist bus trip out to *Hoover Dam* and were thoroughly impressed by the gigantic man-made wonder, even taking an underground tour to inspect the massive subterranean operation of the colossal hydro-electric producing generators. Upon returning to the surface by elevator, the lovers discussed the magnificence of picturesque *Lake Mead.*

"It's hard to believe that something so majestic has been man-made by *Hoover Dam* harnessing the power of the mighty Colorado River," Barker related to Jessica. "This enormous dam supplies electricity to Las Vegas and also to much of Southern California."

"And all of this mammoth construction was admirably accomplished during the *Great Depression* before men had advanced technology and specially-designed-equipment," Jessica Olson Hughs concluded and related as their tour bus passed through Henderson on the trip back to Vegas. "I think I'm going to have students in my class do reports on Hoover Dam and Lake Mead."

Another highlight of the week-long vacation came on Thursday when Fred rented a car and the two adventurers motored-out to the *Painted Desert* where the enthralled pair gazed at and photographed the splendor and the beauty of colorful rock formations and "incomparable raw nature."

"You don't see anything quite like this spectacle back in Jersey," Jessica observed and said. "It's a completely refreshing environment that we're experiencing. No pinelands, boardwalks or beaches anywhere. It seems Fred that civilization and chaos miraculously ends a mile or so outside Vegas."

"True Jessie," her accommodating traveling companion amiably agreed. "It's as if we're the only two people left in the whole-wide-world and we're finally appreciating its total magnificence. It's like this is *Genesis* and we're Adam and Eve reincarnated!"

"That's a very poetic and romantic analogy," Jessica keenly indicated, showing her total satisfaction. "One of your literary ancestors must've been *William Shakespeare*."

On Friday morning Fred and Jessica had breakfast in a classic-themed restaurant inside *Caesar's Palace* and then did some light souvenir shopping in the casino-hotel's gigantic mall, which featured impressive talking statues of classical gods from Roman mythology. The fascinated visitors especially delighted in hearing *Bacchus's* raucous rambling monologue.

"*Bacchus* was the Roman god of wine, a real strange character who lived exclusively for pleasure," Fred informed his spellbound traveling partner, "and the Romans borrowed the idea of *Bacchus* from the worship of *Dionysus,* the Greek god of wine and merriment."

"You really know your Greek and Roman mythology," Jessie admitted. "You could've been a dynamic ancient history professor if you wanted to be!"

Somewhat exhausted from the week's accumulative escapades, the realistic couple finally trekked back to *New York, New York* to relax and unwind. Jessica desired donning a bikini and then sip a tasty pina colada by the hotel's main pool, but Fred preferred to "take a serious nap" and then join his female companion at poolside in "about two hours."

"Is tonight still on in Old Downtown Las Vegas?" Jessica asked. "I can't wait to go there again!"

"Certainly is," Fred affirmatively replied. "I'm anxious to once again feast my eyes and mouth on that giant prime rib over at *Binions*. It's gotta' be the highlight of *my* trip, I just know it! I can almost taste that juicy prime rib' platter right now! And we just gotta' have a repeat performance of that dazzling sound and light display that's shown nightly outside the casinos."

After "Jessie" left the tenth-floor air-conditioned room for her free outdoor "tanning and beverage seminar," Fred was smitten with temporary curiosity. 'Jessie took a twenty dollar bill to buy two pina colidas,' Fred recalled, 'so now's my chance to inspect her wallet, find her driver's license and learn exactly how old *she* really is,' Barker impulsively contemplated.

The highly motivated man rummaged-through the top left drawer of Jessica's bureau and soon located the object of his impetuous quest. Barker quickly removed the woman's pocketbook and after a minute of assiduous frantic fumbling, finally found her New Jersey driver's license. Fred's eyes nearly popped out of their sockets when his hungry pupils closely scrutinized her date of birth.

'My God!' Fred imagined in absolute amazement. 'October 9th, 1931! Jessica is a month older than I am!' the youthful-looking man astonishingly realized about his similarly revitalized partner.

Then a brown paper bag inside the top left bureau drawer caught the searcher's attention. Inside was a bottle of Multi-Vitamins and Minerals that surprisingly had been manufactured by the aforementioned *Eternal Youth Corporation* of Young, Arizona. The stunned man quickly unscrewed the cap and noticed that Jessica's bottle was two-thirds full.

'I only have about a thirty-day supply left in mine,' Fred avariciously estimated. 'I'll cheat a little bit and take one of her capsules right now and then transfer five more into my bottle so that I can extend my happy flirtation with youth revisited and with Mrs. Jessica Olson Hughs.'

The crazed pill pilferer tilted the lady's plastic bottle, popped a tablet into his mouth and then quickly swallowed it down. Fred was completely satisfied at assessing his own sagacity, and the broad smile beaming from his lips and face was accurately reflected in the bureau's mirror. A full minute passed without any change in Fred's joyful demeanor or any noticeable alteration in his standard excellent physical appearance.

Then there was a slow subtle modification in the general appearance of Fred Barker's facial features. Wrinkles began to show, his flesh became flaccid and started sagging heavily under the man's eyes and chin, and soon brown ugly age-marks developed on his arms and hands. The appalled sufferer then immediately felt arthritis and rheumatism rampaging in his knees, elbows, shoulders, hips, wrists, ankles, neck and fingers. Thousands of grayish hairs instantly sprouted from his scalp, and the new undesirable white growths soon easily enveloped and outnumbered their jet-black counterparts. The totally shocked

306

fellow was aging at the rate of a year a second, and after a minute's duration, the pathetic man atrociously looked as if he were a hundred-year-old decrepit invalid turning skeletal.

Ten seconds later the afflicted victim's flimsy anatomy collapsed upon the suite's plush red and blue carpet. Three seconds later Fred Barker's heart stopped beating, and then almost simultaneously, his lungs ceased breathing. The unfortunate man's body quickly disintegrated into two separate dust mounds, the smaller one inside his casual blue denim jeans and the larger heap inside his white cotton shirt.

The *Eternal Youth Corporation* Multi-Vitamin and Mineral bottle had rolled from Fred Barker's right hand and came to a rest upon the red and blue carpet, and the small print facing-up ironically read: '*Important: For Women Only!*'

"The Hotel Delaware"

Superstitious people believe and attest that strange incidents often occur on February 29 of every *Leap Year*. I had never placed too much credence in that unscientific claim until Tuesday, February 29, 2004, which unfortunately is a date I will certainly remember forever. Let me fully explain my accursed dilemma so that all will comprehend the true nature of my misery. The courtesy of another person's sympathy and understanding will be greatly appreciated. I realize that my tale will seem both illogical and incredible to anyone interpreting it, yet I believe I must share its veracity.

A *Leap Year* has three hundred and sixty-six days on the annual calendar, one more twenty-four hour interval than that which exists in a normal year. Greenwich, England scientists and concerned astronomers have adjusted the mechanics of the moon and months to interface with the Earth's revolution around the sun because a quarter of a day is lost each normal year when coordinating those particular solar system relationships. To accurately adjust for the quarter-day time discrepancy in the Earth's elliptical orbit around the sun, February 29 was created on the post medieval *Gregorian Calendar* (developed in the 1580s by Pope Gregory), which we still honor today after the old Julian Calendar (developed in 46 B.C. under the reign of Julius Caesar) had been discarded.

Some *Leap Years* are unluckier than others. Every year divisible by the number four (lets' say the year 2004 or 2008) is generally regarded in common knowledge as a legitimate bona fide *Leap Year*. No problem! So far so good! But every "century year" divisible by a hundred is *not* a *Leap Year* unless that particular year is also divisible by four hundred; then it is still defined as a legitimate, bona fide *Leap Year*. For example, the years 1800, 1900, 2100 and 2200 AD are *not Leap Years* because they can't be divided by four hundred. Conversely, the Year 2000 *was* recognized as a legitimate, bona fide *Leap Year* because it *was* divisible by four hundred.

A person born on this planet Earth has a one in 1,506 chance of being born on February 29 of a *Leap Year,* but nevertheless 4.1 million individuals living around the globe have made their official grand appearance on that weird day and of that large number, 188,000 of them live in the United States. Before February 29, 2004, I had always felt sorry for people born on

February 29 because their birthdays arrive only once every four years. Now I feel sorry for myself' for not staying at home on that ill-starred date. Allow me to fully explain my dilemma.

Some humans residing on this remarkable planet have attempted to conceal the bad omens that are associated with *Leap Year*. For example *Sadie Hawkins Day* is celebrated on February 29 when single women once every four years are permitted to abandon traditional courting practice and chase after or propose marriage to men, thus attempting to make the "unlucky aspects" of that ominous day appear less threatening and more tolerable to the human race. But I can earnestly assert from my own personal experience that February 29, 2004 is a day I feel compelled to remember for all eternity. Soon you'll learn why.

I had made an appointment for Tuesday, February 29, 2004 to meet the book editor of a small publishing company at eleven a.m. at the *Regal Restaurant*, Baltimore Avenue, at the southern end of Ocean City, Maryland. I had been an arcade owner and operator of *Dealers Choice Games* at 410 South Boardwalk, Ocean City, Maryland, from 1967-'81. So naturally I was quite familiar with the city and with the reputable *Regal Restaurant*, which was one of my favorite breakfast and lunch haunts when I had been an industrious summer boardwalk businessman in that popular resort city. From a nostalgia point of view, I was really looking forward to making the business/pleasure trip down to the Maryland shore.

The editor's publishing firm was located in Annapolis, Maryland, and so Ocean City was a convenient halfway destination for us to rendezvous to discuss my book submission that had attracted David Evans' attention. A contract had been signed by me and mailed to the publishing company. All I had to do was drive seventy miles from my Hammonton, New Jersey home to Cape May, catch the 7:30 a.m. ferry across *Delaware Bay* to Lewes, Delaware and then drive another hour down the Atlantic Coast to Ocean City, Maryland. My only regret at the time was that the very busy editor had scheduled our "brunch engagement" at 11 a.m. on the very inauspicious date, February 29, 2004.

My wife wanted to borrow my merlot-colored *Nissan Maxima* to impress some of her friends with *our* new driving machine, so I had to settle driving her light brown *Nissan Altima* from Hammonton seventy miles south down to Cape May, New Jersey. I left my home at six a.m., figuring I had more than sufficient time to make my easy connection with the *Cape May-Lewes Ferry* since I had conducted similar trips hundred of times before from 1967-1981.

310

Driving down Bellevue Avenue in Hammonton, I accidentally ran over a board lying in the street that had nails protruding face-up. I felt the *Altima's* steering wheel wobble when I drove another three miles to the *Atlantic City Expressway* entrance. Five miles in the direction of Atlantic City I frantically veered my wife's brown automobile into the *Frank Farley Rest Area* and quickly inflated the hissing tire with air.

Speeding down the *Expressway* at eighty-miles an hour, I thought I had had a hallucination of sorts. I had an uncanny sensation that I had skidded off the right shoulder of the highly traveled highway and that the light brown *Nissan Altima* had entered a pine barrens' forest and had then slammed into a tree, knocking me unconscious. 'I really didn't get a good night's sleep!' I remember thinking after surviving the rather surreal manifestation that seemingly featured a very real impact. 'I must get to the ferry before this confounded front tire goes flat. Then I will have really *missed the boat*!' my mind mused. 'I mustn't disappoint the editor by having a real collision. That accident was merely a wild figment of my imagination!'

In my wandering mind the same "air injection" of the affected tire was duplicated fifteen miles down the *Expressway* when I exited the toll thoroughfare at Pleasantville and then I again anxiously repeated the nerve-racking inflation procedure. After taking the *Expressway* to the *Garden State Parkway* I had to again stop at a *Parkway Service Area* and fill the tire with air and then desperately continue my extremely harrowing journey south. At Cape May I anxiously drove into a gas station and repeated the left front tire inflation a fourth time until I finally and gratefully made it to the ferry dock at 7:20. My mind was in a very paranoid state from all of the duress that had converted a supposedly pleasant ride into a living nightmare.

When I pulled-up to the *Cape May-Lewes Ferry* tollbooth I turned up the volume on the *Altima's* stereo radio and then paid the unwary grim-faced female collector the exact amount for crossing the bay. She never heard the air hissing and sizzling out of my left front tire. I was too arrogant and proud to understand that the tire traumas were seemingly attempting to warn me not to cross the *Delaware Bay.*

I drove the light brown *Altima* forward and boarded the ferry and at the time I felt haughty and confident that I had cleverly outsmarted a major obstacle (by fooling the apathetic toll collector) caused by unlucky February 29, 2004. The ferry's entrance ramp was raised, the ship's loud horns sounded, and next

I perceived that the huge one-hundred-twenty-vehicle capacity boat had gently slid out of its daily mooring.

I smugly sat in my wife's car, speculating that I would exit it a half-hour later and report my flat tire predicament to the captain when the ferry was halfway across *Delaware Bay*. 'The captain will get several of his crew-members to go down with a can of air-sealant and inflate my front tire so that I can safely make it down to Ocean City without further incident,' I cleverly imagined. 'I've outsmarted the ferry personnel by making my tire problem *their* tire problem to solve! I can always buy a brand new tire and have it mounted at a service station in Ocean City.'

A half-hour finally elapsed on my watch. I casually got out of the *Altima*, inspected the front tire and immediately ascertained that it had indeed gone flat. 'Tires are only flat on the bottom!' I recollect humoring myself' with a familiar overused joke.

My eyes glanced around and extraordinarily observed that the light brown *Altima* was the only car on the ferry, which (as I have mentioned) could easily carry and transport over a hundred similar-sized vehicles across the bay. Furthermore, after ascending the white metal steps to the top-deck, I detected that the ferry was enveloped in a very dense fog. I could barely see the landmark partially sunken concrete ship situated in the distance off of Cape May Point, but the famous *Cape May Lighthouse* was completely shrouded by the heavy veil of dense atmospheric haze that had descended on *Delaware Bay*.

Looking ahead south in the direction of the Delaware shoreline, I couldn't see any signs of land or of man-made structures. 'The fog's as thick as pasta sauce!' I evaluated. 'It's a good thing this ship has an adequate radar system!' I thankfully considered in an effort to allay my heightened anxiety.

Upon entering the main concession area I immediately recognized that something was very abnormal. 'Where are all the other passengers? I'm the only one in the entire room! Where are the waitresses and the food attendants? Nobody's on this cursed ship except me!' I quickly realized.

I wildly clambered up metal stairs to the captain's deck and attempted to open the door to his control room but the doorknob would not turn and the windowless white metal object would not budge. 'This is stranger than peculiar!' I nervously thought. 'This popular ferry has transformed into a mysterious ghost ship of some kind! Damned February 29!' I neurotically blamed that date. "Damned February 29, 2004!" I lustily screamed out into the apathetic dense *Delaware Bay* fog.

I investigated the entire ship and found no evidence of any other human being aboard. I anxiously searched in the Men's Room, in the lounge area, in the engine rooms, and even had the audacity to enter the forbidden "Ladies Room" but much to my disappointment and dismay, apparently I was the only person making the 'supernatural passage.' I recall wishing 'Please Lord, if only I could locate just one petrified passenger to provide me some semblance of comfort from my overwhelming apprehension. Then I'll feel a whole lot better,' I solemnly prayed.

My feet stepped to the ship's bow and I futilely held my left-hand up to my sweaty forehead, endeavoring to get a glimpse of some remote familiar landmark or perhaps hear a *Delaware Bay* oil tanker's horns. 'I've taken this ferry ride at least seven hundred times between 1967 and '81 transporting merchandise from family boardwalk stores in Ocean City, Maryland, Rehoboth Beach, Delaware and Atlantic City, New Jersey,' I remember thinking and analyzing. 'But this misadventure has got to be the most frightening seventeen mile crossing above and beyond any nightmare or seasickness I could ever have experienced!' I concluded as my body trembled and my knees knocked together. 'There just has to be some feasible explanation!'

The ferry's eerie foghorn blasted three times and as I stared off into the distance, my eyes finally were able to identify a nebulous-looking familiar object, the first of two parallel jetties that had been constructed about a mile into the *Delaware Bay* on the Lewes, Delaware side. 'At last, something I know and recognize in this crazy horrifying mental jigsaw puzzle! Now I have some hope! Those jetties had been built to prevent beach erosion,' I recalled.

The captain-less ship then strangely deviated from its normal course (that I had memorized in my head) and slowly cutting through the very palpable fog, it turned left and then entered the channel between the two jetties instead of continuing straight ahead past them to the Lewes, Delaware dock. The vessel was now nearer to Cape Henlopen than to its appointed destination, the Lewes, Delaware terminal.

I felt an intense chill circulating throughout my stunned body. The combination of an overall sinister atmosphere and an accompanying damp mist was comparable in my mind to imagining *me* traveling to a close friend's funeral aboard a mysterious lost ghost ship adrift at sea. At least that was the odd-type of sensation or perception that my consciousness had been rationalizing.

The ferry sounded its loud foghorn one final time and then effortlessly glided and slowly eased into a berth (that was unfamiliar to me) on the Delaware shore. I was quite perturbed and distraught with my heart filled with distinct trepidation, not knowing whether my crazy misadventure was an actual experience or a fantastic arcane delusion. Overhead gears threaded with thick chains suddenly began rotating and next the exit ramp for cars and passengers squeakily descended. 'We've landed near Cape Henlopen and not near Lewes, the ferry's destination,' I recollect thinking. 'This is definitely not where *we're* supposed to be! Something's certainly amiss here!'

My pupils steadfastly gazed through the persistent dense fog and saw a vague illumination directly ahead. A dim light shone from a hand-held lantern and a shadowy figure was silhouetted behind the weak glow. As if my body and spirit had suddenly been magnetized, my legs reflexively began walking in the direction of the obscure figure holding the morbid lantern.

My mind was still aware of the light brown *Nissan Altima* parked near the ferry's bow but my heart and body could not resist the inexplicable potent force that was deliberately pulling and dragging me like an invisible tractor-beam to the ominous figure holding the ancient-looking lantern.

"Welcome to the *Hotel Delaware!*" the old white-bearded man greeted. "Do not be afraid. I'm your host and your guide who will supervise your tenure here. I suppose you have many questions to ask me as most guests initially do."

"Who are you?" I tentatively inquired. "Why am I here? What's going on?"

"I am Diogenes," the ghostly character revealed, "and *you* are here dear visitor obviously because you're dead and your prodigious spirit desperately requires rest, rehabilitation and requiem. Come with me inside your new lodging," the grayish apparition dressed in ancient Greek garb communicated.

"And if I refuse?" I defiantly challenged. "What will be the consequences? What will be my punishment?"

"You have no say in the matter whatsoever," Diogenes grimly uttered. "You had surrendered your free will when your spirit escaped its confinement from inside your body. You have no choice as a dead entity other than to cooperate with my mandates. I can force you to perform any act that I want you to execute so don't resist my standard commands!" my pallid-faced guide

314

explained. "Insolence will not be tolerated. I repeat. You surrendered your free will when your spirit evacuated your body! Do you now comprehend that basic simple truth?"

My emotions were dominated by shock and awe. I remember thinking, '*You've* spent thirty-five years of your life teaching public school kids English grammar, vocabulary, writing and literature, have finally reached retirement age, have begun a promising writing career and have sabotaged it all by suddenly becoming deceased on February 29th!'

My body reluctantly followed Diogenes away from the spooky ferry mooring and then we meandered through the thick fog in the direction of a dilapidated structure situated on a high sand dune directly ahead. My restless spirit (or that element of it which still remained in my consciousness) demanded some plausible explanations from the hoary-looking guide dressed in a wretched-looking ancient mendicant's dull gray robe.

"I must have died in the automobile accident on the *Expressway!*" I gasped in horror. "Diogenes, did I die in an automobile accident? I just have to know *that* detail to alleviate my general nervousness!"

"What is an automobile?" the twenty-four-century old man asked. "It really doesn't matter what that item is," he continued speaking like a verbal cadaver. "You're dead as a doormat and now charged to my professional custody, automobile or no automobile. Do you fathom my words? The ideas and objects of your former world, of *my* former world, no longer interest me. They're both irrelevant and obsolete here!"

We slowly paced forward in the direction of the ominous-looking *Hotel Delaware*, which was now visibly outlined in the very thick mist with a rickety-looking shingle hanging on one hinge indicating my whereabouts. I found my eerie-sounding guide's answer very incomprehensible (let alone reprehensible) but nevertheless quite intriguing. "Diogenes," I boldly said, "are you the ancient Greek known to history as the *Cynic*?"

"You're quite a knowledgeable fellow because not too many souls make that particular association," my spooky host articulated, "and yes Stranger, you are correct in astutely making that connection. You must read books to be aware of that academic fact!"

"But how have you gotten from ancient civilization to the United States in the year 2004, and where did you learn to speak perfect English?" I stammered.

"Please Sir, one annoying question at a time," my new guardian insisted with a stern grimace featured on his ghostly and macabre-looking pale face. "I really don't know or care how I've arrived at *your* distant country. I can only tell you that once every three hundred and eighty-four years I'm moved and re-stationed by the unpredictable *Powers That Be* to a new drab and monotonous assignment in a new odd land. And finally," Diogenes proceeded with his fascinating monologue, "I've learned and conquered your language from conversing with other guests that have stayed or are staying at the *Hotel Delaware*. Does that answer satisfy your rather simplistic primitive curiosity?"

"Well, somewhat!" I marveled and replied. "I had read about you in a college philosophy class," I nervously stated, "and you were notorious for diligently walking the streets with a lantern looking for the face of an honest man. Is that legend actually true? Is that why you're still carrying your lantern?"

"You're most perceptive and appear to be highly educated," my alert guide observed and reluctantly complimented. "Yes it is true, but historical truths are meaningless now, both to you and to me. The only significant fact that really matters is that we're both dead and that *you* must reside by Heaven's decree at the very serene *Hotel Delaware*. That is why the ferryboat delivered you to these obscure premises in that rather intense fog. Every time the mist settles I know I'll be hearing the ship's horns," the old withered specter lethargically related, "and then that ominous blast is my signal to come out from the hotel and cordially escort our latest guest inside. After that task is done my next responsibility is to make my most recent ward as comfortable as possible."

As my famous deceased mentor and I paced up thirteen flimsy steps and gradually arrived at the *Hotel Delaware's* main entrance, the creaky door with un-oiled hinges slowly opened and Diogenes led me inside the musty building, which immediately reminded me of a dingy and despicable murky funeral parlor. Cobwebs, broken windows, bleak-looking dirty chandeliers and layers of dust everywhere suggested that the ramshackle hotel for death-transients was truly a ruinous unkempt *deathtrap*.

"Diogenes, is it true what I've read in encyclopedias that you believed that wealth and honor are of little value because they do not help men lead just and moral lives?" I instinctively asked my laconic host. "I recollect that principle as being the cornerstone to your philosophy."

"All of those seemingly important old ideas are quite immaterial and irrelevant now," Diogenes glumly answered. "Virtue, honor, wealth and morality are no longer essential elements of behavior. If I were you," Diogenes imperatively cautioned, "I would ask fewer questions and then pay strict attention and learn the fundamental elements of *your* new environment. Just remember Sir, you're now dead, and nothing else really matters. Please leave the myriad minuscule problems of the world to the living."

"But didn't you once visit and meet *Alexander the Great*, and he insisted on granting you any wish you wanted," I almost hysterically ranted, "and then you absurdly replied, 'Please move out of my sunlight,' and then *Alexander the Great...*"

"Silence Fool!" Diogenes angrily exclaimed as he held his spectral lantern up, fully exposing his hideous skeletal face. "Any more outbursts from you will surely result in dire consequences for your captured soul. Heed my simple basic commands Stranger, or else you'll certainly be doomed to a far worse eternal fate than mere death! I trust now that I've concisely communicated that stark cause-effect relationship to you."

'*I'm* very much like Diogenes, an avowed cynic and a devout skeptic,' I rationally thought. 'Perhaps that is why I'm assigned here and *he* is here too. The poor Greek scholar has been commanded to teach *me* what I need to know and what years of doubt could not make me realize,' I conjectured.

My heart felt tempted to mentally ask (for *we* were transmitting thoughts and words through a fantastic telepathy and not by using our mouths and voice-boxes) my distinguished escort if he had ever heard of an Athenian named Socrates, but since I didn't desire to antagonize the melancholy morose apparition and subsequently suffer his wrath, I refrained from making the inquiry, for I fathomed that presently *he* had absolute dominion over my weak (and maybe absent) will.

Diogenes solemnly led me through the foyer of the shabby antiquated edifice to a gloomy dusty poorly lit lobby and we passed empty chairs with torn upholstery and several sofas neglected by time and quite apparently in dire need of repair. At the *Hotel Delaware's* front desk my escort solemnly asked me to sign both my real name "John Wiessner" and my pen name "Jay Dubya" in the ledger, which I cooperatively complied while coincidentally and obediently enacting his baneful command.

"How did you know my real name and how did you know I had a pen name?" I requested knowing. "You must be omniscient," I mentally transmitted.

"Knowledge in this afterlife is transparent and not opaque as it is in *our* former world," Diogenes telepathically related, "and it is not exclusively confined to a person's form or body. I simply read your vulnerable mind as if I was reading an elementary book or a tablet. It's quite easy once you learn the knack!"

"Well," I commented in sheer amazement, "what about heaven and hell and purgatory and what about everybody else that's dead and *Jesus* and…"

"Look!" my upset teacher said in an admonishing tone of voice, "the information you're requesting is not available or known on *this* lowly death level. Once you leave this holding area and move on into the greater transcendent after-world," Diogenes carefully enunciated, "then those typical questions that presently riddle your limited comprehension might be satisfactorily answered at the next higher phantom station. Now do you fully evaluate your lowly status on the eternal ladder?"

"But if I died when my car had veered into the woods," I mentally rebutted, "how could I have lived to put air into my front tire several more times before arriving at the ferry terminal?" I desperately argued. "And Diogenes, if my car was wrecked up and if I was dead on impact, how did I manage to drive it all the way to Cape May to take the ferry across the bay to this horrible *Hotel Delaware?*"

"It probably takes about an Earth hour for true death to finally set in," Diogenes theorized and objectively communicated, "and you were still mentally carrying out your trip to the ferry during that delicate hour of transition from your former life to this one. So spiritually, mentally and emotionally," the ancient pessimistic sage cleverly observed and concluded, "you had completed that part of your trip even though your body had perished in the accident you had previously so vividly described."

"Who else is registered here as a guest?" I inquisitively asked. "How many rooms does this place have for occupancy? It looks pre-Victorian in architecture!"

"Please Sir, one appropriate question at a time," Diogenes aggressively chastised. "You have all eternity to learn and decipher what you feel you need to know. You'll soon discover that the *Hotel Delaware* has thirteen guest rooms. And I don't know if that mediocre number is symbolic of anything or not."

I glanced outside a window and the only thing I could discern in the dense fog was the aforementioned unhinged black shutter hanging down from the wooden outside wall that quite evidently needed several serious heavy coats of paint. "Oh," I thought and communicated, "that numerical symbolism makes a lot of sense, having thirteen rooms. Delaware was the first state, and there were thirteen original colonies that had united in the war of independence against England. One room for each colony is a wonderful coincidence! Wouldn't you agree Diogenes?"

I learned from my orientation guide that the other spirit guests residing at the hotel were distinguished personages Benjamin Franklin, George Washington, Thomas Jefferson, Edgar Allan Poe, Abraham Lincoln, Ulysses S. Grant, Mark Twain, Henry Ford, Albert Einstein, Franklin D. Roosevelt, George Herman "Babe" Ruth and Marilyn Monroe.

"But those people are all famous?" I challenged my honorable guide. "What's the meaning of all this? Where do I fit in, a common public school English teacher?"

"You mean they all *were* famous," Diogenes cunningly corrected and clarified.

"But tell me, why am I here with all of these deceased celebrities, inventors and presidents if I'm just an unfortunate ordinary dead person?" I demanded knowing. "Honestly, I certainly lack their accomplishments and their credentials!"

"Maybe you'll become famous after your death just like Herman Melville or William Shakespeare," my ancient Greek ghost page speculated and mentally conveyed. "My senses perceive that you had always wanted to communicate with the dead. Now here's your big chance."

I learned several bizarre things from Diogenes. When Babe Ruth had registered as a guest Christopher Columbus had simultaneously checked out and had been moved to another higher plateau in the afterlife. And when Marilyn Monroe's shade was accepted as an official resident, Henry Hudson's apparition was allowed to move on to loftier post mortem pursuits.

"At the rate of new guests and old ones coming and going," I commented to the stone-faced and generally apathetic Diogenes, "I won't get out of this lackluster *death trap* for another two hundred years judging by how long George Washington has been a prisoner, er, I mean a visitor here."

"That logical assessment seems about right," my ghastly-looking skeptical companion agreed. "But you must remember," Diogenes ruefully clarified, "time as you knew it is meaningless at

319

this place. There is little difference between a minute, a day, a century and a millennium at this splendid and unique hotel. Time here can either expand or it can contract. As that fellow Einstein in Room 1955 once told me, everything including time is relative!" my host mentally related with a very weak-but-irritating smile vaguely reflecting from his countenance.

"Oh," I mentally answered, "now that explanation of yours makes perfectly good sense. When one person moves in, the lucky spirit that has been here the longest is finally eligible to move out. It's sort of like a predictable rotating lottery of sorts!"

"Right you are Sir," Diogenes aptly concurred with my brilliant deduction. "When you moved in, Ben Franklin, according to the established rotation, must step onto the ferry and be taken to the next higher station, wherever that is!"

Just then the ferry horns blasted three times, suggesting that Ben Franklin was obediently ambling up the ramp and happily departing the dismal dreary grounds and sinister vicinity of the *Hotel Delaware* to embark to some new destination in the very bewildering indefinable death realm.

"But why have I been summoned to this morbid death holding station if I'm not famous?" I stubbornly asked my pale pathetic transparent partner. "I think I really don't deserve to be here! The accomplishments of your other guests certainly eclipse and dwarf mine!"

"Maybe you'll finally have become famous when it's time for your departure on yonder ferry," my gruesome-looking ghoulish host imaginatively suggested. "Don't short-change yourself, even after you're certifiably dead!"

"I would rather have led a full normal life as a nobody than to sacrifice twenty-five golden years of retirement for fame after my ill-fated automobile accident!" I strenuously objected. "Life is unfair and now I know that death is too!"

My mind (or what was left of it) was in a complete quandary. I asked to be led to my assigned room, which was the only one situated on the hotel's second floor, ironically Number 2004. Then a certain parallel relationship connected inside my confused, befuddled and disoriented mind. The hotel's room numbers corresponded with the exact year each person had perished. I had died in 2004 and I knew from biographical accounts I had read that Dr. Albert Einstein had died in the year 1955.

"Thank you for showing me my living quarters, or should I say my death quarters!" I mentally said to normally reticent Diogenes. "Are you the only employee here?"

"Why yes," the now guide-turned-butler cerebrally transmitted, still holding his trademark dimly lit lantern. "You'd better keep that exquisite sense of humor of yours," the notorious cynic smartly advised, "because it's guaranteed to raise everyone's *spirits* around here! Ha, ha, ha," he shockingly cackled like an obsessed maniac.

"Why do we have to enter and exit via doors if we're spirits?" I seriously asked. "Why don't we just filter through the walls like ghost vapors?"

"We could, but that would be impolite and too annoying to our other prominent guests," Diogenes reprimanded. "It obviously would infringe on their privacy. You wouldn't want that ferry to *barge* into your room would you? Ha, ha, ha," the ancient Greek wildly cackled. "So, George W., Abe L. or Marilyn M. wouldn't enjoy *you* interrupting *their* privacy or their meditation by *your* intrusively whisking your way through the outer wall, would they? I doubt it!" the now-spirited ghost convincingly argued.

I asked Diogenes to provide me with an abundant supply of pens and writing paper, and to accommodate my requests the specter later rummaged through closets and through desk drawers and eventually located the prescribed requested items. I thanked my new acquaintance, prudently sat at the dusty desk and assiduously began re-writing my manuscript that I had recently sent to my supportive Annapolis publisher. And after meticulously completing that project, which I thoroughly believed far surpassed the original version in quality, I commenced authoring the first of four prodigious novel-length manuscripts that I had felt inspired to write. 'I have two hundred years to write at my leisure,' I intrepidly surmised, 'and this is one labor of love that I feel compelled to perform. I must organize my novels and novellas as carefully as possible and make each page of superior quality. I'll be my own ghostwriter!'

Diogenes had told me that I could export (without penalty) one package into the "physical world" so I was elated when I was able to fill a storage chest with eight thick manuscripts, novels and novella collections. The old chest, loaded to capacity, was then addressed and sent to my publisher in Annapolis, who would be shocked to receive the unanticipated documents authored by a dead writer and surprisingly delivered via conventional parcel post. The details of exactly how this *novel* transaction was done or negotiated had never been disclosed to me, but I had placed implicit faith and trust in the integrity of the sad-faced Diogenes, who incidentally had expertly and expeditiously handled that special favor for me.

It has been a very strange existence for me in this morbid-but-placid afterlife, having no need for either eating or drinking. The desire for biological satisfaction (or for its accompanying pleasures) was totally absent from the *two-dimensional* death world to which I was confined, but I was happy to note that mental pleasure could still be experienced after I had finished the task of writing those assorted "perfect manuscripts."

Feeling exceptionally lonely, I finally summoned sufficient courage to exit my drab and uninspiring room and visit the eldest guest spirit at the *Hotel Delaware*, so I politely knocked on the door of Room 1799. George Washington graciously answered my knocks and the tall pale specter asked me to enter and review post-colonial history events for him.

"It's indeed a distinct honor to meet my country's first President," I anxiously began, "and you look identical to your famous portrait that appears on the one dollar bill."

"Sir," the eminent Founding Father and renowned military general said with his mind, "confidentially, I've never visited anyone else in this confounded hotel. I was afraid that there might be some sort of supernatural reprisal associated with me leaving my humble quarters. Apparently Sir," white-wigged George Washington continued, "you possess great daring to act independently without knowledge of rules and death customs, or without fear of dire consequence."

Then George Washington's specter stated that I too must be a famous person to be confined to the obscure sanctuary of the creepy *Hotel Delaware* even though I was totally unaware of my fame or reputation by virtue of my untimely and premature departure from mortal existence.

I thanked the venerable American for his unsolicited praise and encouragement and then I learned that all of the books in General Washington's room had been printed *before* 1800. The poor fellow thirsted for knowledge about America after his unfortunate death on December 14, 1799.

"Tell me Sir," the tall powder-wigged giant of history mentally said, "has the *Constitution* and the nation adequately survived the past several hundred years?"

I cogently explained to venerable President Washington all that had transpired from his colonial and *Revolutionary War* era up to the year 2004 including the sensational changes associated with the *Industrial Revolution,* the *Civil War*, the invention of the

322

train and the automobile, the *Great Depression*, the two world wars and the atomic and computer ages. I also divulged that the *Constitution* had been *amended* many times, and we discussed those particular modifications in great length.

"Do you mean to tell me that you own a device you call a car that can go up to sixty miles per hour in just six seconds and you have a special gauge you call a speedometer that registers one hundred and forty miles an hour?" Washington marveled and mentally conveyed. "I guess the stagecoach and the horse and wagon are obsolete. These commentaries of yours are quite astounding! Oh I get it!" Washington exclaimed. "The word automobile means that a coach could move all by itself without any horse pulling it! Quite in-genius terminology if I may add!"

"Well, not exactly," I respectfully clarified. "People still go to race tracks and bet on horse races. A big one each May is called the *Kentucky Derby.*"

George Washington was fascinated by all that I told him, for we must have exchanged uninterrupted conversation for at least a full Earth month without the need of sleep, food or drink. I never thought I could be so vociferous as I had been in *his* inimitable company. And when Washington discovered from our lengthy discourse that there were now fifty states instead of thirteen, his pale face produced a proud broad smile.

President Washington became rather disconsolate upon hearing about the notion of "separation of church and state" and how "the establishment clause" had been "misinterpreted" by a sequence of "unfortunate" *Supreme Court* decisions. "National morality cannot last in exclusion of religious principles," our first chief executive lamented and expressed, "and your public schools should not be devoid of teaching morality based on religious principles either," he mentally elaborated. "Your institutions of learning are therefore producing a vile generation of bratty dolts who might have knowledge in subject matter but who lack discipline, resolve and wisdom that come from the practice of simple basic religious morality. The first *Ten Amendments* to the *Constitution* should be predicated upon the *Ten Commandments* handed down to Moses and embodied in the *Bible,*" George Washington adamantly insisted and emphasized.

I humbly informed my perceptive listener about abortion rights, about homosexual marriage and about criminal and animal rights. He nearly blew a fuse arguing, "It's a travesty to believe that such ungodly things have been resulting from the misguided interpretation of a Godly-inspired document such as the sacred

323

United States Constitution. And when you tell me that God has been taken out of your public schools," Washington continued in an emotional state that bordered rage, "then I believe that I had fought the entire *Revolutionary War* in vain. Our nation is doomed to decay from within. Civil rights will ultimately destroy individual morality, which will produce the decadence that will weaken and then eventually erode away the foundational values of *our* great nation. There is no doubt in my mind that *that* catastrophic end will be inevitable!"

On the optimistic side, the first President was elated to know that the country had survived over two centuries of critical challenges since his death in 1799. The great statesman and military strategist found hope in the prospect that a national crisis similar to the *Civil War* or the *Great Depression* might once again shake the country out of apathy after the year 2004. George Washington's spirit explicitly indicated to me that there possibly would emerge a noble crusade to return to the great moral roots and the powerful American traditions strongly embodied in the *Declaration of Independence* and in the *Bill of Rights*. He referred to this phenomenon as "the Phoenix resurrection."

Upon leaving the General's "solitary confinement sanctuary," George Washington's ghost thanked me for my informative visit while regretting that I had conveyed some "distasteful news" about future events and changes in the "established moral codes" that have been over the years erroneously affected by judicial and legislative adaptations in the "legal codes."

I left George Washington's shoddy modest accommodations at the singular *Hotel Delaware* and returned to my own morgue-like second floor room. It again occurred to me that since I had died in the year 2004, I had the only *death quarters* on the second tier. Then an interesting thought flashed through my transparent brain. When additional renowned people would die, more second-floor rooms would have to be added on to the ancient hotel so that the new restless spirits could peacefully dwell until they were allowed to ascend to the next dreadful echelon in the afterlife. 'Or perhaps there are many other death holding stations similar to this *Hotel Delaware* to allow for the other decedents,' I hypothesized.

I stayed dormant in my room for an unspecified interval of time, which to my comprehension remained quite anonymous and mysterious because there were no clocks or wristwatches or views of the sun and the moon from anywhere inside the dreary deplorable hotel. Then I attempted to prepare the outline to a new manuscript but ideas and words eluded me, so I temporarily abandoned that ambitious enterprise.

My mind decided that I would pay a visit to another extraordinary personage trapped in the archaic weather-worn domicile, so I elected to interact with a particular idol of mine from nineteenth century American literature. I had to choose between Edgar Allan Poe and Mark Twain. I chose the former hoping to have an opportunity to speak with Samuel Langhorne Clemens at a future date (even though calendars and dates did not exist anywhere inside the very weird and mystical hotel).

My knuckles rapped on the door of Room 1849 and mused that Edgar Allan Poe would assume that I was an itinerant raven determined to annoy and pester him, all relaxed and pensive in *his* tranquil solitude.

"Hello," I hesitantly greeted the literary master. "May I come in to chat for a while?"

"Certainly," Poe cooperatively-but-cheerlessly replied. "You look harmless although I must laugh at the strange apparel ornamenting your body. I presume you are from a future age? You appear too casual to be dead. Is that how you were buried? Has formality been abandoned entirely?"

"No Sir, er I mean, I don't think I was ever buried and have no knowledge of being buried," I stammered. "This is what I was wearing when I died."

"Well then," my illustrious academic erudite host persisted, "are you from *my* future?"

"Yes Sir," I keenly answered the much-revered genius. "You happen to be a favorite author of mine and I immensely enjoyed teaching my students many of your excellent stories," I sincerely elaborated. "I was a school teacher during most of my life," I clarified, "and your tales of horror and your classic adventure stories were among the best I ever read or analyzed. I especially liked teaching my students your tales 'The Cask of Amontillado' and 'The Fall of the House of Usher'."

Poe was quite flattered by my complimentary remarks and asked me to sit down even though I no longer possessed a body that required rest from its weight or from its exertion. I respectfully honored my literary benefactor's request out of force of habit and out of reverence for past human courtesy customs.

"Well kind Sir," E.A. began, "you must know about my dear Virginia?"

"Your wife Virginia died of tuberculosis in 1847, so in all due deference," I acknowledged, "you know more about her last moments on Earth than I do since you had passed away in 1849."

"I apologize, kind Sir," Edgar Allan Poe mentally transmitted while momentarily exhibiting a rare smile, "but I originally meant the state of Virginia where I grew up and whose memory I have always held dearly inside my miserable heart."

And after I educated Edgar Allan that there were now forty-nine states in the Union besides his precious Virginia, the cheeks on the pale ghost's countenance almost turned from ashen to pink. He had accurately speculated that a bloody forthcoming *Civil War* was imminent after 1849, but a tear seemed to form in his right eye when I explained the tragedy and the widespread suffering in both the American North and the Dixie South. Many painful wounds had to be healed after the devastating conflict between the *Union* and the *Confederacy.* "A period of *Reconstruction* had to be initiated," I very patiently revealed and explained. My listener was just as glad as George Washington had been about the acquisition of additional states to the *Union.*

I immediately identified with the dead man's unique sense of patriotism and with his skeptical outlook on death and its eternal idleness. Much to my surprise, Edgar Allan Poe was amazed that he would become a famous giant in American literature after his untimely death in 1849. The master of the macabre had been found lying outside a Baltimore voting place on October 3 of that year, and he had died in a city hospital four days later without ever regaining consciousness.

"Do you mean to say that my work is read in virtually every high school and college English class in the country?" Poe incredulously mentally asked and marveled. "I knew I would die in poverty and disgrace," he bluntly continued with remorse and disenchantment, "but I never reckoned I would achieve national and international acclaim. You Sir, pardon my aggressive nomenclature," E.A. paused to measure my reaction, "are a most welcomed time courier. In you I see much of me, and I mean this with sincerity when I say that it is most grievously calamitous that you too are deceased and doomed to incarceration in this especially decrepit hotel. Have you attained notoriety during your lifetime?"

"No," I bluntly lamented, "and I really don't know why I've been assigned to and incarcerated here inside the *Hotel Delaware* with such a distinguished group of literary, famous and historical souls occupying the other rooms."

326

"Perhaps you too will be visited by a messenger rapping on your door several hundred years from now and told of your great contributions to civilization," Poe theorized and suggested. "Then *you* will know the pure pristine genuine delight I'm presently feeling at learning that my life's work has achieved honor and prestige in the literary community, a community that vehemently abhorred me and my endeavors and one that I absolutely despised and loathed during my brief tenure on the all-too-mundane Earth."

Then I had the pleasure of discussing with the master most of his outstanding literary gems including "The Cask of Amontillado," "Murders in the Rue Morgue," "The Fall of the House of Usher," "The Tell-Tale Heart," "The Black Cat," "The Pit and the Pendulum" and the "Masque of the Red Death." I was *literally* held spellbound and was thoroughly captivated by Poe's vivid animated descriptions and by his graphic explanations in regard to what critics consider his classic works.

In "The Purloined Letter," I curiously stated, "you had essentially invented the entire theory and methodology of the detective story," I praised the great short story author, "and thousands of writers since your time have imitated the superior model that you've so effectively pioneered. I believe," I respectfully continued, "that you Sir, and I sincerely mean this, have been perhaps the greatest influence on the course of American literature over the past two centuries."

"I always believed that the ideal critic should be objective while slightly leaning toward the negative side," Poe declared while alluding to his own literary reputation at being a premiere reviewer of essays and short stories. "So that's why I get along so well with Diogenes," he humorously added. "But above all else, an author must possess originality, courage of heart and the grammatical skill to efficiently convey *his* intended message to his readers. Otherwise," the disconsolate and totally bored fellow decided, "the author is not an author at all but merely a very ambitious *writer* aspiring to great accomplishments but doomed to failure or in the final analysis, be destined to produce volumes of mediocrity."

I had fathomed and found much merit in Edgar Allan Poe's enlightening commentaries and I only wished at that moment that I could return to my human form and pursue my literary aspirations with the superb knowledge I had absorbed during our most intriguing dialogue. When neither of us had anything additional to relate or to discuss, I bid the prolific genius (possessing a burgeoning vocabulary) "adieu" and next shuffled

327

down the dank dim corridor and then climbed up the rickety wooden steps, ascending back to my non-inspirational room.

My consciousness was gratified by the keen insights that the eminent editorial authority had to share with one of *his* less-talented admirers. Poe's final words remained in my mind and after the comprehensive interview, my energized brain tended to review them incessantly. "Always remember kind Sir," the literary master had imperatively transmitted, "a combination of truth, soul, passion, beauty and creativity is what elevates literature to a higher shelf than the one occupied by traditional newspaper journalism and by ridiculously written political propaganda."

Throughout my humble life I, like Edgar Allan Poe, tended to be reclusive, shy and moody. I never really liked gossip, small talk or was fascinated by glib and garrulous people. 'An introverted nature was also an introspective advantage that both Poe and I cherished and exercised during *our* separate writing sessions,' I realized. "We both like to be alone to ponder and to explore our inner souls and to investigate the deepest secrets lying within our secluded hearts,' I then understood. 'We both quietly loathed obnoxious and ultra-gregarious people.'

And soon a much more enlightening theory entered my troubled mind. I was in one way or another much like all of the inhabitants of the deteriorating non-maintained *Hotel Delaware*. I was diplomatic and gentlemanly like Washington, introverted and emotionally tormented like Poe, and inventive with an *Alpha* (aggressive and determined) personality like Thomas Alva Edison, whom I had selected to be my next hotel resident to interview.

I had by then willfully accepted my possible two-hundred-year confinement in the gloomy *Hotel Delaware* in a rather stoical manner, and frankly, I finally became cognizant of another interesting facet of the complex bizarre puzzle. I was also very much like Diogenes, priding myself on being a skeptic and a cynic about most everything and most anything.

I confidently descended the decrepit staircase to the ground-level corridor and floated (without walking a single step) down to Room 1931 where Thomas Alva Edison's spirit was quietly kept to ruminate. The man's *shade* was a little hard of hearing but after I had introduced myself in a loud clear voice, Edison welcomed me into his disheveled room that had so many cobwebs that it reminded me of a monstrous cocoon. That graphic notion immediately made me contemplate that *we* were indeed trapped in some sort of indefinable chrysalis, waiting to be released into a

328

new existence just as an ugly caterpillar transforms into a beautiful butterfly inside a second *natural* womb.

"I must say I admire your very evident audacity," Edison's ghost remarked as it eagerly greeted me at *his* door. "You demonstrate the daring of an old friend of mine, Henry Ford," he generously praised. "Make yourself comfortable if that's at all possible in this bizarre rudimentary plateau in the afterlife."

"Why Henry Ford!" I exclaimed in a very un-ghostly-like manner. "He's staying in this same hotel in Room 1947. I remember his name and room number from the registry ledger that's kept down in the main lobby."

"Why I'll be giraffe's grandfather!" Thomas A. Edison bellowed in an uncharacteristic and excessive display of emotion. "I've been staying here at this repugnant run-down hotel right down the hall from one of my favorite contemporaries and have been completely ignorant of that fact until *you* came along and informed me. I'll have to garner up enough gumption to mimic your fine example and pay the old coot a belated surprise visit!"

Edison was very anxious to know what had transpired in the world after 1931, and upon hearing about *Bose* sound systems, computer floppy and compact disks, video cassettes, color television, cell phones and the *Internet*, the great inventor, who possessed over a thousand United States' patents, heartily and exuberantly laughed out loud.

"You know," the incomparable genius Thomas Edison responded, "I only wish that I could've lived to see in full operation all that you've so admirably described. I'm so glad and proud that my years of research and experimentation had led to the discovery of these phenomenal creations that you've so wonderfully related," the ingenious fellow mentally said and savored. "Your good news has brought joy to my heart and peace to my restless soul!"

"Yes," I matter-of-factly added, "and Sir, there are high schools, towns and townships named after you all over the United States," I congratulated, "and believe it or not you're still affectionately referred to as the *Wizard of Menlo Park*. And your famous statement 'A genius is one tenth inspiration and nine tenths perspiration' is widely quoted all the time all over the modern world," I sincerely complimented.

"Allow me to modify that if I may," Edison insisted. "It ought to be 'A genius is one-third inspiration, one-third perspiration and one- third desperation!" the great contributor to science and technology aptly joked. "If only I could return to my laboratory in

329

Menlo Park for just one earthly minute! That would be a terrific moment I would definitely cherish for all eternity!"

Thomas Alva Edison and I conversed for the longest time and reviewed just about everything from stereo radios to space satellite communications. Throughout our extended dialogue, the wrinkle-faced man was again a human dynamo exhibiting a great *spirit* and a youthful enthusiasm for all subjects our imaginations touched upon. And when the accomplished inventor heard that his New Jersey research laboratory had been proclaimed a treasured national monument by President Dwight D. Eisenhower in 1956, Edison's sunken eyes seemed to illuminate and his mental articulation became most jubilant.

"You are indeed a Godsend," the creative guru triumphantly declared in appreciation of the intellectual stimulation our conference had provided. "I'm deeply indebted to you for verifying that my life's work has been worthwhile. I now feel that I had laid the foundations for the discovery of more intricate and sophisticated appliances and devices that'll most certainly be beneficial to mankind," the gray-faced spirit gleefully announced. "You have definitely *made my century*!"

Edison and I must have talked for at least several more Earth months without any trace of exhaustion evident in the rhetoric of either of us. Finally, after informing my prestigious host all about the capabilities of the *Hubble Space Telescope* and all about exploratory interplanetary probes to Mars and Jupiter, I left the highly esteemed inventor's company and returned to the quiet sanctuary of my shadowy second floor room.

Several more months must have elapsed before I decided to exit my "dying quarters," slowly amble down to the dark and dreary lobby and initiate a conversation with the sometimes' talkative-but-moody sage Diogenes.

"Well Diogenes," I cunningly began, "I have had the pleasure of meeting the ghosts of George Washington, Edgar Allan Poe and Thomas Edison. Now I can't wait to mingle with Thomas Jefferson, Abraham Lincoln, Mark Twain, Ulysses S. Grant, Albert Einstein, Henry Ford and Marilyn Monroe, if I accurately recall all of the other hotel's spectral guests."

"Kind Sir," Diogenes answered, "please examine the new names listed in the register. I believe almost two centuries have expired in the outside world since your arrival, and now I suspect that *you* are now the senior resident of the *Hotel Delaware*."

I gazed down at the ledger situated on the dusty registration desk and noticed that all of the honorable names I had just enumerated were gone from the list. Instead were unfamiliar appellations such as Sir Hiram Applebee, Salvatore Giovanni, Mildred Carson, Thomas Attanasi, Roseann Celia, Gerald Gares, Arthur Orsi and William Burns.

"Who are these people?" I uttered in sheer protest. "I never heard of any of them! They must all be pedestrian commoners!"

"They are inventors, presidents and entertainers that have become famous during *your* relaxing two-century stay at the *Hotel Delaware*!" Diogenes academically lectured quite nonchalantly. "However, they will certainly recognize your name since your glorious fame has certainly preceded theirs!"

"Do you mean it's already time for me to be transferred to a more enlightening holding area somewhere else in the afterlife?" I sadly asked my aged and withered friend. "I thought I heard the ferry's foghorns several times but I was so engrossed in meditating in my room that I never looked out the window into the dense mist or stepped downstairs to investigate its arrival," I reported to Diogenes in a melancholy tone of voice.

Just then the ferry's whistle blasted three times and I instinctively knew that a new hotel occupant was about to come ashore. Diogenes left me standing in the dingy lobby, and several minutes later the scary-looking apparition reappeared alongside a middle-age spirit still attempting to decipher and define his new gloomy surroundings.

"Hello," I said to the new *Hotel Delaware* guest standing next to me in the dark and dreary lobby. "My name is John Wiessner and I'm glad to meet you!"

"John Wiessner!" the fellow gasped in astonishment. "You mean John Wiessner, alias Jay Dubya! Why you're my favorite author! I've read all of your short stories, *Hammonton Gazette* opinion columns, all of your novellas and all of your novels. This is indeed the highlight of my death experience!"

"And who might you be?" I curiously inquired. "Certainly you must be famous to be invited as a welcomed guest at this temporary holding platform."

"My name is Jason Parsons," the dead fellow's ghost mentally stated, "and I perfected and invented the *Babel Universal Communicator* in 2154. That's indeed my biggest accomplishment."

"What does it do?" I insisted on knowing. "Does it communicate with other planets in the *Milky Way*?"

"*The Babel Universal Communicator* is a hand-held computer device that enables people of different languages to communicate the brain pulses of their thought patterns in *their* language into the words and sentences of a person speaking another language, no matter what it is," Jason Parsons eagerly explained. "A voice simulator I had developed and patented translates the words through a powerful micro-speaker into the second language so that two people of different nationalities or cultures could easily hold an intelligent extensive conversation upon first contact."

"Wow!" I exclaimed with great admiration. "Babel then refers to the *Biblical Tower of Babel* where everyone in the Babylon area suddenly spoke different languages. Jason Parsons, I'm very glad to make your acquaintance," I genuinely expressed, "and don't worry about a thing. Your stay at the *Hotel Delaware* will be both rewarding and soon completed before you know it if you know how to use your time constructively and wisely. Now tell me, how did you happen to die?"

"I think my envious wife poisoned me when she found out I was having an affair with a beautiful and voluptuous *Hollywood* movie star," Jason Parsons disclosed. "But I'm not sure if jealousy was her real motive or whether she simply wanted to inherit my fortune because she was having extra-curricular affairs with the gardener and also with the chauffeur. At any rate," Jason finished with a degree of anguish and distress, "I'm damned dead now and I don't give a Marley's or a Great Caesar's Ghost about it. I just feel extremely betrayed, that's all."

"Women led to *your* demise," Diogenes concluded and insisted as he held *his* dimly lit lantern up to Jason Parsons' honest-looking face. "Both the woman that you desired and the woman that you had, namely your spouse, have each contributed to your eternal fate!"

Then I heard the ferry horn blast three additional times, signaling its intent of disembarking from its mooring and venturing out into the thick *Delaware Bay* fog en route to the second level of enlightenment and emotional growth in the peculiar-but-fascinating vertical death tier hierarchy.

"Maybe now I'll find out about heaven, hell and Jesus and everything else, " I mentioned to Diogenes and to Jason Parsons. "I'm now fully prepared to deal with the attendant duties and responsibilities of the next level of spiritual growth, whatever those specific details might entail!"

Diogenes then adroitly escorted me to the *Hotel Delaware's* lobby door. I warmly shook his cold numb hand, stepped out of the macabre dilapidated structure, descended the thirteen rickety steps and hastened through the dense fog to the awaiting ferry. I

332

enthusiastically ascended the entrance ramp with all the vigor that a veteran ghost could muster. I had no apprehension about or fear of my next surreal destination.

My mind then understood that I was mentally equipped and emotionally mature to sufficiently deal with the elements that would confront me on death's enigmatic second stage of existence. I intuitively also now fully understand that Diogenes had successfully shipped the wooden chest of manuscripts into the past via some wonderful alien method of time compression. The following revelation is now quite lucid in my mind. I now thoroughly comprehend and appreciate a third significant truth, a germane inspiration that currently is quite obvious in its essence. Quite remarkably, I had indeed become Jay Dubya's anonymous *ghostwriter* during my most memorable two-century hiatus at the singular *Hotel Delaware*.

I'm presently placing *this manuscript* describing my death experiences in an empty five-gallon plastic spring water bottle that I've fortunately found inside a remote storage compartment on the deserted ferry. And after inserting the cork tightly into the bottle's neck, I'll carefully toss the container overboard hoping that some lucky mortal will someday discover it and have a brief glimpse of the mystical spirit world awaiting him or her.

"The Bad Old Days"

Last September was very stressful for Hammonton, New Jersey peach and blueberry farmer Richard Jacobs. An irrigation pump caught on fire and the first responder to arrive on the scene was his brother-in-law Charles Garrison. The fireman attempted entering the pit where the pump was situated but the mechanism exploded. Charles Garrison suffered massive burns all over his body and died at a local hospital hours later.

The dead man's family hired an uncompromising high-profile lawyer who immediately sued Richard Jacobs for three million dollars. The plaintiffs easily won the legal case on the grounds that the irrigation pump should have been fenced in so that access to it by the now-deceased Charles Garrison could have been prevented. Richard Jacobs' insurance covered only half of the exorbitant settlement and to make matters worse, the grower could no longer obtain insurance coverage because of his deteriorating credit and poor financial predicament. The result of the expensive litigation had caused additional friction to surface between the bad-luck farmer and his disconsolate wife.

Whenever Richard Jacobs felt distraught or overwhelmed, he would hop into his sparkling red pickup truck and drive from his large gray two-story colonial home down Pine Road to a remote corner of his majestic four-hundred-acre peach and blueberry farm to sit and meditate in seclusion on a giant oak tree stump. Presently the farmer was upset about his lost fortune and also with his nagging wife, who always had the bad habit of treating the formerly prosperous man as if he were henpecked Rip Van Winkle reincarnated. On *this* particular April morning the middle-aged farmer was contemplating his shrinking bank account along with his in jeopardy marital predicament while gazing at the magnificent pink peach blossoms that had budded in one of his twenty-five well-maintained orchards.

'Peggy's now very upset at the loss of her brother and she and I have been relentlessly quarreling for over ten years now,' Richard regretfully considered, 'and with Charles' death, things are rapidly getting much worse. There isn't a marriage counselor in the world with enough skill to make us compatible again! We've been sleeping in separate bedrooms for over a year now and even our grandchildren are becoming aware of the tremendous strain existing between us. Last night was the final straw that broke the proverbial camel's back as far as I'm concerned,' the griever lamented. 'Last night my arrogant wife became inebriated at the Peach Council Convention in Atlantic City, flirted with three receptive out-of-state men and then verbally belittled me in front of my best friends. Her vitriolic remarks are no longer tolerable! That insulting humiliation I had experienced at Harrah's Casino/Hotel last evening had almost destroyed my ego. If it weren't for the cost of an expensive settlement,' Richard imagined, 'I'd launch divorce proceedings first thing tomorrow morning!'

Then the thoroughly distressed plantation owner reviewed certain developments that had formed his relationship with the former Peggy Garrison, the daughter of a prominent local blueberry czar. 'Her haughty father never liked me from the beginning,' Richard recollected, shaking his head in disgust. 'Big Jack Garrison owns the largest cultivated blueberry farm in South Jersey, over fourteen hundred acres, but the major blueberry guys around this town always had a superiority attitude when it came to the lowly peach farmers, especially those like myself that would inherit a mere hundred-acre-estate. But I really showed *him!*'

Jacobs' eyes inspected his familiar surroundings and then the proud man thought about his past before taking a deep breath. 'I expanded my meager peach operations, used my profits to invest in a fine packinghouse and cold storage facility and then diversified my gains into growing blueberries. I now have a four-hundred-acre farm and am the envy of every grower here in Hammonton, New Jersey with the exception of that ruthless tycoon Big Jack Garrison. I believe that Big Jack is actually jealous that I've made it on my own without his lousy assistance! And all I had originally wanted from *him* was the opportunity to be his loyal son-in-law/foreman and eventually run his immense farm! But after dad had died back in 1974 and left me his hundred-acre debt-ridden orchards, I became determined to overcome looming bankruptcy and show Big Jack and his belligerent daughter that I could make it on my own! Thirty-two years and three kids later, my marriage and my dreams of acceptance into the 'Hammonton Agricultural Hierarchy' have hit the skids without any marital remedy in sight!'

And then another ugly thought surfaced in the melancholy man's mind. 'And with Hammonton being in the middle of the New Jersey Pinelands, my property can't be sold to real estate developers. My land has only one-fifth its value now, and I really have trouble getting loans and borrowing money to keep my operation afloat. My four hundred acres are assessed at only a

336

million dollars when they should be worth at least four million under normal economic conditions. Thanks a lot State of New Jersey and your lousy land conservation programs!'

Richard then mentally recalled his three former Hammonton High School girlfriends whom he had dated before the very attractive Peggy Garrison had entered his life during Jacobs' senior year. 'I wonder what my life would've been like today if I had married my freshman sweetheart Angie Genoa, my sophomore doll Carol Sedalia or my junior heartthrob Patty Whittaker? Would I be more happy and content? Instead,' Richard thought with a frown growing upon his countenance, 'I had to be an emotional dunce and settle for Prom Queen and Yearbook Editor Peggy Garrison! How was I to know that beauty is only skin-deep and that my choice for a spouse would eventually evolve into a tyrannical Dame Van Winkle? What a travesty my life has become!'

As the saddened farmer evaluated his romantic adventures while still seated upon the immense tree trunk, a jaunty character, no taller than four-foot in length from toes to head, exited the adjacent woods and stood erect directly beside the very pensive thinker, who was immediately startled upon observing and surveying the general appearance of the odd-looking new arrival.

The little man seemed to be an anachronism, along with being a peculiar combination of a dwarf and a troll. The foreign fellow sported a long grizzled brown beard and wore shoes with silver buckles, dark blue pantaloons accompanied by brown knickers, along with a red medieval-in-appearance hat, a faded green jerkin and a dull black waistcoat somewhat reminiscent of one belonging to a seventeenth century Dutch explorer. The unkempt-looking little gent stood still while staring at the totally amazed farmer, waiting for Richard Jacobs to acknowledge *his* singular presence.

"Who are you?" the shocked landowner finally asked. "You look like you just stepped out of a gruesome children's fairy tale! What's your business trespassing on my land?" Richard then boldly demanded. "Give me a good prompt answer or else I'll dial 911 and summon the local police to come and arrest you!"

"Stop being so foolishly impetuous and presumptuous! One exaggerated question at a time!" the tiny plump fellow insisted. "I repeat! Don't be so impulsive and rambunctious! You're one of the most obnoxious fellows I've met in a long time! And believe me, my journeys have taken me to many of your kind!"

"You still haven't told me your name and your business in being here!" Richard insisted as his face turned florid. "Stop being so evasive and get to the point!"

"Well, since you persist in exercising your silly interrogation, my name is Chaun," the seemingly human-like creature replied. "I'm a magical being of sorts, so therefore any gentleman or lady I stumble across could benefit from my indispensable services. I suppose I'm a bit immortal too besides being an accomplished wizard, although I'm not exactly what you might classify as being a mean-spirited sorcerer. I guess you can call me a sort of mentalist, more specifically, an itinerant clairvoyant with a most extraordinary vocabulary! Kind Sir," the fascinating creature continued, "I won't grant you the usual three wishes as many fanciful fairy tales erroneously portray, but I have the supernatural ability to answer any three questions that you might offer or challenge me with! So go ahead Mr. Richard Jacobs, make any three inquiries of your choosing and I'll then competently satisfy your limited curiosity!"

"How did you know my name?" the still surprised property owner requested knowing. "Surely you can't be supernatural as you've claimed. You must be some kind of impostor! A roving charlatan at best!"

"I can read your mind, your heart and your soul!" the little pudgy fellow confidently articulated. "So be honest and sincere in what you ask, and please, don't you dare try and deceive me. Otherwise," Chaun warned, "you might regret your frivolous attempt at being facetious!"

"Okay Chaun, I'll pretend to believe your words and I'll do my best to be candid with you!" the still nervous man promised as he hesitantly stood-up from the tree stump. "Now then, I'll test your outlandish claims! I had three beautiful girlfriends in high school before I married…"

"Yes indeed, before you wed the voluptuous Peggy Sharon Garrison!" the rascally imp finished his new acquaintance's statement. "And you're quite interested in knowing what your life would've been like if you had married each of them rather than tying the knot with your current wife! Have I accurately interpreted your desire?"

"Why yes, how remarkable!" Richard marveled and exclaimed. "I've often wondered about those particular prospects, and now my mind will finally be at rest. You couldn't have arrived Chaun at a more opportune time!"

"Well then Richard Jacobs, don't congratulate yourself too prematurely! I want you to now direct your attention to the surface of that shallow pond over there to our right. I want you to ponder the pond, ha, ha, ha!" Chaun urged and indulgently chuckled at his ridiculous pun. "There is absolutely nothing esoteric or complicated about this simple process I'm about to demonstrate. The answers to your questions will show up as pictures upon the water as I describe to you in detail the particular knowledge that you seek. I mean, how easier could my instructions be?"

"That all seems quite elementary to follow!" Jacobs amiably agreed. "Now then Chaun, when I was an ambitious freshman in high school, I had dated a knockout girl named Angela Genoa. She was the drum majorette in the Hammonton High Band, was an Italian beauty, had perfect complexion with sensational olive-skin, possessed a terrific body and generally was a very sweet young lady. However, Angie had moved out of town after attending college and I don't know whatever happened to her!"

"Your old flame later graduated from the *University of Pennsylvania Law School*, married a respectable Philadelphia judge and the couple had four healthy children. But in relation to what would've manifested itself if she had married you," Chaun explained and then deliberately paused, "well Richard, I have some bad news to tell. As you might remember from past conversations and secrets shared, Angela's father was a wealthy banker and land developer who would give her the sum of two million dollars upon her marriage to you."

"Wow! That's absolutely right!" Richard enthusiastically remembered. "Then if *that* had materialized, I'd be twice as rich as I am right now!"

"You haven't heard half the story!" Chaun cautioned his excited listener in a very serious and more emphatic tone of voice. "At age thirty-three your beloved Angela would develop a brain tumor and after three years of radiation treatments and subsequent suffering, she'd eventually die of cancer."

"Then I would've gotten her inheritance!" Jacobs avariciously analyzed. "I would then be the fifth wealthiest man in Hammonton, assuming that the generous wedding gift Angie had received from her father accumulated interest over twelve or so years," he haughtily bragged. "Why my fortune could've grown into at least fifteen million dollars by now!"

"Hold your imaginary horses! You're entirely too euphoric and much too selfish for your own good!" Chaun suggested to

Richard. "Now here's the honest-to-heaven truth of the matter, and I hope you don't find this newfound information too disconcerting. When your banker father-in-law, or should I say Angela's father, learned that his only-child daughter had terminal cancer, he used some of his connections with nefarious Hammonton Mafia junkyard dealers and then had the Philadelphia syndicate rub you out. Your very sick lawyer wife would then revise her will and turn all of the money over into trust funds for your son and daughter's college expenses, and whatever was left over would also go to Karen and Joey, for those appellations would've been the names of your two children. So as you can plainly see in the pond's reflection," Chaun disclosed to Richard, "marrying Angela Genoa would've resulted in certain death for you!"

"Yes, I see precisely what you mean!" concurred Jacobs as he stared into the pond with his mouth agape and gazed at his dead body lying prone on the cold concrete floor of his farm's maintenance shop. "Some people are greedy and ruthless when it comes to money! Perhaps I shouldn't be so economically lustful. Quite frankly, I might be a tad…."

"A tad greedy by regular standards but not as ruthless as the Mafia in being so!" Chaun completed Richard's partial confession. "Yes Mr. Jacobs, you certainly do possess that self-destructive propensity of excessive materialism! Your love of mammon is indeed typical of your inferior species. But as the water's reflection has clearly indicated and verified," the extraordinary wayfarer emphasized, "marrying Angela Genoa would have in the end represented a double death sentence: hers and your, truly ironic-but-terrible dual tragedies. Do I make myself clear?"

"That was a rather incredible mind-boggling revelation you just uttered!" the now-relieved farmer admitted as he wiped some excess perspiration from his forehead. "I guess some folks find out the consequences of their decisions a little too late after the fact! I never suspected that Angie's old man would be so wicked, so diabolical!" Richard rationalized and stated. "I would've been just as well off marrying a daughter of Al Capone or John Dillinger if *they* had any female children! Those two wicked gangsters might've been more merciful than Angie's vindictive old man!"

"Yes, sometimes the best of intentions could ultimately turn into ugly scenarios!" Chaun diplomatically philosophized. "Love can become grotesque if contaminated by elements of greed,

340

sickness and death! Yes, a great author once cited that the best laid plans of mice and men could run amuck! Well now, perhaps *that* literary depiction is a little too chauvinistic! Let me be a trifle more accurate! I guess *we* can alter the latter masculine-by-preference analogy to state 'the best laid plans of mice, men and women!"

Richard verbally reminisced to his diminutive comrade how Angie Genoa had been a well-mannered compassionate girl in high school and then Jacobs asked the all-knowing Chaun how her personality could have drastically changed so much to effectively taint *their* relationship in "a past hypothetical marriage." The strange-looking foot traveler seemed puzzled by Jacobs' "naïve nature" and then went on a rant.

"You humans are so inconsistent, always vacillating between right and wrong, between good and evil," Chaun disgustedly declared. "If you Sir thought as much about others as you do about yourself, then I think you'd be more attuned to people in your life and you'd be more lucky in finding and holding a member of the opposite gender. You must be held accountable for aggravating either realistic or theoretical relationships," Chaun vehemently maintained, "obviously making each interactive situation more tempestuous than it really ought to be!"

"Well then Mr. Leprechaun, or whatever you happen to be, what would've happened if I had married my old steady girlfriend Carol Sedalia?" Richard curiously inquired. "She was a peppy cheerleader and the Sicilian beauty rode the same school bus as I did. She never comes to the class reunions but I do know that her family moved away to California right after high school graduation!"

"Oh yes, her full name was Carol Rita Sedalia!" the omniscient corpulent little fellow said before sighing. "Her family moved away from Hammonton to San Diego, Mission Hills section of that fair city if my sometimes faulty cerebrum is functioning and serving me correctly. Carol attended *Fresno State* and eventually became a middle school art teacher. She always had an affinity for helping others, so I suppose that's why she ultimately abandoned your company!"

"That's all fine and dandy," the impatient self-centered farmer declared with a degree of frustration evident in his enunciation, "but you're getting a bit off subject. What would've transpired if Carol and I had gotten hitched?"

"Well now, your life again would have been abundantly filled with strife and difficulty!" Chaun communicated. "First of all,

341

Carol's parents are the meddling type and they would've deluged you with constant criticisms, and yes indeed, conflict with them would not only have been inevitable but also extremely unbearable. Your restless conscience and your short-fused tolerance would be besieged with vitriol day and night without end. You'd be a very unhappy camper in *that* marital arrangement to say the least."

"Well, who would Carol side with during the daily animosity sessions, her parents or me? There is supposed to be some loyalty between husband and wife, you know!"

"Unfortunately, to your chagrin," the weird-looking miniature figure declared, "she would side with her parents nine out of ten times. But then necessity would cause your beloved Carol Sedalia to quit her teaching position. Just as Carol has MS now living out in San Diego, in *your* theoretical marriage I'm now describing, she presently would be confined to a wheelchair and consequently would require constant supervision and care. Either *you* or a nurse would have to dress her every morning, shower her and lift her into your car every time a doctor would have to be visited. You would have to cook her meals and lovingly provide for her every need. I think that your spirit would crack under all that pressure! Basically, in all honesty you aren't a care-giver type of person!"

"I don't know if I could endure such daily self-sacrifice!" Richard confidentially admitted to the tiny stranger. "Perhaps I could adjust to those responsibilities but truthfully Chaun, I'm not that much of a charitable person."

"People often do what they have to do during sudden unexpected emergencies or crises," sternly lectured Chaun. "But in your unique case," the bearded fellow directly admonished, "you're entirely too narcissistic for your own good. However the already mentioned MS problem is not the only travail you would have experienced being married to the former Carol Sedalia."

"Would we have children before the dreadful disease would affect her?" the saddened farmer asked. "Out of all my high school dates, I think I liked Carol the best."

"Well, that sensitive subject was what I was about to expound upon before you so rudely interrupted me!" chastised the all-too-fickle Chaun. "Quite frankly, I advise that you ought to allow this entire conversation be a splendid moral learning lesson to adequately nourish your soul! In your mutual futures together, you and Carol would have had a daughter Jamie who would have to get married out of wedlock during her junior year in high school. Her ill-timed pregnancy would result in triplets after the derelict

342

father of the children ran away from his parental obligations! And next," the woodland roamer continued his revelation, "I don't know if I should divulge to you what catastrophe would soon happen to your son Todd."

"Tell me or else my conscience will not rest," the remorseful peach and blueberry grower implored. "I feel that I just have to know *his* fate even though we're discussing an absurd *fantasy reality* here! I hope that you're an expert grammarian besides being some kind of miniature magician! Now tell me, isn't that some kind of illogical contradiction I just said, *fantasy reality*?"

"In English rhetoric it's called an 'oxymoron' as exemplified in the statement 'the orator Stephen Douglas was referred to as a *little giant*' when it came to the gift of debating people like Abraham Lincoln! But getting back to your son Todd," Chaun pontificated, "he came under the bad influence of a juvenile delinquent friend. Todd would've been crippled in an automobile accident and would've been in and out of a coma during a terrible fifteen year period before finally succumbing to death."

"Was anyone else hurt or killed in this hypothetical accident that never happened?" Richard wondered and elicited. "Doesn't this bizarre painful conversation seem pretty academic?"

"Why yes it does!" Chaun answered in an astonished tone of voice that obviously recognized Jacobs' mounting mental anguish. "A dedicated school principal on his way to work was the unfortunate victim occupying the other car. Todd was a passenger in a speeding auto' being driven by a so-called friend. The boys' vehicle got a flat tire, veered across a dual highway and then collided with the school administrator's automobile, the bleeding man dying an hour later in a nearby hospital. The youth driving the car was wearing a seatbelt and eventually recovered from his injuries," Chaun added. "But your imaginary son Todd was not wearing a safety strap and was a victim of the other kid's carelessness. Indeed Richard Jacobs, should you have married Carol Sedalia your life would've been fraught with hardships, and of course, her nit-picking fault-finding parents naturally would always blame you for not adequately disciplining Todd as he eventually grew into adolescence!"

The short stocky figure clad in the bizarre garb then waved his hand above the pond, thus clearing away the image of Todd lying in bed in a coma, his steady palm acting just like an eraser removing chalk from a schoolroom blackboard. The dwarf's methodical arm motion instantly broke Richard Jacobs' meticulous introspection. Chaun then calmly related to his

343

audience of one what would have occurred in later life if the farmer had married his junior prom sweetheart.

"Patricia Whittaker had become an airline stewardess after high school, moved to Hawaii and currently lives there after being married and divorced three times," Chaun enlightened the now-thoroughly-impressed Richard Jacobs, "but if the two of you had ever eloped and gotten married as you had planned, your life Dear Richard, would definitely be in shambles today!"

"Instead of Dear Richard, I should change my name to Poor Richard and author an almanac," Jacobs responded and jested to lighten his present mental burden. "What negative events would've materialized if Patty and I had gone to the chapel together?"

"The former Patricia Whittaker now has a medical condition called cirrhosis of the liver, which as you are aware is a life-threatening malady caused by drinking an excess of alcohol, in her case hard liquor, scotch to be exact," Chaun confidentially reported. "According to *your* perverted value system, you would instinctively regard Patricia as a detriment, a woman interfering with your freedom to do anything you wished while you would be pursuing your own agenda. By this time in your rocky relationship, divorce would certainly be imminent!"

"We were so intimate and shared so much great fun together our junior year," Richard foolishly romanticized to the all-knowing dwarf. "The summer carnival in downtown Hammonton, the Bellevue Avenue Malt Shop, the Wildwood Boardwalk and beach, Saturday night excursions up to Coney Island, the raucous pool parties and most of all Patty and I enjoying the 'submarine races' out on Snake Road and also at the gravel pits! Those were without a doubt the best times of my life!"

"Yes, time is so ephemeral!" the very wise Chaun expressed to his new acquaintance. "But Julia, your extremely defiant daughter you would have had with Patricia would represent a real problem far worse than juvenile delinquency!"

"What do you mean?" Jacobs skeptically asked. "If I can cope with what's happened in my accursed life since last September, I could adjust to any temperamental teenager's insolence. Nothing could compare to the horrendous irrigation pump fire!"

"That's what you think! Your daughter Julia would constitute a chronic discipline problem that would have even aggravated the Biblical Job!" the grim-faced rascal related. "Julia would have two illegitimate children while still in high school. Then she would later become an alcoholic, a heavy-duty drug addict and finally a desperate adolescent prostitute."

"What a family disaster!" Richard exclaimed. "I think I need to swallow a bottle of aspirins! On second thought, add in a hot water bottle for my throbbing headache too!"

"Julia would be hospitalized three times for serious injuries sustained from brawling with other doomed juvenile hookers over drugs, illicit money and Johns. One day her maniacal pimp would throw her out of his car going thirty miles an hour down Pacific Avenue in Atlantic City," Chaun communicated. "Your daughter would also be arrested for stealing the pimp's car the next week, and after the A.C. police found an unlicensed handgun under the seat, your prospective daughter would be jailed for three years for possession of a stolen weapon after deliberately stealing her pimp's car. And then to make matters even worse, after getting out of jail Julia would…."

"Don't tell me any more ugly details!" pleaded Richard. "I've already heard enough! There's only so much grief the human psyche can endure!"

"Do you now still think that your current life is one continuous train wreck in progress?" Chaun rhetorically challenged. "After all Richard Jacobs, worse things can happen besides financial loss! Money isn't everything' as you've always believed from childhood. Learn to value life over property!" The omnipotent little land-roving man then raised his right hand and almost hypnotically, he motioned it above the pond, his power thus eliminating the distasteful scene of Julia sitting alone weeping inside a dirty jail cell. Jacobs' intense concentration was again broken.

"You're right!" Richard reluctantly concurred, nodding his head. "I guess I'm just too egotistical to appreciate the better things in life along with the small courtesies that seem to make ordinary people happy. And most of my old friends have abandoned me so I speculate that they weren't really my trusted buddies after all. Say Chaun," Richard realized and declared, "I know what I'll do to make amends with Peggy! I'll apologize for all of the unnecessary grief I've caused her, buy her a diamond necklace for our wedding anniversary and after purchasing for her a new silver convertible from my dwindling Merrill Lynch cash management account, we'll re-live our honeymoon! I'll book a cruise to Bermuda in the fall right after peach season ends."

"That's the type of language I wanted to hear from your lips," Chaun commended his newfound contact. "You're exhibiting a true change of heart, a genuine moral metamorphosis so to speak. And now Richard Jacobs, former elite blueberry and peach farmer, it is my expressed and distinct duty to inform you that you must travel with me into another dimension."

And after delivering those stellar remarkable words and without affording his avid listener any viable choice in the matter, a vapor mist quickly enveloped the two entities. The inimitable Chaun was barely visible to his companion, effectively transporting Richard Jacobs to a mysterious destination.

* * * * * * * * * * * *

Moments later the traveling duo appeared inside an ornate palatial corridor decorated with plush wall tapestries, resplendent Oriental rugs, white marble statues and incredible crystal chandeliers suspended from a gold-gilt arched ceiling. Chaun slowly led his apprehensive guest down the impressive hallway and then stopped to open two fabulous-looking immense mahogany doors.

'This reminds me of the Vatican Museum,' Richard thought. 'Yes, my only visit to Rome! The Vatican Museum was very much like this incredible place!'

The unusual pair then very deliberately stepped through opened doors into an opulent marble balcony, which overlooked a large crowded reception hall. Instantaneously the formerly noisy room's attendees became silent as a distant strong baritone voice formally announced, "May I introduce Richard Jacobs, arriving from Hammonton, New Jersey USA." Suddenly a loud ovation permeated the entire chamber below.

"Why this whole astounding experience is absolutely impossible!" Richard gasped while holding a tight grip onto the high balcony's marble railing. "There's my mother and father standing down there', my Aunt Vera and Uncle Henry, my Uncle Leo and my Aunt Marie, my maternal grandparents and oh my God, yes, there's my unfortunate brother-in-law Charles Garrison applauding me. Those people gathered down there have one horrible thing in common: they're all dead!"

The totally astounded guest of honor peered down at Chaun, who no longer was wearing stereotypical medieval peasant clothes but was now a radiant winged angel with a shaved face and a body adorned in a pristine-white satin tunic. The newly expedited soul anxiously waited to hear a feasible explanation from his enigmatic guide. "What's going on here Chaun, if you

346

are still named Chaun?" Jacobs asked the glorious-looking celestial creature. "Have I arrived in Heaven? Have I earned a glimpse of my destiny?"

"Not quite!" the innocent-looking being' nonchalantly replied. "You had died from a massive heart attack after arriving at the tree stump near the pond, which as you remember was situated adjacent to your irrigation pump that had caught on fire and ultimately led to your brother-in-law's traumatic death. This run-of-the-mill assembly hall is really a designated waiting area, a sort of holding tank until your soul is ready to be admitted into Heaven! Ever since Purgatory had been done away with, staging areas like this one' have been put into place to receive all new 'visitors-in-transit' to the Promised Kingdom!"

"They're all still clapping for me down there! They're all still enthusiastically applauding!" yelled Richard above the din. "I feel like I'm a popular celebrity! This is really fantastic! None of my deceased former enemies seem to be holding any animosity towards me!"

"Yes, down there are all of your passed-away acquaintances showing their approval of your' admission to Paradise! If you knew more people during your lifetime, then this event would have had to take place in one of our larger venues," Chaun informed his escorted guest. "Doesn't your spirit feel exhilarated, emancipated from your corrupt body? Tell me Richard, don't you feel exceptionally liberated and rejuvenated?"

"Do you mean that I'm about to go directly to Heaven? My soul has been saved? Say, where are all the clouds with winged beings looking just like you, playing their golden harps?"

"Yes," Chaun the Angel casually answered, featuring a brief smile on his countenance. "But *you* almost didn't make it. Fortunately for you, your heart sort of repented and in the end passed the final litmus test, so to speak. You were contrite, penitent and remorseful about your avarice and thus had reached eternal salvation just before you had expired," the afterlife guide orally conveyed. "To use several common idiomatic expressions, you had made it just in the nick of time and had come to the finish line just under the wire. And finally Richard," the Eternal Guide related, "we don't believe in mundane labels or mindless stereotypes here. You'll find no simpleton cherubs playing harps on floating clouds!"

"This is all rather incomprehensible! I'm hungry and thirsty! Can I go downstairs and get a bite to eat while I'm socializing with my appreciative kith and kin?"

"Unfortunately Richard, that scenario is not possible. I mean, you can socialize all you want, but getting something to eat or drink is not in the rules. For you see," the angelic-looking creature aptly and whimsically explained, "your present existence is midway between a defective human state and an immaculate spirit state, and if I may share a common axiom often used around here, spirits don't require or desire biological necessities such as food or beverage. You're actually in transition Richard, confined to a definite holding pattern, a mobile entity waiting to be transferred onward and upward! In time you'll adjust to the new regulations and become fully assimilated into your new existence, or should I say 'your new environment.' Oh well," the Angel proceeded with his cosmic rhetoric, "I have another important appointment to honor. I hope you don't feel compelled to ask me any more totally boring questions. Have sympathy upon me Richard. I've heard them all at least a million times! I believe it's now the appropriate moment for us to say 'adieu'."

"Where are you going?" the still confused transient soul asked. "Do you have another assignment, is that what you said? Chaun, please don't leave me! I'll feel stranded and alienated!"

"Yes, it does seem that I'm overworked as of late!" the very busy Angel pragmatically complained while ignoring Jacobs' plea. "But just like you, I have no say in the matter. I just go with the flow! And don't worry! You have all of your family and friends down there to reminisce and commiserate with! So long and good luck Richard! It's been a distinct pleasure meeting you and being your personal escort!"

"A Grave Undertaking"

The Hammonton Police Department and the New Jersey State Police were baffled by a wave of a dozen missing persons disappearing from the somnolent South Jersey agricultural community, a town noted for being "The Blueberry Capital of the World." Chief-of-Police Michael Falcone had summoned Detective Fred Arico and Patrolman Samuel Galletta to his downstairs office in the newly constructed Hammonton Town Hall on the corner of Central Avenue and Vine Street. The recent "missing persons' phenomenon" had become a popular topic reported and discussed on Philadelphia and Atlantic City television news broadcasts. Chief Falcone felt personally embarrassed at his department having to solicit outside professional help to engage in solving the complex case currently under investigation.

"As you know men," Chief Falcone began addressing Detective Arico and Patrolman Galletta, "Hammonton has become the focal point of attention throughout the Delaware Valley. One of my major concerns is that I fear the bad publicity our community is receiving is not good for *our* reputation. And I'm quite confused. This missing persons' deal goes far beyond the ordinary issuing of traffic tickets and police reports on auto' accidents!"

"Perhaps the public can assist us in cracking the riddle," Detective Fred Arico constructively suggested. "I meant to say, alert people represent the cornerstone of local law enforcement. Vigilant citizens might just be the key we need to figuring out this very difficult, pardon the expression if I now use a favorite Sherlock Holmes statement, 'this very difficult conundrum'."

"This entire matter requires our full scrutiny and energy twenty-four hours a day seven days a week until we've found all the vital answers," the Chief emphasized to his two honest men. "I do have a certain stake in *this* matter. The timing is absolutely abominable! Only seven months until retirement and pension time and now I have to experience *this* crazy situation. I'm at wits end! These twelve important missing townspeople couldn't all just have vanished into thin air!"

"And as you've just said Chief, according to our files *they* were all prominent members of the community in good standing with the police department," Detective Arico concurred. "Yes, members of the Kiwanis, the Lions, the Rotary, the Women's

349

Civic Club, the Exchange Club, the Sons of Italy, you name it! We're taking a lot of heat over this strange dilemma and that's why the State Police is recommending that the FBI step in and aid us' in our law enforcement activities. It sort of makes us look like a pack of incompetent boobs!"

"Could it be that the missing twelve people have schemed-up a conspiracy just to distract and fool us?" Patrolman Galletta reactively asked Chief Falcone and Detective Arico. "Doesn't this very exceptional debacle have all the markings of a massive prank in progress? I meant to say," Galletta proceeded with his fanciful monologue, "you don't suppose that a mass murderer is on the loose and that specific names are being checked-off his hit list one by one as each additional elimination happens!"

"Nonsense! Totally ridiculous! All of *your* bizarre theories are absolute rubbish!" Chief Michael Falcone vehemently exclaimed. "Hammonton is a decent town of fifteen thousand hard-working ambitious citizens! And besides *that* scenario, we haven't had a murder-type felony committed here in over twenty years. But what bewilders me the most gentlemen is that there hasn't been a trace of evidence discovered anywhere, not one solitary minute clue turning-up! Nobody seems to know anything!"

"What about cause and motive?" Detective Arico inquired. "Let's start there!"

"Extortion doesn't seem to be any motive because no ransom notes have surfaced from any source," the Chief asserted. "It's a lousy annoying *Kind-Un-Drum* as you've just said Fred. But much to my regret it's all happened on our *beat*! Now let's review exactly who has disappeared and perhaps we can connect some dots or establish some relevant links," Chief Falcone indicated to Arico and Galletta. "The worst feature of all this confusion is that just about everybody in Hammonton is somehow related to each other. Our citizens are nervous and quite frankly, they have every right to feel that way unless something gives soon!"

"That's right Chief!" Patrolman Sam Galletta confirmed as he fumbled opening his folder. "For example, you and I Chief are cousins and our wives are second cousins on our mothers' sides! And my second cousins are related to Detective Arico's family if my memory serves me correctly. The townspeople are apprehensive because we haven't made any apprehensions!" the zany young officer quipped, much to Chief Falcone's ire.

After giving Officer Galletta a serious frown (as Detective Fred Arico covered his mouth to avoid overtly laughing), Chief Falcone sternly admonished his comedian subordinate. "Look

350

here Sam! Our department is in a serious predicament, an evolving crisis situation! Let's show the utmost discretion during this informal meeting! Let's try and be more professional even though *that* practical task might be contrary to *your* general nature! This is no time to pretend being Jay Leno or David Letterman! Even Bill O'Reilly is out of your league as a humorist!"

Detective Fred Arico then informed the Chief that Patrolman Galletta would review the first six missing persons in the chronological order of their disappearances and that *he* would present the final six in the same manner in order to see if any direct or remote connections existed that could lead to a primary source of evidence or constitute the basis for a plausible police theory. The department's head interrogator then directed the young officer to commence with *his* background analysis.

"Well Chief, the first victim, er, I mean missing person to vanish was Bernard Norton, who as you know sat, or should I say sits on the Board of Directors of Hammonton Trust Bank. Mr. Norton was on the Parish Council of St. Joseph Church, served in the marines during the *Vietnam War* and is unhappily married to the former Susan Parker, a past Hammonton Peach Queen and also model for newspaper print ads and glossy cover magazines. Mr. Norton's personal vices are Atlantic City casino gambling junkets and having two known affairs outside his unstable marriage. But for the record," the patrolman clarified, "his unfaithful wife Susan is also guilty of those same behaviors, so I guess their unstable marital relationship is, how should I say, is sort of a wash."

"There're no signs of anything illegal being committed although some of Mr. Norton's activities might be a trifle immoral and unethical," the very beleaguered Chief Falcone evaluated. "But this investigation is not a church or marriage counseling matter; it's a police concern! Now then, who was the second individual to become mysteriously absent from the town?"

"Frank Gibson, a rough and tough fruit and produce broker who has his base of operation seventeen miles south of here at the Vineland Produce Auction," Officer Galletta anxiously related. "Mr. Gibson also manages a successful freight company hauling mostly locally grown vegetables all up and down the eastern seaboard from Boston, Massachusetts to Richmond, Virginia. My brother-in-law is a dispatcher for the flourishing trucking company, which I believe has twenty-five tractor-trailers in its fleet. But outside of once being arrested for brawling with another

351

patron outside the Silver Coin Diner and breaking another customer's nose during a fistfight inside the Silver Fox Tavern," Patrolman Galletta summarized, "Frank Gibson's overall police record is pretty clean. He's definitely not the gangster type!"

"Yes, Gibson can become rowdy and pugnacious occasionally, especially when intoxicated, but remember," Chief Falcone austerely reminded Officer Galletta, "he's now a prospective victim of foul play and not a perpetrator of minor or major crime, although I can fully understand why someone on a revenge mission might be seeking retribution against him. Frank Gibson does have a certain reputation for charging higher commission rates to farmers to sell their fruit and vegetables to chain stores than do other produce brokers in the area. We'll bear that particular fact in mind as we try to piece together the details of this difficult investigation and make it more comprehensive. Who's next on our agenda?"

"Well Chief", there's Jack Hines, prosperous blueberry farmer who often did business with the highly volatile Frank Gibson," Officer Sam Galletta read from his oak tag file. "As you know, just like Frank Gibson, Jack Hines is divorced, permanently separated from *your* sister-in-law's niece. Jack likes auto' racing and has sponsored pit-stop teams participating in the Dover Classic and the Daytona 500. Outside of two minor speeding tickets on his otherwise impeccable record, some small town politics are involved! Although Mr. Jack Hines has committed no serious violations, according to our documentation, on two different occasions Hines tried to bribe Officer Hunt and Officer Ambrose with cash to quash his citations before they could reach Judge Philips' bench."

"That association between Jack Hines and Frank Gibson is a definite red flag and might be essential later on," the veteran Chief-of-Police concluded and shared. "But nevertheless, unfortunately nothing mentioned thus far would warrant, let alone justify kidnapping, which as you gentlemen both know, could represent a federal crime, especially if the victims are transported across state lines. Needless to say men," the perplexed Department Czar continued his glib spiel, "I've spent thirty-six years of dedicated service on the force and I don't want to see this very irritating rash of disappearances mar my formerly perfect history of dependability to this community. To me, *that* would be a shameful exit! Now then Sam, who's next on you list? And try being a bit more brief! It's almost lunchtime!"

Officer Galletta then revealed that James Olsen, a chronic alcoholic, was the proprietor of a large winery on the White Horse Pike, that Joseph Spinelli, a reputed Casanova, was a skilled surgeon at Kessler Memorial Hospital and that Thomas Ritter, a shrewd conniving businessman, was also an industrious wealthy real estate broker and charity benefactor. Chief Falcone was worried that all of those "high-repute" missing persons that had been mentioned and reviewed were outstanding citizens of and contributors to the Town of Hammonton.

"This is all very challenging and frustrating!" the bewildered Michael Falcone uttered to his equally pressured underlings. "Why couldn't *this* entire weird fiasco, er, I meant to say 'development' have had happened in Vineland, in Berlin, in Pleasantville or in Egg Harbor City? If we don't bust open this bizarre case soon, the FBI will surely zoom onto our turf and we'll then be the laughingstock of every town and borough in South Jersey. I think I'll be submitting my resignation within the week if we fail to collar any likely suspects. But who might the evil villain or villains be? That's the $64,000.00 dollar question!"

"Well Chief Falcone, this final statement just about completes my presentation," Patrolman Galletta vocalized before taking a deep breath. "James Olsen was having a supposed secret love affair with Joseph Spinelli's wife and the flirtatious surgeon was cheating on his spouse and having another tryst with Thomas Ritter's wife, but since all three men have disappeared like evasive space aliens from the Hammonton map, we can't accuse any of them of anything. Strangely enough," Galletta concluded, "all three can only be classified as missing persons and nothing more!"

Chief Falcone then asked Detective Fred Arico to discuss the six names of missing persons whose records were in *his* police folder. The accommodating civil servant quickly opened his document files and began his narrative.

"Well Chief, Maria Fischer was, or should I say *is* the President of the local Soroptimist Club and is involved in many noteworthy community charities," Detective Arico cited from his records. "As you know, she's a millionaire tens-times-over who owns and runs a very financially solvent clothes manufacturing factory on Fairview Avenue and has several flourishing retail outlet stores in Atlantic City, in Rehoboth Beach, Delaware, in Ocean City, Maryland and on Cape Cod, Massachusetts," Arico added. "It should be cited that Mrs. Fischer's daughter has had a drug problem and was once arrested for cocaine and marijuana

353

possession, and her son had once done some vandalism at the local bowling alleys, but as far as she's concerned, our principal's record is virtually immaculate. There's no doubt in my mind that...."

"That all of these missing persons identified so far have one specific thing in common," Chief Michael Falcone declared as he rubbed his right ear with his forefinger, deliberately interrupting his favorite detective. "They're all millionaires, but remarkably, most of them are multimillionaires! This fact could be the vital connection we're searching for and it's well-worth delving into! Well Fred, who's next on your short list?"

"Jeffrey Stokes is a furniture store operator and also the main influential power member of the Hammonton Democratic Club," the competent detective stated before clearing his throat. "He's been suspected of being implicated in county loan-sharking activities but we never could get anyone to file a written complaint or testify against him. As has been extensively published in South Jersey newspapers," Detective Arico stated, "Mr. Stokes has amassed considerable connections among important politicians throughout the county and the state, and he's believed to be currently circulating a petition for running for a county freeholder seat. He's also a close friend and confidant of several judges sitting on the Superior Court over in the county seat in Mays Landing."

"Jeffrey Stokes does represent a character of interest," the Chief readily acknowledged. "But we must be very careful going forward here. We can't intrude upon his privacy and question his family about his suspected dishonorable relationships and then have the press accuse *us* of practicing guilt by association. That's all I need is the local ACLU sticking its talons in my ribs right before retirement," the Chief cautioned and maintained. "I'll not leave my position in the midst of a firestorm controversy that's guaranteed to fuel the barbershop and hairdresser gossip mills. I'll only leave my post with honor and accomplishment! Who's the next name in your confidential folders?"

"John DiFrancisco is a builder and real estate developer with an esteemed reputation but he's also president of the town's Republican Club," Detective Fred Arico clearly enunciated. "Naturally one would speculate that a certain distinct political difference of opinion would exist between..."

"Between Jeffrey Stokes and John DiFrancisco," the Chief immediately recognized and said, finishing Arico's remark. "And if I recall with any degree of accuracy, Mr. DiFrancisco was supposed to build Jeffrey's Stokes' new furniture store over on Second Road but the whole deal fell through after the two egomaniacs had a bitter argument that required the intervention of our department. I'll bookmark *that* past conflict and keep their antagonism toward each other as something pertinent we'll have to examine more in perspective, but still, no criminal activity, not even a picayune misdemeanor could be attributed to either Mr. Jeffrey Stokes or to Mr. John DiFrancisco. Now then Fred, isn't my old high school sweetheart Barbara DeMarco also a missing person? What information do you have about her?"

"Yes Chief, as you know, Ms. DeMarco never married. She's very creative, owns three dress shops for women at strategic locations throughout the town and has made several million investing in small-cap technology companies on the major stock exchanges. But outside of her being a vocal Scientologist just like Tom Cruise was on the Oprah Show," Fred Arico attested, "your old flame Ms. DeMarco has never been *engaged* in anything illicit or nefarious. What do you think about her Sam?"

"It's too bad Chief that you never married Barbara DeMarco!" Patrolman Galletta opined after he had heard Detective Fred Arico mention the word *engaged*. "Then Chief you wouldn't have to worry about jeopardizing your pension benefits! You'd have it made in the shade with plenty of cash to spare!"

"Look here Sam, I'm not a lame duck police administrator so watch your loose tongue and how it wags!" Chief Falcone reprimanded his somewhat frivolous subordinate. "Any more questionable comments on your part and you might just find yourself getting splinters in your rear end on desk duty instead of merrily cruising town in your patrol car. Now please continue with your briefing Fred. Who's next?"

"Well Chief, as you're fully aware, according to the National Census, Hammonton is the most Italian town in the entire United States, and Officer Galletta's, *yours* and my last names all have Italian heritage," Arico keenly observed and vociferated. "Over fifty-three percent of the town's population is of Italian origin. Our next missing person is Guido Renzi, a notorious Atlantic City gambler and card counter who has been banned from three boardwalk casinos. It's rumored all around town that Guido had inherited five million dollars from his greedy loan sharking old man and that Renzi's more than tripled his fantastic windfall, which incidentally had never been deposited into any bank and was never reported to the IRS."

"Yes, Guido Renzi could be a target of foul play!" Chief Falcone verified as he rubbed his whiskery chin.

"Now as you're keenly aware Chief, good old Guido is a confederate of Stephen Messina, your uncle on your mother's side who as a matter of fact is a conniving junkyard owner with reputed ties to the Philly' Mafia," Fred Arico insinuated. "This guy Renzi is slippery and slick and we can't pin anything substantial on him other than suspecting that his closest friend's retail auto' used parts business is a front for syndicate fencing and drug trafficking activities," Detective Arico elucidated. "But both Renzi and Messina are respected benefactors to many local charities and they're very generous in their contributions and fundraising activities. The congregations of all three Catholic churches in town amply appreciate the donations given by Guido Renzi and *your* benevolent uncle Stephen Messina."

"Yes Fred, every family seems to have its black sheep! Uncle Steve Messina could charm the belly off of a rattlesnake, that's for damned sure!" the Chief reluctantly verified. "I've often had to distance myself from *his* unsavory activities! Last summer during the 16th of July Carnival, I had to leave the Mt. Carmel Hall when *he* showed up so as not to be seen in public mingling with the unscrupulous maniac! And to tell you the truth," Michael Falcone proceeded, "I'd love to wiretap Uncle Steve's phone conversations, despite my dear deceased father being *his* unfortunate brother. But since he's a philanthropist of sorts, the public regards Uncle Steve as a kind of area Robin Hood, cheating the general public and then mercifully and generously assisting the poor and the less fortunate. Because of extenuating circumstances, and I hate sounding too much like a modern-day Eliot Ness, Steve Messina right now is viewed as an 'untouchable' if you know what I mean. But just remember men', Guido Renzi happens to be one of the twelve missing persons and not *his* pal Steve Messina. Isn't there one more name that you've got itemized?"

"Yes, Richard Farinelli, a millionaire produce package supplier to area peach, blueberry and vegetable growers," Detective Arico aptly stated. "Farinelli's a cunning and mean old buzzard who drives a hard bargain, especially since he's the only fertilizer distributor in Hammonton, that's for sure! I could see where someone of Richard Farinelli's ilk could've accumulated hard-boiled enemies over the years, but then again, my name's not Kojak or Perry Mason so perhaps I should keep my unsolicited random conjecturing to myself!"

356

"Excellent self-analysis! It's about time you faced reality and became aware of your shortcomings! " Chief Falcone chided. "But in the future Detective Arico, think before you open your mouth so that you don't have to apologize afterwards upon revealing your all-too-often foolishness! And that needed criticism pertains to you too, Galletta! Now then men, time is of the essence! Get the heck out of my office, stay away from the coffee and doughnut shops and start finding some concrete clues to solve this extremely difficult Kind-Un-Drum!"

* * * * * * * * * * * *

Seven miles north of Hammonton a terrible automobile accident had occurred at the dangerous "S-Curve" above Atsion Lake on *Route 206*, a two-lane highway that is New Jersey's only north-south corridor through the center of the state. A brand new dark blue Cadillac driven by millionaire Jason DeLucca had veered off the road and was instantly demolished after smashing into a forest tree. Jason DeLucca died instantly from injuries sustained in the mishap and the auto's passenger, his brother Nicholas, was immediately transported to Hammonton's Kessler Memorial Hospital for lacerations' treatment and for overnight observation. The following morning a third brother Rocco DeLucca picked up the discharged bandaged patient, his very fortunate younger brother. The two had a meaningful conversation after doctors had examined and released "the lucky rider" from the hospital's emergency ward.

"You know Nick," Rocco said as he drove his black Lexus out of the hospital's nearly empty parking lot, "Jason was really the greatest older brother we could have ever had. It's too bad you guys got into that terrible accident on the way to the Pic-A-Lilli Inn! In my case Jason has financed three of my retail businesses that have failed, insisting that I not repay him one penny," Rocco explained to his surviving brother. "And good old Jay, once he told me that he's goin' to remember both of us in his will along with his wife and three kids. I hate getting misty-eyed and all that but he's certainly going to be missed."

"The whole accident seemed quite strange!" Nick confided. "And it's a good thing I was wearing my seat belt, although Jason's belt didn't matter in his case! After our intended rendezvous with you in the Pic-A-Lilli Inn parking lot, Jay and I were goin' to be on our way to have supper at Izzy's Restaurant over on *541* in Medford. Jay's new Cadillac was in excellent condition, but then we either blew a right front tire on *206* or the wheel came unhinged," Nick told Rocco. "The next thing I knew we had veered off the road at the S-Curve and were barreling straight into the pine-barrens. Then after the air bag inflated, I went unconscious," Nicholas recollected and related. "Thank God for the swift actions of the Hammonton Rescue Squad or else I probably would've bled to death en route to the hospital! I suppose you're going to make arrangements for Jason at the Blake Funeral Home over on Third Street. That's where Mom and Dad had their viewings."

"No Nick," Rocco replied as the traffic light turned green and he stepped on the accelerator making the turn from Central Avenue onto *Route 30*, the White Horse Pike. "At first I was thinking about having the Franklin Mortuary over on Egg Harbor Road doing the funeral. But then again I considered that the Melora Funeral Home over on Central Avenue could better accommodate the massive crowd that's goin' to show-up to pay their last respects. Last night I already had contacted Bill Melora and told him to get in touch with Andrew Blake, who has the keys to the family' mausoleum."

"That sounds like a good idea!" Nicholas DeLucca agreed with Rocco's recommendation. "Melora has a much bigger parlor viewing room than either Franklin or Blake does!"

"But before I take you home, we're gonna' head over to Oak Grove Cemetery to check out the family crypt," Rocco suggested. "The mausoleum might have to be power-washed to get the accumulated algae and green slime off of its façade. We should've never neglected the granite structure so now we'll have to get the ugly mess cleaned-up before Jay's burial. Sometimes I wish I had more foresight."

As Rocco's black Lexus pulled into the Old Forks Road entrance to Oak Grove Cemetery the man behind the wheel noticed something irregular happening a hundred yards down the asphalt lane so he quickly detoured his expensive vehicle onto a dirt road bordered by a hedgerow of pine trees. Nicholas' curiosity had also been stimulated. Immediately the driver's unexpected maneuver had activated the recently injured passenger's wonderment.

"What's this crazy detour all about?" the bandaged younger brother demanded knowing. "Did you forget where the family mausoleum is? Chief Falcone would get your butt hauled into the station for reckless driving!"

"Be quiet and stay still!" Rocco commanded from behind the pine tree cover as he pointed to a familiar distant structure situated under a canopy of tall oak trees. "Look over there at our mausoleum. There's funeral director Andrew Blake and his assistant Phil Ruggeri entering *our* building without our approval or knowledge."

"Maybe they're just inspecting the crypts to make sure everything's in order," Nicholas theorized and said. "You have to give Mr. Blake the benefit of the doubt and not have a rush to judgment and accuse him and his helper of trespassing! There's enough craziness goin' on in Hammonton without us making false allegations!"

"Yes, perhaps you're right!" Rocco acknowledged. "Blake still does have the master entry key since he had conducted Mom and Dad's funerals! But remember, Blake probably already knows that the Melora Funeral Home is going to handle Jason's arrangements. This is very intriguing! Let's just hold tight and witness what's goin' to happen next!"

Ten minutes later the pair of diligent observers was shocked at what their eyes beheld. "Oh my God!" Nicholas exclaimed with the windows rolled up in the air-conditioned luxury automobile. "They're carryin' a body under a black blanket out of the mausoleum! Instead of putting a corpse inside the building two days from now they're taking one out right this minute!"

"This is highly irregular! I don't know if this spectacle we're watchin' is body snatchin' or not, but I gotta' report the suspicious incident to the police," Rocco DeLucca declared. "I'll get in touch with my good pal Detective Fred Arico immediately. I'll make sure he'll get to the bottom of this strange incident and learn exactly what's going on here!"

* * * * * * * * * * * *

The morning after Jason DeLucca's huge funeral and subsequent burial in the family's Oak Grove Cemetery crypt, Detective Fred Arico and Patrolman Samuel Galletta promptly accompanied Rocco and Nicholas DeLucca into Chief Michael Falcone's Town Hall office. The head Hammonton police official was sitting behind his cluttered desk and had acted surprised by the appearance of his four unanticipated visitors. The Chief's skeptical mind wondered what *their* purpose was for barging into his sacred bailiwick without any special invitation.

"What could I do for you gentlemen?" the Chief-of-Police gruffly asked as he noticed (but did not initially address) the presence of the DeLucca brothers. "I've already expressed my deepest condolences to you two distinguished gentlemen last night at the Melora Funeral Home."

"Chief Michael Falcone, it's my unhappy duty to inform you that you're under arrest!" Detective Fred Arico boldly announced. "Thank goodness we don't have too far to go to transport you to the nearest jail cell."

"What did you say? How ludicrous can you be? Don't be ridiculous!" Falcone challenged with obvious indignation apparent in his rather astonished tone of voice. "Are you trying to smear my integrity? I hope that this absurd charade is a joke because it's not a too-funny one! Tell me Detective Arico, on what grounds am I being charged?"

"Your case is being turned-over to the Atlantic County Prosecutor and you'll soon be taken to the Mays Landing jail for interrogation!" Officer Galletta chimed-in. "You have entirely too much influence with the local judges and we don't exactly know how far into the town's government the overall corruption extends. The county seat will be a better venue to hear your trial. Now then," the determined patrolmen continued with his indictment, "you have the right to remain silent and any and all things you say can be held and used as evidence against you! You have a right to an attorney. Do you understand your Miranda Rights?"

"This is absolutely illogical, positively asinine Galletta! Totally preposterous and unwarranted! Put the handcuffs away or else you'll be accused before Town Council of being insubordinate to your superior officer!" Michael Falcone yelled. "Didn't you' hear me! Put the cuffs away or else risk your future!"

Detective Fred Arico then explained the pertinent details of what Rocco and Nicholas DeLucca had witnessed in Oak Grove Cemetery and what funeral director Andrew Blake and his assistant Philip Ruggeri had confessed after being fully questioned at their funeral home. Their' testimonies had next been fully corroborated by statements given by Stephen Messina.

"As soon as I heard Rocco and Nick's bizarre story, I immediately got in touch with Patrolman Galletta," Detective Arico explained the initial chronology of events in an accusatory tone of voice. "Immediately we confiscated Jason DeLucca's dark blue Cadillac and quickly found that the right front wheel had been expertly tampered with, thus eventually causing the car to

360

veer off of *Route 206* right into the Wharton Tract Forest. And so I instantly know that *we* then had a death-by-auto' manslaughter case on our hands!"

"And it seemed mighty peculiar to us Chief that your uncle the reprehensible and belligerent Stephen Messina could dispatch a flatbed truck seven miles north of Hammonton to the S-Curve between Atsion Lake and the Pic-A-Lilli Inn and get it there before any other trucks or flatbeds from nearby *206* gas stations and junkyards could arrive on the accident scene and claim the wrecked vehicle! That oddity had to be definitely looked into!"

"That unique occurrence could've been just a remote coincidence!" Chief Falcone defiantly argued and insisted. "How does a strange combination of events possibly implicate me in your wild-goose-chase amateur investigation? I promise you Arico, your job is in jeopardy!"

Detective Fred Arico calmly explained that the body being removed from the DeLucca Mausoleum in tranquil Oak Grove Cemetery belonged to Richard Farinelli, wealthy produce package distributor and fertilizer merchant who happened to be the twelfth and last missing person to disappear inside Hammonton city limits. Then Officer Galletta provided additional information germane to the alleged grand felony.

"Andrew Blake finally broke-down and told us the missing pieces to the puzzle!" the very responsible patrolman articulated. "Mr. Blake's crematoria had broken-down the week before he thought he would be receiving Jason DeLucca's body for embalming. He couldn't cremate Richard Farinelli because of the crematoria malfunction so Mr. Andrew Blake and Philip Ruggeri temporarily housed the package king's embalmed body in the DeLucca Mausoleum because Blake still had the key to the family's cemetery edifice. And when Andrew Blake suddenly realized that the Melora Funeral Home was to conduct Jason DeLucca's wake and interment, the flustered funeral director had to act fast and…"

"Remove Farinelli's body from the family mausoleum before turning the sepulcher's key over to Mr. Melora," the sleuth-like Detective Fred Arico finished the patrolman's testimony. "Further questioning of the implicated suspects Blake and Ruggeri revealed that the first eleven missing persons were all victims that were heinously murdered and then later intentionally cremated. Mr. Blake had cunningly mixed the victims' ashes in with the ashes of legitimately cremated dearly departed people, and so the embers of the eleven murder victims are now coincidentally

361

preserved in various urns on fireplace mantels all over Hammonton!"

"But how am I involved in this absurd murder caper you've just alluded to?" Michael Falcone demanded knowing. "Your evidence connecting me to these facts is flimsy at best! I know the law! I'm innocent until proven guilty! It'll never stand up in a court room, county or otherwise!"

"You can no longer intimidate *us* with your bullying and gruffness so I'll cut right to the chase Chief! We've already obtained a confession from your Uncle Stephen Messina," Officer Galletta disclosed as Rocco and Nicholas DeLucca attentively listened to the patrolman's vital commentary. "Guido Renzi and your despicable relative by marriage, the unscrupulous Stephen Messina, were secondary henchmen working for the Philadelphia Mafia. When the mob needed to extort some highly desired 'seed money' from a dozen-or-so readily available Hammonton millionaires in order to expand their South Jersey operations," Galletta impressively expounded and then paused, "the ruthless thugs received the exact names and addresses of rich citizens of our fair community from none other than reliable informants Renzi and Messina. The rest of the remarkable story is now modern Hammonton history! But then Messina and Renzi got into an argument over money. According to Mr. Andrew Blake, Stephen Messina had killed Guido Renzi with a hammer and under threat of being murdered, Blake had no alternative other than cremating Renzi soon thereafter."

"But your fairy tale accusations hint at having only circumstantial evidence!" Michael Falcone loudly protested. "You'll never be able to convict me of anything except *your* futilely presenting to the court the usual weak argument of 'guilt by association!' I'll testify that both you Sam and you Fred are looking for promotions at my expense, trying to put feathers in your caps! Yes, I'll accuse you both of impugning my integrity for your own personal gain!"

"On the contrary!" Detective Arico sternly objected. "We've discovered that Mr. Andrew Blake owed the Philly' mob over a million dollars in accumulated gambling debts. And your onerous Uncle Stephen Messina has turned state's evidence and has already entered a convenient plea bargain arrangement with the county prosecutor's office. He's also being considered for entrance into the Witness Protection Program because the County Prosecutor has allied with the FBI and wants to go after the

Philly' mob too!" Arico convincingly indicated. "And as far as your' direct involvement is concerned…."

"Blood is much thicker than water! You knew quite well Chief that all of this perverse illegal activity including the twelve murders was going on while you were covering-up and deliberately ignoring the mess in order to protect your detestable uncle and his mob confederates," Officer Galletta related to his former boss, much to the astonishment and amazement of both Rocco and Nicholas DeLucca. "And furthermore, we have on record valid testimony that you Michael Falcone had also received mob hush money to the amount of two hundred and fifty thousand dollars derived from the total extortion money being obtained from *other* still-alive fearful Hammonton residents of means who had handed-over their precious dough to save their lives," Patrolman Galletta impressively reviewed. "And those unfortunate individuals that refused to participate in the Philly' mob's lethal extortion caper, they were…."

"They were systematically eliminated, cremated and their charred remains placed into jars along with the ashes of other *normally deceased* members of the community," Detective Arico affirmed. "But the one thing that broke the entire case wide open was when Mr. Andrew Blake's crematoria device became inoperable. That's when Mr. Farinelli's body had to be hidden quickly in the Oak Grove Cemetery mausoleum until Blake would get his undependable cremation mechanism fixed and operable again. And finally, if poor Jason DeLucca hadn't coincidentally died in that devastating automobile accident up on *206*, then…."

"Then your police investigation would still be stationary, stalled and sitting on square one!" Rocco DeLucca persuasively concluded and stated. "Nick and I had no idea that our brother's tragic death would spark the beginning of a major crime scene investigation once it emerged from under Michael Falcone's despicable jurisdiction!"

"The Steel Pier"

Atlantic City, New Jersey's famous *Steel Pier* was the *Queen of Resorts* premier showplace for entertainment from its original construction in 1898 (as a Quaker repose) through its heyday during and after *World War II,* leading up to the fabulous "Golden Years" of rock and roll music. In fact the unique extension into the *Atlantic* was a favorite destination for vacationers right through the era of popular variety shows that were prevalent during '50s and '60s pioneering television programming. The revered structure that jutted out over a quarter mile into the ocean had obtained its classic name from the "steel framework" upon which the Pier had been erected. Over the decades many big name stars had performed live shows at the landmark building including the legendary John Philip Sousa, Frank Sinatra, Benny Goodman, Ed Sullivan, Bing Crosby, Jackie Gleason, Dean Martin, Perry Como and comedian Eddie Cantor.

During the 1940s and early '50s, many famous "Big Bands" were featured in the *Pier's* renowned Marine Ballroom, the entertainment venue booking such acclaimed names as Guy Lombardo and his Royal Canadians, Paul Whitman and his Orchestra along with the Tommy and Jimmy Dorsey bands. And in the fabled 1930s and 1940s, such gossip column names as singing sensations Rudy Vallee, Vaughn Monroe and the Andrews Sisters were standard acts appearing often on stage. Even the *Amos N' Andy* radio comedy act graced the *Pier's* outstanding stage in 1939. It is no wonder that the many splendid attractions for the price of "one low admission" gave the glorious Atlantic City *Steel Pier* the well-deserved appellation: "The amusement center at sea."

The legalization of the local casino gambling industry by the State of New Jersey in the late 1970s had sufficiently revitalized a deteriorating Atlantic City, and the impressive economic renaissance has over the past three decades contributed to making the beach resort into a profitable year-round vacation paradise for millions of tourists and gamblers, many of whom' live in East Coast metropolitan areas and are within easy driving distance of South Jersey's most exotic glitzy, ritzy and grandiose hotels.

On July 4th, 2008 Vince DelRossi, a moody, eccentric produce broker from Hammonton, New Jersey was a frequent visitor to Donald Trump's Taj Mahal Casino, situated on the "peaches and cream" boardwalk in Atlantic City. When not thinking or worrying about his fleet of twelve shiny tractor-trailer trucks, his Vineland, New Jersey Commission House or his recent divorce from the former Carolyn DiBona along with the loss of custody of his two teenage children, Vince would habitually drive his luxurious blue Mercedes sedan into the Taj Mahal's concrete high rise parking garage to try his luck at the craps tables.

On July 4th, 2008 the fruit and produce distributor had a very fortunate day, winning a total of $23,500 dollars after the ever-vigilant casino management withheld the appropriate taxes. At least temporarily, gloom and doom no longer dominated the risk-taking man's beleaguered mind. 'Thank goodness the food distribution markets along the East Coast are closed today because of the patriotic holiday, otherwise I could've never made this really unexpected bonanza at the Taj Mahal!' the very thrilled recipient reckoned. 'Long live *Independence Day*!'

'I'll just casually saunter out onto the ageless boardwalk and for old times' sake take a brief refreshing stroll around the present not-too-marvelous *Steel Pier*,' Vince happily thought as he neatly folded his handsome check into his pants' pocket. 'Carolyn will never learn of this fine little windfall so I'll keep my nice little secret cash bonus all to myself. Every once in a blue moon Lady Luck does smile in my direction and thank God no cavities in *her* pearly-white front teeth are evident.'

After exiting the Taj Mahal's front doors and stepping onto the world-famous boardwalk, Vince nostalgically reflected for a moment as he stopped and noticed several wicker roller chairs occupied with passengers being pushed by ambitious self-motivated operators in north and south directions amidst heavy pedestrian foot traffic. Instantly the perceptive man's keen imagination was set into motion. The traditional boardwalk roller chairs along with the distant rolling ocean waves and the fresh summer breeze immediately made DelRossi recollect his many trips and 'double-dates' to Atlantic City as an adventurous carefree youth.

'Mr. Peanut dressed in his odd uniform used to stand right at this very spot greeting intrigued tourists,' Vince remembered with a broad smile, 'and the character was pleasantly representing his retail store Planters Peanuts, which is long gone because of the advent of the Taj Mahal Casino. And oh yes,' DelRossi mused, 'across the wide boardwalk was the incomparable *Steel Pier*, which was paralleled to its right by the *Steeplechase Pier*, owned by the same proprietors as *Steeplechase Park* up in Coney Island,'

DelRossi fondly remembered. 'I once had won Carolyn a giant stuffed giraffe playing a numbers' wheel game there.'

Other memorable thoughts rapidly raced through Vincent's restive mind. 'And oh yes, my teen friends and I would often trek the full mile up and then the full mile back between the *Steel Pier* on Virginia Avenue and the *Million Dollar Pier* on Missouri looking for good-looking girls to meet,' the fruit and vegetable buyer recalled with a broad grin forming on his countenance. 'And during the seasonal spring and fall months my buddies and I would go swimming in the *Ambassador* and also in the *President Hotel's* heated indoor pools and then during the torrid summer months,' the daydreaming gambler recounted, 'we'd splash away in the ocean. And who could ever forget the magnificent architecture evident in the Post-Victorian boardwalk landmark hotels, the *Traymore*, the *Shelbourne*, the *Claridge*, the *Dennis*, the *Marlboro-Blenheim* and the *Chalfonte-Haddon Hall?* Those terrific late '50s and early '60s times were the greatest days for American teenagers to be alive! I'll never forget them as long as I live!'

Vince crossed the boardwalk and eagerly paced onto the present-day *Steel Pier*, which is now an abbreviated length of its former grand self and presently serves as an active amusement center sporting mostly standard children's rides and honky-tonk games. 'The immortal *Pier* had survived a terrible coastal storm in 1962 that had violently smashed away its outermost segment and then in 1970 a huge winter inferno had incinerated the elegant Marine Ballroom with an estimated one million dollars in damage,' DelRossi remembered.

Then the pensive man further evaluated the *Pier's* two major disasters. 'That devastating fire event was an ugly part of Atlantic City history and its memory is deeply ingrained in my mind! But this new 2008 rendition of 'the *Pier*' is very similar in character to what the old neighboring *Steeplechase Pier* used to be!' Vincent concluded. 'I think I'll buy some amusement ride tickets. Yes, that's what I'll do! I'll relive a portion of my childhood by taking a few spins on the ancient carousel, become sentimental and then fancifully reminisce a bit more about the wonderful past.'

Upon finding an adequate seat inside a gold-gilt sleigh firmly anchored upon the *Steel Pier's* colorful merry-go-round, Vincent incidentally found himself sitting opposite a distinguished-looking gentleman who immediately introduced himself to the lucky craps player as "Hermes Messenger." The newcomer felt obligated to reciprocate the stranger's friendly gesture.

"Hi, I'm Vince DelRossi," the cheerful produce broker proudly announced above the "East Side, West Side" calliope music as the gaudy-looking carousel with its menagerie of painted animals began its all-too-familiar rotation. "I used to visit the *Steel Pier* quite often when it was a real showplace," Vince honestly related to Hermes. "I mean back in the '50s and '60s big-name talent would always be on the billet here. The past, or I should say *my* past here in Atlantic City, now seems like it all had happened just yesterday!"

"You seem quite content discussing your many associations with the old *Steel Pier!*" marveled and sympathetically answered Mr. Hermes Messenger. "Over the years you must've had many fond memories of the place! Lots of times people find recollecting and reflecting upon the past much more comfortable than thinking about either the present or the future."

"Yes indeed! There're many terrific memories but one' in particular especially stands out!" Vince instinctively verified. "Back on July 4th, 1958 I had attended the sensational Ricky Nelson concert in the Marine Ballroom. There were...."

"There were over 44,000 people on the *Pier* that hot sultry summer day, easily breaking the former attendance record of around 40,000 previously set by Frank Sinatra," Hermes Messenger remarkably finished Vince's statement. "I too had also been a passionate attendee lost in the raucous crowd on that fabulous 1958 day. I have to admit that it was indeed quite an unbelievable and monumental experience! If my memory serves me properly, the waiting line to buy admission tickets was over four blocks long!"

"And Hermes, I also specifically remember seeing Frankie Avalon, Dion and the Belmonts, Paul Anka, Bobby Rydell and Fabian singing their hit songs on stage," Vince enthusiastically interrupted his newfound carousel companion. "And don't forget the *Steel Pier's* two movie theaters, the great General Motors annual new car shows, the carnival boardwalk games and their boisterous barkers, the circus sideshow acts and the..."

"And the Diving Bell Ride that took visitors plunging under the sea to view murky water in a submarine-type environment," Hermes astutely added, "not to mention the gorgeous lady riders included in the very exciting Diving Horse act at the end of the *Pier*. The brave and highly skilled female equestrian and her steed would adroitly zip down a wet metal slide, fall forty-foot into a deep pool of water and miraculously endure the fantastic ordeal."

"Wow! You really do share my excellent memories of the old *Steel Pier*!" DelRossi abundantly complimented Hermes Messenger. "I had won my teen girlfriends many plush animals and rag doll prizes playing the many games of chance there. And the numerous food vendors sold great hot dogs, frozen custard, pretzels, hamburgers, popcorn, pink lemonade and delicious pizza too!" Vince exclaimed as the mid-twentieth century merry-go-round gradually grinded to a halt. "If only I could do it all again! I mean, everything in Atlantic City seemed so alive and new back then! If only I could return to the excitement of my youth and relive this formerly magnificent *Pier* exactly as it once had been."

"You can and you will!" Hermes dramatically commented and predicted with strong conviction evident in his confident tone of voice. "Now my rambunctious newly acquired Friend, kindly step off the wooden platform. If you'll graciously accompany me, you'll soon see and feel just what I mean!"

"Are you for real?" the produce distributor exclaimed as the two men stepped-down from the amusement relic that the now suspicious DelRossi remembered as a familiar item left over from the fabulous 1950s. "This conversation is rather unorthodox, you know! And Hermes, it's so staggering, almost shocking, that my senses seem to be momentarily distorted."

"Don't feel badly!" Hermes Messenger consoled his newly discovered companion. "For you see Vincent DelRossi, we've just successfully time-traveled back to July 4th, 1958 and yes, we're now walking and talking on the famous *Steel Pier*."

"This is impossible!" Vince shouted above the noise around him. "It defies everything I've ever learned!"

"Listen carefully my skeptical Fellow. Your teen idol Ricky Nelson will be appearing in precisely one hour in the Marine Ballroom. And after his spectacular performance is re-created for your exclusive enjoyment," the knowledgeable guide matter-of-factly revealed to his flabbergasted guest, "you'll have all the time in the world, well anyway, *most* of the time in the world to amply appreciate the Diving Bell experience, the thrilling Diving Horse Show and the *immortal*, and I use *that* very extraordinary terminology loosely, 'the immortal' James Dean movie *Rebel without a Cause*, which as you know also starred beautiful Natalie Wood. And yes Vincent," Hermes nonchalantly elaborated, "at your leisure you can play all the games of chance that you want over and over again, all at my generous expense! How could your avaricious heart desire anything else?"

369

"Why thank you for your fine hospitality Hermes!" Vince gratefully acknowledged as his greedy eyes surveyed his immediate July 4th, 1958 *Steel Pier* environment. "But how is all of this paranormal stuff possible? I meant to say, is this incredible scene all some sort of a phenomenal illusion? Is there some kind of exotic drug in this cup of cola I've been drinking? I mean, I can't even remember purchasing it! Tell me now, are you a mystic or a traveling magician?" the stunned gambler inquired. "And your odd first name, Hermes! Yes, eighth grade English literature class! Doesn't *that* unusual name, Greek in origin I believe, have something to do with mythology?"

"Why yes, very astute observation indeed!" the singular Mr. Hermes Messenger congratulated his new protege. "Hermes was the messenger god portrayed in ancient Greek lore. He often is depicted in museum paintings as having wings on his helmet, and sometimes his sandals are shown having wings too! What an unfortunate travesty of human artistic enterprise your fertile imagination has manufactured! Yes my Friend," Hermes Messenger stated with a frown appearing on his visage, "the fabled courier's facial image now symbolizes fast delivery in the highly competitive florist industry! Don't you perceive *his* particular physical resemblance to me?"

"What do you mean by saying 'travesty'?" the now very apprehensive Vince DelRossi protested and challenged. "Stop being so damned evasive! I'm beginning to wish that I had never met you on that ancient merry-go-round over there! Why must you persist in haunting me?"

"Because, my inquisitive Gambler Friend, I'm an itinerant clairvoyant and I always deliberately use the pseudo-name Hermes Messenger as a cover," the all-too-sublime astral courier informed his astounded listener on the very crowded July 4th, 1958 *Steel Pier*. "And I'm only following instructions from my superiors!"

"Get to the point!" Vincent imperatively insisted. "And don't be so damned facetious in doing so!"

"Many apostates and so-called philosophers and scholars believe that the Hermes from Greek mythology is what Biblical angels are based on, except that the wings on the Olympian god's helmet and sandals have been satisfactorily adapted and transformed into growths on *my* back," Hermes competently explained as he swiftly removed his tawdry suit jacket and exhibited to Vincent a stellar set of dazzling white-feathered wings. "As you can plainly see, I'm your new fine-feathered

370

friend, ha, ha, ha! And I strenuously urge *you* from this moment on to watch your rebellious loose language or else you'll risk suffering some major dire consequences!" The shape-shifter next had a glowing glittery halo appear around his heavenly head to supplement his radiant angelic appearance. DelRossi was absolutely dumbfounded.

"What's this atrocious malarkey all about!" demanded Vincent. "You're violating my free will! Get me out of this despicable vexing fiasco right this minute! You obnoxious Impostor! You wicked Violator! I'll register a grievance, report you to the police or have you punished for deceiving me!"

"Forget uttering all *that* dysfunctional futile verbal nonsense!" ordered the stern-faced angel. "You have no choice in the matter! Sinful Gambler, *you* must be penitent about your abundant trespasses unto others! It's now my explicit duty to inform you that you're officially trapped on this July 4th, 1958' day inside the confines of your highly coveted *Steel Pier*, and you'll have until *Judgment Day* the pleasure of experiencing all that you had amply enjoyed as a youth, over and over again until the repetition makes you nauseous and wanting to regurgitate your repugnant guts out until the End of the World finally arrives. For as you now clearly see, smug and haughty Vincent DelRossi," the extremely serious Messenger from Heaven quite lucidly stated, "I've been assigned to very capably escort you directly into your own personal Purgatory. Repent for your myriad immoral behaviors and transgressions," Hermes commanded, "for Arrogant Fool, you had died of a violent stroke on the carousel and are now temporarily assigned to my custody! Your soul has had its rendezvous with destiny! Partake of the fate that your miserable mediocre life has earned!"

"Well, what if I intentionally escape this horrible nightmare by walking out one of the *Pier's* front exits?" the frustrated time prisoner incredulously asked. "Tell me, what worse penalty would I have accomplished then?"

"You can't just meander off into oblivion!" Hermes adamantly explained. "You can't avoid your already prescribed fate!" Hermes clarified. "The *Pier* entrances and exits are all cleverly warped, by *that* I mean uniquely bent in time! Every attempt you make at escaping, you'll soon discover that you'll just wind-up back at your point of departure," Hermes communicated. "I strongly advise that you don't become constantly disappointed and entirely aggravated by endeavoring such a foolish sophomoric enactment! And besides, when you had died on the familiar

371

merry-go-round you had at *that* very moment surrendered your free will!"

"Well then Hermes, what if I jump off the *Pier* into the *Atlantic*?" the trapped and perplexed victim angrily asked his afterlife guide. "Surely I could swim to shore and upon reaching the beach, eventually get back to my car in the Taj Mahal parking garage." The still-shocked speaker paused for a moment to gather his fleeting thoughts. "Don't be so heartless! You wouldn't deny me *that* second chance at redemption, would you?"

"Preposterous and ludicrous suggestion!" Hermes laughed and chided his mortal companion. "I haven't heard anything so humorous and so idiotic in over a century! Ha, ha, ha! You'll simply drown in the ocean and then show-up again for the already expressed purpose of aimlessly exploring around this July 4th, 1958 *Steel Pier*! It'll all be so outrageously monotonous and redundant! You could repeat your silly desperate suicide by drowning a thousand times or more, all to no avail! Ha, ha, ha!" the inimitable Heavenly Messenger emphasized. "Vincent, are you a slow read or what? Don't you get it? Why can't you get your spatial and temporal abstractions straight! Let's have an on-the-spot reality check! Your stained soul requires purification and you must be purged!" declared Hermes. "Let me review the inflexible facts for you! You're a lost spirit incarcerated here on the *Steel Pier* in 1958 and you're no longer a living mortal traveling around this part of Atlantic City in the year 2008!"

"Wipe that condescending smile off your gloating face! What's so funny and amusing?" the recently deceased soul insisted on knowing. "I'm beginning to despise you more than I had ever hated my estranged wife!"

"Pardon my jocular vernacular and my horrendous play-on-words," the itinerant Angel Hermes guffawed, "but all throughout your celestial experience, you *will* certainly have a monopoly on monotony!"

"You show me no empathy or mercy!" Vincent ineffectively argued. "And you call yourself an Angel from Heaven? I find you as un-inspiring as a funeral casket or as spiritually stimulating as a thrice-used cremation urn!"

"You're dead wrong!" jested the magnificent Winged Messenger. Yes, you're absolutely *dead* wrong!" Hermes reiterated. "It's too late for you to redeem your errant ways! Your many egregious habits have finally caught up with you! Enjoy the remainder of your very judicious and justly deserved penance Vincent DelRossi. I'm sorry, but I can't help but laugh at your unenviable predicament!" the brilliant glowing Angel declared. "I assure you, the world is guaranteed to end within the next thousand years!"

The often-mercurial deceased produce merchant then lost complete control of his mounting temper. Vincent DelRossi felt victimized and duped but could do nothing to modify his new surreal-but-stark surroundings. "This whole situation is positively abominable and totally punitive! Hermes, can't I appeal my fate to a higher authority?"

"You had your chance to demonstrate the proper morality when you had possessed *that* distinct opportunity while you were a typical human being gallivanting all around Hammonton, New Jersey and vicinity," Hermes eloquently articulated. "Just think about your wonderful present environment Vincent, which is actually a vivid rendition of your past surroundings! Just contemplate its totality! You can view and savor the excellent July 4th, 1958 Ricky Nelson *Steel Pier* concert thousands and thousands of times over and over again!" the Angel Hermes emphasized. "That is *your* conferred posthumous reward for awkwardly exercising your free will! But right now I have another important appointment to keep so I'll have to promptly leave your illustrious company! But before I depart your mind's favorite Atlantic City fantasy, I'll grant you one final question for me to answer."

"Before you abandon me to cavort around with these 44,000 other imbecilic zombies, tell me one thing Hermes. Who has died or will be dying right now that you've been assigned to escort *that* unfortunate person into the hereafter?" Vincent asked his temporary mentor with a very stoic expression featured on his very ashen face. "I sincerely hope it's not anyone I had known during my brief tenure as a human being! Is it someone important or just another lackluster soul just like myself?"

"Actually, it's your former wife Carolyn!" Hermes replied rather tongue-in-cheek. "I truly relish this opportunity to convey to you *that* recently occurred good news. And I must also disclose that you'll be reunited right here on the *Steel Pier* with Carolyn and learn to co-exist with her right up until the arrival of *Judgment Day*, whenever that fabled date is finally established! I do believe you'll both have plenty of time to make amends for all of the intense arguments you two have had over the years! And now Vincent DelRossi," Hermes affably expressed, "I'm a very busy overworked Angel and must therefore bid you 'adieu'!"

"Live Free or Die"

Frederick Allen Griffith shuffled into Dr. Augustus Pietropaolo's office at 1237 Paradise Road, Hammonton, New Jersey feeling despondent, sluggish and quite lethargic. Mrs. Elysia Fields, the office receptionist, greeted the new patient and checked his name off her long list. Fred felt a tad insecure in that he was the only person sitting in the large waiting room. The fact that there were no magazines, newspapers or pamphlets on the end tables for him to scrutinize made Griffith feel even more uncomfortable.

"You're a little early for your scheduled appointment," Mrs. Fields stated with a forced smile. "Dr. Pietropaolo will be available to analyze your issues shortly. Nobody has problems any more. If I may use the euphemism, everyone who comes here has *issues*! Anyway, the Dr.'s presently reviewing the records of another eccentric client, or should I say 'unique patient.' Now Mr. Griffith," Mrs. Fields added as she took a glimpse inside Frederick's confidential folder, "you're here to discuss your recent four-day bus trip up to New Hampshire, is that correct?"

"I don't even know why I'm here or how I even got here," the confused man replied, shaking his head in bewilderment as the nervous visitor stared intensely at the nameplate ledger on the woman's neatly organized desk. "My mind must be suffering from acute amnesia or forgetfulness. The only specific things I can remember are that my name is Fred Griffith, I live with my wife Dorothy at 197 North Orchard Street, Hammonton, New Jersey, that we have two grown sons Joseph and Frank and that Dottie and I just got back from a New Hampshire bus trip to the scenic White Mountains. Everything else right now in my mind seems to be drawing a complete blank! Did I have some traumatic experience that I can't recall?"

"Your obvious symptoms are very typical of our average patient!" Mrs. Fields answered, attempting to allay Fred Griffith's very evident anxiety. "I'm sure that after you confer with Dr. Pietropaolo, you'll be able to focus and concentrate better. That's the nature of his practice, you know, and he's the best in his profession at clearing up people's apprehensions and concerns. He's helped many patients just like yourself' make smooth transitions to their lives," the receptionist/secretary assured. "I'm certain Mr. Griffith that you'll be no exception! Now then, your personal file indicates that you had been married to Dorothy for forty years."

"Yes we have been wed for four wonderful decades, and ever since I retired from dentistry in 2006 Dottie and I go on at least three vacations a year," Fred told the very efficient Mrs. Fields. "We never had that much time to travel all those early years because I was so absorbed in my practice and since my wife was a very dedicated budget accountant at the town hospital."

The door to the specialist's office opened and after introducing himself to Fred, the Dr. escorted his latest patient inside and requested that the retired dentist sit in a chair opposite an impressive-looking oak desk. General pleasantries were perfunctorily exchanged and soon thereafter Griffith's "personal interview/consultation" was professionally initiated with a series of delving questions pertaining to Fred and Dorothy's late June New England bus excursion. All the while the affable Dr. Pietropaolo remained polite and cordial.

"Where did your bus trip originate?" the seated Dr. courteously asked as the fingers of his hands touched just below his chin, forming an imperfect isosceles triangle. "And how did you get from Hammonton to your point of departure?"

"Our son Joe picked Dottie and me up in his SUV at 5:30 a.m. last Monday at our Orchard Street home and then drove us and our luggage twenty-five miles east to the Shore Mall on *Route 322*," Fred recalled and shared. "After unloading our two suitcases and a carry-on bag, our bleary-eyed son left, promising to return to the Shore Mall at 8 p.m. on Thursday, June 26th to dutifully transport us back home. We waited fifteen minutes for the bus to arrive with the other thirty-six people, mostly senior citizens, who had also signed-up for the four days and three nights' New Hampshire trip! Everything at the outset seemed normal and copasetic."

"What bus service was conducting the tour?" the Dr. asked as he conscientiously studied the opened file situated on his desk and then clicked his ballpoint pen. "There are at least six decent ones operating out of South Jersey."

"It was Ralph's Bus Tours originating out of Cape May Court House!" Fred recollected and communicated. "The driver, a young fellow named Mike, said the state-of-the-art vehicle cost $450,000.00. It was one of those new ultra-modern 'kneeling buses' that lowers in the front just before the passengers would enter. It even had a sort of spiral staircase entry, suggesting that it offered the riders a bit of transportation class. The only disadvantage to the bus as far as I could see was its gas mileage, only getting about eleven miles per gallon," Fred disclosed, scratching his partially bald head. "But the entire trip cost Dottie and me only around eleven hundred dollars, a considerable value when you include lodging, two excellent side tours and also eight more-than-adequate meals. You know Dr., when an elderly person like myself is living on a fixed income, one has to be frugal."

Fred Griffith next divulged to the seemingly interested Dr. Pietropaolo how the bus trip north to New Hampshire was rather uneventful. As Mike steered the huge vehicle up the heavy-trafficked *Garden State Parkway*, Ralph announced that the group would be stopping at different eateries every two and a half hours with the first passenger exit occurring at the Montvale Rest Area. After a thirty-minute interval, the rejuvenated passengers again boarded and soon Mike drove them into New York State. They soon motored past the gigantic Palisades Center Mall and fifteen minutes thereafter the bus was rumbling by on the *Tappan Zee Bridge* and zipping across the *Hudson* into Tarrytown near Sunnyside, the former home of Washington Irving, the distinguished author of "Rip Van Winkle" and "The Legend of Sleepy Hollow."

"If my knowledge of geography serves me correctly, I suppose you then traveled past White Plains heading northeast toward the *Massachusetts Turnpike*," the Dr. behind the oak desk interrupted his new patient. "I know that particular landscape very well! I used to live in Yonkers, you know."

"Well yes, but first we stopped at a Cracker Barrel Restaurant on the Connecticut/Massachusetts border for a full course breakfast," Fred indicated while neurotically fidgeting around in his leather chair, "and along the way I got to see three state capitals and their golden domed legislative buildings. The first was in Hartford, Connecticut, the second in Springfield, Massachusetts and finally the third one in Concord, New Hampshire. And so, as Ralph narrated various points of interest over the bus's intercom, Dottie and I enjoyed listening to his contemporary history lesson. According to Mike's bus odometer, the trip from the Shore Mall in Pleasantville to our destination, the Beacon Resort in Lincoln, New Hampshire was a total of five hundred and five scenic miles," Griffith glibly vociferated. "Lincoln's located near the end of *Interstate 93* and everyone on the tour arrived safe and sound at 4:40 p.m. without any noticeable or noteworthy incidents. So tell me Dr., why am I here and how did I get here? I never knew that there was a Paradise Road in Hammonton!"

"Your story so far sounds like an ordinary senior citizens' bus tour to me," the somewhat bored Dr. Pietropaolo concluded and said before yawning. "Quite a mundane mediocre tale, I must confess. Oh yes, good old Yankee New Hampshire! I just love the state motto, 'Live Free or Die!' How noble, patriotic and proud that slogan is! It's minted on the new state quarter you know!"

"Well, that's your evaluation and you're entitled to your unbiased opinion," Fred mildly chastised his newfound critic. "I have to tell you that the Beacon Resort is a second-tier type of vacation place that presently caters almost exclusively to senior citizens in the spring and fall and to visiting families in the summer and winter. At any rate, when I was a kid my parents used to often take me to Mt. Airy Lodge and to Pocono Manor up in the mountains near the Delaware River Gap and also a few times up to Grossinger's in the *Catskills*, so I have a good background of experience with which I can compare the Beacon Resort," Griffith conceitedly added. "That first evening my wife and I were eating filet mignon dinners in Dad's Restaurant when all of a sudden I was suffering severe chest pains along with shortness of breath. After the excruciating pain subsided," Fred continued his extended narrative, "a waiter was assigned by the management to accompany my wife and me back to our upstairs suite. The young gent stayed for a full half hour and noticing that I had undergone what seemed to be a miraculous recovery from my 'severe indigestion crisis,' *we* gave the concerned fellow a twenty-dollar tip for his time and effort. As I just said, it seemed as if I had made a miraculous recovery."

"You were lucky that you didn't die on the spot in Dad's Restaurant," the mental health practitioner observed and related. "What happened next?"

"Well, that night I took my clothes off and got into the suite's extra-large *Jacuzzi*, inadvertently slipped on the bottom of the tub and hit my head against the object's ledge," Fred recalled and conveyed. "Perhaps there was a bar of soap that had caused the accident, but that distinct possibility I don't remember. I believe I might've been knocked unconscious for a few seconds, but upon regaining my senses, out of sheer embarrassment, I never told Dottie anything about that awkward mishap! But a throbbing headache stayed with me for a full two hours."

"I suppose you later slept soundly after your first two misadventures at the Beacon," Dr. Pietropaolo speculated and

378

said. "What happened the next day Mr. Griffith? Did your ominous bad-luck streak happen to continue?"

Fred explained that the following morning after breakfast the elderly group from New Jersey boarded the streamlined expensive bus and journeyed north to Our Lady of Grace Shrine in Colebrook. After walking through the property's gardens that featured granite statues commemorating the Stations of the Cross, Fred and Dottie entered the former religious seminary that is still run by the Oblates, a strict order of Roman Catholic priests. "We were preoccupied chatting and ascending the wooden steps to the chapel's choir loft when suddenly I lost my balance and tumbled down six stairs. Well," Fred frowned and then proceeded with relating his graphic rendition, "I again was so mortified from my clumsiness that I got right up onto my feet and stubbornly refused any assistance from other inquisitive people who happened to be in the vicinity. Dottie wanted me to get to a medical facility right away but my obstinate nature prevailed and I refused any suggestion of abandoning the tour in search of a hospital or doctor."

"That's three times you were given explicit warnings but yet you ignored all three," the probing spiritual psychologist diplomatically criticized. "And this last time Mr. Griffith you almost perished at a sacred shrine setting. I suspect that religious symbolism was in play, wouldn't you agree? Didn't *that* odd spiritual coincidence of plunging down the steps at a shrine occur to you?"

"I've never really ever been what you might call a devout church-going person," Fred reluctantly admitted. "I did attend several Catholic schools from grades one through eight, I received all of the necessary sacraments like Communion and Confirmation, but I guess later in life my undergraduate liberal arts college education indoctrinated me into becoming an open-minded apostate and as a result, I regard the church's inflexible teachings as being obsolete and irrelevant. Anyway," Griffith guiltlessly uttered to his newfound all-too-tolerant ego and id advisor, "I still view myself as being a moral and just person even though I've abandoned the strict doctrines, customs and ceremonies advocated by the Catholic Church! Am I to be admonished for that?"

"You don't think of yourself as being too cynical?" the Dr. questioned his new ward. "But in my humble estimation, you seem to be giving the ancient sage Diogenes some serious competition. Do you see yourself as a hypocrite believing in relative values as opposed to absolute traditions?"

"No Dr., I happen to strongly believe in secularism, that man can solve his own problems, or as your receptionist called them *issues*, without the need for Divine Intervention!" Fred obstinately maintained. "Instead of the erroneous Biblical notion that God created man, I subscribe to the theory that man created God in *his* own image!"

"Now let's quickly review the remainder of your New Hampshire trip!" Dr. Pietropaolo assertively replied. "Next in your sequence of events, the people on your bus and you saw a baby moose on a mountain trail along the highway after Mike your driver had pointed the creature out, and then your contingent headed north toward the Balsams Resort in Dixville Notch, just twelve miles or so from the Canadian border."

"How did you know those things? I never revealed them to you!" answered a very astonished Fred Griffith. "Do you gaze into crystal balls as a hobby?"

"Oh, I just get especially lucky every once in a while!" the interviewer/examiner cleverly responded. "Every so often as in your case Mr. Griffith, I believe I do possess ESP powers! Or perhaps I can randomly read my patients' minds!" Dr. Pietropaolo suggested. "Many patients say that my mental faculties seem to transcend common human intuition. Now please proceed with your remotely intriguing story."

"Well then," the rather amazed office visitor proceeded, "the Balsams Resort at Dixville Notch is really a tremendous place that reminded Dottie and me of the fabulous red-roofed Hotel Del Coronado across the bay from San Diego," Fred verbally compared. "Both hotels offer phenomenal amenities to their patrons. The large charming New Hampshire facility is located near two beautiful mountains that touch each other with a gentle stream flowing between them; hence the odd term 'Notch.' The all-inclusive resort is politically famous because that's where eighteen area residents assemble every four years to be the first ones to vote in the United States in any given presidential election. In fact Dr.," Fred academically expounded from knowledge he had learned from Ralph, "the Balsams' at Dixville Notch even has a specially designated voting room that visitors to the grand hotel all tour and marvel at."

"And did you have another serious accident at the Balsams?" the seemingly omniscient interviewer asked. "I don't wish to sound too esoteric but something tells me that you did."

"Now that you mention it, why yes!" Fred said with his mouth agape. "While Dottie was conversing with another woman she had met on the bus tour, I discreetly dismissed myself to use the upstairs men's lavatory. En route I walked through one of many attractive upstairs' lounge areas and then sauntered down a Victorian-décor corridor. A housemaid was busy vacuuming the hallway when her machine's cord popped out of the electric wall socket. I courteously bent down to re-insert the cord back into the hall outlet when I was nearly electrocuted. The wire near the base of the cord had been slightly ripped or spliced," Griffith nervously explained, "and I instantly felt current surging throughout my body. Needless to say, I was knocked to the floor by the unexpected jolt. Then noticing my unfortunate predicament, the alarmed maid helped me to my feet. My mind felt so weird and I was virtually flabbergasted from my horrible ordeal that I immediately left *her* compassionate company and promptly hastened into a nearby men's room," Fred remembered and stated. "Then five minutes later Dr., I warily returned to the hotel's upstairs' dining hall and at lunch never once told my wife or anyone else seated at the table what had just happened."

Griffith next described to his new 'mental health doctor' that the remainder of the day was, much to his relieved satisfaction, "lackluster and uneventful." Later that afternoon the itinerant tour group had passed by *Mt. Washington*, New Hampshire's highest peak famous for its extreme cold winter weather outpost at its summit. And then back in Lincoln a well-appreciated lobster tail supper at Dad's Restaurant had been prepared and subsequently that evening the Beacon Resort guests were treated to an entertaining "Songs From the Musical Grease" show. Then the following morning Ralph's Bus Tours conducted the New Jersey vacationers through nearby Franconia Notch and then on to Loon Mountain, both popular *White Mountains'* ski resorts. The bus then journeyed on to Squam Lake, notable for being the setting for the Hollywood movie *On Golden Pond*. Squam Lake is right next to…."

"Lake Winnipesaukee, which is New Hampshire's most famous resort area!" Dr. Pietropaolo authoritatively declared, showing an increase in enthusiasm. "I've been there countless times and find its exceptional beauty most wondrous! Did you see the many loons that inhabit Squam Lake?"

"Yes, our informative tour-guide Ralph told us that the *loons*, I'm referring to birds and not people, return every spring and can't survive the winter there because their legs are so weak and fragile that they can't land on hard surfaces, especially Squam Lake when it freezes over," Griffith garrulously conveyed. "So then our illustrious tour group was divided in half, and we next motored around placid Squam Lake on two separate pontoon boats."

"Ah yes, *On Golden Pond* was filmed on location there!" Dr. Pietropaolo nostalgically recollected and reminded the somewhat emotionally frustrated Fred Griffith. "I've been *there* numerous times! Katherine Hepburn and…"

"And Henry and Jane Fonda starred in that movie," Fred knowledgeably stated, "with Henry Fonda playing Norman Thayer, Jr. and Katherine Hepburn his wife Ethel. But I can't seem to recall the complete name of their independent-minded daughter that Jane Fonda played."

"Chelsea Thayer Wayne," the sagacious spiritual psychologist enunciated without any sign of hesitation or doubt. "And the elusive enormous trout that Norman and young Billy were trying to catch throughout the movie was affectionately named Walter. Of course, Norman had intentionally named the evasive fish after Ethel's cantankerous brother. And oh yes," Dr. Pietropaolo lectured as he scribbled some notes into Fred's opened folder, "Ethel and Norman always like to play the parlor board game *Parcheesi* whenever they could. The film didn't have a tremendous amount of action but it was very dramatic and heartwarming to the viewer from a sentimental perspective. That's why I'm particularly fond of *On Golden Pond* and to this very day, actually never tire of watching it."

"Yes Dr., Dottie and I saw *On Golden Pond* in a movie theater when the film first came out in the early 1980s and also we've seen it again several times on cable TV," Fred fondly remembered and detailed. "But to this day, I never understood the significance of the medal that Norman had given to Chelsea after she had done the fantastic back-flip into Squam Lake."

"According to the script, Norman had won the diving medal in 1921 while he had been an *Ivy League* student/athlete competing in a tournament at the *University of Pennsylvania*," the doctor/genius very nonchalantly-but-adroitly contributed to the conversation. "In the scene to which you've just alluded, it was *his* special way of rewarding his daughter's courage after performing the difficult back-flip off the dock and into the lake!"

"And I'll bet you even know the year that *On Golden Pond* was made public!" Fred prompted his new spiritual mentor.

"The picture was released in 1981," confidently clarified the encyclopedic guru sitting behind the oak desk. "But tell me Mr.

Griffith, what happened to your pontoon boat in the form of an inferno on the way back to the dock?"

"How did you know about that?" Griffith demanded knowing.

"Adequate professional research on my part!" the all-too-cerebral Dr. Pietropaolo curtly answered.

"There was a loud explosion near the outboard engines and the whole thing caught on fire in a hurry!" Fred exclaimed with a degree of worry apparent on his facial expression. "I was instantly propelled into the water and thank God I was wearing a life vest or else I would've certainly drowned."

"Thank God indeed!" emphasized Dr. Pietropaolo. "Yes, thank God indeed!" the accomplished psychologist very deliberately reiterated. "And of course, your wife experienced a similar fate and outcome."

"Yes she did," the beleaguered and now-paranoid patient confirmed. "We're both extremely lucky to be alive."

Fred then described to Dr. Pietropaolo how *that* unforgettable night he had choked on his rib-eye steak and next was publicly mortified when he vomited-up his meal inside a very crowded Dad's Restaurant. And on the bus trip back to New Jersey, the tour stopped at the Yankee Candle outlet in South Deerfield, Massachusetts and "parsimonious Dottie" bought some bargain-priced knickknacks for the kitchen windowsill. All was fine until the southbound tour bus was crossing the *Tappan Zee Bridge*. A heavy gust of wind swept a bulky recreational vehicle directly into the bus's side lane path. Mike's vehicle swerved and then the rattled driver slammed on the brakes. The two huge objects violently caromed off one another and the tour bus (along with its screaming passengers) crashed through the bridge's retaining barrier and then swiftly plunged into the *Hudson River*.

"Well now Mr. Griffith, I'm glad you've finally reached the end of your rather monotonous narrative because quite frankly I'm fairly exhausted from hearing about your many close brushes with death!" Dr. Pietropaolo complained while clenching his right fist. "It's now time for your sentencing."

"What's this lousy conference all about?" protested Fred. "Is this some sort of colossal hoax I'm involuntarily participating in? Is this farce a wild ruse or some sort of illogical canard? What has happened to American justice?"

"I'm afraid Mr. Griffith that your erratic conscience seems to possess two separate characters, a good-sided one and a sinful alter ego one! I too have a dual personality just like you do!" the enigmatic interviewer verified, his partially opened smile revealing pearly-white teeth. "Haven't you yet deciphered the significance of my last name? 'Pietropaolo' roughly translated from Italian into English means 'Peter and Paul!' I predict Mr. Frederick Allen Griffith that you're about to have your epiphany moment on your individualized 'Road to Damascus'!"

"What? Don't be absurd! This travesty is totally inane! Utter nonsense!" Fred strenuously balked.

"You yourself' by virtue of your own volition had admitted that you didn't know how you had gotten to my private office here on Paradise Road and upon your arrival you had hinted that most of your memory had somehow evaporated into time," Dr. Pietropaolo reviewed for his ill-spirited patient's empirical knowledge and psychological benefit. "This is not an exaggeration! Human life is so ephemeral and needless to say every fleeting second should be cherished as being precious!"

"Well then Dr., what might your first name be?" Griffith defiantly challenged. "All throughout our crazy dialogue I've never learned what it was!"

"Sometimes it's Matthew, sometimes it's Mark, sometimes it's Luke and sometimes it's John, whatever appellation fits my fancy!" the interviewer cryptically explained. "But somehow in our accounting department we had a bureaucratic slip-up in *this* rather disorganized afterlife and *we* now have to establish exactly how you had died on your New Hampshire bus excursion so that I can properly sentence you to your appropriate berth, or should I say *station*, in this, the hereafter! After all Frederick, and I think that *this* testament is quite salient and worthy of mention," Dr. Pietropaolo carefully emphasized with apparent conviction, "New Hampshire's state motto is 'Live Free or Die.' I'm not talking about earthly politics here, Mr. Griffith. I'm specifically talking about afterlife justice that's been earned by virtue of your mortal morality!"

"Where am I? Am I a prisoner in Limbo? Am I in Purgatory?" Fred demanded knowing. "What the Hell's going on here?"

"I'm trying to frame your feeble questions into a discernible pattern of ideas that your limited intelligence can somewhat comprehend. Now then, let's just say that since you had exhibited in your abbreviated life a benevolent nature accompanied by a corresponding nefarious nature too," the ageless eternal Gatekeeper qualified, "then you can reliably presume that you're now contained in a kind of suspended animation that temporarily occupies what could best be described as a parallel dimension. That's about the best way for me to adequately define and portray

384

your present circumstances in easy terms that your finite mind can fathom!" the Being behind the solid oak desk pontificated. "It's too bad that your flawed lame brain has such great trouble interpreting certain elementary abstractions!"

Fredrick Griffith sat there motionless upon his comfortable black leather chair, his heart feeling unjustly cheated and victimized and his addled mind trapped in a complete stupor. Dr. Pietropaolo pressed his intercom button and summoned Mrs. Fields. "Elysia, please come to my office immediately. I know that you're deluged with paperwork just like Noah had been deluged with that great *Old Testament* flood but I require your skilled assistance right away."

After Mrs. Elysia Fields opened the office door and softly stepped inside, Dr. Pietropaolo opened a black curtain that had been concealing a round six-color "Wheel of Misfortune." Upon each surface color and number was painted the words: "Cause of Death." Heart Attack was represented for #1 and color red, Church Fall for #2 and color blue, Electrocution for #3 and color green, Boat Fire for #4 and color purple, Choking for #5 and color orange and Drowning in Hudson for #6 and color brown. A seventh yellow space was evident upon the "Wheel of Misfortune" and Fred curiously asked his "Eternal Prosecutor" what *that* unidentified area meant.

"It's your second *chance* at life!" Dr. Pietropaolo explicitly and matter-of-factly attested. "You definitely didn't die in your *Jacuzzi* fall when you hit your head on the tub's ledge, that 's for sure! Now then, if you spin the wheel and the stopper strap ends on Yellow, then you can survive all of the potentially lethal accidents you had amassed on your tumultuous New Hampshire bus trip and continue living your adult life as a salvaged 'born again' new man! One out of seven is a decent chance at attaining redemption, wouldn't you agree?"

"I refuse to participate in this bizarre charade!" Fred screamed like a virtual maniac. "I won't be subjected to such horrendous abuse, holy, divinely sanctioned or otherwise!"

"How are *we'* ever going to determine how you had died?" Dr. Peter and Paul unconvincingly argued and insisted. "According to the Wheel, either you had died by Heart Attack at the Beacon Resort, by your Stairway Tumble at the Seminary Church, by your Electrocution at the Balsams Resort up in Dixville Notch, by the unexpected Boat Fire on Squam Lake, by Choking at Dad's Restaurant or by Drowning in the *Tappan Zee Bridge/Hudson River* bus disaster, or Frederick, you could gain a second chance at life by luckily spinning the color Yellow! Talk about *free* will! Your eternal destiny is completely in your hands!"

"If I spin #4, Purple, Boat Fire, or #6, Brown, Bus Drowning," Fred conjectured and maintained, "then many people beside myself' would probably die in the terrible catastrophes too. But I definitely don't want to choke to death or be violently electrocuted either! I'm sorry Dr., but I won't play your silly little eternity game! It's against my personal ethics!"

"You have no privileged choice in the matter because you've already surrendered your free will before stepping foot into my office!" the now-irritated soul distributor and destination assigner yelled. "That's the way the cookie crumbles Mr. Griffith. Now Mrs. Fields, since our truculent patient refuses to cooperate, kindly spin the wheel and let's decide our obdurate client's fate for him!"

The obedient receptionist/secretary rotated the wheel and seven seconds later it stopped on #5 Orange, Choking. Dr. Pietropaolo had several last remarks to further perturb the already alienated Frederick Allen Griffith, retired DDS.

"You died by choking to death!" the omnipotent Gatekeeper solemnly announced and confirmed the obvious fact. "Your devoted wife Dorothy attempted saving your life but unfortunately she was unfamiliar with the easy-to-learn Heimlich rescue maneuver. Dottie should've taken a course on that elementary subject. Instead she devotedly worked at your town's hospital in the uninspiring accounting department and hardly ever stepped out of her assigned work area, leaving all medical concerns entirely to the staff!"

"Then where have I been condemned to?" Fred incredulously asked his consultant. "Frankly speaking, I don't handle adversity too well! I hope I'm not permanently doomed!"

"Stop your incessant infantile brooding! This is not a bogus encounter you're witnessing! Accept your fate, Woebegone Man!" the Sentence Issuer commanded.

"What fate are you proclaiming?" Frederick Griffith neurotically questioned. "Be more explicit!"

"You're neither going to be transported to Heaven nor are you destined for Hell!" Dr. Pietropaolo announced to his newly released patient. "You'll be soon stationed at some obscure place securely nestled in between those two distinct polarities. Now Sir, here's the unvarnished truth! You're by far no angel or saint! It's my solemn duty to inform you that your imperfect immortal soul Mr. Frederick Allen Griffith requires much urgent tempering, some special crucial purging before you can successfully ascend into a more exclusive domain of the Eternal Hierarchy!"

"Ignorance Is Bliss"

Ever since his wife Eleanor had died of Lou Gehrig's Disease in March of 2006, James Jefferson Gillespie has been extremely despondent and has gone through the motions of everyday life as a pathetic loner. The twenty-eight year old chemist thought that a change of scenery would certainly diminish his great melancholy, so he visited his Hammonton, New Jersey Bellevue Avenue travel agent and booked a two-week autumn vacation to Athens, Greece. James felt that he needed some fresh stimuli to regenerate his sagging spirit. A stay at the luxurious Grande Bretagne Hotel, conveniently situated in central Athens, was sure to alleviate Gillespie's recent chronic introverted disposition.

'Eleanor's been gone for nearly two whole years now,' James sadly reflected on his tragic loss, 'so perhaps it's time for me to meet and date someone new! I haven't had much luck doing *that* around Hammonton since everyone' in town knows me or knows about me at the bowling alley, at the restaurants and at the all-too-false singles' bars. Yes, October seems like a terrific month to be touring the sights of Athens,' the self-pitying fellow reckoned. 'Maybe my two-week hiatus in Greece will miraculously alter my lousy success at romance. And Room 610 at the Grande Bretagne Hotel seems to be a good luck omen. My three best bowling game scores added together equal *that* number!'

On the morning of October 6th a chauffeur from Rapid Rover Transportation Service drove James Gillespie to Terminal/Concourse C. The lengthy flight from *Philadelphia International Airport* to Athens was both smooth and relaxing. Usually an insomniac, James surprisingly managed to sleep for three hours en route. 'Ah yes,' Gillespie mused while staring out his plane window at the array of cottony clouds. 'I've read on the *Internet* where certain famous guests have stayed at the fine Greek hotel I've booked, some of the more notorious ones being Sophia Loren, Bridget Bardot and Elizabeth Taylor. I have an inkling that I just might get lucky in the love department on this trip!'

The *United Airlines* 747 landed right on schedule and after passing through customs without a hitch, the *Du Pont* laboratory scientist hired a taxi and twenty minutes later checked into the Grande Bretagne at 2 p.m. After tipping the bellboy five Euros for conveying his three heavy suitcases from the lobby up to Room 610, James methodically emptied his luggage and then systematically stored his clothes into the appropriate bureau compartments and closet spaces. Next the successful corporate man rested comfortably on his bed and examined several of the brochures he had randomly obtained from sightseeing racks in the hotel lobby. The ancient history aspects of Athens soon captured his attention.

'Let's see now!' James thought as he concentrated and read the descriptive literature. 'The Acropolis is an absolute must see and it's high on my priority list. And at its summit is the ancient Parthenon, a ruined temple dedicated to the goddess Athena, in antiquity the guardian of the city. That structure is perhaps the most magnificent piece of architecture ever conceived by man!' James deducted.

A minute later the thoroughly intrigued hotel guest examined a second brochure. 'And then there're the winding cobblestone streets of the Plaka District with its many cafes and small shops, which dates back many centuries. And these superb historic landmarks featured in this third colorful city brochure are on and near Syntagma Square and Monastiraki Square and are definitely sites of interest worthy of visiting. There's plenty of fascinations right here in Athens to keep me busy for at least a full week.'

The next morning James ambitiously trekked to the incomparable Acropolis and his pedestrian perseverance was rewarded when he amply appreciated the splendor of the fabulous Parthenon, imagining what the gleaming temple must have looked like during the fabled "Golden Age of Pericles." Although other American vacationers tried initiating casual conversations with James, Gillespie tersely answered their harmless 'trite inquiries,' and the other U.S. travelers instinctively received the impression that *he* was indeed a cold and impersonal individual. After again thinking about and missing his deceased wife, finally the depressed chemist's eyes studied in detail the grandeur of the small Nike Temple, and then becoming fatigued from his many wanderings, James slowly ambled back to the noble Grande Bretagne.

'I guess my main mission in life at this very moment is to feed the hungry pigeons,' James sorrowfully concluded as his persecution complex again surfaced from his subconscious mind and avariciously took command of his psyche. 'Thank goodness these awkward birds pecking away at my feet aren't hawks or eagles or some other aggressive species of aerial predators. God!' the weary American' regretfully considered. 'I've never seen so many ugly-looking women in all my life! Are they sponsoring a

390

Miss Ugly Europe Pageant here in Athens? None of these unglamorous-looking females could ever hold a candle to Eleanor, God rest her soul!' Gillespie lamented. 'Maybe I should've spent my summer vacation off from work frolicking in Atlantic City, Brigantine, Cape May or even Wildwood!'

On James' second day in Athens, he visited the Tomb of the Unknown Soldier, the Parliament Building and then marveled at the architecture of the many excellent hotels that were situated adjacent to Syntagma Square. Out of sheer boredom the restive man next purchased two candy bars from a vendor near Monastiraki Square and then strolled southwest to the busy Plaka, which James immediately evaluated as being quite medieval in appearance. 'The women walking around here are even uglier than the grotesque-looking ones up on the Acropolis,' Gillespie critically analyzed the local members of the opposite gender. 'Oh well, as they say back in the States, tomorrow's another day!'

On his stroll back to the hotel James passed by an attractive-looking flower shop and wished that Eleanor were still alive so that he could buy her the most expensive available arrangement. 'My heart is definitely governed by despair,' the woebegone man ruefully assessed. 'How utterly deplorable my mediocre existence is! I'll always be a prisoner of my contemptible loneliness. I used to enjoy solitude and seclusion before I got married, but now I absolutely abhor those hellish mental conditions!'

That evening James had difficulty going to sleep and the insomniac stayed awake watching an English-speaking television channel until midnight, simply to compensate for his excessive restlessness. The bleary-eyed occupant of Room 610 endeavored reading the *Bible* he had discovered in his hotel desk drawer, but his diversion failed to achieve any satisfactory result. All throughout his mind's anguished state James could only contemplate Eleanor and how her premature departure from the world had left his vulnerable heart feeling most disconsolate. After two grueling hours of tossing and turning upon his bed's hard mattress, James finally made his nocturnal visitation to the Land of Morpheus. Remarkably, soon the sleeper's mind entered into a deep slumber.

In a not-so-benign dream, James Gillespie was contacted by a lovely specter that his subconscious believed was a spiritual manifestation of his cherished Eleanor. The man in his deep repose was undergoing an egotistical and emotional meltdown, thinking that he was rapidly becoming ignorant, suddenly being the possessor of very little empirical or practical knowledge. Soon

391

a mystical telepathic conversation ensued between the luminous female vision and the aggrieved man who was suddenly devoid of self-esteem. The apparition initiated the dialogue.

"James, I've transcended space and time to announce to you that you need not experience a lack of confidence during our little discussion," Eleanor's seemingly supernatural image said. "I'm speaking to you from another dimension, a transcendent time and place! Now James, your limited mental capacity must be able to fathom this one important principle: ordinary spatial and temporal conditions no longer hold me prisoner as they most certainly do you. I know that you're lonely and depressed," the spirit empathetically expressed, "but if you do exactly what I recommend, our souls will again share a common tranquility. You will be liberated from your chains of unhappiness, this I assure you!"

"But right now I don't have confidence in my ability and I've felt quite insecure ever since you had passed away," James sadly confessed to his nocturnal mental visitor, "and I never realized just how much I loved you until your, well, I despise using the word 'death' so I'll have to say since your 'unfortunate departure' from my life. Although I make over $250,000.00 a year from my combined patent royalties and salary," Gillespie confided to his wife's image as he began to toss and turn in his sleep, "Eleanor, ever since you had passed away, I've felt deeply inadequate and insecure."

"I've come to tell you that during my brief stay in your precious company," Eleanor effectively began divulging, "you' will be visited by three female visions, each of whom will offer you a gift. Beware and choose wisely, my dear husband. Heed my warning well and please don't act impulsively! I guarantee that your immortal soul will be weighed in the balance!"

"Wait a minute Eleanor!" Gillespie angrily said to his spectral wife in his all-too-disturbing dream. "I've heard this certain scenario before. Yes, now I remember, in literature, specifically the story 'A Christmas Carol' by Charles Dickens. Ebenezer Scrooge is visited by Marley's Ghost and is told by his former business partner that he'd be haunted by three additional apparitions: the Ghost of Christmas Past, the Ghost of Christmas Present and the Ghost of Christmas Future," James articulated to his wife's very attractive image.

"Are you sure you're making a valid comparison?" Eleanor's spirit questioned.

392

"Why yes I am! The first ghost escorted Scrooge to review certain nostalgic events from *his* youth, the second one conducted him to his poorly paid employee Bob Cratchit's house at Christmastime and the third spirit transported old Ebenezer to the local cemetery where Scrooge saw and cried over his own neglected grave. Is this bizarre dreadful nightmare I'm presently suffering a plagiarism of Charles Dickens story?" James wondered and fearfully asked his wife's specter. "If so Eleanor, then I must surmise that you and this terrible dream are indeed both cruel hoaxes!"

"You are indubitably correct about one thing," the radiant image eloquently declared. "As you've just perceptively alluded, my remarks to you *are* a plagiarism of sorts, but not of Charles Dickens' immortal story 'A Christmas Carol.' Would you like to try again?" the dazzling spirit suggested.

"I can't think of anything else!" James' subconscious mind imagined and transmitted. "Please stop haunting me Eleanor! This emotional agony is excruciating!"

"James, here's a helpful hint," Eleanor's spirit answered, apparently ignoring his discomfort. "The actual source of my three females' reference was not taught to you in eighth grade English class as you had erroneously thought when you had mentioned the classic Ebenezer Scrooge story, although there are several significant parallels between Old Scrooge and you. Think now about college, yes *Rutgers University*, and your sophomore year elective course 'Classical Greek Mythology.' That class with Dr. Spiegel," Eleanor persuasively maintained, "yes, *that* class might offer you' the vital clue you most desperately need to unravel the perplexing plagiarism riddle to which *you* had referred."

"Yes, I think I get the relationship now!" James recognized and mentally stated. "The immortal Ebenezer Scrooge story might've actually been inspired by a famous ancient myth, yes, I can vividly picture it now, the mythological cause of the *Trojan War*. Prince Paris of Troy was selected, or should I say targeted by three goddesses to judge a beauty contest and each deity tried bribing him with a special gift. But Eleanor," Gillespie humbly and dolefully apologized, "I honestly forget which goddess had enticed Paris with which present."

"Let me refresh your weak memory!" Eleanor imperatively advised. "Hera, wife of the supreme Olympian god Zeus, offered Paris great wealth should he choose her over the other two charming contestants. And then Athena, daughter of Zeus offered him wisdom, and finally according to the wonderful fable, Aphrodite, goddess of love and beauty offered Prince Paris as her unique prize the most beautiful woman in the world. Unfortunately, young and naïve Prince Paris selected...."

"Now I remember!" James exclaimed to his wife in his amazing dream. "Paris wrongly chose beautiful Aphrodite, and that terrible decision triggered the entire *Trojan War* because the most beautiful woman in the world happened to be Helen, who was already married to..."

"To the very jealous King Menelaus of Sparta," Eleanor finished her former husband's profound statement. "Yes James, you certainly must recall Dr. Spiegel mentioning that while visiting Sparta, Paris and his bodyguards had kidnapped beautiful Helen and that's how Helen of Sparta became the renowned Helen of Troy, and as the blind bard Homer had later described in his classic *Iliad*, Helen possessed the heavenly face that had launched a thousand Greek ships off to war."

"And I also recall erudite Dr. Spiegel telling the class that the real cause of the *Trojan War* was greed," James recollected and mentally shared. "The raiding Greeks were really cutthroat marauders that wanted to plunder Troy's wealth, but since their true motive seemed too baneful, selfish and wicked, several hundred years later Homer cleverly invented a fairy tale story that tended to make his barbaric Greek ancestors seem idealistic, romantic and brave. What a historical travesty!" Gillespie's subconscious mind observed and emitted. "Homer had made a gruesome war based on pure Greek lust into a fantastic poem!"

"Now then James," Eleanor's apparition continued its incredible narrative, "I've come to your awareness to give you three very distinct choices, but I warn you, don't become arrogant by committing the sin of hubris as young Prince Paris had so destructively done. Behold to your left Husband!" the specter imperatively commanded.

Three magnificent ancient-looking women dressed in stunning pastel-colored gowns and wearing diamond diadems on their heads instantly appeared inside James' subconscious imagination. "Here for your visual delight are Hera, Aphrodite and Athena. Now then," Eleanor dramatically emphasized her key point, "which goddess's gift do you choose: great wealth, great beauty or exceptional wisdom?"

"Unlike the colossal mistake in judgment committed by Paris, I now understand the truth behind the riddle. Eleanor, I must reject fantastic riches and physical beauty and solely seek great

394

wisdom by choosing Athena!" James replied without any palpable hesitation. "Yes, that's my only viable alternative! I seek great wisdom because *that* singular quest will make me understand myself" and the outside world better," Gillespie realized and replied. "It'll also help me cope with *your* absence from my life!"

"You have intelligently chosen your justly earned destiny!" Eleanor's image communicated as the three gorgeous aforementioned goddesses instantly vanished as quickly as they had appeared. "Now before I leave you James, is there anything else you'd like to clarify?"

"Yes, as a matter of fact there is!" the husband confided to his enchanting astral visitor. "Last night I had a terrible dream where I was being savagely slain by a muscular Greek warrior. Now, after speaking with you," James wondered and momentarily paused, "I can fully connect the three goddesses with last evening's nightmare, but could you help me to accurately interpret last night's terrible ordeal?"

"Just look to Homer's *Iliad* for the right answer!" Eleanor hinted. "Think of yourself as King Priam and Queen Hecuba's younger son and you'll then comprehend your exact relevance in the extraordinary scheme of events. You'll then develop the full meaning of last night's nightmare!" And after uttering those cryptic words, Eleanor's shade vanished into thin air, and then James awoke from his distressing slumber, his body in a cold sweat.

"Oh my God!" the panic-stricken man realized and exclaimed to his pallid image in the hotel room's bureau mirror. 'King Priam and Queen Hecuba had two sons, Hector and Paris. Paris was slain by Achilles,' James neurotically remembered, 'the most courageous and the most awesome of the Greek warriors. I wonder if I am Prince Paris of Troy reincarnated? If so,' the worried American sadly thought, 'I know all about Achilles and his legendary heel!'

* * * * * * * * * * * *

The following evening James finally fell asleep upon his bed's hard mattress in Room 610 of the Grande Bretagne Hotel. Soon his body became tense and sweaty and the troubled American began violently tossing and turning. In his stressful dream, Gillespie was wearing a white tunic and walking on a cobblestone path of the Agora, the ancient Athens' central marketplace situated at the foot of the Acropolis. Following a strong emotional compulsion, James wandered through the portal of a marble columned building where three sophisticated Greek scholars were engaging in a philosophical symposium.

"Greetings James!" the first aged intellectual telepathically communicated to the apprehensive new arrival "My name is Socrates and these distinguished gentlemen are my honorable colleagues Plato and Aristotle."

"Please don't get *agora*phobia!" Plato quipped in a humorous mental transmission. "After all, you've just entered *our* marketplace of ideas when you stepped through *that* extraordinary time portal. I do believe that you'll find *our* academic company to be most educational and edifying. Now James," Plato deliberately proceeded with his dialectic, "please have a seat. My good friend Socrates, tell our eminent young guest all about your Cave Allegory. Perhaps then James can correlate your tale, which in essence is really more of a sort of moral parable than an actual mere tale, as I was saying Socrates, James could then parallel your revealing story with events in *his* own life!"

After James Gillespie sat down on a marble bench, he perceptively listened to Socrates' cogent exposition, which the time traveler soon found to be rather illuminating. Within a minute the visitor's anxiety had been lifted as he soon felt a placid peace gradually envelop and then invade and saturate his spirit.

"In my Cave Allegory," Socrates said to James, "a dozen or so people are sitting facing a cavern's wall with their backs to the sun. The bright light entering the cave symbolizes truth, but these people stationed there are slaves to a dominant mass mentality and only see a reflection of the truth being bounced off the cave's stone' wall. Few men have the courage to actually turn around and face the light of truth, which of course is represented by the powerful sun. Now I must emphasize James," Socrates summarized his discourse, "as you can plainly determine, most men, although politically free, are truly mindless slaves imprisoned in their own self-created cave-jail. Now then James," the great philosopher stated with a stern expression evident on his face, "are you the brave one who's not afraid to turn around and look reality squarely in the face, or are you one of the brain-dead masses content to go through your mortal existence living a false life, satisfied in experiencing an illusion that is being artificially deflected off of a stone wall?"

"I suppose I'd rather be the bold fellow who turns around and becomes cognizant of the truth, even if it nearly blinds my eyes," James candidly acknowledged. "But frankly, socially speaking, my shy behavior has always compelled me to be just one of the crowd and nothing more. However Socrates," Gillespie bluntly qualified, "I must admit that I see much merit in the moral to your terrific cave story and will remember its lesson always."

Plato then felt obligated to contribute to the ongoing dialogue. "A Republic is without a doubt the best form of government James," the great political philosopher stated. "But I predict that my friend Socrates here will soon fall victim to the excesses of *democracy* gone amuck. He'll be unjustly accused of corrupting the minds of Athens' youth and then incarcerated, eventually being forced to drink a cup of poisonous hemlock to satisfy the wills of those callous unethical blundering maniacs that will diabolically advance egregious allegations against him. Now my question to you James is simply this," Plato eloquently verbalized. "Would you defend Socrates with your life if given the opportunity?"

"Well, er, yes, I guess I would if I personally knew him!" James equivocated and stammered. "Not to do so would be a violation of my core moral convictions. I've read your *Republic* manuscript while attending *Rutgers University*, which is an academy of higher learning in the land where I had lived," Gillespie pontificated and explained. "In your book, if I remember correctly Plato, you had argued that *democracy* is the weakest form of legal government and that a *republic*, having strong respect and obedience from its citizens for the society's laws, traditions and customs, then logically, a *republic* would obviously constitute the best form of representative government."

"Bravo James!" Socrates mentally transmitted, easily transcending any verbal alphabet or language barrier that ordinarily would exist. "Once I had visited the acclaimed Oracle at Delphi and curiously asked the mystical priestess, 'Who is the most intelligent man in the world?' The prophetess answered in a trance, 'You are Socrates!' Well, I didn't believe the priestess so I spent the next ten years of my adult life traversing all over Greece looking for someone smarter than myself."

"And what did your decade-long exploits discover?" James impetuously asked. "Who was more brilliant than you?"

"Nobody!" the elderly sage telepathically replied. "Everyone that I met and spoke with in my ten-year-long odyssey all throughout the many villages, towns and cities of Greece was selfish, extroverted, egocentric and me-oriented! I was never quite so disappointed in all my life. So James," Socrates philosophized and addressed his avid listener, "I concluded from my grueling research discoveries that the Oracle was absolutely accurate in her stark declaration. I indeed must be the most sagacious person in the world because I'm the only one that had the audacity to admit that I'm basically ignorant and know hardly anything. And so," the savant concluded his exposition, "knowledge of my own mental and behavioral shortcomings allowed me to elevate myself above baneful, ambitious and arrogant men, who right now are conspiring to condemn and prosecute me on false pretenses in our so-called *democracy* gone askew. I wholeheartedly agree with my loyal and meritorious comrade Plato. Athens needs a strong *republic* to ultimately endure and survive."

"Very enlightening!" observed and commented the now intellectually cultivated time traveler dreamer. "Aristotle, up to now you've been very passive during this dynamic exchange of ideas. Do you have any words of wisdom to contribute?"

"As you might know, Socrates is the true expert on morality and good judgment, Plato is the foremost authority on government structure and function, and I'm generally recognized throughout the civilized world as being the gifted one capable of responsibly classifying science into its defining categories: astronomy, biology, botany, chemistry, physics and zoology," Aristotle egotistically remarked. "I've devoted my entire adult life to *that* efficacious pursuit, of course all of *that* tremendous accomplishment happening after I had taught and tutored Alexander the Great in the fundamentals of math' expression and science experimentation. Ah yes, it was Alexander's love for intellectual exploration that activated his quest for world discovery and conquest. If anyone is responsible for his unrivalled reputation outside of Macedonia, then it must certainly be I!"

"Okay, I've learned a lot of powerful ideas just by being here in this Agora meeting place with you three famous philosophers," James genuinely commended his three excellent hosts, "but specifically, what does all of this theoretical stuff have to do with me? I mean, am I a specimen being contained and analyzed in some kind of moral test tube?"

"On the contrary!" Socrates answered with a small grin. "You've mastered the most relevant concept of all, the notion that ignorance is bliss! I need not lecture you any more on what you already know!" And after uttering those profound words, in unison the three ancient geniuses mystically evaporated into thin air.

No sooner had Socrates, Plato and Aristotle vanished into oblivion that Eleanor appeared in James' fantastic dream, the former wife holding a shiny bronze sword in her hand. "Here James, just pretend that you're Prince Paris of Troy about to defend your honor and likewise, just imagine that I'm your cherished Helen whom you wish to protect from harm!"

"What's this insanity all about?" yelled James during the culmination of his very severe nightmare. "Do you want me to join you in the hereafter by committing suicide? I don't know if I'm *that* desperate!" the distraught dreamer mentally communicated.

Just then an awesome-looking Greek warrior entered the marble-pillared building on the Agora and openly challenged James to a death duel. "Paris, I'm your biggest nightmare, your on-a-mission nemesis, exclusively known to mythology and to history as Achilles. Prepare to meet your much-dreaded doom!"

"By dying, your soul will finally be in harmony with the Universe!" Eleanor dressed as Helen of Troy told James. "By attempting to defend yourself, you'll finally achieve your desired unity with my spirit! It's an esoteric cosmic axiom that poetically states: 'To conquer death, you only have to die!' Then James, your shade will follow me down deep inside the Earth, all the way to the daffodil fields of Elysium where together in love we'll rest in serene peace for all eternity!"

The following morning a shocked housemaid discovered James Gillespie's corpse lying upon his Room 610 bed. The hotel desk clerk immediately notified the Athens' Police Department and also the local coroner's office, and a comprehensive autopsy has been scheduled. The examining official presently believes that there are no visible signs of the exact cause of death. After the foreign police investigation and subsequent coroner's inquiry are completed, an obituary will be written and the Marinella Mortuary of Hammonton, New Jersey will have the body shipped back to the United States where detailed funeral arrangements will then be made.

"The Cruisers"

Frederick and Amy Pearl loved to travel internationally, especially enjoying leisurely sea cruises throughout the *Mediterranean* and the *Caribbean*. The residents of 227 Tilton Street, Hammonton, New Jersey preferred taking weeklong ocean and sea voyages to partaking of exotic winter vacations flying to tropical destinations. The medical doctor and his nurse wife believed in working hard and playing hard when not preoccupied with their demanding professions or being busy babysitting their four energetic pre-teen grandchildren, Dan, Karly, Sierra and Lindsey. On December 28th, 2008 the Pearls' oldest son Joseph, a South Jersey insurance and real estate agent, drove the general practitioner and his devoted wife to *Philadelphia International Airport*.

After checking through Terminal C's tight airport security without too much inconvenience, Fred and Amy boarded their *American Airlines* jet bound for sunny San Juan, Puerto Rico, where a seven day cruise on the luxurious and well-appointed state-of-the-art liner *The Winds of Fate* had been booked in early May. Six hours later the delighted sea odyssey tourists were sipping delicious pina coladas aboard the ship's top deck and partaking in the standard gala "bon voyage celebration."

"This leaving port tradition does seem a little bit like a merry *New Year's Eve* party," Fred observed and noted to Amy Pearl. "Everyone seems anxious to get this sea expedition going. What's first on our itinerary?"

"Well, after embarking from San Juan Harbor, we'll glide past that landmark Spanish fort over there, El Morro, I believe. It's supposed to be rich in all sorts of New World history and perhaps we'll visit it later next week. Then after cruising the Caribbean all night we'll wind-up in La Guaira, the beautiful mountainous port of Caracas, Venezuela," the well-organized wife informed her spouse. "Now Fred, we already have tickets for the cable car ride up the mountain to have a breathtaking view of the enchanting *Caribbean*. Then of course we'll bus tour Caracas," Mrs. Pearl matter-of-factly indicated, "because the city's located about ten miles inland from tomorrow's point of origin, the majestic port of La Guaira."

"Sounds rather impressive to me!" Dr. Frederick Pearl agreed. "But let's indulge in all this merriment before we become guilty of wishing our trip away by foolishly thinking about experiencing

Caracas. Maybe we can make some friends while mingling among the other passengers. Everyone on deck is in a pretty festive mood and apparently happy to be island hopping with us," the husband determined. "Claire's never let us down yet! Our travel agent really arranges some very decent vacation packages and this one's no exception! Bartender, our mouths are a little dry. Two more pina coladas please!"

The next morning Fred and Amy heard the ship's engine stacks blast three times and slowly arose from their cabin's bed. Outside the room's sheer white cotton curtain beyond the cabin's balcony was a spectacular view of the verdant mountain peaks seemingly guarding La Guaira. After indulging in a buffet breakfast in the *Winds of Fate's* ornate Juno Dining Room, the passengers eagerly exited the ship and climbed aboard ten modern air-conditioned buses that had been chartered to take the American and European tourists on assigned excursions throughout Caracas, the highlight of each side-trip being the magnificent view of the emerald sea coastline seen from cable car gondolas. At supper that evening the Pearls met and had dinner with Bill and Doris Nelson, retired public school teachers from New York City.

"Where are we heading tomorrow?" Fred asked his new educator friends. "Confidentially, I've always been pretty lousy when it comes to geography."

"The island of Granada," Bill Nelson answered while pouring Doris a glass of merlot. "It's a rather poor place I understand, and its citizens are always either begging for money or trying to sell you some cheap souvenirs in the form of spices, tee-shirts, voodoo dolls or straw hats."

"Well, I don't like being hustled or high-pressured," Amy Pearl added her dissatisfactions to the conversation before sipping *her* dark red wine. "I'm on this trip to relax and I have no particular desire to be hassled, harassed or coaxed into buying junk items I don't really want or need."

"We have acquaintances from Long Island who had taken this same trip last year," Doris contributed to the discussion. "The van driver that the Bronsons had been assigned to stopped at a Granada wood-framed house at the summit of a mountain ridge, and before our friends could blink an eye," Mrs. Nelson added, "the man's entire family exited the ramshackle home carrying musical instruments and began playing some obscure steel drum calypso tune. Our friends the Bronsons felt obligated leaving a five-dollar donation in appreciation of the local song that they had never wished to hear in the first place! How's that for being confronted with some wholesome island fun? Coerced extortion sounds quite nerve-racking to me!"

"Well, let's just go with the flow and not encourage any unfortunate incidents to happen that might mar our vacations," Fred diplomatically suggested. "When in a strange environment, act like you're perfectly content being there and try making the most out of the natives' unsolicited hospitality."

The third day of their *Caribbean* itinerary Fred and Amy accompanied by Bill and Doris toured the island of St. Lucia, a splendid paradise featuring dual volcanic mountains that spiked high into the cloudless azure sky. While sightseeing in a hired van, the couples marveled at the lush rain forest vegetation that was abundant all over and around Castries, the un-frenzied island's capital city. The four aged American explorers soon visited a popular tourist resort and swallowed-down a delectable buffet-style lunch in the hotel's main lodge, their veranda dining area surrounded by fantastic palm trees, indigenous plants and a prodigious array of beautiful jungle foliage. That evening the two couples dressed up for the traditional 'Captain's Dinner,' which was held in the aforementioned crystal chandeliered Juno Dining Room.

"Great vacation so far!" Bill Nelson glibly opined. "I haven't checked our itinerary. Where will we be tomorrow morning? I'll feel inclined to get some sunbathing done up on the main deck if there's nothing too dynamic being planned. The topside pool looks mighty inviting," the New York resident continued his chatter. "I don't want to have this incredible vacation seem too much like nine-to-five work, you know! I had experienced enough daily stress and aggravation patrolling my high school English classroom let alone watching the erratic stock market quotes on the Wall Street ticker tape shown on the cable business channel."

"We'll be in Barbados," Doris informed her gabby husband. "And I'll not allow you to go swimming on this ship when there's so much delightful sightseeing to do on land. I've already purchased our two island tour tickets."

"Well," Amy Pearl sadly said, "I don't think that my husband's going to be able to make it around Barbados without having a degree of discomfort in his right foot."

"What happened?" Doris asked Fred with a concerned expression on her face. "I thought that only doctors' patients suffered pain or discomfort!"

"I'm embarrassed to tell this little story, but since you've asked, here it goes," Fred prefaced his explanation. "Our nine year old grandson Dan had tossed a Frisbee onto our home's side-porch roof. Like an impetuous fool, I boldly climbed up the rungs of an aluminum ladder to retrieve the errant object. It was a freezing cold day, I believe, yes, Monday of last week. No sooner had I thrown down the yellow Frisbee from the roof that I noticed the fact that the strong wind had blown the lightweight ladder onto the lawn. I was helplessly stuck up there on the porch's roof with my teeth clattering and my knees knocking together from the severe cold air! I was almost wishing that I was an Eskimo!"

"Well, what did you do?" Bill Nelson curiously asked before buttering his warm roll. "This sounds like quite a survival story you're revealing. I wish that Amy had been there to capture it all on video! I mean Fred, how did you ever escape your remarkable dilemma and live to tell about it?"

"I tried opening the upstairs' window of my computer room but it was locked," Fred disclosed as his audience of three tried holding back from laughing. "Then Amy drove by the house on her way to her mother's place, completely oblivious to my horrible high altitude predicament. So considering the possibility of getting frost-bitten and hospitalized right before our *Caribbean* cruise," the embarrassed storyteller elaborated, "I felt I had only one alternative and that sole option was to bravely leap twelve feet down from the porch's roof onto the solid frozen turf."

"And obviously you lived through your terrible ordeal!" Bill confirmed and then chuckled. "Did you hurt or injure anything as a result of your courageous deliberate plummet?"

"Yes, I double-sprained my left ankle during the end of my awkward leap when my foot impacted the solid ground," Fred related in a low tone of voice, "and now the swelling comes and goes, depending on how much strain my left foot experiences. It just so happens that it really aches right this very minute from all of the walking we've done around St. Lucia," the now self-conscious Dr. Pearl explained to the thoroughly amused Nelsons, "so I think I'll be sitting out Barbados tomorrow while you three restless vagabonds get to see the glorious sights."

"And ironically, Fred had trained to be an Army paratrooper prior to going to medical school," Amy grinned and then laughed. "I guess my headstrong husband forgot how to jump without the aid of his beloved parachute. Oh well Gang," Mrs. Pearl melodramatically sighed, "I suppose I'll have to miss Fred's illustrious company and scurry all around Barbados with the

Nelsons. Now Honey, don't spend all day tomorrow brooding and playing solitaire down in the card room!" the wife facetiously mentioned to her red-faced spouse, much to the merriment of Bill and Doris Nelson.

"Don't worry *Honey!*" Fred defensively and sarcastically replied. "That's where a little extra *Southern Comfort* will come in handy, you know as *we* highly trained doctors often say, 'For medicinal purposes only,' ha, ha, ha!"

* * * * * * * * * * * *

Two mornings later the ship's mighty stacks blasted three times and Fred and Amy Pearl rose from their comfortable queen-size bed, washed-up and then prepared for enjoying an early breakfast. At 8:00 a.m. sharp the twosome met up with Bill and Doris Nelson in the very casual Brunch Lounge and an hour later, after leaving the *Winds of Fate,* just beyond the wharf the men rented a "cab for four" in Charlotte Amalie, St. Thomas.

After touring Blue Beard's Castle, Meggan's Bay and the regally refurbished Frenchman's Reef Hotel, the hungry-for-adventure couples had lunch at a quaint restaurant overlooking the gorgeous island's enchanting harbor entrance, featuring many scenic islands randomly dotting the picturesque setting.

The warm afternoon was spent taking a short ferry ride over to St. John, another of the U.S. Virgin Islands, a very sedate and tranquil landscape like its sister paradise St. Thomas, the tropical haven flourishing in eye-appealing majestic greenery. A brief-but-informative jeep tour of St. John's was next on the vagabonds' agenda, and then a return ferry shuttle back to bustling St. Thomas was easily accomplished. The women then did some bargain and souvenir hunting in Charlotte Amalie's many "tourist trap" waterfront retail stores while the pensive and fatigued men sat on stools in a quaint terrace bar and reminisced certain highlights from their youth, and finally, the four senior citizen Americans trekked the four final waterfront blocks back to the docked *Winds of Fate.*

At the fancy "Surf and Turf and Baked Alaska Supper" that evening Dr. Pearl told Bill and Doris about how he had once gotten into a heightened argument with an antagonistic peevish van operator in Montego Bay, Jamaica, the difference of opinion being over a wrong-colored hotel-to-airport transport voucher. Out of courtesy the Nelsons listened to all of the details of Fred's peevish-sounding anecdote.

"Well anyway," Dr. Pearl proceeded with *his* rendition of a specific past event, "when we finally arrived back at the Montego Bay Airport to depart for the States, I had gotten the arrogant van driver so riled-up that he sped directly into the parking lot, drove over three high speed bumps and then recklessly slammed on the brakes, the maniac driver's instant reaction causing the van's back compartment doors to suddenly fly open," Fred graphically narrated. "At least a dozen pieces of luggage had tumbled onto the ground and the other American passengers seated in the van wildly cheered the driver's misery, much to the van operator's chagrin and much to his growing animosity for me."

"You're lucky we escaped alive from that horrendous ordeal!" Amy Pearl criticized her rebellious spouse before handing her dinner plate over to the assistant table waiter. "That rather ugly verbal exchange between you and the bad-tempered Jamaican van driver was totally out-of-character for a distinguished former surgeon turned family doctor such as yourself! To tell you the truth Fred," the wife admonished, "that day I was totally shocked at your extremely rude behavior!"

"Somehow I've heard that strange tale of conflict before," Bill Nelson candidly remarked, scratching his forehead. "My memory is becoming more foggy as I get older but I must admit Fred," the retired high school instructor insisted, "I'm quite certain that I've listened to your proud monologue about *that* verbal altercation between you as an irate American passenger and that nasty livid van driver in Montego Bay, Jamaica before."

"And Fred, this might sound totally uncanny but your funny story about jumping off the porch roof back in New Jersey and then spraining your ankle rang mighty familiar to my ears, especially when I had heard you describing how you had suffered great pain," Doris Nelson amiably contributed to the rather strange discourse, "not to mention…."

"Not to mention *you* Fred being a paratrooper before you had entered medical school," Bill Nelson recollected and positively declared. "I don't want to come across as being discourteous or impolite," the former educator turned stocks and bonds' authority sincerely expressed to his equally confused Juno Dining Room meal partners. "Perhaps my aged brain cells are deteriorating at a rapid rate, but those all-too-familiar stories of yours echoed in my mind as if my hollow brain was a deep canyon."

"Maybe I should learn to listen to others more often and not try and dominate dinner conversations," Dr. Pearl humbly apologized. "I must confess, I do have a tendency to become too

406

long-winded and egocentric at times. It's really a very bad habit. I should never presume that my audience is half as interested in my adventures and in my misadventures as I am. I wish that I wasn't such a complete bore! Old age, and even sensational *Caribbean* cruises, all seem to have become quite monotonous and humdrum these days!" Fred maintained in a seldom-heard self-indictment. "I'm afraid that my prattle sounds like drivel and that my drivel sounds too much like prattle! Oh Waiter," Dr. Pearl summoned, motioning with his right hand, "fetch us another bottle of merlot so that I can avoid sounding too repetitious and too overwhelmingly boorish to my wife and friends."

"Perhaps we all should retire early tonight and forget about the variety stage show in the Broadway Follies Theater," Mrs. Pearl constructively suggested. "Fred, your face does appear to be a trifle pallid! Truthfully, I think we're all suffering from senior citizen exhaustion. I had read a good article about *that* widespread phenomenon in a women's magazine at a beauty parlor back in Jersey."

* * * * * * * * * * * *

On the last morning of the incomparable *Caribbean* cruise the stately *Winds of Fate* was scheduled to dock in San Juan, Puerto Rico, the majestic ship's original point of departure. The predictable three blasts from the vessel's enormous stacks awakened the Pearls from their deep slumbers. Fred wiped the sleep from his eyes, climbed out of bed and next opened the purple drapes and followed *that* task with separating the background sheer white curtains to gain a perfect view of the calm harbor and of Old San Juan. But then the good Dr.'s addled mind couldn't believe what his pupils were seeing.

"Amy, this must be some sort of weird optical illusion I'm witnessing!" the suddenly alarmed husband exclaimed. "Just look outside at the city through the sliding glass balcony door! The markings on the buildings and on the wharfs and piers all say 'Barcelona' and not 'San Juan'!"

"That's impossible!" Amy Pearl replied before quickly rising from the mattress to her feet to evaluate her husband's veracity. "Even if the Captain wanted to do so, this cruise ship couldn't cross the *Atlantic* overnight and wind-up docked at a busy port in eastern Spain! This must be some sort of cruel trick! Spain's thousands of nautical miles from Puerto Rico and the West Indies!"

"Look!" the astonished husband said, pointing to the cabin's main bureau top. "Just take a peek at this brochure indicating our trip's week-long itinerary! The first day we'll be staying in and touring Barcelona, the second day Marseilles and Cassis, France, the third day, we'll be strolling around Villefranche and Monaco, and the fourth day…."

"We'll be moored at Livorno, Italy and going by motorbus to Pisa and Florence in Tuscany," the wife read with absolute bewilderment. "We'll even be spending two hours in the medieval town of Volterra where it says in print here Roman ruins still remain. And on the fifth *Mediterranean* cruise day we'll be anchored in…."

"In Civitavecchia, the port leading into Rome," Dr. Pearl incredulously gasped, "and after visiting the Vatican, the Forum, the Pantheon and the Roman Colosseum ruins, we'll return to the ship and be off to…."

"Off to Naples and then there'll be a bus trip down the Amalfi Drive from Sorrento to Salerno with our final stop being the ancient excavations at Pompeii!" Amy Pearl exclaimed. "What's your take on all of this bizarre fantasy Fred? Is this a pernicious nightmare or is it a wild haunting recurring dream come true?"

And then Fred noticed the conspicuous glossy cover of *Nautical Magazine*, which was evident situated on the opposite side of the first class cabin's lengthy bureau. The stunned elderly man leafed through the pages until he came to the periodical's main article that chronicled an analysis of the sinking of the British steamer *Lusitania* off the coast of Ireland on May 7, 1915. According to the magazine story, a German U-Boat had torpedoed the grand ocean-worthy ship, effectively sinking the famous White Star Line vessel in less than twenty minutes. The well-organized article also stated that 1,498 of the passengers and crew had perished in the blatant act of war while 761 had mercifully been rescued.

"The 30,000 ton boat along with its four huge stacks didn't have a chance!' Fred read out loud to his wife. "What an abominable tragedy *that* brutal act of war was! At the time of the destruction, the doomed *Lusitania* was the largest ship in the world! Prior to being maliciously sunk," Dr. Pearl continued his paraphrasing, "the *Lusitania* had already made two hundred and one ocean crossings to and from New York and it had held the speed and time records until the great boat was maliciously targeted, and then it reached its catastrophic end!"

"And now look at this pamphlet I've just discovered under our room's telephone!" Amy excitedly yelled to her stupefied mate. "It's next week's cruising schedule revealing what's in store for us after we arrive back in Barcelona a week from today. We'll be promptly leaving the 55th Street Pier in New York at 7:30 a.m. and voyaging all day and all night to Georgetown and Hamilton, Bermuda and then three days later we'll be sailing off to slated visitations in the Cayman Islands and Antigua. I've always had trouble dealing with the unknown!" the apprehensive and worried wife acknowledged. "Are *we* going insane Fred? What's really going on here?"

The peculiar husband/wife conversation was interrupted with a rapping on their deluxe cabin's door. A very perturbed Dr. Frederick Pearl nervously peered through the peephole, unlocked the safety bolt and then slowly opened the metal barrier to the room. The *Winds of Fate's* vigilant Captain, meticulously clad in his official dress uniform, entered the classy cabin with the intention of making an important announcement.

"It's my distinct duty to inform the two of you that you're required to report up to the main deck in fifteen minutes to witness a very significant sea rendezvous," the all-too-serious Captain articulated. "The *Winds of Fate* will be passing en transit the deceased passengers from the infamous *Titanic* who are presently cruising the high seas aboard *our* superb sister ship, the *Eternal Voyager*. It is hereby requested that *you* Mr. and Mrs. Frederick Pearl show the necessary proper respect and homage to the onboard victims of that horrible disaster!"

"Dead souls from the *Titanic*! Are you kidding? This is so absurd that it's totally preposterous!" Dr. Pearl vehemently protested.

"Yes, those unfortunate souls that had perished on the notorious dates of April 14th and April 15th, 1912," the duty-bound Captain solemnly stated. "The *Titanic* had slammed into an iceberg in the *North Atlantic* on its maiden voyage from England to New York City. The regrettable incident occurred 1,600 miles northeast of Manhattan with the iceberg causing a gaping three hundred foot long gash in the liner's hull," the emotionless Captain almost mechanically lectured. "Half of the passengers and most of the crew died because there happened to be an insufficient number of lifeboats aboard. The proud shipbuilders all thought that the invincible *Titanic* was unsinkable and actually believed that the grand old dame didn't need to have any lifeboats at all!"

Fred glanced out through the cabin's sliding glass door and recognized that the *Winds of Fate* was gently gliding by the *Rock of Gibraltar* and heading out into the deep *Atlantic,* an obvious contradiction of the laws of predictable time and space. "What kind of a mendacious ruse is this?" Fred strenuously balked and objected. "Why do *we* have to salute the dead riders on the other ship? They're already dead Captain! This crazy scenario makes no sense whatsoever!"

"Because the dead *Titanic* passengers riding on the *Eternal Voyager* will be waving at you Dr. Frederick Pearl, and also at your lovely wife Amy. For you see," the cheerless Captain pontificated and then paused, "if you ever have time to find and examine the proper ship registry in the downstairs fifth deck library, a Dr. Frederick Pearl and his wife Amy were indeed passengers on the British ship *Lusitania* that went down off the coast of Old Head of Kinsdale, Ireland in 1915. Your destiny, or should I say your present obligatory existence," the Captain emphasized, "will ultimately be determined by your deportment aboard the *Winds of Fate*, so to speak, all of which will be enacted in a most appropriate symbolic metaphor."

"What is *your* connection to the *Lusitania* and to the *Titanic* sea disasters?" a very aghast Amy Pearl demanded to learn. "Please tell us Captain, because we really have to know the true relationship."

"Well you see," the *Winds of Fate's* chief officer lucidly said, "Captain Edward Smith of the *Titanic* was a good friend of mine back in the early 1900s, and coincidentally, he's presently navigating at the helm of the *Eternal Voyager*. And as far as my personal association with current events is concerned, my name is Captain William Turner. I was innocently piloting the *Lusitania* when it went down on May 7, 1915."

"But I just read in *Nautical Magazine* that you had survived the U-Boat's torpedoing of the *Lusitania,*" Dr. Pearl obstinately insisted. "You had violated the fundamental law of the sea that the captain should go down with his ship!"

"Why must you always be so damned argumentative every time *we* have this conversation?" Captain William Turner indignantly and profoundly reprimanded Dr. Pearl. "Your general arrogance is not at all appreciated! I happen to have survived the historic calamity but you two victims didn't. Now then, to be succinct, your immediate responsibility is to enjoy fifty-two wonderful voyages, one for each week of the year. Just resign yourselves' to cooperate in fulfilling your assigned duty! Learn to

410

love the sea as Captain Edward Smith and I do!" Captain William Turner recommended. "That's *our* prescribed fate until I eventually receive additional instructions from the omnipotent and everlasting Powers-that-Be!"

"Ice Ages"

In early December of 1975 Jeremy Ingram had been an impressionable seventh grader at the Hammonton Middle School where he was greatly influenced by his effervescent social studies teacher Mr. Charles Galinas. The New Jersey history instructor had mentioned to his usually lethargic fifth period students the amazing story of Heinrich Schliemann (1822-1890), a German entrepreneur that had become exceptionally wealthy making lucrative business investments in Russia during the *Crimean War*.

Schliemann had accumulated sufficient expendable wealth to enable the industrious businessman to retire and then energetically pursue *his* greatest childhood ambition: to prove to the world once and for all that Homer's *Iliad* and *Odyssey* had been actual historical events and not mere myths as had been widely believed throughout the Nineteenth Century civilized world. Soon his scientific archeological expeditions confirmed to cynics that *Level VII-a* in Asia Minor was "the Troy of Priam" (that he had against all odds) discovered.

After researching the subject of Heinrich Schliemann more extensively in the middle school library, inspired thirteen-year-old Jeremy Ingram was fascinated to learn more about the life of his new-found hero, the German dreamer turned investor turned amateur archeologist. Young Jeremy discovered that in 1870 relentless Heinrich Schliemann had excavated a mound around four miles from the Hellespont and had officially found the remains of seven cities buried on top of one another.

'The Trojan War had happened around 1184 BC,' Jeremy remembered in 1975 while reading from a library encyclopedia. 'I want to become an even more famous archeologist than Heinrich Schliemann! Who knows what other ancient treasures besides Troy lay under the top layer of Earth's dirt?' the young man conjectured.

And *that* wonderful spark created in 1975 by Mr. Charles Galinas had been the very impetus for Jeremy Ingram to dedicate his entire adult life to pursuing significant breakthroughs in anthropological and also archeological exploration. A decade and a half later the inspired scholar became a revered professor at a major Philadelphia college.

* * * * * * * * * * * * *

"There was no romantic love affair between Paris, Prince of Troy and Helen, wife of King Menelaus of Sparta," Dr. Jeremy Ingram again explained to his fellow accomplished archeologist, University of Pennsylvania Professor Gregory Lawler, who had heard *that* story analysis from his superior's lips at least a dozen times.

"Most every educated person attending the conferences here in Charleston understands *that* elementary truth you just cited," Dr. Lawler readily admitted. "The Achaeans were ruthless marauders and they had invented that fanciful romance story about Paris abducting Helen from Menelaus to make it appear to history textbook writers that the moral and ethical Greeks had justly raided Troy to capture back good old Menelaus's gorgeous wife."

"Yes Greg, your normally suspect logic is basically accurate this time," the internationally acclaimed archeologist complemented his truly affable colleague and assistant. "Agamemnon of Mycenae had efficiently organized a thousand ships to plunder Troy's riches and his design was not to retrieve Menelaus's beautiful wife from sex-starved Prince Paris. That greedy raiding aspect was the real cause of the Trojan War. The popular myth is in reality an ancient rendition of a romantic fairy tale."

The men continued consuming their delicious dinner inside Charleston's Cypress Restaurant on East Bay Street, only several blocks from the South Carolina city's exquisite historic district. After swallowing-down another mouthful of his Maryland-style Crab Soup appetizer, Professor Gregory Lawler gave his take on the Greek heroes of antiquity.

"I'll tell you Jeremy, that's where Odysseus, Achilles, Ajax and the other dauntless-but-egotistical Greek hero-kings collaborated and joined forces with Agamemnon to defeat Troy," Dr. Lawler remarked and then indulgently laughed. "Didn't your incessant-minded idol Schliemann also find Mycenae?"

"Bravo! You're right once again!" the planet's foremost archeologist concurred, waving his right hand above his head to show a more-than-mild degree of animation. "Even way back then the avaricious ancient Greek monarchs unified against a common enemy even though their separate kingdoms functioned as independent and autonomous city-states. And oh yes Greg," Jeremy pompously and facetiously lectured, "old Heinrich was indeed my personal inspiration to become a dedicated archeologist and I owe my entire career and success to my seventh grade social studies teacher who had illuminated my academic
414

path and showed me the light. What goes around comes around I guess! By *that* comment, or should I say 'cliché', I mean that teachers certainly influence confused students, who then eventually evolve into and become future teachers!"

"You're scheduled to deliver the keynote address tomorrow afternoon at the Renaissance Hotel over on Wentwerth Street," Dr. Lawler deliberately said to his traveling *University of Pennsylvania* companion to get off the mundane subject of seventh grade social studies teachers. "According to the city map back at our hotel room, the Renaissance is only five blocks from the Hampton Inn where we're staying over on Meeting Street. It's within easy walking distance if the weather permits, and the casual quarter mile stroll ought to wear off some of tomorrow's high-calorie lunch."

"Right Greg," Jeremy confirmed while checking his wristwatch. "And while we're flitting about downtown Charleston, our very capable graduate school assistant back in Philly', you know, Agnes Ross, well she highly recommended that *we* just have to eat at Hank's Restaurant down near the waterfront not far from the historic marketplace and also we gotta' have a breakfast at the Hominy Grill on the west side of town right after we drive around the *Citadel's* military campus. Agnes says and swears that the really excellent breakfast place absolutely has the best apple cinnamon French toast she's ever sampled."

"And besides cramming our gluttonous stomachs full at those terrific eateries you've just mentioned," Dr. Lawler reminded his fellow Cypress Restaurant diner, "there're plenty of cultural things to see right here in Charleston and vicinity. First of all we have to take the ferry over to Fort Sumter and see where the *Civil War* actually began. And interestingly enough," the overzealous Professor chuckled, "the natives down here still erroneously refer to the War Between the States as 'The War of Northern Aggression,' an odd observation in that the Southern troops aimed and fired their cannons on the Union soldiers defending Fort Sumter. And then," Lawler continued his pretentious monologue without even taking a deep breath, "there's the much-advertised carriage ride that goes around the entire historic district. I especially want to see the antebellum-style stately mansions that line the Battery Park area, including the noteworthy John Calhoun mansion. And the classic architecture in many of the homes, museums and churches in Charleston show a definite Greco-Roman influence with more than a plenteous amount of Doric and Corinthian columns in rich supply."

And after thoroughly discussing how the two rivers that geographically border Charleston were each named after a rich Southern gentleman/settler named *Ashley Cooper*, and after mutually vowing and committing to touring the ancillary sights of interest, namely Sullivan's Island, the Isle of Palms and Folly Beach, the men were finally served their Key Lime pie desserts.

"Yes, Sullivan's Island!" Dr. Lawler robustly exclaimed. "Maybe you don't know this, but I have a master's degree in literature. Sullivan's Island was the setting for Edgar Allan Poe's great novella 'The Gold Bug'."

Jeremy Ingram was not at all impressed with his friend's literary-world braggadocio. "And Greg, there's two other places I want to visit before we depart Charleston," the prestigious archeologist insisted. "Agnes mentioned that the exotic Magnolia Plantation is a must see. It's around twelve miles from downtown on the other side of the *Ashley River*. All we have to do is take the Calhoun Street Bridge to get there in a mere half an hour."

"Yes, I saw a brochure about that semi-tropical garden paradise while perusing the pamphlet rack back at the Hampton Inn lobby," Dr. Lawler added. "It's a scenic thousand acre rice plantation that's still partially operating after all these years. There's also a well-preserved mansion on the premises, not to mention alligators inhabiting the many nearby swamps. I read where the management of the property has had ramps built in the water for the large reptiles to bask in the sun because the gators used to meander out onto the various asphalt tram trails so that the cold-blooded creatures could absorb the heat ascending from the blacktop right into their carnivorous bodies."

"Pretty intelligent solution to the alligator-tourist problem," the renowned guest lecturer stated. "And Greg, did you know that the Spanish moss on all of the live oak and bald cypress trees and also growing on some of the palmettos isn't really a parasitic moss at all. It's really an independent growth that just happens to thrive all by itself on those various kinds of indigenous vegetation, but the term's a definite misnomer. It's not a moss at all."

"You're just a veritable treasury of irrelevant scholarly information!" quipped and laughed Dr. Lawler. "Perhaps you should change your first name to Encyclopedia and your last name to Britannica!"

* * * * * * * * * * * *

That evening Jeremy Ingram was in a rare philosophical mood and the Renaissance Hotel guest lecturer naturally shared his historical sentiments with his affable Hampton Inn roommate, Professor Gregory Lawler. The famed archeologist was in the process of citing how both Charles Darwin and Albert Einstein had dramatically affected and changed the world outside of their separate scientific and mathematical realms.

"Exactly what do you mean Jeremy?" Professor Lawler inquired and mildly challenged. "For instance, how did Charles Darwin impact the world outside the domain of his theory of natural selection? I mean, humans in civil society don't act like animals and don't feel a need to physically survive by being the fittest!"

"After Darwin had made his Evolution Theory public by publishing his classic work, which incidentally had been organized following his tedious study of the unique animal species populating the Galapagos Islands," Ingram said to his educational associate, "social scientists began devising imaginative theories of political development regarding the existence of an *evolutionary theme* advancing throughout history. For example Greg, according to those social revisionists," Ingram staunchly maintained, "in the time of the ancient Greeks, power concentrations *evolved* from aristocracy existing under many city-state rulers to monarchy under King Agamemnon. And then just before the *Revolutionary War*, Thomas Jefferson took the theory one step further when King George's monarchy eventually *evolved* into Constitutional democracy. And then good old Vladimir Lenin…"

"Boldly claimed that democracy would naturally *evolve* into socialism and then the Russian crackpot Joseph Stalin hypothesized that socialism's next alteration would be to characteristically *evolve* into communism. I plainly see now what you're driving at! But Jeremy," Dr. Lawler continued prattling, "what about Albert Einstein's mathematics' equations influencing human society?"

"Well Gregory," the stellar archeologist proceeded with his typically creative discourse, "Einstein's Theory of Relativity really upset the societal apple cart. Mr. Einstein indubitably proved that Isaac Newton's Laws of Gravity were not absolute truths as originally had been thought for several centuries. Instead, everything in the universe, everything in the galaxy and everything in the solar system is *relative* and not absolute. And so as a result of Albert Einstein's revolutionary discovery," the

417

young genius confidently claimed, "your monkey-see-monkey-do social scientists believed that they could engineer a similar cultural theory whereby…"

"Whereby all areas of human behavior and all human values are *relative* and not absolute," Dr. Lawler realized and stated. "Of course, I clearly comprehend your astute observations now, but at first your Einstein statement seemed entirely obscure. Sometimes you impress me with your esoteric and erudite declarations that when thoroughly explained, don't seem so esoteric and so erudite any more, but conversely, your analysis then appears rather simple and easy to understand!"

"Okay Professor, we now have a long and arduous next few days ahead of us. Let's get some sleep before we'll be waking-up the local roosters!"

At 2:15 a.m. Dr. Gregory Lawler woke-up, and while attempting to slightly turn the side table clock so that he could see the correct time, by mistake the man accidentally touched a button on top of the clock and then instantly, loud rock and roll music blasted out of the clock radio, which the absent-minded Professor had thought was only a table timepiece. Then Lawler clumsily fumbled in the dark to activate the table lamp located alongside the clock radio.

"Nice going Indiana Jones!" Jeremy Ingram sleepily chided, holding back his strong inclination to laugh. "Why don't you wake-up the entire second floor while you're at it! Things could've been a lot worse ya' know! You could've had a dissonant rap music station thumping through the speakers!"

"Sorry Boss!" the very embarrassed and florid-faced Dr. Lawler apologized. "The next time I have to use the bathroom I'll do it in the dark without knowing what time of night it is! Who cares if I trip and break my neck?"

Another disruptive interruption occurred an hour later when the wake-up buzzer atop the clock radio unexpectedly blared because Gregory Lawler had accidentally set the timer for 3:15 a.m. when he had been fumbling to turn-off the clamorous rock and roll music an hour earlier.

"If this were amateur night at the local comedy club you'd surely win top prize hands down!" the bleary-eyed archeologist mildly balked and criticized. "Now let's get some much-desired sleep and whatever you do Greg, don't fidget with any more electronic gizmos. Just like good old Rip Van Winkle had aptly thought up in the Catskill Mountains, 'I need my beauty rest'!"

* * * * * * * * * * * * *

Jeremy Ingram's cell phone rang at precisely 7:15 in the morning. Mike Templeton, an enterprising West Coast archeologist affiliated with several top government excavation projects was on the line and happened to be extremely excited about several "unbelievable discoveries" that had just been located.

"Well Mike, at least you had the decency to call me at 7:15 eastern time here in beautiful Charleston, but right now it's only a little after 4 a.m. out there in my favorite U.S. metropolis San Diego," Jeremy deliberately grunted into his hand-held phone, feigning being slightly disturbed. "Listen-up Mike; there's two things I totally despise: exaggeration and hyperbole! Now after telling you those two specific truths, what's so important that you had to call me so early in the morning before I've even had a chance to wash my face, brush my teeth and take two aspirins."

"Jeremy, ya' gotta' hear all of this!" the young man shrieked into his cell phone with a sense of urgency. "Last night several of our advance teams dug-up sensational evidence that you'll never believe in a million years!" Templeton's bass voice boomed. "A replica Parliament Building and an intact Big Ben duplicate have just been unearthed in Antarctica and only two hundred miles away another of our units has found a more-than-marvelous duplicate of the Eiffel Tower, yes, still all in one piece."

"Please forgive my lingering chronic allergies Mike but just yesterday," Jeremy calmly answered before clearing his throat, "one of our select digging groups working in conjunction with the Moscow Natural History Museum located a structure in Siberia very much akin to the Egyptian Sphinx. It's apparently guarding three pyramids that are situated not too far away. These types of phenomena have been occurring all month," Dr. Ingram conveyed to his astonished subordinate, "and the government's been trying to keep the incredible finds out of media scrutiny. What's next? The Hanging Gardens of Babylon being unearthed in Alaska I suppose?"

"But Jeremy, er, I mean Dr. Ingram, what's going on? Why all of this science fiction stuff evidently coming to a culmination? Is the Apocalypse rapidly approaching?" Mike Templeton nervously questioned. "How could civilization, the exact same civilization be occurring, or should I say be reoccurring, that is I mean, being repeated or re-invented, or whatever you want to call it! If my mind had a heart, my brain would be having a major coronary right now!"

"Professor Lawler and I are working on several possible theories," the knowledgeable scientist related and then coughed three times in succession, "and when we have all of the vital details ironed-out, I promise I'll get back to you with some feasible explanation! Just keep me posted Mike about any new significant revelations! Right now my mind is a little fuzzy, sort of in a temporary quandary."

"Okay Boss! Will do! I'm beginning to feel as thrilled as your undaunted hero Heinrich Schliemann probably did over a century ago in Asia Minor! I hope to be in contact with you again real soon! I'll keep burning the midnight coal!" Click.

"More fantastic cultural parallels!" Dr. Lawler exclaimed before yawning heavily and stretching his arms while still lying horizontal in his queen-sized bed. "Now I don't endorse the practice of eavesdropping but I had overheard young Templeton's voice. The neurotic chap was all bent out of shape about a facsimile Big Ben and Parliament Building being identified near the South Pole. Jeremy, I want you to give me your unabridged audacious opinion. What do you make of all of these corroborative remnants of unknown past cultures being dug-up one by one?"

Jeremy slowly explained that "Chuck Darwin" and "Al Einstein" probably had been faced with similar "perplexing conundrums" prior to the scientific wizards formulating their rather incredible theories. Ingram then mentioned to Dr. Lawler how the discovery of the Burgess Shale cliff in Northwestern Canada had completely revolutionized geology and how it had rearranged man's perception of natural history.

"When the fossils of prehistoric clams, huge mollusks and other sea animals were discovered on top of mountain ridges and even in the high Himalayas," Dr. Ingram expressed to Dr. Lawler, "scientists, I mean those researchers of different areas of pursuit such as archeologists, geologists and anthropologists had to radically modify their assumed understandings of not only the Earth's history but also of mankind's brief tenure on this ever-changing Earth!"

"Well Jeremy, many expeditions to various mountain tops have proved that some extraordinarily powerful force had to push sea level up thousands of feet for the ocean animals' fossils to be so high-up on ridges like the Burgess Shale discovery to which you've just alluded. The serious documentation of those dynamic

420

observations eventually led to the modern-day Theory of Plate Techtonics!"

"Correct Greg!" Jeremy promptly confirmed, showing a trace of rare emotion exhibited in his voice. "Any elementary school student studying a bold relief classroom globe a hundred years ago could've seen that South America and Africa could easily fit together like giant jigsaw puzzle pieces. And that's precisely how the Asian mountains rose from the ground or sea level up to the height of Everest in the Himalayas. It was not an isolated find, that's for sure! The sea fossil evidence on the summits of the Himalayas were soon connected to the similar discoveries associated with the fabulous Burgess Shale animal fossils up in Canada's Pacific Northwest!"

"Yes Jeremy," Dr. Lawler appreciatively agreed, finally sitting-up on his bed in his pajamas and nodding his head in the affirmative. "It's a known fact that the plates on which the continents rest move apart about one inch a year, but over the span of millions of years the various land masses sitting upon the floating plates had managed to drift thousands of miles apart. And when two plates carrying a pair of continents collide, that's when...."

"That's when India moving at an inch a year gradually smashed into southeastern Asia and as a result, the Himalayas rose thousands of feet from under the sea into the air, and that's also why ocean animal fossils are quite abundant on those lofty mountaintops," Dr. Ingram finished. "But the whole land-mass grinding/impact process probably took eons to complete!"

"Well then," Professor Lawler frankly proceeded with his evaluation, "what's your outlandish theory about all of these mind-boggling discoveries that your myriad expeditions are digging-up all over the world? Have you managed to combine knowledge from archeology, natural history, geology and anthropology together to synthesize some heretofore unimaginable ingenious hypothesis?"

"Yes Greg, I have, and I'm now ready to share its essence with you!" Jeremy communicated to his eager-to-know traveling companion. "Prepare yourself for something rather alien to traditional thought that might totally defy all human reason! Oh no, there's my blasted cell phone ringing again!"

Cindy Noto, a very conscientious *University of Pennsylvania* archeology doctoral candidate was on the line calling Iceland. She excitedly reported to her supportive thesis paper sponsor that world history was literally repeating itself with the on-the-spot unearthing of an enormous Colossus of Rhodes bronze statue only ten miles outside Reykjavik and that a Temple of Artemis along with an unscathed Acropolis and a splendid Parthenon had just been found in very superb condition in Greenland.

"Just hang in there Cindy," Jeremy encouraged the euphoric doctoral candidate. "Here's something tangible and worthwhile you could write your thesis on. According to testimony given by another of my students, Kelly Greene," Dr. Ingram related to his enthusiastic intern assistant, "replicas of the pyramids and a duplicate Egyptian Sphinx have just been excavated in Siberia. Now confidentially Cindy, I suspect and believe that survivors from the lost civilization of Atlantis had built the Sphinx and that a library housing the secret history of the ancient world is stored inside either the Sphinx's left or right paw, or perhaps there are two separate and distinct archives, one inside each paw. Anyway Cindy," Jeremy objectively elucidated, "the Egyptian government will not allow us to open-up the original Sphinx's paws but I do think we can convince the Russians to cooperate and give us permission to explore what is perhaps the greatest archeological discovery of all time!"

"Gee Jeremy, er, I meant to say Dr. Ingram!" the very beautiful Cindy Noto ecstatically yelled. "My research paper will make me almost as famous as you are! You're a doll for giving me this special once-in-a-lifetime opportunity to make a name for myself!"

"Glad I could help you in earning your doctorate degree!" Dr. Ingram genuinely answered. "I know that your paper will make a great contribution to both science and to general knowledge! If you learn anything else, don't hesitate to get in touch with me! See you in sunny San Francisco next week for the upcoming big Archeology Convention! Bye now Cindy!" Click.

"How about some tasty breakfast over at the Hominy Grill?" Dr. Lawler graphically hinted before hearing his stomach growl. "I'm so hungry I could eat a pregnant stegosaurus!"

"Good idea!" Dr. Ingram replied. "But instead of prehistoric dinosaur meat, I think I'll prefer sampling the apple cinnamon French toast that Agnes Ross had strongly recommended. Then as we academically discuss current developments over our sumptuous breakfasts, I'll merrily share my latest theory with you and then see what you think of it."

* * * * * * * * * * * *

The two famished Charleston conventioneers were cozily seated inside the Hominy Grill indulging in their delectable hotplate orders of apple cinnamon French toast, cornbread, orange juice and savory coffee. Dr. Lawler was glibly commenting about how lucky he and Dr. Ingram were to have arrived at the popular breakfast/brunch place fifteen minutes before a long irregular patrons' line had formed outside the establishment's main entrance.

"Yes Greg, and the shrimp dinners we had enjoyed over at Hank's Restaurant and the fine meals we had gobbled-down at the Fleet Wharf and also at the Cypress Restaurant over on East Bay were terrific dining delights," the normally introspective Dr. Ingram opined. "Now Professor, just think about the many fantastic advancements mankind has made, not only achievements in the food industry but also progress in industry in general. Just twenty-thousand years ago," Dr. Ingram said, "Neanderthal and Cro-Magnon men were crudely drawing animals on cave walls, believing in magic, foolishly thinking that if they drew the animals as perfect as possible, then their artwork would make the two-dimensional ox or the flat-surfaced wild deer appear the next morning in three dimensions to be hunted and killed for food."

"Exactly and very cleverly put," Dr. Lawler amenably agreed, "and humans certainly have been a remarkable species these last ten thousand years, ascending from mere scavengers to the rank of hunters and then moving up to farmers, and finally rising to a nobility where mankind now dominates the entire planet. Science and technology have fantastically led to a plethora of exceptional accomplishments like the invention of the wheel, the bow and arrow, hammers, saws, knives, screwdrivers, shovels, automobiles, forklifts, radios, telescopes, microscopes, televisions, computers, the list goes on and on. And most of those wonderful tools and accessories were specifically created in the last three hundred years."

"Truly impressive but perhaps not totally unprecedented!" Dr. Ingram qualified.

"What do you mean?" Dr. Lawler inquisitively asked. "Is this the introduction to your new Theory of Civilization Regeneration?"

"Why yes it is," the widely-acclaimed archeologist declared. "My latest hypothesis has a lot to do with what I believe is the shifting of the Earth's poles every twenty-five thousand years or so. Now the last ice age ended around 10,000 BC so *that* cessation has given mankind approximately twelve thousand years to get its act together and develop civilization to its present sophisticated level."

"And you claim that before the last catastrophic Ice Age had descended onto the various continents," Dr. Lawler postulated, "similar sophisticated cultures like that of Atlantis had existed?"

"Exactly!" Jeremy argued and maintained. "There have probably been hundreds, maybe thousands of Ice Ages since the world was formed some four and a half billion years ago. And there's substantial concrete geological evidence that as recently as 650 million years ago a mile-thick blanket of ice had covered the entire planet. Then almost miraculously, volcanic action sent heat venting through the ice cover and into the atmosphere, thus creating a novel green house gas that then gradually melted the ice."

"I now see your drift of thought," Gregory Lawler said and paused to gulp down the remainder of his tangy orange juice. "The ice melting eventually caused the great greenery of the planet to happen with the advent of the Cambrian Ecological Period. Colossal swamps similar to today's Okefenokee in Georgia and the Everglades in Florida appeared all over. The lush vegetation in time gave evolving animals a fighting chance to exit the cold seas and then live as voracious reptiles and amphibians on the warm land masses."

Jeremy Ingram was just in the midst of disclosing his scholarly exposition. "Then of course around 200 million years all the way down to 75 million years ago the Earth had its notorious Jurassic Period when scores of plant-eating and carnivorous dinosaurs roamed the continents and ruled over all other animated life forms. And when the much-discussed giant asteroid slammed into the edge of what is now Mexico's Yucatan Peninsula," Dr. Ingram vociferated and emphasized, "then *that* violent collision was the end of the great reptilian era and soon the new environmental reality gave mammals a fair chance at ascension, of course eventually leading-up to the rise of apes and later primitive men."

Much to Dr. Lawler's amazement, Dr. Ingram went on to profoundly discuss the "Mini Ice Age" that had occurred in the 1770s, which remarkably had enabled George Washington and his troops to cross the frozen *Delaware River* to surprise the Hessian soldiers at Trenton and conversely, which also nearly decimated Washington's army at Valley Forge. "During several of those Mini-Ice Age years the sun hardly ever shined brightly in the summer months of July and August. But my principal point Greg

424

is that we've been having Ice Ages of all kinds and of all sizes throughout the entire course of human history."

"Well now Jeremy, you've taken the curious position that the last major Ice Age had ended around twelve thousand years ago, that it in fact actually corresponded to the destruction of Atlantis and that there had been previous human civilizations that had populated the Earth, possibly even long before the last major Ice Age started over 100,000 years ago!"

"You're a quick read Sir Gregory, and definitely a credit to your noble profession!" Dr. Ingram complimented his very savvy colleague. "As you well know, the thick sheet of glacier that had descended down from Canada had slowly traveled as far south to what is now New York City. Then when the massive ice sheet retreated back north, it ripped-out boulders and rocky land above what is now present-day Michigan, thus forming the Great Lakes when the remaining ice masses over time melted inside the deep cavities that had been formed."

"But your theory is advancing the idea that human civilizations have risen and fallen between the major Ice Ages!" Dr. Lawler reiterated. "And you're conjecturing that this ebb and flow of scientific and cultural development has been primarily caused by the Earth shifting on its axis, thus radically changing polarity and playing havoc with geographic climates every twenty-five thousand years or so!"

"Excellent analysis!" Jeremy Ingram commended. "Perhaps *that* pattern recurs every hundred thousand years or so, I'm not quite sure. Now here's an interesting addendum, or should I say 'appendix' to my theory. The Mayan calendar and the French prophet Nostradamus have both predicted that a cataclysmic change is going to alter human life on Earth during the winter solstice, December 21st, 2012. On that targeted day the Earth and the planets of our solar system will be in alignment with the exact center of the Milky Way Galaxy. The gravitational pull on the Earth might be so tremendous that...."

"That the North or the South poles will shift to what is now the Equator because the particular Milky Way-Earth positioning occurs once every twenty-five thousand years," Dr, Lawler gasped before swallowing down some cold water to revive his dizzy thought processes. "Perhaps Mike Templeton was right after all! The Four Horsemen of the Apocalypse might just be galloping their steeds around the closest corner and heading at full speed in our direction!"

"Or perhaps another possibility is that a rather huge celestial object, perhaps a remote planetoid, could approach the Earth and cause the relevant axis shift when acting in unison with the Milky Way alignment!" Jeremy speculated and suggested. "A cosmic magnetic pulse could cause the molten liquid inside the Earth's core to swirl around, thus resulting in a life-threatening polarity shift! Yes Dr. Lawler, I do believe that I like the nomenclature you have cooked-up to describe my new hypothesis: The Theory of Cultural Regeneration! But in the final analysis, I meant to say 'in summary', *we* might all soon fall victim to our own Galaxy's 'Earth destruction timetable' when its set into motion!"

"Move over Newton, Darwin and Einstein!" Dr. Lawler out-of-character yelped, getting the attention of other more disciplined Hominy Grill breakfast patrons. "I had always suspected that you were *bipolar*, ha, ha, ha!"

The archeologists' intense conversation was instantly interrupted with the familiar ringing of Dr. Ingram's cell phone. On the line was one of his more ambitious understudies, Karen Richardson calling from California.

"What's that you're saying?" Jeremy asked the caller above the abundant static being transmitted. "Speak louder please Karen! You say you're having big tremors in San Francisco and you're calling from San Jose?" The telephone communication was then disrupted and within seconds the electronic transmission lost.

"Gregory," Dr. Ingram said with his jaw open and his mouth agape. "Are you ready for survival of the fittest? I think that perhaps December 21st, 2012 is happening a couple of years prematurely!"

"Like Clockwork"

My spirit has been petrified ever since I had experienced what my senses have perceived as a supernatural phenomenon! My consciousness has never been so paranoid in my entire life as it is right this very minute. After I regain a degree of confidence, I plan to seek professional counseling to help my desperate soul grapple with my current unbearable mental predicament. Let me explain the entire dilemma in detail. I promise to be completely thorough in rendering my accurate description of certain events that seemingly defy scientific explanation.

During my very smooth and comfortable United Airlines cross-country flight from Philadelphia to Los Angeles International Airport, my alert mind could not stop thinking about the one-year anniversary of my twin brother Richard Sullivan's unexpected cardiac arrest death on April 14th, 2008. Richard had been an extremely successful lawyer back in Hammonton, New Jersey and both his devoted wife Karen and myself greatly miss his companionship. Besides my wife Susan, Rich had been my trusted confidante, friend, loyal supporter and expert financial adviser. My only brother's keen insight into evolving stock market trends was uncanny, and his shrewd decisions about often-speculative investments were accurate at least eighty percent of the times he had shared his terrific Wall Street recommendations with me.

While flying in the vicinity of Denver, my ever-anxious mind gradually refocused on my important purpose for making my three-thousand-mile week-long transcontinental excursion. 'Enough of this sentimental fantasizing! I'm the regional manager for new product sales of a mid-sized clothing manufacturer and am presently in transit to meet-up with reliable West Coast distributors in L.A., Carlsbad, San Diego and Palm Springs before successfully completing my business odyssey back to good old familiar Hammonton,' I quite practically remembered. 'The truth hurts but Rich is regrettably gone from this Earth and I still must concentrate my full energy on coordinating sales and making an above-average- living! Now I must discard my terrible melancholy and get excited about showing off the company's new line of inventory to prospective buyers and store distributors. I gotta' convert negative emotion into positive drive!'

After the huge jet gracefully landed at LAX I exited the lengthy concourse and then patiently waited for my luggage at

Carousel #2 and upon finally retrieving my two suitcases, as is my responsible habit, I instinctively removed my cell phone from my pants' pocket and called my wife to inform Susan that I had indeed arrived in Los Angeles in one piece without being confronted with any perplexing obstacles or difficulties.

The previous week I had made arrangements to rent a *Ford Taurus* from Hertz and after picking-up the vehicle drove in the direction of the downtown Marriott Hotel located at 333 Figueroa Street, a distance of around seventeen miles northeast of L.A. International. Along the city's all-too-congested main traffic arteries my restless brain contemplated my future trip down scenic coastal U.S. 101 through Oceanside to beautiful Carlsbad, and after meeting with three corporate sales reps' as scheduled, then continuing on further south to my favorite place on the entire planet, majestic La Jolla, California.

'I can almost taste my sumptuous seafood meal at the Crab Catcher Restaurant on Prospect Street and I know I'll find it very relaxing strolling along tranquil Coast Boulevard and observing the idle seals casually basking on ocean rocks without a worry or a care,' I mused as I proceeded onward toward my accommodations' destination. 'Then I'll slowly get back to reality and the monotonous routine of motivating others to sell the company's new fall and winter merchandise lines. If it weren't for Susan and the kids,' I gratefully acknowledged, 'I think I'd be so depressed about Rich's death that I would seriously consider prematurely joining him in the hereafter! Holy Heaven!' I seriously evaluated. 'How preposterously evil! What in the world am I thinking? Since the name printed on my birth certificate reads Carl Sullivan, my often-fanciful mind has deliberately played with the words 'Carl's bad,' which is impishly toying with the identity of the coastal California city Carlsbad.'

At that particular moment my all-too-suspect cerebral activity became more rational as I reflexively stopped for a sudden red light on Figueroa. 'I'll have to squeeze-in the San Diego Zoo, Old Town and the magnificent Hotel Del Coronado while meandering around San Diego,' I imagined and reckoned. 'I suppose I'm rather tired after the stress of traveling coast-to-coast. I'll park my car, check-in at the main desk, get to my reserved room and next take a hot shower to revitalize my senses. Then after a room service meal,' I speculated, 'I'll watch an hour or so of television and later call Susan around 7 p.m. It'll be ten o'clock back in Jersey and my wife will have put our staying-over grandchildren Joey and Debbie to sleep by then so actually, *we* could both enjoy

428

some much-needed mutually beneficial adult conversation. Being away from home for seven days does have its therapeutic value! But in the final analysis,' I aptly concluded, 'it's always good to get back to your wife and family!'

I managed to check into Room 414 without any difficulty and wholeheartedly gave the courteous and affable bellhop a five-dollar tip for carrying my heavy luggage from the lobby to the elevator and next onward down the hallway to my temporary living quarters. After showering and then enjoying a delicious steak and mashed potatoes room service dinner, I decided to divert my attention to some popular television viewing.

As I conveniently channel surfed, I stopped my perusal upon incidentally landing on a re-run of a classic '50s Ed Sullivan Show featuring the premiere TV appearance of Elvis Presley. 'I was a mere ten years old at the time of *this* extraordinary performance,' I fondly recollected. 'Yes, Elvis's hip gyrations earned him the reputation and nickname of 'Elvis the Pelvis' and after his initial sensational appearance, thereafter Presley had to be seen on television screens from the waist up because of bitter outcries from incensed moral protesters, mostly church reverends and Catholic school nuns and priests,' I considered. 'My, how morality has vastly changed since the nostalgic 1950s!'

Soon my astute mental activities associated other salient facts relevant to Elvis's first national network gig. 'Ed Sullivan had been in a bad auto accident and had been hospitalized and *that* evening actor Charles Laughton had been designated the substitute MC,' I observed from my random memory knowledge. 'Although the landmark show had originated in New York, Elvis was wiggling around on stage in Los Angeles at the time singing his hits Love Me Tender, Don't Be Cruel, Hound Dog and Ready Teddy with the Jordanaires providing background harmony. A record TV audience of sixty million Americans watched the show. It truly was one of the most spectacular events of the '50s decade.'

The next thing I knew, a negative thought entered my fine-tuned thinking as I rested under the covers in the soft king-size bed. 'Gee, Elvis Presley and Charles Laughton are both dead along with my twin brother. And I definitely remember that Richard was faithfully sitting there on the living room sofa alongside me and *our* parents, the four of us enthusiastically watching *this* particular entertainment show way back on the memorable date, September 9th, 1956! Oh, if only Richard and I could be somehow reunited, yes, brought together for only a brief moment!'

Fully reclined in the bed with my head propped-up with soft pillows, I became highly-frustrated and frightened with my twin brother reunion contemplation so I abruptly switched channels during an annoying commercial break. 'What a remarkable coincidence!' I amazingly recognized upon noticing the new cable offering. 'A black and white documentary film featuring the life of the late 19th century heavyweight gloved boxing champion John L. Sullivan, the first athlete to earn over a million dollars. First Ed Sullivan, now John L., the fighter's biography all being witnessed by me, the usually unflappable and unfazed Carl Sullivan. The invincible puncher is traveling coast-to-coast arrogantly challenging all comers to brawl in a ring for a handsome five-hundred-dollar prize. Oh my God!' I quickly realized. 'John L. Sullivan is dead too, just like Ed Sullivan and my sibling Rich Sullivan!'

I swiftly grabbed the TV remote control in disgust and then very forcefully again changed the cable channel. My astonished eyes and mind couldn't appreciatively comprehend the next visual sequence, a graphic scene from the award-winning movie "The Miracle Worker." Anne Sullivan was devotedly teaching a blind and deaf Helen Keller how to communicate by establishing code language with her fingers on the blind girl's palm. The revolutionary breakthrough was occurring with Helen's unique understanding of the word "water" when I rapidly and promptly shut-off the aforementioned room television.

'What a bizarre series of events!' I reasoned. 'Ed Sullivan, John L. Sullivan, Anne Sullivan and my brother Richard Sullivan are all deceased! Am I the next one to bite the bullet?' I grievously wondered as sweat beads began cascading down from my forehead. 'Am I the next target in the Grim Reaper's shooting gallery? As a rule I'm not generally superstitious but *these* weird hotel room coincidences are too inexplicable and too exceptional for me to fathom! I really have to close my eyes and get some essential sleep before I become a total basket case! An hour-long catnap will do my psyche good!'

* * * * * * * * * * * *

My deep slumber was rudely interrupted at 9:15 p.m. with the loud ringing of my cell phone. As a steadfast rule, I can only remember a pleasant dream or a reprehensible nightmare if I

430

happen to wake-up in the middle of one. I fumbled with my communications' device and awkwardly answered the call. My ears were truly surprised to hear the exaggerated-but-worried voice of my normally calm sister-in-law, Karen Sullivan. She sounded hysterical, almost delirious.

"Karen, you appear to be alarmed, your sentences almost frantic! What's disturbing you?" I began as my brain revved-up to normal speed. "Are you under some extreme duress?"

"Carl, I just have to talk to you. I'm at my wits' end!" Karen gasped and replied, almost out of breath. "Do you know that beautiful marble clock on my living room mantel?" she rhetorically continued. "You know, the one situated next to the large picture of my late husband."

"Yes," I stated, wiping the excess sleep away from my left eye. "Susan and I have an identical clock on *our* mantel that's right next to an identical picture of Richard. If my memory still serves me, the two facsimile Florentine clocks were expensive souvenirs given to Rich and me after Uncle Jim had visited Italy fifteen years ago," I related. "The pair of handsome-looking made-in-Tuscany items were carefully packaged, neatly gift-wrapped and then specially shipped to the States."

"Well Carl," Karen declared with a heightened degree of exclamation, "the clock above my fireplace chimed twelve times exactly at midnight. As you're quite aware, it's been broken for over two years now. Because of my own negligence, I've never gotten it repaired despite all my good intentions. But Carl, the mystery of the unanticipated chiming has scared the living daylights out of me. You're sensitive enough to know exactly how I feel. I'm scared to death to go back to my bedroom."

"Did Tommy and Billy wake up during the chiming?" I inquired for lack of a better question to ask.

"No, fortunately *my* grand-kids had slept right through the rather strange ordeal. I mean to say Carl, the gorgeous clock is an electric one but its cord and plug had been disconnected from the wall socket behind it ever since it had ceased functioning. As you know, I seldom drink beer or alcohol but I'm so nervous that I intend to take a full shot of *Southern Comfort* after I get off the phone speaking with you."

"Please don't do anything drastic!" I diplomatically cautioned. "Are you sure someone isn't playing a mean prank on you? If they are, it certainly isn't very funny! Tomorrow morning, check your living room for a hidden tape recorder."

431

"Look Carl, I called you to achieve some emotional security, not to encounter some oddball guessing game on your part," Karen effectively reprimanded. "But truthfully, now that I've informed you of the unusual event, I sort of feel a little better. It always pays to express anxiety. It helps clear the mind."

"Get some rest Karen!" I sagely advised. "Broken electric clocks can't tell time or chime, especially when they're not getting any juice from a power outlet. Now then, be sure to take it easy and gulp down a second shot of *Southern Comfort* for me. That seems to be the perfect remedy to quell your temporarily neurotic condition. As long as the clock has stopped its bothersome chiming, you have nothing to worry about. But don't be too dumbfounded if you find out that your visiting grand-kids are naughtily playing a peculiar sadistic joke on you!"

"Okay Carl, thanks for your solicited reassurance," Richard's former wife sincerely conveyed. "I had felt a trifle fidgety so I figured that although it's after midnight here in Hammonton, it's just a quarter after nine out there in L.A. That's what is so remarkable about these modern cell phones. I can reach anyone day or night no matter where they happen to be."

"Yes, they're a distinct advantage over obsolete land-lines in that respect," I concurred. "Now get back to sleep and although it's no easy task, forget all about your apparent paranormal adventure. I pledge I'll call you back tomorrow morning to see if everything is all right!"

"Thanks again Carl! You're just as compassionate and caring as Richard was! Good night and please have a prosperous business trip out West!" Click.

After closing the lid on my cell phone, I pensively thought about Karen's fantastic clock experience and then was finally able to reassemble the various elements of my incredible nightmare that her phone call had trespassed into. 'Oh my word!' I concluded with awe. 'I had been dreaming that Richard and I were Union soldiers during the siege of Fort Sumter, the first battle of the *Civil War*. A powerful cannon ball sent us flying right out of our battle station, and the intense explosion propelled us all the way to Fort Moultrie on nearby Sullivan's Island on the other side of Charleston Harbor. Richard and I weakly staggered to our feet, both of us suffering from shock and bleeding from non-fatal wounds. Richard wrapped his right arm around my shoulder and we began trekking north toward what is now the Isle of Palms when we oddly encountered ashen-faced ghostly likenesses of Ed Sullivan, John L. Sullivan and Anne Sullivan, all refugee

432

anachronisms wandering around *that* particular sector of Sullivan's Island. Yes indeed,' I considered, 'the subconscious mind certainly has the extraordinary propensity of playing imaginative tricks on one's mental health!'

I strolled over to my smaller suitcase, removed a pint of bourbon from its interior and lustily guzzled down several ounces of the delicious warm whiskey. Then I covetously approached my laptop computer to perform some preliminary investigation into the historic Confederate attack on Fort Sumter. The revelations that my dedicated discovery uncovered on Google Search Engine were both fascinating and mind-boggling.

'First of all I had never heard of either the Isle of Palms or Fort Moultrie,' I incredulously realized. 'And according to these vivid color illustrations on my computer screen, the blue uniforms worn in my nightmare by Richard and me were indeed quite authentic and genuine-looking. And Pierre Beauregard, the Confederate general portrayed on the *Internet*, gave the orders to launch an all-out two-day assault on Major Robert Anderson and his Union Garrison defending Fort Sumter. On April 14, 1961,' I read from my trusty computer screen, 'and then the Northern troops reluctantly evacuated Fort Sumter, thus assuring a confidence-building Confederate victory. Hundreds of Charleston residents watched the ongoing conflict from the porches of mansions situated along the city's waterfront battery. And furthermore,' I marveled and comprehended, 'this entire set of circumstances is a bothersome enigma. I've never set foot in the city of Charleston, South Carolina and I personally never desire doing so for the remainder of my life!'

Then a startling and intriguing coincidence momentarily held my mind hostage. I quickly imbibed another healthy swig of sweet bourbon from my glass bottle to provide my faltering mental state with adequate false courage. "April 12 -14th, the Battle of Fort Sumter," I uttered to no one but the lavender sidewall of the well-appointed suite. "Today is April 14th, the one year anniversary of Richard's death! According to my atrocious nightmare, I could be the next candidate to be escorted directly inside the Eternal Hotel! And yes, astoundingly, the numbers on my hotel room suspiciously match the dates of the Battle of Fort Sumter and of Richard's devastating death, 4/14. There isn't enough bourbon in this small bottle to satisfy me!"

I immediately closed my laptop, swallowed-down another mouthful of liquor and then gingerly slid my body into bed. I stubbornly refused to watch any more television out of fear of harvesting additional nightmares from my surfing cable selections, preferring as a much-warranted alternative to shut-off the room's table lamp and to then again journey into the fabled Sandman's Domain. Soon I was dozing-off, trying hard to discard recent unnerving academic disclosures about my haunting relationships with certain television programs, with departed-from-this-earth people having the last name of Sullivan, with famous Fort Sumter and with my deceased twin brother's demise. 'The *Civil War*!' I recall thinking and analyzing. 'What a horrendous oxymoron! What a malicious injustice to logical nomenclature! How in God's Name could any damned war ever be 'civil'?'

* * * * * * * * * * * *

My subsequent venture into dreamland was not a fortuitous mental voyage because it was an ugly repetition of the formerly depicted Fort Sumter disaster with Richard and myself being mutually blasted all the way to Fort Moultrie on Sullivan's Island where we again had our ironic and implausible rendezvous with Ed, John L. and Anne Sullivan. I recollected the same eerie aspects to my reoccurring nightmare because my characteristic deep slumber had been disrupted by a second disturbing call, this time from my very upset spouse. My right hand again wildly searched in the dark for my cell phone while my left appendage tried locating the side table's light switch. After several seconds of frenetic desperation, dual successes were finally achieved. A very familiar voice on the other end of the line initiated the conversation.

"Carl, I just had to call you!" my wife Susan fearfully exclaimed. "Do you know the marble clock on the living room mantel that Uncle Jim had purchased for us in Italy?"

"Susan," I answered as I clumsily flicked on the side table lamp to its 150watt setting. "I had meant to tell you. That mantel clock isn't working. I had noticed that the cord in the back had been slightly spliced since its plug had been placed into the back wall electrical socket at almost a right angle. I guess that over the years' regular wear-and-tear have taken their toll. I had thought that the bent cord might be dangerous so I had disconnected the clock before the potentially hazardous electrical wire caused a house fire. Better safe than sorry, that's what I've always believed."

"Yes Carl, I'm aware of exactly what you had done," Susan confirmed in a rather confused state of mind, "but something very outlandish happened at midnight. The clock had chimed twelve times, which as you know is absolutely impossible without its cord being attached to the rear wall receptacle! To tell you the truth, my nerves are even more frayed than the bent wire in the back of the marble mantel clock is!"

"I know it's really late back in Hammonton, but has Karen been in touch with you within the last half hour?" I honestly interrogated. "A similar mysterious occurrence had happened to our sister-in-law around midnight involving her previously broken mantel clock, which as you know is the twin to ours. You don't suppose that in some uncanny way that Richard is attempting...."

"To communicate with us!" Susan finished my impromptu theorizing in an appalled and nervous tone of voice. "Carl, I'm frightfully rattled. My mind's in big disarray! I wish that you were home here on Eagle Drive and not three thousand miles away at the Downtown L.A. Marriott. Please come back as soon as you can. Can't you cut your trip short a day or two? I'm very jittery and I feel rather nauseous!"

"I suppose I can get out of the Palm Springs meeting later this week if I declare that an unforeseen family emergency has developed. Tell me Susan, did the grandchildren hear the chiming?" I curiously asked. "I've always argued that they watch too many ghost and horror movies as it is."

"No, I haven't heard a peep out of either Joey or Debbie all night long," my wife stated. "They're both exhausted from helping me clean-out the pool and then getting the lawn furniture out of the cellar this afternoon. Our annual Memorial Day weekend backyard barbecue is only six weeks away."

"Well Sue, I suggest you take a few of my heavy-duty sleeping pills from our bathroom medicine cabinet and please get some shut-eye," I recommended. "Karen told me that she planned to settle her nerves with a jigger or two of good old-fashioned *Southern Comfort*. At any rate, get in touch with our sister-in-law early tomorrow morning. Apparently, now you both have something in common. Like I had mentioned to Karen," I paused to collect and separate my fleeting thoughts, "I suspect that someone is playing a not-too-amusing prank on you both. That's the only feasible explanation I can offer. It's all totally beyond reason! But who in tar-nation could the dastardly culprit or instigators be?"

"I just don't know Carl," my very concerned wife replied, the tone of her delivery evidently returning to its normal decibel level. "As you often tell the children, when you think you've seen and heard everything, that's when the ordinary course of events mutate and totally surprise you."

"Take those two sleeping pills and call me in the morning," I said, sounding a little too much like the stereotypical family physician. "I need to get some up-to-now evasive sleep myself to be mentally prepared for tomorrow morning's important power-point presentation. Some of my biggest sales reps' will be attending the conference downstairs in Meeting Room B. I can't allow strange events back in South Jersey to interfere with my informative slide show. In spite of the economic recession," I emphasized, "I gotta' be fully ready to motivate the buyers to purchase the company's fall and winter apparel lines."

"Okay Carl, you've very competently eased my anxiety," Susan assured. "Pardon the expression, but knock 'em dead tomorrow morning with your persuasive style. Call me around noon eastern time and I'll give you an update on the clock mystery once my erratic mind is back to an even keel. The grand-kids will be glad to learn that you'll be coming home a day or two earlier than had been expected. By then the pool should be ready to be christened for the summer!"

"You take care Susan. Love ya' more than words can express." Click.

'The strange episodes that Susan and Karen had perceived were parallel conundrums,' I judged as my vagabond mind imagined words that Sherlock Holmes might have uttered to Dr. Watson on numerous occasions. 'But these dual puzzles are far from being elementary in both scope and nature! Oh well,' I rationalized, 'it's time for some sleep barring me being surreptitiously hexed and vexed by any additional intruding nightmares!'

* * * * * * * * * * * *

Because of the influential teachings of my former ultra-liberal Philosophy, Cultural Anthropology and Contemporary Sociology college professors, I've never in my adult life been a superstitious or a religious person. My contrary "practical disposition" never placed much credence in the occult, in magic, in alchemy or in the arcane. My ordinary approach to the notion of "paranormal" has always been to regard such "remote phenomena" as being childish, insane and basically naïve science fiction.

My skeptical heart along with my very cynical attitude in reference to the off-the-wall stories related by both Susan and Karen were together predisposed and inclined to make my interpretations both biased and dubious. I realized that I needed to have my own 'physical manifestation' occur to fully convince my 'objective scientifically-oriented mind' to penetrate through its 'thick Doubting Thomas shell.' Quite succinctly, I needed to be re-educated and converted back into my superstitious pre-college thinking mode.

Before I fell fast asleep, my erratic brain mulled-over the notion that only a personal 'out-of-this-world' aberration directed exclusively toward *me* would be sufficient cause to affect any specific trepidation that I might in the future feel. When it boiled-down to honoring superstition, my obstinate core character was beyond the shadow of a doubt that of a confirmed apostate.

As my tired mind sank into Sigmund Freud's favorite realm, the same *Civil War* nightmare persisted in dominating my subconscious psyche' as I was generally aware of my tossing and turning during the initial stage of my stressful sleep. According to the recently established pattern, Richard and I had been exploded out of Fort Sumter and we were then violently rocketed across the harbor to the vicinity of Fort Moultrie. Upon rising to our feet, my injured brother and I were again meeting up with Ed, John L. and Anne Sullivan on the extreme tip of Sullivan's Island.

My senses were awakened from my irksome slumber by the sound of Uncle Jim's voice warning me that it was positively imperative for me to regain consciousness or else risk being escorted into the afterlife. My trembling hand managed to flick on the table lamp, thus illuminating Room 414. My strong instinct was to do all that I could to avoid the total permanency of eternal death. I felt that I had to endure and survive for the sake of Susan, my son Stephen and my two grandchildren.

Upon opening my eyes, my pupils were horrified to witness the pallid two-dimensional transparent form of Uncle James Garrison, whose frightening countenance bore an extremely lugubrious expression. Observed from my eyes' bedside perspective, Uncle Jim repeatedly was pointing toward the room's bureau and wall mirror situated directly across the suite.

Throughout the very perplexing frozen-in-time scenario, I dared not move a muscle, feeling almost paralyzed while lying perfectly still under the bed covers. Then amazingly, the visiting specter moved sideways without taking any apparent steps, instantly being absorbed into the locked door and ultimately vanishing out into the fourth floor corridor. My senses were completely befuddled. All of a sudden my throat, esophagus and stomach all felt rather queasy and momentarily, I did feel an urge to regurgitate. I was wholly petrified.

My baffled mind felt rather feeble and my afflicted spirit was not sufficiently prepared to cope with the next sequence of unbelievable events. Upon the empty bureau there gradually appeared a color photograph of my twin brother, the impressive picture being a duplicate of the ones adorning both Karen's and my fireplace mantels back in New Jersey.

Several seconds later, a marble Florentine clock appeared next to the all-too-familiar color photograph. I turned and lifted my wristwatch from the side table to corroborate the time, just as the mystical clock stationed upon the mahogany bureau began chiming twelve times. When I set my watch down upon the lamp table, I hesitantly moved my head and eyes towards the bureau and the slightly elevated wall mirror. Slowly-but-surely the remarkable clock and accompanying picture simultaneously disappeared.

All throughout the frightful experience I had never felt that my life had been in jeopardy from an 'invisible world existential threat', but being a spectator to the anomaly, my vulnerable spirit had been both affected and intimidated. I nervously exited my bed, paced over to my suitcase, removed my precious pint of bourbon and avariciously chugged down the remaining three ounces. I cravenly hopped back into bed, and the next reality I remembered was being awakened by a requested courtesy call from the hotel's main desk at precisely 7 a.m. With the advent of daylight came the hope of continued mortal existence.

Over the course of the next five days, my normally abundant appetite for food had greatly diminished, and much to my utter dismay, I possessed no desire to visit the fabulous Crab Catcher Restaurant on Prospect Street in scenic La Jolla. In fact, I haven't eaten at any New Jersey seafood restaurant since my return from California six months ago. I seem to have altogether lost my desire to consume delectable crabs, lobsters, clams, oysters and scallops. Susan now affectionately calls me "a landlubber!"

Upon shortening my rigorous California business trip by two whole days and then after joyfully returning to 135 Eagle Drive in rural Hammonton, New Jersey, I've never felt any special need to divulge the grotesque supernatural 'weird phantom experience'

438

that my senses had perceived at the L.A. Downtown Marriott to either Susan or Karen. My heart now knows what terror is and I find its mere contemplation to be both alien and excessively repulsive.

I've learned from recent Internet research reading that living twins often have telepathic ability, but my eerie West Coast communication with my dead brother was indeed way beyond standard reasoning. Sometimes a recurrent nightmare reviewing my L.A. hotel room haunting occurs, savagely torturing my fragile psyche. At least once a week I'll awaken from my deep slumber, shivering and trembling. Susan insists that I discuss my dilemma with either my priest or my psychiatrist, but I stubbornly dismiss her sympathetic advice as being "unnecessary."

Just last month I had meticulously labeled the separate ownerships of the two Florentine mantel clocks, took them to a local electrician's shop and had new cords and accompanying wall plugs professionally installed. The splendid mechanisms have worked quite well ever since the essential repairs had been accomplished and I gladly paid the shop's proprietor the handsome sum of three hundred dollars for his invaluable skill and service.

Indeed, in this final contemplation of the bizarre chronology of the triple marble clock events, some matters demand that their inexplicable essence never be shared or further discussed with others, including my wife, my sister-in-law, my priest and my psychiatrist. But quite confidentially, I secretly promised my conscience that I would never again stay as a welcomed guest at the L.A. Downtown Marriott Hotel. As the immortal bard William Shakespeare had once aptly written, "All's Well That Ends Well!" That is, until the next traumatic nightmare violently interrupts and destroys my precious sleep.

"Chiropractic Dreaming"

Every calendar year the time period of February to mid-April is very demanding and stressful for middle-aged Harold DeFelice of 763 Fairview Avenue, Hammonton, NJ. The very thorough and efficient Certified Public Accountant had just mailed the last of his clients' 2008 Federal Income Tax returns at the Third Street Post Office on Wednesday morning, April 15th and now it was time to drive his brand new tuscan red Nissan Maxima to has scheduled appointment at Advanced Chiropractic, 425 White Horse Pike, Atco. Harold preferred patronizing Advanced Chiropractic over its Hammonton counterpart because the Atco office had the latest and most modern professional equipment, so in DeFelice's sage estimation, the seven-mile west drive on four-lane *Route 30* was indeed well-worth the additional time and effort.

'Most of my five hundred customers really go crazy in the six weeks prior to the April 15th tax deadline,' Harold thought as he passed a tractor-trailer while ascending the *Route 30* Ancora Railroad Bridge. 'They persistently call me about deduction trivialities and about every complicated minor change in the tax code as it specifically pertains to them. But now I can relax, get my back and hips adjusted and be pampered by some excellent electrical stimulation, be massaged by the very satisfying roller bed experience and of course babied by my favorite chiropractic indulgence, the invigorating therapeutic aqua-bed.'

Then an aggravating consideration surfaced in the CPA's ever-active mind. 'I'd better watch my speed,' the accountant realized during his momentary behind-the-wheel reverie. 'There're several daily speed traps in Waterford Township and Chesilhurst along this route so I've already been stopped twice this year for exceeding the fifty mile an hour limit. Fortunately my Camden County Police Support Card worked miracles on those two occasions, but I don't want to press my good luck. Some gung-ho on-a-mission rookie cop with something to prove might just pull me over and write me out an expensive citation. But I'd eventually get even with the overly ambitious upstart!' Harold snickered, defensively glancing into his rear-view mirror. 'I know just about every single accountant in this sector of Camden County, many of whom owe me at least one special favor. Come income tax season, I can indirectly get revenge on most any cop!'

Harold casually made the familiar left hand turn from the White Horse Pike onto Coopers Folly Road and then the convenient right behind Woosters Funeral Home and next he slowly motored down the asphalt lane to the rear entrance to Advanced Chiropractic. The business's proprietor Dr. Joe DeClement was just exiting his black Cadillac Escalade and immediately recognized the new arrival in the health center's front parking lot.

"Hi Harold. Got a pretty decent new car I see," Dr. Joe warmly greeted his loyal customer, shaking his right hand. "Nissan Maxima huh! Maybe some day I'll get out of my General Motors habit and purchase one of *those* exotic Japanese models too. I'm due for a change in my automotive taste. I'll bet you get much better gas mileage than my new Cadillac jalopy does."

"Twenty-three miles per gallon and probably twenty-four if I fill-up with premium," Harold boasted, puffing out his skinny chest. "At least that's what the owner's manual claims. Let me show you some of this car's special features. It's really a four-door sports car with a 290 horsepower high torque engine and a unique one-speed transmission that'll take the guy behind the wheel from zero-to-sixty in less than six seconds. This remarkable baby is a classy-chassis if there ever was one!"

Harold proudly demonstrated to a highly impressed Dr. Joe DeClement the amazing key-less entry, ignition and trunk system, the very functional rear window shade screen, the convenient reverse camera view, the accurate GPS viewer, the terrific Sirius-XM radio selector, the standard dual driver and passenger temperature controls, the premier tan leather seats having both heat and air-conditioning luxuries and finally, the separate sun and moon roofs, both concealed and then handily exposed.

"Now I know why General Motors and Chrysler are both on the verge of bankruptcy," Dr. Joe marveled and expressed. "With stiff competition like you've just shown me, I think my next car will be an Infiniti or a Lexus."

"Well Dr. Joe, Nissan produces the Infiniti, Toyota manufactures the Lexus and Honda makes the Acura," Harold academically revealed from his admirable treasury of memorized facts. "I would say that all three manufacturers are comparable, but I might be a trifle biased towards the Infiniti simply because it's a bona fide Nissan automobile. Tell me Dr. Joe, are you gonna' be around to manipulate my spine and hips today or are you on your way to a glitzy Atlantic City Casino as usual?"

"No Harold, my wife and I will be off later this afternoon to the Philly' Airport," Joe DeClement confidentially revealed. "We're spending the next two weeks at our Marco Island home. As you might know, Florida during the summer gets pretty hot so MaryAnn and I decided we'd enjoy a half-month of southern sunshine before the tropical heat and the rainy season moves into the Southern Gulf Coast. But Harold, I know that Dr. Matt will adequately take care of you during my absence. I'm sure he'll introduce you to his new assistant who incidentally specializes in physical therapy. Hope to see you next month here at the clinic Harold. I'll be thinking about you while lying beside the pool and drinking a cold pina colada."

"Thanks Doc!" Harold replied, a bit too sarcastically. "And I'll be thinking about *you* in early June, the next time I wrack my brains out working on your quarterly tax return."

Harold entered the main entrance to Advanced Chiropractic, was immediately greeted by the courteous receptionist, instinctively reached for his wallet and then handed the woman his ten dollar insurance co-payment and next, the jovial patient engaged in several minutes of small-talk with the main desk secretary, who very reliably arranged the CPA's next visitation for three weeks later.

Then according to his normal habit, DeFelice approached the coffee machine, competently poured himself a cup of hot java, added two sugars and an ounce of cream and then automatically stepped over to the Danish counter where the patient began unraveling the cellophane to a delicious cheese-centered snack. The accountant's high-calorie culinary activity was suddenly interrupted by the congenial-but-stern voice of Dr. Matt.

"I again caught you in the act Harold," the highly-skilled husky chiropractor mildly chastised. "I don't know why Dr. Joe has all of these junk food temptations so readily available. We're supposed to be operating a health clinic here for our clients, not a fat farm. This nasty coffee and these harmful pastries seem contrary to the purpose of *our* vital medical mission."

"These wonderful items are here to accommodate the hungry and appreciative clientele," Harold argued in defense of his friend Dr. DeClement. "I humbly suggest Dr. Matt that you discard your impractical idealism for a minute and give your boss Dr. Joe some credit for being a genuinely shrewd businessman. Now here's a bit of undeniably wise philosophy from my lips: Never criticize the hand that feeds you, or in this case, the hand that writes your weekly paychecks."

"You've got a valid point there," Dr. Matt begrudgingly admitted. "Now Harold, I'm goin' to be doing some vital backlogged paperwork this morning so one of our new personnel, Dr. Sue will be taking care of you."

Harold had thought that Dr. Matt had alluded to "Dr. Su," so naturally the "math' figure wizard's" imaginative mind had conjured-up (in a stereotypical manner) the notion that "Dr. Su" was a short fat bald-headed Chinaman. But when a very attractive brunette named Dr. Susan Martin rounded the corner to introduce herself to a blushing Harold DeFelice, the CPA had to chuckle and embarrassingly explain to the vivacious female the true reason for his amusement.

"Just give me five valuable minutes," Harold politely requested. "That's how long I'll need to consume this tasty Danish and wash it down with this extremely hot coffee."

"That's fine with me," Dr. Sue agreeably answered. "I'll use the next five minutes constructively conferring with Dr. Matt about your special chiropractic needs and then I'll be reviewing your case history files in our computer archives. It's been a pleasure to meet you Harold, and please, by all means, don't scald your throat with that steaming hot coffee."

"I just gotta' formally apologize for presuming that you were a corpulent midget male Chinese bone-cruncher when you had been described as 'Dr. Sue' without me seeing you in the flesh," Harold said while maintaining his florid face. "I hope you weren't offended by my unwarranted remark."

"That's perfectly okay Mr. DeFelice! But I believe that you should instead be saying your sorry monologue to that imaginary obese bald-headed chiropractor from Shanghai," Dr. Susan Martin quipped, her grin exhibiting superb pearly white teeth. "I think such a statement would be most appropriate."

"Touche!" the momentarily flustered visitor acknowledged. "I really deserved *that* admonishment!"

Dr. Martin smiled at her new patient and then sauntered around the corner, stepped briskly down the hall and soon stepped into the physical therapy gym area to check on several recuperating people doing their assigned exercises.

* * * * * * * * * * * *

The beleaguered CPA devoured the remainder of his Danish and after his brewed coffee cooled a little bit, the man finished-off the balance. He then met Dr. Susan Martin in the hallway and the

444

newly hired chiropractor escorted her overworked patron into Treatment Room B where she suavely directed DeFelice to lie face down on the adjustment table.

"Where did you go to school?" Harold innocently inquired. "You seem to have a western accent."

"Very perceptive observation on your part! I had graduated from a college out near Denver," Dr. Sue disclosed as her soft hands examined her patient's back muscles. "I had worked out in Colorado for several years before moving east. A good friend of mine was an acquaintance of Dr. Matt, so here I am in metropolitan downtown Atco, population 5,500. What do folks do for fun around here? Watch the Weather Channel on cable? Or maybe the all-exciting Home Shopping Network?"

"Atco is really a part of Waterford Township, but I think you'll like the rustic nature of South Jersey," Harold clarified and assured. "It's relatively close to both Atlantic City and Philadelphia and New York's only a hundred miles north. You'll have the safety and the solitude of the charming countryside and you'll enjoy full access to the cultural benefits of the big cities too."

"Your records show that you have a minor hip rotation that if it goes unattended for several months," Dr. Sue stated, deliberately converting the verbal exchange into a more professional tone, "the accumulative neglect could knock your whole back out of whack. I'll first adjust your spinal vertebrae vertically and then pancake you with my special crunch technique both on your left and right sides. Actually, your problem is quite common but it could become painful without having regular maintenance."

"I know *that* for a fact!" the loyal patient confirmed. "Once it happened when I was busy vacuuming under the living room couch's frame so that my wife could get herself ready to go out to dinner. My back went completely out of kilter and I collapsed face-down upon the rug. My wife entered the room, thought that I was still vacuuming and she yelled out above the loud noise, 'That's right Harold! Be sure to get under the sofa!' Then she left the room totally unaware that I had accidentally injured myself! For a full week I had to crawl from the bed to use the bathroom! How dehumanized can you get?"

"I guess you had to cancel your restaurant reservations," Dr. Sue replied. "It's hard to enjoy a good meal in public with tremendous pain radiating-out from inflamed and damaged discs."

After the pancake manipulations had been successfully accomplished, Dr. Martin applied the two sets of electric stimulus pads to Harold's upper and lower back and then covered his entire upper posterior with soothing heated compresses. She then set the stimulus machine's timer for fifteen minutes and informed Harold that she had to leave his illustrious company to treat another client occupying the adjustment table in Treatment Room D.

Fatigued from coordinating his recent grueling tax accounting workload, Harold DeFelice slowly dozed-off into dreamland. His initial fantasy scene was that he was living in a medieval stone house with odd-looking barefooted people (both male and female) wearing horned Viking helmets on their heads. The primitive-looking men were bearded and quite comical in appearance. The lady occupant of the stone house was vigorously reprimanding her derelict husband for spending too much time associating with his worthless pals at the local tavern. Suddenly a fat lady came out from behind a purple curtain and began obnoxiously singing her tonsils out as if she were the grand finale to a very bad Wagnerian opera.

The next mental tableau in Harold's distorted dream featured two modern-day women gossiping about the remaining narrow field of prospective husbands. Both young ladies were extremely depressed by their obvious inability to find suitable mates to marry. Harold's subconscious awareness felt as if he had been eavesdropping on a confidential conversation. The second potential bride was sobbing and confiding that she'd rather enter a convent than spend a year wed to a grossly undesirable wimpy man. The second depressed marriage candidate next divulged that she would prefer being single for her entire adult life rather than be wickedly mired in a poor in-harmonious relationship with a boring handsome oaf.

The well-defined but segmented dream next creatively shifted to a small apartment with an unkempt scruffy-looking fellow conversing with his agitated articulate dog about how severe the canine's unbearable headache was. The distraught mutt was adamantly protesting that he required more nutritious dog food from his self-indulgent master in order to avoid future mental crises involving preventable chronic suffering from excruciating migraines.

Before Harold could fully fathom the totality of his subconscious manifestations, the apparatus's timer expired and a persistent loud buzzer was sounded. Thirty seconds later Dr. Sue entered Treatment Room B, gently lifted the comforting heating

446

compresses and then expertly detached the four electric stim' pads from her grateful patient's back.

"You must really be exhausted!" Dr. Martin perceptively observed and commented. "I had walked by this room twice in the last quarter hour and you were snoring a bit each time while your preoccupied mind was actively chopping wood. If you want my medical opinion Mr. DeFelice, I think that a lot of rest is the best therapy to rehabilitate a tired mind like yours. Are you now ready to explore the roller bed massage in Treatment Room E?"

"Yes I certainly am!" Harold quite amiably agreed while concealing his deep evaluation of his most recent convoluted dreaming. "I guess my body and my mind both need some requisite R&R. I'll have to remind my wife Helen to call our travel agent and book a cruise out of New York to the Bahamas. I've found that a change in environment often bolsters the flagging spirit. And after being away from Jersey while swimming and dining in the Caribbean for several weeks," Harold contemplated and then shared, "a person usually comes around, returns to his or her town with new-found motivation, puts his or her nose to the grindstone and again appreciates the maxim that there's no place like home!"

The roller bed in Treatment Room E consisted of a moving wheel embedded in a tan leather cushion that made a back and forth motion up and down Harold's spine, each subsequent pass requiring about ten seconds from the base of his neck down to his sacroiliac and then a ten second opposite direction movement back up to his nape. Dr. Sue Martin carefully adjusted the wheel's settings to "maximum" elevation and next declared that Harold was about to receive the ample benefit of "the Full Monty." The entire massage process would take fifteen minutes to complete.

Soon the accountant's overtaxed mind was again drifting into dreamland, the illusion world again featuring a variety of weird characters and situations. A backyard barbecue scene had family and friends amiably chatting around several picnic tables. The majority of the attendees were upset that several uninvited neighbors had crashed the party by climbing over the high fence that separated the adjacent properties. In the next series of events transpiring inside Harold's fertile imagination, an old decrepit man and an elderly woman wearing glasses were sitting at their kitchen table when the gentleman gingerly rose from his chair, patted his insecure wife on the back and then suffered through her complaining that he was just trying to dry his wet hand on her dress while pretending to be comforting her volatile demeanor.

447

The next peculiar interaction in Harold's newsreel-type subconscious trip portrayed two elementary school children restively sitting at their classroom desks. The cheerless kids were criticizing the fact that their female teacher had just left the building before the final bell had rung and was seen out the window entering a car that was being operated by an old man wearing glasses having ultra-thick lenses. In all of the surreal settings, Harold was more of a spectator to the abnormal events than an actual active participant.

Soon the mechanism's timer expired and the confused accountant quickly awoke from his short siesta. Dr. Susan Martin strolled into Treatment Room E and promptly shut-off the roller bed's motor by turning several dials to the left, setting them back to their original positions. Harold DeFelice discreetly opted not to discuss the odd subject matter of his latest dreaming out of fear of being the brunt of several unsolicited jokes from the lips of his new and seemingly opinionated chiropractor.

"Well, there's just one more phase to your appointment today and that's the aqua bed in Treatment Room A," the pretty woman indicated. "That's gotta' be the most relaxing aspect to your Advanced Chiro' visit. You'd think that your Advanced *Chiro'* experience would be happening in Egypt and not here in Atco, New Jersey," jested Dr. Martin.

Ignoring his doctor's sharp wit, Harold humbly explained that he absolutely loved the aqua bed, especially when it made him feel as if he were drifting at sea on a most comfortable raft, gracefully rocking back and forth on calm summer ocean waves. "I hope I don't wind-up in Wildwood or Cape May," the fellow stated with a feigned solemn expression on his face as he awkwardly climbed onto the horizontal machine. "And please don't twist the dial all the way to the right. I might get sea sick."

"How long do you wish to be on the aqua bed?" Dr. Sue asked. "What's your usual time?"

"Thirty-minutes should be just right," DeFelice articulated. Then the patient thought of something additional to enunciate. "Yes, I'm very fickle and fussy in my ways! Thirty-minutes of heavenly bliss is about all the pleasure I can tolerate!"

Once Harold had assumed the standard flat position upon the aqua bed, Dr. Martin set the controls for thirty minutes of pulsating vibration at "maximum heat." Then she nonchalantly departed the room to allow Harold to explore the therapeutic benefits of peace, sanity and privacy. Soon the CPA had succumbed to his need for rest and within minutes his receptive

448

fancy eagerly and voluntarily entered the dark and sinister realm of mythological Morpheus.

The first scene in Harold's new fantasy had a dog attempting to train another dog on how to fetch a ball. The second pooch refused to surrender the round object as the stern instructor canine lifted the student mutt off the ground by grabbing the ball and raising it up to *his* right shoulder. The second escape-from-reality sequence had three adults vociferously debating about the passage of gallstones, giving multiple births in the cab of a backhoe and finally, researching information from a blatantly unreliable *Internet* encyclopedia. Everything seemed fairly logical with the human interactions until personification once again dominated Harold's next Freudian-like mental state. A chicken was obstinately standing on a living room rug protesting to two dogs lying on a davenport that she had been stood-up and ignored by an ugly, egotistical and ill-mannered rooster. The first canine insincerely communicated to his companion dog that he was going antique shopping that afternoon while the second animal was laughing incessantly at the chicken's apparent frustration and at the first canine's very evident ability to adroitly change the subject from the chicken's emotional dilemma to that of seriously going in quest of rare antiques. The fourth vision in Harold's distorted afternoon nap had a hippie-type individual sitting at his desktop computer vehemently arguing with his mother about his lack of success at obtaining a regular job. The very intense feuding pair was aggressively conducting their mutual animosity when the familiar ringing of the aqua bell's timer sounded and Dr. Martin predictably entered Treatment Room A to shut off the marvelous device and then assist Harold in again assuming a vertical standing posture upon the floor.

"I suppose Mr. DeFelice that I'll see you again in three weeks," Dr. Sue suavely communicated. "I hope I've adjusted you as well as you adjust your customers' taxes."

"Please call me Harold," the bewildered and confused patient requested. "Yes Dr. Sue, I'll gladly return in twenty-one days for more therapy and of course, for another delicious Danish. If my wife knew about my diet deviation every time I visit here, she'd forbid me from coming. But what is life without an occasional food delight? Gee whiz, am I philosophical today or what?"

"I'll buy into your simple pleasure hypothesis!" Dr. Martin concurred with a broad grin. "Take care Harold and we'll see you in three weeks. I'll tell Dr. Matt that you were asking about him."

Harold DeFelice heeded the *Route 30* 50 mph speed limit on his seven-mile eastbound ride from Atco back to Hammonton. The Waterford Township and Chesilhurst police had stopped several vehicles with Pennsylvania license plates, the foreign drivers unaware of the notorious local New Jersey speed traps. 'The area cops not only catch in-a-hurry Philly' speeders heading down to the Jersey Shore,' the accountant surmised, shaking his head in sympathy with the unfortunate violators. 'Jersey has a pass left and keep to the right-side lane law and Pennsylvania does not, so the local fuzz is always nabbing Keystone State motorists for a reason other than flagrantly breaking the speed limit.'

After stopping for the traffic signal at the rise of the Ancora Railroad Bridge, the rejuvenated CPA was quite anxious to return home, have supper with Helen and leisurely read the morning edition of the *Atlantic City Press*. 'The paper hadn't been tossed onto the front porch at its normal 6 a.m. time this morning. Must've had a substitute deliveryman performing that monotonous duty. Oh well, there's my Fairview Avenue driveway up ahead. Ah yes, the cellophane-wrapped *Press* is up there right between my porch's white wicker chairs. I'll get caught-up on my reading soon after dinner. I hope that none of my major clients have been arrested for tax evasion.'

Harold wholeheartedly savored Helen's spaghetti and meatballs supper and commended her on the tasty Tuttorosso marinara sauce in which the delicious food had been garnished. As the couple later relished eating the mouth-watering poppy-seeded warm Italian bread, Helen brought-up the topic of how she loved viewing cable re-runs of '50s vintage television shows. Of course the upbeat homemaker had to elaborate on her all-time favorite.

"You know Har," the faithful wife began her narrative, "I was watching a terrific comedy episode of the old 'I Love Lucy Show' this afternoon and I thought it was hilarious. Lucille Ball and Desi Arnes really had a wonderful chemistry going-on between them. Needless to say, I absolutely despise all of the violence and the sexual innuendo that the public is now exposed to in sleazy movies and on mediocre TV soap operas. What ever happened to

450

traditional decency and moral values? I meant to say that television shows don't have to be cruel or dirty to be funny. Do you get my gist Harold, or is it just my prejudiced take on things?"

"Well Helen, everything's radically changed since the black and white, right or wrong, true or false '50s decade," the husband confirmed as he poured a second cup of coffee for himself. "Milton Berle, Jack Benny, Jackie Gleason, Sid Caesar, Perry Como, they were the best. And don't forget the wholesome family shows like *Ozzie and Harriet,....*"

"*Our Miss Brooks, Leave It to Beaver, Dennis the Menace* and *The Life of Riley* starring William Bendix," Helen competently finished her spouse's statement. "The Golden Age of Television will never again be duplicated. We were very lucky growing-up during the best of times, the last Age of Innocence!"

"That reminds me," Harold mentioned before slowly adding an ounce of cream to his coffee. "I still have some of my old baseball cards along with Batman, Superman and The Phantom action comic books up in the attic cedar chest. After all these years, I still treasure those memorabilia!"

"They're all rare collectibles now and probably worth a small fortune," Helen theorized and expressed. "Perhaps you oughta' get them insured!"

"After I help you clear-off the table and clean the dishes," Harold said, deftly avoiding his spouse's expense-oriented suggestion, "I'll go into the den and finally read the morning paper. It was delivered late today so I haven't had the opportunity to see what's happening in Atlantic County. Just like you do, I now get most of my national and international news from *Google* and *Yahoo* along with other pertinent details from cable network news."

"I'll give you a big break tonight about doing your regular kitchen chores," the wife informed her dedicated mate. "You've been burning the midnight coal the last eight weeks so you're entitled to a little free time to recharge your batteries. But tomorrow night," the wife qualified, "you'll be on call again so get the most out of your brief respite from responsibility while you can. But for tonight Har, I want you to know that I do appreciate your sacrifice at work, which you selflessly daily perform, for the good of the order!"

"You're right about the great things that the Fabulous '50s had to offer kids and adults alike," Harold complimented his very intelligent wife. "I never take time to read the newspaper comic strips any more. I mean some of the old cartoon characters are still around like Blondie and Dagwood and Beetle Bailey, but for the most part, what I used to read, items like Buz Sawyer, Little Iodine, Nancy and Sluggo and Dick Tracy are no longer around. I think that even Peanuts is a thing of the past!"

"My father once told me that there was a huge newspaper strike in New York back in the mid-1940s and Mayor Fiorella LaGuardia would read the Sunday rotogravure comics to kids over the radio," Helen declared to her husband. "Dad still claims that that's how he had learned how to read, by following along as the Mayor dramatically read the captioned words and impersonated how the various characters would sound."

"Well Helen, I remember my Dad often talking about shows like The Inner Sanctum and Amos and Andy on the family radio," Harold sentimentally recollected. "It's too bad Dad's gone now. I really liked listening to him describe how hard life was during the *Great Depression* and during *World War II* with gas and certain foods being heavily rationed."

"Why don't you park yourself in your favorite leather chair and peruse the *Press*," Helen aptly suggested. "You've earned the privilege of bumming around this evening. And I saw in the *Hammonton News* last week that Royale Crown just opened for the season yesterday. Maybe later on we can treat ourselves to the first custard hot fudge sundaes of the spring."

Harold slowly wandered into the den, sat in his black leather recliner chair and very deliberately opened the newspaper. 'I haven't read the comics' section in over twenty years,' DeFelice recalled.

On a whim the curious reader thumbed his way to Section B-4, the modern comic strips. The surprised accountant was staggered beyond belief at what his eyes and mind immediately interpreted. The first three comic strips were identical to the three short dreams his mind had envisioned while lying prone on the Advanced Chiropractic manipulation table when he had been connected to the electric stim' machine, and the next seven were parallel to the three dreams on the roller bed and the four that had been synthesized on the incomparable aqua bed.

'This whole phenomenon is totally and absurdly insane!' the amazed fellow determined as sweat beads gradually appeared on his brow. 'There's the barefooted Viking-like personages in the comic strip *Hagar the Horrible*, the gossiping females in *For Better or For Worse*, the unkempt scruffy-looking fellow conversing with his aberrant dog in *Get Fuzzy*, the unwanted
452

neighbors at the backyard barbecue in *Sally Forth* and the elderly woman verbally assaulting the old man for deliberately wiping his wet hand on her dress while pretending to be patting her on the back in *Pickles*.'

After nearly swallowing his tongue during that moment of total consternation, Harold courageously resumed his more-than-casual scrutiny of the *Atlantic City Press's* comic strip page. 'Let me collect my many fleeting thoughts,' Harold systematically decided before he proceeded with his hypothesizing any further. 'Incredibly, the comic strip features are appearing in the exact same chronological order that they had been mentally presented while I had been dozing-off at Atco Chiropractic Associates. Talk about bizarre paranormal experiences!' he conjectured. 'Here's the two elementary school kids complaining about their teacher prematurely leaving the classroom before the final bell sounded in *Curtis*, here's the canine lifting the second uncooperative dog being trained off the ground with the ball in its mouth in *Mutts*, here's the backhoe cab multiple births, the gallstones and the inferior *Internet* encyclopedia research represented in *Dilbert*, here's the chicken and the two haughty dogs lying on the couch fiasco in *Pooch Café* and finally, here's the oddball mother-son employment debate happening right next to the desktop computer in *Doonesbury*.'

It was at that precise moment that CPA Harold DeFelice fully understood what had actually occurred in his uncanny '*Twilight Zone* adventure.' His intelligence had finally profoundly stitched-together the fantastic evolution of events that had recently developed at Atco Chiropractic Associates and at his home. 'This afternoon my subconscious mind had somehow made a four-hour time leap into the future,' Harold conclusively fathomed, 'and I've just seen on the newspaper comic strip page what my time-traveling psyche had envisioned in my three sessions of dozing off at the Atco clinic. In all deference to the Mamas and the Pappas, I'll take Chiropractic dreamin' over California Dreamin' every single time!'

"Harold, are you ready for this year's first hot fudge sundae over at Royale Crown Custard?" Helen bellowed from the kitchen.

The unnerved CPA dared not tell his wife about his extraordinary mental leap forward in time. "No thanks Dear. I think I'll take a rain-check on your kind offer!" the still-rattled husband yelled back.

Then Harold reflected some more about his paranormal experience and hollered a statement into the adjoining room. "Forget Royale Crown this evening! My ravenous hunger has been completely satisfied! Your spaghetti and meatballs happened to be so wonderful Helen that I think I've lost my normally voracious appetite for the rest of the night!"

"Animal Music"

Any fiction writer aptly knows that the absolute ultimate in creativity that the human mind can produce occurs when the dynamic subconscious engages in dreaming and in imagining totally surreal situations during dreadful nightmares. But when ambitious short story and novel authors attempt organizing eccentric tales (that are analogous to capturing fantastic dreams on paper), the writers' manuscripts almost always fall pathetically short of the authors' noble aspirations. Unfortunately, most dreams and nightmares are not fully recollected, but if they could be, then there would exist thousands of additional excellent "soul-inspired" works available for readers' consumption in both World and American literature.

Rick Simon had very serious mental and emotional issues ever since he had graduated as a mediocre student from Hammonton High School. His overwhelming problems began manifesting during the *Vietnam War* era when the want-to-be rock star had attended the Woodstock Music Festival in August of 1969. Soon thereafter the avowed long-haired hippie evaded the Army draft by dodging his military duty to his country, instead opting to live a nomadic existence in Canada. Then in the winter of 1973 the itinerant vagabond married the former Michelle Gibson in Ottawa and the pair eventually had two children, Tommy and Kim.

Rick never earned a recording contract despite his fairly adequate singing voice and his average songwriting and musical versatility, and after seven years of accumulated frustration and failure, the defeated artist surrendered to temptation and became a heroine and cocaine addict. Four years later Michelle filed for a divorce and easily obtained custody of the couple's son and daughter. Rick Simon hadn't seen his former wife and kids since the summer of 1980. The poor despondent fellow's life had really hit the skids and everything was predictably downhill from there on out.

Feeling safe from military prosecution, in 1999 Rick' reluctantly returned to his home state of New Jersey, settling down with a cousin Jack Murphy in the all-too-bland town of Hammonton. But the addict's chronic drug habit, his mental instability and his lack of on-the-job dependability as a handyman always sent the troubled fellow to the back of the unemployment line.

Hampered by shattered hopes and broken dreams, and diagnosed as "potential suicidal" by a panel of state health officials, Rick Simon was finally admitted to South Jersey's Ancora State Hospital in 2007 for "psychiatric examination," for "emotional rehabilitation," and for "an assessed need for the depressed patient to escape the wicked scourge of "dangerous drug dependency." Therapy treatment seemed to be working so the patient was conditionally released back into society but had to check into Ancora once a month for a day's "monitoring and follow-up evaluation."

The one activity that the dejected drug addict really enjoyed was to ride around in an automobile on rural highways while listening to Sirius XM Satellite Radio, his favorite stations being the three that would broadcast lively '50s, '60s and '70s rock and roll music. Those timeless rhythms and lyrics played over the airwaves happened to be the only sounds on Earth that brought pleasure to Rick Simon's ears and a smile to his lips.

In June of 2009 Rick Simon was conditionally released from Ancora, but hospital officials had stipulated the provision that his "improved status" should now be reevaluated every six months. But on August 12th, Jack Murphy experienced the horror of finding his problem-oriented cousin dead sitting inside *his* 2006 Ford Explorer, which the Vineland DJ had lent his emotionally disheveled relative to take for a "pleasant drive" through the pine-barrens along the rustic country roads that encompass downtown Hammonton.

A minuscule obituary of only one paragraph in length appeared in local newspapers. Those gossipy residents dwelling in the vicinity of 431 Peach Street (that were remotely acquainted with the deceased) all regarded Rick Simon as a "genuine born loser." The out-of-luck electric guitar player (who had lived an extremely miserable and woebegone life) was promptly buried in Oak Grove Cemetery with little notoriety or public remorse.

The grim-faced funeral director who presided over the lackluster ceremony recited several prayers because the ministers and the priests that had been contacted wanted no part of a man that never attended any of their sanctimonious church services. Only Jack Murphy and seven other caring relatives attended the brief and uneventful interment. Michelle Simon, Tommy Simon and Kim Simon had been contacted in Canada but all three elected not to witness Rick's cheap wooden casket being lowered into its cold eternal grave.

* * * * * * * * * * * *

Two weeks after Rick Simon's death his "Psychiatric Patient Study Team" consisting of Psychiatrist Dr. Peter Collins, Psychologist Dr. Irene Bennett and Social Worker Janet Owens met in the Ancora Administration Building's second floor conference room to close-out the thick cumulative record file of their deceased subject who had been undergoing *their* mental evaluation. None of the three professional personages had had the decency to attend their' patient's funeral, all three state employees stating that they had other important commitments to pursue on the day of the burial.

"We all know our purpose for being here so let's get this final review of Mr. Rick Simon underway so that we can return to our normal daily activities," Dr. Peter Collins began his introductory narrative. "Now quite succinctly, I'd like for us to get all our ducks in a row to avoid any unnecessary police investigation or any possible intrusive inquiry from the State of New Jersey. As you are aware, we have enough bureaucracy to contend with in regard to our daily busy workloads to have to take time to drive up to Trenton to answer a lot of annoying picayune questions," the committee head prattled, "so if we're all on the same wave length when interviewed by the standard authorities, there won't be any conflicts in our testimonies, especially if we have to give sworn depositions. I understand that a routine autopsy had been performed on Mr. Simon and the cause of death is officially listed as a heart attack. But I don't want the Atlantic County coroner's office coming over here to Camden County to conduct any wild goose chase investigation that'll lead to a bothersome New Jersey Psychiatric Board probe."

"The autopsy report should be sufficient documentation to close Mr. Rick Simon's case once and for all," Psychologist Dr. Irene Bennett concluded and objectively analyzed. "And besides his deadly coronary attack, our former patient's longtime flirtation with marijuana, cocaine and heroine should show-up in the pathology tests and systematically organized as part of the forensic doctor's addendum to the death certificate. But I do concur with you Dr. Collins," the mind examiner declared. "We don't want any foreign investigations interfering with our already overloaded schedules. As a preventive measure, I too believe that it's quite wise to have this routine meeting to avert future aggravating situations."

"I fully agree with Dr. Bennett," Social Worker Janet Owens chimed-in. "Many sociological factors in addition to ongoing emotional distress along with myriad physical problems contributed to our troubled patient's demise. As we all are aware," the extroverted woman expressed, "Rick Simon was alienated from his wife and children for many years and those estranged relationships had to dramatically impact his ability to function effectively in our very demanding culture, or should I say 'our very demanding society'. Mr. Simon's impaired coping mechanisms had diminished considerably prior to his unexpected death but since the patient was under *our* supervision, we have to coordinate our professional opinions just to protect ourselves from any possible litigation that might be lurking out there. Now I don't want to sound too neurotic or paranoid but in this politically correct day and age," Janet Owens expounded, "you never know when a predator attorney wanting to build a reputation at *our* expense is going to come after you."

"I suggest Ms. Owens that you keep your random opinions within the social work domain and leave our former patient's mental challenges up to the professional judgment of Dr. Bennett and me," Dr. Collins politely chastised the lowest ranking member of his study team. "The human psyche is a very fragile and vulnerable thing, and I don't want to sound too simplistic but as the esteemed Sigmund Freud has been reputed to have said, 'The mind is like an iceberg: it exists around one tenth above the surface and functions nine-tenths below. The subconscious brain is frequently unpredictable and oftentimes can be more instrumental in motivating a person's actions than the more obvious conscious cerebrum does," the publish-or-perish psychiatrist continued articulating his lengthy self-important self-defense narrative. "And *we* must not let any overzealous policeman, coroner or state official come into our cozy domain and cause us undeserved grief. Our impeccable reputations as dedicated professionals must be preserved by all means," Dr. Collins convincingly maintained. "Keeping our professional integrity along with our public image is paramount! We don't need any unforeseen dilemma appearing out of the blue and then damaging our professional credibility!"

"I don't know why we call Rick's problems *mental* when they were basically *emotional*, having little to do with logical thinking," Ms. Owens defiantly answered. "I have issues with the descriptive term *mental health*!"

458

"Here's the obvious key *issue* Ms. Owens! The principal tenets of Maslow's Theory of Hierarchal Needs and Drives," Dr. Irene Bennett insisted and added to the professional conversation. "At the base of the matrix everyone has similar physical needs like food, shelter and clothing and also primary drives that must be satisfied like hunger anxiety and of course, sexual fulfillment. Then above *that* foundational *animal level* of human existence there are emotional needs such as love, acceptance, approval, trust and the desire for social interaction. I believe Ms. Owens that this second ascendant structural level of human development was somewhat lacking in Mr. Rick Simon's unhappy childhood and in his out-of-control adult life. The enormous negative factors already alluded to in our preliminary remarks quite evidently show Mr. Rick Simon not being able to..."

"Not being able to ever reach the third essential upward step, namely the rational level of the Maslow Pyramid, which is the individual's ability to perceptively think, to interpret reality, to analyze one's relationship with his or her social and material environments and finally, to logically view the world in an objective *mental* manner," Dr. Peter Collins competently finished the psychologist's statement. "And so, if any pertinent level of the matrix becomes flawed or ruptured, then the person involved never achieves happiness and can never advance to the ultimate plateau of human growth and development, the attainment of self-fulfillment, which as we all know is a sort of Utopian state of mind that's often called and defined as 'self-actualization'. It's a *mental* status Ms. Owens that separates an achiever from his or her peers whereby he or she is independent of and fully above the restrictive forces that exist on the lower three levels of Maslow's reliable matrix. But to explain these intricate theories, or should I say 'intricate principles of psychology' to a layman like a policeman, or to a state prosecutor or to a common coroner's assistant," Dr. Collins persuasively stressed to the social worker, "well, you get my general gist Ms. Owens. The whole complicated ordeal suddenly becomes way above their limited comprehension of the human mind."

"Then in literary terms and correct me if I'm wrong," Dr. Irene Bennett courteously interrupted her authoritative superior, "just like Ralph Waldo Emerson, *you* do believe in Transcendentalism, the idea that emotions should and often do transcend rational thought in the everyday human condition. Feelings over logic should exist as the principal human goal, if I remember correctly."

"Dr. Bennett," the eminent-but-perturbed hospital psychiatrist answered, "I do think that Transcendentalism does govern the behavior of most of *our* patients where certain negative emotions like greed, jealousy, hate, envy, pride and contempt dominate their fragile psyches. But to ascend to true self-actualization as Maslow had so sagaciously postulated and admirably demonstrated in his research," Dr. Collins haughtily emphasized, "then one must advocate and practice Reverse Transcendentalism where the rational mind elevates itself above the standard emotional state of existence and then efficaciously exercises its ability to not let base impulses affect his or her human performance."

"Bravo Dr.," the impressed psychologist commended. "Now since the clock on that wall is rapidly advancing toward lunch time, and since Mr. Rick Simon's cousin Mr. Jack Murphy is slated to soon come in and be interviewed about the circumstances leading-up to his relative's unfortunate death, I recommend that we focus our attention on our patient's permanent record file, which will soon be turned-over to state officials for a cursory examination. Let's start our information sharing with you Ms. Owens."

"Well, when Rick, or should I say Mr. Simon was six years old, he had owned a furry tan teddy bear that he habitually slept with. One day, for no given reason, young Rick Simon exhibited heightened violence by wildly assaulting his treasured possession with an ice pick, ripping the soft object to shreds. Now for some inexplicable reason, *that* bizarre aggressive behavior arose from his subconscious and made the young boy go into a frenzy and engage in extreme unwarranted anti-social misbehavior."

"Yes Ms. Owens," Dr. Collins acknowledged, "the public doesn't understand too much about psychology and psychiatry. These social sciences of ours are not quite as predictable as let's say a classroom experiment in chemistry, biology or physics might be. Our psychology laws are really only weak and flimsy theories. I mean they pertain to many situations and have merit in terms of *general* human needs," the distinguished psychiatrist maintained, "but when it comes down to predicting how and why a particular person performs a specific deed or misdeed, I'm afraid that *our* social science is quite deficient. If psychology or psychiatry were true exact sciences, then murders and all other crimes and felonies could be avoided or stopped because those enactments could have been measured beforehand and would have fallen under the designation of scientific predictability. Now then Ms. Owens, do you have any additional relevant data to reveal to which Dr. Bennett and myself might not be cognizant?"

"Well, Mr. Simon absolutely loved fancy automobiles and oldies rock and roll music," the garrulous social worker orally reviewed from confidential information contained inside the deceased subject's personal folder. "He always desired to be an entertainer but lacked the confidence or the wherewithal to ever succeed in *that* highly competitive field of endeavor. I don't want to delve into our patient's horrible fear of all sorts of animals and his abundant nightmares associated with venomous snakes, with abominable giant insects and with ferocious carnivores because I believe that I'd be recklessly trespassing into Dr. Bennett's realm of expertise and I don't want to selfishly steal any of my respected colleague's thunder or lightning."

The psychiatrist then turned his attention to the psychologist. "Haven't you had Mr. Simon under hypnosis several times?" Dr. Collins asked Dr. Bennett. "If so, I strongly suggest that we expunge those hypnosis sessions from his personal records just in case there's an inquiry about the psychological ramifications associated with Mr. Simon's physical cardio-vascular problems. I don't want to see our reputations becoming a part of any wild all-holds-allowed state orchestrated amateur wrestling match! 'Better safe than sorry' should be our motto in this potentially troubling case!"

"You were right on target about the limitations of psychology as a viable science," Dr. Irene Bennett congratulated Dr. Peter Collins. "As *you* so aptly stated, we psychologists and psychiatrists can identify the general factors, needs and drives that motivate the general public's basic behavior but we can't recognize exactly what compels the specific individual to do a specific thing, like savagely tearing up a cuddly teddy bear for no apparent reason at all!"

"Please Irene, continue with your dissertation about Mr. Simon's various animal nightmares," Dr. Collins implored. "I'm most interested in hearing your revelations and findings."

Dr. Bennett cleared her throat and explained that ever since early childhood Mr. Rick Simon had suffered from frightful nightmares involving all kinds of animals and had a definite inexplicable phobia that adversely affected his mental perception of reality.

"Perhaps he saw a deer with large antlers in the woods just before having his fatal heart seizure," Ms. Owens theorized and expressed, annoyingly interrupting the psychologist. "That event could've been a possible cause-effect relationship. He had taken a drive on back roads through the Wharton State Forest prior to his collapsing inside his cousin's SUV while parked in Jack Murphy's driveway."

"That's rather impossible!" Dr. Peter Collins exclaimed, indirectly admonishing the all-too-impulsive social worker. "Mr. Simon died in mid-August and bucks don't sprout their antlers looking for combat until rutting season begins in November. Now please Ms. Owens, show a little more self-restraint and allow Dr. Bennett to smoothly give her well-documented presentation."

Janet Owens remained reticent while the knowledgeable psychologist thanked the loquacious psychiatrist for extending his "professional support," and then the human brain authority disclosed that Rick Simon's abundant nightmares involving a variety of bellicose animals could be usefully classified into four distinct categories: Life-threatening conflict with human-sized birds and insects, life-threatening conflict with ordinary-sized but especially fierce animals that one might find at a zoo or circus, life threatening conflict with egregious animals that might populate a desert or inhabit a plains' region and finally, life-threatening conflict with voracious animals that could only be grouped together as an aggregate labeled "Others" or "None of the Above." Dr. Bennett had concluded from her accurately compiled data (which she had meticulously gleaned while the patient had been under hypnosis) signified that the confused subject had great difficulty distinguishing fantasy from reality and also differentiating fact from fiction.

"Obviously Mr. Simon's low level of achievement never really reached or met his high level of aspiration, particularly in the music world," Dr. Collins deducted and then expressed to his two conferees. "Dr. Bennett, tell me more details about these intriguing animal nightmares. Of course, as already mentioned, all of *that* confidential information is to be removed from Mr. Simon's file and then conveniently shredded immediately following this rather mundane and fruitless consultation. According to Charles Darwin and possibly even pursuant to Maslow and Freud too," the prestigious psychiatrist egotistically lectured, "the concept of survival starts with the fundamental sense of individual self-preservation! That primitive, or should I say 'primary' survival behavioral trait is characteristically instinctive because it's genetically programmed into all animals and humans including Mr. Rick Simon. Now please Dr. Bennett," Dr. Collins proceeded and deliberately elicited, "kindly continue

462

with your vivid description of our deceased patient's extraordinary phobia about a vicious menagerie of animals in a state of perpetual attack as represented in *his* distorted dreams, and then connect those surreal apprehensions with Mr. Simon's apparent suppressed subconscious linkages and with his widespread emotional turmoil."

Dr. Irene Bennett informed her two participating colleagues that Rick Simon had a profound fear of insects and birds that regularly haunted his nightmares ever since early childhood. Often times the hostile on-the-attack creatures were exaggerated in size and the "imagined molesters" frequently chased the fleeing dreamer to various unfamiliar houses and building that had locked doors.

"Did Mr. Simon ever have an interest in either etymology or ornithology?" Dr. Collins curiously asked. "Did he ever mention being in a panic state when viewing the '50s sci-fi movie 'Them' about giant insects, gargantuan ants I believe, terrorizing Los Angeles, or did he ever discuss with you the Alfred Hitchcock classic horror thriller 'The Birds'?"

"No, the nervous subject never mentioned either of those films during our hypnosis sessions or during our regular meetings and interviews," the now-puzzled psychologist replied. "I don't think that the patient ever enjoyed sitting in dark movie theaters. And also, he was quite afraid of being too confined in a restricted space for too long. I was going to test him for agoraphobia but now *that* sort of psychic exploration is too late to appropriately assess!"

"Continue with your exposition," Dr. Collins entreated. "We want to cover all avenues and angles just to ascertain that we're all singing in the same choir if ever questioned."

"Another unique dimension to Mr. Simon's ongoing terrible nightmares was his extreme dread of ferocious animals like lions, tigers, panthers, gorillas, alligators, elephants and bears," the thorough researcher quantified from her comprehensive notes. "It really didn't matter that those partially-tame creatures would always be fenced in when normally encountered in a standard safe zoo or circus environment. Our paranoid patient was abnormally fearful of them, at least in the depths of his lower mind. Needless to say, the consistent presence of these imaginary predators battered and devastated Mr. Simon's vulnerable psyche almost each and every single night. They constituted a source of perpetual apprehension!"

"Off the record, I know that this discussion is all academic irrelevancy in light of the fact that *our* patient is now dead," Janet Owens interrupted, "but how do we know that Mr. Simon's mental issues had anything to do with his fatal heart attack?"

"Yes indeed Ms. Owens, your skepticism is most justified," the psychiatrist assured his all-too-curious subordinate. "Even if *we* are implicated in some county or state witch-hunt investigation, we'll be exonerated because we'll argue that our psychiatric studies were designed to help Mr. Simon escape his melancholy state of mind and *not* to accelerate his demise. If it weren't for *our* skilled services," the department head sanctimoniously boasted, "our patient might have died four years ago. We had actually extended his life with our advanced therapy methods. Now Dr. Bennett, please finish-up with your commentary."

"The next and final classification pertaining to graphic animal attacks involves creatures native to the plains and the desert," the psychologist reported. "In his rather remarkable nightmares, such indigenous fauna as wild horses, rattlesnakes, wolves, kangaroos and poisonous cobras would chase after Mr. Simon and have him cornered just before he would wake-up in a cold sweat. In fact, our beleaguered patient seldom had any positive dreams. His recollections from his disturbed sleep were always extremely confrontational in nature!"

"Well, if any of us are ever interrogated during a future inquiry or inquest, our patented response should be that our involvement with Mr. Simon had beyond the shadow of a doubt lengthened his dismal life because the subject had been showing signs of improvement just before he had experienced his unfortunate coronary thrombosis. I trust that we're all in perfect agreement on that point?"

Before either Dr. Bennett or Ms. Janet Owens could utter an additional syllable the second floor office secretary announced via the wall speaker that Mr. Jack Murphy had arrived for his scheduled Ancora State Hospital debriefing concerning his cousin's mental health and subsequent "unrelated death."

"Send him in!" Dr. Collins answered back over the intercom. "We're all interested in what Mr. Murphy can add to satisfactorily finalize his cousin's rather extensive cumulative folder."

* * * * * * * * * * * *

464

Vineland disc jockey Jack "the Knack" Murphy stepped into the Ancora State Hospital conference room and caseworker Janet Owens introduced the "down memory lane" oldies' radio station personality to Dr. Peter Collins and Dr. Irene Bennett. After occupying the last remaining leather seat situated around the rectangular table, the friendly social worker initiated the debriefing session.

"How long have you been an area disc jockey Mr. Murphy? I sometimes catch your Friday night rock and roll show on my car's FM dial!"

"For twenty-two glorious years," the record spinner proudly answered. "I've always loved the roots of rock and roll, '50s doo-wop a-cappella street corner harmony. The big sound all started down the Jersey Shore in Wildwood with Bill Haley and His Comets combining black rhythm and blues and country and western beats into dance sensations like 'Shake, Rattle and Roll' and then later the huge explosive blockbuster that created an entirely new music era, 'Rock Around the Clock'. I gotta' tell you folks that I really like my cool radio job a lot but I make most of my dough doin' summer nightclub DJ gigs in Margate, Somers Point and Atlantic City. And as you might already know," Jack Murphy declared with a scintilla of braggadocio evident in his tone of voice, "me and another DJ from the station do three big annual oldies events at the Wildwood Convention Center. You guys oughta' all come out! I wanna' see your face in the place!"

"I suppose you make a decent living doing what you love!" Dr. Irene Bennett encouragingly asked the local radio celebrity. "Indeed, not everyone in America can say the same!"

"The last Wildwood Show was absolutely positively tremendous! It featured Little Anthony and the Imperials, the Coasters, Jay and the Americans and the Cadillacs," Jack "the Knack" Murphy ecstatically boasted. "Louie and I made more cash doin' that huge auditorium event than we did the whole rest of the year put together. Over nine thousand fans packed the place solid that night! What a venue! Ya' couldn't have squeezed another person into the jammed-packed arena with a shoehorn or a crowbar according to the grim-faced Fire Marshal in attendance that night."

The theme of the upbeat civil discussion soon switched to Rick Simon's death behind the Ford Explorer's steering wheel while Jack's SUV had been parked in his Peach Street driveway. Janet Owens was familiar with the general circumstances from a recently held lengthy telephone conversation she had initiated with the exceedingly bodacious DJ.

"Now Jack, tell us about the compact music disc you had made at the radio station for your cousin Rick!" the social worker requested. "We might want to include *that* little anecdote in closing-out Mr. Simon's hospital file. We would appreciate your cooperation in this rather bureaucratic housekeeping responsibility that incidentally, we're obligated to complete for the State."

Jack Murphy recalled and then explained how he had discovered Rick Simon slumped over behind the wheel without any pulse and how the victim's body temperature was well below the usual 98.6F level. "His face was sort of ashen-blue. I got on the horn and called the rescue squad right away and the fellas' were on the scene in five minutes. They couldn't even take Rick to the emergency room at the hospital because he obviously was dead. We had to wait for a medical doctor to come to Peach Street and make the official pronouncement."

"You had mentioned in our last phone conversation something about the special music CD you had put together at your radio studio for Mr. Simon!" Janet Owens reiterated. "Not that it's so important, but if you can Jack, give us some background about the particular selections you had included."

"Well, here it is in two pieces!" Murphy exclaimed as he slowly removed a snapped-in-half CD from his pants' pocket. "I found it layin' on the floor beside my SUV's bucket seat. I can't figure out why Rick had broken the thing in two after I had spent nearly three whole hours puttin' the really neat oldies music on it. But that odd circumstance wasn't important at the time of my cousin's heart attack so I never thought about tellin' the police or the paramedics about it."

"Possibly your cousin was holding the CD when he began having his painful heart attack and then snapped it in half before it fell onto the SUV's floor next to the bucket seat!" theorized and suggested the clear-thinking Dr. Collins. "Can we put the broken CD into your cousin's personal record file!" Dr. Collins alertly asked the visitor. "It'll be sort of a final memento and nothing more."

"Sure, I'll gladly give it to you to finish-out your study," Jack acceded. "I have no special use for a demolished CD! I only wish I could give you a whole one in cherry condition instead of these two useless fragments!"

"Now Mr. Murphy," Dr. Irene Bennett piped-up, "what songs did you arrange on the CD? I'm sort of an oldies' enthusiast myself and would like to know."

"I have a list right here and I've arranged them in the exact …."

"Chronological order of their debut on the Billboard charts?" Janet Owens interrupted.

"Yeah, that's precisely what I meant to say but couldn't think of the proper word 'chronological.' Us dumb radio DJs are basically one and two syllable guys, ya' know!"

"Okay Mr. Murphy, give us the tunes in the time order sequence you had painstakingly created," Dr. Collins insisted. "I'm beginning to become a bit spellbound myself by the mystery of exactly what songs you had chosen from the hundreds, perhaps thousands of hit oldies titles that are available."

The three mental health experts were unprepared for what Jack Murphy had in store to share with them. The "golden oldies" had been seamlessly synthesized with the theme of 'animal titles.' Bill Haley and His Comets 1956 smash 'See You Later Alligator' was first on the CD, Teresa Brewer's 1956 number 'Bo Weevil' was second, Charlie Gracie's 1957 rendition of 'Butterfly' was third, Elvis Presley's 1957 chart-buster 'Hound Dog' was listed fourth, Bobby Day's 1958 song 'Rockin' Robin' was fifth, David Seville's 1958 'The Chipmunk Song' was sixth, Billy and Lillie's 1959 version of 'Lucky Ladybug' was seventh and Chubby Checker's 'Pony Time' was presented as the number eight song on the unique 'Animal Title CD.'

"In the past I had put together other CDs for Rick with certain themes in the titles representing 'Places,' 'Things,' 'Colors,' 'Girl's Names' and 'Days of the Week,' but I figured I would do 'Animals' as the distinct theme this last time," the congenial Vineland DJ innocently divulged.

"Did your deceased cousin ever tell you about the nightmares he often had?" Dr. Bennett incredulously asked the relative of the deranged animal hater. "By *that* direct question I mean, did Rick Simon ever mention the subject matter of his bad dreams?"

"No, he often said he couldn't remember anything in detail about them!" Jack Murphy all-too-honestly answered. "I wish I had known what was botherin' him so that I could've reported it to you so that you guys here at Ancora could've helped him! Besides me, you three folks were the only people that Rick really trusted."

"What other songs were on the CD?" Janet Owens asked the affable DJ as Dr. Peter Collins and Dr. Irene Bennett stared across the table at each other in total awe and amazement.

"Well, next in the series was 'Running Bear' done in 1960 by the versatile Johnny Preston, and then Chubby Checker made the list a second time with his 1961 novelty hit 'The Fly' that he still often dances to," the radio character related to his dumbfounded listeners. "And next also from '61 happened to be the Tokens singing 'The Lion Sleeps Tonight' which was followed by Lou Monte performin' his catchy 1962 tune 'Pepino the Italian Mouse'. And oh yeah," Jack Murphy remembered and elaborated, "how could I not include the 1963 flashy hit 'Mickey's Monkey' by Smoky Robinson and the Miracles and the 1964 California sound blockbuster 'Hey Little Cobra' by the Rip*chords*, which incidentally is a nifty play-on-words with the group's stage name!"

"What were some of the more recent hit songs, like from the '70s?" the shocked Dr. Collins asked the record spinner.

Jack Murphy's eyes again gazed upon his typed song list and related artists. "The remaining tunes are 'A Horse With No Name' by America from 1972, Elton John's 'Crocodile Rock' from 1973, 'Muskrat Love' by the Captain and Tennille from 1976 and then 'Disco Duck' by Rick Dees from that same year. And let's not forget Carly Simon's '74 interpretation of 'Mockingbird' and the Steve Miller Band's 1977 dynamo 'Fly Like An Eagle', not to be outdone by either Duran Duran's 1976 wonder 'Hungry Like the Wolf' or Boy George and the Culture Club's inimitable 'Karma Chameleon'."

"Wow! That's quite a phenomenal collection of animal song titles you had assembled!" praised an astonished and impressed Janet Owens. "Are you sure you hadn't inadvertently forgotten anything?"

"Oh my Lord!" Jack Murphy realized and yelled a little too boisterously for his still shell-shocked audience. "In my rush this morning, I've failed to tell you the name of the last song on the CD that I had added at the end, and unfortunately, it kinda' totally ruined my smooth time-line arrangement. It's Elvis Presley's 1957 cute lively number '(Let Me Be Your) Teddy Bear'."

The three mental health case study professionals sat silent in their black leather chairs and could not utter a word for a full fifteen seconds. Then the usually unfazed Dr. Peter Collins gathered the strength to give Jack some last minute advice.

"Mr. Murphy, I'm sure that you detest government bureaucracy as much as *we* do," the acclaimed psychiatrist prefaced, his left hand slightly trembling as he touched it upon Jack's right shoulder. "Please make it easy on yourself. I personally think that you should remember to tell anyone from the State that might drop by your Peach Street residence inquiring about your cousin's death that Rick had died from suffering a severe coronary thrombosis. Don't volunteer any extra information about the music CD or else you'll be spending a lot of wasted time driving back and forth from Hammonton to Trenton to answer tons of unnecessary questions."

"I know exactly where you're coming from!" the amiable DJ replied, still wondering why his interrogators had pallid-looking faces. "Yes sir Dr. Collins, I know exactly where you're coming from!"

"Poetic Justice"

Every December 1st, FBI Inspector Joe Giralo proudly invites his three loyal agents Salvatore Velardi, Arthur Orsi and Daniel Blachford over to Orchard Street and into his cozy downtown Hammonton, New Jersey home to admire *his* extensive train display and accompanying elaborate village, all spectacularly exhibited on an enormous platform that vitually encompassed the man's entire downstairs "second den."

"I see that you've added several new buildings to complement your intricate Christmas hometown extravaganza," Agent Velardi noted and expressed. "I don't remember *that* dress shop and *that* yogurt and ice cream parlor on the corner ever being in the village last year. You've managed to re-create a miniature scale model of downtown Hammonton! Quite impressive indeed!"

"Thanks for the rather exaggerated kudos Salvatore!" Inspector Giralo genially replied. "Ever since I was a curious toddler I've been infatuated with model trains. This entire project has taken me seven years to complete, and all of the stores and buildings along Bellevue Avenue, Central Avenue, Horton Street along with Second and Third Street I've diligently assembled with my own two hands. The tedious labor was done right here on the premises, with all the items being assiduously built down in my workshop basement."

"I especially like the work you've done on the Post Office Building, the new Town Hall and also on the adjacent St. Joseph High School structure," Agent Orsi commended. "Your meticulous renditions are almost perfect right down to the basic not-so-familiar details! You could've been a terrific architect if you hadn't gone into the FBI."

"Look here Arty!" the now-elated Chief exclaimed, pointing with his preferred left index finger. "I even have *your* house erected over on Tilton Street, and over here is Dan's place located on Pleasant, and oh yes, here's Sal's handsome residence over on Peach."

"I didn't notice those three new additions before you brought them to my exact attention," ordinarily pensive Agent Dan Blachford articulated. "I feel quite honored having my nondescript abode represented on your fantastic town exposition. The craftsmanship is borderline magnificent. And look over there next to Sal's house on Peach Street. You've actually fabricated a tiny duplicate of ..."

"My neighbor Carmen Martino's silver and green Eagles' bus that I drive over to Philadelphia for Sunday home football games," Agent Velardi recognized and promptly declared. "Twelve other guys from Hammonton make the home game pilgrimages with me across the Delaware to 'the Link.' And of course," Inspector Giralo's loyal disciple continued prattling, "two of the season-ticket guys are Arty and Dan, and needless to say, we all enjoy munching on scrumptious barbequed Omaha steaks along with delicious burgers and grilled hot dogs while tailgating with other Eagles' fans two hours before game time."

Suddenly Chief Joe Giralo's contagious grin transformed into a somber, grim frown, which to his three alert subordinates indicated that the specific dialogue was about to change from standard casual folksy levity to serious FBI business that required their immediate addressing and professional problem-solving.

"Salvatore, I know that you've been feeling rather embarrassed lately," the Boss sympathetically indicated. "Please review for Arty and Dan's sake exactly what had transpired on your Peach Street property just a month ago, as a matter of ironic fact, occurring right on Halloween!"

Sal Velardi inhaled a healthy deep breath and then reluctantly related that for essential economic reasons, he had decided to switch his home heating system from oil to gas. The new gas heater had been professionally installed without any snag or snafu, and the subsequent pipe service extending from the street's main gas line to the house had been satisfactorily completed by the always-reliable South Jersey Gas Company. But upon the workmen excavating the old three hundred gallon metal oil tank from the lot's back yard, a truly gruesome observation had been made by the front-end loader operator, a very stark discovery that demanded the immediate services of the New Jersey State Police and the Philadelphia FBI.

"The whole thing was absolutely horrendous besides being totally humiliating for me to personally experience, certainly when happening in a small gossipy town like Hammonton!" Agent Velardi candidly reported. "The talk soon was in every local barbershop and in every hairdresser salon hours before the news ever hit the area papers or TV stations. As you Gentlemen are quite aware, I'm very environmentally conscious about the size of my 'carbon footprint,' and so I had optimistically changed from using an oil furnace and then wisely converting to gas heat. When my ancient rusty oil tank was being dug-up and removed," Velardi recalled and reviewed, "a macabre male skeleton was

472

found crushed underneath the huge oil tank's circumference. It's a good thing my wife was out grocery shopping when the fragmented remains were found. Kathy would've had a French hemorrhage even though she's Italian!"

"But Salvatore, just because you're involved in law enforcement, you shouldn't feel guilty or mortified about the rather bizarre event and the resulting negative community scuttlebutt that automatically developed thereafter! The aged oil tank had already been installed a full decade before you ever moved into your Peach Street home," Chief Giralo plausibly clarified. "The former owners of the house, Mr. and Mrs. Thomas Fallucca, both retired schoolteachers, well, the elderly couple had migrated down to Florida where they both have been deceased since 2010. Obviously, the old oil tank and the unearthed anatomy had been placed into the ground ten years before you ever purchased and occupied the dwelling."

"And the Falluccas are no doubt completely innocent of any wrongdoing and evidently, probably had nothing to do with the alleged crime that had been committed," Agent Orsi relevantly contributed to the conversation. "And furthermore, *you* Sal are simply an unfortunate victim of oddball circumstances, all compounded by unwarranted hearsay community association!"

"Well Chief," Dan Blachford anxiously chimed-in, "I suppose we'll have to separate our subjective emotions from our objective detective skills and conduct a thorough and efficient investigation into this apparent shocking local felony. As you often reiterate Boss, when villains consider themselves as being too clever to ever be apprehended, that's precisely when their tender posteriors are most vulnerable to the legendary long arm of the law."

Introspective Inspector Giralo then initiated a lengthy oral litany that entailed the nature and competence of the FBI, that described the benign forces of good ultimately triumphing over the abundance of world and national evil, and finally, the sage's profound words pontificated about how the suspected crime (that had coincidentally been finalized on Agent Velardi's placid estate) needed to be expertly delved-into "for Salvatore's ultra-sensitive reputation and for his necessary peace of mind."

"Well truthfully Boss," Agent Velardi emphatically stated and soon momentarily hesitated, "I'm looking forward to collaborating with you on cracking-open this premeditated Peach Street burial, and in all sincerity, quite frankly I do believe that it'll be far easier for us four to capture either a phantom Bigfoot or the all-too-elusive Loch Ness Monster than to decipher this very disturbing riddle that had regrettably transpired upon *my* present property over thirty long years ago!"

"You're a positive genius Salvatore!" Inspector Giralo surprisingly complimented his main assistant. "Your exquisite verbosity has just provided me with the tangible clue my tortured mind had been frantically searching for. Thanks to you, my brain has formulated a general hypothesis that's truly worthy of *our* dedicated pursuit! In fact, you might've even afforded me two distinct material ideas!"

Led by inquisitive Sal Velardi's perceptive interrogation, the other two listening agents, being somewhat confused by their Boss's characteristic, enigmatic language, requested learning more pertinent information about the dead man's identity. Inspector Giralo was fairly reasonable and obliging about sharing and conveying the newly gleaned confidential FBI data.

"The victim's name is Jake Sacco, formerly of Hammonton, who had been living in Mays Landing prior to encountering his unenviable fate," the solemn-faced Chief disclosed. "Matt Riley and his crackerjack research team down at DC headquarters were able to determine *his* ID from certain DNA evidence and then later deftly comparing the acquired info' with existing criminal records, since Mr. Jake "the Snake" Sacco had previously been arrested in Massachusetts, in Colorado and in California on assorted burglary charges. Any questions Men?"

"Then this dearly departed crook Jake Sacco was pretty itinerant!" Art Orsi concluded and verbally offered. "Now I've been hanging around you long enough Boss to study and fathom your shrewd analytic methodologies. Exactly what are our specific assignments relative to this nefarious-but-immobilized Jake Sacco fellow?"

"Salvatore, first of all I want *you* to find-out and evaluate every single iota about this thug's chequered-past," Inspector Giralo forcefully commanded. "And secondly Arty, I order that you investigate into the multiple home burglaries performed in Cambridge, Massachusetts, in Fort Collins, Colorado and in Palm Springs, California. And finally Dan," Giralo next austerely instructed Blachford, "see if you can possibly explore some other major crimes besides commonplace burglaries being enacted by our dead diabolical scoundrel, namely this mysterious cross-country wanderlust, Jake Sacco! Are my stated directions clear enough?"

"Will do Chief!" Agent Blachford readily agreed and accepted. "This exploit might amount to one of our more exciting

474

adventures! When will we be meeting again to discuss the fruits of our individual explorations?"

"How about Wednesday, December 11th for breakfast at 9 am sharp. We'll share a booth at the Silver Coin Diner. And Salvatore!" Inspector Giralo added with a contrived smile. "I expect you to drive your white Nissan Murano over to the Silver Coin and not Carmen Martino's silver and green 1981 Ford Eagles fan bus!"

* * * * * * * * * * * *

The four government men informally met inside the foyer of the Route 30 Silver Coin Diner. Inspector Giralo was an acquaintance of "Gus," the establishment's congenial proprietor, who then escorted the federal quartet to a comfortable and secluded red leather booth in the hectic eatery's back dining room. After the standard bacon, eggs, toast, home fries and coffee breakfasts had been ordered, predictably, casual small-talk and cheerful banter had to be exchanged prior to the veteran FBI officials commencing with their intended discussion about the past biography of deceased and disreputable Jake Sacco.

"Sal, I'm glad to see that you didn't drive up here from town to the White Horse Pike in Carmen Martino's green and silver Eagles bus," Chief Giralo humorously chided. "That enormous tin pig looks a little like a Farm Labor Transport vehicle, you know, what the Mexican crewleaders use to drive their hard-working pickers to the big area blueberry farms. The crewleaders have to paint the buses various colors because...."

"Because yellow buses in New Jersey exclusively mean school buses," Art Orsi abruptly interrupted. "Say Sal, do you possess a CDL to drive that two-tone monstrosity to the Sunday home football games? It's really an eyesore because my pupils hurt every time I glance at the archaic menace chugging by!"

"Yes, I had to obtain a Commercial Driver's License from the Motor Vehicle Department," blushing Salvatore Velardi admitted. "And it's even good to use across the Walt Whitman Bridge in Pennsylvania too! But Boss," Velardi blandly stated, switching his attention from Orsi to Giralo, "I want *you* to know that I *don't* also have a New Jersey crewleader's license. Perhaps when I retire from the FBI, I'll apply for one of those babies too!"

"Say Boss," Dan Blachford butted-in, desiring to change the subject to something less ludicrous than an Eagles' fan bus, "Sal, Art and I still believe that you have a particular propensity for

475

being psychic. Could you elaborate on *that* shared speculation of ours?"

"It's more an understanding of the criminal mind, and the alluded-to talent has less to do with the utilization of any noteworthy ESP phenomenon," Chief Giralo modestly lectured. "Actually, what you three students of justice interpret as being 'Psychic,' I understand as being 'Psycho.' Take the 1960 Alfred Hitchcock movie for example, you know, the one starring Anthony Perkins and Janet Leigh filmed at the sinister Bates Motel. The depraved killer was mentally disturbed; demented, so to speak. And the gullible blonde female shower victim, who was soon brutally stabbed, perceived Mr. Norman Bates' twisted personality as simply being odd, peculiar and a trifle weird. Thus she wound-up being terribly murdered by a cold-blooded maniac, never realizing until it was too late that young Mr. Bates had the emotional wherewithal to enact such a heinous act of despicable violence!"

After the courteous and accommodating auburn-hair diner waitress delivered the men's remaining food and beverage orders, gradually the topic of interest evolved from 1960 cinema fiction into the 1970s and 1980s activities of Jake Sacco in Massachusetts, in Colorado and in California. Inspector Giralo asked Agent Velardi to expound on *his* appointed aspect of the investigation.

"Well Chief, according to the police and FBI files I had accessed, this fellow Jake Sacco had a unique method of operation, basically behaving like a common everyday thief in all three states," the senior agent revealed. "First of all, the deceased was an adept locksmith who had graduated from a home instruction course under a mail-order education supplied by the National Locksmith Academy. A year after legitimately receiving his diploma," Agent Velardi accurately declared, "our un-illustrious subject worked with the Diebold Company, conscientiously inspecting and repairing safes and vaults at various Massachusetts' banks. But after turning to a life of redundant illicit acts, Mr. Jake Sacco's new devious pattern was to follow mail delivery vehicles around on rural road routes, especially ones featuring residences' having long-winding tree-shaded driveways set off from the road. Many unwary and usassuming homeowners would nonchalantly amble out to their mailboxes to retrieve their daily mail, exiting their electronic garage doors and then incidentally leaving the portals leading into

476

the houses open. And then this scheming malicious felon Jake Sacco..."

"Would pull into the person's driveway and politely ask the targeted dupe for directions," Art Orsi surmised and contributed. "Then the vile perpetrator would probably pull-out a gun or a knife and tell the startled person to enter the house. Naturally, the alarmed resident would comply with the sudden threatening command."

"Exactly," Agent Velardi concurred with Agent Orsi's random conjecture. "And after tying-up and gagging the still-stunned victim, our nasty Mr. Sacco would rob the house at his leisure, and perhaps with the aid of an accomplice, proceed to steal the victim's car keys and easily pilfer the auto' from the open garage. This relatively creative technique had been employed in all three aforementioned states, and after executing a dozen on so larcenies in each one, eventually, Jake Sacco finally settled-down in Mays Landing."

A moment of silence was sharply broken when Inspector Giralo felt inspired to make a specific lengthy inquiry that was advanced in the form of a declarative statement followed by an exclamatory sentence. "This rather fascinating punk Jake Sacco had been deliberately eliminated and consequently buried under the heavy oil tank in Sal's backyard, furtively terminated from existence, Mafia style! Surely, our Mr. Dead Locksmith must've been engaged in some other surreptitious crimes that were much more risky than him performing mere home robberies via open garage doors! Tell me, is my current assumption correct Dan?"

"Yes, and your insightful comment Chief has directly led to *my* segment of *our* now-complicated multi-state federal investigation," Blachford suavely and diplomatically answered. "I've discovered that this tricky creep Jake Sacco came into contact with the dreaded National Mafia Network, and the greedy neurotic jerk began pilfering jewelry and cash from various millionaires' luxurious mansions in Cambridge, Massachusetts, in Fort Collins, Colorado and in Palm Springs, California. Using his versatile locksmith skills," Blachford continued his pertinent narrative, "cunning Jake "the Snake" deftly manufactured a variety of keys used to gain easy entrance into any designated home or business. The determined trespasser even learned how to dismantle and deactivate burglar alarms, either silent ones or otherwise, and the brazen intruder also was remarkably adroit at neutralizing sophisticated house video cameras along with special home connections to local police stations."

The four government men then conversed about how Jake "the Snake" Sacco had to wear thin plastic or rubber gloves while purloining expensive items from selected mansions in order to stealthily avoid leaving any trace of fingerprint residue, and the four sleuths also considered and related how the slippery felon had to deal with electronic sensors on garage doors that were specifically designed to stop the remote-control objects from fully descending when detecting an obstacle or human form nearby or underneath, thus remaining only half closed to motorists or pedestrians' scrutiny from the nearby street or highway.

"In the case of typical electronic garage door sensors," Sal Velardi reckoned and orally offered, "I suspect that by Mr. Sacco, being an accomplished scheming locksmith, the wily culprit would simply manufacture a house key and then, being able to lock the front or side door, the astute rogue could slickly abandon the targeted mansion unscathed and undetected, that is, if he and a helper didn't plan on also thieving the best available car from the garage."

"But why did the almighty Mafia have Jake Sacco suddenly disappear from the face of the Earth?" Art Orsi wondered and asked. "Did the small-potatoes' locksmith betray any big Philly' or New York City Dons? I mean Fellas', loyalty to evil practices and to the awesome Mob Bosses and their formidable Lieutenants is what keeps absolute discipline alive among the syndicate's ranks! Any noticeable deviation leads to severe reprisal, and ultimately, even a painful death by execeution! Jake Sacco must've known how dangerous it is to fool around with Sicilean fire!"

"Arty, stop your annoying plagiarizing! That's precisely Part II of my intensive Case Summary," Dan Blachford impetuously insisted. "This dead punk Jake Sacco had a reputation for being a Casanova, a habit which turned-out to be *his* principal Achilles Heel. After becoming romantically connected with three separate debutantes in Massachusetts, in Colorado and in California respectively, our dear Mr. Sacco quickly and independently fled those triple locations, his progress swiftly leaving behind three female corpses. Jake was thrice arrested for the brutal murders, but the district attorneys in all three states were unable to convict the clever felon, simply for the lack of non-circumstantial crime scene evidence. Thus," Agent Blachford concluded his graphic revelation, "our man Jake was labeled by local and state authorities as being 'a person of interest' for nearly thirty years until his recent skeletal discovery deep inside Sal's new lawn pit. But the pathetic thug's female victims were all found lying dead

478

inside their homes with all of the doors and windows locked, and now we've learned precisely how the three murdered women had been egregiously eradicated with *their* house keys discovered inside their mansions! Obviously, Mr. Sacco easily duplicated the master keys!"

"Chief, do you think that the vindictive Cosa Nostra guys are really the ones that had our subject murdered?" Art Orsi requested knowing. "This entire Peach Street episode has the markings of gangland activity, no doubt about it! Messing with the mob will more than put someone in jeopardy. It'll send the recipient to a premature grave in Sal's backyard cemetery!"

"Well Arty, I would respond to your sagacious Mafia theory by saying both 'yes and no'," Inspector Giralo very coyly replied. "I had told Salvatore that either Bigfoot or the Loch Ness Monster had given me a definite hunch to further assess events. I've already acknowledged to you my original suspicion about the title Loch Ness Monster, my initial reasoning alluding to the Locksmith Academy and then your mentioning that Jake Sacco had been functioning as an experienced house robber and locksmith."

"Now Boss, what is the second obscure hypothesis that the terms Bigfoot and Loch Ness Monster had elicited your dynamic mind to create?" Agent Blachford boldly questioned his immediate superior. "How are those two special nomenclatures even again remotely germane to our present investigation?"

Chief Giralo slowly swallowed-down the last ounce of his tasty coffee and then quite clearly announced, "Gentlemen, this dastardly-but-crafty dead villain Jake "the Snake" Sacco even was able to construct his own .38 caliber bullets to cruelly kill his three unfortunate rich lovemates. Now Men, your next important bit of homework is to thoroughly read and fully comprehend the classic poem 'Lochinvar,' authored by the distinguished Sir Walter Scott. Now I'm fully confident that *that* piece of popular poetic literature will automatically steer us in the direction of Mr. Sacco's unscrupulous criminal motive, of his advantageous criminal opportunity and of the mob's eventual lethal retribution."

"Logically, maniacal Jake Sacco lived by the pistol and probably, also died by the pistol. That in my estimation is dramatic poetic justice, either with or without 'Lochinvar' ever coming into play. Now then Boss, when will we meet again?" Sal Velardi assertively asked his well-respected mentor. "I hope our next scheduled conclave doesn't interfere with the upcoming Eagles game!"

479

"We'll meet in my Arch Street office at 9 am on Wednesday, December 18th," Inspector Joe Giralo conveyed, recording the date and time into his trusty hand-held computer. "By then I predict that Matt Riley and I should have this entire case successfully wrapped-up and documented."

Agents Sal Velardi, Art Orsi and Dan Blachford could only simultaneously sit there inside their Silver Coin Diner red leather booth, instinctively shrugging their broad shoulders and mutually staring blankly and incredulously at one another in total disbelief.

* * * * * * * * * * * *

At 9 am on Wednesday, December 18th, 2013 a rather fatigued FBI Inspector Joe Giralo seemed abnormally unprepared to eagerly commiserate with his three prime Quaker City agents, Salvatore Velardi, Arthur Orsi and Dan Blachford, who had punctually arrived inside the Chief's eighth floor office, situated inside the all-too-mundane 600 Arch Street Federal Building, downtown Philadelphia, Pennsylvania.

As usual, the curious entrants found their all-too-conspicuous administrator sitting rather comfortably behind his prodigious Canadian oak desk with his large brown eyes seemingly in a self-induced daze, his pupils vaguely scanning the *Philadelphia Inquirer's* morning headlines. The Inspector's ever-vigilant mind was keenly immersed in the process of genuinely contemplating much more challenging crime scenarios than *those* lackluster news' stories that his enviable cerebrum had been correspondingly evaluating.

"Hi Boss," Agent Velardi politely greeted, methodically breaking Inspector Giralo's deep dual concentration. "How about lunch later today at Maggiano's Little Italy over on Filbert Street, you know, the popular fancy restaurant across from the Reading Train Terminal Food Market."

"Sure beats brunch at the corner Dunkin' Donuts!" Agent Orsi opined. "And Boss, the Maggiano's four-cheese ravioli entree is vintage Sicilean. I'd recommend the delectable meal to anyone, even to non-Italians like Blachford here!"

"I prefer good old spaghetti and meatballs," vociferated an already hungry Dan Blachford. "And may I also suggest the traditional Maggiano's family-style salad bowl. That tempting delight is enough to gratify all four of our enormous appetites!"

"Okay Gentlemen," Chief Giralo cooperatively agreed with his always-famished three-member panel. "I'll wholeheartedly

480

endorse Salvatore's sensational recommendation, that is, only if we also enjoy consuming the home-baked luscious cheesecake and fresh-brewed coffee for dessert."

Satisfied that the customary preliminary small-talk had been adequately dispensed with, Chief Giralo maintained that his three underlings should academically explain the essence and the meaning of Sir Walter Scott's romantic poem, "Lochinvar."

Sal Velardi related that Lochinvar had been a young ambitious cavalier who decided to intrepidly enter the castle of a powerful queen and king and quickly demand permission to marry the kingdom's beloved royal princess.

Next, Art Orsi noted that the king and queen were extremely appalled at the obnoxious suitor's urgent request, the unsolicited declaration coming from a bold, insolent wet-behind-the-ears quixotic knight. And then Dan Blachford aptly summarized the story's culmination by citing that Lochinvar avariciously gathered-up the beautiful princess and next, the merry couple, in a wild frenzy, escaped from the ornate throne room seconds before any summoned guards could ever thwart *their* exciting elopement.

"And so Fellas'," Chief Giralo remarked and then paused, "this callow-but-stubborn knight Lord Lochinvar was indeed a sort of medieval gigolo, much like our more contemporary amorous Don Juan, the deceased Jake Sacco had been three decades ago. That rather glaring similarity between the two connivers appears to be a most intriguing parallel being represented here!"

"Alright Boss, I get the significant connections," Sal Velardi ascertained. "Loch Ness Monster, locksmith, Lochinvar! But why did the Mafia rub-out Jake the Snake? Did the itinerant gigolo accidentally double-cross somebody big?"

"For the past several weeks Matt Riley and I have intensely examined the matter and our combined effort finally figured-out the true scope and sequence of meaningful events," Joe Giralo confided. "This amorous-minded gigolo/rogue Jake Sacco had been secretly courting the daughter of a wealthy South Jersey oil baron, Mr. Pasquale Rinaldi, whose prosperous company was centrally based down in Cape May Court House, just outside of Stone Harbor. Anyway," garrulous Joe Giralo resumed his impressive monologue, "the wealthy Mr. Rinaldi didn't savor the ugly notion of a common proletarian flirting with his favorite daughter, and so good old Pasquale, who had certain strong Mafia associations with the ruthless Philly' syndicate, conveniently had dear Mr. Sacco erased right off the planet and propelled right into the hereafter. And much to my satisfaction, the Washington FBI had no difficulty in pinpointing the South Jersey financier of the mob hit by virtue of...."

"By virtue of the Rinaldi Oil Company insignia that had been painted onto the bulky oil tank recently excavated from my own backyard!" Agent Velardi realized and loudly exclaimed. "I now recall seeing the grimy corporate logo on the oil tank's side but thought nothing of it at the time that the metal container was being removed!"

"Do we now arrest and prosecute Mr. Pasquale Rinaldi for authorizing and subsidizing the murder of Jake Sacco?" Art Orsi asked. "I must confess Boss that I do have more than a little mercy and empathy for the venerable elderly aristocrat."

"Such a law enforcement response is completely unnecessary," Joe Giralo respectfully advised. "Mr. Pasquale Rinaldi and his wife Ethel both passed away in 2007, and the pair are buried in the Cape May Court House Cemetery, and so Men," the Boss elucidated with a wide grin, "we can't hold our oil baron suspect responsible for the wicked murder of Jake Sacco, a grisly act surgically performed nearly thirty years ago."

"The mob's hit-men that had committed the barbaric crime are probably also dead too! And thanks to Sir Walter Scott's poetry," Sal Velardi expressed, "unlike the very lucky Dark Ages' rascal knight Lochinvar, our ill-fated Jake Sacco along with the very rich Pasquale Rinaldi did not in the end get off *scot-free* from Next World *heavenly* poetic justice!"

"Sal's right Boss," Art Orsi enunciated, verifying Sal Velardi's keen observation. "With Jake Sacco and Pasquale Rinaldi both dead, it's all sort of like a basic mathematical equation where no common denominator exists after both main factors have been efficiently canceled-out!"

"Einstein couldn't have said it any better," commended Agent Blachford. "The whole formerly complex case is now reduced to a simple veritable wash!"

"But Salvatore, without your knowledge, another perplexing dilemma has recently surfaced in the interim," Inspector Giralo informed his momentarily-euphoric assistant. "This new debacle directly concerns your admirable Philadelphia Eagles' bus neighbor, Mr. Carmen Martino."

"What about Carmen?" Sal Velardi asked with instant anxiety. "Is my good friend injured or hospitalized?"

"Carmen's perfectly okay! Your highly-valued football game amigo had recently contacted South Jersey Gas," the amused

482

Inspector calmly answered. "But your good pal heard that you had switched your home heating system from oil to gas, so Carmen soon contacted South Jersey Gas and had his own line installed and attached to his new cellar heater."

"So what's so incredible or extraordinary about *that* rather mediocre information?" Agent Velardi cynically responded. "Imitation is the sincerest form of flattery', isn't it?"

"Yeah Boss! Let's just focus on relishing our Italian feast over at Maggiano's!" Art Orsi constructively suggested. "I relish pasta even more than I relish ballpark hot dogs!"

"I endorse Art's very intelligent culinary proposal!" Agent Blachford uttered. "Even though I'm a mixture of British and Irish, it's almost time for gobbling-down tasty Italian appetizers!"

"Maybe so!" Chief Giralo indulgently laughed. "But astonishingly enough my dear Salvatore, another anonymous skeleton has since been discovered, the fresh skull and bones being entrenched beneath the Rinaldi Oil Company tank just excavated on Mr. Carmen Martino's Peach Street backyard property. Yes indeed Agent Velardi, it looks like we're all back to the proverbial drawing board and all-too-familiar square one again!"

"Ten Options"

Ever since first grade back in 1949 Ken Keller had aspired to be a Major League pitcher. His father Karl had instilled *that* unrealistic dream in Ken's head. In 1973 Ken Keller had effectively passed-on the love of baseball in general and of pitching in particular to his son Kyle, who in turn in 2009 had effectively conveyed the "family infatuation with baseball" to *his* eleven-year-old son Keith. But the sixty-seven year old retired plumber Ken Keller had never told his son Kyle or his grandson Keith why *he* and his deceased dad Karl had a certain fondness for alliteration using the letter K.

In 1974 Ken Keller inherited his small King Lane Hammonton, New Jersey ranch home a month after his father Karl had passed away. In 1977 Ken's second wife Katherine had also died, leaving the lonely man feeling very disconsolate. But the melancholy widower always kept his well-fertilized lawn properly maintained and Ken was especially proud of the many splendid ewe, rhododendron, rose and hydrangea bushes nestled around his home that were meticulously kept trimmed and looking healthy all summer long. Just the day before Ken had heard an envious neighbor bending the mailman's ear, "Keller's mulch right down to the last black bark chip always appears to be in the exact ideal spot where the little chunk had first been placed. That guy's too much of a perfectionist to suit me!"

'In just five minutes Kyle is going to be dropping off Keith so that *we* can work on the boy's pitching,' Ken remembered as he placed his electric hedge trimmer onto its rightful pegboard prong inside his neat and tidy outside garage. 'This afternoon is my grandson's first Little League game of the season and he's slated to be the starting pitcher. I'll bet Keith's all excited about trying to get his first big win under his belt. Here's my son Kyle now pulling alongside the curb delivering my grandson Keith for *his* pitching lesson, and I can't believe they're right on time.'

"Hi Dad!" Kyle yelled out the driver-side window of his two-year-old mint green Nissan Altima sedan. "I'm goin' to head on over to Al and Rich's and get my car washed and buy a tank of gas. I should be back to pick Keith up in a half an hour. That'll give you enough time to show your totally spoiled grandson a couple of important grips on the ball and how to throw a two seamed fastball and a baffling change-up." And after disclosing those facts to a smiling Ken Keller and after Keith was safely out of the automobile and had slammed the passenger-side front door shut, Kyle Keller gently stepped on the accelerator and headed south in the direction of town.

"Hi Grand-pop!" Keith yelled as he ran up to greet Ken Keller while very carelessly carrying two baseball mitts and a new hard ball. "Let's get started with our game of catch!"

"Good idea!" Ken readily agreed. "We'll go have our little exchange in the rear of your great-grandfather's old tool-shed located right behind the garage. I've already marked off the correct distance from a little mound I've custom-installed just for you and I've also constructed an official-looking home plate that's exactly forty-six-feet away from the authentic-looking pitcher's rubber."

"Grand-pop, are ya' gonna' waste a lot of time this afternoon telling me all about those dead guys like Babe Ruth, Lou Gehrig, Ty Cobb, Chuck Klein and Joe DiMaggio like you always do?" Keith wondered and asked. "I'm tired of hearin' about all those old-timers and how great they were."

"Well Keith," Ken Keller said as the two eventually made their way around the corner of the garage, "your great-grandfather Karl loved those famous players of his day back in the late 1920s, the 1930s and the 1940s. You even have some of *my* valuable baseball trading cards in your big collection," the grandfather reminded the talkative lad. "They're worth plenty of money now. But if you prefer not talkin' about the great stars of the past, I'll chat with you about anything you want as long as the subject involves baseball."

"Okay then," Keith replied as the pair finally reached the vicinity of the well-manicured facsimile Little League mound, "why do all our names begin with a K? There's you and dad and me and my younger brother Kevin. What's with all the dumb Ks?"

"Well Keith, I'm gonna' tell you a major family secret," Ken Keller promised and winked. "When your great-grandfather Karl was alive, he loved going to Big League baseball games in Philadelphia and New York and was thrilled to watch the great hurlers of that era pitch. And according to a story he once told me, he absolutely loved the letter K, which for a long time has been a symbol at baseball games signifying a strikeout," Ken Keller lectured and explained. "That's why even today some loyal fans will hang a new large K sign over a bleacher railing each time their favorite home team pitcher strikes out a player from the opposing squad!"

486

"Wow!" Keith exclaimed with genuine admiration. "Now I got a great new story to tell my teammates on DiDonato's Bowling."

"Ironically Keith, back in 1953 when I was your age I too played in the Hammonton Little League, but it was on the Exchange Club team, which incidentally later became DiDonato's Bowling' in 1954. Then for two whole summers I had been away from New Jersey and lived with my Uncle Kent where I worked on his Pennsylvania dairy farm and as you might've learned from your dad, Uncle Kent also loved baseball. Well, to make a long story short," Ken Keller said to his grandson, "I had played in the Hammonton Little League in 1953, and as you probably know, Hammonton had won the Little League World Series in Williamsport in 1949. But in 1955, I played on a very good Bucks County Little League All-Star squad that was beaten in a close game by an awesome Morrisville, Pa. team that eventually went on to Williamsport, and like Hammonton had done in 1949, Morrisville won the Little League World Series in 1955."

"Geez! Now I have two new really terrific stories to tell my goofy teammates!" Keith gleefully yelled.

After giving his grandson the brief Little League history lesson, the grandfather then held the brand new baseball in his right hand and deftly demonstrated the fastball and the change-up grips. Keith then assumed his position on the simulated Little League mound and Mr. Ken Keller soon crouched down behind the home plate that he had manufactured (along with the pitcher's rubber) in his home's basement. Two standard-sized chalk-outlined rectangles on either side of home plate had been perfectly drawn to represent the common left and right-hand hitters/batters' boxes. The impromptu catch between the two quickly intensified as Keith's arm became more limbered-up. Gradually the velocity of the boy's pitches increased to the ordinary Little League speed level.

"That's the way Keith!" Ken urged and complimented. "Your control is just fine! Now this time really show me your blazing fastball! Buzz it right into my glove Keith! Try to knock the mitt off my hand!"

The grandson let loose with a wicked fastball that was way wide and high of the catcher's target. The errant ball smashed into the old wooden tool-shed's back wall and was instantly lodged inside a partially rotted piece of wood. Ken used all of his strength but couldn't remove the embedded baseball from its unusual location so the determined man pushed the object through the surrounding wood where it promptly plopped down onto an old work counter that hadn't been used since 1974.

"I guess that lost ball concludes our little routine workout," the grandfather told the now-disappointed pitcher. "I don't even know where the key is to get inside your great-grandfather's dingy old work shed. He never mentioned to me what he was mysteriously manufacturing inside but Uncle Kent had once told me that my Dad was workin' on a perpetual motion machine involving metal springs. But a couple of mechanical engineers came here one day to test the apparatus and informed *my* Pop that revolving metal springs eventually will be affected by natural resistance and would in time stop moving."

"There's Dad blowin' his horn in the driveway!" Keith yelled, interrupting Ken Keller's nostalgic perpetual motion machine story. "See ya' at the game Grand-pop! Thanks for showin' me how to grip the ball! We're playin' Varga's Drugs under the lights tonight and I'll try and pitch a no hitter for you! And I'll try to throw more change-ups than fastballs!"

After the fickle grandson scampered around the side of the garage to be reunited with his father, Ken Keller decided to attempt retrieving the brand new baseball from its interior position, the white object situated on the ancient tool-shed's work counter. The baseball hunter slowly removed some splintery pieces of rotted lumber, thus enlarging the hole caused by the off-course baseball. Upon looking downward through the newly formed cavity, Keller could clearly see the circular white sphere, but quite curiously, wedged directly between the workbench and the tool-shed's back wall was a lustrous pulsating second object.

Being very intrigued and fascinated, Ken Keller carefully maneuvered his right hand downward inside the six-inch wide crevice, his arm penetration going all the way up to his shoulder, and by a stroke of good luck, the searcher had successfully grasped the bright 'thing' with his palm and fingers. 'My father loved baseball so much!' Ken recalled. 'He liked to invent things but seldom shared the nature of his projects with anyone. But besides baseball, the only other thing he really enjoyed doing was reading books on medieval alchemy; however, he seldom talked about *that* odd hobby of his!'

Superstitious Ken had never sheared-off the lock to the old abandoned workroom out of deference to *his* fond memories of Mr. Karl Keller. Upon successfully removing the glowing purple round mass from inside the dilapidated tool-shed, the senior-citizen baseball enthusiast was both startled and amazed at what his backyard exploration had discovered: a fabulous talking orb!

"You have by sheer accident found me and activated my wondrous powers!" the still-pulsating purple orb said. "Listen to and follow my instructions to the letter in the exact order that I shall prescribe. First, take me into your house. Then write down on a piece of paper ten unfortunate events in your life that had made you unhappy. Next, light-up your fireplace and burn the paper containing the ten unfortunate memories, for if you do so in a timely manner, the ten negative events will certainly be amended and corrected. Next, carry me' back to your father's tool-shed and deposit me directly down into the exact same space where you had found me. After performing *that* elementary task, get the recently displaced baseball out of its location upon the workbench. again using your long right arm. Finally, repair the hole in the shed's back wall and paint the new wood the same shade of white so that the entire back side looks uniform. Upon finishing that simple work detail, go directly into your home's spare room and be prepared to witness the changes to your life that you presently wish could have been modified. Now then Mr. Kenneth Keller, are there any relevant questions that pertain to what you must do?"

"How long do I have to complete those chores you've just specified?" Keller nervously asked the fantastic sphere, his hands trembling as he anxiously held the magic orb.

"Until six tonight, an hour before your grandson's first baseball game. Now transport me inside your house so that you can copy down the ten events in your life that you desire to see changed. That is all. There will be no further communication!"

* * * * * * * * * * * *

Ken Keller had always been apprehensively cautious when it came to things like palmistry, voodoo, black magic and alchemy, so the anxious recipient of the unearthly orb's predictions labored feverishly, diligently fulfilling the strange commands of the peculiar-but-spectacular purple pulsating oracle. At 5:58 p.m. the exhausted obedient grandfather entered the ranch home's spare room, sat down in one of two identical recently reupholstered rocking chairs (that he had inherited from his father Karl's estate) and stared blankly at the empty white wall situated on the other side of the polished hardwood floor's Oriental rug. 'Thank goodness the orb is safely back inside the tool shed. There used to be some small old family photographs on that opposite wall but I took them down several years ago, removed them from their frames and put them in an album I presently keep on a shelf in the den,' the fidgety man recollected.

At precisely 6 p.m. a short-worded paragraph appeared on the formerly blank white spare room wall and strangely enough, the uncanny message had been authored in the deceased Karl Keller's distinctive handwriting: "My beloved son. Here's what would have happened to the ten incidents you wished you could have altered in your life. Just pretend you are viewing an old silent film in Technicolor, for there will be no audio but only a sequence of visual representations for your eager eyes to behold. Please don't be afraid. Sit back in your favorite rocker and fully comprehend what would have happened should you had made other choices or decisions at critical junctures in your past."

'This is all really pretty eerie!' Ken restlessly imagined as his eyes glanced around the spare room, the same room where Karl Keller had been found dead lying under his bed's blanket and sheet. 'And how could anything be projected onto the wall without a movie projector? It defies explanation! It's as if the paragraph image was being sent from *inside* the wall! This arcane experience is definitely far beyond either alchemy or Merlin's science! It must have something to do with Dad's secret tinkering inside the old work-shed!'

The first scene in the totally bizarre newsreel showed a sad-faced eighteen-year-old Kenneth Keller sitting in the Hammonton High School Auditorium during his class's graduation ceremony. 'I had failed Chemistry and back then, a senior couldn't sit on the stage if he or she had failed one major subject. I couldn't graduate with my class and that distasteful memory has affected my confidence ever since that humiliating 1960 June evening. My first wish on the list was to attend St. Joseph High instead of Hammonton High so that I could be spared the indignity and disgrace of not graduating with my class.' The alternate reality soon replaced the disturbing public school memory evident and graphically exhibited on the opposite wall. Ken was again portrayed sitting in a large hall, but this time as an audience member physically present inside the St. Joseph gymnasium/auditorium because the poor science student had failed Physics. 'It's a wash! Only the curriculum subjects failed and the schools attended have changed but the results would have been identical!' Keller realized and evaluated. 'I should have not fooled around so much my senior year in Mr. Duncan's Chemistry

490

class and I should've been more cooperative and mature. And in the final analysis, I should've taken more responsibility for my lack of motivation and should not have blamed the strict teacher for my own miserable shortcoming.'

The unpleasant second scene presented in the true-to-life personalized supernatural video featured Ken as an eighteen-year-old driver losing control of his vehicle while speeding around a bend on Winslow Road and then violently smashing into an oak tree. 'I had suffered a broken right arm while heading to Williamstown to meet a hot girlfriend!' Keller's mind accurately rehashed. 'I should've been less rambunctious and impetuous!' In the soon-to-follow alternate reality the in-a-hurry impatient 'main character' was parked at a gas pump at a White Horse Pike service station and blowing his horn to attract the attention of an already occupied service attendant. A not-too-bright auto' mechanic spontaneously backed a '55 green and white Chevrolet out of the car repair bay and in an instant unnecessarily crashed into Keller's 'baby blue '54 Ford, the hard impact injuring Ken's left ankle and wrist. The youth was seen upon the white wall screen managing to escape the damaged vehicle just before the engine caught on fire and a minute before the alert gas station owner dashed out of his office with a fire extinguisher and expertly quelled the minor blaze before it ignited the fuel in the gas pumps. 'The alternative outcome at the gas station was even worse than me smashing into the huge oak tree on Winslow Road!' the now-repentant Keller concluded. 'I was better off breaking my arm in the Winslow Road speeding accident!'

The third regrettable past event showed Ken being arrested in the winter of 1964 by Sergeant Hank Rinaldi of the Hammonton Police Department for the possession of marijuana stashed under the front seat of his '54 Ford. In the alternative surreal white wall rendition Ken witnessed himself being taken into custody by two New Jersey State policemen for foolishly selling cocaine to minors. 'It's a good thing I was caught with possession of marijuana back in 1964 by Hank Rinaldi or else I could've been a hostage to a very dangerous life of crime while evilly distributing heavy duty drugs to gullible high school kids and quickly getting deeply involved with the wrong people,' the remorseful man mulled over in his now-guilty mind. 'If it weren't for good old Sergeant Rinaldi, I could still be sitting in a state penitentiary right this minute rather than seated in this family heirloom rocking chair.'

The fourth reality tableau graphically projected onto the opposite wall showed Ken getting married in St. Joseph Catholic Church on North Third Street to the beautiful Karen LeFevre, who four years later filed for divorce after being wooed and courted by a wealthy shopping center developer. 'That bad-judgment 1970 event was an ugly episode in my life that nearly destroyed my ego!' the stubborn remote spectator to *his* own failed marital vows being exchanged reckoned. 'The only positive aspect of *that* frustrating and strained abbreviated relationship was Kyle's birth.' In the subsequent *fantasy* motion picture representation being communicated from the opposite wall, Ken viewed (with growing discomfort) himself being wed in the Williamstown Lutheran Church to the then rather attractive Kristen Lambert, a consummate flirt who later became a bisexual prostitute that preferred short romantic adventures with lesbians over lucrative one night stands with eager-to-pay men. 'I understand now that things could always be worse than they had seemed at the time!' Keller pragmatically theorized. 'And my first wife Karen LeFevre was like a saint when compared to the repulsive adult sexual misbehavior of Kristen Lambert. The major mistakes in my life could've been even bigger dilemmas if I had made other even more unwise choices involving attractive dysfunctional women. Beauty is only skin deep! Thank God I later met and married dear Katherine!'

The fifth negative memory that the hard luck man's eyes scrutinized (being reflected upon the opposite white wall) was of himself attempting to get rich quick investing thirty thousand dollars his rich Aunt Martha had left in her will to her "favorite nephew" in October of '77. 'There I am like a complete idiot investing the whole windfall in a penny stock as part of a doomed scheme that dominated my thinking. But the weakly-founded tip I had received from a distant relative was based on erroneous information and I eventually wound-up blowing away all but five thousand dollars of the entire generous bonanza. If only I could've been more rational and more uncompromising!' In the substitute 1977 scenario conveniently provided by the now-mystical white wall, Ken had poorly invested the thirty thousand dollar surprise inheritance in a Wildwood motel located a block off the highly trafficked boardwalk but *that* risky investment went sour and the entire amount was easily lost when three better and larger motels were built the following summer on the same block as the older facility owned by Ken and his three not-too-brilliant business partners. 'A fool and his money are soon parted!' Keller lamented,

492

his vacillating emotions languishing in his heart's ever-expanding grief.

In the sixth wall setting (of a cold morning in early December of 1981) Kenneth Keller was depicted falling out of a tree because the deer stand on which he had been perched upon suddenly collapsed. 'I was alone in a secluded section of Wharton State Forest up near Atsion Lake,' the viewer recollected. 'I became disoriented in the dense woods and suffered temporary loss of memory. Luckily two hunters came across me and took me to Kessler Hospital. Otherwise I might've perished in the woods right there and then.' The alternative visual rendition showed Ken Keller again tumbling from the flimsy deer stand but this time suffering severe trauma from a head concussion. He was pictured staggering through the forest, limping and experiencing life-threatening hypothermia and debilitating frostbite. A New Jersey game warden miraculously encountered the disabled hunter and heroically salvaged Keller from certain death.

The seventh scene was just as alarming as the sixth. In 1983 Kenneth Keller was swimming in the ocean just to the south of the Ocean City, New Jersey Music Pier when he felt terrible cramps in his abdomen and legs. Two alert lifeguards came to his rescue just before the in-trouble swimmer was about to have a wave slam his body into a pier piling. In the alternate 1983 reality, Ken was making his third solo skydiving attempt and jumping from a small plane in the direction of an open field just north of the Hammonton Airport. An unexpected wind swiftly conducted the novice parachutist in the direction of Paradise Lakes, a campground off of *Route 206* that is completely surrounded by a neck of the Wharton State Forest. The scene culminated with the audacious Keller being removed from a tree limb and then being carried on a stretcher into the rear compartment of an awaiting Hammonton ambulance. 'I was better off nearly drowning in the *Atlantic*!' the distraught witness to his 'fraught with hazards' biography inferred. 'I remember being extremely embarrassed being pulled to the beach and being aware of having artificial respiration being administered. But I suppose swallowing a mouthful of salt water is preferable to being severely injured crashing headfirst into several tall pine trees.'

In the eighth wall-generated incident reviewing Kenneth Keller's accident-laden past, the former high school athlete was playing defensive halfback in a 1985 union workers' flag football game. The out-of-shape plumber had the misfortune of dislocating the thumb of his left hand while endeavoring to separate the two

493

yellow flags from the hip belt of the opposing team's fullback. 'That immense pain was excruciating!' Ken remembered as he cringed in the revered rocking chair he was occupying. 'Kyle was right! I should've known my limitations and never should have participated in *that* physically demanding contest.' In the revised 1985 'pinch-hitting occurrence,' Ken Keller was flashing around the back-court of the Hammonton High gym playing defense in a charity fund-raising basketball game when he had the poor judgment of getting too close to an aggressive offensive player controlling the ball, and the all-too-vigilant frisky guard caught an elbow to the mouth and was coincidentally knocked unconscious. In the following continuation alternative scene Ken was shown to himself seated in a dentist's chair with six of his extracted teeth having been deposited into the oral surgeon's tray.

The ninth incident from the already incinerated written list had Kenneth Keller standing calmly in a convenience store line in February of 1990 when he was caught off-guard and rudely accosted by an armed robber pointing a handgun at the cashier and at him. 'That chance confrontation cost me three hundred dollars from my wallet. I was an absolute imbecile to stupidly enter the Fairview Avenue and *Route 30* WaWa to purchase a candy bar and a newspaper right after leaving the local bank. I suppose I was a human example proving the popular adage, 'Wrong time and wrong place'!' In the consecutive 1990 replacement event, Ken was being savagely stabbed with a knife after handing over four hundred dollars to an ungrateful pair of viperous muggers in the Locust and 10th Street Subway Station in center city Philadelphia. 'I knew I should've stayed in Jersey for my diabetes treatment instead of traveling alone on mass transit to Jefferson Hospital,' Ken assessed. 'Wait a cotton-pickin' minute! That brutal subway assault I just witnessed never occurred in real life! The violence was total fantasy! It only could've happened as a hypothetical option to me being held hostage at gunpoint at the Fairview Avenue WaWa!'

In the tenth and final alteration of past reality, the bad-luck plumber was portrayed in July of 1992 helping his parsimonious cousin Kris move *his* furniture and personal possessions from *his* expensive home in Malvern outside Philadelphia's Main Line to his newly acquired fancy shore residence in Margate, New Jersey. Upon leaping down from a borrowed stake body truck, Ken Keller's diamond-studded ring (conspicuously worn on the third finger of his left hand) became caught on one of the modified pickup truck's pipe supports and the entire finger was painfully

494

yanked from its socket. As the opposite wall video viewer took a glimpse down at his hand missing the important finger, the in-progress wall phenomenon projected-out its next 1992 alternate action-oriented illustration. Ken was shown upon the white wall video helping a peach farmer friend in need of summer help fill thirty-eight pound bushels of fresh fruit from a sorting station on the loud machine's packing line. Keller's left hand inadvertently became caught in a rotating pulley and was instantaneously sheered-off at the wrist. The neurotic viewer grimaced in pain in reaction to his vulnerable mind digesting the imaginary horrible catastrophe that had never occurred.

After taking a deep breath to reconstruct his spirit and again appreciate his regular and predictable June of 2009 reality, the mentally disheveled baseball connoisseur looked directly ahead, staring bewilderingly at the blank white wall situated on the opposite side of the spare room. 'I was never good at coping with adversity!' Ken sadly acknowledged. 'Patience is a virtue in which I've always been lacking!'

* * * * * * * * * * * *

Ken Keller switched his mental concentration from the ordinary white wall to the twin rocking chair that was positioned directly to his right. A transparent two-dimensional ghost of Mr. Karl Keller was perceived sitting and holding a three-D baseball and a pair of 3-D baseball gloves. The ominous-looking macabre visitor was peering directly at his very terrified son.

"I guess you're wondering what this little meeting is all about?" the ghastly specter spoke without his mouth or lips ever moving. "I know the exact location of a heavenly place where you and I can enjoy a nice long catch, just like we used to have! Yes, that'll be our next rendezvous!"

"You mean my time has come?" Ken neurotically asked. "What's this weird séance all about anyway?"

"One mundane question at a time!" insisted the fairly spooky apparition. "Do you remember the last time we had a catch in back of the old tool-shed behind the garage?"

"Why yes!" Ken stammered and then hesitated. "I do remember now. I was throwing you pitches and then one fast ball got away and…."

"And the ball got stuck in the workshop's wooden wall!" Karl's shade said. "After you left to go to the bathroom I tried extracting the baseball. It accidentally fell inside where my eyes noticed a glowing purple orb, the same orb I had been working on perfecting for two whole decades. And it just so happened by coincidence that you've recently discovered that same magical object."

"Then you really weren't a demented charlatan practicing all that crazy tool-shed alchemy as the nosy neighbors all suspected and gossiped," Ken marveled and stated. "You really were a great inventor after all!"

"No Son, I wasn't any delusional charlatan. I suppose I was more like a misguided wizard than a great inventor. But someday Kyle will come across the glowing orb and then be able to join us for a merry three-way catch!" Karl Keller predicted and promised. "And maybe sixty or seventy years later Keith will also join *our* illustrious baseball company. We'll then have our family infield completed!"

"But what if the tool-shed is no longer there? What if it's been knocked down by a hurricane or by a bulldozer? How could you be so sure about the future?"

"Place and space have nothing to do with it!" the ashen-faced haunter insisted. "When the proper time arrives, Kyle will discover the purple orb anywhere that *we* shall designate. Is that fact perfectly clear?"

"Yes Father! I think it is now perfectly clear!" Ken very nervously answered.

"Good then!" Karl Keller exclaimed, showing a bit of emotion. "I've been waiting thirty-five years for us to finally resume our interrupted baseball catch! We'll even have an extended game of pepper! Don't worry, where we're going time is no longer relative to anything!" the ghost cheerfully and persuasively elaborated. "Now I think Ken that you're going to learn to like your new transparent two-dimensional existence! I guarantee you, you'll never feel the sensation of human pain again!"

"Landscapes and Photographs"

On Monday morning September 21st, 2009, the last day of summer, George Rodio had been a bit lucky at Harrah's Casino in Atlantic City. The Hammonton, New Jersey pharmacy owner had just gotten three sevens on a fifty cent slot machine and had merrily won three thousand dollars cash. After leaving the gambling establishment's high-rise parking garage, the perfectly contented slot machine player drove his dark blue *Lexus* south on Brigantine Boulevard heading towards *Route 30*, the White Horse Pike. The recipient of the 'found money' was thinking about how he was going to merrily dispose of his recent 'good fortune bonanza.'

'It's a good thing I honored my hunch and drove to Harrah's to try my luck,' the happy fellow thought. 'I'll call my dependable manager Bill Dawkins after I get home and see if all my help came in to work this morning. But first I'll stop at that new art gallery in Absecon that features works by aspiring South Jersey artists,' George instantly decided. 'If I see a suitable painting that captures my fancy, I'll purchase the Picasso and hang it above the upright piano in the den and then I'll move the ancient collage of the nine family photos' that's now over the piano from the den to the upstairs computer room's blank wall. I think that Barbara will be both surprised and thrilled with the new acquisition, if I ever decide to buy it.'

One Absecon Art Gallery painting in particular had immediately appealed to George's fancy. The five hundred dollar 3' X 3' woods landscape featured a running brook in its center with a stone 'walking bridge' in the background. A clear blue sky had been painted above the many deciduous trees, which appeared quite unique in their stunning portrayal. The trees on the left of the painting exhibited lush green summer foliage while those to the right of the curving stream impressively displayed a variety of red, orange brown and yellow autumnal hues. The totally enamored dispenser of prescription medicines was never one to quibble about price when it came to purchasing something that his instincts desired. Impulsively George cheerfully bought the outstanding canvas landscape, which incidentally was signed in black paint 'Incognito.'

Barbara had left a note on the kitchen table disclosing that she had gone grocery shopping so George immediately removed the family collage from above the den's upright piano and replaced the familiar decoration with the very alluring-and-enchanting 'two season masterpiece.' Then the Cypress Lane homeowner transferred the 3' X 3' golden framed collage from the den to the upstairs computer room wall just in time before Barbara arrived home with her twelve completely-full chain store plastic shopping bags.

"Barb, I want you to check-out the new painting I just bought," the husband politely requested. "I got a little lucky at Harrah's this morning and used some of the new-found money to buy the beautiful scene that's now hanging above the piano. I experienced a tremendous adrenaline rush the very second I saw the mesmerizing landscape at that recently opened Absecon Art Gallery. It's nothing short of spectacular."

"What did you do with the family collage photographs?" Barbara curiously asked. "The kids would be disappointed if you put it up in the attic. That item's really near and dear to *my* heart too! It's got sentimental value, you know!"

"No Honey, I avoided the cellar too. I re-hung it in the computer room," George diplomatically explained. "I mean, *that* picture collection has been on the den wall for over twenty years now and I thought that we were due for a change."

"But what about our three sons' fond opinion of the nostalgic photograph display?" the wife asked. "We could have a family lottery and see if one of our boys would want to keep it."

"Joey's living out in Salt Lake City now, John's got a nice cozy place in Baltimore and Steve's living up near New York. All three of our sons have their own families now so I thought they could reminisce about the collage pictures up in the computer room when we'll all get together here at Thanksgiving!"

"Why it's absolutely beautiful!" Barbara marveled and evaluated upon viewing the splendid rustic-looking landscape. "I've never seen something so unusual, an exquisite combination of summer and fall with the running brook serving as the geographic division! It's really very pleasant to the eyes and quite inspiring too! And the cranberry colored frame with the golden border trim really adds to the painting's enchantment. Your artistic taste is impeccable! I positively adore it!"

"Don't thank me!" George smiled and then grinned. "Thank Mr. Harrah for our delightful new den addition! Eat your jealous heart out Homer Winslow!"

"It's Winslow Homer, not Homer Winslow! Try being a little more accurate when you're pretending to be so artistically knowledgeable!" the schoolteacher wife corrected her pharmacist spouse.

"Whatever!" the husband defensively exclaimed. "Oh yes Barb, there's something of minor importance I had forgot!" the husband apologetically declared as he casually reached his left hand into his pants' pocket. "I'm thoroughly enjoying being in an extremely generous mood today!" George prefaced his next affectionate remark. "Here's a thousand bucks fall season bonus to use at your own discretion!"

* * * * * * * * * * * *

George and Barbara Rodio were anticipating leaving somnolent Hammonton, New Jersey and spending a planned week-long vacation in Las Vegas the first week of November and staying at the luxurious Bellagio Hotel and Casino, centrally situated on the famous "strip," along with partaking in side touring trips already scheduled for Hoover Dam and the Painted Desert.

Over the Columbus Day weekend George was honoring his professional duty, attending a Pharmacists' Convention in downtown Philadelphia and staying at the popular Westin Hotel near Rittenhouse Square. The devoted husband had called his charming wife on Friday evening but she hadn't again heard from him and it was then Sunday night. Becoming a trifle nervous, Barbara called George's cell phone but received only a voice mail response so then the woman checked with the hotel front-desk and five minutes later discovered that her spouse was not in his room or in the lobby. After there were no signs of George's whereabouts again on Monday morning, Barbara notified the Philadelphia Police Department, and Detective Anthony Mason informed the fourth grade instructor that her husband would be put on the "Missing Persons' List" after a preliminary investigation had been initiated.

"How long will that process take?" the apprehensive wife asked. "This is highly irregular for George to be away for so long and not contacting me! I fear that a worst-case scenario is in play here! Can't you give this matter a top priority?"

"We'll keep his name on the appropriate list for three days and if no record or evidence of him turns up," Detective Anthony Mason calmly and methodically qualified over the telephone, "then we'll begin a routine crime investigation into your husband's inexplicable disappearance. That's more or less standard procedure Mrs. Rodio because as you might already suspect, we're deluged with hundreds of similar instances here at the precinct every single day."

"Thank you!" Barbara Rodio hesitantly answered, gathering the emotional strength to hold back her tears. "Maybe I'm jumping the gun here and perhaps my husband's suffering from temporary amnesia or even something less serious. But to say the least," the upset lady said, "this type of behavior or lack thereof is highly inordinate for my all-too-predictable husband George. Thanks again for your time! Good day Detective Mason." Click.

As mild autumn weather dominated the late October calendar all throughout South Jersey, Detective Anthony Mason and Barbara Rodio were constantly in close phone contact but no trace of her husband surfaced anywhere in the contiguous forty-eight states. By mid-fall the wife had become very despondent and not even lengthy telephone conversations with her three distant sons could quell her tremendous anguish. Barbara Rodio had never felt so lonely and abandoned as she had all through October and her overall "weak teaching performance" had also been affected, observed and subsequently reported on a critical written classroom evaluation authored by her stringent grade level supervisor.

'I had to cancel the scheduled Las Vegas trip,' the unnerved woman lamented, 'and still George has not once called or even written me a brief note. And to add to my mounting grief, the town beauty parlors and also the barber shop gossip mills are teeming with all sorts of wild theories ranging from George leaving me for a glamorous Hollywood model to him selling all of our accumulated assets and then irresponsibly blowing it all on a European junket to greedily gamble away our life's savings at the ritzy Monte Carlo Casino in Monaco. Where has all the decency and integrity of this town gone?' the out-of-kilter wife wondered and sobbed. 'Where are my loyal friends when I need their close comfort and sympathy the most? And the Philly' cops haven't uncovered a lousy clue! The whole department is quite apparently bored and overworked!' the distraught wife angrily concluded.

The annual family Thanksgiving Day dinner had been eliminated because of George Rodio's mysterious vanishing from the face of the Earth. But on the morning of Thursday, November 26th, Barbara stepped downstairs, made herself a cup of instant coffee, heated it in the microwave oven and then entered the recently re-furnished den with good intentions of watching the Philadelphia television news and hoping that some vital
500

information about her husband's strange disappearance would be reported. Suddenly Barbara Rodio's attention was drawn to the majestic-looking landscape painting hanging over the upright piano.

'That's totally odd!' the woman instantaneously assessed. 'Both the left and right sides of the running brook are now showing an autumn setting. The former left side summer foliage on the trees has now turned to orange, brown, red and yellow to match perfectly with the trees on the right. Perhaps a slow chemical reaction has happened with the changes in outside and inside temperature from summer to fall!' the astonished woman theorized, nearly spilling her hot coffee on her dress. 'This insane landscape transformation that I'm now observing is definitely more than confusing! The sky in the painting is more of a gray shade, but the stone bridge and the meandering stream look basically the same,' the woman marveled. 'I dare not tell anyone of this weird transition or else they'll think I'm hallucinating it all! I can't even reveal anything about *this* crazy anomaly to Joey, John or Steve!'

Christmas was definitely not the same in the Rodio house. The traditional artificial tree had not been erected and no family dinner was ever organized or prepared. All week the saddened wife had gotten little satisfaction concerning her husband's unknown fate from either the overburdened Philadelphia detectives or the ill-equipped Hammonton Police Department. The mentally disheveled wife again entered the den and thoroughly gazed at the ever-evolving stellar landscape painting.

'Oh my God!' the suddenly scared-to-death woman thought. 'The whole scene has changed from fall colors to a haunting winter setting. All of the trees are now barren, the entire sky is a dull gray and the stream in the middle is frozen with ice. I think that right this second I need the expert services of either the world's most talented psychiatrist or the world's most skilled exorcist!'

Joey, John and Steve were equally concerned about their father's inexplicable disappearance as their now-neurotic mother. The traditional family Easter dinner had been deliberately postponed until Thanksgiving of 2010 but on Easter morning Barbara Rodio stepped into the handsome-looking den and closely peered at the painting still hanging over the upright piano, which had overnight magically and mystically converted from a full winter scene to a more vibrant total springtime setting. Then much to the wife's amassed anxiety, in early July a similar phenomenon occurred when the rejuvenated vernal equinox tree buds represented in the amazing landscape painting miraculously changed to a gorgeous summer leaves' pattern with awesome green vegetation now quite abundant on both sides of the running blue-water brook.

'Let's see what occurs in October on Columbus Day,' the wife's fearful mind contemplated while dreading the rapidly approaching near future date. 'It'll mark the one year anniversary of George's disappearance! And Detective Mason seems to have lost all interest in my husband's rather drab run-of-the-mill 'Missing Person Case'. Could it be that my vanished husband is attempting to communicate with me through this eerily changing landscape painting that he had bought and loved so much? I hope that my already mangled and worn-out mind isn't becoming delusional! I think I'll pour myself a glass of blackberry brandy to help my shrinking courage make it through this extremely difficult emotional crisis!'

* * * * * * * * * * * *

Harry Jackson, a trusted friend and very wealthy owner of a Vineland pharmacy called Barbara on her land-line phone to see if any relevant news had surfaced about George Rodio. The missing man's depressed wife was in the throes of despair and initially felt like talking to no one.

"No Harry, George has not contacted me and the totally overwhelmed Philly' police haven't gleaned any evidence about his disappearance except that he never returned to his room at the Westin Hotel after the first day's business meetings," Barbara related. "It's all quite baffling and bewildering."

"As you might recall Barbara, I had gone to the National Pharmacists' Convention down in Miami, otherwise I would've probably stayed and roomed with George in Philly'," Harry informed his melancholy listener. "I had wanted your husband to go down to Florida with me but he declined my casual offer, saying that he preferred staying closer to New Jersey, especially Hammonton."

"I appreciate you calling to show your concern," Mrs. Rodio told Mr. Jackson. "I gotta' confess that things are getting a little hairy with the help over at the pharmacy and honestly, I don't know too much about how to run the business. Bill Dawkins, our-efficient-but-temperamental manager is starting to feel his oats and is throwing his weight around. Already two good assistants and the daytime cashier have quit."

"Well Barbara, confidentially, I'm always interested in expanding my business and right now I'm willing to go on record saying that I'll buy your Hammonton store from *you* at a reasonable price if George doesn't return to Hammonton within the next year," Harry Jackson offered. "You probably could use the extra cash and then you'll be able to retire from teaching early and still receive your sizable state pension. Perhaps we could discuss the potential deal over dinner at the Maplewood Inn up on *Route 30*," the enterprising entrepreneur proposed. "They have really fantastic pasta dishes. I especially like the terrific veal parmigiana with a side of angel hair spaghetti. Or we could always meet, have dinner and then negotiate a fair deal at Illianos or maybe at the San Rocco Pub downtown."

"We'll see about *that* prospect!" Barbara politely answered with a degree of uncertainty evident in her tone of voice. "Maybe if Bill Dawkins doesn't get his act together soon, I might have to fire him and then do something drastic regarding the pharmacy. I'll take a rain-check on your benign offer right now but you might want to call me back in a month or so. But if I do decide to sell the pharmacy," Barbara Rodio sincerely said, "you'll definitely be the first one in line to take the place over. To tell you the truth, Wal*Mart's been gnawing away, eating into George's gross profits, slowly-but-surely. And the health insurance issue along with complicated Medicare and Medicaid payment problems had been driving him up a wall."

"Okay Barbara, thanks for your sincere vote of confidence," Harry Jackson spontaneously replied. "I'll keep in touch and will be there to help you out of financial trouble whenever the time might arrive."

"Say Harry, would you be interested in buying an oil landscape painting in good condition?" Barbara worriedly asked. "It's about 3' X 3'."

"No, not really," Jackson answered, feigning empathy. "I already have three oil paintings in my house: a bowl with fruit in it is hanging in my living room, a Spanish villa is suspended from the wall above the master bedroom's headboard and then there's a colorful rendition of the Champs Elysees in Paris hanging in my dining room. Stay well Barbara and remember my good offer! Goodbye for now!" Click.

After preparing herself' a blackberry brandy to soothe her frayed nerves, Barbara Rodio again glanced at the totally autumn 'changing landscape' painting and then very deliberately ambled up the steps to do some basic research on the computer. 'I'm getting pretty desperate!' the woman realized and acknowledged, trying hard not to spill any of her blackberry brandy. 'I'll look-up the names of some prominent area psychics to see if I can select one that has proven rare mental abilities, an honest medium who might be able to give me some rather useful concrete information about George's incomprehensible and rather peculiar disappearance.'

After booting-up the high-speed *Internet* computer, Barbara Rodio felt an inclination to take a glimpse at the collage of family pictures situated on the left sidewall, the center oval being of George and her on their April 24, 1975 wedding day and the eight smaller ovals forming a symmetrical ellipse around the perfectly centered black and white marriage photograph.

Noticing that the computer screen had not yet gotten to its Yahoo home page, the highly pressured woman again instinctively looked up to the photo' arrangement contained among the family pictures. Instead of the familiar nine still photographs of her dearly loved family members, the disconsolate viewer was shocked to witness something far more disturbing.

"Oh my goodness! The center photo' is just of me and oh no, George has been completely erased!" the now-paranoid woman observed and gasped. 'And moving clockwise, our three sons are no longer in pictures one through four but instead there're individual color scenes of the four seasons that have been shown on the den landscape painting, first winter, then spring, then summer and finally fall!'

The next four portrayals in the clockwise progression were just as unsettling. 'And where the fifth photo' of *our* three sons standing together had been, there's now a simple pen and ink drawing of Independence Hall. And what's this!' the petrified wife apprehensively thought. 'I know *that* sixth color photograph anywhere; it's the Strawberry Mansion in the city's Fairmount Park section. And oh my,' Mrs. Barbara Rodio reckoned with her hands beginning to tremble, 'the seventh pen and ink drawing is of President Truman and the eighth and final one is the same illustration as that which is represented on the twenty dollar bill, President Andrew Jackson. What's the meaning of all this crazy symbolism?'

Barbara Rodio next closed her eyes for ten seconds to gather her wits and then vigorously shook her head before, out of sheer delirium, her parched mouth and strained vocal cords emitted a

504

very long hysterical scream. Upon opening her eyelids, the lone occupant of the large family home again stared-up in horror at the radically transformed wooden framed gold-gilded collage, which had remarkably returned to again displaying its nine ordinary-looking family photographs.

Then filled with a certain impulsive spiritual inspiration, the panting observer finally became cognizant of exactly what coded message her husband had been trying to communicate both in the landscape canvas and in the nine-picture collage.

'I don't need any competent *Internet* medium! My sixth sense knows what's happening! My beloved husband *is* the medium that I had been seeking! George is sending these explicit idea-graphs to me from the afterlife!' Barbara fearfully recognized and determined. 'He had been brutally murdered at the Four Seasons Hotel at the Logan Circle near the Franklin Institute. That's what the first four picture transformations meant. And then Independence Hall indicates and confirms that my husband had been mercilessly killed in Philadelphia, supposedly the City of Brotherly Love, and he's obviously buried not far from the Strawberry Mansion in Fairmount Park, probably near a running brook, a stone footbridge and a pretty woods' setting.'

Barbara Rodio was now in a state of total mental mayhem. 'And finally,' the weeping widow considered and panted, 'my deceased husband was buried by black-hearted hit-men hired by none other than that unscrupulous avaricious criminal wanting to steal our pharmacy from us at a ridiculously-low bargain basement price, the very despicable and detestable *Harry Jackson*! That evil conniving megalomaniac dirt-bag! And to think,' Barbara speculated and then cried some more. 'I almost was going to go on a dinner date with that ruthless villainous rogue and sell the felonious scoundrel my precious husband's treasured pharmacy!'

"The Pinelands Theatre"

Originally completed and opened in 1914, Hammonton, New Jersey's Pinelands Theatre has had a very long and interesting history. At first the structure functioned as an entertainment venue presenting live vaudeville and variety acts to entertain the local public. Twenty years after its pre-WWI inception, out of sheer economic necessity the landmark Pinelands Theatre switched from showing silent films to innovative "talking movies" in 1930, but in later years competition from the much larger and more elegant Rivoli Theater (at the corner of Bellevue Avenue and Third Street) eventually put the town's first movie house into extinction, forcing the out-of-date building to eventually close its doors in December of 1943, exactly two years after *Pearl Harbor*.

After the Golden Age of Hollywood had passed into posterity, the vacant Second and Vine edifice, located a block east of Bellevue (the town's main thoroughfare), later became a residence in 1951, but then the structure was gutted and converted into a merchants' warehouse in 1957, but in the early 1960s Kennedy-Johnson era, the aged in-need-of-repair skeleton became a convenient storage facility for a Bellevue Avenue department store. Things were looking rather bleak for the once-revered Pinelands Theatre building with the approach of the twenty-first century and its attendant technologies.

In more modern times, Hammonton residents are presently enjoying a sophisticated Performing Arts Center (featuring a fantastic audio system for stage plays and rock concerts) situated inside the new High School at the corner of Old Forks Road and *Route 30*, the White Horse Pike. The contemporary Performing Arts Center is a very comfortable auditorium with over a thousand blue seats tiered on three levels. But with the help of federal and state grant money along with generous private donations, in the spring of 2009 the grand old Pinelands Theatre structure had been thoroughly upgraded, refurbished and renovated. The ninety-five year old relic now easily surpasses its original 1914 majesty. The new luxurious ultra-modern state-of-the-art "playhouse" can adequately accommodate cultural-minded audiences of up to two hundred and fifty classic movie patrons or theatergoers.

On September 11th, 2009, the Main Street Hammonton Organization sponsored its annual '50s-style "Cruisin' Classic Cars Nite." Vintage automobiles and "souped-up" hot-rods sporting chrome-plated flat-head engines (from the nostalgic

507

Fabulous Fifties' decade) were parked all along Bellevue and Central avenues for public inspection, and the entire downtown miraculously changed into a circus/carnival atmosphere with plenty of popcorn, giant pretzels and ice cream cones being street-vended along with colorful balloons and various '50s memorabilia. Hula hoops, DA haircuts, Davy Crockett coonskin hats, poodle skirts, early rock and roll songs spun by area '50s DJs along with a host of Elvis impersonators were prevalent at every downtown intersection, and similar reminiscent phenomena had filled the bustling sidewalks in front of every retail business. For one special night each year the town becomes "retro'."

The Pinelands Theatre committee had cleverly coordinated the scheduling of its "2009 Grand Opening" to coincide with the town's festive "Cruisin' Classic Cars Nite." In keeping with the auspicious '50s theme, the rejuvenated Vine Street theatre would be showing the musical movie *Grease* starring John Travolta and Olivia Newton-John. Tickets for all two hundred and fifty seats for the momentous "motion picture premiere" were in great demand and all admissions had been sold-out a full month in advance.

Citizens throughout the entire community were quite enthusiastic about the much-ballyhooed commemoration of its new 208 Vine Street attraction. Jeffrey and Lorraine Pitale were two of the anxious Hammonton residents who were positively thrilled to patronize the newly reconditioned Pinelands Theatre. The couple had been eagerly anticipating the resurrection of a bygone era.

* * * * * * * * * * * *

Although Jeffrey Pitale had seen the movie *Grease* seven times before at South Jersey cinemas, on VHS tape and on DVD compact disc, at the Pinelands Theatre's opening night he and wife Lorraine were still able to pick-out several nuances in the upbeat film that had previously escaped their attention. The first 2009 audience was very receptive to the theatre's big gala and the Main Street Hammonton committee members that had volunteered their services were greatly encouraged by *Grease's* overwhelming screen success. The Pitales (along with a hundred and twelve other prominent Hammonton families) had already purchased annual memberships to the Pinelands Theatre, which automatically entitled the lucky recipients to twenty percent discounts on all tickets to the next full year's slate of stage productions and "favorite film showings."

On Friday evening, September 18th Lorraine was away from the Pitale's colonial two-story Pleasant Street home, attending a bi-weekly meeting of the Women's Civic Organization at the group's Valley Avenue clubhouse. Meanwhile Jeffrey diligently sat at his den's computer desk using his online banking account to promptly pay several of his monthly utility and credit card bills. After completing those perfunctory tasks, the conscientious electrical engineer suddenly felt compelled to remove several blank sheets from his computer's printer tray, pick up a sharpened pencil and then begin some random drawing.

'I don't know what's actually inspiring me to try and draw something,' the man of the house thought. 'This is really uncharacteristic of me because I never was artistic in high school! The only things I can remember sketching in middle school were crude renditions of jet airplanes and outlines of atomic submarines! Let's see where this weird activity leads me.'

Two hours of assiduous application putting pencil lines upon paper produced the following seemingly unrelated results represented on four separate sheets: the number '1914' exhibited in large six-inch-high illustration, a fairly decent drawing of a turn-of-the-century 'Teddy Roosevelt era' handgun, a mustached early Twentieth Century railroad worker boarding a steam locomotive freight train and finally, a simulated shooting occurring on a playhouse stage. The four spontaneously created diverse drawings addled Pitale's mind.

'What's motivated me to make these four particular drawings, especially when I've always shied away from any artistic endeavors both at home and at school?' Jeffrey curiously wondered. 'It's as if someone from another undefined dimension is actively attempting to communicate with me and then using me as his or her medium! Since I'm done satisfying my bill creditors,' Pitale conjectured, 'and now I have some free time to further explore this odd mystery that's really baffling my sense of reason. Hey, I know what I'll do. I'll research on the *Internet* the gun design that my right hand had just produced. Perhaps I can discover a clue as to exactly what this strange desire to randomly draw remote items on white copying paper is all about. Truthfully, I only love mysteries when they happen on late night television to other people.'

Within a half hour's time searching Google and Yahoo, a photograph of the exact wooden-handled gun Pitale had sketched

509

had been located on a collector's catalog page, and Jeffrey was soon able to identify the weapon as a 1910 Mauser 6.35 mm. pistol that had been manufactured in Germany. 'That's the gun!' the anxious delver realized and confirmed. 'It's not a revolver but it's a pistol! But why hadn't I drawn a revolver? This is all very puzzling! There's something totally eerie and weird about this whole matter that needs clarification. I'll not tell Lorraine about it until I sift through exactly all that has happened to me and then try and develop a plausible explanation as to why it had occurred in the first place. If only I had Alfred Hitchcock, Rod Serling or the brilliant Perry Mason around to help me out here!'

The following Monday afternoon, on the drive back from his Cherry Hill engineering firm's main office, Jeffrey Pitale stopped and parked his black Jaguar in the rear of the *Hammonton News Building* on Twelfth Street and West End Avenue. The visitor's intent was to perform some preliminary investigation into the year 1914. 'I know that the Pinelands Theatre had opened in *that* year and that Europe was preparing for *World War I*, but other than those apparently disconnected facts, my knowledge of *that* bygone time period is quite limited,' Pitale rationally evaluated. 'Let me see if I could intelligently piece together some coherent pattern that could then ingeniously account for the four unique pencil sketches I had produced at my desktop computer.'

"Hi Jane," Jeffrey greeted the elderly woman seated behind the *Hammonton News'* receptionist counter. "I'm interested in looking at some long-forgotten news stories from the year 1914. My son Tommy's taking an important night graduate school history course over at Stockton State College and he needs some relevant information of a local flavor to base his term paper on," Pitale creatively lied. "I mean after all Jane, what are parents for? Could you possible help me help my son? Ever since sixth grade he's always been an A student! I gotta' help him out!"

"Since you and your wife have generously supported the various Pinelands Theatre fundraisers," Mrs. Jane Ruberton amiably and suavely answered, "and since you're a reputable member of the community," she added and joked, "I'll gladly be of assistance."

"Wow! That was a lot easier than I had thought it would be," Jeffrey honestly admitted. "Where do I start?"

"Go over to that third file cabinet on the left and then you can examine the microfiche copies of the *Hammonton News'* weekly editions and editorials for 1914. And when you eventually find what you're looking for," Jane Ruberton patiently explained,
510

"next go to that archaic-looking machine on the back table to your right and use the obsolete-looking contraption to read the appropriate microfiche language in large print. When you're done gleaning your desired data," the proficient newspaper employee further instructed the researcher, "return the microfiche file information to the original shelf location inside the file cabinet from which you had obtained the articles that you had examined."

"I'm quite impressed!" Pitale jested and then grinned. "I believe I'll renew my subscription to this newspaper the next time I get a notice in the mail!"

Jeffrey Pitale's hour-long investigation into the year 1914 in Hammonton and vicinity yielded one extraordinarily intriguing small headline that curiously appeared on page twelve. On the evening of September 14th of that previously ordinary year Shakespearean actor James Pitman had been fatally shot after giving a dramatic one-night performance at the Pinelands Theatre, which had opened to the public in April of that same year.

Astounded by the content of the back page news story, Jeffrey read the remainder of the brief seven-sentence paragraph. He soon learned from subsequent news reports that the murder had not been solved and that no evidence or weapon had ever been uncovered. James Pitman's body had been buried in a Philadelphia cemetery a week after the unsolved murder had been committed.

'Since the theatre management and the town officials probably didn't want too much adverse publicity from the violent incident to circulate,' Jeffrey practically theorized, 'the felony was more or less brushed under the rug after the preliminary Hammonton News article had been published on page twelve. Yes, that's gotta' be what happened. Why else would the short article be on page twelve and not be appearing on page one as a full-scale scandal?' Pitale objectively contemplated. 'The hush-hush murder of actor James Pitman seems to have been a major cover-up. But why did it happen? What was the killer's motive? Revenge? Jealousy? Fear? Greed? A crime of passion?'

"Thanks for your swell cooperation Jane," Jeffrey said at the front receptionist's counter. "Some information just can't be obtained over the *Internet*. You've been most helpful."

"Any time Jeff," the congenial woman replied. "Feel free to come in and study past articles and documents whenever the spirit moves you. I hope your findings will be of benefit to your son's night school grade."

After entering his shiny new car, the downtown visitor had a sudden recollection. 'I need some gray paint to re-do the trellis on the side of the house and to refresh the metal doors leading down to the cellar,' the man about town recalled. 'I'll drive over to Chester's Hardware on Bellevue and see if my always-complaining twin brother has the right color paint in stock. I'll park my wheels in the back lot and go into the store from the rear entrance. I know the place like I know my image in a mirror. The paint department's right there next to the shovels, spades and rakes.'

"Hi Pete," Jeffrey greeted his slightly heavier facsimile. "How's business? Ready to sell this decrepit place and retire to Florida or California?"

"Business hasn't been too good as of late," Peter Pitale reluctantly acknowledged. "Wall*Mart's been crucifying me with all those bargain sales they've been having. The only time my old customers come in here now is for professional advice they can't get from the amateur help over there at that cheap-selling box store," the twin brother griped. "Now I don't have ESP but let me guess. You're in here to purchase some gray paint for your trellis and for your rusty metal cellar doors."

"How did you ever theorize that?" Jeffrey asked, grinning and shaking his head in disbelief.

"Simply because every September you habitually show-up in here with the same redundant request," Peter Pitale replied. "You'd think you'd change the color to black or maybe to silver! You're just too predictable for words to describe!"

"Say Pete, did you ever hear of an old actor named James Pitman? He was shot and killed inside the Pinelands Theatre way back in 1914. I know you're a sort of history buff and maybe that name might register. I know you aren't Quasimodo but the name James Pitman might just ring a bell with you."

"It sure does!" the hardware store proprietor said without thinking twice. "I remember Dad once talking about our bad-luck Great-grandfather, James Pitale, whose stage name was James Pitman because the prejudiced playhouse audiences over in Philadelphia and up in New York frowned upon actors of Italian and Sicilian ethnicity, especially those traveling thespians that pursued dramatic roles in Shakespearean comedies and tragedies."

"Is that all you can tell me?" Jeffrey asked in a contrived disappointed tone of voice. "After all, you *are* the family historian and you always remind me of that fact! What else do you remember? What else *can* you remember?"

512

"Well Jeff, you're testing my brain power but here it goes anyway," Peter Pitale sympathetically related. "I hope you have plenty of patience. Our Great-grandfather was indeed killed in Hammonton in 1914, but since it was believed to be a terrible scandal, Grandfather Ben never really discussed it too often with Dad, and Pop had only casually mentioned James Pitale to me on one or two occasions because he knew that I was interested in acting when I had been participating in the high school plays and also since Pop knew I liked positive family history along with journalism too. It's too bad that I wound-up in retail hardware sales and not in the acting profession or in politics. Ya' know Jeff," Peter imagined and declared, "with my superb oratory talent and above average ambition," the brother bragged and exaggerated, "I could've been governor or senator by now. Most politicians are good actors ya' know!"

Jeffrey was absolutely stunned and staggered at what his almanac-brained twin brother had just revealed. 'Could it be that my Great-grandfather James Pitale, alias James Pitman is on-a-ghostly-mission attempting to communicate to me that he had been murdered on stage at the Pinelands Theatre and had been shot by a mustached man with a German Mauser pistol? Was I experiencing some form of genetic psychic telepathy and inadvertently communicating with the dead when I instinctively drew those four seemingly meaningless and unrelated sketches?"

"Tell me Pete," Jeffrey said, feigning only a shallow interest, "where did our theatrical Great-grandfather work before he studied *Hamlet* and *Macbeth*?"

"I believe he was employed on the old Pennsylvania Railroad that the town had been built around," Peter informed his still emotionally shocked brother. "Now Jeff, I wouldn't be surprised if our on-the-go mobile Great-grandfather hopped freight trains up and down the east coast and rode in empty boxcars when he couldn't afford to buy a ticket to sit in a first-class Pullman car," the hardware store owner evaluated and suggested. "Even several decades before the Great Depression, things were pretty tough economically for struggling itinerant Italian immigrants back then, and my understanding of that long-gone decade is that the area gentry of British descent despised the first influx of Sicilian immigrants more than we can imagine! The dark-skinned Sicilians were regarded as avaricious grease ball locusts invading *their* prized South Jersey territory."

"Thanks for your off-the-beaten-path insights!" Jeffrey genuinely and gratefully exclaimed. "So Pete, our seldom-

513

discussed Great-grandfather was a common laborer for the Pennsy' Railroad! With all your graphic descriptions, perhaps you should've pursued a career in journalism after all! I knew that our Great-grandfather originally was a native of this farming area but that's about all I had ever learned about him. I know Dear Brother that this sounds like total wishful thinking, but it would be nice if our Great-grandfather could come back to life for ten minutes and supernaturally reveal precisely how and why he had been murdered in cold blood!"

* * * * * * * * * * * *

Several weeks later Lorraine Pitale was again away from her Pleasant Street home attending her Women's Civic Organization meeting at the Valley Avenue clubhouse. Her "Alpha personality" husband was again preoccupied at his den's desktop computer paying out more monthly bills including his next rather hefty Jaguar automobile installment.

'These extremely annoying hideous bills appear in my life much too often!' Jeffrey concluded. 'In my next life I hope to be born a multi-millionaire!'

After safely exiting the secure *Internet* banking website, Jeffrey suddenly had an inspiration to again do some random drawing. This time the electrical engineer used two pieces of standard-sized computer copying paper to sketch a black metal box on the first sheet and a cornerstone dated 1914 on the second. A second strange compulsion motivated him to cut out the smaller black box with a scissors and then use Scotch tape to place and hold it inside the middle of the block-shaped cornerstone, dated 1914.

"Could this odd uncanny procedure be the decoding of the 1914 murder mystery?" the excited re-creator whispered to himself. "It's as if I'm a human robot being operated by means of remote control! I do believe that my Great-grandfather's spirit is actually leading me to solve a crime that had been committed almost a century ago. That yellow cornerstone is still cemented inside the building's facade, right in the front of the modernized Vine Street Pinelands Theatre."

The following week the police chief, the mayor, the town's building inspector and the six city council members had all been initially opposed to the idea of breaking-open the yellow 1914 cornerstone until a long-lost newspaper document archived at the *Hammonton News* indicated that a time capsule had been placed

514

inside the hollowed-out cinder-block wall. Much to Jeffrey Pitale and the assembled town officials' surprise, inside the cornerstone shell's black metal box were the following items: a 1914 autographed copy of *Tarzan of the Apes* signed by Edgar Rice Burroughs, a deteriorated and faded 1914 map of Europe, a discolored 1914 calendar, a dull-looking 1914 five dollar Federal Reserve Note and a partially decomposed 1914 front page of the New York Times with the legible headline: "U.S. and Panama Sign Canal Treaty." But in the rear of the black box was a 1910 German Mauser 35 mm. pistol.

"What does this old rusty handgun mean?" the suddenly flabbergasted mayor asked everyone in general and no one in particular. "Why was it hidden inside the black box time capsule?"

"It's a definite clue that means that an old unsolved murder at the Pinelands Theatre in 1914 can now finally be put to rest," Jeffrey Pitale concluded and stated without providing any more essential details. "The gun was the actual murder weapon used nearly a century ago. I'm just glad that the story about the concealed time capsule had been found in the old microfiche newspaper files at the Hammonton News and we all can thank Mrs. Jane Ruberton for excavating that long-forgotten fact. Without a doubt, her indispensable research gave way to getting council's permission for this morning's breaking-open of the original 1914 cornerstone."

"A new cornerstone shouldn't be too hard to install," the mayor announced to his still curious-but-perplexed entourage. "Bill," the mayor said to the stupefied town building inspector, "have a brand new 2009 cornerstone in place as soon as possible!"

* * * * * * * * * * * *

The third Saturday morning in October Jeffrey and Peter Pitale were sitting at a rectangular table inside Mary's Restaurant on *Route 206* enjoying delicious breakfasts of bacon, eggs and pancakes. Midway through the abundant and savory meal, the garrulous brothers analytically discussed the Pinelands Theatre murder of their Great-grandfather, James Pitale, alias vagabond Shakespearean actor James Pitman. Peter had dug-up some additional vital facts from various reliable resources that provided credence and also missing pieces to the whole 1914 felony affair.

"What type of guy was our Great-grandfather?" Jeffrey awkwardly asked. "I meant to say, did he communicate well with

515

the rest of the family? Or was he always sort of a remote personality, a loner out of the loop so to speak?"

"From what *sketchy* information I've gathered, it seems that our beloved Great-grandfather was a sort of Casanova type and often cheated on his wife Martha, our faithful Great-grandmother," Peter disclosed to his curious twin. "Since our rather infamous Great-grandfather's murder had been a pretty huge town scandal at the time, and since his immoral affair with another woman was a second scandal that cast the Pitale name in a bad light among town ministers and their loyal gossip-spreading congregations, Grand-dad Ben hardly ever mentioned the trauma to our Father, who seldom mentioned it at all to either you or me."

"But who was the anonymous woman that the flirtatious James Pitale was having a serious tryst with?" Jeffrey asked. "What's the scuttlebutt on her?"

"Here's what I've recently found out, some of which is naturally surmised," Peter anxiously qualified and explained. "I've concluded that Great-granddad Jim was occasionally seeing an attractive woman named Grayce Corbin, who was also a serious dramatic actress and stage performer back in 1914, the glorious turn-of-the-century O. Henry era. Anyway, this alluring female Grayce Corbin, whose stage name was Jean Eckhardt had been engaged to marry a certain Milton Denninger, a wealthy entrepreneur and part owner of the original Pinelands Theatre. Well, Great-grandfather James and this Jean Eckhardt woman had just finished the famous balcony scene to *Romeo and Juliet* when...."

"When the all-too-covetous Milton Denninger became enraged, and next, *that* anger compelled the jerk to act-out his sheer hatred and jealousy. The livid maniac then deliberately shot our amorous Great-grand-pop with the 1910 German pistol and then the psycho surreptitiously hid the murder weapon in the black box inside the 1914 cornerstone just before the Vine Street building was officially dedicated," an out-of-breath Jeffrey Pitale hypothesized and stated.

"And yes Jeff," Peter continued his impromptu monologue after gulping down another ounce of hot freshly-perked coffee, "this Milton Denninger big shot had plenty of influence in the town and was able to distract and keep the local and state cops off the fundamentals of the case, perhaps by under-the-table payoffs. What a wicked evil conniver!"

"Whatever happened to the woman, the one that probably got our Great-grandfather erased from human existence?" Jeffrey asked.

"From my extensive research delving into the whole complicated matter," Peter expounded and emphasized, "this in-need-of-affection lady Grayce Corbin, alias Jean Eckhardt, probably suspected that the dangerous Mr. Milton Denninger had been responsible for her Romeo's death. Certain confidential papers that I've examined indicate that the woman became distraught over her lover's demise and moved out to San Francisco to escape the clutches of her villainous suitor. Ms. Corbin's sole desire was to start a new life over again out West doing what she loved best, performing with a legitimate Shakespearean acting company."

"Okay Pete," Jeffrey said and solemnly paused, "do you have ten minutes of listening time you can spare? Now it's my turn to tell you all about some very peculiar pencil drawings that I had felt inspired, or should I say 'compelled' to sketch!"

"Sure thing!" the brother answered. "But don't make it sound too much like science fiction. As long as it's not some far-fetched *Twilight Zone* story you're about to relate," Peter stipulated before swallowing-down another gulp of freshly brewed coffee. "I really hate listening to corny phantom and ghost stories! To tell you the truth Jeff, I'd rather sit here and continue chatting about our deceased Great-grandfather's bizarre adventures! But before you talk about drawing," the twin brother seriously stressed to Jeffrey Pitale, "I just gotta' confidentially tell ya' that this 1914 murderer Milton Denninger creep was an ancestor of the present town mayor and also the current chief-of-police!"

"A Second Chance"

Ever since I became an acne-faced teenager back in the mid-1950s, I have always loved fast automobiles, especially ones with chrome-plated flat-head engines. When my family had lived in Bucks County, Pennsylvania from 1953-'59, my tough-guy friends and I would often hitchhike to the Langhorne Speedway on *Route 1* just above Fairless Hills and pay the dollar grandstand admission we had been diligently saving-up for just to sit in the bleachers and watch exciting motorcycle and stock car races. Then my family moved to Hammonton, New Jersey where my addiction to excessive speed persisted right into my junior and senior high school years.

And when I was old enough to drive my father's '55 green and white Chevy, I did surrender to temptation and drag race it on at least a dozen occasions, nearly smashing-up the old jalopy during four separate dangerous racing situations. Because of obstinate pride during those foolish escapades, I never fully comprehended that I had been recklessly putting my own life and the well-being of others in jeopardy.

I must admit that my lust for highway adventure has been radically reformed within the last year and I no longer value what I had once held in great esteem. Please allow me to review what has impacted my conscience (besides contemporary crazed psychos practicing road rage), and what has ultimately demonstrated to me that I really and truly do possess an immortal soul.

This present-time existence that *we* believe is ephemeral is but a "temporary platform dimension." Once the threshold of *our* current reality is fully breached, one's consciousness enters a higher dimension absolutely devoid of physical wants and needs. Based on my recent flirtation with death, I know that there is much veracity in the propitious notion that Divine Law easily transcends man's societal laws in addition to man's scientific laws. But I mustn't get too far ahead of my rather incredible narrative.

This great transformation of mine from "maniacal pride" to "sagacious mental and emotional tranquility" all started with me purchasing a magnificent white 2008 *Infiniti* sedan. But I must confess that when my grandchildren Dan and Karly are riding with me in their car seats, I instinctively abandoned my desire to speed, and subsequently, I drove defensively and cautiously in a conscious effort to protect them from injury and I kept the children safe from aggressive dangerous motorists like myself.

My wife Joanne and I have always enjoyed taking our two hyperactive grandchildren on driving trips, especially when Dan and Karly got commendable grades on their school report cards. Yes, I've always used the "reward excursions" as an incentive for the grand-kids to excel in their academic studies.

Two years ago the four of us had traveled down to Disney World in Orlando and the year before, when both children had made their school honor roll, our itinerary had taken us to four different amusement parks in a two week summer period: Kings Dominion in Virginia, Busch Gardens, also in Virginia, Dorney Park in Allentown, Pennsylvania and then finally winding-up our "East Coast odyssey" at popular Six Flags Great Adventure in Jackson, New Jersey.

Of course, Joanne and I justified all of the roller coaster and fun house rides by balancing-out the amusement activities with educational stops at the Smithsonian Institute in Washington, at Thomas Jefferson's Virginia home Monticello, at Luray Caverns on Skyline Drive, at Harper's Ferry snuggled in a corner of West Virginia, at Gettysburg and finally at Philadelphia's Independence Hall. Since I've always loved to drive, my cooperative wife voluntarily surrendered *that* important responsibility to me, and my body was always the one sitting behind the wheel and piloting the *Infiniti*.

Before June 15, 2009, without my wife and grand-kids riding in the car, my love affair with speed and automobiles continued unabated. Up until that dramatic life changing date, I had been a moody, materialistic, egocentric, money-motivated, Hubris-oriented, capitalistic, power hungry (and generally) introverted individual. All of *those* detrimental "personal cancerous attitudes" have been excised from my spirit as I finally realized that those derelict and selfish pursuits were not essential in *this* transitory life and are totally irrelevant in relation to "the finish line" that we (as a mindless race) are all heading towards.

But is there another (less survival-oriented) mysterious dimension beyond our physical deaths in this life? Yes, there certainly is! Is there a spiritual dimension beyond *this* human existence? The answer to *that* philosophical inquiry is indeed *yes*. All I know with certainty is that there *is* a next existence after our individual abbreviated performances on the stage of this transient world. Yes, another dimension, more of a spiritual than a physical nature, does exist after the final grains of sand fall inside our individual hourglasses.

* * * * * * * * * * * *

In 2002 I had purchased a brand new red fully equipped Nissan Maxima and Joanne and I traveled together on many trips. One was up to the Balsams Resort in Dixville Notch, New Hampshire to admire the gorgeous autumn New England White Mountains' foliage, another trip was up to gawk at scenic Niagara Falls, a third one to tranquil Cape Cod and Boston and a fourth one to Baltimore's Inner Harbor and then touring historic Ft. McHenry. As I've already mentioned, I love to drive, but when alone, unfortunately, I *had* an uncontrollable propensity of throwing caution to the wind and then reflexively pressing my right foot hard on the accelerator.

Early morning on June 15^{th,} 2009 I was craving sampling the first blueberries of the eight-week-long New Jersey harvest season. I dialed and called Atlantic Blueberry Company, the world's largest cultivated blueberry plantation and spoke with the always-courteous office manager Loretta Armstrong.

"Yes, we're picking the first crop today, the Duke variety," Mrs. Armstrong informed me, immediately recognizing my voice since I had in the past been a field manager for the company for eighteen hot summers. "As you know, there're what we call 'the leaders' and they'll be mostly large berries. We'll save you a flat but the wholesale market's bringing twenty-five dollars per twelve pints today so that's what we'll have to charge you. We're selling each loose pint for three dollars retail to our regular customers."

"No big problem!" I politely answered. "Price is not an issue after going eleven months without eating fresh sweet blueberries. I've read in magazine articles that blueberries are about the healthiest food a person can buy."

"That's not just industry propaganda!" Loretta laughed. "It's all true, 'true blue' as you know we like to say here at Atlantic! When are you stopping by?"

"In about an hour!" I replied, already keenly anticipating the savory fresh fruit flavor. "Yes, in an hour," I reiterated.

"Okay, I'll have a flat set aside for you, but don't worry. I promise that we won't run out. We plan to pick and pack around ten thousand crates today!"

After speaking with the very pleasant Atlantic Blueberry Company employee, I drank down the rest of my morning coffee, stepped upstairs, washed my face and shaved, combed the scant hair on my partially bald-head and told Joanne all about my fresh fruit destination. Next I eagerly opened the garage door by remote control, anxiously hopped into my white *Infiniti*, backed-out slowly and then closed the automatic portal, which leads from the garage into the house's laundry room.

Five minutes later I was on the outskirts of Hammonton and motoring south on serpentine-curved Atlantic County #559, better known to local residents as Weymouth Road, the two-lane highway upon which Atlantic Blueberry Company maintains nine hundred of its fourteen hundred fresh fruit acres.

I neglected to honor the vital statistics' data that most automobile accidents occur within a three-mile radius of a person's home. I could not resist the thrill and challenge of driving a powerful *Infiniti* around sharp turns on a very familiar bending road. I remember passing by Sunshine Vegetable Farm and then by Macrie Brothers Blueberry Company before ascending the *Route 559* overpass above the summer-busy *Atlantic City Expressway*.

I had gradually accelerated to a speed of sixty miles an hour, negotiating a challenging wicked curve, when an in-a-hurry eighteen wheel tractor-trailer refrigeration rig was coming from the direction of Atlantic Blueberry and the roaring metallic monster was rounding the same curve heading north. The driver's front wheels crossed the double yellow lines and I frantically attempted swerving to the right, but to no avail. My *Infiniti* collided with (and soon caromed off) the loaded tractor-trailer, skidded off the highway and then zoomed across the narrow shoulder, smashing into a non-yielding telephone pole, which instantly brought my now-demolished new vehicle and me to an abrupt halt. To the best of my knowledge and memory, I had been momentarily knocked unconscious.

My eyes opened and managed to see several feet beyond the inflated airbag and to my right I was certain that I vaguely noticed my Father (who had passed away in September of 1974) sitting in the crumpled-up passenger side, a stern frown showing on his pallid gray two-dimensional countenance. Then much to my mounting consternation, my Father's pale stone face turned into that of a ghostly-looking supernatural personage who, to this very day, I do believe *was* and *is* my Guardian Angel.

'You've again demonstrated contempt for others as well as for your own safe existence,' the being mentally communicated without moving his lips or ever introducing himself to me.

522

'I know that I've been *gravely* injured!' I mentally answered, unaware at that moment of my terrible unintentional pun. 'I don't want to die, not now anyway! I have too much to live for!' I pleaded as my mind considered Joanne, my three grown sons and my exuberant grandchildren Dan and Karly.

'You might be beyond the level of self-redemption!' the mystical being mentally answered. 'You've never learned from near death omens in the past. Yes, you've never learned from treacherous situations and from close-call warnings where you had luckily escaped head-on collisions and near sideswipes, all of which had incidentally occurred rather frequently. You had always erroneously thought that you were invincible!'

Even though the brilliantly illuminated vastly intelligent flat form sitting beside me had no white feathery wings protruding from his back or any accompanying halo floating above his head, at *that* moment I was too frightened to request or question his true identity. 'Please give me another chance to pursue goodness!' I humbly begged as if I was an ancient suppliant in the *Old Testament Bible* or a feeble mendicant in Homer's *Iliad*. 'I now realize how wrong I've been in my past and wish to make amends for my gross wrongdoings. Can't I atone for my misdeeds? I promise you that I'll lead a dignified reformed life! I won't be negligent! I'll fulfill *your* every expectation!'

'Well then, I guess I could make a minor exception in this instance,' the glowing being telepathically stated. 'There's a remote-but-distinct possibility that your present perilous circumstance can be ameliorated. Tell you what I'm going to do, but if you fail the test you're soon to be given,' the superhuman being austerely stipulated, 'then you'll surely die, and consequently, your ultimate fate will be resolved by the supreme judgment of the Heavenly Hierarchy.'

'I think my left leg is broken and that my left lung has collapsed,' my faltering brain transmitted. 'And I fear I'm losing too much blood and that I've sustained a terrible concussion that might result in permanent brain damage. I think I'd rather die than live as a dependent human vegetable!'

'That's all quite reversible,' my spooky other-world companion mentally commented. 'Don't panic! Try to harness your escalating dread!' the specter encouraged. 'If it affords you any comfort, *my* will can control such simple mundane factors as broken arms and excessive loss of blood!'

'What do you want me to do?' my weary waning consciousness mentally communicated. 'What test are you speaking of, er, I mean what sort of test were you *thinking* of?'

'The task you'll be assigned to perform will be satisfactorily defined, for you see,' the sublime apparition attested and expounded, 'the concept of time in *this* awkward border state dimension that you've *accidentally* entered into can be either expanded or contracted, and therefore, it is not bound by any earthly clock or watch,' the erudite being on the front passenger side austerely explained. 'An hour, a day or a month could easily be condensed into a mere second's lapsing, so have no fear that your heart and body will expire before your prescribed project is completed. These unreliable measurements of time, namely minutes, hours, days, weeks, months, years, decades, centuries, millennia, well, they're all just arbitrary standards of expression that mere mortal men have developed over the ages, all based on the rotation of your planet and the revolution of the Earth around the sun.'

'And exactly what *project* must I do?' my weakened mind asked. 'I'm not strong enough to endure anything too strenuous!'

'First you must successfully tell me every car along with its color that you've owned since graduating from high school,' the Guardian Angel explicitly demanded. 'Recite all fifteen vehicles in chronological order!'

'Well now,' I nervously expressed to the extraordinary stone-faced supernatural being, 'after I had cracked the engine block in my father's '55 Chevy....'

'I warn you, don't use grammatically-inferior slang references!' the Guardian Angel sternly chastised. 'Say the word *Chevrolet* instead of the illegitimate terminology Chevy!'

'Sorry Kind Spirit,' I sincerely apologized for my ridiculous impulsiveness. 'After I had cracked the engine in my father's Chevrolet,' I carefully mentally enunciated, 'my first car out of high school was my Dad's white 1961 Chevrolet Impala with a black stripe along both sides. I had been given that nifty auto' for graduating in June of 1965 from Glassboro State Teachers College, which incidentally now is Rowan University.'

'Even though time is not of the essence,' the awesome being mentally declared, 'please refrain in your narrative from engaging in descriptive over-elaboration.'

'Sorry!' I again genuinely apologized. 'Much to my Father's chagrin, in 1966 I traded in the white Chevrolet Impala for a 1967 green British Triumph Spitfire convertible sports car that I loved

524

driving down *Route 559* thirty miles all the way to the college bars in Somers Point, because across the bay, Ocean City, New Jersey has always been a dry town where beer, wine and liquor are frowned upon because that town had a very strict religious origin and....'

'Stop your very annoying rambling! I've already warned you about being too vociferous!' the aggravated Angel again insisted without talking. 'Try being a tad less loquacious when amateurishly employing your lackluster nomenclature!'

'Certainly!' I immediately compromised, my immortal soul's destiny weighing in the balance. 'In 1969 Joanne and I got married and her pop had given us a 1969 green Pontiac LeMans as a wedding gift. Next I believe....'

'You can't believe!' the Angel peevishly reprimanded. 'You must cite your testimony as fact and clearly communicate in concise mental declarative sentences!'

'Okay,' I consented and concurred. 'In 1972 I had purchased a used 1970 yellow Volkswagen convertible from Greg DeCicco, a teaching colleague of mine. And then for car number five, I had bought a green Pontiac station wagon from Frank Celona, and in 1980 I had traded the green wagon in for a brand new blue Pontiac wagon from the same Bellevue Avenue dealer. And in 1983, I had also obtained a brown Pontiac Bonneville from Frank Celona because Joanne and I needed a second car to shuttle our two eldest sons around Hammonton pre-schools during our free preparation periods and during our forty-five minute school lunch periods. According to my count,' I accurately estimated, 'that makes seven cars out of the necessary fifteen.'

'Your memory is more than adequate!' the mentally formidable Guardian Angel complimented me. 'Seven automobiles down and eight more to go!'

'Numbers eight and nine I had bought together as used cars from a dealer in Ocean City, that is Ocean City, New Jersey and not Ocean City, Maryland,' I lucidly clarified. 'The first car was a 1986 red Oldsmobile Toronado and the second was a two-tone brown 1986 Buick Riviera. I had exclusively owned Buick sedans from there on out except when I began preferring to drive Nissan products in the early 2000s.'

'You'll have to be less vague and more specific!' the Angel incisively chided. 'Now that's nine cars that you've recollected and only six more to go.'

'Well, in 1992 I had leased a white Buick Park Avenue from a dealer over in Hurfville just below Glassboro and then in 1996 my four-year lease had expired so then I proudly rented a luxurious 1996 cranberry-colored Park Avenue from the same dealership, Arnold Buick. And I liked *that* car with all its wonderful loaded accessories so much,' I continued mentally transmitting with my extensive automobile litany, 'that then I leased a 2000 metallic powder blue Buick LeSabre. That's twelve down and...'

'And only three to go!' my all-too-patient Heavenly companion mentally replied. 'Let's see if you could make it to the magic finish line without stumbling or defeating yourself.'

'Well now, we're into recent history, which is far easier for me to remember,' I responded with an increased level of confidence. 'In 2002 I decided to switch from General Motors to Nissan products. My first Nissan sports car was a nifty merlot-colored 2002 Maxima. Then in 2006 I had leased a white Maxima with rear wheel drive, but when Nissan returned to manufacturing front wheel drive cars again, I then switched to the motor company's *Infiniti* division over in Turnersville and now have a white *Infiniti*, which apparently I've just totally demolished.'

'Excellent concentration and marvelous presentation!' my immortal gray-faced companion congratulated without ever smiling. 'You've remarkably passed the first qualification. I had wrongly figured that by now I'd be transporting your blemished soul to the overcrowded and bureaucratic 'Spirit Holding and Deployment Area'!'

'Thank goodness my memory didn't fail me!' I expressed with a degree of relief. 'What's the second phase to *this* test that you had mentioned earlier?'

'Ever since you were a young man, you've liked to speed and race your various cars,' the grim-faced Angel recalled and stated. 'Your new task is that you have to race in a hundred-mile-long dangerous demolition derby against the fourteen other cars that you have owned! Are the instructions clear and simple?'

'As clear as a ton of wet mud on an already dirty windshield!' I nastily answered. 'And as simple as Einstein's Theory of Relativity mathematically expressed in reverse!'

* * * * * * * * * * * *

I don't know if I had endured an out-of-body experience during the crisis but the next thing I knew, I was sitting in my undamaged white *Infiniti* in a pack of my fourteen other former cars and waiting for the starter's flag to descend. I immediately recognized that the fifteen automobiles were stationed inside

526

Dover Downs, a large auto-racing stadium and grounds in Dover, Delaware, which I comprehended with amazement, except that the massive grandstands were conspicuously empty. As the engines were started at the public address announcer's command, I impatiently waited for the demolition derby event to commence. My dread intensified when I noticed that all of my rivals' cars had dark-tinted windows and windshields and so, I was unable to observe the faces or forms of any of my determined opponents.

The grueling race designed for the continuation of my human life began and the first three competitive laps were without incident. Then my *Infiniti* careened off of the '59 white Impala, which then rear-ended the red Toronado, with both vehicles smashing into a very solid retaining barrier. Then the driver of the blue Pontiac station wagon sideswiped me on the right rear side and I zipped across the track and knocked the green Pontiac wagon into the infield. I accurately sensed that the other crazed drivers all were keenly focused on specifically eliminating me rather than endeavoring to eradicate or dispose of each other.

The intense competition was very harrowing and nerve-racking, but all throughout the major obstacles I tenaciously persevered. I remember that the yellow Volkswagen convertible was sent rolling over and over into a pit after it had bounced-off my left front wheel's fender. I intrepidly endured all of the hazardous chaos, wanting desperately to continue living my mortal earthly existence.

Apparently my aggressive driving habits had enabled me to prevail throughout that devastating nightmare, if indeed it was a nightmare. At the end of the surreal ordeal all I can nebulously remember is that I had just beaten the merlot 2002 Nissan across the finish line, just before the familiar checkered flag was being waved by a grotesque-looking cadaver.

The next sounds my diminished senses could recollect were the sirens of the Hammonton Rescue Squad ambulance along with a dispatched police car approaching from the south. Incredibly, I woke-up in the emergency room of Atlanticare inside Hammonton's Kessler Memorial Hospital. The doctors and the nurses were positively astounded that I had survived the terrible Weymouth Road collision without a minor scratch anywhere on my body. And I was extremely relieved to learn that the tractor-trailer driver had also escaped injury and that his cargo of delicious blueberries had been completely salvaged.

* * * * * * * * * * * *

The Hammonton Police's investigating officer was extremely puzzled by the unusual condition of my white *Infiniti.* The tractor-trailer cab that I had collided with on Weymouth Road was lavender in color but the many paint scrape marks among the dents and mangled metal on my much-maligned *Infiniti* were green, red, dark blue, yellow, powder blue, merlot and brown.

My Sicilian wife was relieved that I had not perished in the horrible accident and that I had not suffered irreparable injury to any part of my sixty-seven year old anatomy. A week after the near-tragedy Joanne and I had a minor argument in front of her father's mausoleum inside Oak Grove Cemetery. My mercurial-tempered spouse just doesn't appreciate my newly reformed and optimistic personality/character attributes.

"No Joanne, I refuse to spray and kill those meandering ants residing inside your father's geranium pot. My new motto is 'Live and let live'!"

"Don't be absurd!" my irked Sicilian spouse countered. "They're mere ants scooting around we're talking about, not people! I think you're turning into a devout Hindu or something like that. That tiny ant that's scurrying around down there on the bricks is not going to evolve into a Sacred Cow and then come back in a future life reincarnated as a human being!" Joanne loudly maintained. "Don't you get it? This is the United States of America we're living in! Primitive caste systems are only found in foreign distant places like India!"

A second incident validating my psychological and spiritual transformation happened just this morning. I had been reaching on top of the kitchen hutch for my basket of various vitamins and minerals when a sleeping moth was suddenly disturbed and the aroused bug instantly emerged from between the plastic bottles and then flew directly into my right eye. Ordinarily I would have searched for the downstairs fly swatter and would have violently sent the flitting moth directly into insect oblivion.

Instead of killing the small living creature, I slowly opened one of the kitchen's Andersen crank windows, lifted and removed the accompanying screen and then gently ushered the frenetic flying creation out of the house to peacefully enjoy its wonderful freedom.

'God, am I making the most out of my *new lease* on life and I don't even have to obtain a bank loan to further explore it,' I considered and then smiled. 'I'm no longer hedonistic, materialistic and egocentric, but now my most earnest objective in life is to constantly seek requiem and solace. I think I'll have some corn flakes generously sprinkled with delectable fresh blueberries for breakfast. The season only lasts for eight short weeks so I ought to swallow the luscious fruit down while they're still plenteously available for local consumption.'

Then another random thought occurred to my permanently rejuvenated enthusiastic mind. 'I not only have a new lease on life but I also have learned from the guys at the Hammonton Auto Repair Shop that my white 2008 *Infiniti* can be made to look like it's brand new again. I guess I've gotten a *second chance* to participate in life's mysterious raffle, thanks to the glorious intercession of my anonymous-but-trusted extremely benign Guardian Angel!'

"Wolverton Mountain"

Veteran Agents Salvatore Velardi, Arthur Orsi and Dan Blachford stepped into FBI Inspector Joe Giralo's office, loftily situated on the eighth floor of 600 Arch Street, Philadelphia. Each of the conscientious trio was wondering exactly what new investigative matter was of such "urgent and strategic importance," the precise terminology that their reputable Boss had dramatically characterized *their* very next challenging government assignment. As usual, "the Chief" was sitting behind his enormous Canadian oak desk and his brown eyes were carefully examining the front-page articles of the *Philadelphia Inquirer* appearing "above the fold".

"I'm glad that you three easily distracted-but-ambitious junior sleuths have gotten here on time for your scheduled noon appointment, and I'm personally delighted that you're *not* now eating pizza or hoagies down at the crowded Reading Terminal Food Market," the Boss gruffly greeted his loyal subordinates. "I'm also happy to note in my latest report to Matt Riley that you three remarkable gumshoes had easily solved the rather preposterous "Treasure Map Caper" that had been annoying various local police departments in the Pennsylvania, New Jersey, Delaware tri-state area, which had warranted the indispensable services and intervention of the local FBI. Now Men," Inspector Giralo rambled on, "DC headquarters has acknowledged *your* crucial participation in swiftly solving *that* particular regional dilemma."

"At first the Treasure Map Case was pretty mind-boggling and not so routine in either scope or sequence," Agent Sal Velardi honestly attested. "If you recall Chief, Treasure Maps had been mailed only to kids of wealthy parents. The first time each targeted kid went and dug in the indicated bonanza location, the thrilled lad would find a fifty dollar bill deliberately deposited inside a shallowly buried box. The second time around, after receiving another easy-to-read map, the amused parents would usually, out of sheer curiosity, accompany their beloved offspring to the indicated *new* dig site. After merrily excavating a box containing a hundred dollar bill, upon returning home, the entertained well-to-do family would discover that...."

"That their opulent home-sweet-home mansion had been broken-into and that thousands of dollars worth of jewelry, silverware, stashed cash and expensive watches had been criminally pilfered. The Treasure Map Caper represented a very clever ruse, a nifty canard designed to get the parents of ten-year-old boys, usually each one an only child who incidentally has read too many Robert Louis Stevenson sea adventure stories, well my dear Agents," Joe Giralo embellished his monologue, "getting the duped adults out of their residences, allowing enough time for the furtive burglaries to be safely and successfully completed!"

"And so Boss, the wily crooks would audaciously trade a hundred and fifty dollar legal tender loss in exchange for a multi-thousand- dollar illegal gain," Agent Arthur Orsi very capably summarized. "I've learned over the years that the criminal mind could sometimes also be very creative. Too bad that wily felons don't use their ever-scheming cerebrums for enacting constructive pursuits that are beneficial to society."

"As you often remind us Chief," Dan Blachford addressed his well-organized commentary to Inspector Giralo, "many criminals become too cocky and overconfident. The haughty thugs underestimate the competency of law enforcement, and then the dastardly knaves soon fall into redundant behavior patterns that in the end, lead to their swift apprehension and incarceration. The Treasure Map practice became overused and when it did, it was quite an easy task for us to collar the initially imaginative crooks, especially after an alert suburban mayor had notified us that *his* wannabe' pirate son had received a suspicious-looking Treasure Map in the morning post. In the final analysis," Agent Blachford proudly disclosed, "the cunning crooks turned-out to be mere rank amateurs! The quartet of rogues was easily taken into custody while the idiotic dolts were preoccupied staking-out the astute mayor's ritzy suburban palace!"

"Why did you call us into the city today Boss?" Agent Orsi boldly asked his immediate superior. "Are you gonna' again oratorically expound on the ethical merits of ancient Greek philosophers Socrates, Plato and Aristotle like you had so monotonously and so tediously done last week?"

Chief Joe Giralo quickly frowned and then after regaining his normally placid composure, the Inspector effectively lectured his three happy-go-lucky associates that the renowned "Socratic Method" of asking relevant questions had eventually become the sturdy foundation of modern-day police interrogation techniques and that the sage Socrates himself was, in truth, a moral philosopher who had been principally interested in the basic distinction between good and evil and between right and wrong. "In simple historical perspective, erudite Socrates was the teacher of Plato, but in the end, the savant had been falsely accused of corrupting the minds of the Athenian youth and the distinguished master had to drink a poison, hemlock, as his totally unjustified death punishment."

"I really liked the character Socrates in the time-travel movie *Bill and Ted's Excellent Adventure,"* Agent Orsi bizarrely contributed to the rapidly deteriorating conversation. "Particularly when Bill humorously demonstrated the lyrics to the band Kansas' rock and roll song 'Dust in the Wind' by blowing sand from his hand. Despite an obvious language barrier," the FBI speaker elaborated, "the impressed Greek thinker instantly realized that the teen's gesture had been alluding to the frailty of human life on this wonderful planet. The famous teacher Socrates ironically then became Bill's student!"

"And Socrates would often tell the tale of the Cave Allegory," Chief Giralo prattled-on while deliberately ignoring Agent Orsi's fairly facetious remarks, "and in this unique 'Cave Story' the great philosopher described a group of common people, the masses, who were representing most of mankind, sitting with their backs to the sun and spending their entire lives in shackles, only witnessing the reflection of the sun's light, obviously symbolizing truth, being reflected off the cave walls situated in front of them; the daily illusion being experienced by most of humanity every palpable moment of *their* lackluster lives from womb-to tomb!"

"Just like in the song 'Already Gone' often sung by the Eagles," rock and roll enthusiast Sal Velardi impetuously chimed-in. "The lyrics go, 'Often times it happens, that we live our lives in chains, not ever knowing *we* have the keys!'"

"And the Eagles in that same song also sang 'You can see the stars and never see the light'," Agent Dan Blachford added to the oddball discussion, inadvertently fueling Inspector Giralo's mounting chagrin. "And in the song 'Lyin' Eyes, Glenn Frey brilliantly states that 'Every form of refuge has its price!'"

"Enough of your inane ludicrous frivolity!" the mercurial-tempered Chief Inspector affectionately reprimanded his three presently clownish G-men. "I suppose Sal that your next comment will be about Plato being a character shot by the Los Angeles Police in the 1955 movie *Rebel without a Cause* starring James Dean and Natalie Wood while also featuring Sal Mineo as the confused smart kid Plato!"

"Well, er, kinda', Boss," Velardi nervously confessed. "In *that* case you've just cited, I would only be practicing the Associative Law of Thinking like you always encourage us to do! I truly believe that imitation is the sincerest form of flattery, wouldn't you agree?"

"Well, for your education and general information Sal," Chief Giralo orally qualified, "the philosopher Plato often told the story of the Ring of Gyges, a unique tale where the favored owner had the power to become invisible by simply turning the ring around on his or her finger. The crucial paramount question is, my dear Salvatore, 'Would the possessor of the wondrous ring do good things or selfish things while having its supernatural power at his or her command?' And furthermore," Giralo strongly articulated, "the Scientific Method of Reasoning that we, as dedicated detectives, owe to Plato's famous pupil, Aristotle, who not only taught academics to the young Alexander the Great of Macedonia, but later in life, well anyway Men," the Boss paused and reflected, "the adult sage Aristotle also was responsible for classifying science into its primary functioning categories: chemistry, physics, astronomy, botany and biology!"

"Okay Chief, I think you've now satisfactorily exhausted and satisfied the usual mandatory preliminary smalltalk aspect of our current meeting," Sal Velardi courageously insisted, "so let's cut the fat out and finally get to the meat of the matter. Why are *we* three accomplished crime-fighters summoned and assembled here at 600 Arch Street on such abbreviated notice?"

"Strangely enough Sal, the entire ball-of-wax involves rock and roll music, specifically, mostly familiar oldies' tunes from the '50s and '60s," the Boss surprisingly related. "And furthermore Agent Velardi, I believe you still remember the several excellent rock and roll shows I had generously treated you to a few years back, you know, the ones down at the Wildwood Boardwalk Convention Hall!"

"Oh yes, we had the pleasure of seeing Charlie Gracie doing his classic hit 'You Butterfly', and then there was the truly terrific Chubby Checker performance, and still another time we enjoyed the Frankie Avalon, Fabian and Bobby Rydell 'Golden Boys Show'! And who could ever forget Ronnie Spector, former lead singer of the Ronettes. The accompanying small orchestra band played the same introduction over and over again for fifteen full minutes before the temperamental diva eventually came out on stage to sing 'Be My Baby'! Say Boss," Agent Velardi continued with his rambunctious jargon, "did you know that Rydell High School in the movie *Grease* was actually named after Bobby Rydell, who incidentally had starred in the film *Bye, Bye Birdie*?"

Chief Giralo wiggled his nose, slowly shrugged his broad shoulders and then judiciously decided that it was finally time to explain the true purpose of the hastily-arranged conference. The Boss related to his motivated Men that modern songs played by radio station DJs often fit into certain classification themes such as Boys' Names, Girls' Names, Colors, Days of the Week and Animals, but a recently intercepted e-mail obtained from the CIA had "the top brass at the Washington FBI Bureau" rather baffled.

Inspector Giralo deftly reached into his top desk drawer and removed copies of the enigmatic electronic communication, handed the vital "photo-documents" to each of his concerned Men and next asked his three loyal staff members to render "a viable interpretation" of the e-mail after given adequate time to slowly and silently reading the nondescript, ordinary-sounding letter.

August 3, 2013

Dear Mr. Mint Triumph:

I'm having a super time vacationing down here in good old Nassau. The Bahamas are wonderfully warm in August. Anyway, I want to thank you for the well-appreciated home-made CD music disc you had sent me last month. I absolutely love '50s, '60s, '70s and early '80s rock and roll.

After thoroughly listening to all twenty splendid songs, here are my favorite artists arranged from best liked to worst liked. Glen Campbell, Wilbert Harrison, Johnny Rivers, Paper Lace, Bob Seger, Dovells, Manhattan Transfer, Freddie Cannon, Marty Robbins, Elton John, Jan and Dean, Scott McKenzie, Claude King, Harry Belefonte, Gerry and the Pacemakers, The New Vaudeville Band, Big Bopper, Johnny Horton, Bruce Springsteen and Billy Joel.

I can't wait until I receive your next music disc via international courier. Thanks again for so kindly thinking of me.

All the best,

Violet Verdant

"Okay Fellas', I want you to liberally exercise your superlative detective instincts! What's so peculiar about *this* particular e-mail?" Chief Giralo imperatively asked. "Don't be too shy in offering an opinion, any opinion."

"Well Boss, first of all, the given names Mint Triumph and Violet Verdant seem mighty irregular and uncommon," Sal Velardi spoke-up, "but other than *that* weird first name and surname facet, upon initial inspection, quite candidly, the oddball e-mail's general content seems fairly innocuous."

Inspector Giralo proceeded to explain that apparently "Mint Triumph" was a sophisticated code name for the notorious scoundrel "Victor Grenoff," a wealthy European tycoon now living and doing business in Sofia, Bulgaria.

"Sofia Bulgaria!" Sal Velardi exclaimed in amusement. "I think that *that* doll used to be an exotic erotic dancer across the river in Camden over at the Aquarius Strip Club on Route 130."

"Stop being so absurd and so ridiculous!" the now-serious Boss admonished. "Open any mediocre encyclopedia and learn some fundamental geography Salvatore. Sofia is the capital city of Bulgaria, formerly a Soviet Block country that had been languishing for decades behind the Iron Curtain. Now this unscrupulous financier Victor Grenoff, alias Mint Triumph, had made his fantastic fortune in the 1970s bartering purloined goods on the black market, and as a result," Inspector Giralo qualified, "the upwardly mobile social chameleon is now pretending to be a legitimate international corporate mogul, the Bulgarian being heavily invested in the flourishing wind and solar energy business."

"Okay," Arthur Orsi concurred and conceded, "but what about this oldies' song collector basking down in the Bahamas, this Violet Verdant person? Does she have an alias too?"

"Our reliable data base records confirm that Violet Verdant is really a fanatical female anarchist, Viola Greene, who is now a staunch environmental and clean energy activist, a militant radical 'green rights' advocate' at that!" Chief Giralo assertively informed. "But Matt Riley and I just can't seem to connect these two 'persons of interest' with the string of jewelry store robberies along with the skein of power grid explosions and electric company dynamite blasts that have been occurring in recent weeks. Already there's been significant jewelry thefts in New Orleans, in New York, in Chicago, in San Francisco and in Tallahassee, Florida with coincidental power plant explosions violently happening in Allentown and in Bristol Pennsylvania, in Chantilly, France, in Chicago and also most recently in El Paso, Texas. What the heck kind of evil chain reaction is being clandestinely wrought upon our vital free enterprise economic system? How do we get to Square One in order to advance to Square Two?"

"You've always advised us to look for distinct patterns and sequences," Dan Blachford solemnly declared. "Maybe the series of jewelry store thefts and the corresponding electric plant explosions are somehow maliciously connected. You know Chief, perhaps there's a correlation between the two sets of criminal events?"

"Dan might actually be on to something mammoth in magnitude!" Art Orsi automatically agreed. "Maybe the series of jewelry store smash-and grab-operations are somehow financing the massive acts of sabotage being diabolically performed in this country and also in an area of France, Chantilly, I believe."

Just then the desk telephone rang and it was spontaneously recognized that Matt Riley was calling the Philadelphia FBI office from metropolitan downtown DC. After completing an intense two minute dialogue, Chief Giralo briskly hung-up, then gingerly placed his phone into its flat cradle and next, the perplexed Boss meaningfully stared at his three-man-team with a very grim expression formed upon his chubby middle-aged countenance.

"Riley reported that there's just been a huge explosion over at the Egg Harbor Power Plant on the Egg Harbor River in Jersey, not far from Ocean City, and there's also word on the government hot-wire that a tremendous diamond heist has been reported by the nearby Atlantic City Police Department. I now wholly believe that your extraordinary hypothesis is correct Arty! And yours too Dan!" Giralo genuinely commended Agents Orsi and Blachford. "The diamonds and other precious gems purloined in the various jewelry store hits might be financing the TNT and other dangerous materials being subversively used by the pernicious saboteurs, whom I suspect are extremely radical environmentalists maniacally being led by the formidable and despicable Viola Greene, alias *Violet Verdant*, a rather silly appellation, when pronounced out loud; it's essentially a suspicious female I.D. that sounds more like a very poorly designed oxymoron!"

"Boss, you had earlier mentioned that songs often have certain themes like Boys' Names, Girls' Names, Colors, Days of the Week, Animals and so on," Dan Blachford impulsively revealed the nature of his sudden brainstorm. "Well then, what about the names of certain places, cities such as New Orleans, New York, Chicago, San Francisco, Tallahassee and now good old Egg Harbor over in South Jersey."

537

"You're a veritable genius Dan!" Joe Giralo lavishly praised the most laconic member of his effective G-man squad. "I now see a definite developmental pattern being synchronized here. The jewelry stores are evidently not contrived in any special order, but the power plant explosions, at least the five that have been starkly brought to our attention, those affected facilities, now that you've mentioned it Dan," Giralo prattled on, "the five cities whose industries have been struck exist in alphabetical order: Allentown, Bristol, Chantilly, Chicago, and also El Paso almost simultaneously."

"I've heard of *Weird Science,* but now we have weird Geography!" Agent Velardi marveled and exclaimed.

"Salvatore, this whole matter is truly *your* strong suit," the Chief clearly emphasized, pounding his right fist upon the hard flat surface before him. "Do any popular oldies' artists sing any of the songs mentioned in the intercepted e-mail that had been sent from Nassau in the Bahamas to Sofia, Bulgaria?"

"Holy cow herds Boss!" Sal Velardi boisterously bellowed upon recognizing a definite relationship. "Billy Joel does the number 'Allentown', the Dovells do 'Bristol Stomp', the Big Bopper had recorded 'Chantilly Lace', and if my fuzzy memory serves me accurately, a group called Paper Lace did 'The Night Chicago Died', and then, Marty Robbins had performed the big smash 'El Paso', but the recent Egg Harbor power company explosion doesn't seem to mesh with the rest of the evolving big city song pattern!"

"Wait a cotton pickin' minute!" normally reticent Dan Blachford impetuously yelled. "What's *that* fast-paced Bruce Springsteen song about motorcycles roaring down Highway 9. Highway Nine is in New Jersey and I know for a fact that it meanders right past the Egg Harbor Power Plant!"

"Yes! True! Eureka!" bellowed a now-euphoric Agent Velardi, inadvertently mimicking Archimedes. "The lyrics about *Highway 9* are found in the popular Springsteen Song 'Born to Run'!"

"Okay Men, I'm now sufficiently convinced that we're on the right trail!" Inspector Giralo concurred with a healthy sigh of relief. "Tomorrow morning we'll meet at 9 am sharp in the side room at Marcello's Restaurant on Bellevue Avenue in downtown, Hammonton. I want you three zany Einsteins to make a comprehensive list of all twenty recording artists that had been specifically identified in the surreptitious e-mail I had received from Matt Riley, and then thereafter," the Chief proceeded, "I want to know the titles of any songs sung by those same twenty recording stars that deal with a particular city or a particular place. And Men," the rejuvenated Boss concluded his inspirational pontification, "please don't forget to also make a second list of the cities mentioned in the twenty researched tunes, and next, carefully organize the city names into a logical alphabetical order!"

* * * * * * * * * * * *

The following morning Inspector Joe Giralo and his determined agents conveniently met inside the closed-to-the-public adjacent room at Marcello's Restaurant in downtown Hammonton, New Jersey for coffee, Italian pastries and some frank discussion about the enigmatic jewelry store smash-and-grab felonies and the rash of energy installation explosions executed at various strategic settings across the USA, and now, also happening overseas in the vicinity of Chantilly, France, and potentially in Kingston, Jamaica and in Liverpool and Winchester, England as well.

"That Bruce Springsteen song 'Born to Run' really had us four Fed' Guys sniffing our nostrils in the wrong direction," Sal Velardi commented, "but then when it had been mentioned about the Egg Harbor Power Plant being located just outside Atlantic City, immediately, *Highway 9* nicely entered into the difficult equation, and then *we* were able to be more plausible about defining the true reality of our very treacherous new-found enemies, the very ruthless wind and solar panel czar Victor Grenoff, alias Mint Triumph of Sofia, Bulgaria, and his ax-to-grind vindictive accomplice, Viola Greene, stealthily masquerading as Violet Verdant, the female terrorist leisurely sunning herself down in semi-tropical Nassau," the perceptive agent adroitly reviewed and nut-shelled. "And naturally Boss, plenty of loose money is won and lost in nearby Atlantic City casinos, so logically, diamonds, rubies, emeralds and sapphires are always in abundant supply there, available to be stolen in broad daylight during instant surprise-type attacks, the brazen felonies being performed by violent smash-and-grab robbers."

"There are a few obscure bands along with one-hit-wonder recording artists represented and appearing on the twenty songs' list that Sal, Dan and I have so diligently researched and photocopied," Agent Orsi informatively indicated. "For instance Boss, the New Vaudeville Band, Wilbert Harrison, Scott

McKenzie, Paper Lace and finally Claude King, but amazingly, when *those* non-household names were matched-up with their respective familiar song titles," 'Sir Arthur' promptly clarified, "it all quickly made better sense to us researchers."

"Yes, who in the world was, or *is* this fellow Claude King?" Dan Blachford very honestly inquired. "I'm quite aware of the song 'Wolverton Mountain,' but I had never heard of an entertainer having the remote name Claude King."

"Last night I had performed some elementary Google Internet research on Claude King and his main hit 'Wolverton Mountain'," Sal Velardi eagerly communicated, "and this fellow King was a country and western singer, but in 1962, he hit it kinda' big with his catchy tune 'Wolverton Mountain', which in reality is little more than a tall lackluster hill located in the northwestern corner of Arkansas, near a town named...., yes, here it is; I've jotted it down in my notes," Velardi fumbled his notepad and then announced, "an Arkansas town named Morrilton. Columbia Records had produced and marketed Claude King's clever tune to myriad southern radio stations and to Dixie disc jockeys involved in the early rock and roll/country and western '60s era."

"Yes," added Agent Orsi, capitalizing on the momentary slack in Agent Velardi's biographical presentation, "and just this morning I had discovered on the Internet that the song 'Wolverton Mountain' had been based on a certain real-life character, a hillbilly recluse named Clifton Clowers, who had incidentally lived on *that* small unexceptional mountain up in northwestern Arkansas."

"Very interesting info', but fundamentally extraneous to and detached from the parallel jewelry store larcenies and the very damaging ongoing power plant criminal activity," Joe Giralo recounted before indulgently gulping-down a mouthful of Marcello's fresh-brewed coffee. "And Fellas', I also learned during *my* individual computer search analysis that Wolverton is a village or town in England, not too far from London, so having an open mind," the Boss summarized, "I suppose that *this* coincidental connection might also have something germane to do with the targeted British cities of Liverpool and Winchester."

"And Chief," Agent Orsi felt compelled to articulate, "last night I found-out that the song 'Wolverton Mountain' was later covered and re-done in other versions recorded by Dickey Lee and also by Nat King Cole, both in 1962, and later by Bing Crosby in 1965."

"Quite fascinating but otherwise rather immaterial details Arty, and arguably, not-at-all pertinent to *our* proliferating dual crime-wave dilemmas at hand," Joe Giralo evaluated and maintained. "Now Sal, please distribute to us your artist list that had been gleaned from the intercepted e-mail with the city song titles arranged in their original order next to the singers' names. After we thoroughly examine and study your singer/song revised laundry list, we'll then assiduously confer about its content."

"Here guys!" Agent Velardi stated as he slowly disseminated the requested documents to Chief Giralo, to Arthur Orsi and to Dan Blachford. "Let's closely study this original list of singers along with *their* corresponding city song titles and see exactly what can be derived and determined."

	Artist	City and Song Reference
1.	Glen Campbell	Galveston, (Wichita Lineman)
2.	Wilbert Harrison	Kansas City
3.	Johnny Rivers	Memphis
4.	Paper Lace	The Night Chicago Died
5.	Bob Seger	Hollywood Nights
6.	Dovells	Bristol Stomp
7.	Manhattan Transfer	Boy from New York City
8.	Freddie Cannon	Tallahassee Lassie
9.	Marty Robbins	El Paso
10.	Elton John	Philadelphia Freedom
11.	Jan and Dean	Little Old Lady from Pasadena
12.	Scott McKenzie	Going to San Francisco
13.	Claude King	Wolverton Mountain
14.	Harry Belafonte	Jamaica Farewell (Kingston)
15.	Gerry & Pacemakers	Ferry Cross the Mersey (Liverpool)
16.	New Vaudeville Band	Winchester Cathedral
17.	Big Bopper	Chantilly Lace
18.	Johnny Horton	Battle of New Orleans
19.	Bruce Springsteen	Born to Run (N.J. Route 9)
20.	Billy Joel	Allentown

After scrutinizing the original list of twenty singing artists and their respective "Place Songs," persistent Inspector Joe Giralo requested personal observations and reactions from his thoroughly engrossed underlings. "Obviously, Glen Campbell represents a glaring problem for us to consider with two major cities existing in his song titles, Galveston and Wichita," the Chief began the agents' "focus group" interpretation.

"And there's a Kansas City, Kansas and also a Kansas City, Missouri too," Arthur Orsi remembered and shared. "That parallel existence could amount to a thorny problem of sorts. And let's not forget that there's a Hollywood, California and also a Hollywood, Florida!"

"And there's a Bristol, Pennsylvania and also a Bristol, England," Dan Blachford noticed and responsibly disclosed, "but since there's already been destructive power plant explosions in Bristol, Pennsylvania, I suspect that the Dovells' 'Bristol Stomp' has successfully eliminated Bristol, England from the designated endangered cities' target list."

"Some superb reasoning being admirably exhibited!" Inspector Giralo congratulated his illustrious team members. "And let's not forget Victor Grenoff's sinister motive: theoretically, to destroy his competitors' fossil fuel refineries and installations and to vigorously promote wind and solar power throughout the world while simultaneously profiting from his secretive illicit endeavors, and in regard to the desperate anarchist Viola Greene, I presume that *that* wicked *witch* wants to soon rob a well-stocked jewelry store in Wichita! Now Salvatore," Joe Giralo firmly instructed, his graphic speech not missing a syllable, "please distribute the second list I had asked you to put together, you know, the one having the twenty song titles with cities' names now arranged in strict alphabetical order."

"Okay Boss, here it is!" Agent Velardi cooperatively answered. "I trust that the language typed upon *this* piece of paper will somehow enlighten us all!"

The alphabetical list of twenty cities alluded to in the song titles and lyrics were then quietly studied.

1. Allentown, Pennsylvania
2. Bristol, Pennsylvania
3. Chantilly, France
4. Chicago, Illinois
5. Egg Harbor, New Jersey (Route 9)
6. El Paso, Texas
7. Galveston, Texas (or Wichita Kansas)
8. Hollywood (California or Florida)
9. Jamaica Farewell (Kingston)
10. Memphis, Tennessee
11. Mersey (Liverpool, England)

12. New Orleans, Louisiana
13. New York City
14. Pasadena, California
15. Philadelphia, Pennsylvania
16. San Francisco, California
17. Tallahassee, Florida
18. Wichita, Kansas (or Galveston, Texas)
19. Winchester, England
20. Wolverton Mountain (Arkansas)

"Ostensibly Chief," Agent Velardi anxiously stated, "as we all know, the first five cities have already been attacked, at least power plants and refineries operating near them. Allentown, Bristol, Chantilly, Chicago and Egg Harbor, located near Atlantic City; these five specific anarchist targets are no longer in play!"

"And Fellas'," Chief Giralo strongly stressed and then momentarily paused his hoarse voice, "after the giant oil refinery outside El Paso had recently been maliciously destroyed in a colossal conflagration, *that* horrifying catastrophe probably means that the next city of interest is either Galveston or Wichita, according to the two Glen Campbell hit 'city songs' provided on the alphabetical list!"

"Well Boss, which of the pair will it be?" a now-frustrated Agent Orsi demanded knowing a plausible answer. "Use your legendary psychic abilities to intelligently narrow-down the field!"

"Well Arty, alphabetical order would rationally suggest Galveston, but my ordinarily dependable sixth sense gut instinct tells me it's going to be Wichita instead."

"Designed to intentionally throw our investigation off course?" Dan Blachford asked. "How cruelly cunning and deceitful!"

"Possibly Dan," Chief Giralo replied and soon hesitated, "but let's be practical here. To understand the criminal mind, we must seriously adjust our regular thought process and begin thinking like unscrupulous criminals do. The last song appearing in alphabetical order is the classic 'Wolverton Mountain,' which on the U.S. map, in actuality, is geographically closer to Wichita, Kansas than it is to Galveston, Texas."

"But on the revised list Galveston is indicated next, placed right after El Paso, that is, in true alphabetical order!" a still-skeptical Dan Blachford argued. "Wouldn't *that* Texas city be the now-predictable villains' next patterned target?"

"Well Dan, all-too-militant Viola Greene and her indoctrinated green-minded subordinate saboteurs know that Texas has plenty of oil refineries and pipelines that are probably *now* under heavy police and federal surveillance, so if the home-grown terrorists have an ounce of intelligence," Joe Giralo conjectured and persuasively insisted, "they'll instinctively deviate from their established methods and foolishly attempt demolishing a facility that's closest to Wolverton Mountain, Arkansas, and Gentlemen," the veteran FBI Inspector confidently revealed, "the most convenient and closest metropolis to Wolverton Mountain on the 'song city list' is Wichita, Kansas. I'll promptly notify the Galveston cops and the Texas Rangers about keeping a tight guard on Galveston and its numerous oil and electric plants, but I'm going to have *our* brilliant colleague Matt Riley dispatch Colonel Bob Bauers and his highly-skilled commando units to patrol every major jewelry store and every significant power plant operation in and around *that* next designated Kansas city, namely Wichita."

"Wow Boss!" Agent Velardi gleefully exclaimed. "Viola Greene will be apprehended just like those moronic Treasure Map culprits had been easily captured over in suburban Philly'."

"Right Salvatore!" the sagacious FBI Chief readily predicted. "Villainous Victor Grenoff didn't want a traceable paper trail for his cash payments to Viola Greene because the slippery rich European crook was fully aware that the IRS monitors all bank wire transmissions exceeding ten thousand dollars. Then, more than likely," garrulous Inspector Giralo pontificated, "Grenoff's business confederates and his global surrogates in various cities, like Nassau in the Bahamas, paid the ruthless 'save the planet' Ms. Greene off in cash for her hired destructive services. So I currently surmise that Viola Greene was probably operating on her own accord, but had been forced by realistic circumstances to subsidize her national and international power plant explosions by lowering herself to mundanely robbing diamonds and rubies from retail jewelry stores throughout the USA and other nefariously targeted countries like France, Jamaica and England."

"And soon that other diabolical nemesis of ours, Victor Grenoff, will predictably be arrested and taken into custody by Interpol over in Sofia, Bulgaria," Arthur Orsi concluded and added. "Boss, thanks to you capably teaching the three of us how to connect seemingly unrelated details, Sal, Dan and I are quickly becoming psychic human beings just like you! In fact Chief, it's *our* genuine conviction that *you* have impressively become the new paradigm in federal crime-fighting all by yourself! Congratulations!"

"Just relax and swallow-down your delicious coffee!" Chief Giralo sternly recommended, feigning a degree of modesty. "I'll readily concede that all three of you wacky wizards are indeed qualified experts on satisfactorily imbibing large quantities of caffeine! You even have me becoming an addict!"

"You'll have to be admitted into the Maxwell House for immediate rehab'!" Agent Orsi awkwardly jested to his good-natured superior. "Are the Hills Brothers' doctors still practicing experiemental medicine over there?"

"I'll bet that the traitorous and insidious Viola Greene will soon modify and alter her alphabetical list, next starting from Wichita and then possibly proceeding backwards all the way down to Galveston in reverse order, but her futile efforts will all be to no avail," Agent Velardi confidently prognosticated.

"Very true Salvatore," Inspector Joe Giralo verified. "Galveston is probably a planned trigger mechanism to furtively switch to Wichita at the bottom of the alphabetically organized song list. That relevant assumption is more truth than hypothesis!"

"And thanks to Claude King along with his diminutive 'Wolverton Mountain' tune, and also kudos to our ever-maturing collective psychic and detective talents," Agent Sal Velardi concluded and articulated, "this extremely confounding series of dual jewelry store thefts and industrial sabotage crimes has been magnificently and marvelously cracked wide-open. Say Boss, please pass the coffee pot! I think we've all earned a third cup!"

"A Photo' Finish"

At 8 pm sharp a black 2018 Mercedes luxury S 560 sedan entered the secluded U-shaped asphalt driveway enveloping a well-manicured lawn on East First Road, Hammonton NJ. The recently constructed three-million-dollar brick and stone mansion belonged to local wealthy business mogul James Dante Carlino, who that evening was scheduled to meet with the arriving prestigious South-Jersey Central Bank President, Thomas Monastra. In response to recent phone exchanges, the visiting financial executive and the resident real estate guru were slated to discuss an imminent shopping center development project planned for erection just outside Somers Point, across the bay from scenic Ocean City, New Jersey.

"Hello Mr. Monastra," James Carlino warmly greeted. "It's too bad we couldn't meet at the Blue Heron Country Club yesterday for a round of golf. But Mother Nature isn't always cooperative with desired business consultations."

"Very well put!" the bank official aptly answered. "Egg Harbor Township isn't exactly located in Southern California where it seldom rains in the early summer. Living on the West Coast does have its climate advantages. I must admit Mr. Carlino, it's quite a beautiful estate you've imaginatively built here, neatly tucked into the Jersey pines."

"Yes Sir," Carlino appreciatively replied as the investor gestured with his right hand for his guest to enter the spectacular chandeliered foyer that featured a magnificent spiral staircase. "I've designed this home myself. In high school, drafting was my favorite class. In my youth I always aspired to becoming an architect. But I suppose now I'm simply an amateur unlicensed home designer at best."

"Just last week I read in the *South Jersey Gazette* that you had a smalltime robbery happen at the convenience store situated on Fairview Avenue and the Pike, I believe," Mr. Monastra stated with a weak smile. "Hammonton has the reputation of being a rather tranquil rural and agricultural community. I was surprised to read that particular article."

As James Carlino graciously escorted Thomas Monastra into the enormous home's resplendent study, the multi-millionaire explained that the desperate robbers absolutely needed the four-hundred-dollars that the "idiots" had stolen from the startled store cashier to satisfy another debt the armed criminals had amassed.

547

"The full details weren't described in the newspaper account," Mr. Monastra curiously informed. "So much for the mediocre state-of-affairs that's lacking in modern-day journalism. Please if you may, fill-in for me the missing specifics of the ugly misadventure that had apparently boldly occurred in broad daylight."

"Well Sir," seventy-six-year-old James Dante Carlino laughed as the newly-acquainted pair continued conducting their preliminary conversation, "the two lowlife ignoramuses involved in the armed gun heist were caught inside the municipal parking lot in front of Hammonton Town Hall, the ridiculous dummies waiting to have a 3 pm court appearance before the town judge for two speeding tickets along with several other citations for attempting to evade police pursuits. Hammonton Police quickly apprehended the knuckleheaded culprits, who amazingly were intending to use the pilfered money from the convenience store armed felony to pay certain accumulated traffic violation fines that very same day in the Hammonton Municipal Court," explained the all-too-humored speaker. "This incredible oddball story has really become a favorite item shared among the town gossipers sitting in local beauty parlor and barber shop chairs."

"Ha, ha, ha!" guffawed the distinguished and well-dressed banking visitor. "Your terrific story about two imbeciles committing a store heist was a classic example of the all-true aphorism 'Crime doesn't pay'! Those two ambitious moronic fools were really at best dimwitted dunces," the totally amused financial wizard opined. "It's a good thing that Hammonton is not a notorious hotbed for major crime events like Vineland, Millville and Bridgeton are. I'm glad that I live in Mays Landing, which just like Hammonton, is a very placid and serene place to raise a family. But from general knowledge, your wonderful town is such a somnolent small city with a stellar blueberry farm reputation, and its strategically located right in the preserved core area of the pristine Jersey Pinelands."

Before the garrulous duo stepped forward and approached the huge mahogany conference-table occupying the center of the vast study/library room, James Dante Carlino paused for a moment to draw his avid listener's attention to an ordinary-looking vintage waist-high stereo/radio credenza tastefully placed along a side wall, the obsolete object instantly creating a mood of sentimental nostalgia to surface in the homeowner's mind.

"This once-popular early 1970s console was mine when I was a naïve teenager, and to tell you the truth Mr. Monastra, I loved playing rock and roll records and eagerly hearing the radio Top 40 hits during my formative adolescent years. My 97-year-old father gave this marvelous piece of furniture to me five years ago before he had been admitted into the Berlin Rehab' Center, and now my dad Pietro permanently shares a room with my elderly mother Angelina, both of my parents presently being virtual invalids, mom and pop suffering from advanced cases of dementia."

"Sorry to hear such bad news about your folks' declining health!" genuinely sympathized Thomas Monastra. "It's too bad that your mom and dad are unable to enjoy any normal facet of their human existence. My parents have been dead for over a decade now. And I must confess Mr. Carlino, I sure miss them both dearly."

"You can call me Jim," convincingly recommended the rich host. "And let's forget the general formalities that standard etiquette has over-the-years conditioned us with. You don't mind if I drop a cultural norm and call you Tom."

"Not at all!" spontaneously agreed the affable banker. "Before we get down to brass tacks though, please tell me Jim all about these twelve black and white photographs that you've randomly arranged upon the closed lid of your treasured 1970s entertainment console."

* * * * * * * * * * * *

"This first picture to your left is that of Aunt Carmella Carlino, a Hammonton transplant originally from South 'Philly," the mansion dweller confidently told Mr. Thomas Monastra. "Aunt Carmella's husband Uncle Lorenzo Carlino was my father Pietro's younger brother by seven years."

"I presume that your father Pietro and your Uncle Lorenzo were partners on the family farm way back in the 1930s and '40s!" the banker guessed.

"Correct," confirmed James Carlino. "My ambitious father mortgaged everything he owned right after the Great Depression and bought a defunct peach farm from a man named Horace Priestley, who lost his once-thriving agricultural empire after the infamous 1929 stock market collapse. During World War II there was a drastic need for food supplies, so the war actually enabled my father and my uncle to get out of debt."

"When did your family switch from peaches to blueberries?" the bank president inquired? "I've read in the papers where today there are over ten thousand acres of cultivated blueberries harvested in this sandy soil area."

"In the 1950s it was fairly evident that the Hammonton growers were hastily switching from peaches to blueberries," James proudly articulated. "The four-hundred-acre peach and apple farm gradually expanded to eight hundred acres of blueberries. The back section that was newly acquired in the mid-60s was often referred to as 'Texas', and that two-hundred-acre blueberry block was given to Uncle Lorenzo as *his* portion of the Carlino family partnership."

"How did you become directly involved in the farm?" Monastra suavely asked James Carlino. "Was there some sort of rift between your father and his brother Lorenzo?"

"Exactly!" verified and exclaimed the now independently successful entrepreneur. "First my father took a risk and purchased the peach land from Horace Priestley in 1929. Then after my dad and his brother had a major disagreement, my pop bought the 'Texas' ground a second time from Uncle Lorenzo, who then gambled his new-found windfall and went into business as a fertilizer and packages' distributor to area fruit and produce farms, mostly in the Hammonton/Vineland area."

James proceeded to further relate to his all-too-inquisitive guest that in 1972 his father then offered the fertile 'Texas tract' to him and shrewdly took-in the eldest son as a suitable replacement partner. The well-intended arrangement lasted for a dozen years, and in 1984 a truculent Pietro Carlino re-purchased the Texas blueberry block from his son James for the handsome sum of four-hundred-thousand-dollars. "My arrogant father always was an argumentative, stubborn dictator of a man, a sort of unyielding tyrant who never recognized my independent thinking. Pop always wanted to be the boss, whether it was on the farm or playing cards with cronies at the Sons of Italy. In Pop's very limited, narrow-minded understanding, the word *partnership* was only a functional euphemism for *me* being an obedient subordinate to his every command."

"Well now Jim, your father Pietro was definitely aging after you left the farm scene. How did he ever manage operating his huge agricultural empire?"

"Pop immediately made my younger brother Franco his new partner and gave him the aforementioned Texas block as evidence of *his* family commitment and responsibility," James verbally indicated. "But six years later, all-too-sensitive Franco couldn't take the constant daily abuse being administered any longer, so he

550

too departed, being bought-out by Pop for the same remarkable price as I had been. In time my father's mental health eventually diminished to where he exists in his present feeble state. The packinghouse, cold storage and equipment on the once prosperous farm are now in shambles, and the entire operation is debt-ridden."

"And so now Jim, you're standing here and telling me that your obstinate father had obtained the same land four separate times: first from Mr. Horace Priestley, secondly from his brother Lorenzo, thirdly from you and finally, from your younger sibling Franco Carlino. Your dad's once lucrative blueberry empire is now up for auction as I had read last week in the *Atlantic City Press* real estate section," Thomas Monastra accurately expressed. "But please tell me Jim, what ever happened to your attractive Aunt Carmella who is candidly represented smiling in this faded photograph? Is she also deceased?"

"Aunt Carmella became depressed from all of the family bickering being enacted over power and control," James orally conveyed to his astute audience of one. "In 2008 she fell inside her bathroom shower and unfortunately broke her hip. After having a joint replacement operation, Aunt Carmella's troubled-mind went totally haywire. She experienced a severe mental breakdown, became semi-conscious, acting quite erratically, her delirious mind suffering greatly in a heightened state of agitation. I recollect that on her death certificate it had been stated that Aunt Carmella had died of dementia and cardiac arrest."

"Are all of these twelve people depicted in these dozen pictures now dead?"

"Yes indeed," James Carlino softly replied. "And I must mention that I was deeply attached to each and every one of them, and quite frankly, better bonded with a few of them more than the rest. I experience emotional anguish every time I affectionately view these twelve deceased relatives. I only wish I could turn back the hands of time and bring them all back to life and again fully value their support, comfort and love once more!"

"Who is this woman in the second picture?" the banker queried.

"This second black and white photo' is that of my older sister, Bianca Carlino. She was a warty-faced, hideous-looking old maid, and she and I never favorably harmonized on any matter that involved the myriad family businesses, including the very productive blueberry farm!" James Carlino paused for a moment, gauged Mr. Monastra's facial reaction to his negative rhetoric, and then resumed his revealing narrative. "Simply to cause widespread chaos, resentment and disruption, my conniving father deliberately had me work under Bianca's jurisdiction so that I was unable to effectively challenge *his* authority and control. I was the nasty wench's underling in the family packinghouse, on the family roadside market and inside the family cold storage, and I had to endure a litany of belligerent commands from my petulant female superior numerous times each day."

"Then your father obviously perceived you as a direct threat and intentionally empowered your older sister Bianca to neutralize your prowess," Mr. Monastra logically concluded and stated. "He cleverly formed a difficult family alliance against you!"

"That sage assumption you've formulated is right on target!" James Carlino concurred in a melancholy tone of voice. "But outside of the array of family business activities, Bianca was as sweet as could be, especially kind to me during the Thanksgiving and Christmas holidays. That's when the mercurial-tempered witch would bake for me delicious apple and pumpkin pies along with delectable chocolate cakes. My mole-faced sister was like a complicated female version of Dr. Jekyll and Mr. Hyde," James explained. "She was rude and condescending toward me during the summer growing and harvest seasons, but conversely, wonderfully kind and exceptionally courteous to me in November and December. The shrew was neurotic and schizophrenic ever since our early teen years; the nasty hussy was sometimes envious toward me, and at other times, she preferred being dramatically polite and respectful. During the cold winter months," an animated James Carlino expounded, "Bianca's erratic personality was like Mother Teresa in regard to my anemic position in the family enterprises' pecking-order. However, from April to October when she and I had to work together, Bianca's vicious, hostile demeanor was like that of an extremely energized Medusa the Gorgon!"

"How did Bianca die?" Mr. Thomas Monastra wondered and finally asked his ten-million-dollar loan solicitor. "Her overall behavior sounds rather opposed to the well-known maxim, 'Only the good die young'!"

"My mood-changing, hideous-looking elder sister died from advanced lung cancer in April of 2014. Bianca was addicted to nicotine and smoked two packs of cigarettes each and every day, mostly out of perpetual nervousness and tremendous anxiety. Those destructive cancer sticks did her in. I sincerely hope that

552

Bianca's demanding soul is now finally in a passive state and calmly resting in eternal peace!"

James Dante Carlino then used his right index finger to point at the third picture situated atop the waist-high credenza. "This is my Uncle Lorenzo Carlino, married to my Aunt Carmella. As has been mentioned, Uncle Lorenzo left the family plantation and used his new-found profits from the Texas tract deal to own a farm package and fertilizer distribution outlet on West End Avenue in town. His wife Carmella always wanted half of the retail farm market operation, but my mother Angelina refused to share the business with her always-protesting sister-in-law. That was another sticking-point of incessant dispute between my father Pietro and my Uncle Lorenzo. But on the flip side of the coin," James emphasized before taking a deep breath to continue his monologue, "Uncle Lorenzo and Aunt Carmella had a comfortable get-away place in Cape May and allowed me to use it whenever I was having a verbal conflict with my avaricious, egocentric father!"

"How did your Uncle Lorenzo die?" urbane Thomas Monastra deferentially requested learning. "Was it from old age or from natural causes?"

"Uncle Lorenzo was notorious at dining at Hammonton taverns and coincidentally being a chronic alcoholic who after Aunt Carmella had passed away, enjoyed many Southern Comfort Manhattans while having supper, especially at the Maplewood Restaurant over on Route 30. Several times the bar maid had to drive him home in her vehicle while a second bar attendant would follow behind in Lorenzo's trademark red Cadillac," James described and shared. "Cirrhosis of the liver was the principal cause of death as had been documented on the physician's official state certificate. I believe that my seldom-sober uncle drank heavily because of the loss of his devoted Carmella and also, he habitually imbibed liquor as a result of putting-up with my insufferable father's regular abuse!"

"Who is this gorgeous young lady monopolizing this fourth picture? She must have been some sort of beauty queen?"

"Yes Tom, this is my first wife, Lisa Nelson, who was the Hammonton Peach Blossom Queen back in 1960 when peaches were the dominant crop. My father and mother disliked Lisa with a passion because she was not Sicilian but instead, was of British descent. In retrospect, I think I might have married her just to spite my parents, who suspected that Lisa wanted to nail me in matrimony solely for the love of pelf. I must admit that she was obsessed with money, with expensive cars and with our plush La Jolla, California winter vacation home. Regretfully," James sorrowfully related, "Lisa perished in 1968 when her white Bentley lost a wheel and then careened down a steep canyon near Delmar while speeding on Pacific Highway 101. Learning of that devastating tragedy was one of the most horrible, dreadful moments in my entire life!"

The fifth picture on the furniture console was that of Eleanor Davidson, a second cousin to James who lived with her deadbeat husband Robert in Edgewood, just outside Baltimore, Maryland. "Eleanor always kindly remembered my birthday and sent me cards and small gifts. Sometimes Tom, the little things in life are the most important and memorable ones," James Carlino stressed and insisted to his captive listener. "Poor Cousin Eleanor died of ALS, Lou Gehrig's Disease. If I could somehow miraculously bring dear Eleanor back to life for let's say, a mere million dollars, I would gladly do it in a heartbeat!"

"This sixth photo'," deftly interrupted Mr. Monastra. "Is this your younger brother Franco? Genetically speaking, he looks like he possessed several similar facial characteristics to you, particular around the eyes and mouth."

"Yes Sir. My younger brother and I were intense rivals throughout our formative years. Franco was jealous of me because I was a better high school football and basketball player than he was. Clearly," James boasted, "I was the more coordinated and athletic brother. Basically, to put our relationship in context, we merely tolerated each other and had several bloody fistfights in back of the packinghouse, of which naturally I had emerged victorious. But realistically, we were valid stockholders in a number of family enterprises such as the cold storage facility in Vineland and the extensive real estate property in Mays Landing alongside the Atlantic City Expressway. Franco was a poor investor outside the prolific family businesses," the mall developer commented, "and because of the careless mismanagement of his personal funds, the abominable fool declared bankruptcy in 1993 and subsequently died a year later when his ancient airplane crashed inside the Wharton State Forest while approaching the runway at Hammonton Municipal Airport. Although the FAA investigative results into the landing accident were inconclusive, it's my firm conviction that my cowardly brother had committed suicide."

"Is there a small fond memory or perhaps anything good you could remember about Franco?" skillfully interrogated Mr.

554

Monastra. "You seem to give a very pessimistic impression of your younger brother."

"Yes Tom, Franco was better than me in baseball and made the Cape-Atlantic League All Star squad in high school. My mentally capable brother was also more gifted than me academically, and the educated genius graduated from Cornell University with high honors, but my quixotic younger brother lacked corporate acumen and was not at all practical in formulating sound business judgments. Franco was like an isolated Einstein destined for economic bankruptcy when compelled to venture-out on his own and exploring opportunities outside the familiar realm and safety-net of family corporations."

James Dante Carlino then hesitated for a moment to perceptively interpret the impact of his recent statements upon his all-too-pleasant visitor. "Personally Tom, I detest monotony! I hope I'm not boring you with my bizarre family history. I only wish that I could edify and eulogize my brother's memory, but in all candor, I cannot lie and misrepresent the veracity of the actual facts to you!"

"Oh no Jim," Thomas Monastra genteelly replied. "Truthfully, I find your honest revelations to be most refreshing, fascinating and intriguing, and I think that your descriptive anecdotes concerning each photographed person displayed upon your stereo's lid happen to be most authentic; most interesting. It's rather astounding to me how you have over the years become a prominent, legitimate shopping center developer," evaluated and enunciated the amiable banker, "considering all of the very evident negative influences that your tough father, your' elder sister and your vindictive brother must have had on your all-too-vulnerable psychological growth. I wish that you would now elaborate on the other six people whose pictures are sublimely exhibited upon your cherished 1970s music and radio credenza."

* * * * * * * * * * * *

"Jim, you've divulged some fantastic family secrets like your father Pietro spending over a million dollars and buying the Texas block of your family's sprawling farm four separate times. But admirably, you've been able to parlay your consecutive investments into an enormous, enviable financial accomplishment. It's not everyone who is able to present to my bank over ten million bucks of tangible collateral to subsidize a new shopping center!"

"I'll try to be modest and forthright Tom about my series of achievements," the gray-haired financial veteran euphorically maintained, attempting to contribute an element of humility to the ongoing extraordinary dialogue. "There are plenty of farmers in Hammonton who are worth over three million clams, but hidden beneath the surface those same growers have four million in debts. With a little bit of Lady Luck along the way," Carlino pontificated with a broad grin, "I've managed to accumulate a decent fortune by having and utilizing the services of two very competent financial advisers: my CPA William Tomasello and my Stock Account Executive Richard Palmieri, who adroitly manages my stocks and bonds' portfolio. Without their trustworthy, professional guidance, I speculate that I'd probably be several million in arrears rather than thirty million ahead of the game. I can't possibly brag about my holdings without first extending my utmost appreciation and wholehearted kudos to Bill and Rich."

Then signaling his shift in focus for the bank executive to gaze upon the seventh exhibited photo', James Carlino disclosed that the petite female shown inside the silver frame was Barbara Carlino Grillo, the land investor's favored younger sister, his junior by five years. "Barbara was the one family member who truly loved me without seeking any special remuneration in return. She and her husband Steve now live in Ft. Myers, Florida, but the couple made a respectable living flipping houses, mostly in Palm Springs and Palm Desert, California and in South Padre Island, Texas," Carlino lectured to Monastra. "Not only was Barbara very academically smart, being the Valedictorian of her St. Joseph High class, but also she was extremely caring and compassionate toward me. Twice Barbara and Steve flew-up from Florida and visited me in the hospital. First was when I had a polyp surgically removed from my large intestine, and the second occasion was when I had my hip replacement done three years back at Our Lady of Lourdes Hospital in Camden. But I must confess Tom, I'm saddened to relate that my favorite sibling died just last year after courageously battling breast cancer for over a decade."

After taking a very deep breath to demonstrably show his excessive distress, the now-melancholy host next divulged to his indulgent guest that the eighth photo' was that of his second cousin Megyn Carlino Johnson, who had a very tough and miserable early life, being the sixth of seven impoverished children. "Megyn needed a glass eye at the age of five, and I used most of my saved allowance and secretly sent her parents the

556

money to get one. As fate would have it, twenty years later Meg married a construction worker named Fred Johnson, and with my benign help, the industrious pair founded a guardrail business in Glassboro. Over the next twenty years, Meg and Fred eventually lifted themselves out of poverty and did pretty well on the prosperity front. But six years ago, my dearest cousin contracted leukemia and died just last November."

The handsome male depicted in picture number nine was James Dante Carlino's best friend, Gary Testa, who had functioned for twenty-five years as an effective local middle school vice-principal. In terms of recreation, Testa became the land developer's loyal bowling partner twice every week at DiDonato Lanes. "Poor Gary passed away in 2012 of colon cancer, a terrible disease that I fortunately avoided when I had eight inches of large intestine removed from my right-side abdomen at Virtua Hospital on Route 73 in Voorhees. Life can be extremely cruel," the talkative speaker added. "After contributing to Social Security for two and a half decades, Gary's wife Lorraine received a mere 255 dollars towards burial expenses. My bowling chum never collected one penny, succumbing and dying at the tender age of sixty-one years before ever becoming eligible for government benefits."

"And who is this dark-haired beauty in Picture Number Ten? That fabulous face could qualify for Miss Universe?"

"Well Tom, that's Carol Sorrentino Carlino, who was my second wife and a daring and adventurous winter weather person. I had built exclusively for her a magnificent lodge up in the Poconos just outside of Bushkill," the prolific investor communicated. "To make a long story short, Carol loved skiing at several tourist resorts near Camelback Mountain, and one day her defective right ski broke in half and my beloved spouse crashed into a tall pine tree. Much to my sorrow and disenchantment, Carol died from multiple internal injuries sustained in her horrible downhill accident."

"Sorry to learn of your second wife's awful demise," the visiting banker empathized. "I remember reading about the incident in the *Vineland News Journal.* Her family owned several cold storage facilities, didn't they?"

"Yes, and that's the connection of how I had met and courted my second wife!" James revealed. "Her family and mine were fifty-fifty partners in three different fruit and produce cold storages in the Vineland-Newfield area."

Carlino then offered a brief preface on the mustached gentleman represented in Picture Number Eleven. "This very serious-faced gentleman is Ben Lucas, a distant cousin who had a severe gambling problem. I felt sorry for him and gave addicted Ben thousands of dollars from time-to-time to cover his atrocious mounting family debts, hoping that he could somehow eventually be reformed and rehabilitated. But during one notable casino excursion at Harrahs in Atlantic City," James Carlino soberly uttered his exposition, "Ben suffered a wicked heart attack and died shortly thereafter at Mainland Hospital in Pomona."

"And who is the alluring-looking lady shown in this final photo'?"

"She is, or should I say 'was' Josephine Lucas, who was Ben's faithful wife right up to the end," elaborated Carlino. "After her husband unexpectedly departed this Earth, feeling obligated, I provided Josie with food and mortgage money along with additional funds to compensate for her talented daughter's college education at nearby Stockton State University. As you can plainly see Tom," the prospective mall developer resumed, "my personal history has been besieged with both risk and catastrophe. Nothing ventured; nothing gained has always been my motto. But do you want to hear something rather strange and inexplicable about this entire scenario?"

"What is that?" the bank president persuasively insisted.

"Lately, whenever I peer at these twelve flat black and white pictures, I feel as if the individuals' eyes are all staring at me from another indiscernible dimension," the mansion dweller declared. "I'm not ordinarily superstitious, but the entire phenomenal enigma is very eerie and uniquely arcane. And these two-dimensional likenesses situated upon this credenza weirdly project their mysterious eyes at least once a day as of late, and those stares seem to be penetrating right through me, as if the frightening, peculiar gapes are positively surreal, the horrendous, intimidating alien X-ray eyes apparently originating from another world! And sometimes when I turn around quickly, the twenty-four eyes following me are surprisingly caught moving back to their initial positions."

"Well Jim," Thomas Monastra answered with general alarm and mental confusion, "it's often said that the eyes are the windows to the soul! But if you want my honest opinion about your uncanny *Twilight Zone* episodes, I think that your imagination coupled with your emotional anguish are together preventing you from evading your present state of imagination! I think that a few nights of good sleep will replenish your stability. Now then Jim, let's solidify the details of our next meeting on Saturday morning with your corporate CPA and your personal Stockbroker."

* * * * * * * * * * * *

Three days later on Saturday at 9 am a trio of dependable financial gurus assembled upon the expansive curved driveway outside James Dante Carlino's palatial East First Road mansion. Prominent banker Thomas Monastra, reputable Stock and Bond Account Executive Richard Palmieri and reliable CPA William Tomasello were mutually gathered to intelligently finalize James Carlino's longtime aspiration of constructing a multimillion-dollar shopping center complex in pleasant Somers Point, just outside Ocean City, NJ.

"That's odd!" observed and exclaimed the somewhat worried banker. "He's not responding to our doorbell rings. If anything, Mr. Carlino is usually prompt and punctual, especially ready to be available for such an important matter as his shopping center dream coming to fruition. Try ringing the doorbell again Richard! Perhaps our friend is finishing-up his morning coffee in the kitchen."

"Look through this side window!" the now-shocked stockbroker directed his companions. "I see a figure lying face-down on the floor underneath the side-wall drapes!"

"This is a very serious emergency! That's beyond a doubt Mr. Carlino lying there!" ascertained the alarmed-and-upset Certified Public Accountant. "My client has always been an ardent Elvis Presley fan! I would recognize those expensive imported blue suede shoes he's wearing anywhere!"

Nervous William Tomasello instinctively removed his cellphone from his left front pocket and swiftly dialed 911, and the AtlantiCare ambulance squad was instantaneously contacted through the town dispatcher to rush-out and promptly address the crisis. Led by blaring police car sirens, the on-a-mission rescue crew arrived upon the frenzied scene five minutes later. The two frenetic, under-duress on-duty cops violently impacted the dual front doors with a portable battering ram. Then, after several crucial minutes of futilely attempting to resuscitate the fallen victim, the certified EMT captain reluctantly pronounced the rich investor dead.

"James Carlino was undoubtedly one of the wealthiest men in Hammonton just a mere hour ago," CPA William Tomasello asserted and grimly confided, "but now like any other person who becomes deceased, the dead fellow isn't worth a plug nickel!"

* * * * * * * * * * * *

The other-dimension courtroom was gloomily dismal, dingy and obscure. The black-robed, apathetic two-dimensional Devil's Advocate stood before the elevated panel of twelve haunting phantoms, all pathetically gray-robed, similar-in-appearance, solemn-faced specters, and then the Frightful Figure serving as Chief Prosecutor began delivering his introductory announcement.

"I would like to expedite this trial of one James Dante Carlino by having each of you present an abbreviated statement about how this pernicious individual had diabolically harmed you, either physically or emotionally. Your mission is akin to how a Grand Jury presently operates in your former existence. I remind you that you are the twelve appointed prosecuting attorneys as well as being the twelve jurists who will ultimately pronounce a permanent sentence at the completion of this legal formality. In this well-defined procedure, there is no Defense Attorney for the Accused. And after your sagacious verdict has been rendered, I shall determine the precise punishment to be administered and exercised. Needless to say, the Defendant, or should I say 'Accused', will have no means of appeal after this case is evaluated and disposed of. Let us commence this post-life inquisition with testimony from Mrs. Carmella Carlino.

"Thank you, Eminent Prosecutor for recognizing me first," prefaced Mrs. Carmella Carlino. "In July of 1967, my brother-in-law Mr. Pietro Carlino, who incidentally is still barely alive and on life support, now barely breathing in a semi-conscious state, had five-hundred-thousand dollars stashed away in a bedroom wall safe behind a portrait of his wife Angelina. Half of that cash money skimmed primarily from the family farm would have eventually belonged to my husband Lorenzo, Pietro Carlino's younger brother."

Gray-faced Jurist Carmella Carlino paused for a moment to gather her abundant random thoughts. "My nefarious nephew James Carlino had certain Mafia and Cosa Nostra contacts throughout New Jersey. Then four masked thugs broke into Pietro's house, tied Angelina to the bannister with telephone cords, forcefully obtained the safe combination from Pietro, hit

560

my brother-in-law over the head with a pistol and after purloining the stashed cash, quickly abandoned the crime scene with the half-million cold cash in laundry bags; yes, five thousand crisp, hundred-dollar bills were vilely stolen. Evidently, my disgustingly greedy nephew James later used his share of the half-million bucks as seed money to start his own cold storage enterprises. I conclude by stating that James never expressed any remorse or contrition for his many criminal deeds."

Bianca Carlino was the second jurist to prefer charges against the non-penitent 'Accused'. "My evil brother was the Carlino Farm treasurer, and over a ten-year period the despicable felon skimmed and siphoned over one and a half million dollars from the corporation. I never wanted to officially incriminate James because I feared the prospect of public scandal once the charges were published in local newspapers, which sometimes report news as tabloid-type information," Bianca confided and disclosed. "Also, the IRS would have rapidly gotten wind of the secret money withholding, and *that* sort of government investigation could have really exacerbated the whole problem. Fellow Jurists, I realize that I had an ugly mole-laden face during my earthly existence, but my brother James's egregious misconduct was far uglier than my grotesque countenance ever was!"

"Thank you' Bianca for your valuable and insightful input," commended the assigned Devil's Advocate Prosecutor. "We'll now hear from Jurist Number Three, Lorenzo Carlino, Carmella Carlino's exploited husband."

"I despised my covetous nephew James with a wild hateful passion," Lorenzo began his strong indictment. "Besides constantly belittling and abusing me on the family farm in front of employees, my nephew was a crazed womanizer, a sexual predator who frequently abandoned marital fidelity in absurd escapades with at least two dozen whores, prostitutes and promiscuous females. Once I had taken my wife Carmella to a Broadway play and an overnight stay at a Manhattan hotel. After we arrived by taxi to the bustling Port Authority Bus Terminal, Carmella and I noticed James boarding a bus that would be heading to Atlantic City. My egotistical nephew was accompanied by a buxom blonde, who incidentally was not his often-ignored wife Lisa."

"Deplorable deportment indeed!" observed and acknowledged the drab, flat-as-a-billiard-table Devil's Advocate. "Let's now listen to damaging commentary from the specter of Lisa Nelson

Carlino, the Accused Individual's first wife, our Jurist Number Four."

"Forget the provable fact that my heinous husband was a classic womanizer," Lisa Nelson Carlino defiantly stated to her judicial colleagues. "I was casually driving south on Pacific Highway 101 in a leased white Bentley when all of a sudden the right front wheel suspiciously separated from the brand-new car. My vehicle then careened and tumbled down a side ridge and soon caught fire with me inside. My body was severely burned and then deteriorated into an unidentifiable state. I hereby blame my husband James for maliciously causing my grievous death by auto," the former wife attested. "He wanted to dispose of me quickly, used his West Coast Mafia connections to rig my luxury vehicle for impending disaster, and then plotted to collect several hundred-thousand-dollars from a life insurance policy in the process. All of that diabolical California activity had occurred because I had threatened to report my husband's extra-marital affairs to the *Atlantic City Press* if James didn't stop cavorting around with porn stars and also immorally frequenting Atlantic City bordellos."

The fifth designated prosecutor on the Recently Deceased Court Docket was Eleanor Davidson of Edgewood, Maryland, a suburb of Baltimore. "James had offered to pay my hospital expenses for my debilitating ALS condition, but the craven liar never came through on his hollow promises. Instead, my demented cousin and his Mafia allies threatened my boss at the manufacturing plant where I had been employed, falsely claiming that I owed *him* a hundred thousand dollars' promissory note that never existed," Eleanor's apparition intrepidly testified. "The purpose of this illicit behavior on James's part was to recruit my husband Robert into the Baltimore mob syndicate to become a shakedown thug for citizens that had a hard time paying already owed extortion money. And since Rob stands a colossal six foot six in stature and weighs two-hundred and seventy-five pounds, my husband was a prime target for admission into the local Sicilian cartel."

Next on the crowded afterworld agenda happened to be Jurist Number Six, vociferous Franco Carlino, the younger brother and rival of James in the family hierarchy. "My older brother Jimmy was the epitome of harmful wrongdoing," Franco asserted to the other eleven attentive Jury Members and also to the Devil's Advocate Prosecutor. "I believe that James always possessed a distinct aversion to basic human decency. After I had been visited

562

and physically assaulted by three of his Mafia chums, I had to pawn my diamond ring and my wife's jewelry just to make monthly extortion payments to the mob," Franco's shade audaciously stated. "Then I had to donate my fully-equipped late-model Lincoln Continental to the local Mafia so that its parts could go to selected junkyards and to Philly' chop shops for dismantlement and resale. I feared for my endangered life, and now I realize that my unexpected fatal plane crash had occurred because the engine had been spitefully tampered with and expertly sabotaged. Jimmy thought that our father Pietro was gradually liking me more than him, so my black-hearted brother surreptitiously organized my small craft plummet and violent crash into the Wharton State Forest, all happening upon my landing approach to Hammonton Municipal Airport."

"Apparition Number Seven, sister Barbara Carlino, you now have the floor to present a terse dissertation pertaining to the innumerable transgressions of your loathsome brother," the Devil's Advocate instructed. "I believe that your presentation will be the seventh panel recitation."

"Every time I recall my brother James's repulsive self-centered schemes," Barbara Carlino's shade recounted, "I think of the deceiving villain as being both the agony and the ecstasy. His obnoxious behaviors had agonizing consequences for me and for my family, but simultaneously, his misdeeds brought ecstasy to his selfish nature. My husband Steve and I were gaining satisfaction from churning some commendable profits while acquiring and then flipping houses in Palm Springs, California and later in South Padre Island, Texas. But when we set-up shop in Ft. Myers, Florida, my reprehensible older brother threatened us with arson. He effectively practiced extortion by predicting that his treacherous Mafia friends would burn-down our new South Florida home unless we participated in what amounted to a fraudulent Ponzi pyramid conspiracy," Barbara Carlino revealed. "After borrowing our credit cards' money to the limit, Steve and I invested seven-hundred-and-fifty thousand dollars in a real estate trust fund that was designed to pay us 20% interest every year. The first several years went smoothly until the unscrupulous ruse ran-out of newly-duped suckers to draw into the malignant plot. And the initial annual reports were handled by a team of corrupt accountants working for the mob," the taken-advantage-of sister denunciated. "The crooked accomplices' ruthless role was to make all suspect fraudulent records and correspondences appear to be legitimate! When I eventually died of breast cancer, I died broke, and I was in major financial debt!"

"We'll now hear from Prosecutor/Jurist Number Eight, Megyn Carlino Johnson, James Carlino's second cousin who had sacrificed plenty in her early life, growing-up in a destitute family having seven needy children," the Chief Prosecutor dressed in the large black robe carefully cited. "Make it brief so that I can speedily move to terminate this totally bureaucratic process!"

"I died penniless, thanks to the savage effects of being directly associated with my Satanic cousin James Carlino," Megyn Johnson commenced her questionable relative's character analysis. "After establishing a profitable guardrail installation company, Fred, my hard-working husband and I were ordered at gunpoint by James's iniquitous Mafia henchmen to contribute two hundred thousand dollars to be used to bribe three South Jersey mayors to allow for the acquisition and licensing of ten pizza parlors. The newly-created retail businesses were to be utilized for laundering and disguising mob money within the dynamic American capitalistic economic system. To accurately assess this dutiful exact moment in the hereafter," Megyn Johnson's spirit adamantly insisted, "I submit that I still fully resent my uncivilized cousin's destruction and ruination of my formerly happy life that had prevailed prior to me being stricken with full-blown leukemia."

"Thank you' Mrs. Johnson for offering your incisive testimony," the Chief Prosecutor praised. "Our mendacious Mr. James Dante Carlino definitely shows indications of being a prospective candidate for *Dante's Inferno.* Please forgive my flaccid attempt at humor," the slightly embarrassed Chief Prosecutor apologized, "but our subject-in-question shows behavioral propensities for being more of a mendacious *antagonist* than acting as a constructive *protagonist* in enacting his former life. With *that* rational illustration being elucidated, let's now listen to aggrieved Jurist Number Nine, deceased former middle school administrator, Gary Testa."

The school vice-principal, who had died from being painfully defeated by colon cancer, concisely complained that James Dante Carlino had been clandestinely involved in two major drug distribution networks, one in Paramus and the other located in Egg Harbor City, New Jersey. The Ninth Jurist discreetly charged that his underworld bowling buddy had gotten the school official hooked on meth and on crack cocaine. "I was leading a normal life until, who I considered to be my best pal, suddenly betrayed

564

our friendship with drugs," the former educator affirmed. "Once I was addicted, my life went downhill in a hurry. I simply can't forgive this foul menace named James Carlino for the harsh deleterious effect his once-trusted acquaintance has had in dissolving the foundations of all my family relationships. I felt and still feel utter bitterness toward Jim, whom I still think and believe is a dye-in-the-wool psychopath. True, I am partially to blame for my detrimental addiction," Gary Testa's gray ghost realized and stated, "but I warrant and swear that James Dante Carlino is the scoundrel principally responsible for my drug-related decline. I hereby insist that moral justice must be thoroughly implemented by this judicious panel."

Carol Sorrentino Carlino, James's second wife, also showed great enmity towards her "accused gangster former husband". The Tenth Jurist/Shade commenced her commentary by sternly reiterating first wife Lisa Nelson Carlino's boldly proclaimed main allegation. "In addition to being a dedicated womanizer," Carol's vengeful spirit stressed and grieved, "my deranged spouse promised that he would report my family's cold storage businesses to the IRS for owed taxes on siphoned-off money that had been advertently kept concealed from government scrutiny. The isolated Pocono Mountain lodge had been deeded in my name, so under unbelievable pressure exerted by James and his mob collaborators, I deemed it necessary to sell the property and swing the four-hundred-thousand-dollar cash settlement into financing my entrance into James's doomed Ponzi real estate pyramid scheme. And right after *that* implausible expense was made, I experienced the fatal ski accident near Camelback Mountain and consequently, lost my precious life. To sum-up *this* dramatic moment in eternity, I still attribute my painful death to James along with his association with the merciless mob in causing my demise to happen."

"Thank you for your salient and relevant discourse," the Devil's Advocate remarked to the deceased second wife. "Now we'll listen to testimony from Mr. Benjamin Lucas, once regarded as a close confidante of Mr. James Dante Carlino."

The Eleventh Witness/Jurist sat erect in his black two-dimensional chair and calmly addressed his peers and the gruesome-looking Devil's Advocate Prosecutor. "Certainly, when it boiled-down to human values, among them courtesy and fundamental morality, my dysfunctional second cousin regarded himself as being some sort of amoral iconoclast," Benjamin Lucas austerely declared and accused. "Jealous Jim chronically and

565

voluntarily violated the essential premises provided in the Ten Commandments, the lesson taught in the Golden Rule 'Do unto Others', and also the teaching found in the marvelous precept 'Love Thy Neighbor as Thyself'. In my particular case, Mr. James Carlino both encouraged and fueled my gambling habit by perpetually bailing me out of accumulated arrears in order to make me more dependent on his manipulative control over me. My demonic cousin tried to diplomatically make me quit my job as a recognized top-grade automobile mechanic and then illegally operate a mob chop-shop for stolen vehicles, the proposed scam located ten miles southeast of Hammonton in Hamilton Township. But to my credit," Benjamin Lucas clarified, "I refused to be affiliated with the local crime syndicate, but in the interim I became acutely paranoid and fearful that a mob hit squad would arrive at my home and either torture my wife Josephine or assassinate me for not cooperating with James's maniacal, egocentric out-of-control fanaticism. Esteemed Panel, I soon became excessively distraught and emotionally disheveled," Benjamin Lucas related to the perceptive jury. "I claim that the massive heart attack I had suffered was a result of the excruciating mental and emotional discomfort I then experienced, being subjected to periods of fatigue, depression, delirium, continuous apprehension and plenteous bouts of overwhelming hysteria."

Finally, black-robed Justice/Prosecutor Number Twelve, Josephine Lucas, sat erect in her two-dimensional seat and began orating her personal connection to all-too-devious James Dante Carlino. "I must validate the true testimonies of James's first and second wives, corroborating the fact that the guilty subject presently on trial was indeed a deceitful womanizer. Whenever my husband Ben was working at the auto' shop or rolling dice or playing poker in Atlantic City, this parasitic rogue Mr. James Carlino would visit our humble abode and soon attempt being aggressively amorous towards me. It reached a point where I would deliberately have my daughter Eileen staying at home by my side in order to deter the evil fiend from molesting me. But being used to getting what his twisted soul often desired," the aggrieved woman's specter alleged, "wily Mr. James Carlino persisted in his relentless pursuit of sadistic pleasure reflected in the form of sinful adultery."

"I thank all of the contributing Jurists for their convicting renditions relating to the fate and sentencing of Mr. James Dante Carlino's blemished soul, which certainly holds a redundancy of shameful misdeeds. Now then, if you believe that the
566

aforementioned subject is guilty of committing a plethora of mortal and venial sins, I direct that you now raise over your heads the flat black placards located at your feet," the dark figure imperatively instructed. "Fine; I see that the panel is unanimous in its irreversible verdict. As you are well-aware, the stained absent soul on trial has upon death both relinquished and surrendered its free will, so there is no legal objection or appeal to this court's supreme decision or authority. The 'Accused' had enacted multiple trespasses against this unified Jury of Twelve Plaintiffs, and his manifold sins were indeed most malevolent and exceedingly insidious. Therefore, I hereby remand the soul of James Dante Carlino to the custody of St. Peter, Keeper of the Eternal Gates. I herein rule and recommend that the Apostle's formidable angel guards will swiftly conduct Mr. Carlino's impure spirit to a dark, gravel-floored prison cell, and it will remain at *that* punitive destination for a duration of one thousand Earth years, specifically to undergo prescribed and required purification. And then after the millennium period of solitary confinement has expired," the Devil's Advocate emphatically summarized, "the soul of Mr. Carlino will finally be exposed to Perpetual Light shining upon its formerly contaminated existence. This easily resolved trial now stands adjourned. The distinguished panel of qualified Jurists is hereby dismissed."

About the Author

Jay Dubya is author' John Wiessner's pen name and also his initials (J.W.) John is a retired New Jersey public school English teacher and he had taught the subject for thirty-four years. John lives in southern New Jersey with wife Joanne and the couple has three grown sons. John is the creator of thirty-nine published books.

Jay Dubya has written adult satires *Fractured Frazzled Folk Fables and Fairy Farces* and *FFFF and FF, Part II. Black Leather and Blue Denim, A '50s Novel* and its sequel, *The Great Teen Fruit War, A 1960' Novel* and *Frat' Brats, A '60s Novel* are adult-oriented literary endeavors constituting a trilogy.

Pieces of Eight, Pieces of Eight, Part II, Pieces of Eight Part III and *Pieces of Eight, Part IV* are' short story/novella collections featuring science fiction, paranormal and humorous plots and themes. *Nine New Novellas* is the companion book to *Nine New Novellas, Part II, Nine New Novellas, Part III* and *Nine New Novellas, Part IV*. And *So Ya' Wanna' Be A Teacher* is a satirical autobiography describing the author's thirty-four year educational career in American public schools.

Ron Coyote, Man of La Mangia is adult humor and the work is an imaginative satire/parody on Miguel Cervantes' Don Quixote, published in 1605. *Mauled Maimed Mangled Mutilated Mythology* is a work that satires twenty-one famous ancient tales. *The Wholly Book of Genesis* and *The Wholly Book of Exodus* are also adult satirical *humor. Thirteen Sick Tasteless Classics, Thirteen Sick Tasteless Classics, Part II, Thirteen Sick Tasteless Classics, Part III* and *Thirteen Sick Tasteless Classics, Part IV* are adult satirical rewrites of famous short fiction.

John has also authored a trilogy of young adult fantasy novels, *Enchanta, Pot of Gold* and *Space Bugs, Earth Invasion. The Eighteen' Story Gingerbread House* is a new collection of eighteen diverse and creative children's stories.

Jay Dubya likes '50s rock and roll music and he also enjoys pop' songs by the Beach Boys', Fleetwood Mac, the Eagles, the Rolling Stones, ELO, John Mellencamp and by John Fogerty. When not writing or listening to music, Jay Dubya likes watching 76ers basketball and Phillies and Yankees television baseball games.

Author Biography

Born in Hammonton, NJ in 1942, John Wiessner had attended St. Joseph School up to and including Grade 5. After his family moved from Hammonton to Levittown, Pa in 1954, John attended St. Mark School in Bristol, Pa. for Grade 6, St. Michael the Archangel School in Levittown for Grades 7 and 8 and then Immaculate Conception School, Levittown, Pa. for Grade 9. Bishop Egan High School, Levittown Pa was John's educational base for Grades 10 and 11, and later in 1960, the aspiring author graduated from Edgewood Regional High, Tansboro, NJ. John then next attended Glassboro State College, where he was an announcer for the school's baseball games and also read the nightly news and sports over WGLS, GSC's radio station.

John Wiessner had been primarily an English teacher in the Hammonton Public School System for 34 years, specializing in the instruction of middle school language arts. Mr. Wiessner was quite active in the Hammonton Education Association, serving in the capacities of Vice-President, building representative and finally, teachers' head negotiator for 7 years. During his lengthy teaching career, John had been nominated into "Who's Who Among American Teachers" three times. He also was quite active giving professional workshops at schools around South Jersey on the subjects of creative writing and the use of movie videos to motivate students to organize their classroom theme compositions.

John Wiessner was very active in community service, being a past President of the Hammonton Lions Club, where he also functioned for many years as the club's Tail-Twister, Vice-President and Liontamer. John had been named Hammonton Lion of the Year in 1979 and in 2009 received the prestigious Melvin Jones Fellow Award, the highest honor a Lion can receive from Lions International.

John also was a successful businessman, starting with being a Philadelphia Bulletin newspaper delivery boy for two years in the late 1950s in Levittown, Pennsylvania. After his family moved back to New Jersey in 1959, John worked at his grandparents and his parents' farm markets, Square Deal Farm (now Ron's Gardens in Hammonton) and Pete's Farm Market in Elm, respectively. He later managed his wife's parents' farm market, White Horse Farms in Elm for three summers.

Also in a business capacity, for 16 summers starting in 1967 John Wiessner had co-owned Dealers Choice Amusement Arcade on the Ocean City, Maryland boardwalk and also co-owned the New Horizon Tee-Shirt Store for eight summers (1973-'81) on the Rehoboth Beach, Delaware boardwalk. In addition, "Jay Dubya" was a co-owner of Wheel and Deal Amusement Arcade, Missouri Avenue and Boardwalk, Atlantic City. And then, for 18 summers beginning in 1986, John had been the Field Manager in charge of crew-leaders for Atlantic Blueberry Company (the world's largest cultivated blueberry farm), both the Weymouth and Mays Landing Divisions.

After retiring from teaching in 1999, writing under the pen name Jay Dubya (his initials), John Wiessner became the author of 42 books in the genre Action/Adventure Novels, Sci-Fi/Paranormal Story Collections, Adult Satire, Young Adult Fantasy Novels and Non-Fiction Books. His books exist in hardcover, in paperback and in popular Kindle and Nook e-book formats.